EX LIBRIS

VINTAGE CLASSICS

# SELECTED STORIES

Alice Munro was born in 1931. She has received many awards and prizes, including three Governor General's Literary Awards in Canada, two Giller Prizes, the Rea Award for the Short Story, the Lannan Literary Award, the National Book Critics Circle Award, and was shortlisted for the Booker Prize for *The Beggar Maid*. Her stories have appeared in *The New Yorker, Atlantic Monthly, The Paris Review*, and her collections have been translated into thirteen languages. She is the winner of the Man Booker International Prize 2009. She lives with her husband in Ontario, Canada.

ALSO BY ALICE MUNRO

*Dance of the Happy Shades*

*Lives of Girls and Women*

*Something I've Been Meaning to Tell You*

*The Beggar Maid*

*The Moons of Jupiter*

*The Progress of Love*

*Friend of My Youth*

*Open Secrets*

*The Love of a Good Woman*

*Hateship, Friendship, Courtship, Loveship, Marriage*

*The View from Castle Rock*

*Runaway*

*Too Much Happiness*

ALICE MUNRO

# Selected Stories

VINTAGE BOOKS
London

Published by Vintage 2010

2 4 6 8 10 9 7 5 3 1

Copyright © Alice Munro 1996

Alice Munro has asserted her right under the Copyright, Designs
and Patents Act 1988 to be identified as the author of this work

First published in Great Britain by Chatto & Windus 1996
Published in paperback by Vintage 1997

Vintage
Random House, 20 Vauxhall Bridge Road,
London SW1V 2SA

www.vintage-classics.info

Addresses for companies within The Random House Group Limited
can be found at: www.randomhouse.co.uk/offices.htm

The Random House Group Limited Reg. No. 954009

A CIP catalogue record for this book
is available from the British Library

ISBN 9780099541097

The Random House Group Limited supports The Forest
Stewardship Council (FSC), the leading international forest
certification organisation. All our titles that are printed on
Greenpeace approved FSC certified paper carry the FSC logo.
Our paper procurement policy can be found at:
www.rbooks.co.uk/environment

**Mixed Sources**
Product group from well-managed
forests and other controlled sources
www.fsc.org  Cert no. TT-COC-2139
© 1996 Forest Stewardship Council

Printed and bound in Great Britain by
CPI Cox & Wyman, Reading RG1 8EX

*For*
VIRGINIA BARBER

*My essential support and friend for twenty years*

# Contents

Walker Brothers Cowboy 3

Dance of the Happy Shades 16

Postcard 26

Images 40

Something I've Been Meaning to Tell You 50

The Ottawa Valley 67

Material 81

Royal Beatings 96

Wild Swans 115

The Beggar Maid 124

Dulse 152

The Turkey Season 171

Labor Day Dinner 184

The Moons of Jupiter 205

The Progress of Love 219

Lichen 242

Miles City, Montana 261

Fits 278

Friend of My Youth 299

Meneseteung 317

Differently 335

Carried Away 356

Vandals 390

# ACKNOWLEDGEMENTS

Grateful acknowledgement is made to Penguin Books for permission to reproduce the following stories: 'Something I've Been Meaning to Tell You', 'The Ottawa Valley' and 'Material' from *Something I've Been Meaning to Tell You*; 'Royal Beatings', 'Wild Swans' and 'The Beggar Maid' from *The Beggar Maid*; 'Dulse', 'The Turkey Season', 'Labor Day Dinner' and 'The Moons of Jupiter' from *The Moons of Jupiter*.

The other stories appeared in the following collections: 'Walker Brothers Cowboy', 'Dance of the Happy Shades', 'Postcard' and 'Images' in *Dance of the Happy Shades*; 'The Progress of Love', 'Lichen', 'Miles City, Montana' and 'Fits' in *The Progress of Love*; 'Friend of My Youth', 'Meneseteung', and 'Differently' in *Friend of My Youth*; 'Carried Away' and 'Vandals' in *Open Secrets*.

# Walker Brothers Cowboy

AFTER SUPPER my father says, "Want to go down and see if the Lake's still there?" We leave my mother sewing under the dining-room light, making clothes for me against the opening of school. She has ripped up for this purpose an old suit and an old plaid wool dress of hers, and she has to cut and match very cleverly and also make me stand and turn for endless fittings, sweaty, itching from the hot wool, ungrateful. We leave my brother in bed in the little screened porch at the end of the front veranda, and sometimes he kneels on his bed and presses his face against the screen and calls mournfully, "Bring me an ice-cream cone!" but I call back, "You will be asleep," and do not even turn my head.

Then my father and I walk gradually down a long, shabby sort of street, with Silverwoods Ice Cream signs standing on the sidewalk, outside tiny, lighted stores. This is in Tuppertown, an old town on Lake Huron, an old grain port. The street is shaded, in some places, by maple trees whose roots have cracked and heaved the sidewalk and spread out like crocodiles into the bare yards. People are sitting out, men in shirtsleeves and undershirts and women in aprons—not people we know but if anybody looks ready to nod and say, "Warm night," my father will nod too and say something the same. Children are still playing. I don't know them either because my mother keeps my brother and me in our own yard, saying he is too young to leave it and I have to mind him. I am not so sad to watch their evening games because the games themselves are ragged, dissolving. Children, of their own will, draw apart, separate into islands of two or one under the heavy trees, occupying themselves in such solitary ways as I do all day, planting pebbles in the dirt or writing in it with a stick.

Presently we leave these yards and houses behind; we pass a factory with boarded-up windows, a lumberyard whose high wooden gates are locked for the night. Then the town falls away in a defeated jumble of sheds and small junkyards, the sidewalk gives up and we are walking on a sandy path with burdocks, plantains, humble nameless weeds all around. We enter a vacant lot, a kind of park really, for it is kept clear of junk and there is one bench with a slat missing on the back, a place to sit and look at the water. Which is generally gray in the evening, under a lightly overcast sky, no sunsets, the horizon dim. A very quiet, washing noise on the stones of the beach. Further along, towards the main part of town, there is a stretch of sand, a water slide, floats bobbing around the safe swimming area, a lifeguard's rickety throne. Also a long dark-green building, like a roofed veranda, called the Pavilion, full of farmers and their wives, in stiff good clothes, on Sundays. That is the part of the town we used to know when we lived at Dungannon and came here three or four times a summer, to the Lake. That, and the docks where we would go and look at the grain boats, ancient, rusty, wallowing, making us wonder how they got past the breakwater let alone to Fort William.

Tramps hang around the docks and occasionally on these evenings wander up the dwindling beach and climb the shifting, precarious path boys have made, hanging on to dry bushes, and say something to my father which, being frightened of tramps, I am too alarmed to catch. My father says he is a bit hard up himself. "I'll roll you a cigarette if it's any use to you," he says, and he shakes tobacco out carefully on one of the thin butterfly papers, flicks it with his tongue, seals it and hands it to the tramp, who takes it and walks away. My father also rolls and lights and smokes one cigarette of his own.

He tells me how the Great Lakes came to be. All where Lake Huron is now, he says, used to be flat land, a wide flat plain. Then came the ice, creeping down from the North, pushing deep into the low places. Like *that*—and he shows me his hand with his spread fingers pressing the rock-hard ground where we are sitting. His fingers make hardly any impression at all and he says, "Well, the old ice cap had a lot more power behind it than this hand has." And then the ice went back, shrank back towards the North Pole where it came from, and left its fingers of ice in the deep places it had gouged, and ice turned to lakes and there they were today. They were *new*, as time went. I try to see that plain before me, dinosaurs walking on it, but I am not able even to imagine the shore of the Lake when the Indians were there, before Tuppertown. The tiny share we have of time appalls me, though my father seems to regard it with tranquillity. Even my father, who sometimes seems to me to have been at home in the world as long as it has lasted, has really lived on this earth only a little longer than I have, in terms of all the time there has been to live in. He has not known a time, any more than I, when automobiles and electric lights did not at least exist. He was not alive when this century started. I will be barely alive—old, old—when it ends. I do not like to think of it. I wish the Lake to be always just a lake, with the safe-swimming floats marking it, and the breakwater and the lights of Tuppertown.

MY FATHER has a job, selling for Walker Brothers. This is a firm that sells almost entirely in the country, the back country. Sunshine, Boylesbridge, Turnaround—that is all his territory. Not Dungannon where we used to live, Dungannon is too near town and my mother is grateful for that. He sells cough medicine, iron tonic, corn plasters, laxatives, pills for female disorders, mouthwash, shampoo, liniment, salves, lemon and orange and raspberry concentrate for making refreshing drinks, vanilla, food coloring, black and green tea, ginger, cloves, and other spices, rat poison. He has a song about it, with these two lines:

> *And have all liniments and oils,*
> *For everything from corns to boils....*

Not a very funny song, in my mother's opinion. A peddler's song, and that is what he is, a peddler knocking at backwoods kitchens. Up until last winter we had our own business, a fox farm. My father raised silver foxes and sold their pelts to the people who make them into capes and coats and muffs. Prices fell, my father hung on hoping they would get better next year, and they fell again, and he hung on one more year and one more and finally it was not possible to hang on anymore, we owed everything to the feed company. I have heard my mother explain this, several times, to Mrs. Oliphant, who is the only neighbor she talks to. (Mrs. Oliphant also has come down in the world, being a schoolteacher who married the janitor.) We poured all we had into it, my mother says, and we came out with nothing. Many people could say the same thing, these days, but my mother has no time for the national calamity, only ours. Fate has flung us onto a street of poor people (it does not matter that we were poor before; that was a different sort of poverty), and the only way to take this, as she sees it, is with dignity, with bitterness, with no reconciliation. No bathroom with a claw-footed tub and a flush toilet is going to comfort her, nor water on tap and sidewalks past the house and milk in bottles, not even the two movie theatres and the Venus Restaurant and Woolworths so marvellous it has live birds singing in its fan-cooled corners and fish as tiny as fingernails, as bright as moons, swimming in its green tanks. My mother does not care.

In the afternoons she often walks to Simon's Grocery and takes me with her to help carry things. She wears a good dress, navy blue with little flowers, sheer, worn over a navy-blue slip. Also a summer hat of white straw, pushed down on the side of the head, and white shoes I have just whitened on a newspaper on the back steps. I have my hair freshly done in long damp curls which the dry air will fortunately soon loosen, a stiff large hair ribbon on top of my head. This is entirely different from going out after supper with my father. We have not walked past two houses before I feel we have become objects of universal ridicule. Even the dirty words chalked on the sidewalk are laughing at us. My mother does not seem to notice. She walks serenely like a lady shopping, like a *lady* shopping, past the housewives in loose beltless dresses torn under the arms. With me her creation, wretched curls and flaunting hair bow, scrubbed knees and white socks—all I do not want to be. I loathe even my name when she says it in public, in a voice so high, proud, and ringing, deliberately different from the voice of any other mother on the street.

My mother will sometimes carry home, for a treat, a brick of ice cream—pale Neapolitan; and because we have no refrigerator in our house we wake my brother and eat it at once in the dining room, always darkened by the wall of the house next door. I spoon it up tenderly, leaving the chocolate till last, hoping to have some still to eat when my brother's dish is empty. My mother tries then to imitate the conversations we used to have at Dungannon, going back to our earliest, most leisurely days before my brother was born, when she would give me a little tea and a lot of milk in a cup like hers and we would sit out on the step facing the pump, the lilac tree, the fox pens beyond. She is not able to keep from mentioning those days. "Do you remember when we put you in your sled and Major pulled you?" (Major our dog, that we had to leave with neighbors when we moved.) "Do you remember your sandbox outside the kitchen window?" I pretend to remember far less than I do, wary of being trapped into sympathy or any unwanted emotion.

My mother has headaches. She often has to lie down. She lies on my brother's narrow bed in the little screened porch, shaded by heavy branches. "I look up at that tree and I think I am at home," she says.

"What you need," my father tells her, "is some fresh air and a drive in the country." He means for her to go with him, on his Walker Brothers route.

That is not my mother's idea of a drive in the country.

"Can I come?"

"Your mother might want you for trying on clothes."

"I'm beyond sewing this afternoon," my mother says.

"I'll take her then. Take both of them, give you a rest."

What is there about us that people need to be given a rest from? Never mind. I am glad enough to find my brother and make him go to the toilet and get us both into the car, our knees unscrubbed, my hair unringleted. My father brings from the house his two heavy brown suitcases, full of bottles, and sets them on the back seat. He wears a white shirt, brilliant in the sunlight, a tie, light trousers belonging to his summer suit (his other suit is black, for funerals, and belonged to my uncle before he died), and a creamy straw hat. His salesman's outfit, with pencils clipped in the shirt pocket. He goes back once again, probably to say goodbye to my mother, to ask her if she is sure she doesn't want to come, and hear her say, "No. No thanks, I'm better just to lie here with my eyes closed." Then we are backing out of the driveway with the rising hope of adventure, just the little hope that takes you over the bump into the street, the hot air starting to move, turning into a breeze, the houses growing less and less familiar as we follow the shortcut my father knows, the quick way out of town. Yet what is there waiting for us all afternoon but hot hours in stricken farm-yards, perhaps a stop at a country store and three ice-cream cones or bottles of pop, and my father singing? The one he made up about himself has a title—"The Walker Brothers Cowboy"—and it starts out like this:

> *Old Ned Fields, he now is dead,*
> *So I am ridin' the route instead. . . .*

Who is Ned Fields? The man he has replaced, surely, and if so he really is dead; yet my father's voice is mournful-jolly, making his death some kind of nonsense, a comic calamity. "Wisht I was back on the Rio Grande, plungin' through the dusky sand." My father sings most of the time while driving the car. Even now, heading out of town, crossing the bridge and taking the sharp turn onto the highway, he is humming something, mum-bling a bit of a song to himself, just tuning up, really, getting ready to im-provise, for out along the highway we pass the Baptist Camp, the Vacation Bible Camp, and he lets loose:

> *"Where are the Baptists, where are the Baptists,*
> *where are all the Baptists today?*
> *They're down in the water, in Lake Huron water,*
> *with their sins all a-gittin' washed away."*

My brother takes this for straight truth and gets up on his knees trying to see down to the Lake. "I don't see any Baptists," he says accusingly. "Nei-ther do I, son," says my father. "I told you, they're down in the Lake."

No roads paved when we left the highway. We have to roll up the win-dows because of dust. The land is flat, scorched, empty. Bush lots at the back of the farms hold shade, black pine-shade like pools nobody can ever get to. We bump up a long lane and at the end of it what could look more unwelcoming, more deserted than the tall unpainted farmhouse with grass growing uncut right up to the front door, green blinds down, and a door upstairs opening on nothing but air? Many houses have this door, and I have never yet been able to find out why. I ask my father and he says they are for walking in your sleep. *What?* Well, if you happen to be walking in your sleep and you want to step outside. I am offended, seeing too late that he is joking, as usual, but my brother says sturdily, "If they did that they would break their necks."

The 1930s. How much this kind of farmhouse, this kind of afternoon seem to me to belong to that one decade in time, just as my father's hat does, his bright flared tie, our car with its wide running board (an Essex, and long past its prime). Cars somewhat like it, many older, none dustier, sit in the farmyards. Some are past running and have their doors pulled off, their seats removed for use on porches. No living things to be seen, chickens or cattle. Except dogs. There are dogs lying in any kind of shade they can find, dreaming, their lean sides rising and sinking rapidly. They get up when my father opens the car door, he has to speak to them. "Nice boy, there's a boy, nice old boy." They quiet down, go back to their shade. He should know how to quiet animals, he has held desperate foxes with tongs around their necks. One gentling voice for the dogs and another, rousing, cheerful, for calling at doors. "Hello there, missus, it's the Walker Brothers man and what are you out of today?" A door opens, he disappears. Forbidden to follow, forbidden even to leave the car, we can just wait and wonder what he says. Sometimes trying to make my mother laugh, he pretends to be himself in a farm kitchen, spreading out his sample case. "Now then, missus, are you troubled with parasitic life? Your children's scalps, I mean. All those crawly little things we're too polite to mention that show up on the heads of the best of families? Soap alone is useless, kerosene is not too nice a perfume, but I have here—" Or else, "Believe me, sitting and driving all day the way I do I *know* the value of these fine pills. Natural relief. A problem common to old folks too, once their days of activity are over— How about you, Grandma?" He would wave the imaginary box of pills under my mother's nose and she would laugh finally, unwillingly. "He doesn't say that really, does he?" I said, and she said no of course not, he was too much of a gentleman.

One yard after another, then, the old cars, the pumps, dogs, views of gray barns and falling-down sheds and unturning windmills. The men, if they are working in the fields, are not in any fields that we can see. The children are far away, following dry creek beds or looking for blackberries, or else they are hidden in the house, spying at us through cracks in the blinds. The car seat has grown slick with our sweat. I dare my brother to sound the horn, wanting to do it myself but not wanting to get the blame. He knows better. We play I Spy, but it is hard to find many colors. Gray for the barns and sheds and toilets and houses, brown for the yard and fields, black or brown for the dogs. The rusting cars show rainbow patches, in which I strain to pick out purple or green; likewise I peer at doors for shreds of old peeling paint, maroon or yellow. We can't play with letters, which would be better, because my brother is too young to spell. The game disintegrates anyway. He claims my colors are not fair, and wants extra turns.

In one house no door opens, though the car is in the yard. My father knocks and whistles, calls, "Hullo there! Walker Brothers man!" but there is not a stir of reply anywhere. This house has no porch, just a bare, slanting slab of cement on which my father stands. He turns around, searching the barnyard, the barn whose mow must be empty because you can see the sky through it, and finally he bends to pick up his suitcases. Just then a window is opened upstairs, a white pot appears on the sill, is tilted over and its contents splash down the outside wall. The window is not directly above my father's head, so only a stray splash would catch him. He picks up his suitcases with no particular hurry and walks, no longer whistling, to the car. "Do you know what that was?" I say to my brother. *"Pee."* He laughs and laughs.

My father rolls and lights a cigarette before he starts the car. The window has been slammed down, the blind drawn, we never did see a hand or face. "Pee, pee," sings my brother ecstatically. "Somebody dumped down pee!" "Just don't tell your mother that," my father says. "She isn't liable to see the joke." "Is it in your song?" my brother wants to know. My father says no but he will see what he can do to work it in.

I notice in a little while that we are not turning in any more lanes, though it does not seem to me that we are headed home. "Is this the way to Sunshine?" I ask my father, and he answers, "No, ma'am, it's not." "Are we still in your territory?" He shakes his head. "We're going *fast*," my brother says approvingly, and in fact we are bouncing along through dry puddle-holes so that all the bottles in the suitcases clink together and gurgle promisingly.

Another lane, a house, also unpainted, dried to silver in the sun.

"I thought we were out of your territory."

"We are."

"Then what are we going in here for?"

"You'll see."

In front of the house a short, sturdy woman is picking up washing, which had been spread on the grass to bleach and dry. When the car stops she stares at it hard for a moment, bends to pick up a couple more towels to add to the bundle under her arm, comes across to us and says in a flat voice, neither welcoming nor unfriendly, "Have you lost your way?"

My father takes his time getting out of the car. "I don't think so," he says. "I'm the Walker Brothers man."

"George Golley is our Walker Brothers man," the woman says, "and he was out here no more than a week ago. Oh, my Lord God," she says harshly, "it's you."

"It was, the last time I looked in the mirror," my father says.

The woman gathers all the towels in front of her and holds on to them tightly, pushing them against her stomach as if it hurt. "Of all the people I never thought to see. And telling me you were the Walker Brothers man."

"I'm sorry if you were looking forward to George Golley," my father says humbly.

"And look at me, I was prepared to clean the henhouse. You'll think that's just an excuse but it's true. I don't go round looking like this every day." She is wearing a farmer's straw hat, through which pricks of sunlight penetrate and float on her face, a loose, dirty print smock, and canvas shoes. "Who are those in the car, Ben? They're not yours?"

"Well, I hope and believe they are," my father says, and tells our names and ages. "Come on, you can get out. This is Nora, Miss Cronin. Nora, you better tell me, is it still Miss, or have you got a husband hiding in the woodshed?"

"If I had a husband that's not where I'd keep him, Ben," she says, and they both laugh, her laugh abrupt and somewhat angry. "You'll think I got no manners, as well as being dressed like a tramp," she says. "Come on in out of the sun. It's cool in the house."

We go across the yard ("Excuse me taking you in this way but I don't think the front door has been opened since Papa's funeral, I'm afraid the hinges might drop off"), up the porch steps, into the kitchen, which really is cool, high-ceilinged, the blinds of course down, a simple, clean, thread-bare room with waxed worn linoleum, potted geraniums, drinking-pail and dipper, a round table with scrubbed oilcloth. In spite of the cleanness, the wiped and swept surfaces, there is a faint sour smell—maybe of the dishrag or the tin dipper or the oilcloth, or the old lady, because there is one, sitting in an easy chair under the clock shelf. She turns her head slightly in our direction and says, "Nora? Is that company?"

"Blind," says Nora in a quick explaining voice to my father. Then, "You won't guess who it is, Momma. Hear his voice."

My father goes to the front of her chair and bends and says hopefully, "Afternoon, Mrs. Cronin."

"Ben Jordan," says the old lady with no surprise. "You haven't been to see us in the longest time. Have you been out of the country?"

My father and Nora look at each other.

"He's married, Momma," says Nora cheerfully and aggressively. "Married and got two children and here they are." She pulls us forward, makes each of us touch the old lady's dry, cool hand while she says our names in turn. Blind! This is the first blind person I have ever seen close up. Her eyes are closed, the eyelids sunk away down, showing no shape of the eyeball, just hollows. From one hollow comes a drop of silver liquid, a medicine, or a miraculous tear.

"Let me get into a decent dress," Nora says. "Talk to Momma. It's a treat for her. We hardly ever see company, do we, Momma?"

"Not many makes it out this road," says the old lady placidly. "And the ones that used to be around here, our old neighbors, some of them have pulled out."

"True everywhere," my father says.

"Where's your wife then?"

"Home. She's not too fond of the hot weather, makes her feel poorly."

"Well." This is a habit of country people, old people, to say "well," meaning, "Is that so?" with a little extra politeness and concern.

Nora's dress, when she appears again—stepping heavily on Cuban heels down the stairs in the hall—is flowered more lavishly than anything my mother owns, green and yellow on brown, some sort of floating sheer crêpe, leaving her arms bare. Her arms are heavy, and every bit of her skin you can see is covered with little dark freckles like measles. Her hair is short, black, coarse and curly, her teeth very white and strong. "It's the first time I knew there was such a thing as green poppies," my father says, looking at her dress.

"You would be surprised all the things you never knew," says Nora, sending a smell of cologne far and wide when she moves and displaying a change of voice to go with the dress, something more sociable and youthful. "They're not poppies anyway, they're just flowers. You go and pump me some good cold water and I'll make these children a drink." She gets down from the cupboard a bottle of Walker Brothers Orange syrup.

"You telling me you were the Walker Brothers man!"

"It's the truth, Nora. You go and look at my sample cases in the car if you don't believe me. I got the territory directly south of here."

"Walker Brothers? Is that a fact? You selling for Walker Brothers?"

"Yes, ma'am."

"We always heard you were raising foxes over Dungannon way."

"That's what I was doing, but I kind of run out of luck in that business."

"So where're you living? How long've you been out selling?"

"We moved into Tuppertown. I been at it, oh, two, three months. It keeps the wolf from the door. Keeps him as far away as the back fence."

Nora laughs. "Well, I guess you count yourself lucky to have the work. Isabel's husband in Brantford, he was out of work the longest time. I thought if he didn't find something soon I was going to have them all land in here to feed, and I tell you I was hardly looking forward to it. It's all I can manage with me and Momma."

"Isabel married," my father says. "Muriel married too?"

"No, she's teaching school out West. She hasn't been home for five years. I guess she finds something better to do with her holidays. I would if I was her." She gets some snapshots out of the table drawer and starts showing him. "That's Isabel's oldest boy, starting school. That's the baby sitting in her carriage. Isabel and her husband. Muriel. That's her room-mate with her. That's a fellow she used to go around with, and his car. He was working in a bank out there. That's her school, it has eight rooms. She teaches Grade Five." My father shakes his head. "I can't think of her any way but when she was going to school, so shy I used to pick her up on the road—I'd be on my way to see you—and she would not say one word, not even to agree it was a nice day."

"She's got over that."

"Who are you talking about?" says the old lady.

"Muriel. I said she's got over being shy."

"She was here last summer."

"No, Momma, that was Isabel. Isabel and her family were here last summer. Muriel's out West."

"I meant Isabel."

Shortly after this the old lady falls asleep, her head on the side, her mouth open. "Excuse her manners," Nora says. "It's old age." She fixes an afghan over her mother and says we can all go into the front room where our talking won't disturb her.

"You two," my father says. "Do you want to go outside and amuse yourselves?"

Amuse ourselves how? Anyway, I want to stay. The front room is more interesting than the kitchen, though barer. There is a gramophone and a pump organ and a picture on the wall of Mary, Jesus' mother—I know that much—in shades of bright blue and pink with a spiked band of light around her head. I know that such pictures are found only in the homes of Roman Catholics and so Nora must be one. We have never known any Roman Catholics at all well, never well enough to visit in their houses. I think of what my grandmother and my Aunt Tena, over in Dungannon, used to always say to indicate that somebody was a Catholic. *So-and-so digs with the wrong foot,* they would say. *She digs with the wrong foot.* That was what they would say about Nora.

Nora takes a bottle, half full, out of the top of the organ and pours some of what is in it into the two glasses that she and my father have emptied of the orange drink.

"Keep it in case of sickness?" my father says.

"Not on your life," says Nora. "I'm never sick. I just keep it because I keep it. One bottle does me a fair time, though, because I don't care for drinking alone. Here's luck!" She and my father drink and I know what it is. Whisky. One of the things my mother has told me in our talks together is that my father never drinks whisky. But I see he does. He drinks whisky and he talks of people whose names I have never heard before. But after a while he turns to a familiar incident. He tells about the chamberpot that was emptied out the window. "Picture me there," he says, "hollering my heartiest. *Oh, lady, it's your Walker Brothers man, anybody home?*" He does himself hollering, grinning absurdly, waiting, looking up in pleased expectation, and then—oh, ducking, covering his head with his arms, looking as if he begged for mercy (when he never did anything like that, I was watching), and Nora laughs, almost as hard as my brother did at the time.

"That isn't true! That's not a word true!"

"Oh, indeed it is, ma'am. We have our heroes in the ranks of Walker Brothers. I'm glad you think it's funny," he says sombrely.

I ask him shyly, "Sing the song."

"What song? Have you turned into a singer on top of everything else?"

Embarrassed, my father says, "Oh, just this song I made up while I was driving around, it gives me something to do, making up rhymes."

But after some urging he does sing it, looking at Nora with a droll, apologetic expression, and she laughs so much that in places he has to stop and wait for her to get over laughing so he can go on, because she makes him laugh too. Then he does various parts of his salesman's spiel. Nora when she laughs squeezes her large bosom under her folded arms. "You're crazy," she says. "That's all you are." She sees my brother peering into the gramophone and she jumps up and goes over to him. "Here's us sitting enjoying ourselves and not giving you a thought, isn't it terrible?" she says. "You want me to put a record on, don't you? You want to hear a nice record? Can you dance? I bet your sister can, can't she?"

I say no. "A big girl like you and so good-looking and can't dance!" says Nora. "It's high time you learned. I bet you'd make a lovely dancer. Here, I'm going to put on a piece I used to dance to and even your daddy did, in his dancing days. You didn't know your daddy was a dancer, did you? Well, he is a talented man, your daddy!"

She puts down the lid and takes hold of me unexpectedly around the waist, picks up my other hand, and starts making me go backwards. "This is the way, now, this is how they dance. Follow me. This foot, see. One and one-two. One and one-two. That's fine, that's lovely, don't look at your feet! Follow me, that's right, see how easy? You're going to be a lovely dancer! One and one-two. One and one-two. Ben, see your daughter dancing!" *Whispering while you cuddle near me, Whispering so no one can hear me.* . . .

Round and round the linoleum, me proud, intent, Nora laughing and moving with great buoyancy, wrapping me in her strange gaiety, her smell of whisky, cologne, and sweat. Under the arms her dress is damp, and little drops form along her upper lip, hang in the soft black hairs at the corners of her mouth. She whirls me around in front of my father—causing me to stumble, for I am by no means so swift a pupil as she pretends—and lets me go, breathless.

"Dance with me, Ben."

"I'm the world's worst dancer, Nora, and you know it."

"I certainly never thought so."

"You would now."

She stands in front of him, arms hanging loose and hopeful, her breasts, which a moment ago embarrassed me with their warmth and bulk, rising and falling under her loose flowered dress, her face shining with the exercise, and delight.

"Ben."

My father drops his head and says quietly, "Not me, Nora."

So she can only go and take the record off. "I can drink alone but I can't dance alone," she says. "Unless I am a whole lot crazier than I think I am."

"Nora," says my father, smiling. "You're not crazy."

"Stay for supper."

"Oh, no. We couldn't put you to the trouble."

"It's no trouble. I'd be glad of it."

"And their mother would worry. She'd think I'd turned us over in a ditch."

"Oh, well. Yes."

"We've taken a lot of your time now."

"Time," says Nora bitterly. "Will you come by ever again?"

"I will if I can," says my father.

"Bring the children. Bring your wife."

"Yes, I will," says my father. "I will if I can."

When she follows us to the car he says, "You come to see us too, Nora. We're right on Grove Street, left-hand side going in, that's north, and two doors this side—east—of Baker Street."

Nora does not repeat these directions. She stands close to the car in her soft, brilliant dress. She touches the fender, making an unintelligible mark in the dust there.

ON THE WAY home my father does not buy any ice cream or pop, but he does go into a country store and get a package of licorice, which he shares with us. She digs with the wrong foot, I think, and the words seem sad to me as never before, dark, perverse. My father does not say anything to me about not mentioning things at home, but I know, just from the thoughtfulness, the pause when he passes the licorice, that there are things not to be mentioned. The whisky, maybe the dancing. No worry about my brother, he does not notice enough. At most he might remember the blind lady, the picture of Mary.

"Sing," my brother commands my father, but my father says gravely, "I don't know, I seem to be fresh out of songs. You watch the road and let me know if you see any rabbits."

So my father drives and my brother watches the road for rabbits and I feel my father's life flowing back from our car in the last of the afternoon, darkening and turning strange, like a landscape that has an enchantment on it, making it kindly, ordinary and familiar while you are looking at it, but changing it, once your back is turned, into something you will never know, with all kinds of weathers, and distances you cannot imagine.

When we get closer to Tuppertown the sky becomes gently overcast, as always, nearly always, on summer evenings by the Lake.

# Dance of the Happy Shades

∾

MISS MARSALLES is having another party. (Out of musical integrity, or her heart's bold yearning for festivity, she never calls it a recital.) My mother is not an inventive or convincing liar, and the excuses which occur to her are obviously second-rate. The painters are coming. Friends from Ottawa. Poor Carrie is having her tonsils out. In the end all she can say is: Oh, but won't all that be too much trouble, *now*? *Now* being weighted with several troublesome meanings; you may take your choice. Now that Miss Marsalles has moved from the brick-and-frame bungalow on Bank Street, where the last three parties have been rather squashed, to an even smaller place—if she has described it correctly—on Bala Street. (Bala Street, where is that?) Or: now that Miss Marsalles' older sister is in bed, following a stroke; now that Miss Marsalles herself—as my mother says, we must face these things—is simply getting *too old*.

*Now?* asks Miss Marsalles, stung, pretending mystification, or perhaps for that matter really feeling it. And she asks how her June party could ever be too much trouble, at any time, in any place? It is the only entertainment she ever gives anymore (so far as my mother knows it is the only entertainment she ever has given, but Miss Marsalles' light old voice, undismayed, indefatigably social, supplies the ghosts of tea parties, private dances, At Homes, mammoth Family Dinners). She would suffer, she says, as much disappointment as the children, if she were to give it up. Considerably more, says my mother to herself, but of course she cannot say it aloud; she turns her face from the telephone with that look of irritation—as if she had seen something messy which she was unable to clean up—which is her private expression of pity. And she promises to come;

weak schemes for getting out of it will occur to her during the next two weeks, but she knows she will be there.

She phones up Marg French, who like herself is an old pupil of Miss Marsalles and who has been having lessons for her twins, and they commiserate for a while and promise to go together and buck each other up. They remember the year before last when it rained and the little hall was full of raincoats piled on top of each other because there was no place to hang them up, and the umbrellas dripped puddles on the dark floor. The little girls' dresses were crushed because of the way they all had to squeeze together, and the living-room windows would not open. Last year a child had a nosebleed.

"Of course that was not Miss Marsalles' fault."

They giggle despairingly. "No. But things like that did not use to happen."

And that is true; that is the whole thing. There is a feeling that can hardly be put into words about Miss Marsalles' parties; things are getting out of hand, anything may happen. There is even a moment, driving in to such a party, when the question occurs: will anybody else be there? For one of the most disconcerting things about the last two or three parties has been the widening gap in the ranks of the regulars, the old pupils whose children seem to be the only new pupils Miss Marsalles ever has. Every June reveals some new and surely significant dropping-out. Mary Lambert's girl no longer takes; neither does Joan Crimble's. What does this mean? think my mother and Marg French, women who have moved to the suburbs and are plagued sometimes by a feeling that they have fallen behind, that their instincts for doing the right thing have become confused. Piano lessons are not so important now as they once were; everybody knows that. Dancing is believed to be more favorable to the development of the whole child—and the children, at least the girls, don't seem to mind it as much. But how are you to explain that to Miss Marsalles, who says, "All children need music. All children love music in their hearts"? It is one of Miss Marsalles' indestructible beliefs that she can see into children's hearts, and she finds there a treasury of good intentions and a natural love of all good things. The deceits which her spinster's sentimentality has practiced on her original good judgment are legendary and colossal; she has this way of speaking of children's hearts as if they were something holy; it is hard for a parent to know what to say.

In the old days, when my sister Winifred took lessons, the address was in Rosedale; that was where it had always been. A narrow house, built of soot-and-raspberry-colored brick, grim little ornamental balconies curving out from the second-floor windows, no towers anywhere but somehow a turreted effect; dark, pretentious, poetically ugly—the family home. And in Rosedale the annual party did not go off too badly. There was always an awkward little space before the sandwiches, because the woman they had in the kitchen was not used to parties and rather slow, but the sandwiches when they did appear were always very good: chicken, asparagus rolls, wholesome, familiar things—dressed-up nursery food. The performances on the piano were, as usual, nervous and choppy or sullen and spiritless, with the occasional surprise and interest of a lively disaster. It will be understood that Miss Marsalles' idealistic view of children, her tender- or simple-mindedness in that regard, made her almost useless as a teacher; she was unable to criticize except in the most delicate and apologetic way and her praises were unforgivably dishonest; it took an unusually conscientious pupil to come through with anything like a creditable performance.

But on the whole the affair in those days had solidity, it had tradition; in its own serenely out-of-date way it had style. Everything was always as expected; Miss Marsalles herself, waiting in the entrance hall with the tiled floor and the dark, church-vestry smell, wearing rouge, an antique hairdo adopted only on this occasion, and a floor-length dress of plum and pinkish splotches that might have been made out of old upholstery material, startled no one but the youngest children. Even the shadow behind her of another Miss Marsalles, slightly older, larger, grimmer, whose existence was always forgotten from one June to the next, was not discomfiting— though it was surely an arresting fact that there should be not one but two faces like that in the world, both long, gravel-colored, kindly, and grotesque, with enormous noses and tiny, red, sweet-tempered and short-sighted eyes. It must finally have come to seem like a piece of luck to them to be so ugly, a protection against life to be marked in so many ways, *impossible*, for they were gay as invulnerable and childish people are; they appeared sexless, wild, and gentle creatures, bizarre yet domestic, living in their house in Rosedale outside the complications of time.

In the room where the mothers sat, some on hard sofas, some on folding chairs, to hear the children play "The Gypsy Song," "The Harmonious Blacksmith," and the "Turkish March," there was a picture of Mary, Queen of Scots, in velvet, with a silk veil, in front of Holyrood Palace. There were brown misty pictures of historical battles, also the Harvard Classics, iron firedogs, and a bronze Pegasus. None of the mothers smoked, nor were ashtrays provided. It was the same room, exactly the same room, in which they had performed themselves; a room whose dim impersonal style (the flossy bunch of peonies and spirea dropping petals on the piano was Miss Marsalles' own touch, and not entirely happy) was at the same time uncomfortable and reassuring. Here they found themselves year after year— a group of busy, youngish women who had eased their cars impatiently through the archaic streets of Rosedale, who had complained for a week previously about the time lost, the fuss over the children's dresses, and, above all, the boredom, but who were drawn together by a rather implausible allegiance—not so much to Miss Marsalles as to the ceremonies of their childhood, to a more exacting pattern of life which had been breaking apart even then but which survived, and unaccountably still survived, in Miss Marsalles' living room. The little girls in dresses with skirts as stiff as bells moved with a natural awareness of ceremony against the dark walls of books, and their mothers' faces wore the dull, not unpleasant look of acquiescence, the touch of absurd and slightly artificial nostalgia which would carry them through any lengthy family ritual. They exchanged smiles which showed no lack of good manners, and yet expressed a familiar, humorous amazement at the sameness of things, even the selections played on the piano and the fillings of the sandwiches; so they acknowledged the incredible, the wholly unrealistic persistence of Miss Marsalles and her sister and their life.

After the piano-playing came a little ceremony which always caused some embarrassment. Before the children were allowed to escape to the garden—very narrow, a town garden, but still a garden, with hedges, shade, a border of yellow lilies—where a long table was covered with crêpe paper in infants' colors of pink and blue, and the woman from the kitchen set out plates of sandwiches, ice cream, prettily tinted and tasteless sherbet, they were compelled to accept, one by one, a year's-end gift, all wrapped and tied with ribbon, from Miss Marsalles. Except among the most naive new pupils this gift caused no excitement of anticipation. It was apt to be a book, and the question was, where did she find such books? They were of the vintage found in old Sunday-school libraries, in attics and the basements of secondhand stores, but they were all stiff-backed, unread, brand new. *Northern Lakes and Rivers, Knowing the Birds, More Tales by Grey Owl, Little Mission Friends.* She also gave pictures: "Cupid Awake and Cupid Asleep," "After the Bath," "The Little Vigilantes"; most of these seemed to feature that tender childish nudity which our sophisticated prudery found most ridiculous and disgusting. Even the boxed games she gave us proved to be insipid and unplayable—full of complicated rules which allowed everybody to win.

The embarrassment the mothers felt at this time was due not so much to the presents themselves as to a strong doubt whether Miss Marsalles could afford them; it did not help to remember that her fees had gone up only once in ten years (and even when that happened, two or three mothers had quit). They always ended up by saying that she must have other resources. It was obvious—otherwise she would not be living in this house. And then her sister taught—or did not teach anymore; she was retired but she gave private lessons, it was believed, in French and German. They must have enough, between them. If you are a Miss Marsalles your wants are simple and it does not cost a great deal to live.

But after the house in Rosedale was gone, after it had given way to the bungalow on Bank Street, these conversations about Miss Marsalles' means did not take place; this aspect of Miss Marsalles' life had passed into that region of painful subjects which it is crude and unmannerly to discuss.

"I WILL DIE if it rains," my mother says. "I will die of depression at this affair if it rains." But the day of the party it does not rain and in fact the weather is very hot. It is a hot gritty summer day as we drive down into the city and get lost, looking for Bala Street.

When we find it, it gives the impression of being better than we expected, but that is mostly because it has a row of trees, and the other streets we have been driving through, along the railway embankment, have been unshaded and slatternly. The houses here are of the sort that are divided in half, with a sloping wooden partition in the middle of the front porch; they have two wooden steps and a dirt yard. Apparently it is in one of these half-houses that Miss Marsalles lives. They are red brick, with the front door and the window trim and the porches painted cream, gray, oily-green, and yellow. They are neat, kept-up. The front part of the house next to the one where Miss Marsalles lives has been turned into a little store; it has a sign that says: GROCERIES AND CONFECTIONERY.

The door is standing open. Miss Marsalles is wedged between the door, the coatrack, and the stairs; there is barely room to get past her into the living room, and it would be impossible, the way things are now, for anyone to get from the living room upstairs. Miss Marsalles is wearing her rouge, her hairdo, and her brocaded dress, which it is difficult not to tramp on. In this full light she looks like a character in a masquerade, like the feverish, fancied-up courtesan of an unpleasant Puritan imagination. But the fever is only her rouge; her eyes, when we get close enough to see them, are the same as ever, red-rimmed and merry and without apprehension. My mother and I are kissed—I am greeted, as always, as if I were around five years old—and we get past. It seemed to me that Miss Marsalles was looking beyond us as she kissed us; she was looking up the street for someone who has not yet arrived.

The house has a living room and a dining room, with the oak doors pushed back between them. They are small rooms. Mary, Queen of Scots, hangs tremendous on the wall. There is no fireplace so the iron firedogs are not there, but the piano is, and even a bouquet of peonies and spirea from goodness knows what garden. Since it is so small the living room looks crowded, but there are not a dozen people in it, including children. My mother speaks to people and smiles and sits down. She says to me, Marg French is not here yet, could she have got lost too?

The woman sitting beside us is not familiar. She is middle-aged and wears a dress of shot taffeta with rhinestone clips; it smells of the cleaners. She introduces herself as Mrs. Clegg, Miss Marsalles' neighbor in the other half of the house. Miss Marsalles has asked her if she would like to hear the children play, and she thought it would be a treat; she is fond of music in any form.

My mother, very pleasant but looking a little uncomfortable, asks about Miss Marsalles' sister; is she upstairs?

"Oh, yes, she's upstairs. She's not herself though, poor thing."

That is too bad, my mother says.

"Yes, it's a shame. I give her something to put her to sleep for the afternoon. She lost her powers of speech, you know. Her powers of control generally, she lost." My mother is warned by a certain luxurious lowering of the voice that more lengthy and intimate details may follow and she says quickly again that it is too bad.

"I come in and look after her when the other one goes out on her lessons."

"That's very kind of you. I'm sure she appreciates it."

"Oh, well, I feel kind of sorry for a couple of old ladies like them. They're a couple of babies, the pair."

My mother murmurs something in reply but she is not looking at Mrs. Clegg, at her brick-red healthy face or the—to me—amazing gaps in her teeth. She is staring past her into the dining room with fairly well controlled dismay.

What she sees there is the table spread, all ready for the party feast; nothing is lacking. The plates of sandwiches are set out, as they must have been for several hours now; you can see how the ones on top are beginning to curl very slightly at the edges. Flies buzz over the table, settle on the sandwiches, and crawl comfortably across the plates of little iced cakes brought from the bakery. The cut-glass bowl, sitting as usual in the center of the table, is full of purple punch, without ice apparently and going flat.

"I tried to tell her not to put it all out ahead of time," Mrs. Clegg whispers, smiling delightedly, as if she were talking about the whims and errors of some headstrong child. "You know she was up at five o'clock this morning making sandwiches. I don't know what things are going to taste like. Afraid she wouldn't be ready, I guess. Afraid she'd forget something. They hate to forget."

"Food shouldn't be left out in the hot weather," my mother says.

"Oh, well, I guess it won't poison us for once. I was only thinking what a shame to have the sandwiches dry up. And when she put the ginger ale in the punch at noon I had to laugh. But what a waste."

My mother shifts and rearranges her voile skirt, as if she has suddenly become aware of the impropriety, the hideousness even, of discussing a hostess's arrangements in this way in her own living room. "Marg French isn't here," she says to me, in a hardening voice. "She did say she was coming."

"I am the oldest girl here," I say with disgust.

"Shh. That means you can play last. Well. It won't be a very long program this year, will it?"

Mrs. Clegg leans across us, letting loose a cloud of warm unfresh odor from between her breasts. "I'm going to see if she's got the fridge turned up high enough for the ice cream. She'd feel awful if it was all to melt."

My mother goes across the room and speaks to a woman she knows and I can tell that she is saying, Marg French *said* she was *coming*. The women's faces in the room, made up some time before, have begun to show the effects of heat and a fairly general uneasiness. They ask each other when it will begin. Surely very soon now; nobody has arrived for at least a quarter of an hour. How mean of people not to come, they say. Yet in this heat, and the heat is particularly dreadful down here, it must be the worst place in the city—well you can almost see their point. I look around and calculate that there is no one in the room within a year of my age.

The little children begin to play. Miss Marsalles and Mrs. Clegg applaud with enthusiasm; the mothers clap two or three times each, with relief. My mother seems unable, although she makes a great effort, to take her eyes off the dining-room table and the complacent journeys of the marauding flies. Finally she achieves a dreamy, distant look, with her eyes focussed somewhere above the punch bowl, which makes it possible for her to keep her head turned in that direction and yet does not in any positive sense give her away. Miss Marsalles as well has trouble keeping her eyes on the performers; she keeps looking towards the door. Does she expect that even now some of the unexplained absentees may turn up? There are far more than half a dozen presents in the inevitable box beside the piano, wrapped in white paper and tied with silver ribbon—not real ribbon, but the cheap kind that splits and shreds.

It is while I am at the piano, playing the minuet from *Berenice*, that the final arrival, unlooked-for by anybody but Miss Marsalles, takes place. It must seem at first that there has been some mistake. Out of the corner of my eye I see a whole procession of children, eight or ten in all, with a red-haired woman in something like a uniform, mounting the front step. They look like a group of children from a private school on an excursion of some kind (there is that drabness and sameness about their clothes) but their progress is too scrambling and disorderly for that. Or this is the impression I have; I cannot really look. Is it the wrong house, are they really on their way to the doctor for shots, or to Vacation Bible Classes? No, Miss Marsalles has got up with a happy whisper of apology; she has gone to meet them. Behind my back there is a sound of people squeezing together, of folding chairs being opened, there is an inappropriate, curiously unplaceable giggle.

And above or behind all this cautious flurry of arrival there is a peculiarly concentrated silence. Something has happened, something unforeseen, perhaps something disastrous; you can feel such things behind your back. I go on playing. I fill the first harsh silence with my own particularly dogged and lumpy interpretation of Handel. When I get up off the piano bench I almost fall over some of the new children who are sitting on the floor.

One of them, a boy nine or ten years old, is going to follow me. Miss Marsalles takes his hand and smiles at him and there is no twitch of his hand, no embarrassed movement of her head to disown this smile. How peculiar; and a boy too. He turns his head towards her as he sits down; she speaks to him encouragingly. But my attention has been caught by his profile as he looks up at her—the heavy, unfinished features, the abnormally small and slanting eyes. I look at the children seated on the floor and I see the same profile repeated two or three times; I see another boy with a very large head and fair shaved hair, fine as a baby's; there are other children whose features are regular and unexceptional, marked only by an infantile openness and calm. The boys are dressed in white shirts and short gray pants and the girls wear dresses of gray-green cotton with red buttons and sashes.

"Sometimes that kind is quite musical," says Mrs. Clegg.

"Who are they?" my mother whispers, surely not aware of how upset she sounds.

"They're from that class she has out at the Greenhill School. They're nice little things and some of them quite musical but of course they're not all there."

My mother nods distractedly; she looks around the room and meets the trapped, alerted eyes of the other women, but no decision is reached. There is nothing to be done. These children are going to play. Their playing is no worse—not much worse—than ours, but they seem to go slowly, and then there is nowhere to look. For it is a matter of politeness surely not to look closely at such children, and yet where else can you look during a piano performance but at the performer? There is an atmosphere in the room of some freakish inescapable dream. My mother and the others are almost audible saying to themselves: *No, I know it is not right to be repelled by such children and I am not repelled, but nobody told me I was going to come here to listen to a procession of little—little idiots for that's what they are*—WHAT KIND OF A PARTY IS THIS? Their applause, however, has increased, becoming brisk, let-us-at-least-get-this-over-with. But the program shows no signs of being over.

Miss Marsalles says each child's name as if it were a cause for celebration. Now she says, "Dolores Boyle!" A girl as big as I am, a long-legged, rather thin and plaintive-looking girl with blond, almost white, hair, uncoils herself and gets up off the floor. She sits down on the bench and after shifting around a bit and pushing her long hair back behind her ears she begins to play.

We are accustomed to notice performances at Miss Marsalles' parties, but it cannot be said that anyone has ever expected music. Yet this time the music establishes itself so effortlessly, with so little demand for attention, that we are hardly even surprised. What she plays is not familiar. It is something fragile, courtly, and gay, that carries with it the freedom of a great unemotional happiness. And all that this girl does—but this is something you would not think could ever be done—is to play it so that this can be felt, all this can be felt, even in Miss Marsalles' living room on Bala Street on a preposterous afternoon. The children are all quiet, the ones from Greenhill School and the rest. The mothers sit, caught with a look of protest on their faces, a more profound anxiety than before, as if reminded of something that they had forgotten they had forgotten; the white-haired girl sits ungracefully at the piano with her head hanging down, and the music is carried through the open door and the windows to the cindery summer street.

Miss Marsalles sits beside the piano and smiles at everybody in her usual way. Her smile is not triumphant, or modest. She does not look like a magician who is watching people's faces to see the effect of a rather original revelation—nothing like that. You would think, now that at the very end of her life she has found someone whom she can teach—whom she must teach—to play the piano, she would light up with the importance of this discovery. But it seems that the girl's playing like this is something she always expected, and she finds it natural and satisfying; people who believe in miracles do not make much fuss when they actually encounter one. Nor does it seem that she regards this girl with any more wonder than the other children from Greenhill School, who love her, or the rest of us, who do not. To her no gift is unexpected, no celebration will come as a surprise.

The girl is finished. The music is in the room and then it is gone and naturally enough no one knows what to say. For the moment she is finished it is plain that she is just the same as before, a girl from Greenhill School. Yet the music was not imaginary. The facts are not to be reconciled. And so after a few minutes the performance begins to seem, in spite of its innocence, like a trick—a very successful and diverting one, of course, but perhaps—how can it be said?—perhaps not altogether *in good taste.* For the girl's ability, which is undeniable but after all useless, out of place, is not really something that anybody wants to talk about. To Miss Marsalles such a thing is acceptable, but to other people, people who live in the world, it is not. Never mind, they must say something and so they speak gratefully of the music itself, saying how lovely, what a beautiful piece, what is it called?

"The Dance of the Happy Shades," says Miss Marsalles. *Danse des ombres heureuses,* she says, which leaves nobody any the wiser.

BUT THEN driving home, driving out of the hot red-brick streets and out of the city and leaving Miss Marsalles and her no longer possible parties behind, quite certainly forever, why is it that we are unable to say—as we must have expected to say—Poor Miss Marsalles? It is the Dance of the Happy Shades that prevents us, it is that one communiqué from the other country where she lives.

# Postcard

YESTERDAY AFTERNOON, yesterday, I was going along the street to the Post Office, thinking how sick I was of snow, sore throats, the whole dragged-out tail end of winter, and I wished I could pack off to Florida, like Clare. It was Wednesday afternoon, my half-day. I work in King's Department Store, which is nothing but a ready-to-wear and dry goods, in spite of the name. They used to have groceries, but I can just barely recall that. Momma used to take me in and set me on the high stool and old Mr. King would give me a handful of raisins and say, I only give them to the pretty girls. They took the groceries out when he died, old Mr. King, and it isn't even King's Department Store anymore, it belongs to somebody named Kruberg. They never come near it themselves, just send Mr. Hawes in for manager. I run the upstairs, Children's Wear, and put in the Toyland at Christmas. I've been there fourteen years and Hawes doesn't pick on me, knowing I wouldn't take it if he did.

It being Wednesday the wickets in the Post Office were closed, but I had my key. I unlocked our box and took out the Jubilee paper, in Momma's name, the phone bill, and a postcard I very nearly missed. I looked at the picture on it first and it showed me palm trees, a hot blue sky, the front of a motel with a sign out front in the shape of a big husky blond creature, lit up with neon I suppose at night. She was saying *Sleep at my place*—that is, a balloon with those words in it came out of her mouth. I turned it over and read, *I didn't sleep at her place though it was too expensive. Weather could not be better. Mid-seventies. How is the winter treating you in Jubilee? Not bad I hope. Be a good girl. Clare.* The date was ten days back. Well, sometimes postcards are slow, but I bet what happened was he carried this around in his pocket a few days before he remembered to mail it. It was my only card since he left for Florida three weeks ago, and here I was expecting him back in person Friday or Saturday. He made this trip every winter with his sister Porky and her husband, Harold, who lived in Windsor. I had the feeling they didn't like me, but Clare said it was my imagination. Whenever I had to talk to Porky I would make some mistake like saying something was irrevelant to me when I know the word *irrelevant*, and she never let on but I thought about it afterwards and burned. Though I know it serves me right for trying to talk the way I never would normally talk in Jubilee. Trying to impress her because she's a MacQuarrie, after all my lecturing Momma that *we*'re as good as *them*.

I used to say to Clare, write me a *letter* while you're away, and he would say, what do you want me to write about? So I told him to describe the scenery and the people he met, anything would be a pleasure for me to hear about, since I had never been further away from home than Buffalo, for pleasure (I won't count that train trip when I took Momma to Winnipeg to see relatives). But Clare said, I can tell you just as well when I get back. He never did, though. When I saw him again I would say, well, tell me all about your trip, and he would say, what do you want me to tell? That just aggravated me, because how would *I* know?

I saw Momma waiting for me, watching through the little window in the front door. She opened the door when I turned in our walk and called out, "Watch yourself, it's slippery. The milkman nearly took a header this morning."

"There's days when I think I wouldn't mind breaking a leg," I said, and she said, "Don't *say* things like that, it's just asking for punishment."

"Clare sent you a postcard," I said.

"Oh, he did not!" She turned it over and said, "Addressed to you, just as I thought." But she was smiling away. "I don't care for the picture he picked but maybe you don't get much choice down there."

Clare was probably a favorite with old ladies from the time he could walk. To them he was still a nice fat boy, so mannerly, not stuck-up in spite of being a MacQuarrie, and with a way of teasing that perked them up and turned them pink. They had a dozen games going, Momma and Clare, that I could never keep up with. One was him knocking at the door and saying something like, "Good-evening, ma'am, I just wondered if I could interest you in a course in body development I'm selling to put myself through college." And Momma would swallow and put on a stern face and say, "Look here, young man, do I look like I need a course in body development?" Or he would look doleful and say, "Ma'am, I'm here because I'm concerned about your soul." Momma would roar laughing. "You be concerned about your own," she said, and fed him chicken dumplings and lemon-meringue pie, all his favorites. He told her jokes at the table I never thought she'd listen to. "Did you hear about this old gentleman married a young wife and he went to the doctor? Doctor, he says, I'm having a bit of trouble—" "Stop it," Momma said—but she waited till he was through— "you are just embarrassing Helen Louise." I have got rid of the Louise on the end of my name everywhere but at home. Clare picked it up from Momma and I told him I didn't care for it but he went right on. Sometimes I felt like their child, sitting between him and Momma with both of them joking and enjoying their food and telling me I smoked too much and if I didn't straighten up I'd get permanent round shoulders. Clare was—is—twelve years older than I am and I don't ever remember him except as a grown-up man.

I USED to see him on the street and he seemed old to me then, at least old the way almost everybody grown-up did. He is one of those people who look older than they are when they're young and younger than they are when they're old. He was always around the Queen's Hotel. Being a MacQuarrie he never had to work too hard and he had a little office and did some work as a Notary Public and a bit of insurance and real estate. He still has the same place, and the front window is always bleary and dusty and there's a light burning in the back, winter and summer, where a lady about eighty years old, Miss Maitland, does his typing or whatever he gives her to do. If he's not in the Queen's Hotel he has one or two of his friends sitting around the space heater doing a little cardplaying, a little quiet drinking, mostly just talking. There's a certain kind of men in Jubilee and I guess every small town that you might call public men. I don't mean public *figures*, important enough to run for Parliament or even for mayor (though Clare could do that if he wanted to be serious), just men who are always around on the main street and you get to know their faces. Clare and those friends of his are like that.

"He down there with his sister?" Momma said, as if I hadn't told her. A lot of my conversations with Momma are replays. "What is that name they call her?"

"Porky," I said.

"Yes, I remember thinking, That's some name for a grown woman. And I remember her being baptized and her name was Isabelle. Way back before I was married, I was still singing in the choir. They had one of those long, fangle-dangle christening robes on her, you know them." Momma had a soft spot for Clare but not for the MacQuarrie family. She thought they were being stuck-up when they just breathed. I remember a year or two ago, us going past their place, and she said something about being careful not to step on the grass of the *Mansion*, and I told her, "Momma, in a few years' time I am going to be living here, this is going to be *my house*, so you better stop calling it the Mansion in that tone of voice." She and I both looked up at the house with all its dark green awnings decorated with big white Old English *M*'s, and all the verandas and the stained-glass window set in the side wall, like in a church. No sign of life, but upstairs old Mrs. MacQuarrie was lying, and is still, paralyzed down one side and not able to speak, Willa Montgomery tending her by day and Clare by night. Strange voices in the house upset her, and every time Clare took me in we could only whisper so she wouldn't hear me and throw some kind of paralytic fit. After her long look Momma said, "It's a funny thing but I can't imagine your name MacQuarrie."

"I thought you were so fond of Clare."

"Well I am, but I just think of him coming to get you Saturday night, him coming to dinner Sunday night, I don't think of you and him married."

"You wait and see what happens when the old lady passes on."

"Is that what he told you?"

"It's understood."

"Well imagine," Momma said.

"You don't need to act like he's doing me a favor because I can tell you there are plenty of people would consider it the other way round."

"Can't I open my mouth without you taking offense?" said Momma mildly.

Clare and I used to slip in the side door on Saturday nights and make coffee and something to eat in the high, old-fashioned kitchen, being as quiet and sneaky about it as two kids after school. Then we'd tiptoe up the back stairs to Clare's room and turn on the television so she'd think he was by himself, watching that. If she called him I'd lie alone in the big bed watching the program or looking at the old pictures on the wall—him on the high-school hockey team playing goalie, Porky in her graduation outfit, him and Porky and friends I didn't know on holidays. If she kept him a long time and I got bored I would get downstairs under cover of the television and have more coffee. (I never drank anything stronger, left that to Clare.) With just the kitchen light to see by I'd go into the dining room and pull out the drawers and look at her linen and open the china cabinet and the silver chest and feel like a thief. But I'd think, Why shouldn't I have the enjoyment of this and the name MacQuarrie since I wouldn't have to do anything I'm not doing anyway? Clare said, "Marry me," soon after we started going out together and I said, "Don't bother me, I don't want to think about getting married," and he quit. When I brought it up myself, these years later, he seemed pleased. He said, "Well, there's not many old buffalos like me hear a pretty girl like you say she wants to marry them." I thought, Wait till I get married and go into King's Department Store and send Hawes scurrying around waiting on me, the old horse's neck. Wouldn't I like to give him a bad time, but I'd restrain myself, out of good taste.

"I'M GOING to take that postcard now and put it in my box," I said to Momma. "And I can't think of a better way for us to spend this afternoon than for us both to take naps." I went upstairs and put on my dressing gown (Chinese-embroidered, and Clare's present). I creamed my face and got the box I keep postcards and letters and other mementos in, and I put it with the Florida postcards from other years and some from Banff and Jasper and the Grand Canyon and Yellowstone Park. Then just idling away the time I looked at my school pictures and report cards and the program for *H.M.S. Pinafore*, put on by the high school, in which I was the heroine, what's-her-name, the captain's daughter. I remember Clare meeting me on the street and congratulating me on my singing and how pretty I looked and me flirting with him a bit just because he seemed so old and safe and I would as soon flirt as turn around, I was so pleased with myself. Wouldn't I have been surprised if I had seen all of what was going to happen? I hadn't even met Ted Forgie then.

I knew his letter just from looking at the outside, and I never read it anymore, but just out of curiosity I opened it up and started off. *I usually hate to write a typewritten letter because it lacks the personal touch but I am so worn out tonight with all the unfamiliar pressures here that I hope you will forgive me.* Typewritten or not, it used to be that just looking at that letter I would get a feeling of love, if that is what you want to call it, strong enough to pretty near crumple me up and knock me over. Ted Forgie was an announcer at the Jubilee radio station for six months, around the time I was finishing high school. Momma said he was too old for me—she never said that about Clare—but all he was was twenty-four. He had spent two years in a san with t.b. and that had made him old for his years. We used to go up on Sullivan's Hill and he talked about how he had lived with death staring him in the face and he knew the value of being close to one human being, but all he had found was loneliness. He said he wanted to put his head down in my lap and weep, but all the time what he *was* doing was something else. When he went away I just turned into a sleepwalker. I only woke up in the afternoons when I went to the Post Office and opened the box with my knees going hollow, to see if I had a letter. And I never did, after that one. Places bothered me. Sullivan's Hill, the radio station, the coffee shop of the Queen's Hotel. I don't know how many hours I spent in that coffee shop, reciting in my head every conversation we ever had and visualizing every look on his face, not really comprehending yet that wishing wasn't going to drag him through that door again. I got friendly with Clare in there. He said I looked like I needed cheering up and he told me some of his stories. I never let on to him what my trouble was but when we started going out I explained to him that friendship was all I could offer. He said he appreciated that and he would bide his time. And he did.

I read the letter all the way through and I thought, not for the first time, Well, reading this letter any fool can see there is not going to be another. *I want you to know how grateful I am for all your sweetness and understanding.* Sweetness was the only word stuck in my mind then, to give me hope. I thought, When Clare and I get married I am just going to throw this letter away. So why not do it now? I tore it across and across and it was easy, like tearing up notes when school is over. Then because I didn't want Momma commenting on what was in my wastepaper basket, I wadded it up and put it in my purse. That being over I lay down on my bed and thought about several things. For instance, if I hadn't been in a stupor over Ted Forgie, would I have taken a different view of Clare? Not likely. If I hadn't been in that stupor I might have never bothered with Clare at all, I'd have gone off and done something different; but no use thinking about that now. The fuss he made at first made me sorry for him. I used to look down at his round balding head and listen to all his groaning and commotion and think, What can I do now except be polite? He didn't expect anything more of me, never expected anything, but just to lie there and let him, and I got used to that. I looked back and thought, Am I a heartless person, just to lie there and let him grab me and love me and moan around my neck and say the things he did, and never say one loving word back to him? I never wanted to be a heartless person and I was never mean to Clare, and I did let him, didn't I, nine times out of ten?

I HEARD Momma get up from her nap and go and put the kettle on so she could have a cup of tea and read her paper. Then some little time later she gave a yell and I thought somebody had died so I jumped off the bed and ran into the hall, but she was there underneath saying, "Go on back to your nap, I'm sorry I scared you. I made a mistake." I did go back and I heard her using the phone, probably calling one of her old cronies about some news in the paper, and then I guess I fell asleep.

What woke me was a car stopping, somebody getting out and coming up the front walk. I thought, Is it Clare back early? And then, confused and half-asleep, I thought, I already tore up the letter, that's good. But it wasn't his step. Momma opened the door before the bell got a chance to ring and I heard Alma Stonehouse, who teaches at the Jubilee Public School and is my best friend. I went out in the hall and leaned over and called down, "Hey, Alma, are you eating here *again*?" She boards at Bailey's where the food has its ups and downs and when she smells their shepherd's pie she sometimes heads over to our place without an invitation.

Alma started upstairs without taking her coat off, her thin dark face just blazing with excitement, so I knew something had happened. I thought it must have to do with her husband, because they are separated and he writes her terrible letters. She said, "Helen, hi, how are you feeling? Did you just wake up?"

"I heard your car," I said. "I thought for a minute maybe it was Clare but I'm not expecting him for another couple of days."

"Helen. Can you sit down? Come in your room where you can sit down. Are you prepared to get a shock? I wish I wasn't the one had to tell you. Hold yourself steady."

I saw Momma right behind her and I said, "Momma, is this some joke?" Alma said, "Clare MacQuarrie has gotten married."

"What are you two up to?" I said. "Clare MacQuarrie is in Florida and I just today got a postcard from him as Momma well knows."

"He got married in Florida. Helen, be calm."

"How could he get married in Florida, he's on his holidays?"

"They're on their way to Jubilee right now and they're going to live here."

"Alma, wherever you heard that it's a lot of garbage. I just had a postcard from him. Momma—"

Then I saw that Momma was looking at me like I was eight years old and had the measles and a temperature of a hundred and five degrees. She was holding the paper and she spread it out for me to read. "It's in there," she said, probably not realizing she was whispering. "It's written up in the *Bugle-Herald*."

"I don't believe it any more than fly," I said, and I started to read and read all the way through as if the names were ones I'd never heard of before, and some of them were. A quiet ceremony in Coral Gables, Florida, uniting in marriage Clare Alexander MacQuarrie, of Jubilee, son of Mrs. James MacQuarrie of this town and the late Mr. James MacQuarrie, prominent local businessman and long-time Member of Parliament, and Mrs. Margaret Thora Leeson, daughter of the late Mr. and Mrs. Clive Tibbutt of Lincoln, Nebraska. Mr. and Mrs. Harold Johnson, sister and brother-in-law of the bridegroom, were the only attendants. The bride wore a sage green dressmaker suit with dark brown accessories and a corsage of bronze orchids. Mrs. Johnson wore a beige suit with black accessories and green orchids. The couple were at present travelling by automobile to their future home in Jubilee.

"Do you still think it's garbage?" Alma said severely.

I said I didn't know.

"Are you feeling all right?"

All right.

Momma said we would all feel better if we went downstairs and had a cup of tea and something to eat, instead of staying cooped up in this little bedroom. It was about suppertime, anyway. So we all trooped down, me still in my dressing gown, and Momma and Alma together prepared the sort of meal you might eat to keep your strength up when there is sickness in the house and you can't really bother too much about food. Cold meat sandwiches and little dishes of different pickles and sliced cheese and date squares. "Smoke a cigarette if you want to," Momma said to me—the first time she ever said *that* in her life. So I did, and Alma did, and Alma said, "I brought some tranquillizers along in my purse, they're not very strong and you're welcome to one or two." I said no thanks, not yet anyway. I said I couldn't seem to take it in yet.

"He goes to Florida every year, right?"

I said yes.

"Well what I think is this, that he's met this woman before—widow or divorcee or whatever she is—and they have been corresponding and planning this all along."

Momma said it was awfully hard to think that of Clare.

"I'm only saying how it looks to me. And she's his sister's friend, I'll bet. The sister engineered it. They were the attendants, the sister and her husband. She wasn't any friend of yours, Helen, I remember you telling me."

"I didn't hardly know her."

"Helen Louise, you told me you and him were just waiting for the old lady to pass on," Momma said. "Isn't that what he said to you? Clare?"

"Using her for an excuse," Alma said briskly.

"Oh, he wouldn't," Momma said. "Oh, it's so hard to understand it—*Clare!*"

"Men are always out for what they can get," Alma said. There was a pause, both of them looking at me. I couldn't tell them anything. I couldn't tell them what I was thinking, which was about the last Saturday night up at his place, before he went away, him naked as a baby pulling my hair across his face and through his teeth and pretending he was going to bite it off. I didn't relish anybody's saliva in my hair but I let him, just warning him that if he did bite it off he would have to pay for me going to the hairdresser's to get it evened. He didn't act that night like anybody that is going off to be *married*.

Momma and Alma went on talking and speculating and I got sleepier and sleepier. I heard Alma say, "Worse things could happen. I had four years of living hell." And Momma say, "He was always the soul of kindness and he doted on that girl." I wondered how I could possibly be so sleepy, this early in the evening and after having a nap in the afternoon. Alma said, "It's very good you're sleepy, it's Nature's way. Nature's way, just like an anesthetic." They both got me upstairs and into bed and I never heard them go down.

I DIDN'T wake up early, either. I got up when I usually did and got my own breakfast. I could hear Momma stirring but I yelled to her to stay put, like any other morning. She called down, "Are you sure you want to go to work? I could phone Mr. Hawes you're sick." I said, "Why should I give any of them the satisfaction?" I did my makeup at the hall mirror without a light and went out and walked the two and a half blocks to King's, not noticing what kind of a morning it was, beyond the fact that it hadn't turned into spring overnight. Inside the store they were waiting, oh, how nice—good morning, Helen, good morning, Helen—such quiet kind hopeful voices waiting to see if I'm going to fall flat on the floor and start having hysterics. Mrs. McCool, Beryl Allen with her engagement ring, Mrs. Kress that got jilted herself twenty-five years ago and then took up with somebody else—Kress—and *he* vanished. What's she looking at me for? Old Hawes chewing his tongue when he smiles. I said good morning perfectly cheerfully and went on upstairs thanking God I have my own washroom and thinking, I bet this will be a big day for Children's Wear. It was too. I never had a morning with so many mothers in to buy a hair-ribbon or a little pair of socks, willing to climb that stairs for it.

I phoned Momma I wouldn't be home at noon. I thought I'd just go over to the Queen's Hotel and have a hamburger, with all the radio people I hardly know. But at a quarter to twelve in comes Alma. "I wouldn't let you eat by yourself *this* day!" So we have to go to the Queen's Hotel together. She was going to make me eat an egg sandwich, not a hamburger, and a glass of milk not Coke, because she said my digestion was probably in a state, but I vetoed that. She waited till we got our food and were settled down to eating before she said, "Well, they're back."

It took a minute for me to know who. "When?" I said.

"Last night around suppertime. Just when I was driving over to your place to break you the news. I might've run into them."

"Who told you?"

"Well, Beechers live next to MacQuarries, don't they?" Mrs. Beecher teaches Grade 4, Alma Grade 3. "Grace saw them. She had already read the paper so she knew who it was."

"What is she like?" I said in spite of myself.

"She's no juvenile, Grace said. His age, anyway. What did I tell you it was his sister's friend? And she won't win any prizes in the looks department. Mind you she's all *right*."

"Is she big or little?" I couldn't stop now. "Dark or fair?"

"She had a hat on so Grace couldn't see the color of her hair but she thought dark. She's a big woman. Grace said she had a rear end on her like a grand piano. Maybe she has money."

"Did Grace say that too?"

"No. I said it. Just speculating."

"Clare doesn't need to marry anybody with money. *He* has money."

"That's by our standards maybe, but not by his."

I KEPT thinking through the afternoon that Clare would come round, or at least phone me. Then I could start asking him what did he think he had done. I made up in my mind some crazy explanations he might give me, like this poor woman had cancer and only six months to live and she had always been deadly poor (a scrubwoman in his motel) and he wanted to give her a little time of ease. Or that she was blackmailing his brother-in-law about a crooked transaction and he married her to shut her up. But I didn't have time to think up many stories because of the steady stream of customers. Old ladies puffing up the stairs with some story about birthday presents for their grandchildren. Every grandchild in Jubilee must have a birthday in March. They ought to be grateful to me, I thought, haven't I given their day a bit of excitement? Even Alma, she was looking better than she has all winter. I'm not blaming her, I thought, but it's the truth. And who knows, maybe I'd be the same if Don Stonehouse showed up like he threatens to and raped her and left her a mass of purple bruises—his words, not mine—from head to foot. I'd be as sorry as could be, and anything I could do to help her, I'd do, but I might think, Well, awful as it is it's something happening and it's been a long winter.

There was no use even thinking about not going home for supper, that would finish Momma. There she was waiting with a salmon loaf, cabbage and carrot salad with raisins in it, that I like, and Brown Betty. But halfway through this the tears started sliding down over her rouge. "It seems to me like I'm the one ought to do the crying if anybody has to do it," I said. "What's so terrible happened to you?"

"Well I was just so fond of him," she said. "I was that fond of him. At my age there's not too many people that you look forward to them coming all week."

"Well I'm sorry," I said.

"But once a man loses his respect for a girl, he is apt to get tired of her."

"What do you mean by that, Momma?"

"If you don't know am I supposed to tell you?"

"You ought to be ashamed," I said, starting to cry too. "Talking like that to your own daughter." There! And I always thought she didn't know. Never blame Clare, of course, blame me.

"No, I'm not the one that ought to be ashamed," she continued, weeping. "I am an old woman but I know. If a man loses respect for a girl he don't marry her."

"If that was true there wouldn't be hardly one marriage in this town."

"You destroyed your own chances."

"You never said a word of this to me as long as he was coming here and I am not listening to it now," I said, and went upstairs. She didn't come after me. I sat and smoked, hour after hour. I didn't get undressed. I heard her come upstairs, go to bed. Then I went down and watched television for a while, news of car accidents. I put on my coat and went out.

I HAVE a little car Clare gave me a year ago Christmas, a little Morris. I don't use it for work because driving two and a half blocks looks to me silly, and like showing off, though I know people who do it. I went around to the garage and backed it out. This was the first time I had driven it since the Sunday I took Momma to Tuppertown to see Auntie Kay in the nursing home. I use it more in summer.

I looked at my watch and the time surprised me. Twenty after twelve. I felt shaky and weak from sitting so long. I wished now I had one of Alma's pills. I had an idea of just taking off, driving, but I didn't know which direction to go in. I drove around the streets of Jubilee and didn't see another car out but mine. All the houses in darkness, the streets black, the yards pale with the last snow. It seemed to me that in every one of those houses lived people who knew something I didn't. Who understood what had happened and perhaps had known it was going to happen and I was the only one who didn't know.

I drove out Grove Street and on to Minnie Street and saw his house from the back. No lights on there either. I drove around to see it from the front. Did they have to sneak up the stairs and keep the television on? I wondered. No woman with a rear end like a grand piano would settle for that. I bet he took her right up and into the old lady's room and said, "This is the new Mrs. MacQuarrie," and that was that.

I parked the car and rolled down the window. Then without thinking what I was going to do I leaned on the horn and sounded it as long and hard as I could stand.

The sound released me, so I could yell. And I did. "Hey, Clare MacQuarrie, I want to talk to you!"

No answer anywhere. "Clare MacQuarrie!" I shouted up at his dark house. "Clare, come on out!" I sounded the horn again, two, three, I don't know how many times. In between I yelled. I felt as if I was watching myself, way down here, so little, pounding my fist and yelling and leaning on the horn. Carrying on a commotion, doing whatever came into my head. It was enjoyable, in a way. I almost forgot what I was doing it for. I started honking the horn rhythmically and yelling at the same time. "Clare, aren't you ever coming out? Clare MacQuarrie for nuts-in-May, if he don't come we'll pull-him-away—" I was crying as well as yelling, right out in the street, and it didn't bother me one bit.

"Helen, you want to wake everybody up in this whole town?" said Buddy Shields, sticking his head in at the window. He is the night constable and I used to teach him in Sunday school.

"I'm just conducting a shivaree for the newly married couple," I said. "What is the matter with that?"

"I got to tell you to stop that noise."

"I don't feel like stopping."

"Oh yes you do, Helen, you're just a little upset."

"I called and called him and he won't come out," I said. "All I want is him to come out."

"Well you got to be a good girl and stop honking that horn."

"I want him to come out."

"Stop it. Don't honk that horn one more time."

"Will you make him come out?"

"Helen, I can't make a man come out of his own house if he don't want to come."

"I thought you were the Law, Buddy Shields."

"I am but there is a limit to what the Law can do. If you want to see him why don't you come back in the daytime and knock on his door nice the way any lady would do?"

"He is married in case you didn't know."

"Well, Helen, he is married just as much at night as in the daytime."

"Is that supposed to be funny?"

"No it's not, it's supposed to be true. Now why don't you move over and let me drive you home? Lookit the lights on up and down this street. There's Grace Beecher watching us and I can see the Holmses got their windows up. You don't want to give them anything more to talk about, do you?"

"They got nothing to do but talk anyway, they may as well talk about me."

Then Buddy Shields straightened up and moved a little away from the car window and I saw somebody in dark clothes coming across the Mac-Quarries' lawn and it was Clare. He was not wearing a dressing gown or anything, he was all dressed, in shirt and jacket and trousers. He came right up to the car while I sat there waiting to hear what I would say to him. He had not changed. He was a fat, comfortable, sleepy-faced man.

But just his look, his everyday easygoing look, stopped me wanting to cry or yell. I could cry and yell till I was blue in the face and it would not change that look or make him get out of bed and across his yard one little bit faster.

"Helen, go on home," he said, like we had been watching television and so on all evening and now was time to go home and go to bed properly. "Give my love to your momma," he said. "Go on home."

That was all he meant to say. He looked at Buddy and said, "You going to drive her?" and Buddy said yes. I was looking at Clare MacQuarrie and thinking, He is a man that goes his own way. It didn't bother him too much how I was feeling when he did what he did on top of me, and it didn't bother him too much what kind of ruckus I made in the street when he got married. And he was a man who didn't give out explanations, maybe didn't have any. If there was anything he couldn't explain, well, he would just forget about it. Here were all his neighbors watching us, but to-morrow, if he met them on the street, he would tell them a funny story. And what about me? Maybe if he met me on the street one of these days he would just say, "How are you doing, Helen?" and tell me a joke. And if I had really thought about what he was like, Clare MacQuarrie, if I had paid attention, I would have started out a lot differently with him and maybe felt differently too, though heaven knows if that would have mat-tered, in the end.

"Now aren't you sorry you made all this big fuss?" Buddy said, and I slid over on the seat and watched Clare going back to his house, thinking, Yes, that's what I should have done, paid attention. Buddy said, "You're not going to bother him and his wife anymore now, are you, Helen?"

"What?" I said.

"You're not going to bother Clare and his wife anymore? Because now he's married, that's over and done with. And you wake up tomorrow morning, you're going to feel pretty bad over what you done tonight, you won't see how you can go on and face people. But let me tell you things happen all the time, only thing to do is just go along, and remember you're not the only one." It never seemed to occur to him that it was funny for him to be lecturing me, that used to hear his Bible verses and caught him reading Leviticus on the sly.

"Like last week I'll tell you," he said, easing down Grove Street, in no hurry to get me home and have the lecture ended, "last week we got a call and we had to go out to Dunnock Swamp and there's a car stuck in there. This old farmer was waving a loaded gun and talking about shooting this pair for trespassing if they didn't get off of his property. They'd just been following a wagon track after dark, where any idiot would know you'd get stuck this time of year. You would know both of them if I said their names and you'd know they had no business being in that car together. One is a married lady. And worst is, by this time her husband is wondering why she don't come home from choir practice—both these parties sing in the choir, I won't tell you which one—and he has reported her missing. So we got to get a tractor to haul out the car, and leave *him* there sweating, and quieten down this old farmer, and then take her home separate in broad daylight, crying all the way. That's what I mean by things happening. I saw that man and wife downstreet buying their groceries yesterday, and they didn't look too happy but there they were. So just be a good girl, Helen, and go along like the rest of us and pretty soon we'll see spring."

OH, BUDDY Shields, you can just go on talking, and Clare will tell jokes, and Momma will cry, till she gets over it, but why I'll never understand is why, right now, seeing Clare MacQuarrie as an unexplaining man, I felt for the first time that I wanted to reach out my hands and *touch* him.

# Images

NOW THAT Mary McQuade had come, I pretended not to remember her. It seemed the wisest thing to do. She herself said, "If you don't remember me you don't remember much," but let the matter drop, just once adding, "I bet you never went to your grandma's house last summer. I bet you don't remember that either."

It was called, even that summer, my grandma's house, though my grandfather was then still alive. He had withdrawn into one room, the largest front bedroom. It had wooden shutters on the inside of the windows, like the living room and dining room; the other bedrooms had only blinds. Also, the veranda kept out the light so that my grandfather lay in near-darkness all day, with his white hair, now washed and tended and soft as a baby's, and his white nightshirt and pillows, making an island in the room which people approached with diffidence, but resolutely. Mary McQuade in her uniform was the other island in the room, and she sat mostly not moving where the fan, as if it was tired, stirred the air like soup. It must have been too dark to read or knit, supposing she wanted to do those things, and so she merely waited and breathed, making a sound like the fan made, full of old indefinable complaint.

I was so young then I was put to sleep in a crib—not at home but this was what was kept for me at my grandma's house—in a room across the hall. There was no fan there and the dazzle of outdoors—all the flat fields round the house turned, in the sun, to the brilliance of water—made lightning cracks in the drawn-down blinds. Who could sleep? My mother's my grandmother's my aunts' voices wove their ordinary repetitions, on the veranda in the kitchen in the dining room (where with a little brass-handled brush my mother cleaned the white cloth, and the lighting-fixture over the round table hung down unlit flowers of thick, butterscotch glass). All the meals in that house, the cooking, the visiting, the conversation, even someone playing on the piano (it was my youngest aunt, Edith, not married, singing and playing with one hand, *Nita, Juanita, softly falls the southern moon*)—all this life going on. Yet the ceilings of the rooms were very high and under them was a great deal of dim wasted space, and when I lay in my crib too hot to sleep, I could look up and see that emptiness, the stained corners, and feel, without knowing what it was, just what everybody else in the house must have felt—under the sweating heat the fact of death-contained, that little lump of magic ice. And Mary McQuade waiting in her starched white dress, big and gloomy as an iceberg herself, implacable, waiting and breathing. I held her responsible.

So I pretended not to remember her. She had not put on her white uniform, which did not really make her less dangerous but might mean, at least, that the time of her power had not yet come. Out in the daylight, and not dressed in white, she turned out to be freckled all over, everywhere you could see, as if she was sprinkled with oatmeal, and she had a crown of frizzy, glinting, naturally brass-colored hair. Her voice was loud and hoarse, and complaint was her everyday language. "Am I going to have to hang up this wash all by myself?" she shouted at me, in the yard, and I followed her to the clothesline platform where with a groan she let down the basket of wet clothes. "Hand me them clothespins. One at a time. Hand me them right side up. I shouldn't be out in this wind at all, I've got a bronchial condition." Head hung, like an animal chained to her side, I fed her clothespins. Outdoors, in the cold March air, she lost some of her bulk and her smell. In the house I could always smell her, even in the rooms she seldom entered. What was her smell like? It was like metal and like some dark spice (cloves—she did suffer from toothache) and like the preparation rubbed on my chest when I had a cold. I mentioned it once to my mother, who said, "Don't be silly, *I* don't smell anything." So I never told about the taste, and there was a taste too. It was in all the food Mary McQuade prepared and perhaps in all food eaten in her presence—in my porridge at breakfast and my fried potatoes at noon and the slice of bread and butter and brown sugar she gave me to eat in the yard—something foreign, gritty, depressing. How could my parents not know about it? But for reasons of their own they would pretend. This was something I had not known a year ago.

After she had hung out the wash she had to soak her feet. Her legs came straight up, round as drainpipes, from the steaming basin. One hand on each knee, she bent into the steam and gave grunts of pain and satisfaction.

"Are you a nurse?" I said, greatly daring, though my mother had said she was.

"Yes I am and I wish I wasn't."

"Are you my aunt too?"

"If I was your aunt you would call me Aunt Mary, wouldn't you? Well, you don't, do you? I'm your cousin, I'm your father's cousin. That's why they get me instead of getting an ordinary nurse. I'm a practical nurse. And there is always somebody sick in this family and I got to go to them. I never get a rest."

I doubted this. I doubted that she was asked to come. She came, and cooked what she liked and rearranged things to suit herself, complaining about drafts, and let her power loose in the house. If she had never come, my mother would never have taken to her bed.

My mother's bed was set up in the dining room, to spare Mary Mc-Quade climbing the stairs. My mother's hair was done in two little thin dark braids, her cheeks were sallow, her neck warm and smelling of raisins as it always did, but the rest of her under the covers had changed into some large, fragile, and mysterious object, difficult to move. She spoke of herself gloomily in the third person, saying, "Be careful, don't hurt Mother, don't sit on Mother's legs." Every time she said "Mother" I felt chilled, and a kind of wretchedness and shame spread through me as it did at the name of Jesus. This *Mother* that my own real, warm-necked, irascible, and comforting human mother set up between us was an everlastingly wounded phantom, sorrowing like Him over all the wickedness I did not yet know I would commit.

My mother crocheted squares for an afghan, in all shades of purple. They fell among the bedclothes and she did not care. Once they were finished she forgot about them. She had forgotten all her stories which were about princes in the Tower and a queen getting her head chopped off while a little dog was hiding under her dress and another queen sucking poison out of her husband's wound; and also about her own childhood, a time as legendary to me as any other. Given over to Mary's care, she whimpered childishly, "Mary, I'm dying for you to rub my back." "Mary, could you make me a cup of tea? I feel if I drink any more tea I'm going to bob up to the ceiling, just like a big balloon, but you know it's all I want." Mary laughed shortly. "You," she said, "you're not going to bob up anywhere. Take a derrick to move *you*. Come on now, raise up, you'll be worse before you're better!" She shooed me off the bed and began to pull the sheets about with not very gentle jerks. "You been tiring your momma out? What do you want to bother your momma for on this nice a day?" "I think she's lonesome," my mother said, a weak and insincere defense.

"She can be lonesome in the yard just as well as here," said Mary, with her grand, vague, menacing air. "You put your things on, out you go!"

My father too had altered since her coming. When he came in for his meals she was always waiting for him, some joke swelling her up like a bullfrog, making her ferocious-looking and red in the face. She put un-cooked white beans in his soup, hard as pebbles, and waited to see if good manners would make him eat them. She stuck something to the bottom of his water glass to look like a fly. She gave him a fork with a prong missing, pretending it was by accident. He threw it at her, and missed, but startled me considerably. My mother and father, eating supper, talked quietly and seriously. But in my father's family even grownups played tricks with rub-ber worms and beetles, fat aunts were always invited to sit on little rickety chairs, and uncles broke wind in public and said, "Whoa, hold on there!" proud of themselves as if they had whistled a complicated tune. Nobody could ask your age without a rigmarole of teasing. So with Mary McQuade my father returned to family ways, just as he went back to eating heaps of fried potatoes and side meat and thick, floury pies, and drinking tea black and strong as medicine out of a tin pot, saying gratefully, "Mary, you know what it is a man ought to eat!" He followed that up with "Don't you think it's time you got a man of your own to feed?" which earned him, not a fork thrown, but the dishrag.

His teasing of Mary was always about husbands. "I thought up one for you this morning!" he would say. "Now, Mary, I'm not fooling you, you give this some consideration." Her laughter would come out first in little angry puffs and explosions through her shut lips, while her face grew red-der than you would have thought possible and her body twitched and rumbled threateningly in its chair. There was no doubt she enjoyed all this, all these preposterous imagined matings, though my mother would certainly have said it was cruel, cruel and indecent, to tease an old maid about men. In my father's family of course it was what she was always teased about, what else was there? And the heavier and coarser and more impossible she became, the more she would be teased. A bad thing in that family was to have them say you were *sensitive*, as they did of my mother. All the aunts and cousins and uncles had grown tremendously hardened to any sort of personal cruelty, reckless, even proud, it seemed, of a failure or deformity that could make for general laughter.

At suppertime it was dark in the house, in spite of the lengthening days. We did not yet have electricity. It came in soon afterwards, maybe the next summer. But at present there was a lamp on the table. In its light my father and Mary McQuade threw gigantic shadows, whose heads wagged clumsily with their talk and laughing. I watched the shadows instead of the people.

They said, "What are you dreaming about?" but I was not dreaming; I was trying to understand the danger, to read the signs of invasion.

MY FATHER said, "Do you want to come with me and look at the traps?" He had a trapline for muskrats along the river. When he was younger he used to spend days, nights, weeks in the bush, following creeks all up and down Wawanash County, and he trapped not only muskrat then but red fox, wild mink, marten, all animals whose coats are prime in the fall. Muskrat is the only thing you can trap in the spring. Now that he was married and settled down to farming he just kept the one line, and that for only a few years. This may have been the last year he had it.

We went across a field that had been plowed the previous fall. There was a little snow lying in the furrows but it was not real snow, it was a thin crust like frosted glass that I could shatter with my heels. The field went downhill slowly, down to the river flats. The fence was down in some places from the weight of the snow; we could step over it.

My father's boots went ahead. His boots were to me as unique and familiar, as much an index to himself, as his face was. When he had taken them off they stood in a corner of the kitchen, giving off a complicated smell of manure, machine oil, caked black mud, and the ripe and disintegrating material that lined their soles. They were a part of himself, temporarily discarded, waiting. They had an expression that was dogged and uncompromising, even brutal, and I thought of that as part of my father's look, the counterpart of his face, with its readiness for jokes and courtesies. Nor did that brutality surprise me; my father came back to us always, to my mother and me, from places where our judgment could not follow.

For instance, there was a muskrat in the trap. At first I saw it waving at the edge of the water, like something tropical, a dark fern. My father drew it up and the hairs ceased waving, clung together, the fern became a tail with the body of the rat attached to it, sleek and dripping. Its teeth were bared, its eyes wet on top, dead and dull beneath, glinted like washed pebbles. My father shook it and whirled it around, making a little rain of icy river water. "This is a good old rat," he said. "This is a big old king rat. Look at his tail!" Then perhaps thinking that I was worried, or perhaps only wanting to show me the charm of simple, perfect mechanical devices, he lifted the trap out of the water and explained to me how it worked, dragging the rat's head under at once and mercifully drowning him. I did not understand or care. I only wanted, but did not dare, to touch the stiff, soaked body, a fact of death.

My father baited the trap again using some pieces of yellow, winter-wrinkled apple. He put the rat's body in a dark sack which he carried slung over his shoulder, like a peddler in a picture. When he cut the apple, I had seen the skinning knife, its slim bright blade.

Then we went along the river, the Wawanash River, which was high, running full, silver in the middle where the sun hit it and where it arrowed in to its swiftest motion. That is the current, I thought, and I pictured the current as something separate from the water, just as the wind was separate from the air and had its own invading shape. The banks were steep and slippery and lined with willow bushes, still bare and bent over and looking weak as grass. The noise the river made was not loud but deep, and seemed to come from away down in the middle of it, some hidden place where the water issued with a roar from underground.

The river curved, I lost my sense of direction. In the traps we found more rats, released them, shook them and hid them in the sack, replaced the bait. My face, my hands, my feet grew cold, but I did not mention it. I could not, to my father. And he never told me to be careful, to stay away from the edge of the water; he took it for granted that I would have sense enough not to fall in. I never asked how far we were going, or if the trapline would ever end. After a while there was a bush behind us, the afternoon darkened. It did not occur to me, not till long afterwards, that this was the same bush you could see from our yard, a fan-shaped hill rising up in the middle of it with bare trees in wintertime that looked like bony little twigs against the sky.

Now the bank, instead of willows, grew thick bushes higher than my head. I stayed on the path, about halfway up the bank, while my father went down to the water. When he bent over the trap, I could no longer see him. I looked around slowly and saw something else. Further along, and higher up the bank, a man was making his way down. He made no noise coming through the bushes and moved easily, as if he followed a path I could not see. At first I could just see his head and the upper part of his body. He was dark, with a high bald forehead, hair long behind the ears, deep vertical creases in his cheeks. When the bushes thinned I could see the rest of him, his long clever legs, thinness, drab camouflaging clothes, and what he carried in his hand, gleaming where the sun caught it—a little axe, or hatchet.

I never moved to warn or call my father. The man crossed my path somewhere ahead, continuing down to the river. People say they have been paralyzed by fear, but I was transfixed, as if struck by lightning, and what hit me did not feel like fear so much as recognition. I was not surprised. This is the sight that does not surprise you, the thing you have always known was there that comes so naturally, moving delicately and contentedly and in no hurry, as if it was made, in the first place, from a wish of yours, a hope of something final, terrifying. All my life I had known there was a man like this and he was behind doors, around the corner at the dark end of a hall. So now I saw him and just waited, like a child in an old negative, electrified against the dark noon sky, with blazing hair and burned-out Orphan Annie eyes. The man slipped down through the bushes to my father. And I never thought, or even hoped for, anything but the worst.

My father did not know. When he straightened up, the man was not three feet away from him and hid him from me. I heard my father's voice come out, after a moment's delay, quiet and neighborly.

"Hello, Joe. Well. Joe. I haven't seen you in a long time."

The man did not say a word, but edged around my father giving him a close look. "Joe, you know me," my father told him. "Ben Jordan. I been out looking at my traps. There's a lot of good rats in the river this year, Joe."

The man gave a quick not-trusting look at the trap my father had baited.

"You ought to set a line out yourself."

No answer. The man took his hatchet and chopped lightly at the air.

"Too late this year, though. The river is already started to go down."

"Ben Jordan," the man said with a great splurt, a costly effort, like somebody leaping over a stutter.

"I thought you'd recognize me, Joe."

"I never knew it was you, Ben. I thought it was one them Silases."

"Well I been telling you it was me."

"They's down here all the time choppin' my trees and pullin' down my fences. You know they burned me out, Ben. It was them done it."

"I heard about that," my father said.

"I didn't know it was you, Ben. I never knew it was you. I got this axe, I just take it along with me to give them a little scare. I wouldn't of if I'd known it was you. You come on up and see where I'm living now."

My father called me. "I got my young one out following me today."

"Well you and her both come up and get warm."

We followed this man, who still carried and carelessly swung his hatchet, up the slope and into the bush. The trees chilled the air, and underneath them was real snow, left over from winter, a foot, two feet deep. The tree trunks had rings around them, a curious dark space like the warmth you make with your breath.

We came out in a field of dead grass, and took a track across it to another, wider field where there was something sticking out of the ground. It was a roof, slanting one way, not peaked, and out of the roof came a pipe with a cap on it, smoke blowing out. We went down the sort of steps that lead to a cellar, and that was what it was—a cellar with a roof on. My father said, "Looks like you fixed it up all right for yourself, Joe."

"It's warm. Being down in the ground the way it is, naturally it's warm. I thought, What is the sense of building a house up again, they burned it down once, they'll burn it down again. What do I need a house for anyways? I got all the room I need here, I fixed it up comfortable." He opened the door at the bottom of the steps. "Mind your head here. I don't say everybody should live in a hole in the ground, Ben. Though animals do it, and what an animal does, by and large it makes sense. But if you're married, that's another story." He laughed. "Me, I don't plan on getting married."

It was not completely dark. There were the old cellar windows, letting in a little grimy light. The man lit a coal-oil lamp, though, and set it on the table.

"There, you can see where you're at."

It was all one room, an earth floor with boards not nailed together, just laid down to make broad paths for walking, a stove on a sort of platform, table, couch, chairs, even a kitchen cupboard, several thick, very dirty blankets of the type used in sleighs and to cover horses. Perhaps if it had not had such a terrible smell—of coal oil, urine, earth, and stale heavy air—I would have recognized it as the sort of place I would like to live in myself, like the houses I made under snowdrifts, in winter, with sticks of firewood for furniture, like another house I had made long ago under the veranda, my floor the strange powdery earth that never got sun or rain.

But I was wary, sitting on the dirty couch, pretending not to look at anything. My father said, "You're snug here, Joe, that's right." He sat by the table, and there the hatchet lay.

"You should of seen me before the snow started to melt. Wasn't nothing showing but a smokestack."

"Nor you don't get lonesome?"

"Not me. I was never one for lonesome. And I got a cat, Ben. Where is that cat? There he is, in behind the stove. He don't relish company, maybe." He pulled it out, a huge, gray tom with sullen eyes. "Show you what he can do." He took a saucer from the table and a mason jar from the cupboard and poured something into the saucer. He set it in front of the cat.

"Joe, that cat don't drink whisky, does he?"

"You wait and see."

The cat rose and stretched himself stiffly, took one baleful look around, and lowered his head to drink.

"Straight whisky," my father said.

"I bet that's a sight you ain't seen before. And you ain't likely to see it again. That cat'd take whisky ahead of milk any day. A matter of fact he don't get no milk, he's forgot what it's like. You want a drink, Ben?"

"Not knowing where you got that. I don't have a stomach like your cat."

The cat, having finished, walked sideways from the saucer, waited a moment, gave a clawing leap, and landed unsteadily, but did not fall. It swayed, pawed the air a few times, meowing despairingly, then shot forward and slid under the end of the couch.

"Joe, you keep that up, you're not going to have a cat."

"It don't hurt him, he enjoys it. Let's see, what've we got for the little girl to eat?" Nothing, I hoped, but he brought a tin of Christmas candies, which seemed to have melted then hardened then melted again, so the colored stripes had run. They had a taste of nails.

"It's them Silases botherin' me, Ben. They come by day and by night. People won't ever quit botherin' me. I can hear them on the roof at night. Ben, you see them Silases you tell them what I got waitin' for them." He picked up the hatchet and chopped down at the table, splitting the rotten oilcloth. "Got a shotgun too."

"Maybe they won't come and bother you no more, Joe."

The man groaned and shook his head. "They never will stop. No. They never will stop."

"Just try not paying any attention to them, they'll tire out and go away."

"They'll burn me in my bed. They tried to before."

My father said nothing, but tested the axe blade with his finger. Under the couch, the cat pawed and meowed in more and more feeble spasms of delusion. Overcome with tiredness, with warmth after cold, with bewilderment past bearing, I was falling asleep with my eyes open.

MY FATHER set me down. "You're woken up now. Stand up. See. I can't carry you and this sack full of rats both."

We had come to the top of a long hill and that is where I woke. It was getting dark. The whole basin of country drained by the Wawanash River lay in front of us—greenish-brown smudge of bush with the leaves not out yet and evergreens, dark, shabby after winter, showing through, straw-brown fields and the others, darker from last year's plowing, with scales of snow faintly striping them (like the field we had walked across hours, hours earlier in the day) and the tiny fences and colonies of gray barns, and houses set apart, looking squat and small.

"Whose house is that?" my father said, pointing.

It was ours, I knew it after a minute. We had come around in a half-circle and there was the side of the house that nobody saw in winter, the front door that went unopened from November to April and was still stuffed with rags around its edges, to keep out the east wind.

"That's no more'n half a mile away and downhill. You can easy walk home. Soon we'll see the light in the dining room where your momma is."

On the way I said, "Why did he have an axe?"

"Now listen," my father said. "Are you listening to me? He don't mean any harm with that axe. It's just his habit, carrying it around. But don't say anything about it at home. Don't mention it to your momma or Mary, either one. Because they might be scared about it. You and me aren't, but they might be. And there is no use of that."

After a while he said, "What are you not going to mention about?" and I said, "The axe."

"You weren't scared, were you?"

"No," I said hopefully. "Who is going to burn him and his bed?"

"Nobody. Less he manages it himself like he did last time."

"Who is the Silases?"

"Nobody," my father said. "Just nobody."

"We found the one for you today, Mary. Oh, I wisht we could've brought him home."

"We thought you'd fell in the Wawanash River," said Mary McQuade furiously, ungently pulling off my boots and my wet socks.

"Old Joe Phippen that lives up in no-man's-land beyond the bush."

"Him!" said Mary like an explosion. "He's the one burned his house down, I know him!"

"That's right, and now he gets along fine without it. Lives in a hole in the ground. You'd be as cozy as a groundhog, Mary."

"I bet he lives in his own dirt, all right." She served my father his supper and he told her the story of Joe Phippen, the roofed cellar, the boards across the dirt floor. He left out the axe but not the whisky and the cat. For Mary, that was enough.

"A man that'd do a thing like that ought to be locked up."

"Maybe so," my father said. "Just the same I hope they don't get him for a while yet. Old Joe."

"Eat your supper," Mary said, bending over me. I did not for some time realize that I was no longer afraid of her. "Look at her," she said. "Her eyes dropping out of her head, all she's been and seen. Was he feeding the whisky to her too?"

"Not a drop," said my father, and looked steadily down the table at me. Like the children in fairy stories who have seen their parents make pacts with terrifying strangers, who have discovered that our fears are based on nothing but the truth, but who come back fresh from marvellous escapes and take up their knives and forks, with humility and good manners, prepared to live happily ever after—like them, dazed and powerful with secrets, I never said a word.

# Something I've Been
# Meaning to Tell You

~

"Anyway, he knows how to fascinate the women," said Et to Char. She could not tell if Char went paler, hearing this, because Char was pale in the first place as anybody could get. She was like a ghost now, with her hair gone white. But still beautiful, she couldn't lose it.

"No matter to him the age or the size," Et pressed on. "It's natural to him as breathing, I guess. I only hope the poor things aren't taken in by it."

"I wouldn't worry," Char said.

The day before, Et had taken Blaikie Noble up on his invitation to go along on one of his tours and listen to his spiel. Char was asked too, but of course she didn't go. Blaikie Noble ran a bus. The bottom part of it was painted red and the top part was striped, to give the effect of an awning. On the side was painted: LAKESHORE TOURS, INDIAN GRAVES, LIMESTONE GARDENS, MILLIONAIRE'S MANSION, BLAIKIE NOBLE, DRIVER, GUIDE. Blaikie had a room at the hotel, and he also worked on the grounds, with one helper, cutting grass and clipping hedges and digging the borders. What a comedown, Et had said at the beginning of the summer when they first found out he was back. She and Char had known him in the old days.

So Et found herself squeezed into his bus with a lot of strangers, though before the afternoon was over she had made friends with a number of them and had a couple of promises of jackets needing letting out, as if she didn't have enough to do already. That was beside the point, the thing on her mind was watching Blaikie.

And what did he have to show? A few mounds with grass growing on them, covering dead Indians, a plot full of odd-shaped, grayish-white, dismal-looking limestone things—farfetched imitations of plants (there could be the cemetery, if that was what you wanted)—and an old monstrosity of a house built with liquor money. He made the most of it. A historical discourse on the Indians, then a scientific discourse on the Limestone. Et had no way of knowing how much of it was true. Arthur would know. But Arthur wasn't there; there was nobody there but silly women, hoping to walk beside Blaikie to and from the sights, chat with him over their tea in the Limestone Pavilion, looking forward to having his strong hand under their elbows, the other hand brushing somewhere around the waist when he helped them down off the bus ("I'm not a tourist," Et whispered sharply when he tried it on her).

He told them the house was haunted. The first Et had ever heard of it, living ten miles away all her life. A woman had killed her husband, the son of the millionaire, at least it was believed she had killed him.

"How?" cried some lady, thrilled out of her wits.

"Ah, the ladies are always anxious to know the means," said Blaikie, in a voice like cream, scornful and loving. "It was a slow—poison. Or that's what they said. This is all hearsay, all local gossip." (Local my foot, said Et to herself.) "She didn't appreciate his lady friends. The wife didn't. No."

He told them the ghost walked up and down in the garden, between two rows of blue spruce. It was not the murdered man who walked, but the wife, regretting. Blaikie smiled ruefully at the busload. At first Et had thought his attentions were all false, an ordinary commercial flirtation, to give them their money's worth. But gradually she was getting a different notion. He bent to each woman he talked to—it didn't matter how fat or scrawny or silly she was—as if there was one thing in her he would like to find. He had a gentle and laughing but ultimately serious, narrowing look (was that the look men finally had when they made love, that Et would never see?) that made him seem to want to be a deep-sea diver diving down, down through all the emptiness and cold and wreckage to discover the one thing he had set his heart on, something small and precious, hard to locate, as a ruby maybe on the ocean floor. That was a look she would like to have described to Char. No doubt Char had seen it. But did she know how freely it was being distributed?

CHAR AND ARTHUR had been planning a trip that summer to see Yellowstone Park and the Grand Canyon, but they did not go. Arthur suffered a series of dizzy spells just at the end of school, and the doctor put him to bed. Several things were the matter with him. He was anemic, he had an irregular heartbeat, there was trouble with his kidneys. Et worried about leukemia. She woke at night, worrying.

"Don't be silly," said Char serenely. "He's overtired."

Arthur got up in the evenings and sat in his dressing gown. Blaikie Noble came to visit. He said his room at the hotel was a hole above the kitchen, they were trying to steam-cook him. It made him appreciate the cool of the porch. They played the games that Arthur loved, school-teacher's games. They played a geography game, and they tried to see who could make the most words out of the name Beethoven. Arthur won. He got thirty-four. He was immensely delighted.

"You'd think you'd found the Holy Grail," Char said.

They played "Who Am I?" Each of them had to choose somebody to be—real or imaginary, living or dead, human or animal—and the others had to try to guess it in twenty questions. Et got who Arthur was on the thirteenth question. Sir Galahad.

"I never thought you'd get it so soon."

"I thought back to Char saying about the Holy Grail."

*"My strength is as the strength of ten,"* said Blaikie Noble, *"because my heart is pure.* I didn't know I remembered that."

"You should have been King Arthur," Et said. "King Arthur is your namesake."

"I should have. King Arthur was married to the most beautiful woman in the world."

"Ha," said Et. "We all know the end of that story."

Char went into the living room and played the piano in the dark.

> *The flowers that bloom in the spring, tra-la,*
> *Have nothing to do with the case. . . .*

When Et arrived, out of breath, that past June, and said, "Guess who I saw downtown on the street?" Char, who was on her knees picking strawberries, said, "Blaikie Noble."

"You've seen him."

"No," said Char. "I just knew. I think I knew by your voice."

A name that had not been mentioned between them for thirty years. Et was too amazed then to think of the explanation that came to her later. Why did it need to be a surprise to Char? There was a postal service in this country, there had been all along.

"I asked him about his wife," she said. "The one with the dolls." (As if Char wouldn't remember.) "He says she died a long time ago. Not only that. He married another one and she's dead. Neither could have been rich. And where is all the Nobles' money, from the hotel?"

"We'll never know," said Char, and ate a strawberry.

. . .

THE HOTEL had just recently been opened up again. The Nobles had given it up in the twenties and the town had operated it for a while as a hospital. Now some people from Toronto had bought it, renovated the dining room, put in a cocktail lounge, reclaimed the lawns and garden, though the tennis court seemed to be beyond repair. There was a croquet set put out again. People came to stay in the summers, but they were not the sort of people who used to come. Retired couples. Many widows and single ladies. Nobody would have walked a block to see them get off the boat, Et thought. Not that there was a boat anymore.

That first time she met Blaikie Noble on the street she had made a point of not being taken aback. He was wearing a creamy suit and his hair, that had always been bleached by the sun, was bleached for good now, white.

"Blaikie. I knew either it was you or a vanilla ice-cream cone. I bet you don't know who I am."

"You're Et Desmond and the only thing different about you is you cut off your braids." He kissed her forehead, nervy as always.

"So you're back visiting old haunts," said Et, wondering who had seen that.

"Not visiting. Haunting." He told her then how he had got wind of the hotel opening up again, and how he had been doing this sort of thing, driving tour buses, in various places, in Florida and Banff. And when she asked he told her about his two wives. He never asked was she married, taking for granted she wasn't. He never asked if Char was, till she told him.

ET REMEMBERED the first time she understood that Char was beautiful. She was looking at a picture taken of them, of Char and herself and their brother who was drowned. Et was ten in the picture, Char fourteen and Sandy seven, just a couple weeks short of all he would ever be. Et was sitting in an armless chair and Char was behind her, arms folded on the chair back, with Sandy in his sailor suit cross-legged on the floor—or marble terrace, you would think, with the effect made by what had been nothing but a dusty, yellowing screen, but came out in the picture a pillar and draped curtain, a scene of receding poplars and fountains. Char had pinned her front hair up for the picture and was wearing a bright blue, ankle-length silk dress—of course the color did not show—with complicated black velvet piping. She was smiling slightly, with great composure. She could have been eighteen, she could have been twenty-two. Her beauty was not of the fleshy timid sort most often featured on calendars and cigar boxes of the period, but was sharp and delicate, intolerant, challenging.

Et took a long look at this picture and then went and looked at Char, who was in the kitchen. It was washday. The woman who came to help was pulling clothes through the wringer, and their mother was sitting down resting and staring through the screen door (she never got over Sandy; nobody expected her to). Char was starching their father's collars. He had a tobacco and candy store on the Square and wore a fresh collar every day. Et was prepared to find that some metamorphosis had taken place, as in the background, but it was not so. Char, bending over the starch basin, silent and bad-humored (she hated washday, the heat and steam and flapping sheets and chugging commotion of the machine—in fact, she was not fond of any kind of housework), showed in her real face the same almost disdainful harmony as in the photograph. This made Et understand, in some not entirely welcome way, that the qualities of legend were real, that they surfaced where and when you least expected. She had almost thought beautiful women were a fictional invention. She and Char would go down to watch the people get off the excursion boat, on Sundays, walking up to the hotel. So much white it hurt your eyes, the ladies' dresses and parasols and the men's summer suits and panama hats, not to speak of the sun dazzling on the water and the band playing. But looking closely at those ladies, Et found fault. Coarse skin or fat behind or chicken necks or dull nests of hair, probably ratted. Et did not let anything get by her, young as she was. At school she was respected for her self-possession and her sharp tongue. She was the one to tell you if you had been at the blackboard with a hole in your stocking or a ripped hem. She was the one who imitated (but in a safe corner of the schoolyard, out of earshot, always) the teacher reading "The Burial of Sir John Moore."

All the same it would have suited her better to have found one of those ladies beautiful, not Char. It would have been more appropriate. More suitable than Char in her wet apron with her cross expression, bent over the starch basin. Et was a person who didn't like contradictions, didn't like things out of place, didn't like mysteries or extremes.

She didn't like the bleak notoriety of having Sandy's drowning attached to her, didn't like the memory people kept of her father carrying the body up from the beach. She could be seen at twilight, in her gym bloomers, turning cartwheels on the lawn of the stricken house. She made a wry mouth, which nobody saw, one day in the park when Char said, "That was my little brother who was drowned."

THE PARK overlooked the beach. They were standing there with Blaikie Noble, the hotel owner's son, who said, "Those waves can be dangerous. Three or four years ago there was a kid drowned."

And Char said—to give her credit, she didn't say it tragically, but almost with amusement, that he should know so little about Mock Hill people—"That was my little brother who was drowned."

Blaikie Noble was not any older than Char—if he had been, he would have been fighting in France—but he had not had to live all his life in Mock Hill. He did not know the real people there as well as he knew the regular guests at his father's hotel. Every winter he went with his parents to California, on the train. He had seen the Pacific surf. He had pledged allegiance to their flag. His manners were democratic, his skin was tanned. This was at a time when people were not usually tanned as a result of leisure, only work. His hair was bleached by the sun. His good looks were almost as notable as Char's but his were corrupted by charm, as hers were not.

It was the heyday of Mock Hill and all the other towns around the lakes, of all the hotels which in later years would become Sunshine Camps for city children, t.b. sanitoriums, barracks for R.A.F. training pilots in World War II. The white paint on the hotel was renewed every spring, hollowed-out logs filled with flowers were set on the railings, pots of flowers swung on chains above them. Croquet sets and wooden swings were set out on the lawns, the tennis court rolled. People who could not afford the hotel, young workingmen, shop clerks, and factory girls from the city, stayed in a row of tiny cottages, joined by latticework that hid their garbage pails and communal outhouses, stretching far up the beach. Girls from Mock Hill, if they had mothers to tell them what to do, were told not to walk out there. Nobody told Char what to do, so she walked along the boardwalk in front of them in the glaring afternoon, taking Et with her for company. The cottages had no glass in their windows; they had only propped-up wooden shutters that were closed at night. From the dark holes came one or two indistinct sad or drunk invitations, that was all. Char's looks and style did not attract men, perhaps intimidated them. All through high school in Mock Hill she had not one boyfriend. Blaikie Noble was her first, if that was what he was.

What did this affair of Char's and Blaikie Noble's amount to, in the summer of 1918? Et was never sure. He did not call at the house, at least not more than once or twice. He was kept busy working at the hotel. Every afternoon he drove an open excursion wagon, with an awning on top of it, up the lakeshore road, taking people to look at the Indian graves and the limestone garden and to glimpse through the trees the Gothic stone mansion, built by a Toronto distiller and known locally as Grog Castle. He was also in charge of the variety show the hotel put on once a week, with a mixture of local talent, recruited guests, and singers and comedians brought in especially for the performance.

Late mornings seemed to be the time he and Char had. "Come on," Char would say, "I have to go downtown," and she would in fact pick up the mail and walk partway round the Square before veering off into the park. Soon, Blaikie Noble would appear from the side door of the hotel and come bounding up the steep path. Sometimes he would not even bother with the path but jump over the back fence, to amaze them. None of this, the bounding or jumping, was done the way some boy from Mock Hill High School might have done it, awkwardly yet naturally. Blaikie Noble behaved like a man imitating a boy; he mocked himself but was graceful, like an actor.

"Isn't he stuck on himself?" said Et to Char, watching. The position she had taken up right away on Blaikie was that she didn't like him.

"Of course he is," said Char.

She told Blaikie. "Et says you're stuck on yourself."

"What did you say?"

"I told her you had to be, nobody else is."

Blaikie didn't mind. He had taken the position that he liked Et. He would with a quick tug loosen and destroy the arrangement of looped-up braids she wore. He told them things about the concert artists. He told them the Scottish ballad singer was a drunk and wore corsets, that the female impersonator even in his hotel room donned a blue nightgown with feathers, that the lady ventriloquist talked to her dolls—they were named Alphonse and Alicia—as if they were real people, and had them sitting up in bed one on each side of her.

"How would you know that?" Char said.

"I took her up her breakfast."

"I thought you had maids to do that."

"The morning after the show I do it. That's when I hand them their pay envelope and give them their walking papers. Some of them would stay all week if you didn't inform them. She sits up in bed trying to feed them bits of bacon and talking to them and doing them answering back, you'd have a fit if you could see."

"She's cracked, I guess," Char said peacefully.

ONE NIGHT that summer Et woke up and remembered she had left her pink organdie dress on the line, after hand-washing it. She thought she heard rain, just the first few drops. She didn't, it was just leaves rustling, but she was confused, waking up like that. She thought it was far on in the night too, but thinking about it later she decided it might have been only around midnight. She got up and went downstairs, turned on the back kitchen light, and let herself out the back door, and standing on the stoop pulled the clothesline towards her. Then almost under her feet, from the grass right beside the stoop, where there was a big lilac bush that had grown and spread, untended, to the size of a tree, two figures lifted themselves, didn't stand or even sit up, just roused their heads as if from bed, still tangled together some way. The back kitchen light didn't shine directly out but lit the yard enough for her to see their faces. Blaikie and Char.

She never did get a look at what state their clothes were in, to see how far they had gone or were going. She wouldn't have wanted to. To see their faces was enough for her. Their mouths were big and swollen, their cheeks flattened, coarsened, their eyes holes. Et left her dress, she fled into the house and into her bed where she surprised herself by falling asleep. Char never said a word about it to her next day. All she said was "I brought your dress in, Et. I thought it might rain." As if she had never seen Et out there pulling on the clothesline. Et wondered. She knew if she said, "You saw me," Char would probably tell her it had been a dream. She let Char think she had been fooled into believing that, if that was what Char was thinking. That way, Et was left knowing more; she was left knowing what Char looked like when she lost her powers, abdicated. Sandy drowned, with green stuff clogging his nostrils, couldn't look more lost than that.

BEFORE CHRISTMAS the news came to Mock Hill that Blaikie Noble was married. He had married the lady ventriloquist, the one with Alphonse and Alicia. Those dolls, who wore evening dress and had sleek hairdos in the style of Vernon and Irene Castle, were more clearly remembered than the lady herself. The only thing people recalled for sure about her was that she could not have been under forty. A nineteen-year-old boy. It was because he had not been brought up like other boys, had been allowed the run of the hotel, taken to California, let mix with all sorts of people. The result was depravity, and could have been predicted.

Char swallowed poison. Or what she thought was poison. It was laundry blueing. The first thing she could reach down from the shelf in the back kitchen. Et came home after school—she had heard the news at noon, from Char herself, in fact, who had laughed and said, "Wouldn't that kill you?"—and she found Char vomiting into the toilet. "Go get the Medical Book," Char said to her. A terrible involuntary groan came out of her. "Read what it says about poison." Et went instead to phone the doctor. Char came staggering out of the bathroom holding the bottle of bleach they kept behind the tub. "If you don't put up the phone I'll drink the whole bottle," she said in a harsh whisper. Their mother was presumably asleep behind her closed door.

Et had to hang up the phone and look in the ugly old book where she had read long ago about childbirth and signs of death, and had learned about holding a mirror to the mouth. She was under the mistaken impression that Char had been drinking from the bleach bottle already, so she read all about that. Then she found it was the blueing. Blueing was not in the book, but it seemed the best thing to do would be to induce vomiting, as the book advised for most poisons—Char was at it already, didn't need to have it induced—and then drink a quart of milk. When Char got the milk down she was sick again.

"I didn't do this on account of Blaikie Noble," she said between spasms. "Don't you ever think that. I wouldn't be such a fool. A pervert like him. I did it because I'm sick of living."

"What are you sick of about living?" said Et sensibly when Char had wiped her face.

"I'm sick of this town and all the stupid people in it and Mother and her dropsy and keeping house and washing sheets every day. I don't think I'm going to vomit anymore. I think I could drink some coffee. It says coffee."

Et made a pot and Char got out two of the best cups. They began to giggle as they drank.

"I'm sick of Latin," Et said. "I'm sick of Algebra. I think I'll take blueing."

"Life is a burden," Char said. "O Life, where is thy sting?"

"O Death. O Death, where is thy sting?"

"Did I say Life? I meant Death. O Death, where is thy sting? Pardon me."

ONE AFTERNOON Et was staying with Arthur while Char shopped and changed books at the library. She wanted to make him an eggnog, and she went searching in Char's cupboard for the nutmeg. In with the vanilla and the almond extract and the artificial rum she found a small bottle of a strange liquid. ZINC PHOSPHIDE. She read the label and turned it around in her hands. A rodenticide. Rat poison, that must mean. She had not known Char and Arthur were troubled with rats. They kept a cat, old Tom, asleep now around Arthur's feet. She unscrewed the top and sniffed at it, to know what it smelled like. Like nothing. Of course. It must taste like nothing too, or it wouldn't fool the rats.

She put it back where she had found it. She made Arthur his eggnog and took it in and watched him drink it. A slow poison. She remembered that from Blaikie's foolish story. Arthur drank with an eager noise, like a child, more to please her, she thought, than because he was so pleased himself. He would drink anything you handed him. Naturally.

"How are you these days, Arthur?"

"Oh, Et. Some days a bit stronger, and then I seem to slip back. It takes time."

But there was none gone, the bottle seemed full. What awful nonsense. Like something you read about, Agatha Christie. She would mention it to Char and Char would tell her the reason.

"Do you want me to read to you?" she asked Arthur, and he said yes. She sat by the bed and read to him from a book about the Duke of Wellington. He had been reading it by himself but his arms got tired holding it. All those battles, and wars, and terrible things, what did Arthur know about such affairs, why was he so interested? He knew nothing. He did not know why things happened, why people could not behave sensibly. He was too good. He knew about history but not about what went on, in front of his eyes, in his house, anywhere. Et differed from Arthur in knowing that something went on, even if she could not understand why; she differed from him in knowing there were those you could not trust.

She did not say anything to Char after all. Every time she was in the house she tried to make some excuse to be alone in the kitchen, so that she could open the cupboard and stand on tiptoe and look in, to see it over the tops of the other bottles, to see that the level had not gone down. She did think maybe she was going a little strange, as old maids did; this fear of hers was like the absurd and harmless fears young girls sometimes have, that they will jump out a window, or strangle a baby sitting in its buggy. Though it was not her own acts she was frightened of.

ET LOOKED at Char and Blaikie and Arthur, sitting on the porch, trying to decide if they wanted to go in and put the light on and play cards. She wanted to convince herself of her silliness. Char's hair, and Blaikie's too, shone in the dark. Arthur was almost bald now and Et's own hair was thin and dark. Char and Blaikie seemed to her the same kind of animal—tall, light, powerful, with a dangerous luxuriance. They sat apart but shone out together. *Lovers.* Not a soft word, as people thought, but cruel and tearing. There was Arthur in the rocker with a quilt over his knees, foolish as something that hasn't grown its final, most necessary, skin. Yet in a way the people like Arthur were the most troublemaking of all.

"I love my love with an R, because he is ruthless. His name is Rex, and he lives in a—restaurant."

"I love my love with an A, because he is absentminded. His name is Arthur, and he lives in an ash can."

"Why, Et," Arthur said. "I never suspected. But I don't know if I like about the ash can."

"You would think we were all twelve years old," said Char.

· · ·

AFTER THE BLUEING episode Char became popular. She became involved in the productions of the Amateur Dramatic Society and the Oratorio Society, although she was never much of an actress or a singer. She
was always the cold and beautiful heroine in the plays, or the brittle ex-
quisite young society woman. She learned to smoke, because of having to
do it onstage. In one play Et never forgot, she was a statue. Or rather, she
played a girl who had to pretend to be a statue, so that a young man fell in
love with her and later discovered, to his confusion and perhaps disappointment, that she was only human. Char had to stand for eight minutes
perfectly still onstage, draped in white crêpe and showing the audience her
fine indifferent profile. Everybody marvelled at how she did it.

The moving spirit behind the Amateur Dramatic Society and the Oratorio Society was a high-school teacher new to Mock Hill, Arthur Comber.
He taught Et history in her last year. Everybody said he gave her A's
because he was in love with her sister, but Et knew it was because she
worked harder than she ever had before; she learned the history of North
America as she had never learned anything in her life. Missouri Compro-
mise. Mackenzie to the Pacific, 1793. She never forgot.

Arthur Comber was thirty or so, with a high bald forehead, a red face in
spite of not drinking (that later paled), and a clumsy, excited manner. He
knocked a bottle of ink off his desk and permanently stained the History
Room floor. "Oh dear, oh dear," he said, crouching down to the spreading
ink, flapping at it with his handkerchief. Et imitated that. "Oh dear, oh
dear!" "Oh, good heavens!" All his flustery exclamations and miscal-
culated gestures. Then, when he took her essay at the door, his red face
shining with eagerness, giving her work and herself such a welcome, she
felt sorry. That was why she worked so hard, she thought, to make up for
mocking him.

He had a black scholar's gown he wore over his suit, to teach in. Even
when he wasn't wearing it, Et could see it on him. Hurrying along the
street to one of his innumerable, joyfully undertaken obligations, flapping away at the Oratorio singers, jumping onstage—so the whole floor
trembled—to demonstrate something to the actors in a play, he seemed
to her to have those long ridiculous crow's wings flapping after him, to be
as different from other men, as absurd yet intriguing, as the priest from
Holy Cross. Char made him give up the gown altogether, after they were
married. She had heard that he tripped in it, running up the steps of the
school. He had gone sprawling. That finished it, she ripped it up.

"I was afraid one of these days you'd really get hurt."

But Arthur said, "Ah. You thought I looked like a fool."

Char didn't deny it, though his eyes on her, his wide smile, were begging her to. Her mouth twitched at the corners, in spite of herself. Contempt. Fury. Et saw, they both saw, a great wave of that go over her before she could smile at him and say, "Don't be silly." Then her smile and her eyes were trying to hold on to him, trying to clutch onto his goodness (which she saw, as much as anybody else did, but which finally only enraged her, Et believed, like everything else about him, like his sweaty forehead and his galloping optimism), before that boiling wave could come back again, altogether carry her away.

Char had a miscarriage during the first year of her marriage and was sick for a long time afterwards. She was never pregnant again. Et by this time was not living in the house; she had her own place on the Square, but she was there one time on washday, helping Char haul the sheets off the line. Their parents were both dead by that time—their mother had died before and their father after the wedding—but it looked to Et like sheets for two beds.

"It gives you plenty of wash."

"What does?"

"Changing sheets like you do."

Et was often there in the evening, playing rummy with Arthur while Char, in the other room, picked at the piano in the dark. Or talking and reading library books with Char, while Arthur marked his papers. Arthur walked her home. "Why do you have to go off and live by yourself anyway?" he scolded her. "You ought to come back and live with us."

"Three's a crowd."

"It wouldn't be for long. Some man is going to come along someday and fall hard."

"If he was such a fool as to do that I'd never fall for him, so we'd be back where we started."

"I was a fool that fell for Char, and she ended up having me."

Just the way he said her name indicated that Char was above, outside, all ordinary considerations—a marvel, a mystery. No one could hope to solve her, they were lucky just being allowed to contemplate her. Et was on the verge of saying, "She swallowed blueing once over a man that wouldn't have her," but she thought, What would be the good of it, Char would only seem more splendid to him, like a heroine out of Shakespeare. He squeezed Et's waist as if to stress their companionable puzzlement, involuntary obeisance, before her sister. She felt afterwards the bumpy pressure of his fingers as if they had left dents just above where her skirt fastened. It had felt like somebody absentmindedly trying out the keys of a piano.

. . .

ET HAD set up in the dressmaking business. She had a long narrow room on the Square, once a shop, where she did all her fitting, sewing, cutting, pressing, and, behind a curtain, her sleeping and cooking. She could lie in bed and look at the squares of pressed tin on her ceiling, their flower pattern, all her own. Arthur had not liked her taking up dressmaking because he thought she was too smart for it. All the hard work she had done in History had given him an exaggerated idea of her brains. "Besides," she told him, "it takes more brains to cut and fit, if you do it right, than to teach people about the War of 1812. Because, once you learn that, it's learned and isn't going to change you. Whereas every article of clothing you make is an entirely new proposition."

"Still it's a surprise," said Arthur, "to see the way you settle down."

It surprised everybody, but not Et herself. She made the change easily, from a girl turning cartwheels to a town fixture. She drove the other dressmakers out of business. They had been meek, unimportant creatures anyway, going around to people's houses, sewing in back rooms, and being grateful for meals. Only one serious rival appeared in all Et's years, and that was a Finnish woman who called herself a designer. Some people gave her a try, because people are never satisfied, but it soon came out she was all style and no fit. Et never mentioned her, she let people find out for themselves; but afterwards, when this woman had left town and gone to Toronto—where, from what Et had seen on the streets, nobody knew a good fit from a bad—Et did not restrain herself. She would say to a customer she was fitting, "I see you're still wearing that herringbone my foreigner friend tacked together for you. I saw you on the street."

"Oh, I know," the woman would say. "But I do have to wear it out."

"You can't see yourself from behind anyway, what's the difference."

Customers took this kind of thing from Et, came to expect it, even. She's a terror, they said about her, Et's a terror. She had them at a disadvantage, she had them in their slips and corsets. Ladies who looked quite firm and powerful outside were here immobilized, apologetic, exposing such trembly, meek-looking thighs squeezed together by corsets, such long sad breast creases, bellies blown up and torn by children and operations.

Et always closed her front curtains tight, pinning the crack.

"That's to keep the men from peeking."

Ladies laughed nervously.

"That's to keep Jimmy Saunders from stumping over to get an eyeful."

Jimmy Saunders was a World War I veteran who had a little shop next to Et's, harness and leather goods.

"Oh, Et. Jimmy Saunders has a wooden leg."

"He hasn't got wooden eyes. Or anything else that I know of."

"Et, you're terrible."

ET KEPT Char beautifully dressed. The two steadiest criticisms of Char, in Mock Hill, were that she dressed too elegantly, and that she smoked. It was because she was a teacher's wife that she should have refrained from doing either of these things, but Arthur of course let her do anything she liked, even buying her a cigarette holder so she could look like a lady in a magazine. She smoked at a high-school dance, and wore a backless satin evening dress, and danced with a boy who had got a high-school girl pregnant, and it was all the same to Arthur. He did not get to be Principal. Twice the school board passed him over and brought in somebody from outside, and when they finally gave him the job, in 1942, it was only temporarily and because so many teachers were away at war.

Char fought hard all these years to keep her figure. Nobody but Et and Arthur knew what effort that cost her. Nobody but Et knew it all. Both of their parents had been heavy, and Char had inherited the tendency, though Et was always as thin as a stick. Char did exercises and drank a glass of warm water before every meal. But sometimes she went on eating binges. Et had known her to eat a dozen cream puffs one after the other, a pound of peanut brittle, or a whole lemon-meringue pie. Then pale and horrified she took down Epsom salts, three or four or five times the prescribed amount. For two or three days she would be sick, dehydrated, purging her sins, as Et said. During these periods she could not look at food. Et would have to come and cook Arthur's supper. Arthur did not know about the pie or the peanut brittle or whatever it was, or about the Epsom salts. He thought she had gained a pound or two and was going through a fanatical phase of dieting. He worried about her.

"What is the difference, what does it matter?" he would say to Et. "She would still be beautiful."

"She won't do herself any harm," said Et, enjoying her food, and glad to see that worry hadn't put him off his. She always made him good suppers.

IT WAS the week before the Labor Day weekend. Blaikie had gone to Toronto—for a day or two, he said.

"It's quiet without him," said Arthur.

"I never noticed he was such a conversationalist," Et said.

"I only mean in the way that you get used to somebody."

"Maybe we ought to get unused to him," said Et.

Arthur was unhappy. He was not going back to the school; he had obtained a leave of absence until after Christmas. Nobody believed he would go back then.

"I suppose he has his own plans for the winter," he said.

"He may have his own plans for right now. You know, I have my customers from the hotel. I have my friends. Ever since I went on that excursion, I hear things."

She never knew where she got the inspiration to say what she said, where it came from. She had not planned it at all, yet it came so easily, believably.

"I hear he's taken up with a well-to-do woman down at the hotel."

Arthur was the one to take an interest, not Char.

"A widow?"

"Twice, I believe. The same as he is. And she has the money from both. It's been suspected for some time and she was talking about it openly. He never said anything, though. He never said anything to you, did he, Char?"

"No," said Char.

"I heard this afternoon that now he's gone, and she's gone. It wouldn't be the first time he pulled something like this. Char and I remember."

Then Arthur wanted to know what she meant and she told him the story of the lady ventriloquist, remembering even the names of the dolls, though of course she left out all about Char. Char sat through this, even contributing a bit.

"They might come back but my guess is they'd be embarrassed. He'd be embarrassed. He'd be embarrassed to come here, anyway."

"Why?" said Arthur, who had cheered up a little through the ventriloquist story. "We never set down any rule against a man getting married."

Char got up and went into the house. After a while they heard the sound of the piano.

THE QUESTION often crossed Et's mind in later years—what did she mean to do about this story when Blaikie got back? For she had no reason to believe he would not come back. The answer was that she had not made any plans at all. She had not planned anything. She supposed she might have wanted to make trouble between him and Char—make Char pick a fight with him, her suspicions roused even if rumors had not been borne out, make Char read what he might do again in the light of what he had done before. She did not know what she wanted. Only to throw things into confusion, for she believed then that somebody had to, before it was too late.

Arthur made as good a recovery as could be expected at his age; he went back to teaching history to the senior classes, working half-days until it was time for him to retire. Et kept up her own place on the Square and tried to get up and do some cooking and cleaning for Arthur, as well. Finally, after he retired, she moved back into the house, keeping the other place only for business purposes. "Let people jaw all they like," she said. "At our age."

Arthur lived on and on, though he was frail and slow. He walked down to the Square once a day, dropped in on Et, went and sat in the park. The hotel closed down and was sold again. There was a story that it was going to be opened up and used as a rehabilitation center for drug addicts, but the town got up a petition and that fell through. Eventually it was torn down.

Et's eyesight was not as good as it used to be, she had to slow down. She had to turn people away. Still she worked, every day. In the evenings Arthur watched television or read, but she sat out on the porch, in the warm weather, or in the dining room in winter, rocking and resting her eyes. She came and watched the news with him, and made him his hot drink, cocoa or tea.

THERE WAS no trace of the bottle. Et went and looked in the cupboard as soon as she could—having run to the house in response to Arthur's early-morning call, and found the doctor, old McClain, coming in at the same time. She ran out and looked in the garbage, but she never found it. Could Char have found the time to bury it? She was lying on the bed, fully and nicely dressed, her hair piled up. There was no fuss about the cause of death as there is in stories. She had complained of weakness to Arthur the night before, after Et had gone; she had said she thought she was getting the flu. So the old doctor said heart, and let it go. Nor could Et ever know. Would what was in that bottle leave a body undisfigured, as Char's was? Perhaps what was in the bottle was not what it said. She was not even sure that it had been there that last evening; she had been too carried away with what she was saying to go and look, as she usually did. Perhaps it had been thrown out earlier and Char had taken something else, pills maybe. Perhaps it really was her heart. All that purging would have weakened anybody's heart.

Her funeral was on Labor Day and Blaikie Noble came, cutting out his bus tour. Arthur in his grief had forgotten about Et's story, was not surprised to see Blaikie there. He had come back to Mock Hill on the day Char was found. A few hours too late, like some story. Et in her natural confusion could not remember what it was. Romeo and Juliet, she thought later. But Blaikie of course did not do away with himself afterwards; he went back to Toronto. For a year or two he sent Christmas cards, then was not heard of anymore. Et would not be surprised if her story of his marrying had not come true in the end. Only her timing was mistaken.

Sometimes Et had it on the tip of her tongue to say to Arthur, "There's something I've been meaning to tell you." She didn't believe she was going to let him die without knowing. He shouldn't be allowed. He kept a picture of Char on his bureau. It was the one taken of her in her costume for that play, where she played the statue-girl. But Et let it go, day to day. She and Arthur still played rummy and kept up a bit of garden, along with raspberry canes. If they had been married, people would have said they were very happy.

# The Ottawa Valley

~

I THINK of my mother sometimes in department stores. I don't know why, I was never in one with her; their plenitude, their sober bustle, it seems to me, would have satisfied her. I think of her of course when I see somebody on the street who has Parkinson's disease, and more and more often lately when I look in the mirror. Also in Union Station, Toronto, because the first time I was there I was with her, and my little sister. It was one summer during the War, we waited between trains; we were going home with her, with my mother, to her old home in the Ottawa Valley.

A cousin she was planning to meet, for a between-trains visit, did not show up. "She probably couldn't get away," said my mother, sitting in a leather chair in the darkly panelled Ladies' Lounge, which is now boarded up. "There was probably something to do that she couldn't leave to any-body else." This cousin was a legal secretary, and she worked for a senior partner in what my mother always called, in her categorical way, "the city's leading law firm." Once, she had come to visit us, wearing a large black hat and a black suit, her lips and nails like rubies. She did not bring her husband. He was an alcoholic. My mother always mentioned that her husband was an alcoholic, immediately after she had stated that she held an important job with the city's leading law firm. The two things were seen to balance each other, to be tied together in some inevitable and fore-boding way. In the same way, my mother would say of a family we knew that they had everything money could buy but their only son was an epileptic, or that the parents of the only person from our town who had become moderately famous, a pianist named Mary Renwick, had said that they would give all their daughter's fame for a pair of baby hands. *A pair of baby hands?* Luck was not without its shadow, in her universe.

My sister and I went out into the station, which was like a street with its lighted shops and like a church with its high curved roof and great windows at each end. It was full of the thunder of trains hidden, it seemed, just behind the walls, and an amplified voice, luxuriant, powerful, reciting place names that could not quite be understood. I bought a movie magazine and my sister bought chocolate bars with the money we had been given. I was going to say to her, "Give me a bite or I won't show you the way back," but she was so undone by the grandeur of the place, or subdued by her dependence on me, that she broke off a piece without being asked.

Late in the afternoon we got on the Ottawa train. We were surrounded by soldiers. My sister had to sit on my mother's knee. A soldier sitting in front of us turned around and joked with me. He looked very much like Bob Hope. He asked me what town I came from, and then he said, "Have they got the second story on there yet?" in just the sharp, unsmiling, smart-alecky way that Bob Hope would have said it. I thought that maybe he really was Bob Hope, travelling around incognito in a soldier's uniform. That did not seem unlikely to me. Outside of my own town—this far outside it, at least—all the bright and famous people in the world seemed to be floating around free, ready to turn up anywhere.

Aunt Dodie met us at the station in the dark and drove us to her house, miles out in the country. She was small and sharp-faced and laughed at the end of every sentence. She drove an old square-topped car with a running board.

"Well, did Her Majesty show up to see you?"

She was referring to the legal secretary, who was in fact her sister. Aunt Dodie was not really our aunt at all but our mother's cousin. She and her sister did not speak.

"No, but she must have been busy," said my mother neutrally.

"Oh, busy," said Aunt Dodie. "She's busy scraping the chicken dirt off her boots. Eh?" She drove fast, over washboard and potholes.

My mother waved at the blackness on either side of us. "Children! Children, this is the Ottawa Valley!"

IT WAS no valley. I looked for mountains, or at least hills, but in the morning all it was was fields and bush, and Aunt Dodie outside the window holding a milk pail for a calf. The calf was butting its head into the pail so hard it slopped the milk out, and Aunt Dodie was laughing and scolding and hitting it, trying to make it slow down. She called it a bugger. "Greedy little bugger!"

She was dressed in her milking outfit, which was many-layered and -colored and ragged and flopping like the clothes a beggarwoman might wear in a school play. A man's hat without a crown was shoved—for what purpose?—on her head.

My mother had not led me to believe we were related to people who dressed like that or who used the word *bugger*. "I will not tolerate filth," my mother always said. But apparently she tolerated Aunt Dodie. She said they had been like sisters when they were growing up. (The legal secretary, Bernice, had been older and had left home early.) Then my mother usually said that Aunt Dodie had had a tragic life.

Aunt Dodie's house was bare. It was the poorest house I had ever been in, to stay. From this distance, our own house—which I had always thought poor, because we lived too far out of town to have a flush toilet or running water, and certainly we had no real touches of luxury, like Venetian blinds—looked very comfortably furnished, with its books and piano and good set of dishes and one rug that was bought, not made out of rags. In Aunt Dodie's front room there was one overstuffed chair and a magazine rack full of old Sunday-school papers. Aunt Dodie lived off her cows. Her land was not worth farming. Every morning, after she finished milking and separating, she loaded the cans in the back of her pickup truck and drove seven miles to the cheese factory. She lived in dread of the milk inspector, who went around declaring cows tubercular, we understood, for no reason but spite, and to put poor farmers out of business. Big dairy interests paid him off, Aunt Dodie said.

The tragedy in her life was that she had been jilted. "Did you know," she said, "that I was jilted?" My mother had said we were never to mention it, and there was Aunt Dodie in her own kitchen, washing the noon dishes, with me wiping and my sister putting away (my mother had to go and have her rest), saying "jilted" proudly, as somebody would say "Did you know I had polio?" or some such bad important disease.

"I had my cake baked," she said. "I was in my wedding dress."

"Was it satin?"

"No, it was a nice dark-red merino wool, because of it being a late-fall wedding. We had the minister here. All prepared. My dad kept running out to the road to see if he could see him coming. It got dark, and I said, 'Time to go out and do the milking!' I pulled off my dress and I never put it back on. I gave it away. Lots of girls would've cried, but me, I laughed."

My mother telling the same story said, "When I went home two years after that, and I was staying with her, I used to wake up and hear her crying in the night. Night after night."

> *"There was I*
> *Waiting at the church,*
> *Waiting at the church,*
> *Waiting at the church.*
> *And when I found*
> *He'd left me in the lurch,*
> *Oh, how it did upset me."*

Aunt Dodie sang this at us, washing the dishes at her round table covered with scrubbed oilcloth. Her kitchen was as big as a house, with a back door and a front door; always a breeze blew through. She had a homemade icebox, such as I had never seen, with a big chunk of ice in it that she would haul in a child's wagon from the ice-house. The ice-house itself was remarkable, a roofed dugout where ice cut from the lake in winter lasted the summer, in sawdust.

"Of course it wasn't," she said, "in my case, it wasn't the church."

Across the fields from Aunt Dodie on the next farm lived my mother's brother, Uncle James, and his wife, Aunt Lena, and their eight children. That was the house where my mother had grown up. It was a bigger house with more furniture but still unpainted outside, dark gray. The furniture was mostly high wooden beds, with feather ticks and dark carved headboards. Under the beds were pots not emptied every day. We visited there but Aunt Dodie did not come with us. She and Aunt Lena did not speak. But Aunt Lena did not speak much to anybody. She had been a sixteen-year-old girl, straight out of the backwoods, said my mother and Aunt Dodie (which left you to wonder, Where was this?), when Uncle James married her. At this time, she would have been married ten or twelve years. She was tall and straight, flat as a board front and back—even though she would bear her ninth child before Christmas—darkly freckled, with large dark slightly inflamed eyes, animal's eyes. All the children had got those, instead of Uncle James's mild blue ones.

"When your mother was dying," said Aunt Dodie, "oh, I can hear her. Don't touch that towel! Use your own towel! Cancer, she thought you could catch it like the measles. She was that ignorant."

"I can't forgive her."

"And wouldn't let any of the kids go near her. I had to go over myself and give your mother her wash. I saw it all."

"I can never forgive her."

Aunt Lena was stiff all the time with what I now recognize as terror. She would not let her children swim in the lake for fear they would drown, she would not let them go tobogganing in winter for fear they would fall off the toboggan and break their necks, she would not let them learn to skate for fear they would break their legs and be crippled for life. She beat them all the time for fear they would grow up to be lazy, or liars, or clumsy people who broke things. They were not lazy but they broke things anyway; they were always darting and grabbing; and, of course, they were all liars, even the little ones, brilliant, instinctive liars who lied even when it was not necessary, just for the practice, and maybe the pleasure, of it. They were always telling and concealing, making and breaking alliances; they had the most delicate and ruthless political instincts. They howled when they were beaten. Pride was a luxury they had discarded long ago, or never considered. If you did not howl for Aunt Lena, when would she ever stop? Her arms were as long and strong as a man's, her face set in an expression of remote unanswerable fury. But five minutes, three minutes, afterwards, her children would have forgotten. With me, such a humiliation could last for weeks, or forever.

Uncle James kept the Irish accent my mother had lost and Aunt Dodie had halfway lost. His voice was lovely, saying the children's names. Marie, Ron-ald, Ru-thie. So tenderly, comfortingly, reproachfully he said their names, as if the names, or the children themselves, were jokes played on him. But he never held them back from being beaten, never protested. You would think all this had nothing to do with him. You would think Aunt Lena had nothing to do with him.

The youngest child slept in the parents' bed until a new baby displaced it.

"He used to come over and see me," Aunt Dodie said. "We used to have some good laughs. He used to bring two, three of the kids but he quit that. I know why. They'd tell on him. Then he quit coming himself. She lays down the law. But he gets it back on her, doesn't he?"

Aunt Dodie did not get a daily paper, just the weekly that was published in the town where she had picked us up.

"There's a mention in here about Allen Durrand."

"Allen Durrand?" said my mother doubtfully.

"Oh, he's a big Holstein man now. He married a West."

"What's the mention?"

"It's the Conservative Association. I bet he wants to get nominated. I bet."

She was in the rocker, with her boots off, laughing. My mother was sitting with her back against a porch post. They were cutting up yellow beans, to can.

"I was thinking about the time we gave him the lemonade," Aunt Dodie said, and turned to me. "He was just a French Canadian boy then, working here for a couple of weeks in the summer."

"Only his name was French," my mother said. "He didn't even speak it."

"You'd never know now. He turned his religion too, goes to St. John's."

"He was always intelligent."

"You bet he is. Oh, intelligent. But we got him with the lemonade.

"You picture the hottest possible day in summer. Your mother and I didn't mind it so much, we could stay in the house. But Allen had to be in the mow. You see they were getting the hay in. My dad was bringing it in and Allen was spreading it out. I bet James was over helping too."

"James was pitching on," my mother said. "Your dad was driving, and building the load."

"And they put Allen in the mow. You've no idea what a mow is like on that kind of a day. It's a hell on earth. So we thought it would be a nice idea to take him some lemonade— No. I'm getting ahead of myself. I meant to tell about the overalls first.

"Allen had brought me these overalls to fix just when the men were sitting down to dinner. He had a heavy pair of old suit pants on, and a work shirt, must have been killing him, though the shirt I guess he took off when he got in the barn. But he must've wanted the overalls on because they'd be cooler, you know, the circulation. I forget what had to be fixed on them, just some little thing. He must have been suffering bad in those old pants just to bring himself to ask, because he was awful shy. He'd be— what, then?"

"Seventeen," my mother said.

"And us two eighteen. It was the year before you went away to Normal. Yes. Well, I took and fixed his pants, just some little thing to do to them while you served up dinner. There I was sitting in the corner of the kitchen at the sewing machine when I had my inspiration, didn't I? I called you over. Pretended I was calling you to hold the material straight for me. So's you could see what I was doing. And neither one of us cracked a smile or dared look sideways at each other, did we?"

"No."

"Because my inspiration was to sew up his fly!

"So then, you see, a little bit on in the afternoon, with them out to work again, we got the idea for the lemonade. We made two pailfuls. One we took out to the men working in the field; we yelled to them and set it under a tree. And the other we took up to the mow and offered it to him. We'd used up every lemon we had, and even so it was weak. I remember we had to put vinegar in. But he wouldn't've noticed. I never saw a person so thirsty in my life as him. He drank by the dipperful, and then he just tipped up the pail. Drank it all down. Us standing there watching. How did we keep a straight face?"

"I'll never know," my mother said.

"Then we took the pail and made for the house and waited about two seconds before we came sneaking back. We hid ourselves up in the granary. That was like an oven too. I don't know how we stood it. But we climbed up on the sacks of feed and each found ourselves a crack or knothole or something to look through. We knew the corner of the barn the men always peed in. They peed down the shovel if they were upstairs. Down in the stable I guess they peed in the gutter. And soon enough, soon enough, he starts strolling over in that direction. Dropped his fork and starts strolling over. Puts his hand up to himself as he went. Sweat running down our faces from the heat and the way we had to keep from laughing. Oh, the cruelty of it! First he was just going easy, wasn't he? Then thinking about it I guess the need gets stronger; he looked down wondering what was the matter, and soon he's fairly clawin' and yankin' every which way, trying all he can to get himself free. But I'd sewed him up good and strong. I wonder when it hit him what'd been done?"

"Right then, I'd think. He was never stupid."

"He never was. So he must've put it all together. The lemonade and all. The one thing I don't guess he ever thought of was us hid up in the granary. Or else would he've done what he did next?"

"He wouldn't have," said my mother firmly.

"I don't know, though. He might've been past caring. Eh? He just finally went past caring and gave up and ripped down his overalls altogether and let 'er fly. We had the full view."

"He had his back to us."

"He did not! When he shot away there wasn't a thing we couldn't see. He turned himself sideways."

"I don't remember that."

"Well, I do. I haven't seen so many similar sights that I can afford to forget."

"Dodie!" said my mother, as if at this too-late point to issue a warning. (Another thing my mother quite often said was "I will never listen to smut.")

"Oh, you! You didn't run away yourself. Did you? Kept your eye to the knothole!"

My mother looked from me to Aunt Dodie and back with an unusual expression on her face: helplessness. I won't say she laughed. She just looked as if there was a point at which she might give up.

*The onset is very slow and often years may pass before the patient or his family observes that he is becoming disabled. He shows slowly increasing bodily rigidity, associated with tremors of the head and limbs. There may be various tics, twitches, muscle spasms, and other involuntary movements. Salivation increases and drooling is common. Scientifically the disease is known as paralysis agitans. It is also called Parkinson's disease or shaking palsy. Paralysis agitans affects first a single arm or leg, then the second limb on the same side and finally those on the other side. The face begins to lose its customary expressiveness and changes slowly or not at all with passing moods. The disease is typically one of elderly people, striking mostly persons in their sixties and seventies. No recoveries are recorded. Drugs are available to control the tremor and excess salivation. The benefits of these, however, are limited.* [Fishbein, *Medical Encyclopedia.*]

My mother, during this summer, would have been forty-one or forty-two years old, I think, somewhere around the age that I am now.

Just her left forearm trembled. The hand trembled more than the arm. The thumb knocked ceaselessly against the palm. She could, however, hide it in her fingers, and she could hold the arm still by stiffening it against her body.

UNCLE JAMES drank porter after supper. He let me taste it, black and bitter. Here was a new contradiction. "Before I married your father," my mother had told me, "I asked him to promise me that he would never drink, and he never has." But Uncle James, her brother, could drink without apologies.

On Saturday night we all went into town. My mother and my sister went in Aunt Dodie's car. I was with Uncle James and Aunt Lena and the children. The children claimed me. I was a little older than the oldest of them, and they treated me as if I were a trophy, someone for whose favor they could jostle and compete. So I was riding in their car, which was high and old and square-topped, like Aunt Dodie's. We were coming home, we had the windows rolled down for coolness, and unexpectedly Uncle James began to sing.

He had a fine voice, of course, a fine sad, lingering voice. I can remember perfectly well the tune of the song he sang, and the sound of his voice rolling out the black windows, but I can remember only bits of the words, here and there, though I have often tried to remember more, because I liked the song so well.

"*As I was a-goen over Kil-i-kenny Mountain . . .*"

I think that was the way it started.

Then further along something about *pearly*, or *early*, and *Some take delight in*—various things, and finally the strong but sad-sounding line:

"*But I take delight in the water of the barley.*"

There was silence in the car while he was singing. The children were not squabbling and being hit, some of them were even falling asleep. Aunt

Lena, with the youngest on her knee, was an unthreatening dark shape. The car bounced along as if it would go forever through a perfectly black night with its lights cutting a frail path; and there was a jackrabbit on the road, leaping out of our way, but nobody cried out to notice it, nobody broke the singing, its booming tender sadness.

*"But I take delight in THE WATER OF THE BARLEY."*

WE GOT to church early, so that we could go and look at the graves. St. John's was a white wooden church on the highway, with the graveyard behind it. We stopped at two stones, on which were written the words *Mother* and *Father*. Underneath in much smaller letters the names and dates of my mother's parents. Two flat stones, not very big, lying like paving stones in the clipped grass. I went off to look at things more interesting—urns and praying hands and angels in profile.

Soon my mother and Aunt Dodie came too.

"Who needs all this fancy folderol?" said Aunt Dodie, waving.

My sister, who was just learning to read, tried reading the inscriptions.

*"Until the Day Break"*

*"He is not Dead but Sleepeth"*

*"In Pacem"*

"What is *pacem*?"

"Latin," said my mother approvingly.

"A lot of these people put up these fancy stones and it is all show, they are still paying for them. Some of them still trying to pay for the plots and not even started on the stones. Look at that, for instance." Aunt Dodie pointed to a large cube of dark-blue granite, flecked white like a cooking pot, balanced on one corner.

"How modern," said my mother absently.

"That is Dave McColl's. Look at the size of it. And I know for a fact they told her if she didn't hurry up and pay something on the plot, they were going to dig him up and pitch him out on the highway."

"Is that Christian?" my mother wondered.

"Some people don't deserve Christian."

I felt something slithering down from my waist and realized that the elastic of my underpants had broken. I caught my hands to my sides in time—I had no hips then to hold anything up—and said to my mother in an angry whisper, "I have to have a safety pin."

"What do you want a safety pin for?" said my mother, in a normal or louder-than-normal voice. She could always be relied upon to be obtuse at such moments.

I would not answer, but glared at her beseechingly, threateningly.

"I bet her panties bust." Aunt Dodie laughed.

"Did they?" said my mother sternly, still not lowering her voice.

"*Yes.*"

"Well, take them off then," said my mother.

"Not right here, though," said Aunt Dodie. "There is the Ladies."

Behind St. John's Church, as behind a country school, were two wooden toilets.

"Then I wouldn't have anything on," I said to my mother, scandalized. I couldn't imagine walking into church in a blue taffeta dress and no pants. Rising to sing the hymns, sitting down, in *no pants.* The smooth cool boards of the pew and *no pants.*

Aunt Dodie was looking through her purse. "I wish I had one to give you but I haven't. You just run and take them off and nobody's going to know the difference. Lucky there's no wind."

I didn't move.

"Well, I do have one pin," said my mother doubtfully. "But I can't take it out. My slip strap broke this morning when I was getting dressed and I put a pin in to hold it. But I can't take that out."

My mother was wearing a soft gray dress covered with little flowers which looked as if they had been embroidered on, and a gray slip to match, because you could see through the material. Her hat was a dull rose color, matching the color of some of the flowers. Her gloves were almost the same rose and her shoes were white, with open toes. She had brought this whole outfit with her, had assembled it, probably, especially to wear when she walked into St. John's Church. She might have imagined a sunny morning, with St. John's bell ringing, just as it was ringing now. She must have planned this and visualized it just as I now plan and visualize, sometimes, what I will wear to a party.

"I can't take it out for you or my slip will show."

"People going in," Aunt Dodie said.

"Go to the Ladies and take them off. If you won't do that, go sit in the car."

I started for the car. I was halfway to the cemetery gate when my mother called my name. She marched ahead of me to the ladies' toilet, where without a word she reached inside the neck of her dress and brought out the pin. Turning my back—and not saying thank-you, because I was too deep in my own misfortune and too sure of my own rights—I fastened together the waistband of my pants. Then my mother walked ahead of me up the toilet path and around the side of the church. We were late, everybody had gone in. We had to wait while the choir, with the minister trailing, got themselves up the aisle at their religious pace.

> *"All things bright and beautiful,*
> *All creatures great and small,*
> *All things wise and wonderful,*
> *The Lord God made them all."*

When the choir was in place and the minister had turned to face the congregation, my mother set out boldly to join Aunt Dodie and my sister in a pew near the front. I could see that the gray slip had slid down half an inch and was showing in a slovenly way at one side.

After the service my mother turned in the pew and spoke to people. People wanted to know my name and my sister's name and then they said, "She does look like you"; "No, maybe this one looks more like you"; or, "I see your own mother in this one." They asked how old we were and what grade I was in at school and whether my sister was going to school. They asked her when she was going to start and she said, "I'm not," which was laughed at and repeated. (My sister often made people laugh without meaning to; she had such a firm way of publicizing her misunderstandings. In this case it turned out that she really did think she was not going to school because the primary school near where we lived was being torn down, and nobody had told her she would go on a bus.)

Two or three people said to me, "Guess who taught me when *I* went to school? Your momma!"

"She never learned me much," said a sweaty man, whose hand I could tell she did not want to shake, "but she was the best-lookin' one I ever had!"

"Did my slip show?"

"How could it? You were standing in the pew."

"When I was walking down the aisle, I wonder?"

"Nobody could see. They were still standing for the hymn."

"They could have seen, though."

"Only one thing surprises me. Why didn't Allen Durrand come over and say hello?"

"Was he there?"

"Didn't you see him? Over in the Wests' pew, under the window they put in for the father and mother."

"I didn't see him. Was his wife?"

"Ah, you must have seen *her*! All in blue with a hat like a buggy wheel. She's very dressy. But not to be compared to you, today."

Aunt Dodie herself was wearing a navy-blue straw hat with some droopy cloth flowers, and a button-down-the-front slub rayon dress.

"Maybe he didn't know me. Or didn't see me."

"He couldn't very well not have seen you."

"Well."

"And he's turned out such a good-looking man. That counts if you go into politics. And the height. You very seldom see a short man get elected."

"What about Mackenzie King?"

"I meant around here. We wouldn't've elected *him*, from around here."

"YOUR mother's had a little stroke. She says not, but I've seen too many like her.

"She's had a little one, and she might have another little one, and another, and another. Then someday she might have the big one. You'll have to learn to be the mother then.

"Like me. My mother took sick when I was only ten. She died when I was fifteen. In between, what a time I had with her! She was all swollen up; what she had was dropsy. They came one time and took it out of her by the pailful."

"Took what out?"

"*Fluid.*

"She sat up in her chair till she couldn't anymore, she had to go to bed. She had to lie on her right side all the time to keep the fluid pressure off her heart. What a life. She developed bedsores, she was in misery. So one day she said to me, 'Dodie, please, just turn me onto my other side for just a little while, just for the relief.' She begged me. I got hold of her and turned her—she was a weight! I turned her on her heart side, and the minute I did, she died.

"What are you crying about? I never meant to make you cry! Well, you are a big baby, if you can't stand to hear about Life."

Aunt Dodie laughed at me, to cheer me up. In her thin brown face her eyes were large and hot. She had a scarf around her head that day and looked like a gypsy woman, flashing malice and kindness at me, threatening to let out more secrets than I could stand.

"DID you have a stroke?" I said sullenly.

"What?"

"Aunt Dodie said you had a stroke."

"Well, I didn't. I told her I didn't. The doctor says I didn't. She thinks she knows everything, Dodie does. She thinks she knows better than a doctor."

"Are you going to have a stroke?"

"No. I have low blood pressure. That is just the opposite of what gives you strokes."

"So, are you not going to get sick at all?" I said, pushing further. I was very much relieved that she had decided against strokes, and that I would not have to be the mother, and wash and wipe and feed her lying in bed, as Aunt Dodie had had to do with her mother. For I did feel it was she who decided, she gave her consent. As long as she lived, and through all the changes that happened to her, and after I had received the medical explanations of what was happening, I still felt secretly that she had given her consent. For her own purposes, I felt she did it: display, of a sort; revenge of a sort as well. More, that nobody could ever understand.

She did not answer me, but walked on ahead. We were going from Aunt Dodie's place to Uncle James's, following a path through the humpy cow pasture that made the trip shorter than going by the road.

"Is your arm going to stop shaking?" I pursued recklessly, stubbornly.

I demanded of her now, that she turn and promise me what I needed.

But she did not do it. For the first time she held out altogether against me. She went on as if she had not heard, her familiar bulk ahead of me turning strange, indifferent. She withdrew, she darkened in front of me, though all she did in fact was keep on walking along the path that she and Aunt Dodie had made when they were girls running back and forth to see each other; it was still there.

ONE NIGHT my mother and Aunt Dodie sat on the porch and recited poetry. How this started I forget; with one of them thinking of a quotation, likely, and the other one matching it. Uncle James was leaning against the railing, smoking. Because we were visiting, he had permitted himself to come.

"*How can a man die better,*" cried Aunt Dodie cheerfully,

> "*Than facing fearful odds,*
> *For the ashes of his fathers*
> *And the temples of his gods?*"

"*And all day long the noise of battle rolled,*" my mother declared,

> "*Among the mountains by the winter sea.*
>
> "*Not a drum was heard, not a funeral note,*
> *As his corpse to the ramparts we hurried. . . .*
>
> "*For I am going a long way*
> *To the island-valley of Avalon*
> *Where falls not hail, or rain, or any snow. . . .*"

My mother's voice had taken on an embarrassing tremor, so I was glad when Aunt Dodie interrupted.

"Heavens, wasn't it all sad, the stuff they put in the old readers?"

"I don't remember a bit of it," said Uncle James. "Except—" and he recited without a break:

> *"Along the line of smoky hills*
> *The crimson forest stands*
> *And all day long the bluejay calls*
> *Throughout the autumn lands."*

"Good for you," said Aunt Dodie, and she and my mother joined in, so they were all reciting together, and laughing at each other:

> *"Now by great marshes wrapped in mist,*
> *Or past some river's mouth,*
> *Throughout the long still autumn day*
> *Wild birds are flying south."*

"Though when you come to think of it, even that has kind of a sad ring," Aunt Dodie said.

If I had been making a proper story out of this, I would have ended it, I think, with my mother not answering and going ahead of me across the pasture. That would have done. I didn't stop there, I suppose, because I wanted to find out more, remember more. I wanted to bring back all I could. Now I look at what I have done and it is like a series of snapshots, like the brownish snapshots with fancy borders that my parents' old camera used to take. In these snapshots Aunt Dodie and Uncle James and even Aunt Lena, even her children, come out clear enough. (All these people dead now except the children, who have turned into decent friendly wage earners, not a criminal or as far as I know even a neurotic among them.) The problem, the only problem, is my mother. And she is the one of course that I am trying to get; it is to reach her that this whole journey has been undertaken. With what purpose? To mark her off, to describe, to illumine, to celebrate, to *get rid of* her; and it did not work, for she looms too close, just as she always did. She is heavy as always, she weighs everything down, and yet she is indistinct, her edges melt and flow. Which means she has stuck to me as close as ever and refused to fall away, and I could go on, and on, applying what skills I have, using what tricks I know, and it would always be the same.

# *Material*

I DON'T KEEP up with Hugo's writing. Sometimes I see his name, in the library, on the cover of some literary journal that I don't open—I haven't opened a literary journal in a dozen years, praise God. Or I read in the paper or see on a poster—this would be in the library too, or in a bookstore—an announcement of a panel discussion at the university, with Hugo flown in to discuss the state of the novel today, or the contemporary short story, or the new nationalism in our literature. Then I think, Will people really go, will people who could be swimming or drinking or going for a walk really take themselves out to the campus to find the room and sit in rows listening to those vain quarrelsome men? Bloated, opinionated, untidy men, that is how I see them, cosseted by the academic life, the literary life, by women. People will go to hear them say that such and such a writer is not worth reading anymore, and that some writer must be read; to hear them dismiss and glorify and argue and chuckle and shock. People, I say, but I mean women, middle-aged women like me, alert and trembling, hoping to ask intelligent questions and not be ridiculous; soft-haired young girls awash in adoration, hoping to lock eyes with one of the men on the platform. Girls, and women too, fall in love with such men; they imagine there is power in them.

The wives of the men on the platform are not in that audience. They are buying groceries or cleaning up messes or having a drink. Their lives are concerned with food and mess and houses and cars and money. They have to remember to get the snow tires on and go to the bank and take back the beer bottles, because their husbands are such brilliant, such talented incapable men, who must be looked after for the sake of the words that will come from them. The women in the audience are married to engineers or doctors or businessmen. I know them, they are my friends. Some of them have turned to literature frivolously, it is true, but most come shyly, and with enormous transitory hope. They absorb the contempt of the men on the platform as if they deserved it; they half-believe they do deserve it, because of their houses and expensive shoes, and their husbands who read Arthur Hailey.

I am married to an engineer myself. His name is Gabriel, but he prefers the name Gabe. In this country he prefers the name Gabe. He was born in Romania; he lived there until the end of the war, when he was sixteen. He has forgotten how to speak Romanian. How can you forget, how can you forget the language of your childhood? I used to think he was pretending to forget, because the things he had seen and lived through when he spoke that language were too terrible to remember. He told me this was not so. He told me his experience of the war was not so bad. He described the holiday uproar at school when the air-raid sirens sounded. I did not quite believe him. I required him to be an ambassador from bad times as well as distant countries. Then I thought he might not be Romanian at all, but an impostor.

This was before we were married, when he used to come and see me in the apartment on Clark Road where I lived with my little daughter, Clea. Hugo's daughter too, of course, but he had to let go of her. Hugo had grants, he travelled, he married again and his wife had three children; he divorced and married again, and his next wife, who had been his student, had three more children, the first born to her while he was still living with his second wife. In such circumstances a man can't hang on to everything. Gabriel used to stay all night sometimes on the pullout couch I had for a bed in this tiny, shabby apartment; and I would look at him sleeping and think that for all I knew he might be a German or a Russian or even of all things a Canadian faking a past and an accent to make himself interesting. He was mysterious to me. Long after he became my lover and after he became my husband he remained, remains, mysterious to me. In spite of all the things I know about him, daily and physical things. His face curves out smoothly and his eyes, set shallowly in his head, curve out too under the smooth pink lids. The wrinkles he has are traced on top of this smoothness, this impenetrable surface; they are of no consequence. His body is substantial, calm. He used to be a fine, rather lazy-looking skater. I cannot describe him without a familiar sense of capitulation. I cannot describe him. I could describe Hugo, if anybody asked me, in great detail—Hugo as he was eighteen, twenty years ago, crew-cut and skinny, with the bones of his body and even of his skull casually, precariously, joined and knitted together, so that there was something uncoordinated, unexpected about the shifting planes of his face as well as the movements, often dangerous, of his limbs. "He's held together by nerves," a friend of mine at college said when I first brought him around, and it was true; after that I could almost see the fiery strings.

Gabriel told me when I first knew him that he enjoyed life. He did not say that he believed in enjoying it; he said that he did. I was embarrassed for him. I never believed people who said such things and anyway, I associated this statement with gross, self-advertising, secretly unpleasantly restless men. But it seems to be the truth. He is not curious. He is able to take pleasure and give off smiles and caresses and say softly, "Why do you worry about that? It is not a problem of yours." He has forgotten the language of his childhood. His lovemaking was strange to me at first, because it was lacking in desperation. He made love without emphasis, so to speak, with no memory of sin or hope of depravity. He does not watch himself. He will never write a poem about it, never, and indeed may have forgotten it in half an hour. Such men are commonplace, perhaps. It was only that I had not known any. I used to wonder if I would have fallen in love with him if his accent and his forgotten, nearly forgotten, past had been taken away; if he had been, say, an engineering student in my own year at college. I don't know, I can't tell. What holds anybody in a man or a woman may be something as flimsy as a Romanian accent or the calm curve of an eyelid, some half-fraudulent mystery.

No mystery of this sort about Hugo. I did not miss it, did not know about it, maybe would not have believed in it. I believed in something else, then. Not that I knew him all the way through, but the part I knew was in my blood and from time to time would give me a poison rash. None of that with Gabriel; he does not disturb me, any more than he is disturbed himself.

It was Gabriel who found me Hugo's story. We were in a bookstore, and he came to me with a large, expensive paperback, a collection of short stories. There was Hugo's name on the cover. I wondered how Gabriel had found it, what he had been doing in the fiction section of the store anyway; he never reads fiction. I wondered if he sometimes went and looked for things by Hugo. He is interested in Hugo's career as he would be interested in the career of a magician or popular singer or politician with whom he had, through me, a plausible connection, a proof of reality. I think it is because he does such anonymous work himself, work intelligible only to his own kind. He is fascinated by people who work daringly out in the public eye, without the protection of any special discipline—it must seem so, to an engineer—just trying to trust themselves, and elaborating their bag of tricks, and hoping to catch on.

"Buy it for Clea," he said.

"Isn't it a lot of money for a paperback?"

He smiled.

"There's your father's picture, your real father, and he has written this story you might like to read," I said to Clea, who was in the kitchen making toast. She is seventeen. Some days she eats toast and honey and peanut butter and Oreos, and cream cheese and chicken sandwiches and fried potatoes. If anybody comments on what she is eating or not eating, she may run upstairs and slam the door of her room.

"He looks overweight," said Clea, and put the book down. "You always said he was skinny." Her interest in her father is all from the point of view of heredity, and what genes he might have passed on to herself. Did he have a bad complexion, did he have a high I.Q., did the women in his family have big breasts?

"He was when I knew him," I said. "How was I to know what had happened to him since?"

He looked, however, very much as I would have thought he would look by now. When I saw his name in the newspaper or on a poster, I had pictured somebody much like this; I had foreseen the ways in which time and his life would have changed him. It did not surprise me that he had got fat but not bald, that he had let his hair grow wild and had grown a full, curly beard. Pouches under his eyes, a dragged-down look to the cheeks even when he is laughing. He is laughing, into the camera. His teeth have gone from bad to worse. He hated dentists, said his father died of a heart attack in the dentist's chair. A lie, like so much else, or at least an exaggeration. He used to smile crookedly for photographs to hide the right top incisor, dead since somebody at high school pushed him into a drinking fountain. Now he doesn't care, he laughs, he bares those rotting stumps. He looks, at the same time, woebegone and cheerful. A Rabelaisian writer. Checked wool shirt open at the top to show his undershirt; he didn't use to wear one. Do you wash, Hugo? Do you have bad breath, with those teeth? Do you call your girl students fond exasperated dirty names, are there phone calls from insulted parents, does the Dean or somebody have to explain that no harm is meant, that writers are not as other men are? Probably not, probably no one minds. Outrageous writers may bounce from one blessing to another nowadays, bewildered, as permissively reared children are said to be, by excess of approval.

I have no proof. I construct somebody from this one smudgy picture, I am content with such clichés. I have not the imagination or good will to proceed differently; and I have noticed anyway, everybody must have noticed as we go further into middle age, how shopworn and simple, really, are the disguises, the identities if you like, that people take up. In fiction, in Hugo's business, such disguises would not do, but in life they are all we seem to want, all anybody can manage. Look at Hugo's picture, look at the undershirt, listen to what it says about him.

> *Hugo Johnson was born and semi-educated in the bush, and in the mining and lumbering towns of Northern Ontario. He has worked as a lumberjack, beer-slinger, counterman, telephone lineman, and sawmill foreman, and has been sporadically affiliated with various academic communities. He lives now most of the time on the side of a mountain above Vancouver, with his wife and six children.*

The student wife, it seems, got stuck with all the children. What happened to Mary Frances, did she die, is she liberated, did he drive her crazy? But listen to the lies, the half-lies, the absurdities. *He lives on the side of a mountain above Vancouver.* It sounds as if he lives in a wilderness cabin, and all it means, I'm willing to bet, is that he lives in an ordinary comfortable house in North or West Vancouver, which now stretch far up the mountain. He has been *sporadically affiliated with various academic communities.* What does that mean? If it means he has taught for years, most of his adult life, at universities, that teaching at universities has been the only steady well-paid job he has ever had, why doesn't it say so? You would think he came out of the bush now and then to fling them scraps of wisdom, to give them a demonstration of what a real male *writer*, a creative *artist*, is like; you would never think he was a practicing *academic*. I don't know if he was a lumberjack or a beer-slinger or a counterman, but I do know that he was not a telephone lineman. He had a job painting telephone poles. He quit that job in the middle of the second week because the heat and the climbing made him sick. It was a broiling June, just after we had both graduated. Fair enough. The sun really did make him sick; twice he came home and vomited. I have quit jobs myself that I could not stand. The same summer I quit my job folding bandages at Victoria Hospital, because I was going mad with boredom. But if I was a writer, and was listing all my varied and colorful occupations, I don't think I would put down *bandage folder*, I don't think I would find that entirely honest.

After he quit, Hugo found a job marking Grade 12 examination papers. Why didn't he put that down? *Examination marker.* He liked marking examination papers better than he liked climbing telephone poles, and probably better than he liked lumberjacking or beer-slinging or any of those other things if he ever did them; why couldn't he put it down? *Examination marker.*

Nor has he, to my knowledge, ever been the foreman in a sawmill. He worked in his uncle's mill the summer before I met him. What he did all day was load lumber and get sworn at by the real foreman, who didn't like him because of his uncle being the boss. In the evenings, if he was not too tired, he used to walk half a mile to a little creek and play his recorder. Blackflies bothered him, but he did it anyway. He could play "Morning," from *Peer Gynt*, and some Elizabethan airs whose names I have forgotten. Except for one: "Wolsey's Wilde." I learned to play it on the piano so we could play a duet. Was that meant for Cardinal Wolsey, and what was a *wilde*, a dance? Put that down, Hugo. *Recorder player*. That would be quite all right, quite in fashion now; as I understand things, recorder-playing and such fey activities are not out of favor now, quite the contrary. Indeed, they may be more acceptable than all that lumberjacking and beer-slinging. Look at you, Hugo, your image is not only fake but out-of-date. You should have said you'd meditated for a year in the mountains of Uttar Pradesh; you should have said you'd taught Creative Drama to autistic children; you should have shaved your head, shaved your beard, put on a monk's cowl; you should have shut up, Hugo.

When I was pregnant with Clea we lived in a house on Argyle Street in Vancouver. It was such a sad gray stucco house on the outside, in the rainy winter, that we painted the inside, all the rooms, vivid ill-chosen colors. Three walls of the bedrooms were Wedgwood blue, one was magenta. We said it was an experiment to see if color could drive anybody mad. The bathroom was a deep orange-yellow. "It's like being inside a cheese," Hugo said when we finished it. "That's right, it is," I said. "That's very good, phrase-maker." He was pleased but not as pleased as if he'd written it. After that he said, every time he showed anybody the bathroom, "See the color? It's like being inside a cheese." Or, "It's like peeing inside a cheese." Not that I didn't do the same thing, save things up and say them over and over. Maybe I said that about peeing inside a cheese. We had many phrases in common. We both called the landlady the Green Hornet, because she had worn, the only time we had seen her, a poison-green outfit with bits of rat fur and a clutch of violets, and had given off a venomous sort of buzz. She was over seventy and she ran a downtown boarding-house for men. Her daughter Dotty we called the harlot-in-residence. I wonder why we chose to say "harlot"; that was not, is not, a word in general use. I suppose it had a classy sound, a classy depraved sound, contrasting ironically—we were strong on irony—with Dotty herself.

She lived in a two-room apartment in the basement of the house. She was supposed to pay her mother forty-five dollars monthly rent and she told me she meant to try to make the money baby-sitting.

"I can't go out to work," she said, "on account of my nerves. My last husband, I had him six months dying down at Mother's, dying with his kidney disease, and I owe her three hundred dollars board still on that.

She made me make him his eggnog with skim milk. I'm broke every day of my life. They say it's all right not having wealth if you got health, but what if you never had either one? Bronchial pneumonia from the time I was three years old. Rheumatic fever at twelve. Sixteen I married my first husband, he was killed in a logging accident. Three miscarriages. My womb is in shreds. I use up three packs of Kotex every month. I married a dairy farmer out in the Valley and his herd got the fever. Wiped us out. That was the one who died with his kidneys. No wonder. No wonder my nerves are shot."

I am condensing. This came out at greater length and by no means dolefully, indeed with some amazement and pride, at Dotty's table. She asked me down for cups of tea, then for beer. This is life, I thought, fresh from books, classes, essays, discussions. Unlike her mother, Dotty was flat-faced, soft, doughy, fashioned for defeat, the kind of colorless puzzled woman you see carrying a shopping bag, waiting for the bus. In fact, I had seen her once on a bus downtown, and not recognized her at first in her dull blue winter coat. Her rooms were full of heavy furniture salvaged from her marriage—an upright piano, overstuffed chesterfield and chairs, walnut-veneer china cabinet and dining-room table, where we sat. In the middle of the table was a tremendous lamp, with a painted china base and a pleated dark-red silk shade, held out at an extravagant angle, like a hoop skirt.

I described it to Hugo. "That is a whorehouse lamp," I said. Afterwards I wanted to be congratulated on the accuracy of this description. I told Hugo he ought to pay more attention to Dotty if he wanted to be a writer. I told him about her husbands and her womb and her collection of souvenir spoons, and he said I was welcome to look at them all by myself. He was writing a verse play.

Once when I went down to put coal on the furnace, I found Dotty in her pink chenille dressing gown saying goodbye to a man in a uniform, some sort of deliveryman or gas-station attendant. It was the middle of the afternoon. She and this man were not parting in any way that suggested either lechery or affection and I would not have understood anything about it, I would probably have thought he was some relative, if she had not begun at once a long complicated slightly drunk story about how she had got wet in the rain and had to leave her clothes at her mother's house and worn home her mother's dress which was too tight and that was why she was now in her dressing gown. She said that first Larry had caught her in it delivering some sewing he wanted her to do for his wife, and now me, and she didn't know what we would think of her. This was strange, as I had seen her in her dressing gown many times before. In the middle of her laughing and explaining, the man, who had not looked at me, not smiled or said a word or in any way backed up her story, simply ducked out the door.

"Dotty has a lover," I said to Hugo.

"You don't get out enough. You're trying to make life interesting."

The next week I watched to see if this man came back. He did not. But three other men came, and one of them came twice. They walked with their heads down, quickly, and did not have to wait at the basement door. Hugo couldn't deny it. He said it was life imitating art again, it was bound to happen, after all the fat varicose-veined whores he'd met in books. It was then we named her the harlot-in-residence and began to brag about her to our friends. They stood behind the curtains to catch a glimpse of her going in or out.

"That's not her!" they said. "Is that her? Isn't she disappointing? Doesn't she have any professional clothes?"

"Don't be so naive," we said. "Did you think they all wore spangles and boas?"

Everybody hushed to hear her play the piano. She sang or hummed along with her playing, not steadily, but loudly, in the rather defiant, self-parodying voice people use when they are alone, or think they are alone. She sang "Yellow Rose of Texas," and "You Can't Be True, Dear."

"Whores should sing hymns."

"We'll get her to learn some."

"You're all such voyeurs. You're all so mean," said a girl named Mary Frances Shrecker, a big-boned, calm-faced girl with black braids down her back. She was married to a former mathematical prodigy, Elsworth Shrecker, who had had a breakdown. She worked as a dietician. Hugo said he could not look at her without thinking of the word *lumpen*, but he supposed she might be nourishing, like oatmeal porridge. She became his second wife. I thought she was the right wife for him, I thought she would stay forever, nourishing him, but the student evicted her.

The piano-playing was an entertainment for our friends, but disastrous on the days when Hugo was home trying to work. He was supposed to be working on his thesis but he really was writing his play. He worked in our bedroom, at a card table in front of the window, facing a board fence. When Dotty had been playing for a bit, he might come out to the kitchen and stick his face into mine and say in low, even tones of self-consciously controlled rage, "You go down and tell her to cut that out."

"You go."

"Bloody hell. She's your friend. You cultivate her. You encourage her."

"I never told her to play the piano."

"I arranged so that I could have this afternoon free. That did not just happen. I arranged it. I am at a crucial point, I am at the point where this play *lives or dies*. If I go down there I'm afraid I might strangle her."

"Well, don't look at *me*. Don't strangle *me*. Excuse my breathing and everything."

I always did go down to the basement, of course, and knock on Dotty's door and ask her if she would mind not playing the piano now, because my husband was at home and was trying to work. I never said the word *write*, Hugo had trained me not to, that word was like a bare wire to us. Dotty apologized every time; she was scared of Hugo and respectful of his work and his intelligence. She left off playing but the trouble was she might forget, she might start again in an hour, half an hour. The possibility made me nervous and miserable. Because I was pregnant I always wanted to eat, and I would sit at the kitchen table greedily, unhappily, eating something like a warmed-up plateful of Spanish rice. Hugo felt the world was hostile to his writing; he felt not only all its human inhabitants but its noises and diversions and ordinary clutter were linked against him, maliciously, purposefully, diabolically thwarting and maiming him and keeping him from his work. And I, whose business it was to throw myself between him and the world, was failing to do so, by choice perhaps as much as ineptitude for the job. I did not believe in him. I had not understood how it would be necessary to believe in him. I believed that he was clever and talented, whatever that might mean, but I was not sure he would turn out to be a writer. He did not have the authority I thought a writer should have. He was too nervous, too touchy with everybody, too much of a show-off. I believed that writers were calm, sad people, knowing too much. I believed that there was a difference about them, some hard and shining, rare intimidating quality they had from the beginning, and Hugo didn't have it. I thought that someday he would recognize this. Meanwhile, he lived in a world whose rewards and punishments were as strange, as hidden from me, as if he had been a lunatic. He would sit at supper, pale and disgusted; he would clench himself over the typewriter in furious paralysis when I had to get something from the bedroom, or he would leap around the living room asking me what he was (a rhinoceros who thinks he is a gazelle, Chairman Mao dancing a war dance in a dream dreamt by John Foster Dulles) and then kiss me all over the neck and throat with hungry gobbling noises. I was cut off from the source of these glad or bad moods, I did not affect them.

I teased him sourly: "Suppose after we have the baby the house is on fire and the baby and the play are both in there, which would you save?"

"Both."

"But supposing you can just save one? Never mind the baby, suppose *I* am in there, no, suppose I am drowning *here* and you are *here* and cannot possibly reach us both—"

"You're making it tough for me."

"I know I am. I know I am. Don't you hate me?"

"Of course I hate you." After this we might go to bed, playful, squealing, mock-fighting, excited. All our life together, the successful part of our life together, was games. We made up conversations to startle people on the bus. Once we sat in a beer parlor and he berated me for going out with other men and leaving the children alone while he was off in the bush working to support us. He pleaded with me to remember my duty as a wife and as a mother. I blew smoke in his face. People around us were looking stern and gratified. When we got outside we laughed till we had to hold each other up, against the wall. We played in bed that I was Lady Chatterley and he was Mellors.

"Where be that little rascal John Thomas?" he said thickly. "I canna find John Thomas!"

"Frightfully sorry, I think I must have swallowed him," I said, ladylike.

THERE WAS a water pump in the basement. It made a steady, thumping noise. The house was on fairly low-lying ground not far from the Fraser River, and during the rainy weather the pump had to work most of the time to keep the basement from being flooded. We had a dark rainy January, as is usual in Vancouver, and this was followed by a dark rainy February. Hugo and I felt gloomy. I slept a lot of the time. Hugo couldn't sleep. He claimed it was the pump that kept him awake. He couldn't work because of it in the daytime and he couldn't sleep because of it at night. The pump had replaced Dotty's piano-playing as the thing that most enraged and depressed him in our house. Not only because of its noise, but because of the money it was costing us. Its entire cost went onto our electricity bill, though it was Dotty who lived in the basement and reaped the benefits of not being flooded. He said I should speak to Dotty and I said Dotty could not pay the expenses she already had. He said she could turn more tricks. I told him to shut up. As I became more pregnant, slower and heavier and more confined to the house, I got fonder of Dotty, used to her, less likely to store up and repeat what she said. I felt more at home with her than I did sometimes with Hugo and our friends.

All right, Hugo said, I ought to phone the landlady. I said he ought. He said he had far too much to do. The truth was we both shrank from a confrontation with the landlady, knowing in advance how she would confuse and defeat us with shrill evasive prattle.

In the middle of the night in the middle of a rainy week I woke up and wondered what had wakened me. It was the silence.

"Hugo, wake up. The pump's broken. I can't hear the pump."

"I am awake," Hugo said.

"It's still raining and the pump isn't going. It must be broken."

"No, it isn't. It's shut off. I shut it off."

I sat up and turned on the light. He was lying on his back, squinting and trying to give me a hard look at the same time.

"You didn't turn it off."

"All right, I didn't."

"You did."

"I could not stand the goddamn expense anymore. I could not stand thinking about it. I could not stand the noise either. I haven't had any sleep in a week."

"The basement will flood."

"I'll turn it on in the morning. A few hours' peace is all I want."

"That'll be too late, it's raining torrents."

"It is not."

"You go to the window."

"It's raining. It's not raining torrents."

I turned out the light and lay down and said in a calm stern voice, "Listen to me, Hugo, you have to go and turn it on, Dotty will be flooded out."

"In the morning."

"You have to go and turn it on *now*."

"Well I'm not."

"If you're not, I am."

"No, you're not."

"I am."

But I didn't move.

"Don't be such an alarmist."

"*Hugo*."

"Don't *cry*."

"Her stuff will be ruined."

"Best thing could happen to it. Anyway, it won't." He lay beside me stiff and wary, waiting, I suppose, for me to get out of bed, go down to the basement, and figure out how to turn the pump on. Then what would he have done? He could not have hit me, I was too pregnant. He never did hit me, unless I hit him first. He could have gone and turned it off again, and I could have turned it on, and so on, how long could that last? He could have held me down, but if I struggled he would have been afraid of hurting me. He could have sworn at me and left the house, but 've had no car,

and it was raining too hard for him to stay out very long. He would probably have just raged and sulked, alternately, and I could have taken a blan-
ket and gone to sleep on the living-room couch for the rest of the night. I
think that is what a woman of firm character would have done. I think
that is what a woman who wanted that marriage to last would have done.
But I did not do it. Instead, I said to myself that I did not know how the
pump worked, I did not know where to turn it on. I said to myself that I
was afraid of Hugo. I entertained the possibility that Hugo might be right,
nothing would happen. But I wanted something to happen, I wanted
Hugo to crash.

When I woke up, Hugo was gone and the pump was thumping as
usual. Dotty was pounding on the door at the top of the basement stairs.

"You won't believe your eyes what's down here. I'm up to my knees in
water. I just put my feet out of bed and up to my knees in water. What
happened? You hear the pump go off?"

"No," I said.

"I don't know what could've gone wrong, I guess it could've got over-
worked. I had a couple of beers before I went to bed elst I would've known
there was something wrong. I usually sleep light. But I was sleeping like
the dead and I put my feet out of bed and Jesus, it's a good thing I didn't
pull on the light switch at the same time, I would have been electrocuted.
Everything's floating."

Nothing was floating and the water would not have come to any grown
person's knees. It was about five inches deep in some places, only one
or two in others, the floor being so uneven. It had soaked and stained
the bottom of her chesterfield and chairs and got into the bottom of her
piano. The floor tiles were loosened, the rugs soggy, the edges of her bed-
spread dripping, her floor heater ruined.

I got dressed and put on a pair of Hugo's boots and took a broom
downstairs. I started sweeping the water towards the drain outside the
door. Dotty made herself a cup of coffee in my kitchen and sat for a while
on the top step watching me, going over the same monologue about having a couple of beers and sleeping more soundly than usual, not hearing
the pump go off, not understanding why it should go off, if it had gone
off, not knowing how she was going to explain to her mother, who would
certainly make it out to be her fault and charge her. We were in luck, I
saw. (*We* were?) Dotty's expectation and thrifty relish of misfortune made
her less likely than almost anyone else would have been to investigate just
what had gone wrong. After the water level went down a bit, she went into
her bedroom, put on some clothes and some boots which she had to drain
first, got her broom, and helped me.

"The things that don't happen to me, eh? I never get my fortune told.

I've got these girlfriends that are always getting their fortune told and I say, never mind me, there's one thing I know and I know it ain't good."

I went upstairs and phoned the university, trying to get Hugo. I told them it was an emergency and they found him in the library.

"It did flood."

"What?"

"It did flood. Dotty's place is underwater."

"I turned the pump on."

"Like hell you did. This morning you turned it on."

"This morning there was a downpour and the pump couldn't handle it. That was after I turned it on."

"The pump couldn't handle it last night because the pump wasn't on last night and don't talk to me about any downpour."

"Well there was one. You were asleep."

"You have no idea what you've done, do you? You don't even stick around to look at it. I have to look. I have to cope. I have to listen to that poor woman."

"Plug your ears."

"Shut up, you filthy moral idiot."

"I'm sorry. I was kidding. I'm sorry."

"Sorry. You're bloody sorry. This is the mess you made and I told you you'd make and you're bloody sorry."

"I have to go to a seminar. I am sorry. I can't talk now, it's no good talking to you now, I don't know what you're trying to get me to say."

"I'm just trying to get you to *realize*."

"All right, I realize. Though I still think it happened this morning."

"You don't realize. You never realize."

"You dramatize."

"*I* dramatize!"

Our luck held. Dotty's mother was not so likely as Dotty to do without explanations and it was, after all, her floor tiles and wallboard that were ruined. But Dotty's mother was sick, the cold wet weather had undermined her too, and she was taken to hospital with pneumonia that very morning. Dotty went to live in her mother's house, to look after the boarders. The basement had a disgusting, moldy smell. We moved out too, a short time later. Just before Clea was born we took over a house in North Vancouver, belonging to some friends who had gone to England. The quarrel between us subsided in the excitement of moving; it was never really resolved. We did not move much from the positions we had taken on the phone. I said you don't realize, you never realize, and he said, what do you want me to say? Why do you make such a fuss over this, he asked reasonably. Anybody might wonder. Long after I was away from him, I wondered too. I could have turned on the pump, as I have said, taking responsibility for both of us, as a patient realistic woman, a really married woman, would have done, as I am sure Mary Frances would have done, did, many times, during the ten years she lasted. Or I could have told Dotty the truth, though she was not a very good choice to receive such information. I could have told somebody, if I thought it was that important, pushed Hugo out into the unpleasant world and let him taste trouble. But I didn't, I was not able fully to protect or expose him, only to flog him with blame, desperate sometimes, feeling I would claw his head open to pour my vision into it, my notion of what had to be understood. What presumptuousness, what cowardice, what bad faith. Unavoidable. "You have a problem of incompatibility," the marriage counsellor said to us a while later. We laughed till we cried in the dreary municipal hall of the building in North Vancouver where the marriage counselling was dispensed. That is our problem, we said to each other, what a relief to know it, incompatibility.

I DID NOT read Hugo's story that night. I left it with Clea and she as it turned out did not read it either. I read it the next afternoon. I got home about two o'clock from the girls' private school where I have a part-time job teaching history. I made tea as I usually do and sat down in the kitchen to enjoy the hour before the boys, Gabriel's sons, get home from school. I saw the book still lying on top of the refrigerator and I took it down and read Hugo's story.

The story is about Dotty. Of course, she has been changed in some unimportant ways and the main incident concerning her has been invented, or grafted on from some other reality. But the lamp is there, and the pink chenille dressing gown. And something about Dotty that I had forgotten: When you were talking she would listen with her mouth slightly open, nodding, then she would chime in on the last word of your sentence with you. A touching and irritating habit. She was in such a hurry to agree, she hoped to understand. Hugo has remembered this, and when did Hugo ever talk to Dotty?

That doesn't matter. What matters is that this story of Hugo's is a very good story, as far as I can tell, and I think I can tell. How honest this is and how lovely, I had to say as I read. I had to admit. I was moved by Hugo's story; I was, I am, glad of it, and I am not moved by tricks. Or if I am, they have to be good tricks. Lovely tricks, honest tricks. There is Dotty, lifted out of life and held in light, suspended in the marvellous clear jelly that Hugo has spent all his life learning how to make. It is an act of magic, there is no getting around it; it is an act, you might say, of a special, unsparing, unsentimental love. A fine and lucky benevolence. Dotty was a lucky person, people who understand and value this act might say (not everybody, of course, does understand and value this act); she was lucky to live in that basement for a few months and eventually to have this done to her, though she doesn't know what has been done and wouldn't care for it, probably, if she did know. She has passed into Art. It doesn't happen to everybody.

Don't be offended. Ironical objections are a habit with me. I am half-ashamed of them. I respect what has been done. I respect the intention and the effort and the result. Accept my thanks.

I did think that I would write a letter to Hugo. All the time I was preparing dinner, and eating it, and talking to Gabriel and the children, I was thinking of a letter. I was thinking I would tell him how strange it was for me to realize that we shared, still shared, the same bank of memory, and that what was all scraps and oddments, useless baggage, for me, was ripe and usable, a paying investment, for him. Also I wanted to apologize, in some not-outright way, for not having believed he would be a writer. Acknowledgment, not apology; that was what I owed him. A few graceful, a few grateful, phrases.

At the same time, at dinner, looking at my husband Gabriel, I decided that he and Hugo are not really so unalike. Both of them have managed something. Both of them have decided what to do about everything they run across in this world, what attitude to take, how to ignore or use things. In their limited and precarious ways they both have authority. They are not *at the mercy*. Or think they are not. I can't blame them for making whatever arrangements they can make.

After the boys had gone to bed and Gabriel and Clea had settled to watch television, I found a pen and got the paper in front of me, to write my letter, and my hand jumped. I began to write short jabbing sentences that I had never planned:

*This is not enough, Hugo. You think it is, but it isn't. You are mistaken, Hugo.*

That is not an argument to send through the mail.

I do blame them. I envy and despise.

Gabriel came into the kitchen before he went to bed, and saw me sitting with a pile of test papers and my marking pencils. He might have meant to talk to me, to ask me to have coffee, or a drink, with him, but he respected my unhappiness as he always does; he respected the pretense that I was not unhappy but preoccupied, burdened with these test papers; he left me alone to get over it.

# Royal Beatings

~

Royal Beating. That was Flo's promise. You are going to get one Royal Beating.

The word "Royal" lolled on Flo's tongue, took on trappings. Rose had a need to picture things, to pursue absurdities, that was stronger than the need to stay out of trouble, and instead of taking this threat to heart she pondered: How is a beating royal? She came up with a tree-lined avenue, a crowd of formal spectators, some white horses and black slaves. Someone knelt, and the blood came leaping out like banners. An occasion both savage and splendid. In real life they didn't approach such dignity, and it was only Flo who tried to supply the event with some high air of necessity and regret. Rose and her father soon got beyond anything presentable.

Her father was king of the royal beatings. Those Flo gave never amounted to much; they were quick cuffs and slaps dashed off while her attention remained elsewhere. You get out of my road, she would say. You mind your own business. You take that look off your face.

They lived behind a store in Hanratty, Ontario. There were four of them: Rose, her father, Flo, Rose's young half brother, Brian. The store was really a house, bought by Rose's father and mother when they married and set up here in the furniture- and upholstery-repair business. Her mother could do upholstery. From both parents Rose should have inherited clever hands, a quick sympathy with materials, an eye for the nicest turns of mending, but she hadn't. She was clumsy, and when something broke she couldn't wait to sweep it up and throw it away.

Her mother had died. She said to Rose's father during the afternoon, "I have a feeling that is so hard to describe. It's like a boiled egg in my chest, with the shell left on." She died before night, she had a blood clot on her lung. Rose was a baby in a basket at the time, so of course could not remember any of this. She heard it from Flo, who must have heard it from her father. Flo came along soon afterward, to take over Rose in the basket, marry her father, open up the front room to make a grocery store. Rose, who had known the house only as a store, who had known only Flo for a mother, looked back on the sixteen or so months her parents spent here as an orderly, far gentler and more ceremonious time, with little touches of affluence. She had nothing to go on but some eggcups her mother had bought, with a pattern of vines and birds on them, delicately drawn as if with red ink; the pattern was beginning to wear away. No books or clothes or pictures of her mother remained. Her father must have got rid of them, or else Flo would. Flo's only story about her mother, the one about her death, was oddly grudging. Flo liked the details of a death: the things people said, the way they protested or tried to get out of bed or swore or laughed (some did those things), but when she said that Rose's mother mentioned a hard-boiled egg in her chest she made the comparison sound slightly foolish, as if her mother really was the kind of person who might think you could swallow an egg whole.

Her father had a shed out behind the store, where he worked at his furniture repairing and restoring. He caned chair seats and backs, mended wickerwork, filled cracks, put legs back on, all most admirably and skillfully and cheaply. That was his pride: to startle people with such fine work, such moderate, even ridiculous charges. During the Depression people could not afford to pay more, perhaps, but he continued the practice through the war, through the years of prosperity after the war, until he died. He never discussed with Flo what he charged or what was owing. After he died she had to go out and unlock the shed and take all sorts of scraps of paper and torn envelopes from the big wicked-looking hooks that were his files. Many of these she found were not accounts or receipts at all but records of the weather, bits of information about the garden, things he had been moved to write down.

> *Ate new potatoes 25th June. Record.*
> *Dark Day, 1880's, nothing supernatural. Clouds of ash from forest*
> *fires.*
> *Aug 16, 1938. Giant thunderstorm in evng. Lightning str. Pres. Church,*
> *Turberry Twp. Will of God?*
> *Scald strawberries to remove acid.*
> *All things are alive. Spinoza.*

Flo thought Spinoza must be some new vegetable he planned to grow, like broccoli or eggplant. He would often try some new thing. She showed the scrap of paper to Rose and asked, did she know what Spinoza was? Rose did know, or had an idea—she was in her teens by that time—but she replied that she did not. She had reached an age where she thought she could not stand to know any more, about her father, or about Flo; she pushed any discovery aside with embarrassment and dread.

There was a stove in the shed, and many rough shelves covered with cans of paint and varnish, shellac and turpentine, jars of soaking brushes and also some dark sticky bottles of cough medicine. Why should a man who coughed constantly, whose lungs took in a whiff of gas in the war (called, in Rose's earliest childhood, not the First, but the Last, War), spend all his days breathing fumes of paint and turpentine? At the time, such questions were not asked as often as they are now. On the bench outside Flo's store several old men from the neighborhood sat gossiping, drowsing, in the warm weather, and some of these old men coughed all the time too. The fact is they were dying, slowly and discreetly, of what was called, without any particular sense of grievance, "the foundry disease." They had worked all their lives at the foundry in town, and now they sat still, with their wasted yellow faces, coughing, chuckling, drifting into aimless obscenity on the subject of women walking by, or any young girl on a bicycle.

From the shed came not only coughing but speech, a continual muttering, reproachful or encouraging, usually just below the level at which separate words could be made out. Slowing down when her father was at a tricky piece of work, taking on a cheerful speed when he was doing something less demanding, sandpapering or painting. Now and then some words would break through and hang clear and nonsensical on the air. When he realized they were out, there would be a quick bit of cover-up coughing, a swallowing, an alert, unusual silence.

"Macaroni, pepperoni, Botticelli, beans—"

What could that mean? Rose used to repeat such things to herself. She could never ask him. The person who spoke these words and the person who spoke to her as her father were not the same, though they seemed to occupy the same space. It would be the worst sort of taste to acknowledge the person who was not supposed to be there; it would not be forgiven. Just the same, she loitered and listened.

The cloud-capped towers, she heard him say once.

"The cloud-capped towers, the gorgeous palaces."

That was like a hand clapped against Rose's chest, not to hurt, but astonish her, to take her breath away. She had to run then, she had to get away. She knew that was enough to hear, and besides, what if he caught her? It would be terrible.

This was something the same as bathroom noises. Flo had saved up and had a bathroom put in, but there was no place to put it except in a corner of the kitchen. The door did not fit, the walls were only beaverboard. The result was that even the tearing of a piece of toilet paper, the shifting of a haunch, was audible to those working or talking or eating in the kitchen. They were all familiar with each other's nether voices, not only in their more explosive moments but in their intimate sighs and growls and pleas and statements. And they were all most prudish people. So no one ever seemed to hear, or be listening, and no reference was made. The person creating the noises in the bathroom was not connected with the person who walked out.

They lived in a poor part of town. There was Hanratty and West Hanratty, with the river flowing between them. This was West Hanratty. In Hanratty the social structure ran from doctors and dentists and lawyers down to foundry workers and factory workers and draymen; in West Hanratty it ran from factory workers and foundry workers down to large improvident families of casual bootleggers and prostitutes and unsuccessful thieves. Rose thought of her own family as straddling the river, belonging nowhere, but that was not true. West Hanratty was where the store was and they were, on the straggling tail end of the main street. Across the road from them was a blacksmith shop, boarded up about the time the war started, and a house that had been another store at one time. The Salada Tea sign had never been taken out of the front window; it remained as a proud and interesting decoration though there was no Salada Tea for sale inside. There was just a bit of sidewalk, too cracked and tilted for roller-skating, though Rose longed for roller skates and often pictured herself whizzing along in a plaid skirt, agile and fashionable. There was one streetlight, a tin flower; then the amenities gave up and there were dirt roads and boggy places, front-yard dumps and strange-looking houses. What made the houses strange-looking were the attempts to keep them from going completely to ruin. With some the attempt had never been made. These were gray and rotted and leaning over, falling into a landscape of scrub hollows, frog ponds, cattails and nettles. Most houses, however, had been patched up with tarpaper, a few fresh shingles, sheets of tin, hammered-out stovepipes, even cardboard. This was, of course, in the days before the war, days of what would later be legendary poverty, from which Rose would remember mostly low-down things—serious-looking anthills and wooden steps, and a cloudy, interesting, problematical light on the world.

THERE WAS a long truce between Flo and Rose in the beginning. Rose's nature was growing like a prickly pineapple, but slowly, and secretly, hard pride and skepticism overlapping, to make something surprising even to herself. Before she was old enough to go to school, and while Brian was still in the baby carriage, Rose stayed in the store with both of them—Flo sitting on the high stool behind the counter, Brian asleep by the window; Rose knelt or lay on the wide creaky floorboards, working with crayons on pieces of brown paper too torn or irregular to be used for wrapping.

People who came to the store were mostly from the houses around. Some country people came too, on their way home from town, and a few people from Hanratty, who walked across the bridge. Some people were always on the main street, in and out of stores, as if it was their duty to be always on display and their right to be welcomed. For instance, Becky Tyde.

Becky Tyde climbed up on Flo's counter, made room for herself beside an open tin of crumbly jam-filled cookies.

"Are these any good?" she said to Flo, and boldly began to eat one. "When are you going to give us a job, Flo?"

"You could go and work in the butcher shop," said Flo innocently. "You could go and work for your brother."

"Roberta?" said Becky with a stagey sort of contempt. "You think I'd work for him?" Her brother who ran the butcher shop was named Robert but often called Roberta, because of his meek and nervous ways. Becky Tyde laughed. Her laugh was loud and noisy like an engine bearing down on you.

She was a big-headed loud-voiced dwarf, with a mascot's sexless swagger, a red velvet tam, a twisted neck that forced her to hold her head on one side, always looking up and sideways. She wore little polished high-heeled shoes, real lady's shoes. Rose watched her shoes, being scared of the rest of her, of her laugh and her neck. She knew from Flo that Becky Tyde had been sick with polio as a child, that was why her neck was twisted and why she had not grown any taller. It was hard to believe that she had started out differently, that she had ever been normal. Flo said she was not cracked, she had as much brains as anybody, but she knew she could get away with anything.

"You know I used to live out here?" Becky said, noticing Rose. "Hey! What's-your-name! Didn't I used to live out here, Flo?"

"If you did it was before my time," said Flo, as if she didn't know anything.

"That was before the neighborhood got so downhill. Excuse me saying so. My father built his house out here and he built his slaughterhouse and we had half an acre of orchard."

"Is that so?" said Flo, using her humoring voice, full of false geniality, humility even. "Then why did you ever move away?"

"I told you, it got to be such a downhill neighborhood," said Becky. She would put a whole cookie in her mouth if she felt like it, let her cheeks puff out like a frog's. She never told any more.

Flo knew anyway, and who didn't. Everyone knew the house, red brick with the veranda pulled off and the orchard, what was left of it, full of the usual outflow—car seats and washing machines and bedsprings and junk. The house would never look sinister, in spite of what had happened in it, because there was so much wreckage and confusion all around.

Becky's old father was a different kind of butcher from her brother, according to Flo. A bad-tempered Englishman. And different from Becky in the matter of mouthiness. His was never open. A skinflint, a family tyrant. After Becky had polio he wouldn't let her go back to school. She was seldom seen outside the house, never outside the yard. He didn't want people gloating. That was what Becky said, at the trial. Her mother was dead by that time and her sisters married. Just Becky and Robert at home. People would stop Robert on the road and ask him, "How about your sister, Robert? Is she altogether better now?"

"Yes."

"Does she do the housework? Does she get your supper?"

"Yes."

"And is your father good to her, Robert?"

The story being that the father beat them, had beaten all his children and beaten his wife as well, beat Becky more now because of her deformity, which some people believed he had caused (they did not understand about polio). The stories persisted and got added to. The reason that Becky was kept out of sight was now supposed to be her pregnancy, and the father of the child was supposed to be her own father. Then people said it had been born, and disposed of.

"What?"

"Disposed of," Flo said. "They used to say go and get your lamb chops at Tyde's, get them nice and tender! It was all lies in all probability," she said regretfully.

Rose could be drawn back—from watching the wind shiver along the old torn awning, catch in the tear—by this tone of regret, caution, in Flo's voice. Flo telling a story—and this was not the only one, or even the most lurid one, she knew—would incline her head and let her face go soft and thoughtful, tantalizing, warning.

"I shouldn't even be telling you this stuff."

More was to follow.

Three useless young men, who hung around the livery stable, got together—or were got together, by more influential and respectable men in town—and prepared to give old man Tyde a horsewhipping, in the interests of public morality. They blacked their faces. They were provided with whips and a quart of whisky apiece, for courage. They were: Jelly Smith, a horse-racer and a drinker; Bob Temple, a ball-player and strongman; and Hat Nettleton, who worked on the town dray, and had his nickname from a bowler hat he wore, out of vanity as much as for the comic effect. He still worked on the dray, in fact; he had kept the name if not the hat, and could often be seen in public—almost as often as Becky Tyde—delivering sacks of coal, which blackened his face and arms. That should have brought to mind his story, but didn't. Present time and past, the shady melodramatic past of Flo's stories, were quite separate, at least for Rose. Present people could not be fitted into the past. Becky herself, town oddity and public pet, harmless and malicious, could never match the butcher's prisoner, the cripple daughter, a white streak at the window: mute, beaten, impregnated. As with the house, only a formal connection could be made.

The young men primed to do the horsewhipping showed up late, outside Tyde's house, after everybody had gone to bed. They had a gun, but they used up their ammunition firing it off in the yard. They yelled for the butcher and beat on the door; finally they broke it down. Tyde concluded they were after his money, so he put some bills in a handkerchief and sent Becky down with them, maybe thinking those men would be touched or scared by the sight of a little wry-necked girl, a dwarf. But that didn't content them. They came upstairs and dragged the butcher out from under his bed, in his nightgown. They dragged him outside and stood him in the snow. The temperature was four below zero, a fact noted later in court. They meant to hold a mock trial but they could not remember how it was done. So they began to beat him and kept beating him until he fell. They yelled at him, *Butcher's meat!* and continued beating him while his nightgown and the snow he was lying in turned red. His son Robert said in court that he had not watched the beating. Becky said that Robert had watched at first but had run away and hid. She herself had watched all the way through. She watched the men leave at last and her father make his delayed bloody progress through the snow and up the steps of the veranda. She did not go out to help him, or open the door until he got to it. Why not? she was asked in court, and she said she did not go out because she just had her nightgown on, and she did not open the door because she did not want to let the cold into the house.

Old man Tyde then appeared to have recovered his strength. He sent Robert to harness the horse, and made Becky heat water so that he could wash. He dressed and took all the money and with no explanation to his children got into the cutter and drove to Belgrave where he left the horse tied in the cold and took the early-morning train to Toronto. On the train he behaved oddly, groaning and cursing as if he was drunk. He was picked up on the streets of Toronto a day later, out of his mind with fever, and was taken to a hospital, where he died. He still had all the money. The cause of death was given as pneumonia.

But the authorities got wind, Flo said. The case came to trial. The three men who did it all received long prison sentences. A farce, said Flo. Within a year they were all free, had all been pardoned, had jobs waiting for them. And why was that? It was because too many higher-ups were in on it. And it seemed as if Becky and Robert had no interest in seeing justice done. They were left well-off. They bought a house in Hanratty. Robert went into the store. Becky after her long seclusion started on a career of public sociability and display.

That was all. Flo put the lid down on the story as if she was sick of it. It reflected no good on anybody.

"Imagine," Flo said.

Flo at this time must have been in her early thirties. A young woman. She wore exactly the same clothes that a woman of fifty, or sixty, or seventy, might wear: print housedresses loose at the neck and sleeves as well as the waist; bib aprons, also of print, which she took off when she came from the kitchen into the store. This was a common costume, at the time, for a poor though not absolutely poverty-stricken woman; it was also, in a way, a scornful deliberate choice. Flo scorned slacks, she scorned the outfits of people trying to be in style, she scorned lipstick and permanents. She wore her own black hair cut straight across, just long enough to push behind her ears. She was tall but fine-boned, with narrow wrists and shoulders, a small head, a pale, freckled, mobile, monkeyish face. If she had thought it worthwhile, and had the resources, she might have had a black-and-pale, fragile, nurtured sort of prettiness; Rose realized that later. But she would have to have been a different person altogether; she would have to have learned to resist making faces, at herself and others.

Rose's earliest memories of Flo were of extraordinary softness and hardness. The soft hair, the long, soft, pale cheeks, soft almost invisible fuzz in front of her ears and above her mouth. The sharpness of her knees, hardness of her lap, flatness of her front.

When Flo sang:

> *"Oh the buzzin' of the bees in the cigarette trees*
> *And the soda-water fountain . . ."*

Rose thought of Flo's old life before she married her father, when she worked as a waitress in the coffee shop in Union Station, and went with her girlfriends Mavis and Irene to Centre Island, and was followed by men on dark streets and knew how pay phones and elevators worked. Rose heard in her voice the reckless dangerous life of cities, the gum-chewing sharp answers.

And when she sang:

> "Then slowly, slowly, she got up
> And slowly she came nigh him
> And all she said, that she ever did say,
> Was young man, I think you're dyin'!"

Rose thought of a life Flo seemed to have had beyond that, earlier than that, crowded and legendary, with Barbara Allan and Becky Tyde's father and all kinds of outrages and sorrows jumbled up together in it.

THE ROYAL beatings. What got them started?

Suppose a Saturday, in spring. Leaves not out yet but the doors open to the sunlight. Crows. Ditches full of running water. Hopeful weather. Often on Saturdays Flo left Rose in charge of the store—it's a few years now, these are the years when Rose was nine, ten, eleven, twelve—while she herself went across the bridge to Hanratty (going uptown they called it) to shop and see people, and listen to them. Among the people she listened to were Mrs. Lawyer Davies, Mrs. Anglican Rector Henley-Smith, and Mrs. Horse-Doctor McKay. She came home and imitated their flibberty voices. Monsters, she made them seem, of foolishness, and showiness, and self-approbation.

When she finished shopping she went into the coffee shop of the Queen's Hotel and had a sundae. What kind? Rose and Brian wanted to know when she got home, and they would be disappointed if it was only pineapple or butterscotch, pleased if it was a Tin Roof, or Black and White. Then she smoked a cigarette. She had some ready-rolled that she carried with her, so that she wouldn't have to roll one in public. Smoking was the one thing she did that she would have called showing off in anybody else. It was a habit left over from her working days, from Toronto. She knew it was asking for trouble. Once, the Catholic priest came over to her right in the Queen's Hotel, and flashed his lighter at her before she could get her matches out. She thanked him but did not enter into conversation, lest he should try to convert her.

Another time, on the way home, she saw at the town end of the bridge a boy in a blue jacket, apparently looking at the water. Eighteen, nineteen years old. Nobody she knew. Skinny, weakly-looking, something the matter with him, she saw at once. Was he thinking of jumping? Just as she came up even with him, what does he do but turn and display himself, holding his jacket open, also his pants. What he must have suffered from the cold, on a day that had Flo holding her coat collar tight around her throat.

When she first saw what he had in his hand, Flo said, all she could think of was What is he doing out here with a baloney sausage?

She could say that. It was offered as truth; no joke. She maintained that she despised dirty talk. She would go out and yell at the old men sitting in front of her store.

"If you want to stay where you are you better clean your mouths out!"

Saturday, then. For some reason Flo is not going uptown, has decided to stay home and scrub the kitchen floor. Perhaps this has put her in a bad mood. Perhaps she was in a bad mood anyway, due to people not paying their bills, or the stirring-up of feelings in spring. The wrangle with Rose has already commenced, has been going on forever, like a dream that goes back and back into other dreams, over hills and through doorways, maddeningly dim and populous and familiar and elusive. They are carting all the chairs out of the kitchen preparatory to the scrubbing, and they have also got to move some extra provisions for the store, some cartons of canned goods, tins of maple syrup, coal-oil cans, jars of vinegar. They take these things out to the woodshed. Brian, who is five or six by this time, is helping drag the tins.

"Yes," says Flo, carrying on from our lost starting point. "Yes, and that filth you taught to Brian."

"What filth?"

"And he doesn't know any better."

There is one step down from the kitchen to the woodshed, a bit of carpet on it so worn Rose can't ever remember seeing the pattern. Brian loosens it, dragging a tin.

"Two Vancouvers," she says softly.

Flo is back in the kitchen. Brian looks from Flo to Rose and Rose says again in a slightly louder voice, an encouraging singsong, "Two Vancouvers—"

"Fried in snot!" finishes Brian, not able to control himself any longer.

"Two pickled arseholes—"

"—tied in a knot!"

There it is. The filth.

> *Two Vancouvers fried in snot!*
> *Two pickled arseholes tied in a knot!*

Rose has known that for years, learned it when she first went to school. She came home and asked Flo, what is a Vancouver?

"It's a city. It's a long ways away."

"What else besides a city?"

Flo said, what did she mean, what else? How could it be fried, Rose said, approaching the dangerous moment, the delightful moment, when she would have to come out with the whole thing.

"Two Vancouvers fried in snot!/Two pickled arseholes tied in a knot!"

"You're going to get it!" cried Flo in a predictable rage. "Say that again and you'll get a good clout!"

Rose couldn't stop herself. She hummed it tenderly, tried saying the innocent words aloud, humming through the others. It was not just the words *snot* and *arsehole* that gave her pleasure, though of course they did. It was the pickling and tying and the unimaginable Vancouvers. She saw them in her mind shaped rather like octopuses, twitching in the pan. The tumble of reason; the spark and spit of craziness.

Lately she has remembered it again and taught it to Brian, to see if it has the same effect on him, and of course it has.

"Oh, I heard you!" says Flo. "I heard that! And I'm warning you!"

So she is. Brian takes the warning. He runs away, out the woodshed door, to do as he likes. Being a boy, free to help or not, involve himself or not. Not committed to the household struggle. They don't need him anyway, except to use against each other, they hardly notice his going. They continue, can't help continuing, can't leave each other alone. When they seem to have given up they really are just waiting and building up steam.

Flo gets out the scrub pail and the brush and the rag and the pad for her knees, a dirty red rubber pad. She starts to work on the floor. Rose sits on the kitchen table, the only place left to sit, swinging her legs. She can feel the cool oilcloth, because she is wearing shorts, last summer's tight faded shorts dug out of the summer-clothes bag. They smell a bit moldy from winter storage.

Flo crawls underneath, scrubbing with the brush, wiping with the rag. Her legs are long, white, and muscular, marked all over with blue veins as if somebody had been drawing rivers on them with an indelible pencil. An abnormal energy, a violent disgust, is expressed in the chewing of the brush at the linoleum, the swish of the rag.

What do they have to say to each other? It doesn't really matter. Flo speaks of Rose's smart-aleck behavior, rudeness and sloppiness and conceit. Her willingness to make work for others, her lack of gratitude. She mentions Brian's innocence, Rose's corruption. Oh, don't you think you're somebody, says Flo, and a moment later, Who do you think you are? Rose contradicts and objects with such poisonous reasonableness and mildness, displays theatrical unconcern. Flo goes beyond her ordinary scorn and self-possession and becomes amazingly theatrical herself, saying it was for Rose that she sacrificed her life. She saw her father saddled with a baby daughter and she thought, What is that man going to do? So she married him, and here she is, on her knees.

At that moment the bell rings, to announce a customer in the store. Because the fight is on, Rose is not permitted to go into the store and wait on whoever it is. Flo gets up and throws off her apron, groaning—but not communicatively; it is not a groan whose exasperation Rose is allowed to share—and goes in and serves. Rose hears her using her normal voice.

"About time! Sure is!"

She comes back and ties on her apron and is ready to resume.

"You never have a thought for anybody but your ownself! You never have a thought for what I'm doing."

"I never asked you to do anything. I wish you never had. I would have been a lot better off."

Rose says this smiling directly at Flo, who has not yet gone down on her knees. Flo sees the smile, grabs the scrub rag that is hanging on the side of the pail, and throws it at her. It may be meant to hit her in the face but instead it falls against Rose's leg and she raises her foot and catches it, swinging it negligently against her ankle.

"All right," says Flo. "You've done it this time. All right."

Rose watches her go to the woodshed door, hears her tramp through the woodshed, pause in the doorway, where the screen door hasn't yet been hung, and the storm door is standing open, propped with a brick. She calls Rose's father. She calls him in a warning, summoning voice, as if against her will preparing him for bad news. He will know what this is about.

The kitchen floor has five or six different patterns of linoleum on it. Ends, which Flo got for nothing and ingeniously trimmed and fitted together, bordering them with tin strips and tacks. While Rose sits on the table waiting, she looks at the floor, at this satisfying arrangement of rectangles, triangles, some other shape whose name she is trying to remember. She hears Flo coming back through the woodshed, on the creaky plank walk laid over the dirt floor. She is loitering, waiting too. She and Rose can carry this no further by themselves.

Rose hears her father come in. She stiffens, a tremor runs through her legs, she feels them shiver on the oilcloth. Called away from some peaceful, absorbing task, away from the words running in his head, called out of himself, her father has to say something. He says, "Well? What's wrong?"

Now comes another voice of Flo's. Enriched, hurt, apologetic, it seems to have been manufactured on the spot. She is sorry to have called him from his work. Would never have done it if Rose was not driving her to distraction. How to distraction? With her back talk and impudence and her terrible tongue. The things Rose has said to Flo are such that if Flo had said them to her mother, she knows her father would have thrashed her into the ground.

Rose tries to butt in, to say this isn't true.

What isn't true?

Her father raises a hand, doesn't look at her, says, "Be quiet."

When she says it isn't true, Rose means that she herself didn't start this, only responded, that she was goaded by Flo, who is now, she believes, telling the grossest sort of lies, twisting everything to suit herself. Rose puts aside her other knowledge that whatever Flo has said or done, whatever she herself has said or done, does not really matter at all. It is the struggle itself that counts, and that can't be stopped, can never be stopped, short of where it has got to now.

Flo's knees are dirty, in spite of the pad. The scrub rag is still hanging over Rose's foot.

Her father wipes his hands, listening to Flo. He takes his time. He is slow at getting into the spirit of things, tired in advance, maybe, on the verge of rejecting the role he has to play. He won't look at Rose, but at any sound or stirring from Rose, he holds up his hand.

"Well, we don't need the public in on this, that's for sure," Flo says, and she goes to lock the door of the store, putting in the store window the sign that says BACK SOON, a sign Rose made for her with a great deal of fancy curving and shading of letters in black and red crayon. When she comes back she shuts the door to the store, then the door to the stairs, then the door to the woodshed.

Her shoes have left marks on the clean wet part of the floor.

"Oh, I don't know," she says now, in a voice worn down from its emotional peak. "I don't know what to do about her." She looks down and sees her dirty knees (following Rose's eyes) and rubs at them viciously with her bare hands, smearing the dirt around.

"She humiliates me," she says, straightening up. There it is, the explanation. "She humiliates me," she repeats with satisfaction. "She has no respect."

"I do not!"

"Quiet, you!" says her father.

"If I hadn't called your father you'd still be sitting there with that grin on your face! What other way is there to manage you?"

Rose detects in her father some objections to Flo's rhetoric, some embarrassment and reluctance. She is wrong, and ought to know she is wrong, in thinking that she can count on this. The fact that she knows about it, and he knows she knows, will not make things any better. He is beginning to warm up. He gives her a look. This look is at first cold and challenging. It informs her of his judgment, of the hopelessness of her position. Then it clears, it begins to fill up with something else, the way a

spring fills up when you clear the leaves away. It fills with hatred and pleasure. Rose sees that and knows it. Is that just a description of anger,
should she see his eyes filling up with anger? No. Hatred is right. Pleasure
is right. His face loosens and changes and grows younger, and he holds up
his hand this time to silence Flo.

"All right," he says, meaning that's enough, more than enough, this
part is over, things can proceed. He starts to loosen his belt.

Flo has stopped anyway. She has the same difficulty Rose does, a difficulty in believing that what you know must happen really will happen,
that there comes a time when you can't draw back.

"Oh, I don't know, don't be too hard on her." She is moving around
nervously as if she has thoughts of opening some escape route. "Oh, you
don't have to use the belt on her. Do you have to use the belt?"

He doesn't answer. The belt is coming off, not hastily. It is being
grasped at the necessary point. *All right you.* He is coming over to Rose.
He pushes her off the table. His face, like his voice, is quite out of character. He is like a bad actor, who turns a part grotesque. As if he must savor
and insist on just what is shameful and terrible about this. That is not to
say he is pretending, that he is acting, and does not mean it. He is acting,
and he means it. Rose knows that, she knows everything about him.

She has since wondered about murders, and murderers. Does the thing
have to be carried through, in the end, partly for the effect, to prove to the
audience of one—who won't be able to report, only register, the lesson—
that such a thing can happen, that there is nothing that can't happen, that
the most dreadful antic is justified, feelings can be found to match it?

She tries again looking at the kitchen floor, that clever and comforting
geometrical arrangement, instead of looking at him or his belt. How can
this go on in front of such daily witnesses—the linoleum, the calendar
with the mill and creek and autumn trees, the old accommodating pots
and pans?

*Hold out your hand!*

Those things aren't going to help her, none of them can rescue her.
They turn bland and useless, even unfriendly. Pots can show malice, the
patterns of linoleum can leer up at you, treachery is the other side of
dailiness.

At the first, or maybe the second, crack of pain, she draws back. She will
not accept it. She runs around the room, she tries to get to the doors. Her
father blocks her off. Not an ounce of courage or of stoicism in her, it
would seem. She runs, she screams, she implores. Her father is after her,
cracking the belt at her when he can, then abandoning it and using his
hands. Bang over the ear, then bang over the other ear. Back and forth, her

head ringing. Bang in the face. Up against the wall and bang in the face again. He shakes her and hits her against the wall, he kicks her legs. She is incoherent, insane, shrieking. *Forgive me! Oh please, forgive me!*

Flo is shrieking too. *Stop, stop!*

Not yet. He throws Rose down. Or perhaps she throws herself down. He kicks her legs again. She has given up on words but is letting out a noise, the sort of noise that makes Flo cry, *Oh, what if people can hear her?* The very last-ditch willing sound of humiliation and defeat it is, for it seems Rose must play her part in this with the same grossness, the same exaggeration, that her father displays, playing his. She plays his victim with a self-indulgence that arouses, and maybe hopes to arouse, his final, sickened contempt.

They will give this anything that is necessary, it seems, they will go to any lengths.

Not quite. He has never managed really to injure her, though there are times, of course, when she prays that he will. He hits her with an open hand, there is some restraint in his kicks.

Now he stops, he is out of breath. He allows Flo to move in, he grabs Rose up and gives her a push in Flo's direction, making a sound of disgust. Flo retrieves her, opens the stair door, shoves her up the stairs.

"Go on up to your room now! Hurry!"

Rose goes up the stairs, stumbling, letting herself stumble, letting herself fall against the steps. She doesn't bang her door because a gesture like that could still bring him after her, and anyway, she is weak. She lies on the bed. She can hear through the stovepipe hole Flo snuffling and remonstrating, her father saying angrily that Flo should have kept quiet then, if she did not want Rose punished she should not have recommended it. Flo says she never recommended a hiding like that.

They argue back and forth on this. Flo's frightened voice is growing stronger, getting its confidence back. By stages, by arguing, they are being drawn back into themselves. Soon it's only Flo talking; he will not talk anymore. Rose has had to fight down her noisy sobbing, so as to listen to them, and when she loses interest in listening, and wants to sob some more, she finds she can't work herself up to it. She has passed into a state of calm, in which outrage is perceived as complete and final. In this state events and possibilities take on a lovely simplicity. Choices are mercifully clear. The words that come to mind are not the quibbling, seldom the conditional. "Never" is a word to which the right is suddenly established. She will never speak to them, she will never look at them with anything but loathing, she will never forgive them. She will punish them; she will finish them. Encased in these finalities, and in her bodily pain, she floats in curious comfort, beyond herself, beyond responsibility.

Suppose she dies now? Suppose she commits suicide? Suppose she runs away? Any of these things would be appropriate. It is only a matter of choosing, of figuring out the way. She floats in her pure superior state as if kindly drugged.

And just as there is a moment, when you are drugged, in which you feel perfectly safe, sure, unreachable, and then without warning and right next to it a moment in which you know the whole protection has fatally cracked, though it is still pretending to hold soundly together, so there is a moment now—the moment, in fact, when Rose hears Flo step on the stairs—that contains for her both present peace and freedom and a sure knowledge of the whole down-spiralling course of events from now on.

Flo comes into the room without knocking, but with a hesitation that shows it might have occurred to her. She brings a jar of cold cream. Rose is hanging on to advantage as long as she can, lying face down on the bed, refusing to acknowledge or answer.

"Oh, come on," Flo says uneasily. "You aren't so bad off, are you? You put some of this on and you'll feel better."

She is bluffing. She doesn't know for sure what damage has been done. She has the lid off the cold cream. Rose can smell it. The intimate, babyish, humiliating smell. She won't allow it near her. But in order to avoid it, the big ready clot of it in Flo's hand, she has to move. She scuffles, resists, loses dignity, and lets Flo see there is not really much the matter.

"All right," Flo says. "You win. I'll leave it here and you can put it on when you like."

Later still a tray will appear. Flo will put it down without a word and go away. A large glass of chocolate milk on it, made with Vita-Malt from the store. Some rich streaks of Vita-Malt around the bottom of the glass. Little sandwiches, neat and appetizing. Canned salmon of the first quality and reddest color, plenty of mayonnaise. A couple of butter tarts from a bakery package, chocolate biscuits with a peppermint filling. Rose's favorites, in the sandwich, tart, and cookie line. She will turn away, refuse to look, but left alone with these eatables will be miserably tempted; roused and troubled and drawn back from thoughts of suicide or flight by the smell of salmon, the anticipation of crisp chocolate, she will reach out a finger, just to run it around the edge of one of the sandwiches (crusts cut off!) to get the overflow, get a taste. Then she will decide to eat one, for strength to refuse the rest. One will not be noticed. Soon, in helpless corruption, she will eat them all. She will drink the chocolate milk, eat the tarts, eat the cookies. She will get the malty syrup out of the bottom of the glass with her finger, though she sniffles with shame. Too late.

Flo will come up and get the tray. She may say, "I see you got your appetite still," or, "Did you like the chocolate milk, was it enough syrup in it?" depending on how chastened she is feeling, herself. At any rate, all advantage will be lost. Rose will understand that life has started up again, that they will all sit around the table eating again, listening to the radio news. Tomorrow morning, maybe even tonight. Unseemly and unlikely as that may be. They will be embarrassed, but rather less than you might expect considering how they have behaved. They will feel a queer lassitude, a convalescent indolence, not far off satisfaction.

One night after a scene like this they were all in the kitchen. It must have been summer, or at least warm weather, because her father spoke of the old men who sat on the bench in front of the store.

"Do you know what they're talking about now?" he said, and nodded his head toward the store to show who he meant, though of course they were not there now, they went home at dark.

"Those old coots," said Flo. "What?"

There was about them both a geniality not exactly false but a bit more emphatic than was normal, without company.

Rose's father told them then that the old men had picked up the idea somewhere that what looked like a star in the western sky, the first star that came out after sunset, the evening star, was in reality an airship hovering over Bay City, Michigan, on the other side of Lake Huron. An American invention, sent up to rival the heavenly bodies. They were all in agreement about this, the idea was congenial to them. They believed it to be lit by ten thousand electric light bulbs. Her father had ruthlessly disagreed with them, pointing out that it was the planet Venus they saw, which had appeared in the sky long before the invention of an electric light bulb. They had never heard of the planet Venus.

"Ignoramuses," said Flo. At which Rose knew, and knew her father knew, that Flo had never heard of the planet Venus either. To distract them from this, or even apologize for it, Flo put down her teacup, stretched out with her head resting on the chair she had been sitting on and her feet on another chair (somehow she managed to tuck her dress modestly between her legs at the same time), and lay stiff as a board, so that Brian cried out in delight, "Do that! Do that!"

Flo was double-jointed and very strong. In moments of celebration or emergency she would do tricks.

They were silent while she turned herself around, not using her arms at all but just her strong legs and feet. Then they all cried out in triumph, though they had seen it before.

Just as Flo turned herself Rose got a picture in her mind of that airship, an elongated transparent bubble, with its strings of diamond lights, floating in the miraculous American sky.

"The planet Venus!" her father said, applauding Flo. "Ten thousand electric lights!"

There was a feeling of permission, relaxation, even a current of happiness, in the room.

YEARS LATER, many years later, on a Sunday morning, Rose turned on the radio. This was when she was living by herself in Toronto.

*Well, sir.*

*It was a different kind of place in our day. Yes, it was.*

*It was all horses then. Horses and buggies. Buggy races up and down the main street on the Saturday nights.*

"Just like the chariot races," says the announcer's, or interviewer's, smooth encouraging voice.

*I never seen a one of them.*

"No, sir, that was the old Roman chariot races I was referring to. That was before your time."

*Musta been before my time. I'm a hunerd and two years old.*

"That's a wonderful age, sir."

*It is so.*

She left it on, as she went around the apartment kitchen, making coffee for herself. It seemed to her that this must be a staged interview, a scene from some play, and she wanted to find out what it was. The old man's voice was so vain and belligerent, the interviewer's quite hopeless and alarmed, under its practiced gentleness and ease. You were surely meant to see him holding the microphone up to some toothless, reckless, preening centenarian, wondering what in God's name he was doing here, and what would he say next?

"They must have been fairly dangerous."

*What was dangerous?*

"Those buggy races."

*They was. Dangerous. Used to be the runaway horses. Used to be a-plenty of accidents. Fellows was dragged along on the gravel and cut their face open. Wouldna matter so much if they was dead. Heh.*

*Some of them horses was the high-steppers. Some, they had to have the mustard under their tail. Some wouldn step out for nothin. That's the thing it is with the horses. Some'll work and pull till they drop down dead and some wouldn pull your cock out of a pail of lard. Hehe.*

It must be a real interview after all. Otherwise they wouldn't have put that in, wouldn't have risked it. It's all right if the old man says it. Local color. Anything rendered harmless and delightful by his hundred years.

*Accidents all the time then. In the mill. Foundry. Wasn't the precautions.*

"You didn't have so many strikes then, I don't suppose? You didn't have so many unions?"

*Everybody taking it easy nowadays. We worked and we was glad to get it. Worked and was glad to get it.*

"You didn't have television."

*Didn't have no TV. Didn't have no radio. No picture show.*

"You made your own entertainment."

*That's the way we did.*

"You had a lot of experiences young men growing up today will never have."

*Experiences.*

"Can you recall any of them for us?"

*I eaten groundhog meat one time. One winter. You wouldna cared for it. Heh.*

There was a pause, of appreciation, it would seem, then the announcer's voice saying that the foregoing had been an interview with Mr. Wilfred Nettleton of Hanratty, Ontario, made on his hundred and second birthday, two weeks before his death, last spring. A living link with our past. Mr. Nettleton had been interviewed in the Wawanash County Home for the Aged.

Hat Nettleton.

Horsewhipper into centenarian. Photographed on his birthday, fussed over by nurses, kissed no doubt by a girl reporter. Flashbulbs popping at him. Tape recorder drinking in the sound of his voice. Oldest resident. Oldest horsewhipper. Living link with our past.

Looking out from her kitchen window at the cold lake, Rose was longing to tell somebody. It was Flo who would enjoy hearing. She thought of her saying *Imagine!* in a way that meant she was having her worst suspicions gorgeously confirmed. But Flo was in the same place Hat Nettleton had died in, and there wasn't any way Rose could reach her. She had been there even when that interview was recorded, though she would not have heard it, would not have known about it. After Rose put her in the Home, a couple of years earlier, she had stopped talking. She had removed herself, and spent most of her time sitting in a corner of her crib, looking crafty and disagreeable, not answering anybody, though she occasionally showed her feelings by biting a nurse.

# *Wild Swans*

~

FLO SAID to watch for White Slavers. She said this was how they operated: an old woman, a motherly or grandmotherly sort, made friends
while riding beside you on a bus or train. She offered you candy, which
was drugged. Pretty soon you began to droop and mumble, were in no
condition to speak for yourself. Oh, help, the woman said, my daughter
(granddaughter) is sick, please somebody help me get her off so that she
can recover in the fresh air. Up stepped a polite gentleman, pretending to
be a stranger, offering assistance. Together, at the next stop, they hustled
you off the train or bus, and that was the last the ordinary world ever saw
of you. They kept you a prisoner in the White Slave place (to which you
had been transported drugged and bound so you wouldn't even know
where you were), until such time as you were thoroughly degraded and in
despair, your insides torn up by drunken men and invested with vile disease, your mind destroyed by drugs, your hair and teeth fallen out. It took
about three years for you to get to this state. You wouldn't want to go
home then; maybe couldn't remember home, or find your way if you did.
So they let you out on the streets.

Flo took ten dollars and put it in a little cloth bag, which she sewed to
the strap of Rose's slip. Another thing likely to happen was that Rose
would get her purse stolen.

Watch out, Flo said as well, for people dressed up as ministers. They
were the worst. That disguise was commonly adopted by White Slavers, as
well as those after your money.

Rose said she didn't see how she could tell which ones were disguised.

Flo had worked in Toronto once. She had worked as a waitress in a coffee shop in Union Station. That was how she knew all she knew. She never saw sunlight, in those days, except on her days off. But she saw plenty else. She saw a man cut another man's stomach with a knife, just pull out his shirt and do a tidy cut, as if it was a watermelon not a stomach. The stomach's owner just sat looking down surprised, with no time to protest. Flo implied that that was nothing, in Toronto. She saw two bad women (that was what Flo called whores, running the two words together, like badminton) get into a fight, and a man laughed at them, other men stopped and laughed and egged them on, and they had their fists full of each other's hair. At last the police came and took them away, still howling and yelping.

She saw a child die of a fit too. Its face was black as ink.

"Well, I'm not scared," said Rose provokingly. "There's the police, anyway."

"Oh, them! They'd be the first ones to diddle you!"

She did not believe anything Flo said on the subject of sex. Consider the undertaker.

A little bald man, very neatly dressed, would come into the store sometimes and speak to Flo with a placating expression.

"I only wanted a bag of candy. And maybe a few packages of gum. And one or two chocolate bars. Could you go to the trouble of wrapping them?"

Flo in her mock-deferential tone would assure him that she could. She wrapped them in heavy-duty white paper, so they were something like presents. He took his time with the selection, humming and chatting, then dawdled for a while. He might ask how Flo was feeling. And how Rose was, if she was there.

"You look pale. Young girls need fresh air." To Flo he would say, "You work too hard. You've worked hard all your life."

"No rest for the wicked," Flo would say agreeably.

When he went out she hurried to the window. There it was—the old black hearse with its purple curtains.

"He'll be after them today!" Flo would say as the hearse rolled away at a gentle pace, almost a funeral pace. The little man had been an undertaker, but he was retired now. The hearse was retired too. His sons had taken over the undertaking and bought a new one. He drove the old hearse all over the country, looking for women. So Flo said. Rose could not believe it. Flo said he gave them the gum and the candy. Rose said he probably ate them himself. Flo said he had been seen, he had been heard. In mild weather he drove with the windows down, singing, to himself or to somebody out of sight in the back.

*"Her brow is like the snowdrift
Her throat is like the swan . . ."*

Flo imitated him singing. Gently overtaking some woman walking on a back road, or resting at a country crossroads. All compliments and courtesy and chocolate bars, offering a ride. Of course every woman who reported being asked said she had turned him down. He never pestered anybody, drove politely on. He called in at houses, and if the husband was home he seemed to like just as well as anything to sit and chat. Wives said that was all he ever did anyway but Flo did not believe it.

"Some women are taken in," she said. "A number." She liked to speculate on what the hearse was like inside. Plush. Plush on the walls and the roof and the floor. Soft purple, the color of the curtains, the color of dark lilacs.

All nonsense, Rose thought. Who could believe it, of a man that age?

ROSE WAS going to Toronto on the train for the first time by herself. She had been once before, but that was with Flo, long before her father died. They took along their own sandwiches and bought milk from the vendor on the train. It was sour. Sour chocolate milk. Rose kept taking tiny sips, unwilling to admit that something so much desired could fail her. Flo sniffed it, then hunted up and down the train until she found the old man in his red jacket, with no teeth and the tray hanging around his neck. She invited him to sample the chocolate milk. She invited people nearby to smell it. He let her have some ginger ale for nothing. It was slightly warm.

"I let him know," Flo said, looking around after he had left. "You have to let them know."

A woman agreed with her but most people looked out the window. Rose drank the warm ginger ale. Either that, or the scene with the vendor, or the conversation Flo and the agreeing woman now got into about where they came from, why they were going to Toronto, and Rose's morning constipation which was why she was lacking color, or the small amount of chocolate milk she had got inside her, caused her to throw up in the train toilet. All day long she was afraid people in Toronto could smell vomit on her coat.

This time Flo started the trip off by saying, "Keep an eye on her, she's never been away from home before!" to the conductor, then looking around and laughing, to show that was jokingly meant. Then she had to get off. It seemed the conductor had no more need for jokes than Rose had, and no intention of keeping an eye on anybody. He never spoke to Rose except to ask for her ticket. She had a window seat, and was soon extraordinarily happy. She felt Flo receding, West Hanratty flying away from her, her own wearying self discarded as easily as everything else. She loved the towns less and less known. A woman was standing at her back door in her nightgown, not caring if everybody on the train saw her. They were travelling south, out of the snowbelt, into an earlier spring, a tenderer sort of landscape. People could grow peach trees in their back yards.

Rose collected in her mind the things she had to look for in Toronto. First, things for Flo. Special stockings for her varicose veins. A special kind of cement for sticking handles on pots. And a full set of dominoes.

For herself Rose wanted to buy hair-remover to put on her arms and legs, and if possible an arrangement of inflatable cushions, supposed to reduce your hips and thighs. She thought they probably had hair-remover in the drugstore in Hanratty, but the woman in there was a friend of Flo's and told everything. She told Flo who bought hair dye and slimming medicine and French safes. As for the cushion business, you could send away for it but there was sure to be a comment at the Post Office, and Flo knew people there as well. She also planned to buy some bangles, and an angora sweater. She had great hopes of silver bangles and powder-blue angora. She thought they could transform her, make her calm and slender and take the frizz out of her hair, dry her underarms and turn her complexion to pearl.

The money for these things, as well as the money for the trip, came from a prize Rose had won, for writing an essay called "Art and Science in the World of Tomorrow." To her surprise, Flo asked if she could read it, and while she was reading it, she remarked that they must have thought they had to give Rose the prize for swallowing the dictionary. Then she said shyly, "It's very interesting."

She would have to spend the night at Cela McKinney's. Cela McKinney was her father's cousin. She had married a hotel manager and thought she had gone up in the world. But the hotel manager came home one day and sat down on the dining-room floor between two chairs and said, "I am never going to leave this house again." Nothing unusual had happened, he had just decided not to go out of the house again, and he didn't, until he died. That had made Cela McKinney odd and nervous. She locked her doors at eight o'clock. She was also very stingy. Supper was usually oatmeal porridge, with raisins. Her house was dark and narrow and smelled like a bank.

The train was filling up. At Brantford a man asked if she would mind if he sat down beside her.

"It's cooler out than you'd think," he said. He offered her part of his newspaper. She said no thanks.

Then, lest he think her rude, she said it really was cooler. She went on looking out the window at the spring morning. There was no snow left, down here. The trees and bushes seemed to have a paler bark than they did at home. Even the sunlight looked different. It was as different from home, here, as the coast of the Mediterranean would be, or the valleys of California.

"Filthy windows, you'd think they'd take more care," the man said. "Do you travel much by train?"

She said no.

Water was lying in the fields. He nodded at it and said there was a lot this year.

"Heavy snows."

She noticed his saying "snows," a poetic-sounding word. Anyone at home would have said "snow."

"I had an unusual experience the other day. I was driving out in the country. In fact, I was on my way to see one of my parishioners, a lady with a heart condition—"

She looked quickly at his collar. He was wearing an ordinary shirt and tie and a dark-blue suit.

"Oh, yes," he said. "I'm a United Church minister. But I don't always wear my uniform. I wear it for preaching in. I'm off duty today.

"Well, as I said, I was driving through the country and I saw some Canada geese down on a pond, and I took another look, and there were some swans down with them. A whole great flock of swans. What a lovely sight they were. They would be on their spring migration, I expect, heading up North. What a spectacle. I never saw anything like it."

Rose was unable to think appreciatively of the wild swans because she was afraid he was going to lead the conversation from them to Nature in general and then to God, the way a minister would feel obliged to do. But he did not, he stopped with the swans.

"A very fine sight. You would have enjoyed them."

He was between fifty and sixty years old, Rose thought. He was short, and energetic-looking, with a square ruddy face and bright waves of gray hair combed straight up from his forehead. When she realized he was not going to mention God she felt she ought to show her gratitude.

She said they must have been lovely.

"It wasn't even a regular pond, it was only some water lying in a field. It was just luck the water was lying there and they came down and I came driving by at the right time. Just luck. They come in at the east end of Lake Erie, I think. But I never was lucky enough to see them before."

She turned by degrees to the window, and he returned to his paper. She remained slightly smiling, so as not to seem rude, not to seem to be rejecting conversation altogether. The morning really was cool, and she had taken down her coat off the hook where she put it when she first got on the train; she had spread it over herself, like a lap robe. She had set her purse on the floor when the minister sat down, to give him room. He took the sections of the paper apart, shaking and rustling them in a leisurely, rather showy way. He seemed to her the sort of person who does everything in a showy way. A ministerial way. He brushed aside the sections he didn't want at the moment. A corner of newspaper touched her leg, just at the edge of her coat.

She thought for some time that it was the paper. Then she said to herself, What if it is a hand? That was the kind of thing she could imagine. She would sometimes look at men's hands, at the fuzz on their forearms, their concentrating profiles. She would think about everything they could do. Even the stupid ones. For instance, the driver-salesman who brought the bread to Flo's store. The ripeness and confidence of manner, the settled mixture of ease and alertness with which he handled the bread truck. A fold of mature belly over the belt did not displease her. Another time she had her eye on the French teacher at school. Not a Frenchman at all, really, his name was McLaren, but Rose thought teaching French had rubbed off on him, made him look like one. Quick and sallow; sharp shoulders; hooked nose and sad eyes. She saw him lapping and coiling his way through slow pleasures, a perfect autocrat of indulgences. She had a considerable longing to be somebody's object. Pounded, pleasured, reduced, exhausted.

But what if it was a hand? What if it really was a hand? She shifted slightly, moved as much as she could toward the window. Her imagination seemed to have created this reality, a reality she was not prepared for at all. She found it alarming. She was concentrating on that leg, that bit of skin with the stocking over it. She could not bring herself to look. Was there a pressure, or was there not? She shifted again. Her legs had been, and remained, tightly closed. It was. It was a hand. It was a hand's pressure.

*Please don't.* That was what she tried to say. She shaped the words in her mind, tried them out, then couldn't get them past her lips. Why was that? The embarrassment, was it, the fear that people might hear? People were all around them, the seats were full.

It was not only that.

She did manage to look at him, not raising her head but turning it cautiously. He had tilted his seat back and closed his eyes. There was his dark-blue suit sleeve, disappearing under the newspaper. He had arranged the paper so that it overlapped Rose's coat. His hand was underneath, simply resting, as if flung out in sleep.

Now, Rose could have shifted the newspaper and removed her coat. If he was not asleep, he would have been obliged to draw back his hand. If he was asleep, if he did not draw it back, she could have whispered *Excuse me* and set his hand firmly on his own knee. This solution, so obvious and foolproof, did not occur to her. And she would have to wonder, Why not? The minister's hand was not, or not yet, at all welcome to her. It made her feel uncomfortable, resentful, slightly disgusted, trapped and wary. But she could not take charge of it, to reject it. She could not insist that it was there, when he seemed to be insisting that it was not. How could she declare him responsible, when he lay there so harmless and trusting, resting himself before his busy day, with such a pleased and healthy face? A man older than her father would be, if he were living, a man used to deference, an appreciator of Nature, delighter in wild swans. If she did say *Please don't* she was sure he would ignore her, as if overlooking some silliness or impoliteness on her part. She knew that as soon as she said it she would hope he had not heard.

But there was more to it than that. Curiosity. More constant, more imperious, than any lust. A lust in itself, that will make you draw back and wait, wait too long, risk almost anything, just to see what will happen. *To see what will happen.*

The hand began, over the next several miles, the most delicate, the most timid, pressures and investigations. Not asleep. Or if he was, his hand wasn't. She did feel disgust. She felt a faint, wandering nausea. She thought of flesh: lumps of flesh, pink snouts, fat tongues, blunt fingers, all on their way trotting and creeping and lolling and rubbing, looking for their comfort. She thought of cats in heat rubbing themselves along the top of board fences, yowling with their miserable complaint. It was pitiful, infantile, this itching and shoving and squeezing. Spongy tissues, inflamed membranes, tormented nerve-ends, shameful smells; humiliation.

All that was starting. His hand, that she wouldn't ever have wanted to hold, that she wouldn't have squeezed back, his stubborn patient hand was able, after all, to get the ferns to rustle and the streams to flow, to waken a sly luxuriance.

Nevertheless, she would rather not. She would still rather not. Please remove this, she said out the window. Stop it, please, she said to the stumps and barns. The hand moved up her leg past the top of her stocking to her bare skin, had moved higher, under her suspender, reached her underpants and the lower part of her belly. Her legs were still crossed, pinched together. While her legs stayed crossed she could lay claim to innocence, she had not admitted anything. She could still believe that she would stop this in a minute. Nothing was going to happen, nothing more. Her legs were never going to open.

But they were. They were. As the train crossed the Niagara Escarpment above Dundas, as they looked down at the preglacial valley, the silver-wooded rubble of little hills, as they came sliding down to the shores of Lake Ontario, she would make this slow, and silent, and definite declaration, perhaps disappointing as much as satisfying the hand's owner. He would not lift his eyelids, his face would not alter, his fingers would not hesitate, but would go powerfully and discreetly to work. Invasion, and welcome, and sunlight flashing far and wide on the lake water; miles of bare orchards stirring round Burlington.

This was disgrace, this was beggary. But what harm in that, we say to ourselves at such moments, what harm in anything, the worse the better, as we ride the cold wave of greed, of greedy assent. A stranger's hand, or root vegetables or humble kitchen tools that people tell jokes about; the world is tumbling with innocent-seeming objects ready to declare themselves, slippery and obliging. She was careful of her breathing. She could not believe this. Victim and accomplice she was borne past Glassco's Jams and Marmalades, past the big pulsating pipes of oil refineries. They glided into suburbs where bedsheets, and towels used to wipe up intimate stains, flapped leeringly on the clotheslines, where even the children seemed to be frolicking lewdly in the schoolyards, and the very truck drivers stopped at the railway crossings must be thrusting their thumbs gleefully into curled hands. Such cunning antics now, such popular visions. The gates and towers of the Exhibition Grounds came into view, the painted domes and pillars floated marvellously against her eyelids' rosy sky. Then flew apart in celebration. You could have had such a flock of birds, wild swans, even, wakened under one big dome together, exploding from it, taking to the sky.

She bit the edge of her tongue. Very soon the conductor passed through the train, to stir the travellers, warn them back to life.

In the darkness under the station the United Church minister, refreshed, opened his eyes and got his paper folded together, then asked if she would like some help with her coat. His gallantry was self-satisfied, dismissive. No, said Rose, with a sore tongue. He hurried out of the train ahead of her. She did not see him in the station. She never saw him again in her life. But he remained on call, so to speak, for years and years, ready to slip into place at a critical moment, without even any regard, later on, for husband or lovers. What recommended him? She could never understand it. His simplicity, his arrogance, his perversely appealing lack of handsomeness, even of ordinary grown-up masculinity? When he stood up she saw that he was shorter even than she had thought, that his face was pink and shiny, that there was something crude and pushy and childish about him.

Was he a minister, really, or was that only what he said? Flo had mentioned people who were not ministers, dressed up as if they were. Not real ministers dressed as if they were not. Or, stranger still, men who were not real ministers pretending to be real but dressed as if they were not. But that she had come as close as she had, to what could happen, was an unwelcome thing. Rose walked through Union Station feeling the little bag with the ten dollars rubbing at her, knew she would feel it all day long, rubbing its reminder against her skin.

She couldn't stop getting Flo's messages, even with that. She remembered, because she was in Union Station, that there was a girl named Mavis working here, in the gift shop, when Flo was working in the coffee shop. Mavis had warts on her eyelids that looked like they were going to turn into sties but they didn't, they went away. Maybe she had them removed, Flo didn't ask. She was very good-looking, without them. There was a movie star in those days she looked a lot like. The movie star's name was Frances Farmer.

Frances Farmer. Rose had never heard of her.

That was the name. And Mavis went and bought herself a big hat that dipped over one eye and a dress entirely made of lace. She went off for the weekend to Georgian Bay, to a resort up there. She booked herself in under the name of Florence Farmer. To give everybody the idea she was really the other one, Frances Farmer, but calling herself Florence because she was on holiday and didn't want to be recognized. She had a little cigarette holder that was black and mother-of-pearl. She could have been arrested, Flo said. For the *nerve*.

Rose almost went over to the gift shop to see if Mavis was still there and if she could recognize her. She thought it would be an especially fine thing to manage a transformation like that. To dare it; to get away with it, to enter on preposterous adventures in your own, but newly named, skin.

# *The Beggar Maid*

~

PATRICK BLATCHFORD was in love with Rose. This had become a fixed, even furious, idea with him. For her, a continual surprise. He wanted to marry her. He waited for her after classes, moved in and walked beside her, so that anybody she was talking to would have to reckon with his presence. He would not talk when these friends or classmates of hers were around, but he would try to catch her eye, so that he could indicate by a cold incredulous look what he thought of their conversation. Rose was flattered, but nervous. A girl named Nancy Falls, a friend of hers, mispronounced Metternich in front of him. He said to her later, "How can you be friends with people like that?"

Nancy and Rose had gone and sold their blood together, at Victoria Hospital. They each got fifteen dollars. They spent most of the money on evening shoes, tarty silver sandals. Then because they were sure the bloodletting had caused them to lose weight, they had hot fudge sundaes at Boomers. Why was Rose unable to defend Nancy to Patrick?

Patrick was twenty-four years old, a graduate student, planning to be a history professor. He was tall, thin, fair, and good-looking, though he had a long pale-red birthmark, dribbling like a tear down his temple and his cheek. He apologized for it, but said it was fading as he got older. When he was forty, it would have faded away. It was not the birthmark that cancelled out his good looks, Rose thought. (Something did cancel them out, or at least diminish them, for her; she had to keep reminding herself they were there.) There was something edgy, jumpy, disconcerting about him. His voice would break under stress—with her, it seemed he was always under stress—he knocked dishes and cups off tables, spilled drinks and bowls of peanuts, like a comedian. He was not a comedian; nothing could be further from his intentions. He came from British Columbia. His family was rich.

He arrived early to pick Rose up, when they were going to the movies. He wouldn't knock, he knew he was early. He sat on the step outside Dr. Henshawe's door. This was in the winter, it was dark out, but there was a little coach lamp beside the door.

"Oh, Rose! Come and look!" called Dr. Henshawe, in her soft, amused voice, and they looked down together from the dark window of the study. "The poor young man," said Dr. Henshawe tenderly. Dr. Henshawe was in her seventies. She was a former English professor, fastidious and lively. She had a lame leg, but a still youthfully, charmingly tilted head, with white braids wound around it.

She called Patrick poor because he was in love, and perhaps also because he was a male, doomed to push and blunder. Even from up here he looked stubborn and pitiable, determined and dependent, sitting out there in the cold.

"Guarding the door," Dr. Henshawe said. "Oh, Rose!"

Another time she said disturbingly, "Oh, dear, I'm afraid he is after the wrong girl."

Rose didn't like her saying that. She didn't like her laughing at Patrick. She didn't like Patrick sitting out on the steps that way, either. He was asking to be laughed at. He was the most vulnerable person Rose had ever known; he made himself so, didn't know anything about protecting himself. But he was also full of cruel judgments, he was full of conceit.

"YOU ARE a scholar, Rose," Dr. Henshawe would say. "This will interest you." Then she would read aloud something from the paper, or, more likely, something from *Canadian Forum* or the *Atlantic Monthly*. Dr. Henshawe had at one time headed the city's school board, she was a founding member of Canada's Socialist Party. She still sat on committees, wrote letters to the paper, reviewed books. Her father and mother had been medical missionaries; she had been born in China. Her house was small and perfect. Polished floors, glowing rugs, Chinese vases, bowls, and landscapes, black carved screens. Much that Rose could not appreciate, at the time. She could not really distinguish between the little jade animals on Dr. Henshawe's mantelpiece and the ornaments displayed in the jewelry-store window in Hanratty, though she could now distinguish between either of these and the things Flo bought from the five-and-ten.

She could not really decide how much she liked being at Dr. Henshawe's. At times she felt discouraged, sitting in the dining room with a linen napkin on her knee, eating from fine white plates on blue placemats.

For one thing, there was never enough to eat, and she had taken to buying doughnuts and chocolate bars and hiding them in her room. The canary swung on its perch in the dining-room window and Dr. Henshawe directed conversation. She talked about politics, about writers. She mentioned Frank Scott and Dorothy Livesay. She said Rose must read them. Rose must read this, she must read that. Rose became sullenly determined not to. She was reading Thomas Mann. She was reading Tolstoy.

Before she came to Dr. Henshawe's, Rose had never heard of the working class. She took the designation home.

"This would have to be the last part of town where they put the sewers," Flo said.

"Of course," Rose said coolly. "This is the working-class part of town."

"*Working* class?" said Flo. "Not if the ones around here can help it."

Dr. Henshawe's house had done one thing. It had destroyed the naturalness, the taken-for-granted background, of home. To go back there was to go quite literally into a crude light. Flo had put fluorescent lights in the store and the kitchen. There was also, in a corner of the kitchen, a floor lamp Flo had won at Bingo; its shade was permanently wrapped in wide strips of cellophane. What Dr. Henshawe's house and Flo's house did best, in Rose's opinion, was discredit each other. In Dr. Henshawe's charming rooms there was always for Rose the raw knowledge of home, an indigestible lump, and at home now her sense of order and modulation elsewhere exposed such embarrassing sad poverty in people who never thought themselves poor. Poverty was not just wretchedness, as Dr. Henshawe seemed to think, it was not just deprivation. It meant having those ugly tube lights and being proud of them. It meant continual talk of money and malicious talk about new things people had bought and whether they were paid for. It meant pride and jealousy flaring over something like the new pair of plastic curtains, imitating lace, that Flo had bought for the front window. That as well as hanging your clothes on nails behind the door and being able to hear every sound from the bathroom. It meant decorating your walls with a number of admonitions, pious and cheerful and mildly bawdy.

THE LORD IS MY SHEPHERD
BELIEVE IN THE LORD JESUS CHRIST AND THOU SHALL BE SAVED

Why did Flo have those, when she wasn't even religious? They were what people had, common as calendars.

THIS IS MY KITCHEN AND I WILL DO AS I DARNED PLEASE
MORE THAN TWO PERSONS TO A BED IS DANGEROUS AND UNLAWFUL

Billy Pope had brought that one. What would Patrick have to say about them? What would someone who was offended by a mispronunciation of Metternich think of Billy Pope's stories?

Billy Pope worked in Tyde's Butcher Shop. What he talked about most frequently now was the D.P., the Belgian, who had come to work there, and got on Billy Pope's nerves with his impudent singing of French songs and his naive notions of getting on in this country, buying a butcher shop of his own.

"Don't you think you can come over here and get yourself ideas," Billy Pope said to the D.P. "It's *youse* workin' for *us*, and don't think that'll change into *us* workin' for *youse*." That shut him up, Billy Pope said.

Patrick would say from time to time that since her home was only fifty miles away he ought to come up and meet Rose's family.

"There's only my stepmother."

"It's too bad I couldn't have met your father."

Rashly, she had presented her father to Patrick as a reader of history, an amateur scholar. That was not exactly a lie, but it did not give a truthful picture of the circumstances.

"Is your stepmother your guardian?"

Rose had to say she did not know.

"Well, your father must have appointed a guardian for you in his will. Who administers his estate?"

His *estate*. Rose thought an estate was land, such as people owned in England.

Patrick thought it was rather charming of her to think that.

"No, his money and stocks and so on. What he left."

"I don't think he left any."

"Don't be silly," Patrick said.

AND SOMETIMES Dr. Henshawe would say, "Well, you are a scholar, you are not interested in that." Usually she was speaking of some event at the college: a pep rally, a football game, a dance. And usually she was right; Rose was not interested. But she was not eager to admit it. She did not seek or relish that definition of herself.

On the stairway wall hung graduation photographs of all the other girls, scholarship girls, who had lived with Dr. Henshawe. Most of them had got to be teachers, then mothers. One was a dietician, two were librarians, one was a professor of English, like Dr. Henshawe herself. Rose did not care for the look of them, for their soft-focussed meekly smiling gratitude, their large teeth and maidenly rolls of hair. They seemed to be urging on her some deadly secular piety. There were no actresses among them, no brassy magazine journalists; none of them had latched on to the sort of life Rose wanted for herself. She wanted to perform in public. She thought she wanted to be an actress but she never tried to act, was afraid to go near the college drama productions. She knew she couldn't sing or dance. She would really have liked to play the harp, but she had no ear for music. She wanted to be known and envied, slim and clever. She told Dr. Henshawe that if she had been a man she would have wanted to be a foreign correspondent.

"Then you must be one!" cried Dr. Henshawe alarmingly. "The future will be wide open for women. You must concentrate on languages. You must take courses in political science. And economics. Perhaps you could get a job on the paper for the summer. I have friends there."

Rose was frightened at the idea of working on a paper, and she hated the introductory economics course; she was looking for a way of dropping it. It was dangerous to mention things to Dr. Henshawe.

SHE HAD GOT to live with Dr. Henshawe by accident. Another girl had been picked to move in but she got sick; she had t.b., and went instead to a sanitorium. Dr. Henshawe came up to the college office on the second day of registration to get the names of some other scholarship freshmen.

Rose had been in the office just a little while before, asking where the meeting of the scholarship students was to be held. She had lost her notice. The Bursar was giving a talk to the new scholarship students, telling them of ways to earn money and live cheaply and explaining the high standards of performance to be expected of them here if they wanted their payments to keep coming.

Rose found out the number of the room, and started up the stairs to the first floor. A girl came up beside her and said, "Are you on your way to three-oh-twelve, too?"

They walked together, telling each other the details of their scholarships. Rose did not yet have a place to live, she was staying at the Y. She did not really have enough money to be here at all. She had a scholarship for her tuition and the county prize to buy her books and a bursary of three hundred dollars to live on; that was all.

"You'll have to get a job," the other girl said. She had a larger bursary, because she was in science (that's where the money is, the money's all in science, she said seriously), but she was hoping to get a job in the cafeteria. She had a room in somebody's basement. How much does your room cost? How much does a hot plate cost? Rose asked her, her head swimming with anxious calculations.

This girl wore her hair in a roll. She wore a crêpe blouse, yellowed and shining from washing and ironing. Her breasts were large and sagging. She probably wore a dirty-pink hooked-up-the-side brassiere. She had a scaly patch on one cheek.

"This must be it," she said.

There was a little window in the door. They could look through at the other scholarship winners already assembled and waiting. It seemed to Rose that she saw four or five girls of the same stooped and matronly type as the girl who was beside her, and several bright-eyed, self-satisfied, babyish-looking boys. It seemed to be the rule that girl scholarship winners looked about forty and boys about twelve. It was not possible, of course, that they all looked like this. It was not possible that in one glance through the windows of the door Rose could detect traces of eczema, stained underarms, dandruff, moldy deposits on the teeth, and crusty flakes in the corners of the eyes. That was only what she thought. But there was a pall over them, she was not mistaken, there was a true terrible pall of eagerness and docility. How else could they have supplied so many right answers, so many pleasing answers, how else distinguished themselves and got themselves here? And Rose had done the same.

"I have to go to the john," she said.

She could see herself working in the cafeteria. Her figure, broad enough already, broadened out still more by the green cotton uniform, her face red and her hair stringy from the heat. Dishing up stew and fried chicken for those of inferior intelligence and handsomer means. Blocked off by the steam tables, the uniform, by decent hard work that nobody need be ashamed of, by publicly proclaimed braininess and poverty. Boys could get away with that, barely. For girls it was fatal. Poverty in girls is not attractive unless combined with sweet sluttishness, stupidity. Braininess is not attractive unless combined with some signs of elegance; *class*. Was this true, and was she foolish enough to care? It was; she was.

She went back to the first floor where the halls were crowded with ordinary students who were not on scholarships, who would not be expected to get A's and be grateful and live cheap. Enviable and innocent, they milled around the registration tables in their new purple-and-white blazers, their purple Frosh beanies, yelling reminders to each other, confused information, nonsensical insults. She walked among them feeling bitterly superior and despondent. The skirt of her green corduroy suit kept falling back between her legs as she walked. The material was limp; she should have spent more and bought the heavier weight. She thought now that the jacket was not properly cut either, though it had looked all right at home. The whole outfit had been made by a dressmaker in Hanratty, a friend of Flo's, whose main concern had been that there should be no revelations of the figure. When Rose asked if the skirt couldn't be made tighter this woman had said, "You wouldn't want your b.t.m. to show, now would you?" and Rose hadn't wanted to say she didn't care.

Another thing the dressmaker said was "I thought now you was through school you'd be getting a job and help out at home."

A woman walking down the hall stopped Rose.

"Aren't you one of the scholarship girls?"

It was the Registrar's secretary. Rose thought she was going to be reprimanded for not being at the meeting, and she was going to say she felt sick. She prepared her face for this lie. But the secretary said, "Come with me, now. I've got somebody I want you to meet."

Dr. Henshawe was making a charming nuisance of herself in the office. She liked poor girls, bright girls, but they had to be fairly good-looking girls.

"I think this could be your lucky day," the secretary said, leading Rose. "If you could put a pleasanter expression on your face."

Rose hated being told that, but she smiled obediently.

Within the hour she was taken home with Dr. Henshawe, installed in the house with the Chinese screens and vases, and told she was a scholar.

SHE GOT a job working in the library of the college, instead of in the cafeteria. Dr. Henshawe was a friend of the Head Librarian. Rose worked on Saturday afternoons. She worked in the stacks, putting books away. On Saturday afternoons in the fall the library was nearly empty, because of the football games. The narrow windows were open to the leafy campus, the football field, the dry fall country. The distant songs and shouts came drifting in.

The college buildings were not old at all, but they were built to look old. They were built of stone. The Arts Building had a tower, and the library had casement windows, which might have been designed for shooting arrows through. The buildings and the books in the library were what pleased Rose most about the place. The life that usually filled it, and that was now drained away, concentrated around the football field, letting loose those noises, seemed to her inappropriate and distracting. The cheers and songs were idiotic, if you listened to the words. What did they want to build such dignified buildings for if they were going to sing songs like that?

She knew enough not to reveal these opinions. If anybody said to her, "It's awful you have to work Saturdays and can't get to any of the games," she would fervently agree.

Once a man grabbed her bare leg, between her sock and her skirt. It happened in the Agriculture section, down at the bottom of the stacks.

Only the faculty, graduate students, and employees had access to the stacks, though someone could have hoisted himself through a ground-floor window if he was skinny. She had seen a man crouched down looking at the books on a low shelf, further along. As she reached up to push a book into place he passed behind her. He bent and grabbed her leg, all in one smooth startling motion, and then was gone. She could feel for quite a while where his fingers had dug in. It didn't seem to her a sexual touch; it was more like a joke, though not at all a friendly one. She heard him run away, or felt him running; the metal shelves were vibrating. Then they stopped. There was no sound of him. She walked around looking between the stacks, looking into the carrels. Suppose she did see him, or bumped into him around a corner, what did she intend to do? She did not know. It was simply necessary to look for him, as in some tense childish game. She looked down at the sturdy pinkish calf of her leg. Amazing, that out of the blue somebody had wanted to blotch and punish it.

There were usually a few graduate students working in the carrels, even on Saturday afternoons. More rarely, a professor. Every carrel she looked into was empty, until she came to one in the corner. She poked her head in freely, by this time not expecting anybody. Then she had to say she was sorry.

There was a young man with a book on his lap, books on the floor, papers all around him. Rose asked him if he had seen anybody run past. He said no.

She told him what had happened. She didn't tell him because she was frightened or disgusted, as he seemed afterward to think, but just because she had to tell somebody; it was so odd. She was not prepared at all for his response. His long neck and face turned red, the flush entirely absorbing a birthmark down the side of his cheek. He was thin and fair. He stood up without any thought for the book in his lap or the papers in front of him. The book thumped on the floor. A great sheaf of papers, pushed across the desk, upset his ink bottle.

"How vile," he said.

"Grab the ink," Rose said. He leaned to catch the bottle and knocked it onto the floor. Fortunately the top was on, and it did not break.

"Did he hurt you?"

"No, not really."

"Come on upstairs. We'll report it."

"Oh, no."

"He can't get away with that. It shouldn't be allowed."

"There isn't anybody to report to," Rose said with relief. "The librarian goes off at noon on Saturdays."

"It's disgusting," he said in a high-pitched, excitable voice. Rose was sorry now that she had told him anything, and said she had to get back to work.

"Are you really all right?"

"Oh, yes."

"I'll be right here. Just call me if he comes back."

That was Patrick. If she had been trying to make him fall in love with her, there was no better way she could have chosen. He had many chivalric notions, which he pretended to mock, by saying certain words and phrases as if in quotation marks. "The fair sex," he would say, and "damsel in distress." Coming to his carrel with that story, Rose had turned herself into a damsel in distress. The pretended irony would not fool anybody; it was clear that he did wish to operate in a world of knights and ladies; outrages; devotions.

She continued to see him in the library, every Saturday, and often she met him walking across the campus or in the cafeteria. He made a point of greeting her with courtesy and concern, saying, "How are you?" in a way that suggested she might have suffered a further attack, or might still be recovering from the first one. He always flushed deeply when he saw her, and she thought that this was because the memory of what she had told him so embarrassed him. Later she found out it was because he was in love.

He discovered her name, and where she lived. He phoned her at Dr. Henshawe's house and asked her to go to the movies. At first when he said, "This is Patrick Blatchford speaking," Rose could not think who it was, but after a moment she recognized the high, rather aggrieved and tremulous voice. She said she would go. This was partly because Dr. Henshawe was always saying she was glad Rose did not waste her time running around with boys.

Rather soon after she started to go out with him, she said to Patrick, "Wouldn't it be funny if it was you grabbed my leg that day in the library?"

He did not think it would be funny. He was horrified that she would think such a thing.

She said she was only joking. She said she meant that it would be a good twist in a story, maybe a Maugham story, or a Hitchcock movie. They had just been to see a Hitchcock movie.

"You know, if Hitchcock made a movie out of something like that, you could be a wild insatiable leg-grabber with one half of your personality, and the other half could be a timid scholar."

He didn't like that either.

"Is that how I seem to you, a timid scholar?" It seemed to her he deepened his voice, introduced a few growling notes, drew in his chin, as if for a joke. But he seldom joked with her; he didn't think joking was suitable when you were in love.

"I didn't say you were a timid scholar or a leg-grabber. It was just an idea."

After a while he said, "I suppose I don't seem very manly."

She was startled and irritated by such an exposure. He took such chances; had nothing ever taught him not to take such chances? But maybe he didn't, after all. He knew she would have to say something reassuring. Though she was hoping not to, she longed to say judiciously, "Well, no. You don't."

But that would not actually be true. He did seem masculine to her. Because he took those chances. Only a man could be so careless and demanding.

"We come from two different worlds," she said to him, on another occasion. She felt like a character in a play, saying that. "My people are poor people. You would think the place I lived in was a dump."

Now she was the one who was being dishonest, pretending to throw herself on his mercy, for of course she did not expect him to say, "Oh, well, if you come from poor people and live in a dump, then I will have to withdraw my offer."

"But I'm glad," said Patrick. "I'm glad you're poor. You're so lovely. You're like the Beggar Maid."

"Who?"

" 'King Cophetua and the Beggar Maid.' You know. The painting. Don't you know that painting?"

Patrick had a trick—no, it was not a trick, Patrick had no tricks—Patrick had a way of expressing surprise, fairly scornful surprise, when people did not know something he knew, and similar scorn, similar surprise, whenever they had bothered to know something he did not. His arrogance and humility were both oddly exaggerated. The arrogance, Rose decided in time, must come from being rich, though Patrick was never arrogant about that in itself. His sisters, when she met them, turned out to be the same way, disgusted with anybody who did not know about horses or sailing, and just as disgusted by anybody knowing about music, say, or politics. Patrick and they could do little together but radiate disgust. But wasn't Billy Pope as bad, wasn't Flo as bad, when it came to arrogance? Maybe. There was a difference, though, and the difference was that Billy Pope and Flo were not protected. Things could get at them: D.P.'s; people speaking French on the radio; changes. Patrick and his sisters behaved as if things could never get at them. Their voices, when they quarrelled at the table, were astonishingly childish; their demands for food they liked, their petulance at seeing anything on the table they didn't like, were those of children. They had never had to defer and polish themselves and win favor in the world, they never would have to, and that was because they were rich.

Rose had no idea at the beginning how rich Patrick was. Nobody believed that. Everybody believed she had been calculating and clever, and she was so far from clever, in that way, that she really did not mind if they believed it. It turned out that other girls had been trying, and had not struck, as she had, the necessary note. Older girls, sorority girls, who had never noticed her before began to look at her with puzzlement and respect. Even Dr. Henshawe, when she saw that things were more serious than she had supposed, and settled Rose down to have a talk about it, assumed that she would have an eye on the money.

"It is no small triumph to attract the attentions of the heir to a mercantile empire," said Dr. Henshawe, being ironic and serious at the same time. "I don't despise wealth," she said. "Sometimes I wish I had some of it." (Did she really suppose she had not?) "I am sure you will learn how to put it to good uses. But what about your ambitions, Rose? What about your studies and your degree? Are you going to forget all that so soon?"

"Mercantile empire" was a rather grand way of putting it. Patrick's family owned a chain of department stores in British Columbia. All Patrick had said to Rose was that his father owned some stores. When she said *two different worlds* to him she was thinking that he probably lived in some substantial house like the houses in Dr. Henshawe's neighborhood. She was thinking of the most prosperous merchants in Hanratty. She could not realize what a coup she had made because it would have been a coup for her if the butcher's son had fallen for her, or the jeweller's; people would say she had done well.

She had a look at that painting. She looked it up in an art book in the library. She studied the Beggar Maid, meek and voluptuous, with her shy white feet. The milky surrender of her, the helplessness and gratitude. Was that how Patrick saw Rose? Was that how she could be? She would need that king, sharp and swarthy as he looked, even in his trance of passion, clever and barbaric. He could make a puddle of her, with his fierce desire. There would be no apologizing with him, none of that flinching, that lack of faith, that seemed to be revealed in all transactions with Patrick.

She could not turn Patrick down. She could not do it. It was not the amount of money but the amount of love he offered that she could not ignore; she believed that she felt sorry for him, that she had to help him out. It was as if he had come up to her in a crowd carrying a large, simple, dazzling object—a huge egg, maybe, of solid silver, something of doubtful use and punishing weight—and was offering it to her, in fact thrusting it at her, begging her to take some of the weight of it off him. If she thrust it back, how could he bear it? But that explanation left something out. It left out her own appetite, which was not for wealth but for worship. The size, the weight, the shine, of what he said was love (and she did not doubt him) had to impress her, even though she had never asked for it. It did not seem likely such an offering would come her way again. Patrick himself, though worshipful, did in some oblique way acknowledge her luck.

She had always thought this would happen, that somebody would look at her and love her totally and helplessly. At the same time she had thought that nobody would, nobody would want her at all, and up until now nobody had. What made you wanted was nothing you did, it was something you had, and how could you ever tell whether you had it? She would look at herself in the glass and think: Wife, sweetheart. Those mild lovely words. How could they apply to her? It was a miracle; it was a mistake. It was what she had dreamed of; it was not what she wanted.

She grew very tired, irritable, sleepless. She tried to think admiringly of Patrick. His lean, fair-skinned face was really very handsome. He must know a number of things. He graded papers, presided at examinations, he was finishing his thesis. There was a smell of pipe tobacco and rough wool about him that she liked. He was twenty-four. No other girl she knew who had a boyfriend had one as old as that.

Then without warning she thought of him saying, "I suppose I don't seem very manly." She thought of him saying, "Do you love me? Do you really love me?" He would look at her in a scared and threatening way. Then when she said yes he said how lucky he was, how lucky they were; he mentioned friends of his and their girls, comparing their love affairs unfavorably to his and Rose's. Rose would shiver with irritation and misery. She was sick of herself as much as him, she was sick of the picture they made at this moment, walking across a snowy downtown park, her bare hand snuggled in Patrick's, in his pocket. Some outrageous and cruel things were being shouted inside her. She had to do something, to keep them from getting out. She started tickling and teasing him.

Outside Dr. Henshawe's back door, in the snow, she kissed him, tried to make him open his mouth, she did scandalous things to him. When he kissed her his lips were soft; his tongue was shy; he collapsed over rather than held her, she could not find any force in him.

"You're lovely. You have lovely skin. Such fair eyebrows. You're so delicate."

She was pleased to hear that, anybody would be. But she said warningly, "I'm not so delicate, really. I'm quite large."

"You don't know how I love you. There's a book I have called *The White Goddess*. Every time I look at the title it reminds me of you."

She wriggled away from him. She bent down and got a handful of snow from the drift by the steps and clapped it on his head.

"My White God."

He shook the snow out. She scooped up some more and threw it at him. He didn't laugh; he was surprised and alarmed. She brushed the snow off his eyebrows and licked it off his ears. She was laughing, though she felt desperate rather than merry. She didn't know what made her do this.

"Dr. *Hen*-shawe," Patrick hissed at her. The tender poetic voice he used for rhapsodizing about her could entirely disappear, could change to remonstrance, exasperation, with no steps at all between.

"Dr. Henshawe will hear you!"

"Dr. Henshawe says you are an honorable young man," Rose said dreamily. "I think she's in love with you." It was true; Dr. Henshawe had said that. And it was true that he was. He couldn't bear the way Rose was talking. She blew at the snow in his hair. "Why don't you go in and deflower her? I'm sure she's a virgin. That's her window. Why don't you?" She rubbed his hair, then slipped her hand inside his overcoat and rubbed the front of his pants. "You're hard!" she said triumphantly. "Oh, Patrick! You've got a hard-on for Dr. Henshawe!" She had never said anything like this before, never come near behaving like this.

"Shut up!" said Patrick, tormented. But she couldn't. She raised her head and in a loud whisper pretended to call toward an upstairs window, "Dr. Henshawe! Come and see what Patrick's got for you!" Her bullying hand went for his fly.

To stop her, to keep her quiet, Patrick had to struggle with her. He got a hand over her mouth, with the other hand beat her away from his zipper. The big loose sleeves of his overcoat beat at her like floppy wings. As soon as he started to fight she was relieved—that was what she wanted from him, some sort of action. But she had to keep resisting, until he really proved himself stronger. She was afraid he might not be able to.

But he was. He forced her down, down, to her knees, face down in the snow. He pulled her arms back and rubbed her face in the snow. Then he let her go, and almost spoiled it.

"Are you all right? Are you? I'm sorry. Rose?"

She staggered up and shoved her snowy face into his. He backed off.

"Kiss me! Kiss the snow! I love you!"

"Do you?" he said plaintively, and brushed the snow from a corner of her mouth and kissed her, with understandable bewilderment. "*Do* you?"

Then the light came on, flooding them and the trampled snow, and Dr. Henshawe was calling over their heads.

"Rose! Rose!"

She called in a patient, encouraging voice, as if Rose was lost in a fog nearby, and needed directing home.

· · ·

"Do you love him, Rose?" said Dr. Henshawe. "No, think about it. Do you?" Her voice was full of doubt and seriousness. Rose took a deep breath and answered as if filled with calm emotion, "Yes, I do."

"Well, then."

In the middle of the night Rose woke up and ate chocolate bars. She craved sweets. Often in class or in the middle of a movie she started thinking about fudge cupcakes, brownies, some kind of cake Dr. Henshawe bought at the European Bakery; it was filled with dollops of rich bitter chocolate that ran out on the plate. Whenever she tried to think about herself and Patrick, whenever she made up her mind to decide what she really felt, these cravings intervened.

She was putting on weight, and had developed a nest of pimples between her eyebrows.

Her bedroom was cold, being over the garage, with windows on three sides. Otherwise it was pleasant. Over the bed hung framed photographs of Greek skies and ruins, taken by Dr. Henshawe herself on her Mediterranean trip.

She was writing an essay on Yeats's plays. In one of the plays a young bride is lured away by the fairies from her sensible unbearable marriage.

"Come away, O human child . . ." Rose read, and her eyes filled up with tears for herself, as if she was that shy elusive virgin, too fine for the bewildered peasants who have entrapped her. In actual fact she was the peasant, shocking high-minded Patrick, but he did not look for escape.

She took down one of those Greek photographs and defaced the wallpaper, writing the start of a poem which had come to her while she ate chocolate bars in bed and the wind from Gibbons Park banged at the garage walls.

> *Heedless in my dark womb*
> *I bear a madman's child . . .*

She never wrote any more if it, and wondered sometimes if she had meant headless. She never tried to rub it out, either.

PATRICK shared an apartment with two other graduate students. He lived plainly, did not own a car or belong to a fraternity. His clothes had an ordinary academic shabbiness. His friends were the sons of teachers and ministers. He said his father had all but disowned him for becoming an intellectual. He said he would never go into business.

They came back to the apartment in the early afternoon when they knew both the other students would be out. The apartment was cold. They undressed quickly and got into Patrick's bed. Now was the time. They clung together, shivering and giggling. Rose was doing the giggling. She felt a need to be continually playful. She was terrified that they would not manage it, that there was a great humiliation in store, a great exposure of their poor deceits and stratagems. But the deceits and stratagems were only hers. Patrick was never a fraud; he managed, in spite of gigantic embarrassment, apologies; he passed through some amazed pantings and flounderings, to peace. Rose was no help, presenting instead of an honest passivity much twisting and fluttering eagerness, unpracticed counterfeit of passion. She was pleased when it was accomplished; she did not have to counterfeit that. They had done what others did, they had done what lovers did. She thought of celebration. What occurred to her was something delicious to eat, a sundae at Boomers, apple pie with hot cinnamon sauce. She was not at all prepared for Patrick's idea, which was to stay where they were and try again.

When pleasure presented itself, the fifth or sixth time they were together, she was thrown out of gear entirely, her passionate carrying-on was silenced.

Patrick said, "What's the matter?"

"Nothing!" Rose said, turning herself radiant and attentive once more. But she kept forgetting, the new developments interfered, and she had finally to give in to that struggle, more or less ignoring Patrick. When she could take note of him again she overwhelmed him with gratitude; she was really grateful now, and she wanted to be forgiven, though she could not say so, for all her pretended gratitude, her patronizing, her doubts.

Why should she doubt so much, she thought, lying comfortably in the bed while Patrick went to make some instant coffee. Might it not be possible, to feel as she pretended? If this sexual surprise was possible, wasn't anything? Patrick was not much help; his chivalry and self-abasement, next door to his scoldings, did discourage her. But wasn't the real fault hers? Her conviction that anyone who could fall in love with her must be hopelessly lacking, must finally be revealed as a fool? So she took note of anything that was foolish about Patrick, even though she thought she was looking for things that were masterful, admirable. At this moment, in his bed, in his room, surrounded by his books and clothes, his shoe brushes and typewriter, some tacked-up cartoons—she sat up in bed to look at them, and they really were quite funny, he must allow things to be funny when she was not here—she could see him as a likable, intelligent, even humorous person; no hero; no fool. Perhaps they could be ordinary. If only, when he came back in, he would not start thanking and fondling and worshipping her. She didn't like worship, really; it was only the idea of it she liked. On the other hand, she didn't like it when he started to correct and criticize her. There was much he planned to change.

Patrick loved her. What did he love? Not her accent, which he was trying hard to alter, though she was often mutinous and unreasonable, declaring in the face of all evidence that she did not have a country accent, everybody talked the way she did. Not her jittery sexual boldness (his relief at her virginity matched hers at his competence). She could make him flinch at a vulgar word, a drawling tone. All the time, moving and speaking, she was destroying herself for him, yet he looked right through her, through all the distractions she was creating, and loved some obedient image that she herself could not see. And his hopes were high. Her accent could be eliminated, her friends could be discredited and removed, her vulgarity could be discouraged.

What about all the rest of her? Energy, laziness, vanity, discontent, ambition? She concealed all that. He had no idea. For all her doubts about him, she never wanted him to fall out of love with her.

They made two trips.

They went to British Columbia, on the train, during the Easter holidays. His parents sent Patrick money for his ticket. He paid for Rose, using up what he had in the bank and borrowing from one of his roommates. He told her not to reveal to his parents that she had not paid for her own ticket. She saw that he meant to conceal that she was poor. He knew nothing about women's clothes, or he would not have thought that possible. Though she had done the best she could. She had borrowed Dr. Henshawe's raincoat for the coastal weather. It was a bit long, but otherwise all right, due to Dr. Henshawe's classically youthful tastes. She had sold more blood and bought a fuzzy angora sweater, peach-colored, which was extremely messy and looked like a small-town girl's idea of dressing up. She always realized things like that as soon as a purchase was made, not before.

Patrick's parents lived on Vancouver Island, near Sidney. About half an acre of clipped green lawn—green in the middle of winter; March seemed like the middle of winter to Rose—sloped down to a stone wall and a narrow pebbly beach and salt water. The house was half stone, half stucco-and-timber. It was built in the Tudor style, and others. The windows of the living room, the dining room, the den, all faced the sea, and because of the strong winds that sometimes blew onshore, they were made of thick glass, plate glass Rose supposed, like the windows of the automobile showroom in Hanratty. The seaward wall of the dining room was all windows, curving out in a gentle bay; you looked through the thick curved glass as through the bottom of a bottle. The sideboard too had a curving, gleaming belly, and seemed as big as a boat. Size was noticeable everywhere and particularly thickness. Thickness of towels and rugs and handles of knives and forks, and silences. There was a terrible amount of luxury and unease. After a day or so there Rose became so discouraged that her wrists and ankles felt weak. Picking up her knife and fork was a chore; cutting and chewing the perfect roast beef was almost beyond her; she got short of breath climbing the stairs. She had never known before how some places could choke you off, choke off your very life. She had not known this in spite of a number of very unfriendly places she had been in.

The first morning, Patrick's mother took her for a walk on the grounds, pointing out the greenhouse, the cottage where "the couple" lived: a charming, ivied, shuttered cottage, bigger than Dr. Henshawe's house. The couple, the servants, were more gentle-spoken, more discreet and dignified, than anyone Rose could think of in Hanratty, and indeed they were superior in these ways to Patrick's family.

Patrick's mother showed her the rose garden, the kitchen garden. There were many low stone walls.

"Patrick built them," said his mother. She explained anything with an indifference that bordered on distaste. "He built all these walls."

Rose's voice came out full of false assurance, eager and inappropriately enthusiastic.

"He must be a true Scot," she said. Patrick was a Scot, in spite of his name. The Blatchfords had come from Glasgow. "Weren't the best stone-masons always Scotsmen?" (She had learned quite recently not to say "Scotch.") "Maybe he had stonemason ancestors."

She cringed afterward, thinking of these efforts, the pretense of ease and gaiety, as cheap and imitative as her clothes.

"No," said Patrick's mother. "No. I don't think they were stonemasons." Something like fog went out from her: affront, disapproval, dismay. Rose thought that perhaps she had been offended by the suggestion that her husband's family might have worked with their hands. When she got to know her better—or had observed her longer; it was impossible to get to know her—she understood that Patrick's mother disliked anything fanciful, speculative, abstract, in conversation. She would also, of course, dislike Rose's chatty tone. Any interest beyond the factual consideration of the matter at hand—food, weather, invitations, furniture, servants—seemed to her sloppy, ill-bred, and dangerous. It was all right to say, "This is a warm day," but not, "This day reminds me of when we used to—" She hated people being *reminded*.

She was the only child of one of the early lumber barons of Vancouver Island. She had been born in a vanished northern settlement. But whenever Patrick tried to get her to talk about the past, whenever he asked her for the simplest sort of information—what steamers went up the coast, what year was the settlement abandoned, what was the route of the first logging railway—she would say irritably, "I don't know. How would I know about that?" This irritation was the strongest note that ever got into her words.

Neither did Patrick's father care for this concern about the past. Many things, most things, about Patrick seemed to strike him as bad signs.

"What do you want to know all that for?" he shouted down the table. He was a short square-shouldered man, red-faced, astonishingly belligerent. Patrick looked like his mother, who was tall, fair, and elegant in the most muted way possible, as if her clothes, her makeup, her style, were chosen with an ideal neutrality in mind.

"Because I am interested in history," said Patrick in an angry, pompous, but nervously breaking voice.

"Because-I-am-interested-in-history," said his sister Marion in an immediate parody, break and all. "History!"

The sisters Joan and Marion were younger than Patrick, older than Rose. Unlike Patrick they showed no nervousness, no cracks in self-satisfaction. At an earlier meal they had questioned Rose.

"Do you ride?"

"No."

"Do you sail?"

"No."

"Play tennis? Play golf? Play badminton?"

No. No. No.

"Perhaps she is an intellectual genius, like Patrick," the father said. And Patrick, to Rose's horror and embarrassment, began to shout at the table in general an account of her scholarships and prizes. What did he hope for? Was he so witless as to think such bragging would subdue them, would bring out anything but further scorn? Against Patrick, against his shouted boasts, his contempt for sports and television, his so-called intellectual interests, the family seemed united. But this alliance was only temporary. The father's dislike of his daughters was minor only in comparison with his dislike of Patrick. He railed at them too, when he could spare a moment; he jeered at the amount of time they spent at their games, complained about the cost of their equipment, their boats, their horses. And they wrangled with each other on obscure questions of scores and borrowings and damages. All complained to the mother about the food, which was plentiful and delicious. The mother spoke as little as possible to anyone and to tell the truth Rose did not blame her. She had never imagined so much true malevolence collected in one place. Billy Pope was a bigot and a grumbler, Flo was capricious, unjust, and gossipy, her father, when he was alive, had been capable of cold judgments and unremitting disapproval; but compared to Patrick's family, all Rose's people seemed jovial and content.

"Are they always like this?" she said to Patrick. "Is it me? They don't like me."

"They don't like you because I chose you," said Patrick with some satisfaction.

They lay on the stony beach after dark, in their raincoats, hugged and kissed and uncomfortably, unsuccessfully, attempted more. Rose got seaweed stains on Dr. Henshawe's coat. Patrick said, "You see why I need you? I need you so much!"

SHE TOOK him to Hanratty. It was just as bad as she had thought it would be. Flo had gone to great trouble, and cooked a meal of scalloped potatoes, turnips, big country sausages which were a special present from Billy Pope, from the butcher shop. Patrick detested coarse-textured food, and made no pretense of eating it. The table was spread with a plastic cloth, they ate under the tube of fluorescent light. The centerpiece was new and especially for the occasion. A plastic swan, lime green in color, with slits in the wings, in which were stuck folded, colored paper napkins. Billy Pope, reminded to take one, grunted, refused. Otherwise he was on dismally good behavior. Word had reached him, word had reached both Flo and Billy, of Rose's triumph. It had come from their superiors in Hanratty; otherwise they could not have believed it. Customers in the butcher shop—formidable ladies, the dentist's wife, the veterinarian's wife—had said to Billy Pope that they heard Rose had picked herself up a millionaire. Rose knew Billy Pope would go back to work tomorrow with stories of the millionaire, or millionaire's son, and that all these stories would focus on his—Billy Pope's—forthright and unintimidated behavior in the situation.

"We just set him down and give him some sausages, don't make no difference to us what he comes from!"

She knew Flo would have her comments too, that Patrick's nervousness would not escape her, that she would be able to mimic his voice and his flapping hands that had knocked over the ketchup bottle. But at present they both sat hunched over the table in miserable eclipse. Rose tried to start some conversation, talking brightly, unnaturally, rather as if she was an interviewer trying to draw out a couple of simple local people. She felt ashamed on more levels than she could count. She was ashamed of the food and the swan and the plastic tablecloth; ashamed for Patrick, the gloomy snob, who made a startled grimace when Flo passed him the toothpick-holder; ashamed for Flo with her timidity and hypocrisy and pretensions; most of all ashamed for herself. She didn't even have any way that she could talk, and sound natural. With Patrick there, she couldn't slip back into an accent closer to Flo's, Billy Pope's, and Hanratty's. That accent jarred on her ears now, anyway. It seemed to involve not just a different pronunciation but a whole different approach to talking. Talking was shouting; the words were separated and emphasized so that people could bombard each other with them. And the things people said were like lines from the most hackneyed rural comedy. *Wal, if a feller took a notion to,* they said. They really said that. Seeing them through Patrick's eyes, hearing them through his ears, Rose too had to be amazed.

She was trying to get them to talk about local history, some things she thought Patrick might be interested in. Presently, Flo did begin to talk; she could only be held in so long, whatever her misgivings. The conversation took another line from anything Rose had intended.

"The line I lived on when I was just young," Flo said, "it was the worst place ever created for suiciding."

"A line is a concession road. In the township," Rose said to Patrick. She had doubts about what was coming, and rightly so, for then Patrick got to hear about a man who cut his own throat, *his own throat,* from ear to ear; a man who shot himself the first time and didn't do enough damage, so he loaded up and fired again and managed it; another man who hanged himself using a chain, the kind of chain you hook on a tractor with, so it was a wonder his head was not torn off.

*Tore off,* Flo said.

She went on to a woman who, though not a suicide, had been dead in her house a week before she was found, and that was in the summer. She asked Patrick to imagine it. All this happened, said Flo, within five miles of where she herself was born. She was presenting credentials, not trying to horrify Patrick, at least not more than was acceptable in a social way; she did not mean to disconcert him. How could he understand that?

"You were right," said Patrick as they left Hanratty on the bus. "It is a dump. You must be glad to get away."

Rose felt immediately that he should not have said that.

"Of course that's not your real mother," Patrick said. "Your real parents can't have been like that." Rose did not like his saying that either, though it was what she believed herself. She saw that he was trying to provide for her a more genteel background, perhaps something like the homes of his poor friends: a few books about, a tea tray, and mended linen, worn good taste; proud, tired, educated people. What a coward he was, she thought angrily, but she knew that she herself was the coward, not knowing any way to be comfortable with her own people or the kitchen or any of it. Years later she would learn how to use it, she would be able to amuse or intimidate right-thinking people at dinner parties with glimpses of her early home. At the moment she felt confusion, misery.

Nevertheless her loyalty was starting. Now that she was sure of getting away, a layer of loyalty and protectiveness was hardening around every memory she had, around the store and the town, the flat, somewhat scrubby, unremarkable countryside. She would oppose this secretly to Patrick's views of mountains and ocean, his stone-and-timbered mansion. Her allegiances were far more proud and stubborn than his.

But it turned out he was not leaving anything behind.

PATRICK gave her a diamond ring and announced that he was giving up being a historian for her sake. He was going into his father's business.

She said she thought he hated his father's business. He said that he could not afford to take such an attitude now that he would have a wife to support.

It seemed that Patrick's desire to marry, even to marry Rose, had been taken by his father as a sign of sanity. Great streaks of bounty were mixed in with all the ill will in that family. His father at once offered a job in one of the stores, offered to buy them a house. Patrick was as incapable of turning down this offer as Rose was of turning down Patrick's, and his reasons were as little mercenary as hers.

"Will we have a house like your parents'?" Rose said. She really thought it might be necessary to start off in that style.

"Well, maybe not at first. Not quite so—"

"I don't want a house like that! I don't want to live like that!"

"We'll live however you like. We'll have whatever kind of house you like."

Provided it's not a dump, she thought nastily.

Girls she hardly knew stopped and asked to see her ring, admired it, wished her happiness. When she went back to Hanratty for a weekend, alone this time, thank God, she met the dentist's wife on the main street.

"Oh, Rose, isn't it wonderful! When are you coming back again? We're going to give a tea for you, the ladies in town all want to give a tea for you!"

This woman had never spoken to Rose, never given any sign before of knowing who she was. Paths were opening now, barriers were softening. And Rose—oh, this was the worst, this was the shame of it—Rose, instead of cutting the dentist's wife, was blushing and skittishly flashing her diamond and saying yes, that would be a lovely idea. When people said how happy she must be she did think herself happy. It was as simple as that. She dimpled and sparkled and turned herself into a fiancée with no trouble at all. Where will you live, people said, and she said, Oh, in British

Columbia! That added more magic to the tale. Is it really beautiful there, they said, is it never winter?

"Oh, yes!" cried Rose. "Oh, no!"

SHE WOKE up early, got up and dressed, and let herself out the side door of Dr. Henshawe's garage. It was too early for the buses to be running. She walked through the city to Patrick's apartment. She walked across the park. Around the South African War Memorial a pair of greyhounds were leaping and playing, an old woman standing by, holding their leashes. The sun was just up, shining on their pale hides. The grass was wet. Daffodils and narcissus in bloom.

Patrick came to the door, tousled, frowning sleepily, in his gray-and-maroon striped pajamas.

"Rose! What's the matter?"

She couldn't say anything. He pulled her into the apartment. She put her arms around him and hid her face against his chest and, in a stagy voice, said, "Please, Patrick. Please let me not marry you."

"Are you sick? What's the matter?"

"Please let me not marry you," she said again, with even less conviction.

"You're crazy."

She didn't blame him for thinking so. Her voice sounded so unnatural, wheedling, silly. As soon as he opened the door and she faced the fact of him, his sleepy eyes, his pajamas, she saw that what she had come to do was enormous, impossible. She would have to explain everything to him, and of course she could not do it. She could not make him see her necessity. She could not find any tone of voice, any expression of the face, that would serve her.

"Are you upset?" said Patrick. "What's happened?"

"Nothing."

"How did you get here anyway?"

"Walked."

She had been fighting back a need to go to the bathroom. It seemed that if she went to the bathroom she would destroy some of the strength of her case. But she had to. She freed herself. She said, "Wait a minute, I'm going to the john."

When she came out Patrick had the electric kettle going, was measuring out instant coffee. He looked decent and bewildered.

"I'm not really awake," he said. "Now. Sit down. First of all, are you premenstrual?"

"No." But she realized with dismay that she was, and that he might be able to figure it out, because they had been worried last month.

"Well, if you're not premenstrual, and nothing's happened to upset you, then what is all this about?"

"I don't want to get married," she said, backing away from the cruelty of *I don't want to marry you.*

"When did you come to this decision?"

"Long ago. This morning."

They were talking in whispers. Rose looked at the clock. It was a little after seven.

"When do the others get up?"

"About eight."

"Is there milk for the coffee?" She went to the refrigerator.

"Quiet with the door," said Patrick, too late.

"I'm sorry," she said, in her strange silly voice.

"We went for a walk last night and everything was fine. You come this morning and tell me you don't want to get married. *Why* don't you want to get married?"

"I just don't. I don't want to be married."

"What else do you want to do?"

"I don't know."

Patrick kept staring at her sternly, drinking his coffee. He who used to plead with her *do you love me, do you really*, did not bring the subject up now.

"Well, I know."

"What?"

"I know who's been talking to you."

"Nobody has been talking to me."

"Oh, no. Well, I bet Dr. Henshawe has."

"No."

"Some people don't have a very high opinion of her. They think she has an influence on girls. She doesn't like the girls who live with her to have boyfriends. Does she? You even told me that. She doesn't like them to be normal."

"That's not it."

"What did she say to you, Rose?"

"She didn't say anything." Rose began to cry.

"Are you sure?"

"Oh, Patrick, listen, please, I can't marry you, please, I don't know why, I can't, please, I'm sorry, believe me, I can't," Rose babbled at him, weeping, and Patrick saying, "Shh! You'll wake them up!" lifted or dragged her out of the kitchen chair and took her to his room, where she sat on the bed. He shut the door. She held her arms across her stomach, and rocked back and forth.

"What is it, Rose? What's the matter? Are you sick?"

"It's just so hard to tell you!"

"Tell me what?"

"What I just did tell you!"

"I mean have you found out you have t.b. or something?"

"No!"

"Is there something in your family you haven't told me about? Insanity?" said Patrick encouragingly.

"No!" Rose rocked and wept.

"So what is it?"

"I don't love you!" she said. "I don't love you. I don't love you." She fell on the bed and put her head in the pillow. "I'm so sorry. I'm so sorry. I can't help it."

After a moment or two Patrick said, "Well. If you don't love me you don't love me. I'm not forcing you to." His voice sounded strained and spiteful, against the reasonableness of what he was saying. "I just wonder," he said, "if you know what you do want. I don't think you do. I don't think you have any idea what you want. You're just in a state."

"I don't have to know what I want to know what I don't want!" Rose said, turning over. This released her. "I never loved you."

"Shh. You'll wake them. We have to stop."

"I never loved you. I never wanted to. It was a mistake."

"All right. All right. You made your point."

"Why am I supposed to love you? Why do you act as if there was something wrong with me if I didn't? You despise me. You despise my family and my background and you think you are doing me a *great favor*—"

"I fell in love with you," Patrick said. "I don't despise you. Oh, Rose. I worship you."

"You're a sissy," Rose said. "You're a prude." She jumped off the bed with great pleasure as she said this. She felt full of energy. More was coming. Terrible things were coming.

"You don't even know how to make love right. I always wanted to get out of this from the very first. I felt sorry for you. You won't look where you're going, you're always knocking things over, just because you can't be bothered, you can't be bothered noticing anything, you're wrapped up in yourself, and you're always bragging, it's so stupid, you don't even know how to brag right, if you really want to impress people you'll never do it, the way you do it all they do is laugh at you!"

Patrick sat on the bed and looked up at her, his face open to whatever she would say. She wanted to beat and beat him, to say worse and worse, uglier and crueller, things. She took a breath, drew in air, to stop the things she felt rising in her from getting out.

"I don't want to see you, ever!" she said viciously. But at the door she turned and said in a normal and regretful voice, "Goodbye."

Patrick wrote her a note: *I don't understand what happened the other day and I want to talk to you about it. But I think we should wait for two weeks and not see or talk to each other and find out how we feel at the end of that time.*

Rose had forgotten all about giving him back his ring. When she came out of his apartment building that morning she was still wearing it. She couldn't go back, and it seemed too valuable to send through the mail. She continued to wear it, mostly because she did not want to have to tell Dr. Henshawe what had happened. She was relieved to get Patrick's note. She thought that she could give him back the ring then.

She thought about what Patrick had said about Dr. Henshawe. No doubt there was some truth in that, else why should she be so reluctant to tell Dr. Henshawe she had broken her engagement, so unwilling to face her sensible approval, her restrained, relieved congratulations?

She told Dr. Henshawe that she was not seeing Patrick while she studied for her exams. Rose could see that even that pleased her.

She told no one that her situation had changed. It was not just Dr. Henshawe she didn't want knowing. She didn't like giving up being envied; the experience was so new to her.

She tried to think what to do next. She could not stay on at Dr. Henshawe's. It seemed clear that if she escaped from Patrick, she must escape from Dr. Henshawe too. And she did not want to stay on at the college, with people knowing about her broken engagement, with the girls who now congratulated her saying they had known all along it was a fluke, her getting Patrick. She would have to get a job.

The Head Librarian had offered her a job for the summer but that was perhaps at Dr. Henshawe's suggestion. Once she moved out, the offer might not hold. She knew that instead of studying for her exams she ought to be downtown, applying for work as a filing clerk at the insurance offices, applying at Bell Telephone, at the department stores. The idea frightened her. She kept on studying. That was the one thing she really knew how to do. She was a scholarship student after all.

On Saturday afternoon, when she was working at the library, she saw Patrick. She did not see him by accident. She went down to the bottom floor, trying not to make noise on the spiralling metal staircase. There was a place in the stacks where she could stand, almost in darkness, and see into his carrel. She did that. She couldn't see his face. She saw his long pink neck and the old plaid shirt he wore on Saturdays. His long neck. His bony shoulders. She was no longer irritated by him, no longer frightened by him; she was free. She could look at him as she would look at anybody. She could appreciate him. He had behaved well. He had not tried to rouse her pity, he had not bullied her, he had not molested her with pitiful telephone calls and letters. He had not come and sat on Dr. Henshawe's doorstep. He was an honorable person, and he would never know how she acknowledged that, how she was grateful for it. The things she had said to him made her ashamed now. And they were not even true. Not all of them. He did know how to make love. She was so moved, made so gentle and wistful, by the sight of him, that she wanted to give him something, some surprising bounty, she wished to undo his unhappiness.

Then she had a compelling picture of herself. She was running softly into Patrick's carrel, she was throwing her arms around him from behind, she was giving everything back to him. Would he take it from her, would he still want it? She saw them laughing and crying, explaining, forgiving. *I love you. I do love you, it's all right, I was terrible, I didn't mean it, I was just crazy, I love you, it's all right.* This was a violent temptation for her; it was barely resistible. She had an impulse to hurl herself. Whether it was off a cliff or into a warm bed of welcoming grass and flowers, she really could not tell.

It was not resistible, after all. She did it.

WHEN ROSE afterward reviewed and talked about this moment in her life—for she went through a period, like most people nowadays, of talking freely about her most private decisions, to friends and lovers and party acquaintances whom she might never see again, while they did the same—she said that comradely compassion had overcome her, she was not proof against the sight of a bare bent neck. Then she went further into it, and said greed, greed. She said she had run to him and clung to him and overcome his suspicions and kissed and cried and reinstated herself simply because she did not know how to do without his love and his promise to look after her; she was frightened of the world and she had not been able to think up any other plan for herself. When she was seeing life in economic terms, or was with people who did, she said that only middle-class people had choices anyway, that if she had had the price of a train ticket to Toronto her life would have been different.

Nonsense, she might say later, never mind that, it was really vanity, it was vanity pure and simple, to resurrect him, to bring him back his happiness. To see if she could do that. She could not resist such a test of power. She explained then that she had paid for it. She said that she and Patrick had been married ten years, and that during that time the scenes of the first breakup and reconciliation had been periodically repeated, with her saying again all the things she had said the first time, and the things she had held back, and many other things which occurred to her. She hopes she did not tell people (but thinks she did) that she used to beat her head against the bedpost, that she smashed a gravy boat through a dining-room window; that she was so frightened, so sickened by what she had done that she lay in bed, shivering, and begged and begged for his forgiveness. Which he granted. Sometimes she flew at him; sometimes he beat her. The next morning they would get up early and make a special breakfast; they would sit eating bacon and eggs and drinking filtered coffee, worn out, bewildered, treating each other with shamefaced kindness.

What do you think triggers the reaction? they would say.

Do you think we ought to take a holiday? A holiday together? Holidays alone?

A waste, a sham, those efforts, as it turned out. But they worked for the moment. Calmed down, they would say that most people probably went through the same things like this, in a marriage, and indeed they seemed to know mostly people who did. They could not separate until enough damage had been done, until nearly mortal damage had been done, to keep them apart. And until Rose could get a job and make her own money, so perhaps there was a very ordinary reason after all.

What she never said to anybody, never confided, was that she sometimes thought it had not been pity or greed or cowardice or vanity but something quite different, like a vision of happiness. In view of everything else she had told she could hardly tell that. It seems very odd; she can't justify it. She doesn't mean that they had perfectly ordinary, bearable times in their marriage, long busy stretches of wallpapering and vacationing and meals and shopping and worrying about a child's illness, but that sometimes, without reason or warning, happiness, the possibility of happiness, would surprise them. Then it was as if they were in different though identical-seeming skins, as if there existed a radiantly kind and innocent Rose and Patrick, hardly ever visible, in the shadow of their usual selves. Perhaps it was that Patrick she saw when she was free of him, invisible to him, looking into his carrel. Perhaps it was. She should have left him there.

SHE KNEW that was how she had seen him; she knows it, because it happened again. She was in Toronto Airport, in the middle of the night. This was about nine years after she and Patrick were divorced. She had become fairly well known by this time, her face was familiar to many people in this country. She did a television program on which she interviewed politicians, actors, writers, *personalities*, and many ordinary people who were angry about something the government or the police or a union had done to them. Sometimes she talked to people who had seen strange sights,

UFOs, or sea monsters, or who had unusual accomplishments or collections, or kept up some obsolete custom.

She was alone. No one was meeting her. She had just come in on a delayed flight from Yellowknife. She was tired and bedraggled. She saw Patrick standing with his back to her, at a coffee bar. He wore a raincoat. He was heavier than he had been, but she knew him at once. And she had the same feeling that this was a person she was bound to, that by a certain magical yet possible trick, they could find and trust each other, and that to begin this all that she had to do was go up and touch him on the shoulder, surprise him with his happiness.

She did not do this, of course, but she did stop. She was standing still when he turned around, heading for one of the little plastic tables and curved seats grouped in front of the coffee bar. All his skinniness and academic shabbiness, his look of prim authoritarianism, was gone. He had smoothed out, filled out, into such a modish and agreeable, responsible, slightly complacent-looking man. His birthmark had faded. She thought how haggard and dreary she must look, in her rumpled trenchcoat, her long, graying hair fallen forward around her face, old mascara smudged under her eyes.

He made a face at her. It was a truly hateful, savagely warning, face; infantile, self-indulgent, yet calculated; it was a timed explosion of disgust and loathing. It was hard to believe. But she saw it.

Sometimes when Rose was talking to someone in front of the television cameras she would sense the desire in them to make a face. She would sense it in all sorts of people, in skillful politicians and witty liberal bishops and honored humanitarians, in housewives who had witnessed natural disasters and in workmen who had performed heroic rescues or been cheated out of disability pensions. They were longing to sabotage themselves, to make a face or say a dirty word. Was this the face they all wanted to make? To show somebody, to show everybody? They wouldn't do it, though; they wouldn't get the chance. Special circumstances were required. A lurid unreal place, the middle of the night, a staggering unhinging weariness, the sudden, hallucinatory appearance of your true enemy.

She hurried away then, down the long varicolored corridor, shaking. She had seen Patrick; Patrick had seen her; he had made that face. But she was not really able to understand how she could be an enemy. How could anybody hate Rose so much, at the very moment when she was ready to come forward with her good will, her smiling confession of exhaustion, her air of diffident faith in civilized overtures?

Oh, Patrick could. Patrick could.

# Dulse

AT THE END of the summer Lydia took a boat to an island off the southern coast of New Brunswick, where she was going to stay overnight. She had just a few days left until she had to be back in Ontario. She worked as an editor, for a publisher in Toronto. She was also a poet, but she did not refer to that unless it was something people knew already. For the past eighteen months she had been living with a man in Kingston. As far as she could see, that was over.

She had noticed something about herself on this trip to the Maritimes. It was that people were no longer so interested in getting to know her. It wasn't that she had created such a stir before, but something had been there that she could rely on. She was forty-five, and had been divorced for nine years. Her two children had started on their own lives, though there were still retreats and confusions. She hadn't got fatter or thinner, her looks had not deteriorated in any alarming way, but nevertheless she had stopped being one sort of woman and had become another, and she had noticed it on this trip. She was not surprised because she was in a new, strange condition at the time. She made efforts, one after the other. She set little blocks on top of one another and she had a day. Sometimes she almost could not do this. At other times the very deliberateness, the seeming arbitrariness, of what she was doing, the way she was living, exhilarated her.

She found a guesthouse overlooking the docks, with their stacks of lobster traps, and the few scattered stores and houses that made up the village. A woman of about her own age was cooking dinner. This woman took her to a cheap, old-fashioned room upstairs. There were no other guests around, though the room next door was open and seemed to be occupied, perhaps by a child. Whoever it was had left several comic books on the floor beside the bed.

She went for a walk up the steep lane behind the guesthouse. She occupied herself by naming shrubs and weeds. The goldenrod and wild aster were in bloom, and Japanese boxwood, a rarity in Ontario, seemed commonplace here. The grass was long and coarse and the trees were small. The Atlantic coast, which she had never seen before, was just as she had expected it to be. The bending grass; the bare houses; the sea light. She started wondering what it would be like to live there, whether the houses were still cheap or if people from the outside had started to buy them up. Often on this trip she had busied herself with calculations of this kind, and also with ideas of how she could make a living in some new way, cut off from everything she had done before. She did not think of making a living writing poetry, not only because the income would be so low but because she thought, as she had thought innumerable times in her life, that probably she would not write any more poems. She was thinking that she could not cook well enough to do it for pay but she could clean. There was at least one other guesthouse besides the one where she was staying, and she had seen a sign advertising a motel. How many hours' cleaning could she get if she cleaned all three places, and how much an hour did cleaning pay?

There were four small tables in the dining room, but only one man was sitting there, drinking tomato juice. He did not look at her. A man who was probably the husband of the woman she had met earlier came in from the kitchen. He had a grayish-blond beard, and a downcast look. He asked Lydia's name and took her to the table where the man was sitting. The man stood up, stiffly, and Lydia was introduced. The man's name was Mr. Stanley and Lydia took him to be about sixty. Politely, he asked her to sit down.

Three men in work clothes came in and sat down at another table. They were not noisy in any self-important or offensive way, but just coming in and disposing themselves around the table, they created an enjoyable commotion. That is, they enjoyed it, and looked as if they expected others to. Mr. Stanley bowed in their direction. It really was a little bow, not just a nod of the head. He said good evening. They asked him what there was for supper, and he said he believed it was scallops, with pumpkin pie for dessert.

"These gentlemen work for the New Brunswick Telephone Company," he said to Lydia. "They are laying a cable to one of the smaller islands, and they stay here during the week."

He was older than she had thought at first. It did not show in his voice, which was precise and American, or in the movements of his hands, but in his small, separate, brownish teeth, and in his eyes, which had a delicate milky skin over the light-brown iris.

The husband brought their food, and spoke to the workmen. He was an efficient waiter, but rather stiff and remote, rather like a sleepwalker, in fact, as if he did not perform this job in his real life. The vegetables were served in large bowls, from which they helped themselves. Lydia was glad to see so much food: broccoli, mashed turnips, potatoes, corn. The American took small helpings of everything and began to eat in a very deliberate way, giving the impression that the order in which he lifted forkfuls of food to his mouth was not haphazard, that there was a reason for the turnip to follow the potatoes, and for the deep-fried scallops, which were not large, to be cut neatly in half. He looked up a couple of times as if he thought of saying something, but he did not do it. The workmen were quiet now too, laying into the food.

Mr. Stanley spoke at last. He said, "Are you familiar with the writer Willa Cather?"

"Yes." Lydia was startled, because she had not seen anybody reading a book for the past two weeks; she had not even noticed any paperback racks.

"Do you know, then, that she spent every summer here?"

"Here?"

"On this island. She had her summer home here. Not more than a mile away from where we are sitting now. She came here for eighteen years, and she wrote many of her books here. She wrote in a room that had a view of the sea, but now the trees have grown up and blocked it. She was with her great friend, Edith Lewis. Have you read *A Lost Lady*?"

Lydia said that she had.

"It is my favorite of all her books. She wrote it here. At least, she wrote a great part of it here."

Lydia was aware of the workmen listening, although they did not glance up from their food. She felt that even without looking at Mr. Stanley or each other they might manage to communicate an indulgent contempt. She thought she did not care whether or not she was included in this contempt, but perhaps it was for that reason that she did not find anything much to say about Willa Cather, or tell Mr. Stanley that she worked for a publisher, let alone that she was any sort of writer herself. Or it could have been just that Mr. Stanley did not give her much of a chance.

"I have been her admirer for over sixty years," he said. He paused, holding his knife and fork over his plate. "I read and reread her, and my admiration grows. It simply grows. There are people here who remember her. Tonight, I am going to see a woman, a woman who knew Willa, and had conversations with her. She is eighty-eight years old but they say she has not forgotten. The people here are beginning to learn of my interest and they will remember someone like this and put me in touch.

"It is a great delight to me," he said solemnly.

All the time he was talking, Lydia was trying to think what his conversational style reminded her of. It didn't remind her of any special person, though she might have had one or two teachers at college who talked like that. What it made her think of was a time when a few people, just a few people, had never concerned themselves with being democratic, or ingratiating, in their speech; they spoke in formal, well-thought-out, slightly self-congratulating sentences, though they lived in a country where their formality, their pedantry, could bring them nothing but mockery. No, that was not the whole truth. It brought mockery, and an uncomfortable admiration. What he made Lydia think of, really, was the old-fashioned culture of provincial cities long ago (something she of course had never known, but sensed from books); the high-mindedness, the propriety; hard plush concert seats and hushed libraries. And his adoration of the chosen writer was of a piece with this; it was just as out-of-date as his speech. She thought that he could not be a teacher; such worship was not in style for teachers, even of his age.

"Do you teach literature?"

"No. Oh, no. I have not had that privilege. No. I have not even studied literature. I went to work when I was sixteen. In my day there was not so much choice. I have worked on newspapers."

She thought of some absurdly discreet and conservative New England paper with a fusty prose style.

"Oh. Which paper?" she said, then realized her inquisitiveness must seem quite rude, to anyone so circumspect.

"Not a paper you would have heard of. Just the daily paper of an industrial town. Other papers in the earlier years. That was my life."

"And now, would you like to do a book on Willa Cather?" This question seemed not so out of place to her, because she was always talking to people who wanted to do books about something.

"No," he said austerely. "My eyes do not permit me to do any reading or writing beyond what is necessary."

That was why he was so deliberate about his eating.

"No," he went on, "I don't say that at one time I might not have thought of that, doing a book on Willa. I would have written something just about her life here on the island. Biographies have been done, but not so much on that phase of her life. Now I have given up the idea. I do my investigating just for my own pleasure. I take a camp chair up there, so I can sit underneath the window where she wrote and looked at the sea. There is never anybody there."

"It isn't being kept up? It isn't any sort of memorial?"

"Oh, no indeed. It isn't kept up at all. The people here, you know, while they were very impressed with Willa, and some of them recognized her genius—I mean the genius of her personality, for they would not be able to recognize the genius of her work—others of them thought her unfriendly and did not like her. They took offense because she was unsociable, as she had to be, to do her writing."

"It could be a project," Lydia said. "Perhaps they could get some money from the government. The Canadian government and the Americans too. They could preserve the house."

"Well, that isn't for me to say." He smiled; he shook his head. "I don't think so. No."

He did not want any other worshippers coming to disturb him in his camp chair. She should have known that. What would this private pilgrimage of his be worth if other people got into the act, and signs were put up, leaflets printed; if this guesthouse, which was now called Sea View, had to be renamed Shadows on the Rock? He would let the house fall down and the grass grow over it sooner than see that.

AFTER LYDIA'S last attempt to call Duncan, the man she had been living with in Kingston, she had walked along the street in Toronto, knowing that she had to get to the bank, she had to buy some food, she had to get on the subway. She had to remember directions, and the order in which to do things: to open her checkbook, to move forward when it was her turn in line, to choose one kind of bread over another, to drop a token in the slot. These seemed to be the most difficult things she had ever done. She had immense difficulty reading the names of the subway stations, and getting off at the right one, so that she could go to the apartment where she was staying. She would have found it hard to describe this difficulty. She knew perfectly well which was the right stop, she knew which stop it came after; she knew where she was. But she could not make the connection between herself and things outside herself, so that getting up and leaving the car, going up the steps, going along the street all seemed to involve a bizarre effort. She thought afterwards that she had been seized up, as machines are said to be. Even at the time she had an image of herself. She saw herself as something like an egg carton, hollowed out in back.

When she reached the apartment she sat down on a chair in the hall. She sat for an hour or so; then she went to the bathroom, undressed, put on her nightgown, and got into bed. In bed she felt triumph and relief, that she had managed all the difficulties and got herself to where she was supposed to be and would not have to remember anything more.

She didn't feel at all like committing suicide. She couldn't have managed the implements, or aids, she couldn't even have thought which to use. It amazed her to think that she had chosen the loaf of bread and the cheese, which were now lying on the floor in the hall. How had she imagined she was going to chew and swallow them?

AFTER DINNER Lydia sat out on the veranda with the woman who had cooked the meal. The woman's husband did the cleaning up.

"Well, of course we have a dishwasher," the woman said. "We have two freezers and an oversized refrigerator. You have to make an investment. You get the crews staying with you, you have to feed them. This place soaks up money like a sponge. We're going to put in a swimming pool next year. We need more attractions. You have to run to stay in the same place. People think what an easy nice life. Boy."

She had a strong, lined face, and long straight hair. She wore jeans and an embroidered smock and a man's sweater.

"Ten years ago I was living in a commune in the States. Now I'm here. I work sometimes eighteen hours a day. I have to pack the crew's lunch yet tonight. I cook and bake, cook and bake. John does the rest."

"Do you have someone to clean?"

"We can't afford to hire anybody. John does it. He does the laundry— everything. We had to buy a mangle for the sheets. We had to put in a new furnace. We got a bank loan. I thought that was funny, because I used to be married to a bank manager. I left him."

"I'm on my own now too."

"Are you? You can't be on your own forever. I met John, and he was in the same boat."

"I was living with a man in Kingston, in Ontario."

"Were you? John and I are extremely happy. He used to be a minister. But when I met him he was doing carpentry. We both had sort of dropped out. Did you talk to Mr. Stanley?"

"Yes."

"Had you ever heard of Willa Cather?"

"Yes."

"That'd make him happy. I don't read hardly at all, it doesn't mean anything to me. I'm a visual person. But I think he's a wonderful character, old Mr. Stanley. He's a real old scholar."

"Has he been coming here for a long time?"

"No, he hasn't. This is just his third year. He says he's wanted to come here all his life. But he couldn't. He had to wait till some relative died, that he was looking after. Not a wife. A brother, maybe. Anyway he had to wait. How old do you think he is?"

"Seventy? Seventy-five?"

"That man is eighty-one. Isn't that amazing? I really admire people like that. I really do. I admire people that keep going."

"THE MAN I was living with—that is, the man I used to live with, in Kingston," said Lydia, "was putting some boxes of papers in the trunk of his car once, this was out in the country, at an old farmhouse, and he felt something nudge him and he glanced down. It was about dusk, on a pretty dark day. So he thought this was a big friendly dog, a big black dog giving him a nudge, and he didn't pay much attention. He just said go on, now, boy, go away now, good boy. Then when he got the boxes arranged he turned around. And he saw it was a bear. It was a black bear."

She was telling this later that same evening, in the kitchen.

"So what did he do then?" said Lawrence, who was the boss of the telephone work crew. Lawrence and Lydia and Eugene and Vincent were playing cards.

Lydia laughed. "He said, *Excuse me.* That's what he claims he said."

"Papers all he had in the boxes? Nothing to eat?"

"He's a writer. He writes historical books. This was some material he needed for his work. Sometimes he has to go and scout out material from people who are very strange. That bear hadn't come out of the bush. It was a pet, actually, that had been let off its chain, for a joke. There were two old brothers there, that he got the papers from, and they just let it off its chain to give him a scare."

"That's what he does, collects old stuff and writes about it?" Lawrence said. "I guess that's interesting."

She immediately regretted having told this story. She had brought it up because the men were talking about bears. But there wasn't much point to it unless Duncan told it. He could show you himself, large and benign and civilized, with his courtly apologies to the bear. He could make you see the devilish old men behind their tattered curtains.

"You'd have to know Duncan" was what she almost said. And hadn't she told this simply to establish that she had known Duncan—that she had recently had a man, and an interesting man, an amusing and adventurous man? She wanted to assure them that she was not always alone, going on her aimless travels. She had to show herself attached. A mistake. They were not likely to think a man adventurous who collected old papers from misers and eccentrics, so that he could write books about things that had happened a hundred years ago. She shouldn't even have said that

Duncan was a man she had lived with. All that could mean, to them, was that she was a woman who had slept with a man she was not married to.

Lawrence the boss was not yet forty, but he was successful. He was glad to tell about himself. He was a free-lance labor contractor and owned two houses in St. Stephen. He had two cars and a truck and a boat. His wife taught school. Lawrence was getting a thick waist, a trucker's belly, but he still looked alert and vigorous. You could see that he would be shrewd enough, in most situations, for his purposes; sure enough, ruthless enough. Dressed up, he might turn flashy. And certain places and people might be capable of making him gloomy, uncertain, contentious.

Lawrence said it wasn't all true—all the stuff they wrote about the Maritimes. He said there was plenty of work for people who weren't afraid to work. Men or women. He said he was not against women's lib, but the fact was, and always would be, that there was work men did better than women and work women did better than men, and if they would both settle down and realize that they'd be happier.

His kids were cheeky, he said. They had it too soft. They got everything—that was the way nowadays, what could you do? The other kids got everything too. Clothes, bikes, education, records. He hadn't had anything handed to him. He had got out and worked, driven trucks. He had got to Ontario, got as far as Saskatchewan. He had only got to Grade 10 in school but he hadn't let that hold him back. Sometimes he wished, though, that he did have more of an education.

Eugene and Vincent, who worked for Lawrence, said they had never got past Grade 8, when that was as far as you could go in the country schools. Eugene was twenty-five and Vincent was fifty-two. Eugene was French-Canadian from northern New Brunswick. He looked younger than his age. He had a rosy color, a downy, dreamy look—a masculine beauty that was nevertheless soft-edged, sweet-tempered, bashful. Hardly any men or boys have that look nowadays. Sometimes you see it in an old photograph—of a bridegroom, a basketball player: the thick water-combed hair, the blooming boy's face on the new man's body. Eugene was not very bright, or perhaps not very competitive. He lost money at the game they were playing. It was a card game that the men called Skat. Lydia remembered playing it when she was a child, and calling it Thirty-one. They played for a quarter a game.

Eugene permitted Vincent and Lawrence to tease him about losing at cards, about getting lost in St. John, about women he liked, and about being French-Canadian. Lawrence's teasing amounted to bullying. Lawrence wore a carefully good-natured expression, but he looked as if something hard and heavy had settled inside him—a load of self-esteem that weighed him down instead of buoying him up. Vincent had no such extra weight, and though he too was relentless in his teasing—he teased Lawrence as well as Eugene—there was no sense of cruelty or danger. You could see that his natural tone was one of rumbling, easy mockery. He was sharp and sly but not insistent; he would always be able to say the most pessimistic things and not sound unhappy.

Vincent had a farm—it was his family's farm, where he had grown up, near St. Stephen. He said you couldn't make enough to keep you nowadays, just from farming. Last year he put in a potato crop. There was frost in June, snow in September. Too short a season by a long shot. You never knew, he said, when you might get it like that. And the market is all controlled now; it is all run by the big fellows, the big interests. Everybody does what he can, rather than trust to farming. Vincent's wife works too. She took a course and learned to do hair. His sons are not hard-working like their parents. All they want to do is roar around in cars. They get married and the first thing their wives want is a new stove. They want a stove that practically cooks the dinner by itself and puts it on the table.

It didn't use to be that way. The first time Vincent ever had boots of his own—new boots that hadn't been worn by anybody before him—was when he joined the army. He was so pleased he walked backwards in the dirt to see the prints they made, fresh and whole. Later on, after the war, he went to St. John to look for work. He had been working at home on the farm for a while and he had worn out his army clothes—he had just one pair of decent pants left. In a beer parlor in St. John a man said to him, "You want to pick up a good pair of pants cheap?" Vincent said yes, and the man said, "Follow me." So Vincent did. And where did they end up? At the undertaker's! For the fact was that the family of a dead man usually bring in a suit of clothes to dress him in, and he only needs to be dressed from the waist up, that's all that shows in the coffin. The undertaker sold the pants. That was true. The army gave Vincent his first pair of new boots and a corpse donated the best pair of pants he ever wore, up to that time.

Vincent had no teeth. This was immediately apparent, but it did not make him look unattractive; it simply deepened his look of secrecy and humor. His face was long and his chin tucked in, his glance unchallenging but unfooled. He was a lean man, with useful muscles, and graying black hair. You could see all the years of hard work on him, and some years of it ahead, and the body just equal to it until he turned into a ropy-armed old man, shrunken, uncomplaining, hanging on to a few jokes.

While they played Skat the talk was boisterous and interrupted all the time by exclamations, joking threats to do with the game, laughter. Afterwards it became more serious and personal. They had been drinking a local beer called Moose, but when the game was over Lawrence went out to the truck and brought in some Ontario beer, thought to be better. They called it "the imported stuff." The couple who owned the guesthouse had long ago gone to bed, but the workmen and Lydia sat on in the kitchen, just as if it belonged to one of them, drinking beer and eating dulse, which Vincent had brought down from his room. Dulse was a kind of seaweed, greenish brown, salty and fishy-tasting. Vincent said it was what he ate last thing at night and first thing in the morning—nothing could beat it. Now that they had found out it was so good for you, they sold it in the stores, done up in little wee packages at a criminal price.

The next day was Friday, and the men would be leaving the island for the mainland. They talked about trying to get the two-thirty boat instead of the one they usually caught, at five-thirty, because the forecast was for rough weather; the tail end of one of the tropical hurricanes was due to hit the Bay of Fundy before night.

"But the ferries won't run if it's too rough, will they?" said Lydia. "They won't run if it's dangerous?" She thought that she would not mind being cut off, she wouldn't mind not having to travel again in the morning.

"Well, there's a lot of fellows waiting to get off the island on a Friday night," Vincent said.

"Wanting to get home to their wives," said Lawrence sardonically. "There's always crews working over here, always men away from home." Then he began to talk in an unhurried but insistent way about sex. He talked about what he called the immorality on the island. He said that at one time the authorities had been going to put a quarantine around the whole island, on account of the V.D. Crews came over here to work and stayed at the motel, the Ocean Wave, and there'd be parties there all night every night, with drinking and young girls turning up offering themselves for sale. Girls fourteen and fifteen—oh, thirteen years of age. On the island, he said, it was getting so a woman of twenty-five could practically be a grandmother. The place was famous. Those girls would do anything for a price, sometimes for a beer.

"And sometimes for nothing," said Lawrence. He luxuriated in the telling.

They heard the front door open.

"Your old boyfriend," Lawrence said to Lydia.

She was bewildered for a moment, thinking of Duncan.

"The old fellow at the table," said Vincent.

Mr. Stanley did not come into the kitchen. He crossed the living room and climbed the stairs.

"Hey? Been down to the Ocean Wave?" said Lawrence softly, raising his head as if to call through the ceiling. "Old bugger wouldn't know what to do with it," he said. "Wouldn't've known fifty years ago any better than now. I don't let any of my crews go near that place. Do I, Eugene?"

Eugene blushed. He put on a solemn expression, as if he was being badgered by a teacher at school.

"Eugene, now, he don't have to," Vincent said.

"Isn't it true what I'm saying?" said Lawrence urgently, as if somebody had been disputing with him. "It's true, isn't it?"

He looked at Vincent, and Vincent said, "Yeah. Yeah." He did not seem to relish the subject as much as Lawrence did.

"You'd think it was all so innocent here," said Lawrence to Lydia. "Innocent! Oh, boy!"

Lydia went upstairs to get a quarter that she owed Lawrence from the last game. When she came out of her room into the dark hall, Eugene was standing there, looking out the window.

"I hope it don't storm too bad," he said.

Lydia stood beside him, looking out. The moon was visible, but misty.

"You didn't grow up near the water?" she said.

"No, I didn't."

"But if you get the two-thirty boat it'll be all right, won't it?"

"I sure hope so." He was quite childlike and unembarrassed about his fear. "One thing I don't like the idea of is getting drownded."

Lydia remembered that as a child she had said "drownded." Most of the adults and all the children she knew then said that.

"You won't," she said, in a firm, maternal way. She went downstairs and paid her quarter.

"Where's Eugene?" Lawrence said. "He upstairs?"

"He's looking out the window. He's worried about the storm."

Lawrence laughed. "You tell him to go to bed and forget about it. He's right in the room next to you. I just thought you ought to know in case he hollers in his sleep."

LYDIA had first seen Duncan in a bookstore, where her friend Warren worked. She was waiting for Warren to go out to lunch with her. He had gone to get his coat. A man asked Shirley, the other clerk in the store, if she could find him a copy of *Persian Letters*. That was Duncan. Shirley walked ahead of him to where the book was kept, and in the quiet store Lydia heard him saying that it must be difficult to know where to shelve *Persian Letters*. Should it be classed as fiction or as a political essay? Lydia felt that he revealed something, saying this. He revealed a need that she supposed was common to customers in the bookstore, a need to distinguish himself, appear knowledgeable. Later on she would look back on this moment and try to imagine him again so powerless, slightly ingratiating, showing a bit of neediness. Warren came back with his coat on, greeted Duncan, and as he and Lydia went outside Warren said under his breath, "The Tin Woodman." Warren and Shirley livened up their days with nicknames for customers; Lydia had already heard of Marble-Mouth, and Chickpea and the Colonial Duchess. Duncan was the Tin Woodman. Lydia thought they must call him that because of the smooth gray overcoat he wore, and his hair, a bright gray which had obviously once been blond. He was not thin or angular and he did not look as if he would be creaky in the joints. He was supple and well-fleshed and dignified and pleasant; fair-skinned, freshly groomed, glistening.

She never told him about that name. She never told him that she had seen him in the bookstore. A week or so later she met him at a publisher's party. He did not remember ever seeing her before, and she supposed he had not seen her, being occupied with chatting with Shirley.

Lydia trusts what she can make of things, usually. She trusts what she thinks about her friend Warren, or his friend Shirley, and about chance acquaintances, like the couple who run the guesthouse, and Mr. Stanley, and the men she has been playing cards with. She thinks she knows why people behave as they do, and she puts more stock than she will admit in her own unproven theories and unjustified suspicions. But she is stupid and helpless when contemplating the collision of herself and Duncan. She has plenty to say about it, given the chance, because explanation is her habit, but she doesn't trust what she says, even to herself; it doesn't help her. She might just as well cover her head and sit wailing on the ground.

She asks herself what gave him his power. She knows who did. But she asks what, and when—when did the transfer take place, when was the abdication of all pride and sense?

SHE READ for half an hour after getting into bed. Then she went down the hall to the bathroom. It was after midnight. The rest of the house was in darkness. She had left her door ajar, and coming back to her room, she did not turn on the hall light. The door of Eugene's room was also ajar, and as she was passing she heard a low, careful sound. It was like a moan, and also like a whisper. She remembered Lawrence saying Eugene hollered in his sleep, but this sound was not being made in sleep. She knew he was awake. He was watching from the bed in his dark room and he was inviting her. The invitation was amorous and direct and helpless-sounding as his confession of fear when he stood by the window. She went on into her own room and shut the door and hooked it. Even as she did this, she knew she didn't have to. He would never try to get in; there was no bullying spirit in him.

Then she lay awake. Things had changed for her; she refused adventures. She could have gone to Eugene, and earlier in the evening she could have given a sign to Lawrence. In the past she might have done it. She might, or she might not have done it, depending on how she felt. Now it seemed not possible. She felt as if she were muffled up, wrapped in layers and layers of dull knowledge, well protected. It wasn't altogether a bad thing—it left your mind unclouded. Speculation can be more gentle, can take its time, when it is not driven by desire.

She thought about what those men would have been like as lovers. It was Lawrence who would have been her reasonable choice. He was near-est to her own age, and predictable, and probably well used to the discreet encounter. His approach was vulgar, but that would not necessarily have put her off. He would be cheerful, hearty, prudent, perhaps a bit self-congratulatory, attentive in a businesslike way, and he would manage in the middle of his attentions to slip in a warning: a joke, a friendly insult, a reminder of how things stood.

Eugene would never feel the need to do that, though he would have a shorter memory even than Lawrence (much shorter, for Lawrence, though not turning down opportunities, would carry afterward the thought of some bad consequence, for which he must keep ready a sharp line of de-fense). Eugene would be no less experienced than Lawrence; for years, girls and women must have been answering the kind of plea Lydia had heard, the artless confession. Eugene would be generous, she thought. He would be a grateful, self-forgetful lover, showing his women such kind-ness that when he left they would never make trouble. They would not try to trap him; they wouldn't whine after him. Women do that to the men who have held back, who have contradicted themselves, promised, lied, mocked. These are the men women get pregnant by, send desperate letters to, preach their own superior love to, take their revenge on. Eugene would go free, he would be an innocent, happy prodigy of love, until he decided it was time to get married. Then he would marry a rather plain, maternal sort of girl, perhaps a bit older than himself, a bit shrewder. He would be faithful, and good to her, and she would manage things; they would raise a large Catholic family.

What about Vincent? Lydia could not imagine him as she easily imag-ined the others: their noises and movements and bare shoulders and pleasing warm skin; their power, their exertions, their moments of help-lessness. She was shy of thinking any such things about him. Yet he was the only one whom she could think of now with real interest. She thought of his courtesy and reticence and humor, his inability to better his luck. She liked him for the very things that made him different from Lawrence and insured that all his life he would be working for Lawrence—or for somebody like Lawrence—never the other way round. She liked him also for the things that made him different from Eugene: the irony, the pa-tience, the self-containment. He was the sort of man she had known when she was a child living on a farm not so different from his, the sort of man who must have been in her family for hundreds of years. She knew his life. With him she could foresee doors opening to what she knew and had forgotten; rooms and landscapes opening; *there*. The rainy evenings, a country with creeks and graveyards, and chokecherry and finches in the fence-corners. She had to wonder if this was what happened, after the years of appetite and greed—did you drift back into tenderhearted fantasies? Or was it just the truth about what she needed and wanted; should she have fallen in love with, and married, a man like Vincent years ago; should she have concentrated on the part of her that would have been content with such an arrangement, and forgotten about the rest?

That is, should she have stayed in the place where love is managed for you, not gone where you have to invent it, and reinvent it, and never know if these efforts will be enough?

DUNCAN spoke about his former girlfriends. Efficient Ruth, pert Judy, vivacious Diane, elegant Dolores, wifely Maxine. Lorraine the golden-haired, full-breasted beauty; Marian the multilingual; Caroline the neurotic; Rosalie who was wild and gypsylike; gifted, melancholy Louise; serene socialite Jane. What description would do now for Lydia? Lydia the poet. Morose, messy, unsatisfactory Lydia. The unsatisfactory poet.

One Sunday, when they were driving in the hills around Peterborough, he talked about the effects of Lorraine's beauty. Perhaps the voluptuous countryside reminded him. It was almost like a joke, he said. It was almost silly. He stopped for gas in a little town and Lydia went across the street to a discount store that was open Sundays. She bought makeup in tubes off a rack. In the cold and dirty toilet of the gas station she attempted a transformation, slapping buff-colored liquid over her face and rubbing green paste on her eyelids.

"What have you done to your face?" he said when she came back to the car.

"Makeup. I put some makeup on so I'd look more cheerful."

"You can see where the line stops, on your neck."

At such times she felt strangled. It was frustration, she said to the doctor later. The gap between what she wanted and what she could get. She believed that Duncan's love—love for her—was somewhere inside him, and that by gigantic efforts to please, or fits of distress which obliterated all those efforts, or tricks of indifference, she could claw or lure it out.

What gave her such an idea? He did. At least he indicated that he could love her, that they could be happy, if she could honor his privacy, make no demands upon him, and try to alter those things about her person and behavior which he did not like. He listed these things precisely. Some were

very intimate in nature and she howled with shame and covered her ears
and begged him to take them back or to say no more.

"There is no way to have a discussion with you," he said. He said he hated
hysterics, emotional displays, beyond anything, yet she thought she saw a
quiver of satisfaction, a deep thrill of relief, that ran through him when she
finally broke under the weight of his calm and detailed objections.

"Could that be?" she said to the doctor. "Could it be that he wants a
woman close but is so frightened of it he has to try to wreck her? Is that
oversimplified?" she said anxiously.

"What about you?" said the doctor. "What do you want?"

"For him to love me?"

"Not for you to love him?"

She thought about Duncan's apartment. There were no curtains; he
was higher than the surrounding buildings. No attempt had been made to
arrange things to make a setting; nothing was in relation to anything else.
Various special requirements had been attended to. A certain sculpture
was in a corner behind some filing cabinets because he liked to lie on the
floor and look at it in shadow. Books were in piles beside the bed, which
was crossways in the room in order to catch the breeze from the window.
All disorder was actually order, carefully thought out and not to be interfered with. There was a beautiful little rug at the end of the hall, where he
sat and listened to music. There was one great, ugly armchair, a master-
piece of engineering, with all its attachments for the head and limbs. Lydia
asked about his guests—how were they accommodated? He replied that
he did not have any. The apartment was for himself. He was a popular
guest, witty and personable, but not a host, and this seemed reasonable to
him, since social life was other people's requirement and invention.

Lydia brought flowers, and there was nowhere to put them except in
a jar on the floor by the bed. She brought presents from her trips to
Toronto: records, books, cheese. She learned pathways around the apartment and found places where she could sit. She discouraged old friends,
or any friends, from phoning or coming to see her, because there was too
much she couldn't explain. They saw Duncan's friends sometimes, and
she was nervous with them, thinking they were adding her to a list, speculating. She didn't like to see how much he gave them of that store of
presents—anecdotes, parodies, flattering wit—which were also used to
delight her. He could not bear dullness. She felt that he despised people
who were not witty. You needed to be quick to keep up with him in conversation, you needed energy. Lydia saw herself as a dancer on her toes,
trembling delicately all over, afraid of letting him down on the next turn.

"Do you mean you think I don't love him?" she said to the doctor.

"How do you know you do?"

"Because I suffer so when he's fed up with me. I want to be wiped off the earth. It's true. I want to hide. I go out on the streets and every face I look at seems to despise me for my failure."

"Your failure to make him love you."

Now Lydia must accuse herself. Her self-absorption equals Duncan's, but is more artfully concealed. She is in competition with him as to who can love best. She is in competition with all other women, even when it is ludicrous for her to be so. She cannot stand to hear them praised or know they are well remembered. Like many women of her generation, she has an idea of love which is ruinous but not serious in some way, not respectful. She is greedy. She talks intelligently and ironically and in this way covers up her indefensible expectations. The sacrifices she made with Duncan—in living arrangements, in the matter of friends, as well as in the rhythm of sex and the tone of conversations—were violations, committed not seriously but flagrantly. That is what was not respectful, that was what was indecent. She made him a present of such power, then complained relentlessly to herself and finally to him, that he had got it. She was out to defeat him.

That is what she says to the doctor. But is it the truth?

"The worst thing is not knowing what is true about any of this. I spend all my waking hours trying to figure out about him and me and I get nowhere. I make wishes. I even pray. I throw money into those wishing wells. I think that there's something in him that's an absolute holdout. There's something in him that has to get rid of me, so he'll find reasons. But he says that's rubbish, he says if I could stop overreacting we'd be happy. I have to think maybe he's right, maybe it is all me."

"When are you happy?"

"When he's pleased with me. When he's joking and enjoying himself. No. No. I'm never happy. What I am is relieved, it's as if I'd overcome a challenge, it's more triumphant than happy. But he can always pull the rug out."

"So, why are you with somebody who can always pull the rug out?"

"Isn't there always somebody? When I was married it was me. Do you think it helps to ask these questions? Suppose it's just pride? I don't want to be alone, I want everybody to think I've got such a desirable man? Suppose it's the humiliation, I want to be humiliated? What good will it do me to know that?"

"I don't know. What do you think?"

"I think these conversations are fine when you're mildly troubled and interested but not when you're desperate."

"You're desperate?"

She felt suddenly tired, almost too tired to speak. The room where she and the doctor were talking had a dark-blue carpet, blue-and-green-striped upholstery. There was a picture of boats and fishermen on the wall. Collusion somewhere, Lydia felt. Fake reassurance, provisional comfort, earnest deceptions.

"No."

It seemed to her that she and Duncan were monsters with a lot of heads, in those days. Out of the mouth of one head could come insult and accusation, hot and cold, out of another false apologies and slimy pleas, out of another just such mealy, reasonable, true-and-false chat as she had practiced with the doctor. Not a mouth would open that had a useful thing to say, not a mouth would have the sense to shut up. At the same time she believed—though she didn't know she believed it—that these monster heads with their cruel and silly and wasteful talk could all be drawn in again, could curl up and go to sleep. Never mind what they'd said; never mind. Then she and Duncan with hope and trust and blank memories could reintroduce themselves, they could pick up the undamaged delight with which they'd started, before they began to put each other to other uses.

When she had been in Toronto a day she tried to retrieve Duncan, by phone, and found that he had acted quickly. He had changed to an unlisted number. He wrote to her, in care of her employer, that he would pack and send her things.

LYDIA had breakfast with Mr. Stanley. The telephone crew had eaten and gone off to work before daylight.

She asked Mr. Stanley about his visit with the woman who had known Willa Cather.

"Ah," said Mr. Stanley, and wiped a corner of his mouth after a bite of poached egg. "She was a woman who used to run a little restaurant down by the dock. She was a good cook, she said. She must have been, because Willa and Edith used to get their dinners from her. She would send it up with her brother, in his car. But sometimes Willa would not be pleased with the dinner—perhaps it would not be quite what she wanted, or she would think it was not cooked as well as it might be—and she would send it back. She would ask for another dinner to be sent." He smiled, and said in a confidential way, "Willa could be imperious. Oh, yes. She was not perfect. All people of great abilities are apt to be impatient in daily matters."

Rubbish, Lydia wanted to say, she sounds a proper bitch.

Sometimes waking up was all right, and sometimes it was very bad. This morning she had wakened with the cold conviction of a mistake—something avoidable and irreparable.

"But sometimes she and Edith would come down to the café," Mr.

Stanley continued. "If they felt they wanted some company, they would have dinner there. On one of these occasions Willa had a long talk with the woman I was visiting. They talked for over an hour. The woman was considering marriage. She had to consider whether to make a marriage that she gave me to understand was something of a business proposition. Companionship. There was no question of romance, she and the gentleman were not young and foolish. Willa talked to her for over an hour. Of course she did not advise her directly to do one thing or the other, she talked to her in general terms very sensibly and kindly and the woman still remembers it vividly. I was happy to hear that but I was not surprised."

"What would she know about it, anyway?" Lydia said.

Mr. Stanley lifted his eyes from his plate and looked at her in grieved amazement.

"Willa Cather lived with a woman," Lydia said.

When Mr. Stanley answered he sounded flustered, and mildly upbraiding.

"They were devoted," he said.

"She never lived with a man."

"She knew things as an artist knows them. Not necessarily by experience."

"But what if they don't know them?" Lydia persisted. "What if they don't?"

He went back to eating his egg as if he had not heard that. Finally he said, "The woman considered Willa's conversation was very helpful to her."

Lydia made a sound of doubtful assent. She knew she had been rude, even cruel. She knew she would have to apologize. She went to the sideboard and poured herself another cup of coffee.

The woman of the house came in from the kitchen.

"Is it keeping hot? I think I'll have a cup too. Are you really going today? Sometimes I think I'd like to get on a boat and go too. It's lovely here and I love it but you know how you get."

They drank their coffee standing by the sideboard. Lydia did not want to go back to the table, but knew that she would have to. Mr. Stanley looked frail and solitary, with his narrow shoulders, his neat bald head, his brown checked sports jacket which was slightly too large. He took the trouble to be clean and tidy, and it must have been a trouble, with his eyesight. Of all people he did not deserve rudeness.

"Oh, I forgot," the woman said.

She went into the kitchen and came back with a large brown-paper bag.

"Vincent left you this. He said you liked it. Do you?"

Lydia opened the bag and saw long, dark, ragged leaves of dulse, oily-looking even when dry.

"Well," she said.

The woman laughed. "I know. You have to be born here to have the taste."

"No, I do like it," said Lydia. "I was getting to like it."

"You must have made a hit."

Lydia took the bag back to the table and showed it to Mr. Stanley. She tried a conciliatory joke.

"I wonder if Willa Cather ever ate dulse?"

"Dulse," said Mr. Stanley thoughtfully. He reached into the bag and pulled out some leaves and looked at them. Lydia knew he was seeing what Willa Cather might have seen. "She would most certainly have known about it. She would have known."

But was she lucky or was she not, and was it all right with that woman? How did she live? That was what Lydia wanted to say. Would Mr. Stanley have known what she was talking about? If she had asked how did Willa Cather live, would he not have replied that she did not have to find a way to live, as other people did, that she was Willa Cather?

What a lovely, durable shelter he had made for himself. He could carry it everywhere and nobody could interfere with it. The day may come when Lydia will count herself lucky to do the same. In the meantime, she'll be up and down. "Up and down," they used to say in her childhood, talking of the health of people who weren't going to recover. "Ah. She's up and down."

Yet look how this present slyly warmed her, from a distance.

# The Turkey Season

TO JOE RADFORD

When I was fourteen I got a job at the Turkey Barn for the Christmas season. I was still too young to get a job working in a store or as a part-time waitress; I was also too nervous.

I was a turkey gutter. The other people who worked at the Turkey Barn were Lily and Marjorie and Gladys, who were also gutters; Irene and Henry, who were pluckers; Herb Abbott, the foreman, who superintended the whole operation and filled in wherever he was needed. Morgan Elliott was the owner and boss. He and his son, Morgy, did the killing.

Morgy I knew from school. I thought him stupid and despicable and was uneasy about having to consider him in a new and possibly superior guise, as the boss's son. But his father treated him so roughly, yelling and swearing at him, that he seemed no more than the lowest of the workers. The other person related to the boss was Gladys. She was his sister, and in her case there did seem to be some privilege of position. She worked slowly and went home if she was not feeling well, and was not friendly to Lily and Marjorie, although she was, a little, to me. She had come back to live with Morgan and his family after working for many years in Toronto, in a bank. This was not the sort of job she was used to. Lily and Marjorie, talking about her when she wasn't there, said she had had a nervous breakdown. They said Morgan made her work in the Turkey Barn to pay for her keep. They also said, with no worry about the contradiction, that she had taken the job because she was after a man, and that the man was Herb Abbott.

All I could see when I closed my eyes, the first few nights after working there, was turkeys. I saw them hanging upside down, plucked and stiff-ened, pale and cold, with the heads and necks limp, the eyes and nostrils clotted with dark blood; the remaining bits of feathers—those dark and bloody too—seemed to form a crown. I saw them not with aversion but with a sense of endless work to be done.

Herb Abbott showed me what to do. You put the turkey down on the table and cut its head off with a cleaver. Then you took the loose skin around the neck and stripped it back to reveal the crop, nestled in the cleft between the gullet and the windpipe.

"Feel the gravel," said Herb encouragingly. He made me close my fingers around the crop. Then he showed me how to work my hand down behind it to cut it out, and the gullet and windpipe as well. He used shears to cut the vertebrae.

"Scrunch, scrunch," he said soothingly. "Now, put your hand in."

I did. It was deathly cold in there, in the turkey's dark insides.

"Watch out for bone splinters."

Working cautiously in the dark, I had to pull the connecting tissues loose.

"Ups-a-daisy." Herb turned the bird over and flexed each leg. "Knees up, Mother Brown. Now." He took a heavy knife and placed it directly on the knee knuckle joints and cut off the shank.

"Have a look at the worms."

Pearly-white strings, pulled out of the shank, were creeping about on their own.

"That's just the tendons shrinking. Now comes the nice part!"

He slit the bird at its bottom end, letting out a rotten smell.

"Are you educated?"

I did not know what to say.

"What's that smell?"

"Hydrogen sulfide."

"Educated," said Herb, sighing. "All right. Work your fingers around and get the guts loose. Easy. Easy. Keep your fingers together. Keep the palm inwards. Feel the ribs with the back of your hand. Feel the guts fit into your palm. Feel that? Keep going. Break the strings—as many as you can. Keep going. Feel a hard lump? That's the gizzard. Feel a soft lump? That's the heart. Okay? Okay. Get your fingers around the gizzard. Easy. Start pulling this way. That's right. That's right. Start to pull her out."

It was not easy at all. I wasn't even sure what I had was the gizzard. My hand was full of cold pulp.

"Pull," he said, and I brought out a glistening, liverish mass.

"Got it. There's the lights. You know what they are? Lungs. There's the heart. There's the gizzard. There's the gall. Now, you don't ever want to break that gall inside or it will taste the entire turkey." Tactfully, he scraped out what I had missed, including the testicles, which were like a pair of white grapes.

"Nice pair of earrings," Herb said.

Herb Abbott was a tall, firm, plump man. His hair was dark and thin, combed straight back from a widow's peak, and his eyes seemed to be slightly slanted, so that he looked like a pale Chinese or like pictures of the Devil, except that he was smooth-faced and benign. Whatever he did around the Turkey Barn—gutting, as he was now, or loading the truck, or hanging the carcasses—was done with efficient, economical movements, quickly and buoyantly. "Notice about Herb—he always walks like he had a boat moving underneath him," Marjorie said, and it was true. Herb worked on the lake boats, during the season, as a cook. Then he worked for Morgan until after Christmas. The rest of the time he helped around the poolroom, making hamburgers, sweeping up, stopping fights before they got started. That was where he lived: he had a room above the pool-room on the main street.

In all the operations at the Turkey Barn it seemed to be Herb who had the efficiency and honor of the business continually on his mind; it was he who kept everything under control. Seeing him in the yard talking to Morgan, who was a thick, short man, red in the face, an unpredictable bully, you would be sure that it was Herb who was the boss and Morgan the hired help. But it was not so.

If I had not had Herb to show me, I don't think I could have learned turkey gutting at all. I was clumsy with my hands and had been shamed for it so often that the least show of impatience on the part of the person instructing me could have brought on a dithering paralysis. I could not stand to be watched by anybody but Herb. Particularly, I couldn't stand to be watched by Lily and Marjorie, two middle-aged sisters, who were very fast and thorough and competitive gutters. They sang at their work and talked abusively and intimately to the turkey carcasses.

"Don't you nick me, you old bugger!"

"Aren't you the old crap factory!"

I had never heard women talk like that.

Gladys was not a fast gutter, though she must have been thorough; Herb would have talked to her otherwise. She never sang and certainly she never swore. I thought her rather old, though she was not as old as Lily and Marjorie; she must have been over thirty. She seemed offended by everything that went on and had the air of keeping plenty of bitter judgments to herself. I never tried to talk to her, but she spoke to me one day in the cold little washroom off the gutting shed. She was putting pancake makeup on her face. The color of the makeup was so distinct from the color of her skin that it was as if she were slapping orange paint over a whitewashed, bumpy wall.

She asked me if my hair was naturally curly.

I said yes.

"You don't have to get a permanent?"

"No."

"You're lucky. I have to do mine up every night. The chemicals in my system won't allow me to get a permanent."

There are different ways women have of talking about their looks. Some women make it clear that what they do to keep themselves up is for the sake of sex, for men. Others, like Gladys, make the job out to be a kind of housekeeping, whose very difficulties they pride themselves on. Gladys was genteel. I could see her in the bank, in a navy-blue dress with the kind of detachable white collar you can wash at night. She would be grumpy and correct.

Another time, she spoke to me about her periods, which were profuse and painful. She wanted to know about mine. There was an uneasy, prudish, agitated expression on her face. I was saved by Irene, who was using the toilet and called out, "Do like me, and you'll be rid of all your problems for a while." Irene was only a few years older than I was, but she was recently—tardily—married, and heavily pregnant.

Gladys ignored her, running cold water on her hands. The hands of all of us were red and sore-looking from the work. "I can't use that soap. If I use it, I break out in a rash," Gladys said. "If I bring my own soap in here, I can't afford to have other people using it, because I pay a lot for it—it's a special anti-allergy soap."

I think the idea that Lily and Marjorie promoted—that Gladys was after Herb Abbott—sprang from their belief that single people ought to be teased and embarrassed whenever possible, and from their interest in Herb, which led to the feeling that somebody ought to be after him. They wondered about him. What they wondered was, How can a man want so little? No wife, no family, no house. The details of his daily life, the small preferences, were of interest. Where had he been brought up? (Here and there and all over.) How far had he gone in school? (Far enough.) Where was his girlfriend? (Never tell.) Did he drink coffee or tea if he got the choice? (Coffee.)

When they talked about Gladys's being after him they must have really wanted to talk about sex—what he wanted and what he got. They must have felt a voluptuous curiosity about him, as I did. He aroused this feeling by being circumspect and not making the jokes some men did, and at the same time by not being squeamish or gentlemanly. Some men, showing me the testicles from the turkey, would have acted as if the very existence of testicles were somehow a bad joke on me, something a girl could be taunted about; another sort of man would have been embarrassed and would have thought he had to protect me from embarrassment. A man who didn't seem to feel one way or the other was an oddity—as much to older women, probably, as to me. But what was so welcome to me may have been disturbing to them. They wanted to jolt him. They even wanted Gladys to jolt him, if she could.

There wasn't any idea then—at least in Logan, Ontario, in the late forties—about homosexuality's going beyond very narrow confines. Women, certainly, believed in its rarity and in definite boundaries. There were homosexuals in town, and we knew who they were: an elegant, light-voiced, wavy-haired paperhanger who called himself an interior decorator; the minister's widow's fat, spoiled only son, who went so far as to enter baking contests and had crocheted a tablecloth; a hypochondriacal church organist and music teacher who kept the choir and his pupils in line with screaming tantrums. Once the label was fixed, there was a good deal of tolerance for these people, and their talents for decorating, for crocheting, and for music were appreciated—especially by women. "The poor fellow," they said. "He doesn't do any harm." They really seemed to believe—the women did—that it was the penchant for baking or music that was the determining factor, and that it was this activity that made the man what he was—not any other detours he might take, or wish to take. A desire to play the violin would be taken as more a deviation from manliness than would a wish to shun women. Indeed, the idea was that any manly man would wish to shun women but most of them were caught off guard, and for good.

I don't want to go into the question of whether Herb was homosexual or not, because the definition is of no use to me. I think that probably he was, but maybe he was not. (Even considering what happened later, I think that.) He is not a puzzle so arbitrarily solved.

THE OTHER plucker, who worked with Irene, was Henry Streets, a neighbor of ours. There was nothing remarkable about him except that he was eighty-six years old and still, as he said of himself, a devil for work. He had whisky in his thermos, and drank it from time to time through the day. It was Henry who said to me, in our kitchen, "You ought to get yourself a job at the Turkey Barn. They need another gutter." Then my father said at once, "Not her, Henry. She's got ten thumbs," and Henry said he was just joking—it was dirty work. But I was already determined to try it—I had a great need to be successful in a job like that. I was almost in the condition of a grown-up person who is ashamed of never having learned to read, so much did I feel my ineptness at manual work. Work, to everybody I knew, meant doing things I was no good at doing, and work was what people prided themselves on and measured each other by. (It goes without saying that the things I was good at, like schoolwork, were suspect or held in plain contempt.) So it was a surprise and then a triumph for me not to get fired, and to be able to turn out clean turkeys at a rate that was not dis- graceful. I don't know if I really understood how much Herb Abbott was responsible for this, but he would sometimes say, "Good girl," or pat my waist and say, "You're getting to be a good gutter—you'll go a long ways in the world," and when I felt his quick, kind touch through the heavy sweater and bloody smock I wore, I felt my face glow and I wanted to lean back against him as he stood behind me. I wanted to rest my head against his wide, fleshy shoulder. When I went to sleep at night, lying on my side, I would run my cheek against the pillow and think of that as Herb's shoulder.

I was interested in how he talked to Gladys, how he looked at her or noticed her. This interest was not jealousy. I think I wanted something to happen with them. I quivered in curious expectation, as Lily and Marjorie did. We all wanted to see the flicker of sexuality in him, hear it in his voice, not because we thought it would make him seem more like other men but because we knew that with him it would be entirely different. He was kinder and more patient than most women, and as stern and remote, in some ways, as any man. We wanted to see how he could be moved.

If Gladys wanted this too, she didn't give any signs of it. It is impossible for me to tell with women like her whether they are as thick and deadly as they seem, not wanting anything much but opportunities for irritation and contempt, or if they are all choked up with gloomy fires and useless passions.

Marjorie and Lily talked about marriage. They did not have much good to say about it, in spite of their feeling that it was a state nobody should be allowed to stay out of. Marjorie said that shortly after her marriage she had gone into the woodshed with the intention of swallowing Paris green.

"I'd have done it," she said. "But the man came along in the grocery truck and I had to go out and buy the groceries. This was when we lived on the farm."

Her husband was cruel to her in those days, but later he suffered an ac- cident—he rolled the tractor and was so badly hurt he would be an invalid all his life. They moved to town, and Marjorie was the boss now.

"He starts to sulk the other night and say he don't want his supper. Well, I just picked up his wrist and held it. He was scared I was going to twist his arm. He could see I'd do it. So I say, 'You *what*?' And he says, 'I'll eat it.' "

They talked about their father. He was a man of the old school. He had a noose in the woodshed (not the Paris green woodshed—this would be an earlier one, on another farm), and when they got on his nerves he used to line them up and threaten to hang them. Lily, who was the younger, would shake till she fell down. This same father had arranged to marry Marjorie off to a crony of his when she was just sixteen. That was the husband who had driven her to the Paris green. Their father did it because he wanted to be sure she wouldn't get into trouble.

"Hot blood," Lily said.

I was horrified, and asked, "Why didn't you run away?"

"His word was law," Marjorie said.

They said that was what was the matter with kids nowadays—it was the kids that ruled the roost. A father's word should be law. They brought up their own kids strictly, and none had turned out bad yet. When Marjorie's son wet the bed she threatened to cut off his dingy with the butcher knife. That cured him.

They said ninety percent of the young girls nowadays drank, and swore, and took it lying down. They did not have daughters, but if they did and caught them at anything like that they would beat them raw. Irene, they said, used to go to the hockey games with her ski pants slit and nothing under them, for convenience in the snowdrifts afterward. Terrible.

I wanted to point out some contradictions. Marjorie and Lily themselves drank and swore, and what was so wonderful about the strong will of a father who would insure you a lifetime of unhappiness? (What I did not see was that Marjorie and Lily were not unhappy altogether—could not be, because of their sense of consequence, their pride and style.) I could be enraged then at the lack of logic in most adults' talk—the way they held to their pronouncements no matter what evidence might be presented to them. How could these women's hands be so gifted, so delicate and clever—for I knew they would be as good at dozens of other jobs as they were at gutting; they would be good at quilting and darning and painting and papering and kneading dough and setting out seedlings— and their thinking so slapdash, clumsy, infuriating?

Lily said she never let her husband come near her if he had been drinking. Marjorie said since the time she nearly died with a hemorrhage she never let her husband come near her, period. Lily said quickly that it was only when he'd been drinking that he tried anything. I could see that it was a matter of pride not to let your husband come near you, but I couldn't quite believe that "come near" meant "have sex." The idea of Marjorie and Lily being sought out for such purposes seemed grotesque. They had bad teeth, their stomachs sagged, their faces were dull and spotty. I decided to take "come near" literally.

THE TWO weeks before Christmas was a frantic time at the Turkey Barn. I began to go in for an hour before school as well as after school and on weekends. In the morning, when I walked to work, the streetlights would still be on and the morning stars shining. There was the Turkey Barn, on the edge of a white field, with a row of big pine trees behind it, and always, no matter how cold and still it was, these trees were lifting their branches and sighing and straining. It seems unlikely that on my way to the Turkey Barn, for an hour of gutting turkeys, I should have experienced such a sense of promise and at the same time of perfect, impenetrable mystery in the universe, but I did. Herb had something to do with that, and so did the cold snap—the series of hard, clear mornings. The truth is, such feelings weren't hard to come by then. I would get them but not know how they were to be connected with anything in real life.

One morning at the Turkey Barn there was a new gutter. This was a boy eighteen or nineteen years old, a stranger named Brian. It seemed he was a relative, or perhaps just a friend, of Herb Abbott's. He was staying with Herb. He had worked on a lake boat last summer. He said he had got sick of it, though, and quit.

What he said was "Yeah, fuckin' boats, I got sick of that."

Language at the Turkey Barn was coarse and free, but this was one word never heard there. And Brian's use of it seemed not careless but flaunting, mixing insult and provocation. Perhaps it was his general style that made it so. He had amazing good looks: taffy hair, bright blue eyes, ruddy skin, well-shaped body—the sort of good looks nobody disagrees about for a moment. But a single, relentless notion had got such a hold on him that he could not keep from turning all his assets into parody. His mouth was wet-looking and slightly open most of the time, his eyes were half shut, his expression a hopeful leer, his movements indolent, exaggerated, inviting. Perhaps if he had been put on a stage with a microphone and a guitar and let grunt and howl and wriggle and excite, he would have seemed a true celebrant. Lacking a stage, he was unconvincing. After a while he seemed just like somebody with a bad case of hiccups—his insistent sexuality was that monotonous and meaningless.

If he had toned down a bit, Marjorie and Lily would probably have enjoyed him. They could have kept up a game of telling him to shut his filthy mouth and keep his hands to himself. As it was, they said they were sick of him, and meant it. Once, Marjorie took up her gutting knife. "Keep your distance," she said. "I mean from me and my sister and that kid."

She did not tell him to keep his distance from Gladys, because Gladys wasn't there at the time and Marjorie would probably not have felt like protecting her anyway. But it was Gladys Brian particularly liked to bother. She would throw down her knife and go into the washroom and stay there ten minutes and come out with a stony face. She didn't say she was sick anymore and go home, the way she used to. Marjorie said Morgan was mad at Gladys for sponging and she couldn't get away with it any longer.

Gladys said to me, "I can't stand that kind of thing. I can't stand people mentioning that kind of thing and that kind of—gestures. It makes me sick to my stomach."

I believed her. She was terribly white. But why, in that case, did she not complain to Morgan? Perhaps relations between them were too uneasy, perhaps she could not bring herself to repeat or describe such things. Why did none of us complain—if not to Morgan, at least to Herb? I never thought of it. Brian seemed just something to put up with, like the freezing cold in the gutting shed and the smell of blood and waste. When Marjorie and Lily did threaten to complain, it was about Brian's laziness.

He was not a good gutter. He said his hands were too big. So Herb took him off gutting, told him he was to sweep and clean up, make packages of giblets, and help load the truck. This meant that he did not have to be in any one place or doing any one job at a given time, so much of the time he did nothing. He would start sweeping up, leave that and mop the tables, leave that and have a cigarette, lounge against the table bothering us until Herb called him to help load. Herb was very busy now and spent a lot of time making deliveries, so it was possible he did not know the extent of Brian's idleness.

"I don't know why Herb don't fire you," Marjorie said. "I guess the answer is he don't want you hanging around sponging on him, with no place to go."

"I know where to go," said Brian.

"Keep your sloppy mouth shut," said Marjorie. "I pity Herb. Getting saddled."

ON THE LAST school day before Christmas we got out early in the afternoon. I went home and changed my clothes and came in to work at about three o'clock. Nobody was working. Everybody was in the gutting shed, where Morgan Elliott was swinging a cleaver over the gutting table and yelling. I couldn't make out what the yelling was about, and thought someone must have made a terrible mistake in his work; perhaps it had been me. Then I saw Brian on the other side of the table, looking very sulky and mean, and standing well back. The sexual leer was not altogether gone from his face, but it was flattened out and mixed with a look of impotent bad temper and some fear. That's it, I thought, Brian is getting fired for being so sloppy and lazy. Even when I made out Morgan saying "pervert" and "filthy" and "maniac," I still thought that was what was happening. Marjorie and Lily, and even brassy Irene, were standing around with downcast, rather pious looks, such as children get when somebody is suffering a terrible bawling out at school. Only old Henry seemed able to keep a cautious grin on his face. Gladys was not to be seen. Herb was standing closer to Morgan than anybody else. He was not interfering but was keeping an eye on the cleaver. Morgy was blubbering, though he didn't seem to be in any immediate danger.

Morgan was yelling at Brian to get out. "And out of this town—I mean it—and don't you wait till tomorrow if you still want your arse in one piece! Out!" he shouted, and the cleaver swung dramatically towards the door. Brian started in that direction but, whether he meant to or not, he made a swaggering, taunting motion of the buttocks. This made Morgan break into a roar and run after him, swinging the cleaver in a stagy way. Brian ran, and Morgan ran after him, and Irene screamed and grabbed her stomach. Morgan was too heavy to run any distance and probably could not have thrown the cleaver very far, either. Herb watched from the doorway. Soon Morgan came back and flung the cleaver down on the table.

"All back to work! No more gawking around here! You don't get paid for gawking! What are you getting under way at?" he said, with a hard look at Irene.

"Nothing," Irene said meekly.

"If you're getting under way get out of here."

"I'm not."

"All right, then!"

We got to work. Herb took off his blood-smeared smock and put on his jacket and went off, probably to see that Brian got ready to go on the suppertime bus. He did not say a word. Morgan and his son went out to the yard, and Irene and Henry went back to the adjoining shed, where they did the plucking, working knee-deep in the feathers Brian was supposed to keep swept up.

"Where's Gladys?" I said softly.

"Recuperating," said Marjorie. She too spoke in a quieter voice than usual, and *recuperating* was not the sort of word she and Lily normally used. It was a word to be used about Gladys, with a mocking intent.

They didn't want to talk about what had happened, because they were afraid Morgan might come in and catch them at it and fire them. Good workers as they were, they were afraid of that. Besides, they hadn't seen anything. They must have been annoyed that they hadn't. All I ever found out was that Brian had either done something or shown something to Gladys as she came out of the washroom and she had started screaming and having hysterics.

Now she'll likely be laid up with another nervous breakdown, they said. And he'll be on his way out of town. And good riddance, they said, to both of them.

. . .

I HAVE a picture of the Turkey Barn crew taken on Christmas Eve. It was taken with a flash camera that was someone's Christmas extravagance. I think it was Irene's. But Herb Abbott must have been the one who took the picture. He was the one who could be trusted to know or to learn immediately how to manage anything new, and flash cameras were fairly new at the time. The picture was taken about ten o'clock on Christmas Eve, after Herb and Morgy had come back from making the last delivery and we had washed off the gutting table and swept and mopped the cement floor. We had taken off our bloody smocks and heavy sweaters and gone into the little room called the lunchroom, where there was a table and a heater. We still wore our working clothes: overalls and shirts. The men wore caps and the women kerchiefs, tied in the wartime style. I am stout and cheerful and comradely in the picture, transformed into someone I don't ever remember being or pretending to be. I look years older than fourteen. Irene is the only one who has taken off her kerchief, freeing her long red hair. She peers out from it with a meek, sluttish, inviting look, which would match her reputation but is not like any look of hers I remember. Yes, it must have been her camera; she is posing for it, with that look, more deliberately than anyone else is. Marjorie and Lily are smiling, true to form, but their smiles are sour and reckless. With their hair hidden, and such figures as they have bundled up, they look like a couple of tough and jovial but testy workmen. Their kerchiefs look misplaced; caps would be better. Henry is in high spirits, glad to be part of the work force, grinning and looking twenty years younger than his age. Then Morgy, with his hangdog look, not trusting the occasion's bounty, and Morgan very flushed and bosslike and satisfied. He has just given each of us our bonus turkey. Each of these turkeys has a leg or a wing missing, or a malformation of some kind, so none of them are salable at the full price. But Morgan has been at pains to tell us that you often get the best meat off the gimpy ones, and he has shown us that he's taking one home himself.

We are all holding mugs or large, thick china cups, which contain not the usual tea but rye whisky. Morgan and Henry have been drinking since suppertime. Marjorie and Lily say they only want a little, and only take it at all because it's Christmas Eve and they are dead on their feet. Irene says she's dead on her feet as well but that doesn't mean she only wants a little. Herb has poured quite generously not just for her but for Lily and Marjorie too, and they do not object. He has measured mine and Morgy's out at the same time, very stingily, and poured in Coca-Cola. This is the first drink I have ever had, and as a result I will believe for years that rye-and-Coca-Cola is a standard sort of drink and will always ask for it, until I notice that few other people drink it and that it makes me sick. I didn't get sick that Christmas Eve, though; Herb had not given me enough. Except for an odd taste, and my own feeling of consequence, it was like drinking Coca-Cola.

I don't need Herb in the picture to remember what he looked like. That is, if he looked like himself, as he did all the time at the Turkey Barn and the few times I saw him on the street—as he did all the times in my life when I saw him except one.

The time he looked somewhat unlike himself was when Morgan was cursing out Brian and, later, when Brian had run off down the road. What was this different look? I've tried to remember, because I studied it hard at the time. It wasn't much different. His face looked softer and heavier then, and if you had to describe the expression on it you would have to say it was an expression of shame. But what would he be ashamed of? Ashamed of Brian, for the way he had behaved? Surely that would be late in the day; when had Brian ever behaved otherwise? Ashamed of Morgan, for carrying on so ferociously and theatrically? Or of himself, because he was famous for nipping fights and displays of this sort in the bud and hadn't been able to do it here? Would he be ashamed that he hadn't stood up for Brian? Would he have expected himself to do that, to stand up for Brian?

All this was what I wondered at the time. Later, when I knew more, at least about sex, I decided that Brian was Herb's lover, and that Gladys really was trying to get attention from Herb, and that that was why Brian had humiliated her—with or without Herb's connivance and consent. Isn't it true that people like Herb—dignified, secretive, honorable people—will often choose somebody like Brian, will waste their helpless love on some vicious, silly person who is not even evil, or a monster, but just some importunate nuisance? I decided that Herb, with all his gentleness and carefulness, was avenging himself on us all—not just on Gladys but on us all—with Brian, and that what he was feeling when I studied his face must have been a savage and gleeful scorn. But embarrassment as well— embarrassment for Brian and for himself and for Gladys, and to some degree for all of us. Shame for all of us—that is what I thought then.

Later still, I backed off from this explanation. I got to a stage of backing off from the things I couldn't really know. It's enough for me now just to think of Herb's face with that peculiar, stricken look; to think of Brian monkeying in the shade of Herb's dignity; to think of my own mystified concentration on Herb, my need to catch him out, if I could ever get the chance, and then move in and stay close to him. How attractive, how delectable, the prospect of intimacy is, with the very person who will never grant it. I can still feel the pull of a man like that, of his promising and refusing. I would still like to know things. Never mind facts. Never mind theories, either.

When I finished my drink I wanted to say something to Herb. I stood beside him and waited for a moment when he was not listening to or talking with anyone else and when the increasingly rowdy conversation of the others would cover what I had to say.

"I'm sorry your friend had to go away."

"That's all right."

Herb spoke kindly and with amusement, and so shut me off from any further right to look at or speak about his life. He knew what I was up to. He must have known it before, with lots of women. He knew how to deal with it.

Lily had a little more whisky in her mug and told how she and her best girlfriend (dead now, of liver trouble) had dressed up as men one time and gone into the men's side of the beer parlor, the side where it said MEN ONLY, because they wanted to see what it was like. They sat in a corner drinking beer and keeping their eyes and ears open, and nobody looked twice or thought a thing about them, but soon a problem arose.

"Where were we going to go? If we went around to the other side and anybody seen us going into the ladies', they would scream bloody murder. And if we went into the men's somebody'd be sure to notice we didn't do it the right way. Meanwhile the beer was going through us like a bugger!"

"What you don't do when you're young!" Marjorie said.

Several people gave me and Morgy advice. They told us to enjoy ourselves while we could. They told us to stay out of trouble. They said they had all been young once. Herb said we were a good crew and had done a good job but he didn't want to get in bad with any of the women's husbands by keeping them there too late. Marjorie and Lily expressed indifference to their husbands, but Irene announced that she loved hers and that it was not true that he had been dragged back from Detroit to marry her, no matter what people said. Henry said it was a good life if you didn't weaken. Morgan said he wished us all the most sincere Merry Christmas.

When we came out of the Turkey Barn it was snowing. Lily said it was like a Christmas card, and so it was, with the snow whirling around the streetlights in town and around the colored lights people had put up outside their doorways. Morgan was giving Henry and Irene a ride home in the truck, acknowledging age and pregnancy and Christmas. Morgy took a shortcut through the field, and Herb walked off by himself, head down and hands in his pockets, rolling slightly, as if he were on the deck of a lake boat. Marjorie and Lily linked arms with me as if we were old comrades.

"Let's sing," Lily said. "What'll we sing?"

" 'We Three Kings'?" said Marjorie. " 'We Three Turkey Gutters'?"

" 'I'm Dreaming of a White Christmas.' "

"Why dream? You got it!"

So we sang.

# *Labor Day Dinner*

~

JUST BEFORE six o'clock in the evening, George and Roberta and Angela and Eva get out of George's pickup truck—he traded his car for a pickup when he moved to the country—and walk across Valerie's front yard, under the shade of two aloof and splendid elm trees that have been expensively preserved. Valerie says those trees cost her a trip to Europe. The grass underneath them has been kept green all summer, and is bordered by fiery dahlias. The house is of pale-red brick, and around the doors and windows there is a decorative outline of lighter-colored bricks, originally white. This style is often found in Grey County; perhaps it was a specialty of one of the early builders.

George is carrying the folding lawn chairs Valerie asked them to bring. Roberta is carrying a dessert, a raspberry bombe made from raspberries picked on their own farm—George's farm—earlier in the summer. She has packed it in ice cubes and wrapped it in dish towels, but she is eager to get it into the freezer. Angela and Eva carry bottles of wine. Angela and Eva are Roberta's daughters. It has been arranged between Roberta and her husband that they spend the summers with her and George and the school year in Halifax with him. Roberta's husband is in the Navy. Angela is seventeen, Eva is twelve.

These four people are costumed in a way that would suggest they were going to different dinner parties. George, who is a stocky, dark, barrel-chested man, with a daunting, professional look of self-assurance and impatience (he used to be a teacher), wears a clean T-shirt and nondescript pants. Roberta is wearing faded tan cotton pants and a loose raw-silk top of mud-brick color—a color that suits her dark hair and pale skin well enough when she is at her best, but she is not at her best today. When she made herself up in the bathroom, she thought her skin looked like a piece of waxed paper that had been crumpled into a tight ball and then smoothed out. She was momentarily pleased with her thinness and had planned to wear a slinky silver halter top she owns—a glamorous joke— but at the last minute she changed her mind. She is wearing dark glasses, and the reason is that she has taken to weeping in spurts, never at the really bad times but in between; the spurts are as unbidden as sneezes.

As for Angela and Eva, they are dramatically arrayed in outfits contrived from a box of old curtains found in the upstairs of George's house. Angela wears emerald-green damask with long, sun-faded stripes, draped so as to leave one golden shoulder bare. She has cut vine leaves out of the same damask, pasted them on cardboard, and arranged them in her hair. Angela is tall and fair-haired, and embarrassed by her recently acquired beauty. She will go to great trouble to flaunt it, as she does now, and then will redden and frown and look stubbornly affronted when somebody tells her she looks like a goddess. Eva is wearing several fragile, yellowed lace curtains draped and bunched up, and held together with pins, ribbons, and nosegays of wild phlox already drooping and scattering. One of the curtains is pinned across her forehead and flows behind her, like a 1920s bridal veil. She has put her shorts on underneath, in case anybody should glimpse underpants through the veiling. Eva is puritanical, outrageous—an acrobat, a parodist, an optimist, a disturber. Her face, under the pinned veil, is lewdly painted with green eye shadow and dark lipstick and rouge and mascara. The violent colors emphasize her childish look of recklessness and valor.

Angela and Eva have ridden here in the back of the truck, stretched out on the lawn chairs. It is only three miles from George's place to Valerie's, but Roberta did not think riding like that was safe—she wanted them to get down and sit on the truck bed. To her surprise, George spoke up on their behalf, saying it would be ignominious for them to have to huddle down on the floor in their finery. He said he would drive slowly and avoid bumps; so he did. Roberta was a little nervous, but she was relieved to see him sympathetic and indulgent about the very things—self-dramatization, self-display—that she had expected would annoy him. She herself has given up wearing long skirts and caftans because of what he has said about disliking the sight of women trailing around in such garments, which announce to him, he says, not only a woman's intention of doing no serious work but her persistent wish to be admired and courted. This is a wish George has no patience with and has spent some energy, throughout his adult life, in thwarting.

Roberta thought that after speaking in such a friendly way to the girls, and helping them into the truck, he might speak to her when he got into the cab, might even take her hand, brushing away her undisclosed crimes, but it did not happen. Shut up together, driving over the hot gravel roads at an almost funereal pace, they are pinned down by a murderous silence. On the edge of it, Roberta feels herself curling up like a jaundiced leaf. She knows this to be a hysterical image. Also hysterical is the notion of screaming and opening the door and throwing herself on the gravel. She ought to make an effort not to be hysterical, not to exaggerate. But surely it is hatred—what else can it be?—that George is steadily manufacturing and wordlessly pouring out at her, and surely it is a deadly gas. She tries to break the silence herself, making little clucks of worry as she tightens the towels over the bombe and then sighing—a noisy imitation sigh meant to sound tired, pleased, and comfortable. They are driving between high stands of corn, and she thinks how ugly the corn looks—a monotonous, coarse-leaved crop, a foolish army. How long has this been going on? Since yesterday morning: she felt it in him before they got out of bed. They went out and got drunk last night to try to better things, but the relief didn't last.

Before they left for Valerie's, Roberta was in the bedroom, fastening her halter top, and George came in and said, "Is that what you're wearing?"

"I thought I would, yes. Doesn't it look all right?"

"Your armpits are flabby."

"Are they? I'll put on something with sleeves."

In the truck, now that she knows he isn't going to make up, she lets herself hear him say that. A harsh satisfaction in his voice. The satisfaction of airing disgust. He is disgusted by her aging body. That could have been foreseen. She starts humming something, feeling the lightness, the freedom, the great tactical advantage of being the one to whom the wrong has been done, the bleak challenge offered, the unforgivable thing said.

But suppose he doesn't think it's unforgivable, suppose in his eyes she's the one who's unforgivable? She's always the one; disasters overtake her daily. It used to be that as soon as she noticed some deterioration she would seek strenuously to remedy it. Now the remedies bring more problems. She applies cream frantically to her wrinkles, and her face breaks out in spots, like a teenager's. Dieting until her waist was thin enough to please produced a haggard look about her cheeks and throat. Flabby armpits—how can you exercise the armpits? What is to be done? Now the payment is due, and what for? For vanity. Hardly even for that. Just for having those pleasing surfaces once, and letting them speak for you; just for allowing an arrangement of hair and shoulders and breasts to have its effect. You don't stop in time, don't know what to do instead; you lay yourself open to humiliation. So thinks Roberta, with self-pity—what she knows to be self-pity—rising and sloshing around in her like bitter bile.

She must get away, live alone, wear sleeves.

VALERIE calls to them from a darkened window under the vines, "Go on in, go in. I'm just putting on my panty hose."

"Don't put on your panty hose!" cry George and Roberta together. You would think from the sound of their voices that all the way over here they had been engaged in tender and lively conversation.

"Don't put on your *panty* hose," wail Angela and Eva.

"Oh, all right, if there's all that much prejudice against panty hose," says Valerie behind her window. "I won't even put on a dress. I'll come as I am."

"Not that!" cries George, and staggers, holding the lawn chairs up in front of his face.

But Valerie, appearing in the doorway, is dressed beautifully, in a loose gown of green and gold and blue. She doesn't have to worry about George's opinion of long dresses. She is absolved of blame anyway, because you could never say that Valerie is looking to be courted or admired. She is a tall, flat-chested woman, whose long, plain face seems to be crackling with welcome, eager understanding, with humor and intelligence and appreciation. Her hair is thick, gray-black, and curly. This summer she recklessly cut it off, so that all that is left is a curly crew cut, revealing her long, corded neck and the creases at the edge of her cheeks, and her large, flat ears.

"I think it makes me look like a goat," she has said. "I like goats. I love their eyes. Wouldn't it be wonderful to have those horizontal pupils. Bizarre!"

Her children tell her she is bizarre enough already.

Here come Valerie's children now, as George and Roberta and Angela and Eva crowd into the hall, Roberta saying that she is dripping ice and must get this pretentious concoction into the freezer. First, Ruth, who is twenty-five and nearly six feet tall and looks a lot like her mother. She has given up wanting to be an actress and is learning to teach disturbed children. Her arms are full of goldenrod and Queen Anne's lace and dahlias— weeds and flowers all mixed up together—and she throws them on the hall floor with a theatrical gesture and embraces the bombe.

"Dessert," she says lovingly. "Oh, bliss! Angela, you look incredibly lovely! Eva too. I know who Eva is. She's the Bride of Lammermoor!"

Angela will allow, even delight in, such open praise from Ruth, because Ruth is the person she admires most in the world—possibly the only person she admires.

"The Bride of who?" Eva is asking happily. "The Bride of *who*?"

David, Valerie's twenty-one-year-old son, a history student, is standing in the living-room doorway, smiling tolerantly and affectionately at the excitement. David is tall and lean, dark-haired and dark-skinned, like his mother and sister, but he is deliberate, low-voiced, never rash. In this household of many delicate checks and balances it is noticeable that the lively, outspoken women defer to David in some ceremonial way, seeming to ask for the gesture of his protection, though protection itself is something they are not likely to need.

When the greetings die down David says, "This is Kimberly," and introduces them each in turn to the young woman standing under his arm. She is very clean and trim, in a white skirt and a short-sleeved pink shirt. She wears glasses and no makeup; her hair is short and straight and tidy, and a pleasant light-brown color. She shakes hands with each of them and looks each of them in the eye, through her glasses, and though her manner is entirely polite, even subdued, there is a slight feeling of an official person greeting the members of an unruly, outlandish delegation.

Valerie has known both George and Roberta for years. She knew them long before they knew each other. She and George were on the staff of the same Toronto high school. George was head of the art department; Valerie was school counsellor. She knew George's wife, a jittery, well-dressed woman, who was killed in a plane crash in Florida. George and his wife were separated by that time.

And, of course, Valerie knew Roberta because Roberta's husband, Andrew, is her cousin. They never cared much for each other—Valerie and Roberta's husband—and each of them has described the other to Roberta as a stick. Andrew used to say that Valerie was a queer-looking stick and utterly sexless, and when Roberta told Valerie that she was leaving him Valerie said, "Oh, good. He is such a stick." Roberta was pleased to find such sympathy and pleased that she wouldn't have to dredge up acceptable reasons; apparently Valerie thought his being a stick was reason enough. At the same time, Roberta had a wish to defend her husband and to inquire how on earth Valerie could presume to know whether he was a stick or wasn't. She can't get over wishing to defend him; she feels he had such bad luck marrying her.

When Roberta moved out and left Halifax, she came and stayed with Valerie in Toronto. There she met George, and he took her off to see his farm. Now Valerie says they are her creation, the result of her totally inadvertent matchmaking.

"It was the first time I ever saw love bloom at close quarters," she says. "It was like watching an amaryllis. Astounding."

But Roberta has the idea that, much as she likes them both and wishes them well, love is really something Valerie could do without being reminded of. In Valerie's company you do wonder sometimes what all the fuss is about. Valerie wonders. Her life and her presence, more than any opinion she expresses, remind you that love is not kind or honest and does not contribute to happiness in any reliable way.

When she talked to Roberta about George (this was before she knew Roberta was in love with him), Valerie said, "He's a mysterious man, really. I think he's very idealistic, though he'd hate to hear me say that. This farm he's bought. This self-sufficient, remote, productive life in the country." She went on to talk about how he had grown up in Timmins, the son of a Hungarian shoemaker, youngest of six children and the first to finish high school, let alone go to university. "He's the sort of person who would know what to do in a street fight but doesn't know how to swim. He brought his old crabby, bent-over father down to Toronto and took care of him till he died. I think he drops women rather hard."

Roberta listened to all this with great interest and a basic disregard, because what other people knew about George already seemed unessential to her. She was full of alarm and delight. Being in love was nothing she had counted on. The most she'd hoped for was a life like Valerie's. She had illustrated a couple of children's books and thought she could get more commissions; she could rent a room out in the Beaches, in East Toronto, paint the walls white, sit on cushions instead of chairs, and learn to be self-disciplined and self-indulgent, as she thought solitary people must be.

VALERIE and Roberta walk through the house, carrying a bottle of cold wine and two of Valerie's grandmother's water goblets. Roberta thinks Valerie's house is exactly what people have in mind when they say longingly "a house in the country" or, more particularly, "an old brick farmhouse." The warm, pale-red brick with the light brick trim, the vines and elms, the sanded floors and hooked rugs and white walls, the chipped wash-jug set on a massive chest of drawers in front of a dim mirror. Of course, Valerie has had fifteen years to bring this about. She and her husband bought the house as a summer place, and then when he died she sold their city house and moved to an apartment and put her money and her energy into this. George bought his house and land two years ago, having been introduced to this part of the country by Valerie, and fourteen months ago he left his teaching job and moved up here for good. On the heels of that move came his first meeting with Roberta. Last December she came to live with him. She thought that it would take them about a year to get the place fixed up, and then George could get back to doing his sculpting. A sculptor is what he really wants to be. That is why he wanted to give up teaching and live cheaply in the country—raise a lot of vegetables, keep chickens. He hasn't started on the chickens yet.

Roberta meant to keep busy illustrating books. Why hasn't she done this? No time, nowhere to work: no room, no light, no table. No clear moments of authority, now that life has got this new kind of grip on her.

What they have done so far—what George has done, mostly, while Roberta sweeps and cooks—is put a new roof on the house, put in aluminum-frame windows, pour bag after bag of dusty pebble-like insulation into the space behind the walls, fit batts of yellow, woolly-looking fiberglass against the attic roof, clean all the stovepipes and replace some of them and rebrick part of the chimney, replace the rotting eaves. After all these essential and laborious repairs the house is still unattractive on the outside, with its dark-red imitation-brick covering and its sagging porch heaped with drying new lumber and salvaged old lumber and extra batts of fiberglass and other useful debris. And it is dark and sour-smelling within. Roberta would like to rip up the linoleum and tear down the dismal wallpaper, but everything must be done in order, and George has figured out the order; it is no use ripping up and tearing down until the wiring and insulating have been finished and the shell of the house reconstructed. Lately he has been saying that before he starts on the inside of the house or puts the siding on the outside he must do a major job on the barn; if he doesn't get the beam structure propped and strengthened the whole building may come down in next winter's storms.

As well as this there is the garden: the apple and cherry trees, which have been pruned; the raspberry canes, which have been cleaned out; the lawn, which has been reseeded, reclaimed from patches of long wild grass and patches of bare ground and rubble under the shade of some ragged pines. At first Roberta kept an idea of the whole place in her mind—all the things that had been done, that were being done, and that were yet to do. Now she doesn't think of the work that way—she has no general picture of it—but stays in the kitchen and does jobs as they arise. Dealing with the produce of the garden—making chili sauce, preparing tomatoes and peppers and beans and corn for the freezer, making tomato juice, making cherry jam—has taken up a lot of her time. Sometimes she looks into the freezer and wonders who will eat all this—George and who else? She can feel her own claims shrinking.

THE TABLE is laid on the long screened veranda at the back of the house. Valerie and Roberta go out a door at the end of the veranda, down some shallow steps, and into a little brick-walled, brick-paved area that Valerie has had made this summer but does not like to call a patio. She says you can't have a patio on a farmhouse. She hasn't decided yet what she does like to call it. She hasn't decided, either, whether to get heavy wooden lawn chairs, which she likes the look of, or comfortable lightweight metal-and-plastic chairs, like those which George and Roberta brought.

They pour the wine and lift their glasses, the capacious old water goblets they love to drink wine from. They can hear Ruth and Eva and Angela laughing in Ruth's bedroom. Ruth has said they must help her get into costume too—she is going to think of something that will outdo them all. And they can hear the swish of George's scythe, which he has brought to cut the long grass and burdocks around Valerie's little stone dairy house.

"The dairy house would make a lovely studio," Valerie says. "I should rent it to an artist. George? You? I'd rent it for the scything and a raspberry bombe. George is going to make a studio in the barn, though, isn't he?"

"Eventually," says Roberta. At present all George's work is in the front of the house, in the old parlor. Some half-finished and nearly finished pieces are there, covered up with dusty sheets, and also some blocks of wood (George works only in wood)—a big chunk of seasoned oak and pieces of kiln-dried butternut and cherry. His ripsaw, his chisels and gouges, his linseed oil and turpentine and beeswax and resins are all there, the lids dusty and screwed tight. Eva and Angela used to go around and, standing on tiptoe in the rubble and weeds, peer in the front window at the shrouded shapes.

"Ugh, they look spooky," Eva said to George. "What are they underneath?"

"Wooden doughnuts," George said. "Pop sculpt."

"Really?"

"A potato and a two-headed baby."

Next time they went to look they found a sheet tacked up over the window. This was a grayish-colored sheet, torn at the top. To anybody driving by it made the house look even more bleak and neglected.

"Do you know I had cigarettes all the time?" Valerie says. "I have half a carton. I hid them in the cupboard in my room."

She has sent David and Kimberly into town, telling them she's out of cigarettes. Valerie can't stop smoking, though she takes vitamin pills and is careful not to eat anything with red food coloring in it. "I couldn't think of anything else to say I was out of, and I had to have them clear off for a while. Now I don't dare smoke one or they'll smell it when they get back and know I was a liar. And I want one."

"Drink instead," says Roberta. When she got here she thought she couldn't talk to anybody—she was going to say her head ached and ask if she could lie down. But Valerie steadies her, as always. Valerie makes what isn't bearable interesting.

"So how are you?" Valerie says.

"Ohhh," says Roberta.

"Life would be grand if it weren't for the people," says Valerie moodily. "That sounds like a quotation, but I think I just made it up. The problem is that Kimberly is a Christian. Well, that's fine. We could use a Christian or two. For that matter, I am not an un-Christian. But she is very noticeably a Christian, don't you think? I'm amazed how mean she makes me feel."

GEORGE is enjoying the scything. For one thing, he likes working without spectators. Whenever he works at home these days, he is aware of a crowd of female spectators. Even if they're nowhere in sight, he feels as if they're watching—taking their ease, regarding his labors with mystification and amusement. He admits, if he thinks about it, that Roberta does do some work, though she has done nothing to earn money as far as he knows; she hasn't been in touch with her publishers, and she hasn't worked on ideas of her own. She permits her daughters to do nothing all day long, all summer long. Yesterday morning he got up feeling tired and disheartened— he had gone to sleep thinking of the work he had to do on the barn, and this preoccupation had seeped into his dreams, which were full of collapses, miscalculations, structural treacheries—and he went out to the deck off the kitchen, thinking to eat his eggs there and brood about the day's jobs. This deck is the only thing he had built as yet, the only change he has made in the house. He built it last spring in response to Roberta's complaints about the darkness of the house and the bad ventilation. He told her that the people who built these houses did so much work in the sun that they never thought of sitting in it.

He came out on the deck, then, carrying his plate and mug, and all three of them were already there. Angela was dressed in a sapphire-blue leotard; she was doing ballet exercises by the deck railing. Eva was sitting with her back against the wall of the house, spooning up bran flakes out of a soup bowl; she did this with such enthusiasm that many were spilled on the deck floor. Roberta, in a deck chair, had the everlasting mug of coffee clasped in both hands. She had one knee up and her back hunched, and with her dark glasses on she looked tense and mournful. He knows she weeps behind those glasses. It seems to him that she has let the children draw the sap right out of her body. She spends her time placating them, picking up after them; she has to beg them to make their beds and clean up their rooms; he has heard her pleading with them to collect their dirty dishes, so that she can wash them. Or that is what it sounds like to him. Is this the middle-class fashion of bringing up children? Here she was admiring Angela, meekly admiring her own daughter—the naked, lifted, golden leg, the disdainful profile. If either of his sisters had ventured on such a display, his mother would have belted them.

Angela lowered her leg and said, "Greetings, Master!"

"I don't see you bumping your head on the ground," said George. He usually joked with the girls no matter what he felt like. Rough joking was his habit, and it had been hugely successful in the classroom, where he had maintained a somewhat overdrawn, occasionally brutal, consistently entertaining character. He had done this with most of the other teachers as well, expressing his contempt for them so colorfully that they could not believe he meant it.

Eva loved to act out any suggestion of this sort. She stretched herself full length on the deck and knocked her head hard on the boards.

"You'll get a concussion," Roberta said.

"No, I won't. I'll just give myself a lobotomy."

"George, do you realize that in four brief days we will be gone?" said Angela. "Isn't your heart broken?"

"In twain."

"But will you let Mom take care of Diana when we're gone?" said Eva, sitting upright and feeling her head for bruises. Diana was a stray cat she was feeding in the barn.

"What do you mean, *let*?" said Roberta, and George at the same time said, "Certainly not. I'll tie her to the bedpost if she ever tries to go near the barn."

This cat is a sore point. If Angela sees the farm as a stage for herself, or sometimes as Nature—a begetter of thoughts and poems, to which she yields herself, wandering and dreaming—Eva sees it as a place to look for animals, with some of her attention left over for insects, minnows, rocks, and slugs. Both of them see it, certainly, as vacationland, spread out before them for whatever use or pleasure they can get out of it; neither sees the jobs waiting to be done under their noses. Eva has spent the summer stalking groundhogs and rabbits, trapping frogs and letting them go, catching minnows in a jar, trying to figure out how various animals could be housed in the barn. George holds her responsible—out of the very strength of her desire—for luring the deer out of the bush, so that he had to stop everything else that he was doing and build an eight-foot-high wire fence around the garden. The only animal she has managed to install in the barn is Diana, rail-thin, ugly, and half wild, whose dangling teats show that she is maintaining a family of kittens elsewhere. Much of Eva's time has been spent trying to discover the whereabouts of these kittens.

George sees the cat as a freeloader, a potential great nuisance, an invader of his property. By feeding it and encouraging it, Eva has embarked on a course of minor but significant treachery, which Roberta has implicitly supported. He knows his feelings on this matter are exaggerated, even comical; that does not help him. One of the things he has never wanted to be, and has avoided being, is a comic dad, a fulminator, a bungler. But it is Roberta's behavior that bothers him, more than Eva's. Here Roberta shows most plainly the mistake she has made in bringing up her children. In his mind he can hear Roberta talking to somebody at a party. "Eva has adopted a horrible cat, a really nasty-looking vagabond—that's her summer achievement. And Angela spends the whole day doing jetés and sulking at us." He has not actually heard Roberta say this—they have not been to any parties—but he can well imagine it. She would summon her children up for the entertainment of others; she would make them into characters from whom nothing serious was to be expected. This seems to George not only frivolous but heartless. Roberta, who is so indulgent with her children, who worries constantly that they may find her insufficiently loving, interested, understanding, is nevertheless depriving them. She is not taking them seriously; she is not bringing them up. And what is George to do in the face of this? They are not his children. One of the reasons he has not had children is that he doubts if he could give his attention unreservedly, and for as long as would be needed, to this very question of bringing them up. As a teacher, he knows how to make a lot of noise and keep several steps ahead of them, but it is exhausting to have to do that on the home front. And it was boys, chiefly, whom he learned to outmaneuver; boys were the threat in a class. The girls he never bothered much about, beyond some careful sparring with the sexy ones. That is not in order here.

Aside from all this, he often can't help liking Angela and Eva. They seem to him confused and appealing. They think him highly amusing, which irks him sometimes and pleases him at other times. His way with people is to be very reserved or very entertaining, and he believes that his preference is to be reserved. Therefore, he likes the entertainment to be appreciated.

But when he finished his breakfast and got two six-quart baskets and went down to the garden to pick the tomatoes, nobody stirred to help him. Roberta continued her moody thinking and her coffee-drinking. Angela had finished her exercises and was writing in the notebook she uses for a journal. Eva had taken off for the barn.

ANGELA sits down at the piano in Valerie's living room. There is no piano in George's house, and she misses one. Doesn't her mother miss one? Her mother has become a person who doesn't ask for anything.

*I have seen her change,* Angela has written in her journal, *from a person I deeply respected into a person on the verge of being a nervous wreck. If this is love I want no part of it. He wants to enslave her and us all and she walks a tightrope trying to keep him from getting mad. She doesn't enjoy anything and if you gave her the choice she would like best to lie down in a dark room with a cloth over her eyes and not see anybody or do anything. This is an intelligent woman who used to believe in freedom.*

She starts to play the "Turkish March," which brings to her mind the picture of a house her parents sold when she was five. There was a little shelf up near the ceiling in the dining room, where her mother had set the dessert plates for decoration. A tree, or bush, in the yard had lettuce-colored leaves as big as plates.

She has written in her journal: *I know nostalgia is a futile emotion. Sometimes I feel like tearing out some things I have written where perhaps I have been too harsh in judging certain people or situations but I have decided to leave everything because I want to have a record of what I really felt at the time. I want to have a truthful record of my whole life. How to keep oneself from lying I see as the main problem everywhere.*

During the summer Angela has spent a lot of time reading. She has read *Anna Karenina, The Second Sex, Emily of New Moon, The Norton Anthology of Poetry, The Autobiography of W. B. Yeats, The Happy Hooker, The Act of Creation, Seven Gothic Tales.* Some of these, to be accurate, she has not read all the way through. Her mother used to read all the time too. Angela would come home from school at noon, and again in the afternoon, and find her mother reading. Her mother read about the conquest of Mexico, she read *The Tale of Genji.* Angela marvels at how safe her mother seemed then.

Angela has one picture in her mind of Eva before Eva was born. The three of them—Angela, her mother, and her father—are on a beach. Her father is scooping out a large hole in the sand. Her father is a gifted builder of sand castles with road and irrigation systems, so Angela watches with interest any projects he undertakes. But the hole has nothing to do with a sand castle. When it is finished her mother rolls over, giggling, and fits her stomach into it. In her stomach is Eva, and the hollow is like a spoon for an egg. The beach is wide, mile after mile of white sand sloping delicately into the blue-green water. No rocky lakefront or stingy bit of cove. A radiant, generous place. Where could it have been?

She proceeds from the "Turkish March" to a try at "Eine kleine Nachtmusik." Roberta, listening to the piano at the same time she's listening to Valerie talking humorously and despairingly about her fear of Kimberly, her dislike of intruders, her indefensible reluctance to relinquish her children, thinks, No, it wasn't a mistake. What does she mean by that? She means it wasn't a mistake to leave her husband. Whatever happens, it wasn't a mistake. It was necessary. Otherwise she wouldn't have known.

"This is a bad time for you," Valerie says judiciously. "There is just a spectacular lot of strain."

"That's what I say to myself," says Roberta. "But sometimes I think that's not it. It's not the house, it's not the children. It's just something black that rises."

"Oh, there's always something black," says Valerie, grumbling.

"I think about Andrew—what was I doing to him? Setting things up to find the failure in him, railing at him, then getting cold feet and making up. Gradually the need to get rid of him would build again, but I was always sure it was his fault—if he'd just do this or that I could love him. So horrible for him that he turned into—remember what you said he was? A stick."

"He was a stick," says Valerie. "He always was. You're not responsible for everything."

"I think about it, because I wonder if that's what George is doing to me. He wants to be rid of me, then he doesn't, then he does, then he can't admit that, even to himself; he has to set up failures. I feel I know what Andrew went through. Not that I'd go back. Never. But I see it."

"I doubt if things happen so symmetrically."

"I don't think so either, really. I don't think you get your punishment in such a simple way. Isn't it funny how you're attracted—I am—to the idea of a pattern like that? I mean, the idea is attractive, of there being that balance. But not the experience. I'd like to avoid them."

"You forget how happy you are when you're happy."

"And vice versa. It's like childbirth."

GEORGE has finished scything and is cleaning the blade. He can hear the piano through the open windows of Valerie's house, and erratic streams of sweet, cold air are coming up from the river. He feels much better now, either because of the simple exercise or from the relief of feeling unobserved; perhaps it's just good to get away from the mountainous demands of his own place. He wonders if it's Roberta playing. The music fits in nicely with what he's doing: first the cheerful, workaday "Turkish March," to go along with the scything; now, as he stands cleaning the blade and smelling the cut grass, the subtle congratulations—even if a bit uncertainly delivered—of "Eine kleine Nachtmusik." As always, when his mood truly lifts, when the dawn breaks, he wants to go and find Roberta and envelop her, assure her—assure himself—that no real damage has been done. He hoped to be able to do that last night when they went drinking, but he couldn't; something still held him back.

He recalls Roberta's first visit to his house. That was in late August or early September, about a year ago now. They staged an indecorous sort of picnic, cooking feasts and playing records, hauling a mattress out into the yard. Clear nights, with Roberta pointing out to him the unlikely ways the stars tie up into their constellations, and every day pure gold. Roberta saying he must get it all straight now: she is forty-three years old, which is six years too old for him; she has left her husband because everything between them seemed artificial; but she hates saying that, because it may be just cant, she isn't sure what she means, and above all, she doesn't know what she's capable of. She seemed to him courageous, truthful, without vanity. How out of this could come such touchiness, tearfulness, weariness, such a threat of collapse, he cannot imagine.

But the first impression is worth respecting, he thinks.

EVA AND RUTH are decorating the dinner table on the veranda. Ruth is wearing a white shirt belonging to her brother, his striped pajama bottoms, and a monumental black turban. She looks like a proud but good-natured Sikh.

"I think the table ought to be strewn," says Ruth. "Subtlety is out, Eva."

At intervals they set orange and gold dahlias and beautifully striped pepper squash, zucchini, yellow gourds, Indian corn.

Under cover of the music Eva says, "Angela has more problems living here than I do. She thinks that whenever they fight it's about her."

"Do they fight?" says Ruth softly. Then she says, "It's none of my business." She was in love with George when she was thirteen or fourteen. It was when her mother first became friends with him. She used to hate his wife, and was glad when they separated. She remembers that the wife was the daughter of a gynecologist, and that this was cited by her mother as a reason George and his wife could never get on. It was probably the father's prosperity her mother was talking about, or the way the daughter had been brought up. But to Ruth the word *gynecologist* seemed sharp and appalling, and she saw the gynecologist's daughter dressed in an outfit of cold, jagged metal.

"They have silent fights. We can tell. Angela is so self-interested she thinks everything revolves around her. That's what happens when you become an adolescent. I don't want it to happen to me."

There is a pause in Angela's playing, and Eva says sharply, "Oh, I don't want to leave! I hate leaving."

"Do you?"

"I hate to leave Diana. I don't know what will happen to her. I don't know if I'll ever see her again. I don't think I'll ever see the deer again. I hate having to leave things."

Now that the piano is silent, Eva can be heard outside, where Valerie and Roberta are sitting. Roberta hears what Eva says, and waits, expecting to hear her say something about next summer. She braces herself to hear it.

Instead, Eva says, "You know, I understand George. I don't mind about him the way Angela does. I know how to be jokey. I understand him."

Roberta and Valerie look at each other, and Roberta smiles, shakes her head, and shivers. She has been afraid, sometimes, that George would hurt her children, not physically but by some turnabout, some revelation of dislike, that they could never forget. It seems to her that she has instructed them, by example, that he is to be accommodated, his silences respected, his joking responded to. What if he should turn, within this safety, and deal them a memorable blow? If it happened, it would be she who would have betrayed them into it. And she can feel a danger. For instance, when George was pruning the apple trees she heard Angela say, "My father's got an apple tree and a cherry tree now."

(That was information. Would he take it as competition?)

"I suppose he has some minions come and prune them for him?" George said.

"He has hundreds," said Angela cheerfully. "Dwarfs. He makes them all wear little Navy uniforms."

Angela was on thin ice at that moment. But Roberta thinks now that the real danger is not to Angela, who would find a way to welcome insult, would be ready to reap some advantage. (Roberta has read parts of the journal.) It is Eva, with her claims of understanding, her hopes of all-round conciliation, who could be smashed and stranded.

OVER COLD apple-and-watercress soup Eva has switched back to her *enfant terrible* style to tell the table, "They went out and got drunk last night. They were polluted."

David says he hasn't heard that expression in a long time.

Valerie says, "How awful for you little ones."

"We considered phoning the Children's Aid," says Angela, looking very unchildlike in the candlelight—looking like a queen, in fact—and aware that David is watching her, though with David it's hard to say whether he's watching with approval or with reservations. It seems as if it might be approval. Kimberly has taken over his reservations.

"Did you have a dissolute time?" says Valerie. "Roberta, you never told me. Where did you go?"

"It was highly respectable," says Roberta. "We went to the Queen's Hotel in Logan. To the Lounge—that's what they call it. The posh place to drink."

"George wouldn't take you out to any old beer parlor," says Ruth. "George is a closet conservative."

"It's true," says Valerie. "George believes you should take ladies only to nice places."

"And children should be seen and not heard," says Angela.

"Not seen, either," says George.

"Which is confusing to everyone, because he comes on like a raving radical," says Ruth.

"This is a treat," says George, "getting a free analysis. Actually, it was quite dissolute, and Roberta probably doesn't remember, on account of being so polluted, as Eva says. She bewitched a fellow who did tooth-pick tricks."

Roberta says it was a game where you made a word out of toothpicks, then took a toothpick away or rearranged what was there and made another word, and so on.

"I hope not dirty words?" says Eva.

"I never talked like that when I was her age," Angela says. "I was your pre-permissive child."

"And after we got tired of the game, or after he did, because I was tired of it quite soon, he showed me pictures of his wife and himself on their Mediterranean cruise. He was with another lady last night, because his wife is dead now, and if he forgot where the pictures were taken this lady reminded him. She said she didn't think he'd ever get over it."

"The cruise or his wife?" says Ruth, while George is saying that he had a conversation with a couple of Dutch farmers who wanted to take him for a ride in their plane.

"I don't think I went," George adds.

"I dissuaded you," says Roberta, not looking at him.

" 'Dissuaded' sounds so lovely," says Ruth. "It's so smooth. I must be thinking of suede."

Eva asks what it means.

"Persuaded not to," says Roberta. "I persuaded George not to go for a plane ride at one o'clock in the morning with the rich Dutch farmers. In-stead, we all had an adventure getting the man from the Mediterranean cruise into his car so his girlfriend could drive him home."

Ruth and Kimberly get up to remove the soup bowls, and David goes to put on a record of Dvořák's *New World* Symphony. This is his mother's request. David says it's syrupy.

They are quiet, waiting for the music to start. Eva says, "How did you guys fall in love anyway? Was it a physical attraction?"

Ruth knocks her gently on the head with a soup bowl. "You ought to have your jaws wired shut," she says. "Don't forget I'm learning how to cope with disturbed children."

"Didn't it bother you, Mom being so much older?"

"You see what I mean about her?" Angela says.

"What do you know about love?" says George grandly. "Love suffereth long, and is kind. Similar to myself in that respect. Love is not puffed up . . ."

"I think that is a particular kind of love," says Kimberly, setting down the vegetables. "If you're quoting."

Under cover of a conversation about translation and the meanings of words (a subject of which George knows little but about which he is soon making sweeping, provocative statements, true to his classroom technique), Roberta says to Valerie, "The man's girlfriend said that the wonderful thing was that his wife had done the whole Mediterranean cruise with a front-end loader."

"A what?"

"Front-end loader. I looked blank too, so she said, 'You know, his wife had one of those operations and she had to wear one of those bag things.' "

"Oh, God help us."

"She had big fat arms and a sprayed blond hairdo. The wife did, in the pictures. The girlfriend was something the same, but trimmer. The wife had such a lewd, happy look. A good-times look."

"And a front-end loader."

So you see against what odds, and with what unpromising-looking persons, love takes root and flourishes, and I myself have no front-end loader, merely some wrinkles and slackness and sallowness and subtle withering. This is what Roberta is saying to herself. It's not my fault, she says to herself, as she has said so often before. Usually when she says it, it's a whine, a plea, a whimper. Now it says itself matter-of-factly in her head; the tone in which it is stated is bored and tired. It seems as if this could be the truth.

BY DESSERT the conversation has shifted to architecture. The only light on the veranda is from the candles on the table. Ruth has taken the big candles away and set in front of each place a single small candle in a black metal holder with a handle, like the candle in the nursery rhyme. Valerie and Roberta say it together: " 'Here comes a candle to light you to bed. Here comes a chopper to chop off your head!' "

Neither of them taught that rhyme to her children, and their children have never heard it before.

"I've heard it," says Kimberly.

"The pointed arch, for instance—that was just a fad," George is saying. "It was an architectural fashion, very like fashions today."

"Well, it wasn't only that," says David, temporizing. "It was more than a fashion. The people who built the cathedrals were not entirely like us."

"They were very unlike us," Kimberly says.

"I'm sure I was always taught, if I was taught at all in those far-off days," says Valerie, "that the pointed arch was a development of the Romanesque arch. It suddenly occurred to them to carry it further. And it looked more religious."

"Bull," says George happily. "Beggin' your pardon. I know that's what they used to say, but in fact the pointed arch is the most primitive. It's the easiest arch; it's not a development from the round arch at all—how could it be? They had pointed arches in Egypt. The round arch, the keystone arch, is the most sophisticated arch you can build. The whole thing has been reported ass backwards to favor Christianity."

"Well, it may be sophisticated, but I think it's depressing," says Ruth. "I think they're very depressing, those round arches. They're monotonous; they just go along blah-blah-blah—they don't exactly make your spirits soar."

"It must have expressed something the people deeply wanted," Kimberly says. "You can hardly call that a fad. They built those cathedrals, the people did; the plan wasn't dictated by some architect."

"A misconception. They did have architects. In some cases we even know who they were."

"Nevertheless, I think Kimberly's right," says Valerie. "In those cathedrals you feel so much of the aspirations of those people; you feel the Christian emotion in the architecture—"

"Never mind what you feel. The fact is, the Crusaders brought the pointed arch back from the Arab world. Just as they brought back a taste for spicy food. It wasn't dreamed up by the collective unconscious to honor Jesus any more than I was. It was the latest style. The earliest examples you can see are in Italy, and then it worked north."

Kimberly is very pink in the face but is benignly, tightly smiling. Valerie, just because she so much dislikes Kimberly, is feeling a need to say anything at all to come to her rescue. Valerie never minds if she sounds silly; she will throw herself headlong into any conversation to turn it off its contentious course, to make people laugh and calm down. Ruth also has a knack for lightening things, though in her case it seems to be done not so deliberately but serenely and almost inadvertently, as a result of her faithful following of her own line of thought. What about David? At this moment David is caught up by Angela and not paying as much attention as he might be. Angela is trying out her powers; she will try them out even on a cousin she has known since she was child. Kimberly is endangered on two sides, Roberta thinks. But she will manage. She is strong enough to hold on to David through any number of Angelas, and strong enough to hold her smile in the face of George's attack on her faith. Does her smile foresee how he will burn? Not likely. She foresees, instead, how all of them will stumble and wander around and tie themselves in knots; what does it matter who wins the argument? For Kimberly, all the arguments have already been won.

Thinking this, pinning them all down this way, Roberta feels competent, relieved. Indifference has rescued her. The main thing is to be indifferent to George—that's the great boon. But her indifference flows past him; it's generous, it touches everybody. She is drunk enough to feel like reporting some findings. "Sexual abdication is not enough," she might say to Valerie. She is sober enough to keep quiet.

Valerie has got George talking about Italy. Ruth and David and Kimberly and Angela have started talking about something else. Roberta hears Angela's voice speaking with impatience and authority, and with an eagerness, a shyness, only she can detect.

"Acid rain . . ." Angela is saying.

Eva flicks her fingers against Roberta's arm. "What are you thinking?" she says.

"I don't know."

"You can't not know. What are you thinking?"

"About life."

"What about life?"

"About people."

"What about people."

"About the dessert."

Eva flicks harder, giggling. "What about the dessert?"

"I thought it was okay."

Sometime later Valerie has occasion to say that she was not born in the nineteenth century, in spite of what David may think. David says that everybody born in this country before the Second World War was to all intents and purposes brought up in the nineteenth century, and that their thinking is archaic.

"We are more than products of our upbringing," Valerie says. "As you yourself must hope, David." She says that she has been listening to all this talk about overpopulation, ecological disaster, nuclear disaster, this and that disaster, destroying the ozone layer—it's been going on and on, on and on for years, talk of disaster—but here they sit, all healthy, relatively sane, with a lovely dinner and lovely wine inside them, in the beautiful, undestroyed countryside.

"The Incas eating off gold plates while Pizarro was landing on the coast," says David.

"Don't talk as if there's no solution," says Kimberly.

"I think maybe we're destroyed already," Ruth says dreamily. "I think maybe we're anachronisms. No, that's not what I mean. I mean relics. In some way we are already. Relics."

Eva raises her head from her folded arms on the table. Her curtain veil is pulled down over one eye; her makeup has leaked beyond its boundaries, so that her whole face is a patchy flower. She says in a loud, stern voice, "I am not a relic," and they all laugh.

"Certainly not!" says Valerie, and then begins the yawning, the pushing back of chairs, the rather sheepish and formal smiles, the blowing out of candles: time to go home.

"Smell the river now!" Valerie tells them. Her voice sounds forlorn and tender, in the dark.

"A GIBBOUS MOON."

It was Roberta who told George what a gibbous moon was, and so his saying this is always an offering. It is an offering now, as they drive between the black cornfields.

"So there is."

Roberta doesn't reject the offering with silence, but she doesn't welcome it, either. She is polite. She yawns, and there is a private sound to her yawn. This isn't tactics, though she knows indifference is attractive. The real thing is. He can spot an imitation; he can always withstand tactics. She has to go all the way, to where she doesn't care. Then he feels how light and distant she is and his love revives. She has power. But the minute she begins to value it, it will begin to leave her. So she is thinking, as she yawns and wavers on the edge of caring and not caring. She'd stay on this edge if she could.

The half-ton truck bearing George and Roberta, with Eva and Angela in the back, is driving down the third concession road of Weymouth Township, known locally as the Telephone Road. It is a gravel road, fairly wide and well travelled. They turned onto it from the River Road, a much narrower road, which runs past Valerie's place. From the corner of the River Road to George's gate is a distance of about two and a quarter miles. Two side roads cut this stretch of the Telephone Road at right angles. Both these roads have stop signs; the Telephone Road is a through road. The first crossroad they have already passed. Along the second crossroad, from the west, a dark-green 1969 Dodge is travelling at between eighty and ninety miles an hour. Two young men are returning from a party to their home in Logan. One has passed out. The other is driving. He hasn't remembered to put the lights on. He sees the road by the light of the moon.

There isn't time to say a word. Roberta doesn't scream. George doesn't touch the brake. The big car flashes before them, a huge, dark flash, without lights, seemingly without sound. It comes out of the dark corn and fills the air right in front of them the way a big flat fish will glide into view suddenly in an aquarium tank. It seems to be no more than a yard in front of their headlights. Then it's gone—it has disappeared into the corn on the other side of the road. They drive on. They drive on down the Telephone Road and turn in to the lane and come to a stop and are sitting in the truck in the yard in front of the dark shape of the half-improved house. What they feel is not terror or thanksgiving—not yet. What they feel is strangeness. They feel as strange, as flattened out and borne aloft, as unconnected with previous and future events as the ghost car was, the black fish. The shaggy branches of the pine trees are moving overhead, and under those branches the moonlight comes clear on the hesitant grass of their new lawn.

"Are you guys dead?" Eva says, rousing them. "Aren't we home?"

# The Moons of Jupiter

~

I FOUND MY FATHER in the heart wing, on the eighth floor of Toronto General Hospital. He was in a semi-private room. The other bed was empty. He said that his hospital insurance covered only a bed in the ward, and he was worried that he might be charged extra.

"I never asked for a semi-private," he said.

I said the wards were probably full.

"No. I saw some empty beds when they were wheeling me by."

"Then it was because you had to be hooked up to that thing," I said. "Don't worry. If they're going to charge you extra, they tell you about it."

"That's likely it," he said. "They wouldn't want those doohickeys set up in the wards. I guess I'm covered for that kind of thing."

I said I was sure he was.

He had wires taped to his chest. A small screen hung over his head. On the screen a bright jagged line was continually being written. The writing was accompanied by a nervous electronic beeping. The behavior of his heart was on display. I tried to ignore it. It seemed to me that paying such close attention—in fact, dramatizing what ought to be a most secret activity—was asking for trouble. Anything exposed that way was apt to flare up and go crazy.

My father did not seem to mind. He said they had him on tranquillizers. You know, he said, the happy pills. He did seem calm and optimistic.

It had been a different story the night before. When I brought him into the hospital, to the emergency room, he had been pale and closemouthed. He had opened the car door and stood up and said quietly, "Maybe you better get me one of those wheelchairs." He used the voice he always used in a crisis. Once, our chimney caught on fire; it was on a Sunday afternoon and I was in the dining room pinning together a dress I was making. He came in and said in that same matter-of-fact, warning voice, "Janet. Do you know where there's some baking powder?" He wanted it to throw on the fire. Afterwards he said, "I guess it was your fault—sewing on Sunday."

I had to wait for over an hour in the emergency waiting room. They summoned a heart specialist who was in the hospital, a young man. He called me out into the hall and explained to me that one of the valves of my father's heart had deteriorated so badly that there ought to be an immediate operation.

I asked him what would happen otherwise.

"He'd have to stay in bed," the doctor said.

"How long?"

"Maybe three months."

"I meant, how long would he live?"

"That's what I meant too," the doctor said.

I went to see my father. He was sitting up in bed in a curtained-off corner. "It's bad, isn't it?" he said. "Did he tell you about the valve?"

"It's not as bad as it could be," I said. Then I repeated, even exaggerated, anything hopeful the doctor had said. "You're not in any immediate danger. Your physical condition is good, otherwise."

"Otherwise," said my father gloomily.

I was tired from the drive—all the way up to Dalgleish, to get him, and back to Toronto since noon—and worried about getting the rented car back on time, and irritated by an article I had been reading in a magazine in the waiting room. It was about another writer, a woman younger, better-looking, probably more talented than I am. I had been in England for two months and so I had not seen this article before, but it crossed my mind while I was reading that my father would have. I could hear him saying, Well, I didn't see anything about you in *Maclean's*. And if he had read something about me he would say, Well, I didn't think too much of that write-up. His tone would be humorous and indulgent but would produce in me a familiar dreariness of spirit. The message I got from him was simple: Fame must be striven for, then apologized for. Getting or not getting it, you will be to blame.

I was not surprised by the doctor's news. I was prepared to hear something of the sort and was pleased with myself for taking it calmly, just as I would be pleased with myself for dressing a wound or looking down from the frail balcony of a high building. I thought, Yes, it's time; there has to be something, here it is. I did not feel any of the protest I would have felt twenty, even ten, years before. When I saw from my father's face that he felt it—that refusal leapt up in him as readily as if he had been thirty or forty years younger—my heart hardened, and I spoke with a kind of badgering cheerfulness. "Otherwise is plenty," I said.

THE NEXT day he was himself again.

That was how I would have put it. He said it appeared to him now that the young fellow, the doctor, might have been a bit too eager to operate. "A bit knife-happy," he said. He was both mocking and showing off the hospital slang. He said that another doctor had examined him, an older man, and had given it as his opinion that rest and medication might do the trick.

I didn't ask what trick.

"He says I've got a defective valve, all right. There's certainly some damage. They wanted to know if I had rheumatic fever when I was a kid. I said I didn't think so. But half the time then you weren't diagnosed what you had. My father was not one for getting the doctor."

The thought of my father's childhood, which I always pictured as bleak and dangerous—the poor farm, the scared sisters, the harsh father—made me less resigned to his dying. I thought of him running away to work on the lake boats, running along the railway tracks, toward Goderich, in the evening light. He used to tell about that trip. Somewhere along the track he found a quince tree. Quince trees are rare in our part of the country; in fact, I have never seen one. Not even the one my father found, though he once took us on an expedition to look for it. He thought he knew the crossroad it was near, but we could not find it. He had not been able to eat the fruit, of course, but he had been impressed by its existence. It made him think he had got into a new part of the world.

The escaped child, the survivor, an old man trapped here by his leaky heart. I didn't pursue these thoughts. I didn't care to think of his younger selves. Even his bare torso, thick and white—he had the body of a working-man of his generation, seldom exposed to the sun—was a danger to me; it looked so strong and young. The wrinkled neck, the age-freckled hands and arms, the narrow, courteous head, with its thin gray hair and mustache, were more what I was used to.

"Now, why would I want to get myself operated on?" said my father reasonably. "Think of the risk at my age, and what for? A few years at the outside. I think the best thing for me to do is go home and take it easy. Give in gracefully. That's all you can do, at my age. Your attitude changes, you know. You go through some mental changes. It seems more natural."

"What does?" I said.

"Well, death does. You can't get more natural than that. No, what I mean, specifically, is not having the operation."

"That seems more natural?"

"Yes."

"It's up to you," I said, but I did approve. This was what I would have expected of him. Whenever I told people about my father I stressed his independence, his self-sufficiency, his forbearance. He worked in a factory, he worked in his garden, he read history books. He could tell you about the Roman emperors or the Balkan wars. He never made a fuss.

JUDITH, my younger daughter, had come to meet me at Toronto Airport two days before. She had brought the boy she was living with, whose name was Don. They were driving to Mexico in the morning, and while I was in Toronto I was to stay in their apartment. For the time being, I live in Vancouver. I sometimes say I have my headquarters in Vancouver.

"Where's Nichola?" I said, thinking at once of an accident or an overdose. Nichola is my older daughter. She used to be a student at the Conservatory, then she became a cocktail waitress, then she was out of work. If she had been at the airport, I would probably have said something wrong. I would have asked her what her plans were, and she would have gracefully brushed back her hair and said, "Plans?"—as if that was a word I had invented.

"I knew the first thing you'd say would be about Nichola," Judith said.

"It wasn't. I said hello and I—"

"We'll get your bag," Don said neutrally.

"Is she all right?"

"I'm sure she is," said Judith, with a fabricated air of amusement. "You wouldn't look like that if I was the one who wasn't here."

"Of course I would."

"You wouldn't. Nichola is the baby of the family. You know, she's four years older than I am."

"I ought to know."

Judith said she did not know where Nichola was exactly. She said Nichola had moved out of her apartment (that dump!) and had actually telephoned (which is quite a deal, you might say, Nichola phoning) to say she wanted to be incommunicado for a while but she was fine.

"I told her you would worry," said Judith more kindly on the way to their van. Don walked ahead carrying my suitcase. "But don't. She's all right, believe me."

Don's presence made me uncomfortable. I did not like him to hear these things. I thought of the conversations they must have had, Don and Judith. Or Don and Judith and Nichola, for Nichola and Judith were sometimes on good terms. Or Don and Judith and Nichola and others whose names I did not even know. They would have talked about me. Judith and Nichola comparing notes, relating anecdotes; analyzing, regretting, blaming, forgiving. I wished I'd had a boy and a girl. Or two boys. They wouldn't have done that. Boys couldn't possibly know so much about you.

I did the same thing at that age. When I was the age Judith is now I talked with my friends in the college cafeteria or, late at night, over coffee in our cheap rooms. When I was the age Nichola is now I had Nichola herself in a carry-cot or squirming in my lap, and I was drinking coffee again all the rainy Vancouver afternoons with my one neighborhood friend, Ruth Boudreau, who read a lot and was bewildered by her situation, as I was. We talked about our parents, our childhoods, though for some time we kept clear of our marriages. How thoroughly we dealt with our fathers and mothers, deplored their marriages, their mistaken ambitions or fear of ambition, how competently we filed them away, defined them beyond any possibility of change. What presumption.

I looked at Don walking ahead. A tall ascetic-looking boy, with a St. Francis cap of black hair, a precise fringe of beard. What right did he have to hear about me, to know things I myself had probably forgotten? I decided that his beard and hairstyle were affected.

Once, when my children were little, my father said to me, "You know those years you were growing up—well, that's all just a kind of a blur to me. I can't sort out one year from another." I was offended. I remembered each separate year with pain and clarity. I could have told how old I was when I went to look at the evening dresses in the window of Benbow's Ladies' Wear. Every week through the winter a new dress, spotlit—the sequins and tulle, the rose and lilac, sapphire, daffodil—and me a cold worshipper on the slushy sidewalk. I could have told how old I was when I forged my mother's signature on a bad report card, when I had measles, when we papered the front room. But the years when Judith and Nichola were little, when I lived with their father—yes, *blur* is the word for it. I remember hanging out diapers, bringing in and folding diapers; I can recall the kitchen counters of two houses and where the clothesbasket sat. I remember the television programs—*Popeye the Sailor*, *The Three Stooges*, *Funorama*. When *Funorama* came on it was time to turn on the lights and cook supper. But I couldn't tell the years apart. We lived outside Vancouver in a dormitory suburb: Dormir, Dormer, Dormouse—something like that. I was sleepy all the time then; pregnancy made me sleepy, and the night feedings, and the west coast rain falling. Dark dripping cedars, shiny dripping laurel; wives yawning, napping, visiting, drinking coffee, and folding diapers; husbands coming home at night from the city across the water. Every night I kissed my homecoming husband in his wet Burberry and hoped he might wake me up; I served up meat and potatoes and one of the four vegetables he permitted. He ate with a violent appetite, then fell asleep on the living-room sofa. We had become a cartoon couple, more middle-aged in our twenties than we would be in middle age.

Those bumbling years are the years our children will remember all their lives. Corners of the yards I never visited will stay in their heads.

"Did Nichola not want to see me?" I said to Judith.

"She doesn't want to see anybody, half the time," she said. Judith moved ahead and touched Don's arm. I knew that touch—an apology, an anxious reassurance. You touch a man that way to remind him that you are grateful, that you realize he is doing for your sake something that bores him or slightly endangers his dignity. It made me feel older than grandchildren would to see my daughter touch a man—a boy—this way. I felt her sad jitters, could predict her supple attentions. My blunt and stocky, blond and candid child. Why should I think she wouldn't be susceptible, that she would always be straightforward, heavy-footed, self-reliant? Just as I go around saying that Nichola is sly and solitary, cold, seductive. Many people must know things that would contradict what I say.

In the morning Don and Judith left for Mexico. I decided I wanted to see somebody who wasn't related to me, and who didn't expect anything in particular from me. I called an old lover of mine, but his phone was answered by a machine: "This is Tom Shepherd speaking. I will be out of town for the month of September. Please record your message, name, and phone number."

Tom's voice sounded so pleasant and familiar that I opened my mouth to ask him the meaning of this foolishness. Then I hung up. I felt as if he had deliberately let me down, as if we had planned to meet in a public place and then he hadn't shown up. Once, he had done that, I remembered.

I got myself a glass of vermouth, though it was not yet noon, and I phoned my father.

"Well, of all things," he said. "Fifteen more minutes and you would have missed me."

"Were you going downtown?"

"Downtown Toronto."

He explained that he was going to the hospital. His doctor in Dalgleish wanted the doctors in Toronto to take a look at him, and had given him a letter to show them in the emergency room.

"Emergency room?" I said.

"It's not an emergency. He just seems to think this is the best way to handle it. He knows the name of a fellow there. If he was to make me an appointment, it might take weeks."

"Does your doctor know you're driving to Toronto?" I said.

"Well, he didn't say I couldn't."

The upshot of this was that I rented a car, drove to Dalgleish, brought my father back to Toronto, and had him in the emergency room by seven o'clock that evening.

Before Judith left I said to her, "You're sure Nichola knows I'm staying here?"

"Well, I told her," she said.

Sometimes the phone rang, but it was always a friend of Judith's.

"WELL, IT LOOKS like I'm going to have it," my father said. This was on the fourth day. He had done a complete turnaround overnight. "It looks like I might as well."

I didn't know what he wanted me to say. I thought perhaps he looked to me for a protest, an attempt to dissuade him.

"When will they do it?" I said.

"Day after tomorrow."

I said I was going to the washroom. I went to the nurses' station and found a woman there who I thought was the head nurse. At any rate, she was gray-haired, kind, and serious-looking.

"My father's having an operation the day after tomorrow?" I said.

"Oh, yes."

"I just wanted to talk to somebody about it. I thought there'd been a sort of decision reached that he'd be better not to. I thought because of his age."

"Well, it's his decision and the doctor's." She smiled at me without condescension. "It's hard to make these decisions."

"How were his tests?"

"Well, I haven't seen them all."

I was sure she had. After a moment she said, "We have to be realistic. But the doctors here are very good."

When I went back into the room my father said, in a surprised voice, "*Shore*-less seas."

"What?" I said. I wondered if he had found out how much, or how little, time he could hope for. I wondered if the pills had brought on an untrustworthy euphoria. Or if he had wanted to gamble. Once, when he was talking to me about his life, he said, "The trouble was I was always afraid to take chances."

I used to tell people that he never spoke regretfully about his life, but that was not true. It was just that I didn't listen to it. He said that he should have gone into the Army as a tradesman—he would have been better off. He said he should have gone on his own, as a carpenter, after the war. He should have got out of Dalgleish. Once, he said, "A wasted life, eh?" But he was making fun of himself, saying that, because it was such a dramatic thing to say. When he quoted poetry too, he always had a scoffing note in his voice, to excuse the showing-off and the pleasure.

"Shoreless seas," he said again. " 'Behind him lay the gray Azores, / Behind the Gates of Hercules; / Before him not the ghost of shores, / Before him only shoreless seas.' That's what was going through my head last night. But do you think I could remember what kind of seas? I could not. Lonely seas? Empty seas? I was on the right track but I couldn't get it. But there now when you came into the room and I wasn't thinking about it at all, the word popped into my head. That's always the way, isn't it? It's not all that surprising. I ask my mind a question. The answer's there, but I can't see all the connections my mind's making to get it. Like a computer. Nothing out of the way. You know, in my situation the thing is, if there's anything you can't explain right away, there's a great temptation to—well, to make a mystery out of it. There's a great temptation to believe in—You know."

"The soul?" I said, speaking lightly, feeling an appalling rush of love and recognition.

"Oh, I guess you could call it that. You know, when I first came into this room there was a pile of papers here by the bed. Somebody had left them here—one of those tabloid sort of things I never looked at. I started reading them. I'll read anything handy. There was a series running in them on personal experiences of people who had died, medically speaking—heart arrest, mostly—and had been brought back to life. It was what they remembered of the time when they were dead. Their experiences."

"Pleasant or un-?" I said.

"Oh, pleasant. Oh, yes. They'd float up to the ceiling and look down on themselves and see the doctors working on them, on their bodies. Then float on further and recognize some people they knew who had died before them. Not see them exactly but sort of sense them. Sometimes there would be a humming and sometimes a sort of—what's that light that there is or color around a person?"

"Aura?"

"Yes. But without the person. That's about all they'd get time for; then they found themselves back in the body and feeling all the mortal pain and so on—brought back to life."

"Did it seem—convincing?"

"Oh, I don't know. It's all in whether you want to believe that kind of thing or not. And if you are going to believe it, take it seriously, I figure you've got to take everything else seriously that they print in those papers."

"What else do they?"

"Rubbish—cancer cures, baldness cures, bellyaching about the younger generation and the welfare bums. Tripe about movie stars."

"Oh, yes. I know."

"In my situation you have to keep a watch," he said, "or you'll start playing tricks on yourself." Then he said, "There's a few practical details we ought to get straight on," and he told me about his will, the house, the cemetery plot. Everything was simple.

"Do you want me to phone Peggy?" I said. Peggy is my sister. She is married to an astronomer and lives in Victoria.

He thought about it. "I guess we ought to tell them," he said finally. "But tell them not to get alarmed."

"All right."

"No, wait a minute. Sam is supposed to be going to a conference the end of this week, and Peggy was planning to go along with him. I don't want them wondering about changing their plans."

"Where is the conference?"

"Amsterdam," he said proudly. He did take pride in Sam, and kept track of his books and articles. He would pick one up and say, "Look at that, will you? And I can't understand a word of it!" in a marvelling voice that managed nevertheless to have a trace of ridicule.

"Professor Sam," he would say. "And the three little Sams." This is what he called his grandsons, who did resemble their father in braininess and in an almost endearing pushiness—an innocent energetic showing-off. They went to a private school that favored old-fashioned discipline and started calculus in Grade 5. "And the dogs," he might enumerate further, "who have been to obedience school. And Peggy . . ."

But if I said, "Do you suppose she has been to obedience school too?" he would play the game no further. I imagine that when he was with Sam and Peggy he spoke of me in the same way—hinted at my flightiness just as he hinted at their stodginess, made mild jokes at my expense, did not quite conceal his amazement (or pretended not to conceal his amazement) that people paid money for things I had written. He had to do this so that he might never seem to brag, but he would put up the gates when the joking got too rough. And of course I found later, in the house, things of mine he had kept—a few magazines, clippings, things I had never bothered about.

Now his thoughts travelled from Peggy's family to mine. "Have you heard from Judith?" he said.

"Not yet."

"Well, it's pretty soon. Were they going to sleep in the van?"

"Yes."

"I guess it's safe enough, if they stop in the right places."

I knew he would have to say something more and I knew it would come as a joke.

"I guess they put a board down the middle, like the pioneers?"

I smiled but did not answer.

"I take it you have no objections?"

"No," I said.

"Well, I always believed that too. Keep out of your children's business. I tried not to say anything. I never said anything when you left Richard."

"What do you mean, 'said anything'? Criticize?"

"It wasn't any of my business."

"No."

"But that doesn't mean I was pleased."

I was surprised—not just at what he said but at his feeling that he had any right, even now, to say it. I had to look out the window and down at the traffic to control myself.

"I just wanted you to know," he added.

A long time ago, he said to me in his mild way, "It's funny. Richard when I first saw him reminded me of what my father used to say. He'd say if that fellow was half as smart as he thinks he is, he'd be twice as smart as he really is."

I turned to remind him of this, but found myself looking at the line his heart was writing. Not that there seemed to be anything wrong, any difference in the beeps and points. But it was there.

He saw where I was looking. "Unfair advantage," he said.

"It is," I said. "I'm going to have to get hooked up too."

We laughed, we kissed formally; I left. At least he hadn't asked me about Nichola, I thought.

THE NEXT afternoon I didn't go to the hospital, because my father was having some more tests done, to prepare for the operation. I was to see him in the evening instead. I found myself wandering through the Bloor Street dress shops, trying on clothes. A preoccupation with fashion and my own appearance had descended on me like a raging headache. I looked at the women in the street, at the clothes in the shops, trying to discover how a transformation might be made, what I would have to buy. I recognized this obsession for what it was but had trouble shaking it. I've had people tell me that waiting for life-or-death news they've stood in front of an open refrigerator eating anything in sight—cold boiled potatoes, chili sauce, bowls of whipped cream. Or have been unable to stop doing crossword puzzles. Attention narrows in on something—some distraction—grabs on, becomes fanatically serious. I shuffled clothes on the racks, pulled them on in hot little changing rooms in front of cruel mirrors. I was sweating; once or twice I thought I might faint. Out on the street again, I thought I must remove myself from Bloor Street, and decided to go to the museum.

I remembered another time, in Vancouver. It was when Nichola was going to kindergarten and Judith was a baby. Nichola had been to the doctor about a cold, or maybe for a routine examination, and the blood test revealed something about her white blood cells—either that there were too many of them or that they were enlarged. The doctor ordered further tests, and I took Nichola to the hospital for them. Nobody mentioned leukemia but I knew, of course, what they were looking for. When I took Nichola home I asked the baby-sitter who had been with Judith to stay for the afternoon and I went shopping. I bought the most daring dress I ever owned, a black silk sheath with some laced-up arrangement in front. I remembered that bright spring afternoon, the spike-heeled shoes in the department store, the underwear printed with leopard spots.

I also remembered going home from St. Paul's Hospital over the Lions Gate Bridge on the crowded bus and holding Nichola on my knee. She suddenly recalled her baby name for *bridge* and whispered to me, "Whee—over the whee." I did not avoid touching my child—Nichola was slender and graceful even then, with a pretty back and fine dark hair—but realized I was touching her with a difference, though I did not think it could ever be detected. There was a care—not a withdrawal exactly but a care—not to feel anything much. I saw how the forms of love might be maintained with a condemned person but with the love in fact measured and disciplined, because you have to survive. It could be done so discreetly that the object of such care would not suspect, any more than she would suspect the sentence of death itself. Nichola did not know, would not know. Toys and kisses and jokes would come tumbling over her; she would never know, though I worried that she would feel the wind between the cracks of the manufactured holidays, the manufactured normal days. But all was well. Nichola did not have leukemia. She grew up—was still alive, and possibly happy. Incommunicado.

I could not think of anything in the museum I really wanted to see, so I walked past it to the planetarium. I had never been to a planetarium. The show was due to start in ten minutes. I went inside, bought a ticket, got in line. There was a whole class of schoolchildren, maybe a couple of classes, with teachers and volunteer mothers riding herd on them. I looked around to see if there were any other unattached adults. Only one—a man with a red face and puffy eyes, who looked as if he might be here to keep himself from going to a bar.

Inside, we sat on wonderfully comfortable seats that were tilted back so that you lay in a sort of hammock, attention directed to the bowl of the ceiling, which soon turned dark blue, with a faint rim of light all around the edge. There was some splendid, commanding music. The adults all around were shushing the children, trying to make them stop crackling their potato-chip bags. Then a man's voice, an eloquent professional voice, began to speak slowly, out of the walls. The voice reminded me a little of the way radio announcers used to introduce a piece of classical music or describe the progress of the Royal Family to Westminster Abbey on one of their royal occasions. There was a faint echo-chamber effect.

The dark ceiling was filling with stars. They came out not all at once but one after another, the way the stars really do come out at night, though more quickly. The Milky Way appeared, was moving closer; stars swam into brilliance and kept on going, disappearing beyond the edges of the sky-screen or behind my head. While the flow of light continued, the voice presented the stunning facts. A few light-years away, it announced, the sun appears as a bright star, and the planets are not visible. A few dozen light-years away, the sun is not visible, either, to the naked eye. And that distance—a few dozen light-years—is only about a thousandth part of the distance from the sun to the center of our galaxy, one galaxy, which itself contains abut two hundred billion suns. And is, in turn, one of millions, perhaps billions, of galaxies. Innumerable repetitions, innumerable variations. All this rolled past my head too, like balls of lightning.

Now realism was abandoned, for familiar artifice. A model of the solar system was spinning away in its elegant style. A bright bug took off from the earth, heading for Jupiter. I set my dodging and shrinking mind sternly to recording facts. The mass of Jupiter two and a half times that of all the other planets put together. The Great Red Spot. The thirteen moons. Past Jupiter, a glance at the eccentric orbit of Pluto, the icy rings of Saturn. Back to Earth and moving in to hot and dazzling Venus. Atmospheric pressure ninety times ours. Moonless Mercury rotating three times while circling the sun twice; an odd arrangement, not as satisfying as what they used to tell us—that it rotated once as it circled the sun. No perpetual darkness after all. Why did they give out such confident information, only to announce later that it was quite wrong? Finally, the picture already familiar from magazines: the red soil of Mars, the blooming pink sky.

When the show was over I sat in my seat while the children clambered across me, making no comments on anything they had just seen or heard. They were pestering their keepers for eatables and further entertainments. An effort had been made to get their attention, to take it away from canned pop and potato chips and fix it on various knowns and unknowns and horrible immensities, and it seemed to have failed. A good thing too, I thought. Children have a natural immunity, most of them, and it shouldn't be tampered with. As for the adults who would deplore it, the ones who promoted this show, weren't they immune themselves to the extent that they could put in the echo-chamber effects, the music, the churchlike solemnity, simulating the awe that they supposed they ought to feel? Awe—what was that supposed to be? A fit of the shivers when you looked out the window? Once you know what it was, you wouldn't be courting it.

Two men came with brooms to sweep up the debris the audience had left behind. They told me that the next show would start in forty minutes. In the meantime, I had to get out.

"I went to the show at the planetarium," I said to my father. "It was very exciting—about the solar system." I thought what a silly word I had used: *exciting*. "It's like a slightly phony temple," I added.

He was already talking. "I remember when they found Pluto. Right where they thought it had to be. Mercury, Venus, Earth, Mars," he recited. "Jupiter, Saturn, Nept—no, Uranus, Neptune, Pluto. Is that right?"

"Yes," I said. I was just as glad he hadn't heard what I said about the phony temple. I had meant that to be truthful, but it sounded slick and superior. "Tell me the moons of Jupiter."

"Well, I don't know the new ones. There's a bunch of new ones, isn't there?"

"Two. But they're not new."

"New to us," said my father. "You've turned pretty cheeky now I'm going under the knife."

" 'Under the knife.' What an expression."

He was not in bed tonight, his last night. He had been detached from his apparatus, and was sitting in a chair by the window. He was bare-legged, wearing a hospital dressing gown, but he did not look self-conscious or out of place. He looked thoughtful but good-humored, an affable host.

"You haven't even named the old ones," I said.

"Give me time. Galileo named them. Io."

"That's a start."

"The moons of Jupiter were the first heavenly bodies discovered with the telescope." He said this gravely, as if he could see the sentence in an old book. "It wasn't Galileo named them, either; it was some German. Io, Europa, Ganymede, Callisto. There you are."

"Yes."

"Io and Europa, they were girlfriends of Jupiter's, weren't they? Ganymede was a boy. A shepherd? I don't know who Callisto was."

"I think she was a girlfriend too," I said. "Jupiter's wife—Jove's wife—changed her into a bear and stuck her up in the sky. Great Bear and Little Bear. Little Bear was her baby."

The loudspeaker said that it was time for visitors to go.

"I'll see you when you come out of the anesthetic," I said.

"Yes."

When I was at the door, he called to me, "Ganymede wasn't any shepherd. He was Jove's cupbearer."

WHEN I left the planetarium that afternoon, I had walked through the museum to the Chinese garden. I saw the stone camels again, the warriors, the tomb. I sat on a bench looking toward Bloor Street. Through the evergreen bushes and the high grilled iron fence I watched people going by in the late-afternoon sunlight. The planetarium show had done what I wanted it to after all—calmed me down, drained me. I saw a girl who reminded me of Nichola. She wore a trenchcoat and carried a bag of groceries. She was shorter than Nichola—not really much like her at all—but I thought that I might see Nichola. She would be walking along some street maybe not far from here—burdened, preoccupied, alone. She was one of the grown-up people in the world now, one of the shoppers going home.

If I did see her, I might just sit and watch, I decided. I felt like one of those people who have floated up to the ceiling, enjoying a brief death. A relief, while it lasts. My father had chosen and Nichola had chosen. Someday, probably soon, I would hear from her, but it came to the same thing.

I meant to get up and go over to the tomb, to look at the relief carvings, the stone pictures, that go all the way around it. I always mean to look at them and I never do. Not this time, either. It was getting cold out, so I went inside to have coffee and something to eat before I went back to the hospital.

# The Progress of Love

I GOT A CALL at work, and it was my father. This was not long after I was divorced and started in the real-estate office. Both of my boys were in school. It was a hot enough day in September.

My father was so polite, even in the family. He took time to ask me how I was. Country manners. Even if somebody phones up to tell you your house is burning down, they ask first how you are.

"I'm fine," I said. "How are you?"

"Not so good, I guess," said my father, in his old way—apologetic but self-respecting. "I think your mother's gone."

I knew that *gone* meant *dead*. I knew that. But for a second or so I saw my mother in her black straw hat setting off down the lane. The word *gone* seemed full of nothing but a deep relief and even an excitement—the excitement you feel when a door closes and your house sinks back to normal and you let yourself loose into all the free space around you. That was in my father's voice too—behind the apology, a queer sound like a gulped breath. But my mother hadn't been a burden—she hadn't been sick a day—and far from feeling relieved at her death, my father took it hard. He never got used to living alone, he said. He went into the Netterfield County Home quite willingly.

He told me how he found my mother on the couch in the kitchen when he came in at noon. She had picked a few tomatoes, and was setting them on the windowsill to ripen; then she must have felt weak, and lain down. Now, telling this, his voice went wobbly—meandering, as you would expect—in his amazement. I saw in my mind the couch, the old quilt that protected it, right under the phone.

"So I thought I better call you," my father said, and he waited for me to say what he should do now.

MY MOTHER prayed on her knees at midday, at night, and first thing in the morning. Every day opened up to her to have God's will done in it. Every night she totted up what she'd done and said and thought, to see how it squared with Him. That kind of life is dreary, people think, but they're missing the point. For one thing, such a life can never be boring. And nothing can happen to you that you can't make use of. Even if you're wracked by troubles, and sick and poor and ugly, you've got your soul to carry through life like a treasure on a platter. Going upstairs to pray after the noon meal, my mother would be full of energy and expectation, seriously smiling.

She was saved at a camp meeting when she was fourteen. That was the same summer that her own mother—my grandmother—died. For a few years, my mother went to meetings with a lot of other people who'd been saved, some who'd been saved over and over again, enthusiastic old sinners. She could tell stories about what went on at those meetings, the singing and hollering and wildness. She told about one old man getting up and shouting, "Come down, O Lord, come down among us now! Come down through the roof and I'll pay for the shingles!"

She was back to being just an Anglican, a serious one, by the time she got married. She was twenty-five then, and my father was thirty-eight. A tall good-looking couple, good dancers, good cardplayers, sociable. But serious people—that's how I would try to describe them. Serious the way hardly anybody is anymore. My father was not religious in the way my mother was. He was an Anglican, an Orangeman, a Conservative, because that's what he had been brought up to be. He was the son who got left on the farm with his parents and took care of them till they died. He met my mother, he waited for her, they married; he thought himself lucky then to have a family to work for. (I have two brothers, and I had a baby sister who died.) I have a feeling that my father never slept with any woman before my mother, and never with her until he married her. And he had to wait, because my mother wouldn't get married until she had paid back to her own father every cent he had spent on her since her mother died. She had kept track of everything—board, books, clothes—so that she could pay it back. When she married, she had no nest egg, as teachers usually did, no hope chest, sheets, or dishes. My father used to say, with a sombre, joking face, that he had hoped to get a woman with money in the bank. "But you take the money in the bank, you have to take the face that goes with it," he said, "and sometimes that's no bargain."

. . .

THE HOUSE we lived in had big, high rooms, with dark-green blinds on the windows. When the blinds were pulled down against the sun, I used to like to move my head and catch the light flashing through the holes and cracks. Another thing I liked looking at was chimney stains, old or fresh, which I could turn into animals, people's faces, even distant cities. I told my own two boys about that, and their father, Dan Casey, said, "See, your mom's folks were so poor, they couldn't afford TV, so they got these stains on the ceiling—your mom had to watch the stains on the ceiling!" He always liked to kid me about thinking poor was anything great.

WHEN my father was very old, I figured out that he didn't mind people doing new sorts of things—for instance, my getting divorced—as much as he minded them having new sorts of reasons for doing them.

Thank God he never had to know about the commune.

"The Lord never intended," he used to say. Sitting around with the other old men in the Home, in the long, dim porch behind the spirea bushes, he talked about how the Lord never intended for people to tear around the country on motorbikes and snowmobiles. And how the Lord never intended for nurses' uniforms to be pants. The nurses didn't mind at all. They called him "Handsome," and told me he was a real old sweetheart, a real old religious gentleman. They marvelled at his thick black hair, which he kept until he died. They washed and combed it beautifully, wet-waved it with their fingers.

Sometimes, with all their care, he was a little unhappy. He wanted to go home. He worried about the cows, the fences, about who was getting up to light the fire. A few flashes of meanness—very few. Once, he gave me a sneaky, unfriendly look when I went in; he said, "I'm surprised you haven't worn all the skin off your knees by now."

I laughed. I said, "What doing? Scrubbing floors?"

"Praying!" he said, in a voice like spitting.

He didn't know who he was talking to.

I DON'T remember my mother's hair being anything but white. My mother went white in her twenties, and never saved any of her young hair, which had been brown. I used to try to get her to tell what color brown.

"Dark."

"Like Brent, or like Dolly?" Those were two workhorses we had, a team.

"I don't know. It wasn't horsehair."

"Was it like chocolate?"

"Something like."

"Weren't you sad when it went white?"

"No. I was glad."

"Why?"

"I was glad that I wouldn't have hair anymore that was the same color as my father's."

Hatred is always a sin, my mother told me. Remember that. One drop of hatred in your soul will spread and discolor everything like a drop of black ink in white milk. I was struck by that and meant to try it, but knew I shouldn't waste the milk.

ALL THESE things I remember. All the things I know, or have been told, about people I never even saw. I was named Euphemia, after my mother's mother. A terrible name, such as nobody has nowadays. At home they called me Phemie, but when I started to work, I called myself Fame. My husband, Dan Casey, called me Fame. Then in the bar of the Shamrock Hotel, years later, after my divorce, when I was going out, a man said to me, "Fame, I've been meaning to ask you, just what is it you are famous for?"

"I don't know," I told him. "I don't know, unless it's for wasting my time talking to jerks like you."

After that I thought of changing it altogether, to something like Joan, but unless I moved away from here, how could I do that?

IN THE summer of 1947, when I was twelve, I helped my mother paper the downstairs bedroom, the spare room. My mother's sister, Beryl, was coming to visit us. These two sisters hadn't seen each other for years. Very soon after their mother died, their father married again. He went to live in Minneapolis, then in Seattle, with his new wife and his younger daughter, Beryl. My mother wouldn't go with them. She stayed on in the town of Ramsay, where they had been living. She was boarded with a childless couple who had been neighbors. She and Beryl had met only once or twice since they were grown up. Beryl lived in California.

The paper had a design of cornflowers on a white ground. My mother had got it at a reduced price, because it was the end of a lot. This meant we had trouble matching the pattern, and behind the door we had to do some tricky fitting with scraps and strips. This was before the days of pre-pasted wallpaper. We had a trestle table set up in the front room, and we mixed the paste and swept it onto the back of the paper with wide brushes, watching for lumps. We worked with the windows up, screens fitted under them, the front door open, the screen door closed. The country we could see through the mesh of screens and the wavery old window glass was all hot and flowering—milkweed and wild carrot in the pastures, mustard rampaging in the clover, some fields creamy with the buckwheat people grew then. My mother sang. She sang a song she said her own mother used to sing when she and Beryl were little girls.

> "*I once had a sweetheart, but now I have none.*
> *He's gone and he's left me to weep and to moan.*
> *He's gone and he's left me, but contented I'll be,*
> *For I'll get another one, better than he!*"

I was excited because Beryl was coming, a visitor, all the way from California. Also because I had gone to town in late June to write the Entrance Examinations, and was hoping to hear soon that I had passed with honors. Everybody who had finished Grade 8 in the country schools had to go into town to write those examinations. I loved that—the rustling sheets of foolscap, the important silence, the big stone high-school building, all the old initials carved in the desks, darkened with varnish. The first burst of summer outside, the green and yellow light, the townlike chestnut trees, and honeysuckle. And all it was was this same town, where I have lived now more than half my life. I wondered at it. And at myself, drawing maps with ease and solving problems, knowing quantities of answers. I thought I was so clever. But I wasn't clever enough to understand the simplest thing. I didn't even understand that examinations made no difference in my case. I wouldn't be going to high school. How could I? That was before there were school buses; you had to board in town. My parents didn't have the money. They operated on very little cash, as many farmers did then. The payments from the cheese factory were about all that came in regularly. And they didn't think of my life going in that direction, the high-school direction. They thought that I would stay at home and help my mother, maybe hire out to help women in the neighborhood who were sick or having a baby. Until such time as I got married. That was what they were waiting to tell me when I got the results of the examinations.

You would think my mother might have a different idea, since she had been a schoolteacher herself. But she said God didn't care. God isn't interested in what kind of job or what kind of education anybody has, she told me. He doesn't care two hoots about that, and it's what He cares about that matters.

This was the first time I understood how God could become a real opponent, not just some kind of nuisance or large decoration.

MY MOTHER'S name as a child was Marietta. That continued to be her name, of course, but until Beryl came I never heard her called by it. My father always said Mother. I had a childish notion—I knew it was childish—that Mother suited my mother better than it did other mothers. Mother, not Mama. When I was away from her, I could not think what my mother's face was like, and this frightened me. Sitting in school, just over a hill from home, I would try to picture my mother's face. Sometimes I thought that if I couldn't do it, that might mean my mother was dead. But I had a sense of her all the time, and would be reminded of her by the most unlikely things—an upright piano, or a tall white loaf of bread. That's ridiculous, but true.

Marietta, in my mind, was separate, not swallowed up in my mother's grown-up body. Marietta was still running around loose up in her town of Ramsay, on the Ottawa River. In that town, the streets were full of horses and puddles, and darkened by men who came in from the bush on weekends. Loggers. There were eleven hotels on the main street, where the loggers stayed, and drank.

The house Marietta lived in was halfway up a steep street climbing from the river. It was a double house, with two bay windows in front, and a wooden trellis that separated the two front porches. In the other half of the house lived the Sutcliffes, the people Marietta was to board with after her mother died and her father left town. Mr. Sutcliffe was an Englishman, a telegraph operator. His wife was German. She always made coffee instead of tea. She made strudel. The dough for the strudel hung down over the edges of the table like a fine cloth. It sometimes looked to Marietta like a skin.

Mrs. Sutcliffe was the one who talked Marietta's mother out of hanging herself.

Marietta was home from school that day, because it was Saturday. She woke up late and heard the silence in the house. She was always scared of that—a silent house—and as soon as she opened the door after school she would call, "Mama! Mama!" Often her mother wouldn't answer. But she would be there. Marietta would hear with relief the rattle of the stove grate or the steady slap of the iron.

That morning, she didn't hear anything. She came downstairs, and got herself a slice of bread and butter and molasses, folded over. She opened the cellar door and called. She went into the front room and peered out the window, through the bridal fern. She saw her little sister, Beryl, and some other neighborhood children rolling down the bit of grassy terrace to the sidewalk, picking themselves up and scrambling to the top and rolling down again.

"Mama?" called Marietta. She walked through the house to the back yard. It was late spring, the day was cloudy and mild. In the sprouting vegetable gardens, the earth was damp, and the leaves on the trees seemed suddenly full-sized, letting down drops of water left over from the rain of the night before.

"Mama?" calls Marietta under the trees, under the clothesline.

At the end of the yard is a small barn, where they keep firewood, and some tools and old furniture. A chair, a straight-backed wooden chair, can be seen through the open doorway. On the chair, Marietta sees her mother's feet, her mother's black laced shoes. Then the long, printed cotton summer work dress, the apron, the rolled-up sleeves. Her mother's shiny-looking white arms, and neck, and face.

Her mother stood on the chair and didn't answer. She didn't look at Marietta, but smiled and tapped her foot, as if to say, "Here I am, then. What are you going to do about it?" Something looked wrong about her, beyond the fact that she was standing on a chair and smiling in this queer, tight way. Standing on an old chair with back rungs missing, which she had pulled out to the middle of the barn floor, where it teetered on the bumpy earth. There was a shadow on her neck.

The shadow was a rope, a noose on the end of a rope that hung down from a beam overhead.

"Mama?" says Marietta, in a fainter voice. "Mama. Come down, please." Her voice is faint because she fears that any yell or cry might jolt her mother into movement, cause her to step off the chair and throw her weight on the rope. But even if Marietta wanted to yell she couldn't. Nothing but this pitiful thread of a voice is left to her—just as in a dream when a beast or a machine is bearing down on you.

"Go and get your father."

That was what her mother told her to do, and Marietta obeyed. With terror in her legs, she ran. In her nightgown, in the middle of a Saturday morning, she ran. She ran past Beryl and the other children, still tumbling down the slope. She ran along the sidewalk, which was at that time a boardwalk, then on the unpaved street, full of last night's puddles. The street crossed the railway tracks. At the foot of the hill, it intersected the main street of the town. Between the main street and the river were some warehouses and the buildings of small manufacturers. That was where Marietta's father had his carriage works. Wagons, buggies, sleds were made there. In fact, Marietta's father had invented a new sort of sled to carry logs in the bush. It had been patented. He was just getting started in Ramsay. (Later on, in the States, he made money. A man fond of hotel bars, barbershops, harness races, women, but not afraid of work—give him credit.)

Marietta did not find him at work that day. The office was empty. She ran out into the yard where the men were working. She stumbled in the fresh sawdust. The men laughed and shook their heads at her. No. Not here. Not a-here right now. No. Why don't you try upstreet? Wait. Wait a minute. Hadn't you better get some clothes on first?

They didn't mean any harm. They didn't have the sense to see that something must be wrong. But Marietta never could stand men laughing. There were always places she hated to go past, let alone into, and that was the reason. Men laughing. Because of that, she hated barbershops, hated their smell. (When she started going to dances later on with my father, she asked him not to put any dressing on his hair, because the smell reminded her.) A bunch of men standing out on the street, outside a hotel, seemed to Marietta like a clot of poison. You tried not to hear what they were saying, but you could be sure it was vile. If they didn't say anything, they laughed and vileness spread out from them—poison—just the same. It was only after Marietta was saved that she could walk right past them. Armed by God, she walked through their midst and nothing stuck to her, nothing scorched her; she was safe as Daniel.

Now she turned and ran, straight back the way she had come. Up the hill, running to get home. She thought she had made a mistake leaving her mother. Why did her mother tell her to go? Why did she want her father? Quite possibly so that she could greet him with the sight of her own warm body swinging on the end of a rope. Marietta should have stayed—she should have stayed and talked her mother out of it. She should have run to Mrs. Sutcliffe, or any neighbor, not wasted time this way. She hadn't thought who could help, who could even believe what she was talking about. She had the idea that all families except her own lived in peace, that threats and miseries didn't exist in other people's houses, and couldn't be explained there.

A train was coming into town. Marietta had to wait. Passengers looked out at her from its windows. She broke out wailing in the faces of those strangers. When the train passed, she continued up the hill—a spectacle, with her hair uncombed, her feet bare and muddy, in her nightgown, with a wild, wet face. By the time she ran into her own yard, in sight of the barn, she was howling. "Mama!" she was howling. "Mama!"

Nobody was there. The chair was standing just where it had been before. The rope was dangling over the back of it. Marietta was sure that her mother had gone ahead and done it. Her mother was already dead—she had been cut down and taken away.

But warm, fat hands settled down on her shoulders, and Mrs. Sutcliffe said, "Marietta. Stop the noise. Marietta. Child. Stop the crying. Come inside. She is well, Marietta. Come inside and you will see."

Mrs. Sutcliffe's foreign voice said, "Mari-et-cha," giving the name a rich, important sound. She was as kind as could be. When Marietta lived with the Sutcliffes later, she was treated as the daughter of the household, and it was a household just as peaceful and comfortable as she had imagined other households to be. But she never felt like a daughter there.

In Mrs. Sutcliffe's kitchen, Beryl sat on the floor eating a raisin cookie and playing with the black-and-white cat, whose name was Dickie. Marietta's mother sat at the table, with a cup of coffee in front of her.

"She was silly," Mrs. Sutcliffe said. Did she mean Marietta's mother or Marietta herself? She didn't have many English words to describe things.

Marietta's mother laughed, and Marietta blacked out. She fainted, after running all that way uphill, howling, in the warm, damp morning. Next thing she knew, she was taking black, sweet coffee from a spoon held by Mrs. Sutcliffe. Beryl picked Dickie up by the front legs and offered him as a cheering present. Marietta's mother was still sitting at the table.

HER HEART was broken. That was what I always heard my mother say. That was the end of it. Those words lifted up the story and sealed it shut. I never asked, Who broke it? I never asked. What was the men's poison talk? What was the meaning of the word *vile*?

Marietta's mother laughed after not hanging herself. She sat at Mrs. Sutcliffe's kitchen table long ago and laughed. Her heart was broken.

I always had a feeling, with my mother's talk and stories, of something swelling out behind. Like a cloud you couldn't see through, or get to the end of. There was a cloud, a poison, that had touched my mother's life. And when I grieved my mother, I became part of it. Then I would beat my head against my mother's stomach and breasts, against her tall, firm front, demanding to be forgiven. My mother would tell me to ask God. But it wasn't God, it was my mother I had to get straight with. It seemed as if she knew something about me that was worse, far worse, than ordinary lies and tricks and meanness; it was a really sickening shame. I beat against my mother's front to make her forget that.

My brothers weren't bothered by any of this. I don't think so. They seemed to me like cheerful savages, running around free, not having to learn much. And when I just had the two boys myself, no daughters, I felt as if something could stop now—the stories, and griefs, the old puzzles you can't resist or solve.

AUNT BERYL said not to call her Aunt. "I'm not used to being any-body's aunt, honey. I'm not even anybody's momma. I'm just me. Call me Beryl."

Beryl had started out as a stenographer, and now she had her own typing and bookkeeping business, which employed many girls. She had arrived with a man friend, whose name was Mr. Florence. Her letter had said that she would be getting a ride with a friend, but she hadn't said whether the friend would be staying or going on. She hadn't even said if it was a man or a woman.

Mr. Florence was staying. He was a tall, thin man with a long, tanned face, very light-colored eyes, and a way of twitching the corner of his mouth that might have been a smile.

He was the one who got to sleep in the room that my mother and I had papered, because he was the stranger, and a man. Beryl had to sleep with me. At first we thought that Mr. Florence was quite rude, because he wasn't used to our way of talking and we weren't used to his. The first morning, my father said to Mr. Florence, "Well, I hope you got some kind of a sleep on that old bed in there?" (The spare-room bed was heavenly, with a feather tick.) This was Mr. Florence's cue to say that he had never slept better.

Mr. Florence twitched. He said, "I slept on worse."

His favorite place to be was in his car. His car was a royal-blue Chrysler, from the first batch turned out after the war. Inside it, the upholstery and floor covering and roof and door padding were all pearl gray. Mr. Florence kept the names of those colors in mind and corrected you if you said just "blue" or "gray."

"Mouse skin is what it looks like to me," said Beryl rambunctiously. "I tell him it's just mouse skin!"

The car was parked at the side of the house, under the locust trees. Mr. Florence sat inside with the windows rolled up, smoking, in the rich new-car smell.

"I'm afraid we're not doing much to entertain your friend," my mother said.

"I wouldn't worry about him," said Beryl. She always spoke about Mr. Florence as if there was a joke about him that only she appreciated. I wondered long afterward if he had a bottle in the glove compartment and took a nip from time to time to keep his spirits up. He kept his hat on.

Beryl herself was being entertained enough for two. Instead of staying in the house and talking to my mother, as a lady visitor usually did, she demanded to be shown everything there was to see on a farm. She said that I was to take her around and explain things, and see that she didn't fall into any manure piles.

I didn't know what to show. I took Beryl to the icehouse, where chunks of ice the size of dresser drawers, or bigger, lay buried in sawdust. Every few days, my father would chop off a piece of ice and carry it to the kitchen, where it melted in a tin-lined box and cooled the milk and butter.

Beryl said she had never had any idea ice came in pieces that big. She seemed intent on finding things strange, or horrible, or funny.

"Where in the world do you get ice that big?"

I couldn't tell if that was a joke.

"Off of the lake," I said.

"Off of the lake! Do you have lakes up here that have ice on them all summer?"

I told her how my father cut the ice on the lake every winter and hauled it home, and buried it in sawdust, and that kept it from melting.

Beryl said, "That's amazing!"

"Well, it melts a little," I said. I was deeply disappointed in Beryl.

"That's really amazing."

Beryl went along when I went to get the cows. A scarecrow in white slacks (this was what my father called her afterward), with a white sun hat tied under her chin by a flaunting red ribbon. Her fingernails and toenails—she wore sandals—were painted to match the ribbon. She wore the small, dark sunglasses people wore at that time. (Not the people I knew— they didn't own sunglasses.) She had a big red mouth, a loud laugh, hair of an unnatural color and a high gloss, like cherry wood. She was so noisy and shiny, so glamorously got up, that it was hard to tell whether she was good-looking, or happy, or anything.

We didn't have any conversation along the cowpath, because Beryl kept her distance from the cows and was busy watching where she stepped. Once I had them all tied in their stalls, she came closer. She lit a cigarette. Nobody smoked in the barn. My father and other farmers chewed tobacco there instead. I didn't see how I could ask Beryl to chew tobacco.

"Can you get the milk out of them or does your father have to?" Beryl said. "Is it hard to do?"

I pulled some milk down through the cow's teat. One of the barn cats came over and waited. I shot a thin stream into its mouth. The cat and I were both showing off.

"Doesn't that hurt?" said Beryl. "Think if it was you."

I had never thought of a cow's teat as corresponding to any part of myself, and was shaken by this indecency. In fact, I could never grasp a warm, warty teat in such a firm and casual way again.

BERYL SLEPT in a peach-colored rayon nightgown trimmed with écru lace. She had a robe to match. She was just as careful about the word *écru* as Mr. Florence was about his royal blue and pearl gray.

I managed to get undressed and put on my nightgown without any part of me being exposed at any time. An awkward business. I left my underpants on, and hoped that Beryl had done the same. The idea of sharing my bed with a grownup was a torment to me. But I did get to see the contents of what Beryl called her beauty kit. Hand-painted glass jars contained puffs of cotton wool, talcum powder, milky lotion, ice-blue astringent. Little pots of red and mauve rouge—rather greasy-looking. Blue and black pencils. Emery boards, a pumice stone, nail polish with an overpowering smell of bananas, face powder in a celluloid box shaped like a shell, with the name of a dessert—Apricot Delight.

I had heated some water on the coal-oil stove we used in summertime. Beryl scrubbed her face clean, and there was such a change that I almost expected to see makeup lying in strips in the washbowl, like the old wallpaper we had soaked and peeled. Beryl's skin was pale now, covered with fine cracks, rather like the shiny mud at the bottom of puddles drying up in early summer.

"Look what happened to my skin," she said. "Dieting. I weighed a hundred and sixty-nine pounds once, I took it off too fast and my face fell in on me. Now I've got this cream, though. It's made from a secret formula and you can't even buy it commercially. Smell it. See, it doesn't smell all perfumy. It smells serious."

She was patting the cream on her face with puffs of cotton wool, patting away until there was nothing to be seen on the surface.

"It smells like lard," I said.

"Christ Almighty, I hope I haven't been paying that kind of money to rub lard on my face. Don't tell your mother I swear."

She poured clean water into the drinking glass and wet her comb, then combed her hair wet and twisted each strand round her finger, clamping the twisted strand to her head with two crossed pins. I would be doing the same myself, a couple of years later.

"Always do your hair wet, else it's no good doing it up at all," Beryl said. "And always roll it under even if you want it to flip up. See?"

When I was doing my hair up—as I did for years—I sometimes thought of this, and thought that of all the pieces of advice people had given me, this was the one I had followed most carefully.

We put the lamp out and got into bed, and Beryl said, "I never knew it could get so dark. I've never known a dark that was as dark as this." She was whispering. I was slow to understand that she was comparing country nights to city nights, and I wondered if the darkness in Netterfield County could really be greater than that in California.

"Honey?" whispered Beryl. "Are there any animals outside?"

"Cows," I said.

"Yes, but wild animals? Are there bears?"

"Yes," I said. My father had once found bear tracks and droppings in the bush, and the apples had all been torn off a wild apple tree. That was years ago, when he was a young man.

Beryl moaned and giggled. "Think if Mr. Florence had to go out in the night and he ran into a bear!"

NEXT DAY was Sunday. Beryl and Mr. Florence drove my brothers and me to Sunday school in the Chrysler. That was at ten o'clock in the morning. They came back at eleven to bring my parents to church.

"Hop in," Beryl said to me. "You too," she said to the boys. "We're going for a drive."

Beryl was dressed up in a satiny ivory dress with red dots, and a red-lined frill over the hips, and red high-heeled shoes. Mr. Florence wore a pale-blue summer suit.

"Aren't you going to church?" I said. That was what people dressed up for, in my experience.

Beryl laughed. "Honey, this isn't Mr. Florence's kind of religion."

I was used to going straight from Sunday school into church, and sitting for another hour and a half. In summer, the open windows let in the cedary smell of the graveyard and the occasional, almost sacrilegious sound of a car swooshing by on the road. Today we spent this time driving through country I had never seen before. I had never seen it, though it was less than twenty miles from home. Our truck went to the cheese factory, to church, and to town on Saturday nights. The nearest thing to a drive was when it went to the dump. I had seen the near end of Bell's Lake, because that was where my father cut the ice in winter. You couldn't get close to it in summer; the shoreline was all choked up with bulrushes. I had thought that the other end of the lake would look pretty much the same, but when we drove there today, I saw cottages, docks and boats, dark water reflecting the trees. All this and I hadn't known about it. This too was Bell's Lake. I was glad to have seen it at last, but in some way not altogether glad of the surprise.

Finally, a white frame building appeared, with verandas and potted flowers, and some twinkling poplar trees in front. The Wildwood Inn. Today the same building is covered with stucco and done up with Tudor beams and called the Hideaway. The poplar trees have been cut down for a parking lot.

On the way back to the church to pick up my parents, Mr. Florence turned in to the farm next to ours, which belonged to the McAllisters. The McAllisters were Catholics. Our two families were neighborly but not close.

"Come on, boys, out you get," said Beryl to my brothers. "Not you," she said to me. "You stay put." She herded the little boys up to the porch, where some McAllisters were watching. They were in their raggedy home clothes, because their church, or Mass, or whatever it was, got out early. Mrs. McAllister came out and stood listening, rather dumbfounded, to Beryl's laughing talk.

Beryl came back to the car by herself. "There," she said. "They're going to play with the neighbor children."

Play with McAllisters? Besides being Catholics, all but the baby were girls.

"They've still got their good clothes on," I said.

"So what? Can't they have a good time with their good clothes on? I do!"

My parents were taken by surprise as well. Beryl got out and told my father he was to ride in the front seat, for the legroom. She got into the back, with my mother and me. Mr. Florence turned again onto the Bell's Lake road, and Beryl announced that we were all going to the Wildwood Inn for dinner.

"You're all dressed up, why not take advantage?" she said. "We dropped the boys off with your neighbors. I thought they might be too young to appreciate it. The neighbors were happy to have them." She said with a further emphasis that it was to be their treat. Hers and Mr. Florence's.

"Well, now," said my father. He probably didn't have five dollars in his pocket. "Well, now. I wonder do they let the farmers in?"

He made various jokes along this line. In the hotel dining room, which was all in white—white tablecloths, white painted chairs—with sweating glass water pitchers and high, whirring fans, he picked up a table napkin the size of a diaper and spoke to me in a loud whisper, "Can you tell me what to do with this thing? Can I put it on my head to keep the draft off?"

Of course he had eaten in hotel dining rooms before. He knew about table napkins and pie forks. And my mother knew—she wasn't even a country woman, to begin with. Nevertheless this was a huge event. Not exactly a pleasure—as Beryl must have meant it to be—but a huge, unsettling event. Eating a meal in public, only a few miles from home, eating in a big room full of people you didn't know, the food served by a stranger, a snippy-looking girl who was probably a college student working at a summer job.

"I'd like the rooster," my father said. "How long has he been in the pot?" It was only good manners, as he knew it, to joke with people who waited on him.

"Beg your pardon?" the girl said.

"Roast chicken," said Beryl. "Is that okay for everybody?"

Mr. Florence was looking gloomy. Perhaps he didn't care for jokes when it was his money that was being spent. Perhaps he had counted on something better than ice water to fill up the glasses.

The waitress put down a dish of celery and olives, and my mother said, "Just a minute while I give thanks." She bowed her head and said quietly but audibly, "Lord, bless this food to our use, and us to Thy service, for Christ's sake. Amen." Refreshed, she sat up straight and passed the dish to me, saying, "Mind the olives. There's stones in them."

Beryl was smiling around at the room.

The waitress came back with a basket of rolls.

"Parker House!" Beryl leaned over and breathed in their smell. "Eat them while they're hot enough to melt the butter!"

Mr. Florence twitched, and peered into the butter dish. "Is that what this is—butter? I thought it was Shirley Temple's curls."

His face was hardly less gloomy than before, but it was a joke, and his making it seemed to convey to us something of the very thing that had just been publicly asked for—a blessing.

"When he says something funny," said Beryl—who often referred to Mr. Florence as "he" even when he was right there—"you notice how he always keeps a straight face? That reminds me of Mama. I mean of our mama, Marietta's and mine. Daddy, when he made a joke you could see it coming a mile away—he couldn't keep it off his face—but Mama was another story. She could look so sour. But she could joke on her deathbed. In fact, she did that very thing. Marietta, remember when she was in bed in the front room the spring before she died?"

"I remember she was in bed in that room," my mother said. "Yes."

"Well, Daddy came in and she was lying there in her clean nightgown, with the covers off, because the German lady from next door had just been helping her take a wash, and she was still there tidying up the bed. So Daddy wanted to be cheerful, and he said, 'Spring must be coming. I saw a crow today.' This must have been in March. And Mama said quick as a shot, 'Well, you better cover me up then, before it looks in that window and gets any ideas!' The German lady—Daddy said she just about dropped the basin. Because it was true, Mama was skin and bones; she was dying. But she could joke."

Mr. Florence said, "Might as well when there's no use to cry."

"But she could carry a joke too far, Mama could. One time, one time, she wanted to give Daddy a scare. He was supposed to be interested in some girl that kept coming around to the works. Well, he was a big good-looking man. So Mama said, 'Well, I'll just do away with myself, and you can get on with her and see how you like it when I come back and haunt you.' He told her not to be so stupid, and he went off downtown. And Mama went out to the barn and climbed on a chair and put a rope around her neck. Didn't she, Marietta? Marietta went looking for her and she found her like that!"

My mother bent her head and put her hands in her lap, almost as if she was getting ready to say another grace.

"Daddy told me all about it, but I can remember anyway. I remember Marietta tearing off down the hill in her nightie, and I guess the German lady saw her go, and she came out and was looking for Mama, and somehow we all ended up in the barn—me too, and some kids I was playing with—and there was Mama up on a chair preparing to give Daddy the fright of his life. She'd sent Marietta after him. And the German lady starts wailing, 'Oh, missus, come down missus, think of your little *kindren*'—'*kindren*' is the German for 'children'—'think of your *kindren*,' and so on. Until it was me standing there—I was just a little squirt, but I was the one noticed that rope. My eyes followed that rope up and up and I saw it was just hanging over the beam, just flung there—it wasn't tied at all! Marietta hadn't noticed that, the German lady hadn't noticed it. But I just spoke up and said, 'Mama, how are you going to manage to hang yourself without that rope tied around the beam?' "

Mr. Florence said, "That'd be a tough one."

"I spoiled her game. The German lady made coffee and we went over there and had a few treats, and, Marietta, you couldn't find Daddy after all, could you? You could hear Marietta howling, coming up the hill, a block away."

"Natural for her to be upset," my father said.

"Sure it was. Mama went too far."

"She meant it," my mother said. "She meant it more than you give her credit for."

"She meant to get a rise out of Daddy. That was their whole life together. He always said she was a hard woman to live with, but she had a lot of character. I believe he missed that, with Gladys."

"I wouldn't know," my mother said, in that particularly steady voice with which she always spoke of her father. "What he did say or didn't say."

"People are dead now," said my father. "It isn't up to us to judge."

"I know," said Beryl. "I know Marietta's always had a different view."

My mother looked at Mr. Florence and smiled quite easily and radiantly. "I'm sure you don't know what to make of all these family matters."

The one time that I visited Beryl, when Beryl was an old woman, all knobby and twisted up with arthritis, Beryl said, "Marietta got all Daddy's looks. And she never did a thing with herself. Remember her wearing that old navy-blue crêpe dress when we went to the hotel that time? Of course, I know it was probably all she had, but did it have to be all she had? You know, I was scared of her somehow. I couldn't stay in a room alone with her. But she had outstanding looks." Trying to remember an occasion when I had noticed my mother's looks, I thought of the time in the hotel, my mother's pale-olive skin against the heavy white, coiled hair, her open, handsome face smiling at Mr. Florence—as if he was the one to be forgiven.

I DIDN'T HAVE a problem right away with Beryl's story. For one thing,

I was hungry and greedy, and a lot of my attention went to the roast chicken and gravy and mashed potatoes laid on the plate with an ice-cream scoop and the bright diced vegetables out of a can, which I thought much superior to those fresh from the garden. For dessert, I had a butter-scotch sundae, an agonizing choice over chocolate. The others had plain vanilla ice cream.

Why shouldn't Beryl's version of the same event be different from my mother's? Beryl was strange in every way—everything about her was slanted, seen from a new angle. It was my mother's version that held, for a time. It absorbed Beryl's story, closed over it. But Beryl's story didn't vanish; it stayed sealed off for years, but it wasn't gone. It was like the knowledge of that hotel and dining room. I knew about it now, though I didn't think of it as a place to go back to. And indeed, without Beryl's or Mr. Florence's money, I couldn't. But I knew it was there.

The next time I was in the Wildwood Inn, in fact, was after I was married. The Lions Club had a banquet and dance there. The man I had married, Dan Casey, was a Lion. You could get a drink there by that time. Dan Casey wouldn't have gone anywhere you couldn't. Then the place was remodelled into the Hideaway, and now they have strippers every night but Sunday. On Thursday nights, they have a male stripper. I go there with people from the real-estate office to celebrate birthdays or other big events.

THE FARM was sold for five thousand dollars in 1965. A man from Toronto bought it, for a hobby farm or just an investment. After a couple of years, he rented it to a commune. They stayed there, different people drifting on and off, for a dozen years or so. They raised goats and sold the milk to the health-food store that had opened up in town. They painted a rainbow across the side of the barn that faced the road. They hung tie-dyed sheets over the windows, and let the long grass and flowering weeds reclaim the yard. My parents had finally got electricity in, but these people didn't use it. They preferred oil lamps and the woodstove, and taking their dirty clothes to town. People said they wouldn't know how to handle lamps or wood fires, and they would burn the place down. But they didn't. In fact, they didn't manage badly. They kept the house and barn in some sort of repair and they worked a big garden. They even dusted their pota-toes against blight—though I heard that there was some sort of row about this and some of the stricter members left. The place actually looked a lot better than many of the farms round about that were still in the hands of the original families. The McAllister son had started a wrecking business on their place. My own brothers were long gone.

I knew I was not being reasonable, but I had the feeling that I'd rather see the farm suffer outright neglect—I'd sooner see it in the hands of hoodlums and scroungers—than see that rainbow on the barn, and some letters that looked Egyptian painted on the wall of the house. They seemed a mockery. I even disliked the sight of those people when they came to town—the men with their hair in ponytails, and with holes in their overalls that I believed were cut on purpose, and the women with long hair and no makeup and their meek, superior expressions. What do you know about life, I felt like asking them. What makes you think you can come here and mock my father and mother and their life and their poverty? But when I thought of the rainbow and those letters, I knew they weren't trying to mock or imitate my parents' life. They had displaced that life, hardly knowing it existed. They had set up in its place these beliefs and customs of their own, which I hoped would fail them.

That happened, more or less. The commune disintegrated. The goats disappeared. Some of the women moved to town, cut their hair, put on makeup, and got jobs as waitresses or cashiers to support their children. The Toronto man put the place up for sale, and after about a year it was sold for more than ten times what he had paid for it. A young couple from Ottawa bought it. They have painted the outside a pale gray with oyster trim, and have put in skylights and a handsome front door with carriage lamps on either side. Inside, they've changed it around so much that I've been told I'd never recognize it.

I did get in once, before this happened, during the year that the house was empty and for sale. The company I work for was handling it, and I had a key, though the house was being shown by another agent. I let myself in on a Sunday afternoon. I had a man with me, not a client but a friend—Bob Marks, whom I was seeing a lot at the time.

"This is that hippie place," Bob Marks said when I stopped the car. "I've been by here before."

He was a lawyer, a Catholic, separated from his wife. He thought he wanted to settle down and start up a practice here in town. But there already was one Catholic lawyer. Business was slow. A couple of times a week, Bob Marks would be fairly drunk before supper.

"It's more than that," I said. "It's where I was born. Where I grew up." We walked through the weeds, and I unlocked the door.

He said that he had thought, from the way I talked, that it would be farther out.

"It seemed farther then."

All the rooms were bare, and the floors swept clean. The woodwork was freshly painted—I was surprised to see no smudges on the glass. Some new panes, some old wavy ones. Some of the walls had been stripped of their paper and painted. A wall in the kitchen was painted a deep blue, with an enormous dove on it. On a wall in the front room, giant sunflowers appeared, and a butterfly of almost the same size.

Bob Marks whistled. "Somebody was an artist."

"If that's what you want to call it," I said, and turned back to the kitchen. The same woodstove was there. "My mother once burned up three thousand dollars," I said. "She burned three thousand dollars in that stove."

He whistled again, differently. "What do you mean? She threw in a check?"

"No, no. It was in bills. She did it deliberately. She went into town to the bank and she had them give it all to her, in a shoebox. She brought it home and put it in the stove. She put it in just a few bills at a time, so it wouldn't make too big a blaze. My father stood and watched her."

"What are you talking about?" said Bob Marks. "I thought you were so poor."

"We were. We were very poor."

"So how come she had three thousand dollars? That would be like thirty thousand today. Easily. More than thirty thousand today."

"It was her legacy," I said. "It was what she got from her father. Her father died in Seattle and left her three thousand dollars, and she burned it up because she hated him. She didn't want his money. She hated him."

"That's a lot of hate," Bob Marks said.

"That isn't the point. Her hating him, or whether he was bad enough for her to have a right to hate him. Not likely he was. That isn't the point."

"Money," he said. "Money's always the point."

"No. My father letting her do it is the point. To me it is. My father stood and watched and he never protested. If anybody had tried to stop her, he would have protected her. I consider that love."

"Some people would consider it lunacy."

I remember that that had been Beryl's opinion, exactly.

I went into the front room and stared at the butterfly, with its pink-and-orange wings. Then I went into the front bedroom and found two human figures painted on the wall. A man and a woman holding hands and facing straight ahead. They were naked, and larger than life size.

"It reminds me of that John Lennon and Yoko Ono picture," I said to Bob Marks, who had come in behind me. "That record cover, wasn't it?" I didn't want him to think that anything he had said in the kitchen had upset me.

Bob Marks said, "Different color hair."

That was true. Both figures had yellow hair painted in a solid mass, the way they do it in the comic strips. Horsetails of yellow hair curling over their shoulders and little pigtails of yellow hair decorating their not so private parts. Their skin was a flat beige pink and their eyes a staring blue, the same blue that was on the kitchen wall.

I noticed that they hadn't quite finished peeling the wallpaper away before making this painting. In the corner, there was some paper left that matched the paper on the other walls—a modernistic design of intersecting pink and gray and mauve bubbles. The man from Toronto must have put that on. The paper underneath hadn't been stripped off when this new paper went on. I could see an edge of it, the cornflowers on a white ground.

"I guess this was where they carried on their sexual shenanigans," Bob Marks said, in a tone familiar to me. That thickened, sad, uneasy, but determined tone. The not particularly friendly lust of middle-aged respectable men.

I didn't say anything. I worked away some of the bubble paper to see more of the cornflowers. Suddenly I hit a loose spot, and ripped away a big swatch of it. But the cornflower paper came too, and a little shower of dried plaster.

"Why is it?" I said. "Just tell me, why is it that no man can mention a place like this without getting around to the subject of sex in about two seconds flat? Just say the words *hippie* or *commune* and all you guys can think about is screwing! As if there wasn't anything at all behind it but orgies and fancy combinations and non-stop screwing! I get so sick of that— it's all so stupid it just makes me sick!"

IN THE CAR, on the way home from the hotel, we sat as before—the men in the front seat, the women in the back. I was in the middle, Beryl and my mother on either side of me. Their heated bodies pressed against me, through cloth; their smells crowded out the smells of the cedar bush we passed through, and the pockets of bog, where Beryl exclaimed at the water lilies. Beryl smelled of all those things in pots and bottles. My mother smelled of flour and hard soap and the warm crêpe of her good dress and the kerosene she had used to take the spots off.

"A lovely meal," my mother said. "Thank you, Beryl. Thank you, Mr. Florence."

"I don't know who is going to be fit to do the milking," my father said. "Now that we've all ate in such style."

"Speaking of money," said Beryl—though nobody actually had been— "do you mind my asking what you did with yours? I put mine in real estate. Real estate in California—you can't lose. I was thinking you could get an electric stove, so you wouldn't have to bother with a fire in summer or fool with that coal-oil thing, either one."

All the other people in the car laughed, even Mr. Florence.

"That's a good idea, Beryl," said my father. "We could use it to set things on till we get the electricity."

"Oh, Lord," said Beryl. "How stupid can I get?"

"And we don't actually have the money, either," my mother said cheerfully, as if she was continuing the joke.

But Beryl spoke sharply. "You wrote me you got it. You got the same as me."

My father half turned in his seat. "What money are you talking about?" he said. "What's this money?"

"From Daddy's will," Beryl said. "That you got last year. Look, maybe I shouldn't have asked. If you had to pay something off, that's still a good use, isn't it? It doesn't matter. We're all family here. Practically."

"We didn't have to use it to pay anything off," my mother said. "I burned it."

Then she told how she went into town in the truck, one day almost a year ago, and got them to give her the money in a box she had brought along for the purpose. She took it home, and put it in the stove and burned it.

My father turned around and faced the road ahead.

I could feel Beryl twisting beside me while my mother talked. She was twisting, and moaning a little, as if she had a pain she couldn't suppress. At the end of the story, she let out a sound of astonishment and suffering, an angry groan.

"So you burned up money!" she said. "You burned up money in the stove."

My mother was still cheerful. "You sound as if I'd burned up one of my children."

"You burned their chances. You burned up everything the money could have got for them."

"The last thing my children need is money. None of us need his money."

"That's criminal," Beryl said harshly. She pitched her voice into the front seat: "Why did you let her?"

"He wasn't there," my mother said. "Nobody was there."

My father said, "It was her money, Beryl."

"Never mind," Beryl said. "That's criminal."

"Criminal is for when you call in the police," Mr. Florence said. Like other things he had said that day, this created a little island of surprise and a peculiar gratitude.

Gratitude not felt by all.

"Don't you pretend this isn't the craziest thing you ever heard of,"

Beryl shouted into the front seat. "Don't you pretend you don't think so! Because it is, and you do. You think just the same as me!"

MY FATHER did not stand in the kitchen watching my mother feed the money into the flames. It wouldn't appear so. He did not know about it— it seems fairly clear, if I remember everything, that he did not know about it until that Sunday afternoon in Mr. Florence's Chrysler, when my mother told them all together. Why, then, can I see the scene so clearly, just as I described it to Bob Marks (and to others—he was not the first)? I see my father standing by the table in the middle of the room—the table with the drawer in it for knives and forks, and the scrubbed oilcloth on top—and there is the box of money on the table. My mother is carefully dropping the bills into the fire. She holds the stove lid by the blackened lifter in one hand. And my father, standing by, seems not just to be permitting her to do this but to be protecting her. A solemn scene, but not crazy. People doing something that seems to them natural and necessary. At least, one of them is doing what seems natural and necessary, and the other believes that the important thing is for that person to be free, to go ahead. They understand that other people might not think so. They do not care.

How hard it is for me to believe that I made that up. It seems so much the truth it is the truth; it's what I believe about them. I haven't stopped believing it. But I have stopped telling that story. I never told it to anyone again after telling it to Bob Marks. I don't think so. I didn't stop just because it wasn't, strictly speaking, true. I stopped because I saw that I had to give up expecting people to see it the way I did. I had to give up expecting them to approve of any part of what was done. How could I even say that I approved of it myself? If I had been the sort of person who approved of that, who could do it, I wouldn't have done all I have done—run away from home to work in a restaurant in town when I was fifteen, gone to night school to learn typing and bookkeeping, got into the real-estate office, and finally become a licensed agent. I wouldn't be divorced. My father wouldn't have died in the county home. My hair would be white, as it has been naturally for years, instead of a color called Copper Sunrise. And not one of these things would I change, not really, if I could.

Bob Marks was a decent man—good-hearted, sometimes with imagination. After I had lashed out at him like that, he said, "You don't need to be so tough on us." In a moment, he said, "Was this your room when you were a little girl?" He thought that was why the mention of the sexual shenanigans had upset me.

And I thought it would be just as well to let him think that. I said yes, yes, it was my room when I was a little girl. It was just as well to make up right away. Moments of kindness and reconciliation are worth having, even if the parting has to come sooner or later. I wonder if those moments aren't more valued, and deliberately gone after, in the setups some people like myself have now, than they were in those old marriages, where love and grudges could be growing underground, so confused and stubborn, it must have seemed they had forever.

# *Lichen*

~

STELLA'S FATHER built the place as a summer house, on the clay bluffs overlooking Lake Huron. Her family always called it "the summer cottage." David was surprised when he first saw it, because it had none of the knotty-pine charm, the battened-down coziness, that those words suggested. A city boy, from what Stella's family called "a different background," he had no experience of summer places. It was and is a high, bare wooden house, painted gray—a copy of the old farmhouses nearby, though perhaps less substantial. In front of it are the steep bluffs—they are not so substantial, either, but have held so far—and a long flight of steps down to the beach. Behind it is a small fenced garden, where Stella grows vegetables with considerable skill and coaxing, a short sandy lane, and a jungle of wild blackberry bushes.

As David turns the car in to the lane, Stella steps out of these bushes, holding a colander full of berries. She is a short, fat, white-haired woman, wearing jeans and a dirty T-shirt. There is nothing underneath these clothes, as far as he can see, to support or restrain any part of her.

"Look what's happened to Stella," says David, fuming. "She's turned into a troll."

Catherine, who has never met Stella before, says decently, "Well. She's older."

"Older than what, Catherine? Older than the house? Older than Lake Huron? Older than the cat?"

There is a cat asleep on the path beside the vegetable garden. A large ginger tom with ears mutilated in battle, and one grayed-over eye. His name is Hercules and he dates from David's time.

"She's an older woman," says Catherine in a flutter of defiance. Even defiant, she's meek. "You know what I mean."

David thinks that Stella has done this on purpose. It isn't just an acceptance of natural deterioration—oh, no, it's much more. Stella would always dramatize. But it isn't just Stella. There's the sort of woman who has to come bursting out of the female envelope at this age, flaunting fat or an indecent scrawniness, sprouting warts and facial hair, refusing to cover pasty veined legs, almost gleeful about it, as if this was what she'd wanted to do all along. Man-haters, from the start. You can't say a thing like that out loud nowadays.

He has parked too close to the berry bushes—too close for Catherine, who slides out of the car on the passenger side and is immediately in trouble. Catherine is slim enough, but her dress has a full skirt and long, billowy sleeves. It's a dress of cobwebby cotton, shading from pink to rose, with scores of tiny, irregular pleats that look like wrinkles. A pretty dress but hardly a good choice for Stella's domain. The blackberry bushes catch it everywhere, and Catherine has to keep picking herself loose.

"David, really, you could have left her some room," says Stella.

Catherine laughs at her predicament. "I'm all right, I'm okay, really."

"Stella, Catherine," says David, introducing.

"Have some berries, Catherine," says Stella sympathetically. "David?"

David shakes his head, but Catherine takes a couple. "Lovely," she says. "Warm from the sun."

"I'm sick of the sight of them," says Stella.

Close up, Stella looks a bit better—with her smooth, tanned skin, childishly cropped hair, wide brown eyes. Catherine, drooping over her, is a tall, frail, bony woman with fair hair and sensitive skin. Her skin is so sensitive it won't stand any makeup at all, and is easily inflamed by colds, foods, emotions. Lately she has taken to wearing blue eye shadow and black mascara, which David thinks is a mistake. Blackening those sparse wisps of lashes emphasizes the watery blue of her eyes, which look as if they couldn't stand daylight, and the dryness of the skin underneath. When David first met Catherine, about eighteen months ago, he thought she was a little over thirty. He saw many remnants of girlishness; he loved her fairness and tall fragility. She has aged since then. And she was older than he thought to start with—she is nearing forty.

"But what will you do with them?" Catherine says to Stella. "Make jam?"

"I've made about five million jars of jam already," Stella says. "I put them in little jars with those artsy-fartsy gingham tops on them and I give them away to all my neighbors who are too lazy or too smart to pick their own. Sometimes I don't know why I don't just let Nature's bounty rot on the vine."

"It isn't on the vine," says David. "It's on those god-awful thornbushes, which ought to be cleaned out and burned. Then there'd be room to park a car."

Stella says to Catherine, "Listen to him, still sounding like a husband."

Stella and David were married for twenty-one years. They have been separated for eight.

"It's true, David," says Stella contritely. "I should clean them out. There's a long list of things I never get around to doing. Come on in and I'll get changed."

"We'll have to stop at the liquor store," says David. "I didn't get a chance."

Once every summer, he makes this visit, timing it as nearly as he can to Stella's father's birthday. He always brings the same present—a bottle of Scotch whisky. This birthday is his father-in-law's ninety-third. He is in a nursing home a few miles away, where Stella can visit him two or three times a week.

"I just have to wash," Stella says. "And put on something bright. Not for Daddy, he's completely blind now. But I think the others like it, the sight of me dressed in pink or blue or something cheers them up the way a balloon would. You two have time for a quick drink. Actually, you can make me one too."

She leads them, single file, up the path to the house. Hercules doesn't move.

"Lazy beast," says Stella. "He's getting about as bad as Daddy. You think the house needs painting, David?"

"Yes."

"Daddy always said every seven years. I don't know—I'm considering putting on siding. I'd get more protection from the wind. Even since I winterized, it sometimes feels as if I'm living in an open crate."

Stella lives here all year round. In the beginning, one or the other of the children would often be with her. But now Paul is studying forestry in Oregon and Deirdre is teaching at an English-language school in Brazil.

"But could you get anything like that color in siding?" says Catherine. "It's so nice, that lovely weather-beaten color."

"I was thinking of cream," says Stella.

ALONE in this house, in this community, Stella leads a busy and sometimes chaotic life. Evidence of this is all around them as they progress through the back porch and the kitchen to the living room. Here are some plants she has been potting, and the jam she mentioned—not all given away but waiting, she explains, for bake sales and the fall fair. Here is her winemaking apparatus; then, in the long living room, overlooking the lake, her typewriter, surrounded by stacks of books and papers.

"I'm writing my memoirs," says Stella. She rolls her eyes at Catherine. "I'll stop for a cash payment. No, it's okay, David, I'm writing an article on the old lighthouse." She points the lighthouse out to Catherine. "You can see it from this window if you squeeze right down to the end. I'm doing a piece for the historical society and the local paper. Quite the budding authoress."

Besides the historical society, she says, she belongs to a play-reading group, a church choir, the winemakers' club, and an informal group in which the members entertain one another weekly at dinner parties that have a fixed (low) cost.

"To test our ingenuity," she says. "Always testing something."

And that is only the more or less organized part of it. Her friends are a mixed bag. People who have retired here, who live in remodelled farm-houses or winterized summer cottages; younger people of diverse back-ground who have settled on the land, taking over rocky old farms that born-and-bred farmers won't bother about anymore. And a local dentist and his friend, who are gay.

"We're marvellously tolerant around here now," shouts Stella, who has gone into the bathroom and is conveying her information over the sound of running water. "We don't insist on matching up the sexes. It's nice for us pensioned-off wives. There are about half a dozen of us. One's a weaver."

"I can't find the tonic," yells David from the kitchen.

"It's in cans. The box on the floor by the fridge. This woman has her own sheep. The weaver woman. She has her own spinning wheel. She spins the wool and then she weaves it into cloth."

"Holy shit," says David thoughtfully.

Stella has turned the tap off, and is splashing.

"I thought you'd like that. See, I'm not so far gone. I just make jam."

In a moment, she comes out with a towel wrapped around her, saying, "Where's my drink?" The top corners of the towel are tucked together under one arm, the bottom corners are flapping dangerously free. She accepts a gin-and-tonic.

"I'll drink it while I dress. I have two new summer outfits. One is flamingo and one is turquoise. I can mix and match. Either way, I look stupendous."

Catherine comes from the living room to get her drink, and takes the first two gulps as if it were a glass of water.

"I love this house," she says with a soft vehemence. "I really do. It's so primitive and unpretentious. It's full of light. I've been trying to think what it reminds me of, and now I know. Did you ever see that old Ing-mar Bergman movie where there is a family living in a summer house on an island? A lovely shabby house. The girl was going crazy. I remember thinking at the time, That's what summer houses should be like, and they never are."

"That was the one where God was a helicopter," David says. "And the girl fooled around with her brother in the bottom of a boat."

"We never had anything quite so interesting going on around here, I'm afraid," says Stella over the bedroom wall. "I can't say I ever really appreciated Bergman movies. I always thought they were sort of bleak and neurotic."

"Conversations tend to be widespread around here," says David to Catherine. "Notice how none of the partitions go up to the ceiling? Except the bathroom, thank God. It makes for a lot of family life."

"Whenever David and I wanted to say something private, we had to put our heads under the covers," Stella says. She comes out of the bedroom wearing a pair of turquoise stretch pants and a sleeveless top. The top has turquoise flowers and fronds on a white background. At least, she seems to have put on a brassiere. A light-colored strap is visible, biting the flesh of her shoulder.

"Remember one night we were in bed," she says, "and we were talking about getting a new car, saying we wondered what kind of mileage you got with a such-and-such, I forget what. Well, Daddy was always mad about cars, he knew everything, and all of a sudden we heard him say, 'Twenty-eight miles to the gallon,' or whatever, just as if he were right there on the other side of the bed. Of course, he wasn't—he was lying in bed in his own room. David was quite blasé about it; he just said, 'Oh, thank you, sir,' as if we'd been including Daddy all along!"

WHEN David comes out of the liquor store, in the village, Stella has rolled down the car window and is talking to a couple she introduces as Ron and Mary. They are in their mid-sixties probably, but very tanned and trim. They wear matching plaid pants and white sweatshirts and plaid caps.

"Glad to meet you," says Ron. "So you're up here seeing how the smart folks live!" He has the sort of jolly voice that suggests boxing feints, playful punches. "When are you going to retire and come up here and join us?"

That makes David wonder what Stella has been telling them about the separation.

"It's not my turn to retire yet."

"Retire early! That's what a lot of us up here did! We got ourselves out of the whole routine. Toiling and moiling and earning and spending."

"Well, I'm not in that," says David. "I'm just a civil servant. We take the taxpayers' money and try not to do any work at all."

"That's not true," says Stella, scolding—wifely. "He works in the Department of Education and he works hard. He just will never admit it."

"A simple serpent!" says Mary, with a crow of pleasure. "I used to work in Ottawa—that was eons ago—and we used to call ourselves simple serpents! Civil serpents. Servants."

Mary is not in the least fat, but something has happened to her chin that usually happens to the chins of fat women. It has collapsed into a series of terraces flowing into her neck.

"Kidding aside," says Ron. "This is a wonderful life. You wouldn't believe how much we find to do. The day is never long enough."

"You have a lot of interests?" says David. He is perfectly serious now, respectful and attentive.

This is a tone that warns Stella, and she tries to deflect Mary. "What are you going to do with the material you brought back from Morocco?"

"I can't decide. It would make a gorgeous dress but it's hardly me. I might just end up putting it on a bed."

"There's so many activities, you can just keep up forever," Ron says. "For instance, skiing. Cross-country. We were out nineteen days in the month of February. Beautiful weather this year. We don't have to drive anywhere. We just go down the back lane—"

"I try to keep up my interests too," says David. "I think it keeps you young."

"There is no doubt it does!"

David has one hand in the inner pocket of his jacket. He brings out something he keeps cupped in his palm, shows it to Ron with a deprecating smile.

"One of my interests," he says.

"WANT to see what I showed Ron?" David says later. They are driving along the bluffs to the nursing home.

"No, thank you."

"I hope Ron liked it," David says pleasantly.

He starts to sing. He and Stella met while singing madrigals at university. Or that's what Stella tells people. They sang other things too, not just madrigals. "David was a skinny innocent bit of a lad with a pure sweet tenor and I was a stocky little brute of a girl with a big deep alto," Stella likes to say. "There was nothing he could do about it. Destiny."

"O, Mistress mine, where are you roaming?" sings David, who has a fine tenor voice to this day:

> *"O, Mistress mine, where are you roaming?*
> *O, Mistress mine, where are you roaming?*
> *O, stay and hear, your true love's coming,*
> *O, stay and hear, your true love's coming,*
> *Who can sing, both High and Low."*

. . .

Down on the beach, at either end of Stella's property, there are long, low walls of rocks that have been stacked in baskets of wire, stretching out into the water. They are there to protect the beach from erosion. On one of these walls, Catherine is sitting, looking out at the water, with the lake breeze blowing her filmy dress and her long hair. She could be posed for a picture. She might be advertising something, Stella thinks—either something very intimate, and potentially disgusting, or something truly respectable and rather splendid, like life insurance.

"I've been meaning to ask you," says Stella. "Is there anything the matter with her eyes?"

"Eyes?" says David.

"Her eyesight. It's just that she doesn't seem to be quite focussing, close up. I don't know how to describe it."

Stella and David are standing at the living-room window. Returned from the nursing home, they each hold a fresh, restorative drink. They have hardly spoken on the way home, but the silence has not been hostile. They are feeling chastened and reasonably companionable.

"There isn't anything wrong with her eyesight that I know of."

Stella goes into the kitchen, gets out the roasting pan, rubs the roast of pork with cloves of garlic and fresh sage leaves.

"You know, there's a smell women get," says David, standing in the living-room doorway. "It's when they know you don't want them anymore. Stale."

Stella slaps the meat over.

"Those groins are going to have to be rewired entirely," she says. "The wire is just worn to cobwebs in some places. You should see. The power of water. It can wear out tough wire. I'll have to have a work party this fall. Just make a lot of food and ask some people over and make sure enough of them are able-bodied. That's what we all do."

She puts the roast in the oven and rinses her hands.

"It was Catherine you were telling me about last summer, wasn't it? She was the one you said was inclined to be fey."

David groans. "I said what?"

"Inclined to be fey." Stella bangs around, getting out apples, potatoes, onions.

"All right, tell me," says David, coming into the kitchen to stand close to her. "Tell me what I said?"

"That's all, really. I don't remember anything else."

"Stella. Tell me all I said about her."

"I don't, really. I don't remember."

Of course she remembers. She remembers the exact tone in which he said "inclined to be fey." The pride and irony in his voice. In the throes of love, he can be counted on to speak of the woman with tender disparagement—with amazement, even. He likes to say that it's crazy, he does not understand it, he can plainly see that this person isn't his kind of person at all. And yet, and yet, and yet. And yet it's beyond him, irresistible. He told Stella that Catherine believed in horoscopes, was a vegetarian, and painted weird pictures in which tiny figures were enclosed in plastic bubbles.

"The roast," says Stella, suddenly alarmed. "Will she eat meat?"

"What?"

"Will Catherine eat meat?"

"She may not eat anything. She may be too spaced out."

"I'm making an apple-and-onion casserole. It'll be quite substantial. Maybe she'll eat that."

Last summer he said, "She's a hippie survivor, really. She doesn't even know those times are gone. I don't think she's ever read a newspaper. She hasn't the remotest idea of what's going on in the world. Unless she's heard it from a fortune-teller. That's her idea of reality. I don't think she can read a map. She's all instinct. Do you know what she did? She went to Ireland to see the Book of Kells. She'd heard the Book of Kells was in Ireland. So she just got off the plane at Shannon Airport, and asked somebody the way to the Book of Kells. And you know what, she found it!"

Stella asked how this fey creature earned the money for trips to Ireland.

"Oh, she has a job," David said. "Sort of a job. She teaches art, part time. God knows what she teaches them. To paint by their horoscopes, I think."

Now he says, "There's somebody else. I haven't told Catherine. Do you think she senses it? I think she does. I think she senses it."

He is leaning against the counter, watching Stella peel apples. He reaches quickly into his inside pocket, and before Stella can turn her head away he is holding a Polaroid snapshot in front of her eyes.

"That's my new girl," he says.

"It looks like lichen," says Stella, her paring knife halting. "Except it's rather dark. It looks to me like moss on a rock."

"Don't be dumb, Stella. Don't be cute. You can see her. See her legs?"

Stella puts the paring knife down and squints obediently. There is a flattened-out breast far away on the horizon. And the legs spreading into the foreground. The legs are spread wide—smooth, golden, monumental: fallen columns. Between them is the dark blot she called moss, or lichen. But it's really more like the dark pelt of an animal, with the head and tail and feet chopped off. Dark silky pelt of some unlucky rodent.

"Well, I can see now," she says, in a sensible voice.

"Her name is Dina. Dina without an 'h.' She's twenty-two years old."

Stella won't ask him to put the picture away, or even to stop holding it in front of her face.

"She's a bad girl," says David. "Oh, she's a bad girl! She went to school to the nuns. There are no bad girls like those convent-school girls, once they decide to go wild! She was a student at the art college where Catherine teaches. She quit. Now she's a cocktail waitress."

"That doesn't sound so terribly depraved to me. Deirdre was a cocktail waitress for a while when she was at college."

"Dina's not like Deirdre."

At last, the hand holding the picture drops, and Stella picks up her knife and resumes peeling the apples. But David doesn't put the picture away. He starts to, then changes his mind.

"The little witch," he says. "She torments my soul."

His voice when he talks about this girl seems to Stella peculiarly artificial. But who is she to say, with David, what is artificial and what is not? This special voice of his is rather high-pitched, monotonous, insistent, with a deliberate, cruel sweetness. Whom does he want to be cruel to— Stella, Catherine, the girl, himself? Stella gives a sigh that is noisier and more exasperated than she meant it to be and puts down an apple half-peeled. She goes into the living room and looks out the window.

Catherine is climbing off the wall. Or she's trying to. Her dress is caught in the wire.

"That pretty li'l old dress is giving her all sorts of trouble today," Stella says, surprising herself with the bad accent and a certain viciousness of tone.

"Stella. I wish you'd keep this picture for me."

"Me keep it?"

"I'm afraid I'll show it to Catherine. I keep wanting to. I'm afraid I will."

Catherine has disengaged herself, and has spotted them at the window. She waves, and Stella waves back.

"I'm sure you have others," says Stella. "Pictures."

"Not with me. It's not that I want to hurt her."

"Then don't."

"She makes me want to hurt her. She hangs on me with her weepy looks. She takes pills. Mood elevators. She drinks. Sometimes I think the best thing to do would be to give her the big chop. *Coup de grâce. Coup de grâce*, Catherine. Here you are. Big chop. But I worry about what she'll do."

"Mood elevator," says Stella. "Mood elevator, going up!"

"I'm serious, Stella. Those pills are deadly."

"That's your affair."

"Very funny."

"I didn't even mean it to be. Whenever something slips out like that, I always pretend I meant it, though. I'll take all the credit I can get!"

THESE THREE people feel better at dinnertime than any of them might have expected. David feels better because he has remembered that there is a telephone booth across from the liquor store. Stella always feels better when she has cooked a meal and it has turned out so well. Catherine's reasons for feeling better are chemical.

Conversation is not difficult. Stella tells stories that she has come across in doing research for her article, about wrecks on the Great Lakes. Catherine knows something about wrecks. She has a boyfriend—a former boyfriend—who is a diver. David is gallant enough to assert that he is jealous of this fellow, does not care to hear about his deep-water prowess. Perhaps this is the truth.

After dinner, David says he needs to go for a walk. Catherine tells him to go ahead. "Go on," she says merrily. "We don't need you here. Stella and I will get along fine without you!"

Stella wonders where this new voice of Catherine's comes from, this pert and rather foolish and flirtatious voice. Drink wouldn't do it. Whatever Catherine has taken has made her sharper, not blunter. Several layers of wispy apology, tentative flattery, fearfulness, or hopefulness have simply blown away in this brisk chemical breeze.

But when Catherine gets up and tries to clear the table it becomes apparent that the sharpening is not physical. Catherine bumps into a corner of the counter. She makes Stella think of an amputee. Not much cut off, just the tips of her fingers and maybe her toes. Stella has to keep an eye on her, relieving her of the dishes before they slide away.

"Did you notice the hair?" says Catherine. Her voice goes up and down like a Ferris wheel; it dips and sparkles. "He's dyeing it!"

"David is?" says Stella, in genuine surprise.

"Every time he'd think of it, he'd tilt his head back, so you couldn't get too close a look. I think he was afraid you'd say something. He's slightly afraid of you. Actually, it looks very natural."

"I really didn't notice."

"He started a couple of months ago. I said, 'David, what does it matter—your hair was getting gray when I fell in love with you, do you think it's going to bother me now?' Love is strange, it does strange things. David is actually a sensitive person—he's a vulnerable person." Stella rescues a wineglass that is drooping from Catherine's fingers. "It can make you mean. Love can make you mean. If you feel dependent on somebody, then you can be mean to them. I understand that in David."

They drink mead at dinner. This is the first time Stella has tried this batch of homemade mead and she thinks now how good it was, dry and sparkling. It looked like champagne. She checks to see if there is any left in the bottle. About half a glass. She pours it out for herself, sets her glass behind the blender, rinses the bottle.

"You have a good life here," Catherine says.

"I have a fine life. Yes."

"I feel a change coming in my life. I love David, but I've been submerged in this love for so long. Too long. Do you know what I mean? I was down looking at the waves and I started saying, 'He loves me, he loves me not.' I do that often. Then I thought, Well, there isn't any end to the waves, not like there is to a daisy. Or even like there is to my footsteps, if I start counting them to the end of the block. I thought, The waves never, ever come to an end. So then I knew, this is a message for me."

"Just leave the pots, Catherine. I'll deal with them later."

Why doesn't Stella say, "Sit down, I can manage better by myself"? It's a thing she has said often to helpers less inept than Catherine. She doesn't say it because she's wary of something. Catherine's state seems so brittle and delicate. Tripping her up could have consequences.

"He loves me, he loves me not," says Catherine. "That's the way it goes. It goes forever. That's what the waves were trying to tell me."

"Just out of curiosity," says Stella, "do you believe in horoscopes?"

"You mean have I had mine done? No, not really. I know people who have. I've thought about it. I guess I don't quite believe in it enough to spend the money. I look at those things in the newspapers sometimes."

"You read the newspapers?"

"I read parts. I get one delivered. I don't read it all."

"And you eat meat? You ate pork for dinner."

Catherine doesn't seem to mind being interrogated, or even to notice that this is an interrogation.

"Well, I can live on salads, particularly at this time of year. But I do eat meat from time to time. I'm a sort of very lackadaisical vegetarian. It was fantastic, that roast. Did you put garlic on it?"

"Garlic and sage and rosemary."

"It was delicious."

"I'm glad."

Catherine sits down suddenly, and spreads out her long legs in a tomboyish way, letting her dress droop between them. Hercules, who has slept all through dinner on the fourth chair, at the other side of the table, takes a determined leap and lands on what there is of her lap.

Catherine laughs. "Crazy cat."

"If he bothers you, just bat him off."

Freed now of the need to watch Catherine, Stella gets busy scraping and stacking the plates, rinsing glasses, cleaning off the table, shaking the cloth, wiping the counters. She feels well satisfied and full of energy. She takes a sip of the mead. Lines of a song are going through her head, and she doesn't realize until a few words of this song reach the surface that it's the same one David was singing, earlier in the day. "What's to come is still unsure!"

Catherine gives a light snore, and jerks her head up. Hercules doesn't take fright, but tries to settle himself more permanently, getting his claws into her dress.

"Was that me?" says Catherine.

"You need some coffee," Stella says. "Hang on. You probably shouldn't go to sleep right now."

"I'm tired," says Catherine stubbornly.

"I know. But you shouldn't go to sleep right now. Hang on, and we'll get some coffee into you."

Stella takes a hand towel from the drawer, soaks it in cold water, holds it to Catherine's face.

"There, now," says Stella. "You hold it, I'll start the coffee. We're not going to have you passing out here, are we? David would carry on about it. He'd say it was my mead or my cooking or my company, or something. Hang on, Catherine."

DAVID, in the phone booth, begins to dial Dina's number. Then he remembers that it's long distance. He must dial the operator. He dials the operator, asks how much the call will cost, empties his pockets of change. He picks out a dollar and thirty-five cents in quarters and dimes, stacks it ready on the shelf. He starts dialling again. His fingers are shaky, his palms sweaty. His legs, gut, and chest are filled with a rising commotion. The first ring of the phone, in Dina's cramped apartment, sets his innards bubbling. This is craziness. He starts to feed in quarters.

"I will tell you when to deposit your money," says the operator. "Sir? I will tell you when to deposit it." His quarters clank down into the change return and he has trouble scooping them out. The phone rings again, on Dina's dresser, in the jumble of makeup, panty hose, beads and chains, long feathered earrings, a silly cigarette holder, an assortment of windup toys. He can see them: the green frog, the yellow duck, the brown bear— all the same size. Frogs and bears are equal. Also some space monsters, based on characters in a movie. When set going, these toys will lurch and clatter across Dina's floor or table, spitting sparks out of their mouths. She likes to set up races, or put a couple of them on a collision course. Then she squeals, and even screams with excitement, as they go their unpredictable ways.

"There doesn't seem to be any answer, sir."

"Let it ring a few more times."

Dina's bathroom is across the hall. She shares it with another girl. If she is in the bathroom, even in the bathtub, how long will it take her to decide whether to answer it at all? He decides to count ten rings more, starting now.

"Still no answer, sir."

Ten more.

"Sir, would you like to try again later?"

He hangs up, having thought of something. Immediately, energetically, he dials information.

"For what place, sir?"

"Toronto."

"Go ahead, sir."

He asks for the phone number of a Michael Read. No, he does not have a street address. All he has is the name—the name of her last, and perhaps not quite finished with, boyfriend.

"I have no listing for a Michael Read."

"All right. Try Reade, R-E-A-D-E."

There is indeed an M. Reade, on Davenport Road. Not a Michael but at least an M. Check back and see, then. Is there an M. Read? Read? Yes. Yes, there is an M. Read, living on Simcoe Street. And another M. Read, R-E-A-D, living on Harbord. Why didn't she say that sooner?

He picks Harbord on a hunch. That's not too far from Dina's apartment. The operator tells him the number. He tries to memorize it. He has nothing to write with. He feels it's important not to ask the operator to repeat the number more than once. He should not reveal that he is here in a phone booth without a pen or pencil. It seems to him that the desperate, furtive nature of his quest is apparent, and that at any moment he may be shut off, not permitted to acquire any further information about M. Read, or M. Reade, on Harbord or Simcoe or Davenport, or wherever.

Now he must start all over again. The Toronto area code. No, the operator. The memorized number. Quick, before he loses his nerve, or loses the number. If she should answer, what is he going to say? But it isn't likely that she will answer, even if she is there. M. Read will answer. Then David must ask for Dina. But perhaps not in his own voice. Perhaps not in a man's voice at all. He used to be able to do different voices on the phone. He could even fool Stella at one time.

Perhaps he could do a woman's voice, squeaky. Or a child's voice, a little-sister voice. *Is Dina there?*

"I beg your pardon, sir?"

"Nothing. Sorry."

"It's ringing now. I will let you know when to deposit your money."

What if M. Read is a woman? Not Michael Read at all. Mary Read. Old-age pensioner. Career girl. What are you phoning me for? Sexual harassment. Back to information, then. Try M. Read on Simcoe. Try M. Reade on Davenport. Keep trying.

"I'm sorry. I can't seem to get an answer."

The phone rings again and again in M. Read's apartment, or house, or room. David leans against the metal shelf, where his change is waiting. A car has parked in the liquor-store lot. The couple in it are watching him. Obviously waiting to use the phone. With any luck, Ron and Mary will drive up next.

Dina lives above an Indian-import shop. Her clothes and hair always have a smell of curry powder, nutmeg, incense, added to what David thinks of as her natural smell, of cigarettes and dope and sex. Her hair is dyed dead black. Her cheeks bear a slash of crude color and her eyelids are sometimes brick red. She tried out once for a part in a movie some people she knew about were making. She failed to get the part because of some squeamishness about holding a tame rat between her legs. This failure humiliated her.

David sweats now, trying not to catch her out but to catch her any way at all, to hear her harsh young voice, with its involuntary tremor and insistent obscenities. Even if hearing it, at this moment, means that she has betrayed him. Of course she has betrayed him. She betrays him all the time. If only she would answer (he has almost forgotten it's M. Read who is supposed to answer), he could howl at her, berate her, and if he felt low enough—he *would* feel low enough—he could plead with her. He would welcome the chance. Any chance. At dinner, talking in a lively way to Stella and Catherine, he kept writing the name Dina with his finger on the underside of the wooden table.

People don't have any patience with this sort of suffering, and why should they? The sufferer must forgo sympathy, give up on dignity, cope with the ravages. And on top of that, people will take time out to tell you that this isn't real love. These bouts of desire and dependence and worship and perversity, willed but terrible transformations—they aren't real love.

Stella used to tell him he wasn't interested in love. "Or sex, even. I don't think you're even interested in sex, David. I think all you're interested in is being a big bad boy."

Real love—that would be going on living with Stella, or taking on

Catherine. A person presumed to know all about Real Love might be Ron, of Ron-and-Mary.

David knows what he's doing. This is the interesting part of it, he thinks, and has said. He knows that Dina is not really so wild, or so avid, or doomed, as he pretends she is, or as she sometimes pretends she is. In ten years' time, she won't be wrecked by her crazy life, she won't be a glamorous whore. She'll be a woman tagged by little children in the laundromat. The delicious, old-fashioned word *trollop*, which he uses to describe her, doesn't apply to her, really—has no more to do with her than *hippie* had to do with Catherine, a person he cannot now bear to think about. He knows that sooner or later, if Dina allows her disguise to crack, as Catherine did, he will have to move on. He will have to do that anyway—move on.

He knows all this and observes himself, and such knowledge and observation has no effect at all on his quaking gut, zealous sweat glands, fierce prayers.

"Sir? Do you want to keep on trying?"

THE NURSING home that they visited, earlier in the day, is called the Balm of Gilead Home. It is named after the balm-of-Gilead trees, a kind of poplar, that grow plentifully near the lake. A large stone mansion built by a nineteenth-century millionaire, it is now disfigured by ramps and fire escapes.

Voices summoned Stella, from the clusters of wheelchairs on the front lawn. She called out various names in answer, detoured to press hands and drop kisses. Vibrating here and there like a fat hummingbird.

She sang when she rejoined David:

> "I'm your little sunbeam, short and stout,
> Turn me over, pour me out!"

Out of breath, she said, "Actually it's *teapot*. I don't think you'll see much change in Daddy. Except the blindness is total now."

She led him through the green-painted corridors, with their low false ceilings (cutting the heating costs), their paint-by-number pictures, their disinfectant—and other—smells. Out on a back porch, alone, her father sat wrapped in blankets, strapped into his wheelchair so that he wouldn't fall out.

Her father said, "David?"

The sound seemed to come from a wet cave deep inside him, to be unshaped by lips or jaws or tongue. These could not be seen to move. Nor did he move his head.

Stella went behind the chair and put her arms around his neck. She touched him very lightly.

"Yes, it's David, Daddy," she said. "You knew his step!"

Her father didn't answer. David bent to touch the old man's hands, which were not cold, as he expected, but warm and very dry. He laid the whisky bottle in them.

"Careful. He can't hold it," said Stella softly. David kept his own hands on the bottle while Stella pushed up a chair, so that he could sit down opposite her father.

"Same old present," David said.

His father-in-law made an acknowledging sound.

"I'm going to get some glasses," Stella said. "It's against the rules to drink outside, but I can generally get them to bend the rules a bit. I'll tell them it's a celebration."

To get used to looking at his father-in-law, David tried to think of him as a post-human development, something new in the species. Survival hadn't just preserved, it had transformed him. Bluish-gray skin, with dark-blue spots, whitened eyes, a ribbed neck with delicate deep hollows, like a smoked-glass vase. Up through this neck came further sounds, a conversational offering. It was the core of each syllable that was presented, a damp vowel barely held in shape by surrounding consonants.

"Traffic—bad?"

David described conditions on the freeway and on the secondary highways. He told his father-in-law that he had recently bought a car, a Japanese car. He told how he had not, at first, been able to get anything close to the advertised mileage. But he had complained, he had persisted, had taken the car back to the dealer. Various adjustments had been tried, and now the situation had improved and the figure was satisfactory, if not quite what had been promised.

This conversation seemed welcome. His father-in-law appeared to follow it. He nodded, and on his narrow, elongated, bluish, post-human face there were traces of old expressions. An expression of shrewd and dignified concern, suspicion of advertising and of foreign cars and car dealers. There was even a suggestion of doubt—as in the old days—that David could be trusted to handle such things well. And relief that he had done so. In his father-in-law's eyes David would always be somebody learning how to be a man, somebody who might never learn, might never achieve the steadfastness and control, the decent narrowness of range. David, who preferred gin to whisky, read novels, didn't understand the stock market, talked to women, and had started out as a teacher. David, who had always driven small cars, foreign cars. But that was all right now. Small cars were not a sign of any of the things they used to be a sign of. Even here on the bluffs above Lake Huron at the very end of life, certain shifts had registered, certain changes had been understood, by a man who couldn't grasp or see.

"Hear anything about—Lada?"

It happens luckily that David has a colleague who drives a Lada, and many boring lunch and coffee breaks have been taken up with the discussion of this car's strengths and failings and the difficulty of getting parts. David recounted these, and his father-in-law seemed satisfied.

"Gray. Dort. Gray-Dort. First car—ever drove. Yonge Street. Sixty miles. Sixty miles. Uh. Uh. Hour."

"He certainly never drove a Gray-Dort down Yonge Street at sixty miles an hour," said Stella when they had got her father and his bottle back to his room, had said goodbye, and were walking back through the green corridors. "Never. Whose Gray-Dort? They were out of production long before he had the money to buy a car. And he'd never have taken the risk with anybody else's. It's his fantasy. He's reached the stage where that's his big recreation—fixing up the past so anything he wishes had happened did happen. Wonder if we'll get to that stage? What would your fantasy be, David? No. Don't tell me!"

"What would yours be?" said David.

"That you didn't leave? That you didn't want to leave? I bet that's what you think mine would be, but I'm not so sure! Daddy was so pleased to see you, David. A man just means more, for Daddy. I suppose if he thought about you and me he'd have to be on my side, but that's all right, he doesn't have to think about it."

Stella, at the nursing home, seemed to have regained some sleekness and suppleness of former times. Her attentions to her father, and even to the wheelchair contingent, brought back a trace of deferential grace to her movements, a wistfulness to her voice. David had a picture of her as she had been twelve or fifteen years before. He saw her coming across the lawn at a suburban party, carrying a casserole. She was wearing a sundress. She always claimed in those days that she was too fat for pants, though she was not half so fat as now. Why did this picture please him so much? Stella coming across the lawn, with her sunlit hair—the gray in it then merely made it ash blond—and her bare toasted shoulders, crying out greetings to her neighbors, laughing, protesting about some cooking misadventure. Of course the food she brought would be wonderful, and she brought not only food but the whole longed-for spirit of the neighborhood party. With her overwhelming sociability, she gathered everybody in. And David felt quite free of irritation, though there were times, certainly, when these gifts of Stella's had irritated him. Her vivacious exasperation, her exaggeration, her wide-eyed humorous appeals for sympathy had irritated him. For others' entertainment he had heard her shaping stories out of their life—the children's daily mishaps and provocations, the cat's visit to the vet, her son's first hangover, the perversity of the power lawnmower, the papering of the upstairs hall. A charming wife, a wonderful person at a party, she has such a funny way of looking at things. Sometimes she was a riot. *Your wife's a riot.*

Well, he forgave her—he loved her—as she walked across the lawn. At that moment, with his bare foot, he was stroking the cold, brown, shaved, and prickly calf of another neighborhood wife, who had just come out of the pool and had thrown on a long, concealing scarlet robe. A dark-haired, childless, chain-smoking woman, given—at least at that stage in their relationship—to tantalizing silences. (His first, that one, the first while married to Stella. Rosemary. A sweet dark name, though finally a shrill trite woman.)

It wasn't just that. The unexpected delight in Stella just as she was, the unusual feeling of being at peace with her, didn't come from just that—the illicit activity of his big toe. This seemed profound, this revelation about himself and Stella—how they were bound together after all, and how as long as he could feel such benevolence toward her, what he did secretly and separately was somehow done with her blessing.

That did not turn out to be a notion Stella shared at all. And they weren't so bound, or if they were it was a bond he had to break. We've been together so long, couldn't we just tough it out, said Stella at the time, trying to make it a joke. She didn't understand, probably didn't understand yet, how that was one of the things that made it impossible. This white-haired woman walking beside him through the nursing home dragged so much weight with her—a weight not just of his sexual secrets but of his middle-of-the-night speculations about God, his psychosomatic chest pains, his digestive sensitivity, his escape plans, which once included her and involved Africa or Indonesia. All his ordinary and extraordinary life—even some things it was unlikely she knew about—seemed stored up in her. He could never feel any lightness, any secret and victorious expansion, with a woman who knew so much. She was bloated with all she knew. Nevertheless he put his arms around Stella. They embraced, both willingly.

A young girl, a Chinese or Vietnamese girl, slight as a child in her pale-green uniform, but with painted lips and cheeks, was coming along the corridor, pushing a cart. On the cart were paper cups and plastic containers of orange and grape juice.

"Juice time," the girl was calling, in her pleasant and indifferent singsong. "Juice time. Orange. Grape. Juice." She took no notice of David and Stella, but they let go of each other and resumed walking. David did feel a slight, very slight, discomfort at being seen by such a young and pretty girl in the embrace of Stella. It was not an important feeling—it simply brushed him and passed—but Stella, as he held the door open for her, said, "Never mind, David. I could be your sister. You could be comforting your sister. *Older* sister."

"Madam Stella, the celebrated mind reader."

It was strange, the way they said these things. They used to say bitter and wounding things, and pretend, when they said them, to be mildly amused, dispassionate, even kindly. Now this tone that was once a pretense had soaked down, deep down, through all their sharp feelings, and the bitterness, though not transformed, seemed stale, useless and formal.

A WEEK or so later, when she is tidying up the living room, getting ready for a meeting of the historical society that is to take place at her house, Stella finds the picture, a Polaroid snapshot. David has left it with her after all—hiding it, but not hiding it very well, behind the curtains at one end of the long living-room window, at the spot where you stand to get a view of the lighthouse.

Lying in the sun had faded it, of course. Stella stands looking at it, with a dust cloth in her hand. The day is perfect. The windows are open, her house is pleasantly in order, and a good fish soup is simmering on the stove. She sees that the black pelt in the picture has changed to gray. It's a bluish or greenish gray now. She remembers what she said when she first saw it. She said it was lichen. No, she said it looked like lichen. But she knew what it was at once. It seems to her now that she knew what it was even when David put his hand to his pocket. She felt the old cavity opening up in her. But she held on. She said, "Lichen." And now, look, her words have come true. The outline of the breast has disappeared. You would never know that the legs were legs. The black has turned to gray, to the soft, dry color of a plant mysteriously nourished on the rocks.

This is David's doing. He left it there, in the sun.

Stella's words have come true. This thought will keep coming back to her—a pause, a lost heartbeat, a harsh little break in the flow of the days and nights as she keeps them going.

# Miles City, Montana

~

MY FATHER came across the field carrying the body of the boy who had been drowned. There were several men together, returning from the search, but he was the one carrying the body. The men were muddy and exhausted, and walked with their heads down, as if they were ashamed. Even the dogs were dispirited, dripping from the cold river. When they all set out, hours before, the dogs were nervy and yelping, the men tense and determined, and there was a constrained, unspeakable excitement about the whole scene. It was understood that they might find something horrible.

The boy's name was Steve Gauley. He was eight years old. His hair and clothes were mud-colored now and carried some bits of dead leaves, twigs, and grass. He was like a heap of refuse that had been left out all winter. His face was turned in to my father's chest, but I could see a nostril, an ear, plugged up with greenish mud.

I don't think so. I don't think I really saw all this. Perhaps I saw my father carrying him, and the other men following along, and the dogs, but I would not have been allowed to get close enough to see something like mud in his nostril. I must have heard someone talking about that and imagined that I saw it. I see his face unaltered except for the mud—Steve Gauley's familiar, sharp-honed, sneaky-looking face—and it wouldn't have been like that; it would have been bloated and changed and perhaps muddied all over after so many hours in the water.

To have to bring back such news, such evidence, to a waiting family, particularly a mother, would have made searchers move heavily, but what was happening here was worse. It seemed a worse shame (to hear people talk) that there was no mother, no woman at all—no grandmother or aunt, or even a sister—to receive Steve Gauley and give him his due of grief. His father was a hired man, a drinker but not a drunk, an erratic man without being entertaining, not friendly but not exactly a trouble-maker. His fatherhood seemed accidental, and the fact that the child had been left with him when the mother went away, and that they continued living together, seemed accidental. They lived in a steep-roofed, gray-shingled hillbilly sort of house that was just a bit better than a shack—the father fixed the roof and put supports under the porch, just enough and just in time—and their life was held together in a similar manner; that is, just well enough to keep the Children's Aid at bay. They didn't eat meals together or cook for each other, but there was food. Sometimes the father would give Steve money to buy food at the store, and Steve was seen to buy quite sensible things, such as pancake mix and macaroni dinner.

I had known Steve Gauley fairly well. I had not liked him more often than I had liked him. He was two years older than I was. He would hang around our place on Saturdays, scornful of whatever I was doing but un-able to leave me alone. I couldn't be on the swing without him wanting to try it, and if I wouldn't give it up he came and pushed me so that I went crooked. He teased the dog. He got me into trouble—deliberately and maliciously, it seemed to me afterward—by daring me to do things I wouldn't have thought of on my own: digging up the potatoes to see how big they were when they were still only the size of marbles, and pushing over the stacked firewood to make a pile we could jump off. At school, we never spoke to each other. He was solitary, though not tormented. But on Saturday mornings, when I saw his thin, self-possessed figure sliding through the cedar hedge, I knew I was in for something and he would de-cide what. Sometimes it was all right. We pretended we were cowboys who had to tame wild horses. We played in the pasture by the river, not far from the place where Steve drowned. We were horses and riders both, screaming and neighing and bucking and waving whips of tree branches beside a little nameless river that flows into the Saugeen in southern Ontario.

The funeral was held in our house. There was not enough room at Steve's father's place for the large crowd that was expected because of the circumstances. I have a memory of the crowded room but no picture of Steve in his coffin, or of the minister, or of wreaths of flowers. I remember that I was holding one flower, a white narcissus, which must have come from a pot somebody forced indoors, because it was too early for even the forsythia bush or the trilliums and marsh marigolds in the woods. I stood in a row of children, each of us holding a narcissus. We sang a children's hymn, which somebody played on our piano: "When He Cometh, When He Cometh, to Make Up His Jewels." I was wearing white ribbed stock-ings, which were disgustingly itchy, and wrinkled at the knees and ankles.

The feeling of these stockings on my legs is mixed up with another feeling in my memory. It is hard to describe. It had to do with my parents. Adults in general but my parents in particular. My father, who had carried Steve's body from the river, and my mother, who must have done most of the arranging of this funeral. My father in his dark-blue suit and my mother in her brown velvet dress with the creamy satin collar. They stood side by side opening and closing their mouths for the hymn, and I stood removed from them, in the row of children, watching. I felt a furious and sickening disgust. Children sometimes have an access of disgust concerning adults. The size, the lumpy shapes, the bloated power. The breath, the coarseness, the hairiness, the horrid secretions. But this was more. And the accompanying anger had nothing sharp and self-respecting about it. There was no release, as when I would finally bend and pick up a stone and throw it at Steve Gauley. It could not be understood or expressed, though it died down after a while into a heaviness, then just a taste, an occasional taste— a thin, familiar misgiving.

TWENTY years or so later, in 1961, my husband, Andrew, and I got a brand-new car, our first—that is, our first brand-new. It was a Morris Oxford, oyster-colored (the dealer had some fancier name for the color)—a big small car, with plenty of room for us and our two children. Cynthia was six and Meg three and a half.

Andrew took a picture of me standing beside the car. I was wearing white pants, a black turtleneck, and sunglasses. I lounged against the car door, canting my hips to make myself look slim.

"Wonderful," Andrew said. "Great. You look like Jackie Kennedy." All over this continent probably, dark-haired, reasonably slender young women were told, when they were stylishly dressed or getting their pictures taken, that they looked like Jackie Kennedy.

Andrew took a lot of pictures of me, and of the children, our house, our garden, our excursions and possessions. He got copies made, labelled them carefully, and sent them back to his mother and his aunt and uncle in Ontario. He got copies for me to send to my father, who also lived in Ontario, and I did so, but less regularly than he sent his. When he saw pictures he thought I had already sent lying around the house, Andrew was perplexed and annoyed. He liked to have this record go forth.

That summer, we were presenting ourselves, not pictures. We were driving back from Vancouver, where we lived, to Ontario, which we still called "home," in our new car. Five days to get there, ten days there, five days back. For the first time, Andrew had three weeks' holiday. He worked in the legal department at B. C. Hydro.

On a Saturday morning, we loaded suitcases, two thermos bottles—one filled with coffee and one with lemonade—some fruit and sandwiches, picture books and coloring books, crayons, drawing pads, insect repellent, sweaters (in case it got cold in the mountains), and our two children into the car. Andrew locked the house, and Cynthia said ceremoniously, "Goodbye, house."

Meg said, "Goodbye, house." Then she said, "Where will we live now?"

"It's not goodbye forever," said Cynthia. "We're coming back. Mother! Meg thought we weren't ever coming back!"

"I did not," said Meg, kicking the back of my seat.

Andrew and I put on our sunglasses, and we drove away, over the Lions Gate Bridge and through the main part of Vancouver. We shed our house, the neighborhood, the city, and—at the crossing point between Washington and British Columbia—our country. We were driving east across the United States, taking the most northerly route, and would cross into Canada again at Sarnia, Ontario. I don't know if we chose this route because the Trans-Canada Highway was not completely finished at the time or if we just wanted the feeling of driving through a foreign, a very slightly foreign, country—that extra bit of interest and adventure.

We were both in high spirits. Andrew congratulated the car several times. He said he felt so much better driving it than our old car, a 1951 Austin that slowed down dismally on the hills and had a fussy-old-lady image. So Andrew said now.

"What kind of image does this one have?" said Cynthia. She listened to us carefully and liked to try out new words such as *image*. Usually she got them right.

"Lively," I said. "Slightly sporty. It's not show-off."

"It's sensible, but it has class," Andrew said. "Like my image."

Cynthia thought that over and said with a cautious pride, "That means like you think you want to be, Daddy?"

As for me, I was happy because of the shedding. I loved taking off. In my own house, I seemed to be often looking for a place to hide—sometimes from the children but more often from the jobs to be done and the phone ringing and the sociability of the neighborhood. I wanted to hide so that I could get busy at my real work, which was a sort of wooing of distant parts of myself. I lived in a state of siege, always losing just what I wanted to hold on to. But on trips there was no difficulty. I could be talking to Andrew, talking to the children and looking at whatever they wanted me to look at—a pig on a sign, a pony in a field, a Volkswagen on a revolving stand—and pouring lemonade into plastic cups, and all the time those bits and pieces would be flying together inside me. The essential composition would be achieved. This made me hopeful and lighthearted. It was being a watcher that did it. A watcher, not a keeper.

We turned east at Everett and climbed into the Cascades. I showed Cynthia our route on the map. First I showed her the map of the whole United States, which showed also the bottom part of Canada. Then I turned to the separate maps of each of the states we were going to pass through. Washington, Idaho, Montana, North Dakota, Minnesota, Wisconsin. I showed her the dotted line across Lake Michigan, which was the route of the ferry we would take. Then we would drive across Michigan to the bridge that linked the United States and Canada at Sarnia, Ontario. Home.

Meg wanted to see too.

"You won't understand," said Cynthia. But she took the road atlas into the back seat.

"Sit back," she said to Meg. "Sit still. I'll show you."

I could hear her tracing the route for Meg, very accurately, just as I had done it for her. She looked up all the states' maps, knowing how to find them in alphabetical order.

"You know what that line is?" she said. "It's the road. That line is the road we're driving on. We're going right along this line."

Meg did not say anything.

"Mother, show me where we are right this minute," said Cynthia.

I took the atlas and pointed out the road through the mountains, and she took it back and showed it to Meg. "See where the road is all wiggly?" she said. "It's wiggly because there are so many turns in it. The wiggles are the turns." She flipped some pages and waited a moment. "Now," she said, "show me where we are." Then she called to me, "Mother, she understands! She pointed to it! Meg understands maps!"

It seems to me now that we invented characters for our children. We had them firmly set to play their parts. Cynthia was bright and diligent, sensitive, courteous, watchful. Sometimes we teased her for being too conscientious, too eager to be what we in fact depended on her to be. Any reproach or failure, any rebuff, went terribly deep with her. She was fair-haired, fair-skinned, easily showing the effects of the sun, raw winds, pride, or humiliation. Meg was more solidly built, more reticent—not rebellious but stubborn sometimes, mysterious. Her silences seemed to us to show her strength of character, and her negatives were taken as signs of an imperturbable independence. Her hair was brown, and we cut it in straight bangs. Her eyes were a light hazel, clear and dazzling.

We were entirely pleased with these characters, enjoying their contradictions as well as the confirmations of them. We disliked the heavy, the uninventive, approach to being parents. I had a dread of turning into a certain kind of mother—the kind whose body sagged, who moved in a woolly-smelling, milky-smelling fog, solemn with trivial burdens. I believed that all the attention these mothers paid, their need to be burdened,

was the cause of colic, bed-wetting, asthma. I favored another approach—
the mock desperation, the inflated irony of the professional mothers who
wrote for magazines. In those magazine pieces, the children were splen-
didly self-willed, hard-edged, perverse, indomitable. So were the mothers,
through their wit, indomitable. The real-life mothers I warmed to were
the sort who would phone up and say, "Is my embryo Hitler by any
chance over at your house?" They cackled clear above the milky fog.

We saw a dead deer strapped across the front of a pickup truck.

"Somebody shot it," Cynthia said. "Hunters shoot the deer."

"It's not hunting season yet," Andrew said. "They may have hit it on
the road. See the sign for deer crossing?"

"I would cry if we hit one," Cynthia said sternly.

I had made peanut-butter-and-marmalade sandwiches for the children
and salmon-and-mayonnaise for us. But I had not put any lettuce in, and
Andrew was disappointed.

"I didn't have any," I said.

"Couldn't you have got some?"

"I'd have had to buy a whole head of lettuce just to get enough for
sandwiches, and I decided it wasn't worth it."

This was a lie. I had forgotten.

"They're a lot better with lettuce."

"I didn't think it made that much difference." After a silence, I said,
"Don't be mad."

"I'm not mad. I like lettuce on sandwiches."

"I just didn't think it mattered that much."

"How would it be if I didn't bother to fill up the gas tank?"

"That's not the same thing."

"Sing a song," said Cynthia. She started to sing:

> *"Five little ducks went out one day,*
> *Over the hills and far away.*
> *One little duck went*
> *'Quack-quack-quack.'*
> *Four little ducks came swimming back."*

Andrew squeezed my hand and said, "Let's not fight."

"You're right. I should have got lettuce."

"It doesn't matter that much."

I wished that I could get my feelings about Andrew to come together
into a serviceable and dependable feeling. I had even tried writing two
lists, one of things I liked about him, one of things I disliked—in the caul-
dron of intimate life, things I loved and things I hated—as if I hoped by
this to prove something, to come to a conclusion one way or the other.

But I gave it up when I saw that all it proved was what I already knew—that I had violent contradictions. Sometimes the very sound of his footsteps seemed to me tyrannical, the set of his mouth smug and mean, his hard, straight body a barrier interposed—quite consciously, even dutifully, and with a nasty pleasure in its masculine authority—between me and whatever joy or lightness I could get in life. Then, with not much warning, he became my good friend and most essential companion. I felt the sweetness of his light bones and serious ideas, the vulnerability of his love, which I imagined to be much purer and more straightforward than my own. I could be greatly moved by an inflexibility, a harsh propriety, that at other times I scorned. I would think how humble he was, really, taking on such a ready-made role of husband, father, breadwinner, and how I myself in comparison was really a secret monster of egotism. Not so secret, either—not from him.

At the bottom of our fights, we served up what we thought were the ugliest truths. "I know there is something basically selfish and basically untrustworthy about you," Andrew once said. "I've always known it. I also know that that is why I fell in love with you."

"Yes," I said, feeling sorrowful but complacent.

"I know that I'd be better off without you."

"Yes. You would."

"You'd be happier without me."

"Yes."

And finally—finally—wracked and purged, we clasped hands and laughed, laughed at those two benighted people, ourselves. Their grudges, their grievances, their self-justification. We leapfrogged over them. We declared them liars. We would have wine with dinner, or decide to give a party.

I haven't seen Andrew for years, don't know if he is still thin, has gone completely gray, insists on lettuce, tells the truth, or is hearty and disappointed.

WE STAYED the night in Wenatchee, Washington, where it hadn't rained for weeks. We ate dinner in a restaurant built about a tree—not a sapling in a tub but a tall, sturdy cottonwood. In the early-morning light, we climbed out of the irrigated valley, up dry, rocky, very steep hillsides that would seem to lead to more hills, and there on the top was a wide plateau, cut by the great Spokane and Columbia rivers. Grainland and grassland, mile after mile. There were straight roads here, and little farming towns with grain elevators. In fact, there was a sign announcing that this county we were going through, Douglas County, had the second-highest wheat yield of any county in the United States. The towns had planted shade trees. At least, I thought they had been planted, because there were no such big trees in the countryside.

All this was marvellously welcome to me. "Why do I love it so much?" I said to Andrew. "Is it because it isn't scenery?"

"It reminds you of home," said Andrew. "A bout of severe nostalgia." But he said this kindly.

When we said "home" and meant Ontario, we had very different places in mind. My home was a turkey farm, where my father lived as a widower, and though it was the same house my mother had lived in, had papered, painted, cleaned, furnished, it showed the effects now of neglect and of some wild sociability. A life went on in it that my mother could not have predicted or condoned. There were parties for the turkey crew, the gutters and pluckers, and sometimes one or two of the young men would be living there temporarily, inviting their own friends and having their own impromptu parties. This life, I thought, was better for my father than being lonely, and I did not disapprove, had certainly no right to disapprove. Andrew did not like to go there, naturally enough, because he was not the sort who could sit around the kitchen table with the turkey crew, telling jokes. They were intimidated by him and contemptuous of him, and it seemed to me that my father, when they were around, had to be on their side. And it wasn't only Andrew who had trouble. I could manage those jokes, but it was an effort.

I wished for the days when I was little, before we had the turkeys. We had cows, and sold the milk to the cheese factory. A turkey farm is nothing like as pretty as a dairy farm or a sheep farm. You can see that the turkeys are on a straight path to becoming frozen carcasses and table meat. They don't have the pretense of a life of their own, a browsing idyll, that cattle have, or pigs in the dappled orchard. Turkey barns are long, efficient buildings—tin sheds. No beams or hay or warm stables. Even the smell of guano seems thinner and more offensive than the usual smell of stable manure. No hints there of hay coils and rail fences and songbirds and the flowering hawthorn. The turkeys were all let out into one long field, which they picked clean. They didn't look like great birds there but like fluttering laundry.

Once, shortly after my mother died, and after I was married—in fact, I was packing to join Andrew in Vancouver—I was at home alone for a couple of days with my father. There was a freakishly heavy rain all night. In the early light, we saw that the turkey field was flooded. At least, the low-lying parts of it were flooded—it was like a lake with many islands. The turkeys were huddled on these islands. Turkeys are very stupid. (My father would say, "You know a chicken? You know how stupid a chicken is? Well, a chicken is an Einstein compared with a turkey.") But they had managed to crowd to higher ground and avoid drowning. Now they might push each other off, suffocate each other, get cold and die. We couldn't wait for the water to go down. We went out in an old rowboat we had. I rowed and my father pulled the heavy, wet turkeys into the boat and we took them to the barn. It was still raining a little. The job was difficult and absurd and very uncomfortable. We were laughing. I was happy to be working with my father. I felt close to all hard, repetitive, appalling work, in which the body is finally worn out, the mind sunk (though sometimes the spirit can stay marvellously light), and I was homesick in advance for this life and this place. I thought that if Andrew could see me there in the rain, red-handed, muddy, trying to hold on to turkey legs and row the boat at the same time, he would only want to get me out of there and make me forget about it. This raw life angered him. My attachment to it angered him. I thought that I shouldn't have married him. But who else? One of the turkey crew?

And I didn't want to stay there. I might feel bad about leaving, but I would feel worse if somebody made me stay.

Andrew's mother lived in Toronto, in an apartment building looking out on Muir Park. When Andrew and his sister were both at home, his mother slept in the living room. Her husband, a doctor, had died when the children were still too young to go to school. She took a secretarial course and sold her house at Depression prices, moved to this apartment, managed to raise her children, with some help from relatives—her sister Caroline, her brother-in-law Roger. Andrew and his sister went to private schools and to camp in the summer.

"I suppose that was courtesy of the Fresh Air Fund?" I said once, scornful of his claim that he had been poor. To my mind, Andrew's urban life had been sheltered and fussy. His mother came home with a headache from working all day in the noise, the harsh light of a department-store office, but it did not occur to me that hers was a hard or admirable life. I don't think she herself believed that she was admirable—only unlucky. She worried about her work in the office, her clothes, her cooking, her children. She worried most of all about what Roger and Caroline would think.

Caroline and Roger lived on the east side of the park, in a handsome stone house. Roger was a tall man with a bald, freckled head, a fat, firm stomach. Some operation on his throat had deprived him of his voice—he spoke in a rough whisper. But everybody paid attention. At dinner once in the stone house—where all the dining-room furniture was enormous, darkly glowing, palatial—I asked him a question. I think it had to do with Whittaker Chambers, whose story was then appearing in the *Saturday Evening Post*. The question was mild in tone, but he guessed its subversive intent and took to calling me Mrs. Gromyko, referring to what he alleged to be my "sympathies." Perhaps he really craved an adversary, and could not find one. At that dinner, I saw Andrew's hand tremble as he lit his mother's cigarette. His Uncle Roger had paid for Andrew's education, and was on the board of directors of several companies.

"He is just an opinionated old man," Andrew said to me later. "What is the point of arguing with him?"

Before we left Vancouver, Andrew's mother had written, *Roger seems quite intrigued by the idea of your buying a small car!* Her exclamation mark showed apprehension. At that time, particularly in Ontario, the choice of a small European car over a large American car could be seen as some sort of declaration—a declaration of tendencies Roger had been sniffing after all along.

"It isn't that small a car," said Andrew huffily.

"That's not the point," I said. "The point is, it isn't any of his business!"

WE SPENT the second night in Missoula. We had been told in Spokane, at a gas station, that there was a lot of repair work going on along Highway 2, and that we were in for a very hot, dusty drive, with long waits, so we turned onto the interstate and drove through Coeur d'Alene and Kellogg into Montana. After Missoula, we turned south toward Butte, but detoured to see Helena, the state capital. In the car, we played Who Am I?

Cynthia was somebody dead, and an American, and a girl. Possibly a lady. She was not in a story. She had not been seen on television. Cynthia had not read about her in a book. She was not anybody who had come to the kindergarten, or a relative of any of Cynthia's friends.

"Is she human?" said Andrew, with a sudden shrewdness.

"No! That's what you forgot to ask!"

"An animal," I said reflectively.

"Is that a question? Sixteen questions!"

"No, it is not a question. I'm thinking. A dead animal."

"It's the deer," said Meg, who hadn't been playing.

"That's not fair!" said Cynthia. "She's not playing!"

"What deer?" said Andrew.

I said, "Yesterday."

"The day before," said Cynthia. "Meg wasn't playing. Nobody got it."

"The deer on the truck," said Andrew.

"It was a lady deer, because it didn't have antlers, and it was an American and it was dead," Cynthia said.

Andrew said, "I think it's kind of morbid, being a dead deer."

"I got it," said Meg.

Cynthia said, "I think I know what morbid is. It's depressing."

Helena, an old silver-mining town, looked forlorn to us even in the morning sunlight. Then Bozeman and Billings, not forlorn in the slightest—energetic, strung-out towns, with miles of blinding tinsel fluttering over used-car lots. We got too tired and hot even to play Who Am I? These busy, prosaic cities reminded me of similar places in Ontario, and I thought about what was really waiting there—the great tombstone furniture of Roger and Caroline's dining room, the dinners for which I must iron the children's dresses and warn them about forks, and then the other table a hundred miles away, the jokes of my father's crew. The pleasures I had been thinking of—looking at the countryside or drinking a Coke in an old-fashioned drugstore with fans and a high, pressed-tin ceiling—would have to be snatched in between.

"Meg's asleep," Cynthia said. "She's so hot. She makes me hot in the same seat with her."

"I hope she isn't feverish," I said, not turning around.

What are we doing this for, I thought, and the answer came—to show off. To give Andrew's mother and my father the pleasure of seeing their grandchildren. That was our duty. But beyond that we wanted to show them something. What strenuous children we were, Andrew and I, what relentless seekers of approbation. It was as if at some point we had received an unforgettable, indigestible message—that we were far from satisfactory, and that the most commonplace success in life was probably beyond us. Roger dealt out such messages, of course—that was his style—but Andrew's mother, my own mother and father couldn't have meant to do so. All they meant to tell us was "Watch out. Get along." My father, when I was in high school, teased me that I was getting to think I was so smart I would never find a boyfriend. He would have forgotten that in a week. I never forgot it. Andrew and I didn't forget things. We took umbrage.

"I wish there was a beach," said Cynthia.

"There probably is one," Andrew said. "Right around the next curve."

"There isn't any curve," she said, sounding insulted.

"That's what I mean."

"I wish there was some more lemonade."

"I will just wave my magic wand and produce some," I said. "Okay, Cynthia? Would you rather have grape juice? Will I do a beach while I'm at it?"

She was silent, and soon I felt repentant. "Maybe in the next town there might be a pool," I said. I looked at the map. "In Miles City. Anyway, there'll be something cool to drink."

"How far is it?" Andrew said.

"Not so far," I said. "Thirty miles, about."

"In Miles City," said Cynthia, in the tones of an incantation, "there is a beautiful blue swimming pool for children, and a park with lovely trees."

Andrew said to me, "You could have started something."

But there was a pool. There was a park too, though not quite the oasis of Cynthia's fantasy. Prairie trees with thin leaves—cottonwoods and poplars—worn grass, and a high wire fence around the pool. Within this fence, a wall, not yet completed, of cement blocks. There were no shouts or splashes; over the entrance I saw a sign that said the pool was closed every day from noon until two o'clock. It was then twenty-five after twelve.

Nevertheless I called out, "Is anybody there?" I thought somebody must be around, because there was a small truck parked near the entrance. On the side of the truck were these words: *We have Brains, to fix your Drains. (We have Roto-Rooter too.)*

A girl came out, wearing a red lifeguard's shirt over her bathing suit. "Sorry, we're closed."

"We were just driving through," I said.

"We close every day from twelve until two. It's on the sign." She was eating a sandwich.

"I saw the sign," I said. "But this is the first water we've seen for so long, and the children are awfully hot, and I wondered if they could just dip in and out—just five minutes. We'd watch them."

A boy came into sight behind her. He was wearing jeans and a T-shirt with the words *Roto-Rooter* on it.

I was going to say that we were driving from British Columbia to Ontario, but I remembered that Canadian place names usually meant nothing to Americans. "We're driving right across the country," I said. "We haven't time to wait for the pool to open. We were just hoping the children could get cooled off."

Cynthia came running up barefoot behind me. "Mother. Mother, where is my bathing suit?" Then she stopped, sensing the serious adult negotiations. Meg was climbing out of the car—just wakened, with her top pulled up and her shorts pulled down, showing her pink stomach.

"Is it just those two?" the girl said.

"Just the two. We'll watch them."

"I can't let any adults in. If it's just the two, I guess I could watch them. I'm having my lunch." She said to Cynthia, "Do you want to come in the pool?"

"Yes, please," said Cynthia firmly.

Meg looked at the ground.

"Just a short time, because the pool is really closed," I said. "We appreciate this very much," I said to the girl.

"Well, I can eat my lunch out there, if it's just the two of them." She looked toward the car as if she thought I might try to spring some more children on her.

When I found Cynthia's bathing suit, she took it into the changing room. She would not permit anybody, even Meg, to see her naked. I changed Meg, who stood on the front seat of the car. She had a pink cotton bathing suit with straps that crossed and buttoned. There were ruffles across the bottom.

"She *is* hot," I said. "But I don't think she's feverish."

I loved helping Meg to dress or undress, because her body still had the solid unself-consciousness, the sweet indifference, something of the milky smell, of a baby's body. Cynthia's body had long ago been pared down, shaped and altered, into Cynthia. We all liked to hug Meg, press and nuzzle her. Sometimes she would scowl and beat us off, and this forthright independence, this ferocious bashfulness, simply made her more appealing, more apt to be tormented and tickled in the way of family love.

Andrew and I sat in the car with the windows open. I could hear a radio playing, and thought it must belong to the girl or her boyfriend. I was thirsty, and got out of the car to look for a concession stand, or perhaps a soft-drink machine, somewhere in the park. I was wearing shorts, and the backs of my legs were slick with sweat. I saw a drinking fountain at the other side of the park and was walking toward it in a roundabout way, keeping to the shade of the trees. No place became real till you got out of the car. Dazed with the heat, with the sun on the blistered houses, the pavement, the burnt grass, I walked slowly. I paid attention to a squashed leaf, ground a Popsicle stick under the heel of my sandal, squinted at a trash can strapped to a tree. This is the way you look at the poorest details of the world resurfaced, after you've been driving for a long time—you feel their singleness and precise location and the forlorn coincidence of your being there to see them.

*Where are the children?*

I turned around and moved quickly, not quite running, to a part of the fence beyond which the cement wall was not completed. I could see some of the pool. I saw Cynthia, standing about waist-deep in the water, fluttering her hands on the surface and discreetly watching something at the end of the pool, which I could not see. I thought by her pose, her discretion, the look on her face, that she must be watching some byplay between the lifeguard and her boyfriend. I couldn't see Meg. But I thought she must be playing in the shallow water—both the shallow and deep ends of the pool were out of my sight.

"Cynthia!" I had to call twice before she knew where my voice was coming from. "Cynthia! Where's Meg?"

It always seems to me, when I recall this scene, that Cynthia turns very gracefully toward me, then turns all around in the water—making me think of a ballerina on pointe—and spreads her arms in a gesture of the stage. "Dis-ap-peared!"

Cynthia was naturally graceful, and she did take dancing lessons, so these movements may have been as I have described. She did say "Disappeared" after looking all around the pool, but the strangely artificial style of speech and gesture, the lack of urgency, is more likely my invention. The fear I felt instantly when I couldn't see Meg—even while I was telling myself she must be in the shallower water—must have made Cynthia's movements seem unbearably slow and inappropriate to me, and the tone in which she could say "Disappeared" before the implications struck her (or was she covering, at once, some ever-ready guilt?) was heard by me as quite exquisitely, monstrously self-possessed.

I cried out for Andrew, and the lifeguard came into view. She was pointing toward the deep end of the pool, saying, "What's that?"

There, just within my view, a cluster of pink ruffles appeared, a bouquet, beneath the surface of the water. Why would a lifeguard stop and point, why would she ask what that was, why didn't she just dive into the water and swim to it? She didn't swim; she ran all the way around the edge of the pool. But by that time Andrew was over the fence. So many things seemed not quite plausible—Cynthia's behavior, then the lifeguard's—and now I had the impression that Andrew jumped with one bound over this fence, which seemed about seven feet high. He must have climbed it very quickly, getting a grip on the wire.

I could not jump or climb it, so I ran to the entrance, where there was a sort of lattice gate, locked. It was not very high, and I did pull myself over it. I ran through the cement corridors, through the disinfectant pool for your feet, and came out on the edge of the pool.

The drama was over.

Andrew had got to Meg first, and had pulled her out of the water. He just had to reach over and grab her, because she was swimming somehow, with her head underwater—she was moving toward the edge of the pool. He was carrying her now, and the lifeguard was trotting along behind. Cynthia had climbed out of the water and was running to meet them. The only person aloof from the situation was the boyfriend, who had stayed on the bench at the shallow end, drinking a milkshake. He smiled at me, and I thought that unfeeling of him, even though the danger was past. He may have meant it kindly. I noticed that he had not turned the radio off, just down.

Meg had not swallowed any water. She hadn't even scared herself. Her hair was plastered to her head and her eyes were wide open, golden with amazement.

"I was getting the comb," she said. "I didn't know it was deep."

Andrew said, "She was swimming! She was swimming by herself. I saw her bathing suit in the water and then I saw her swimming."

"She nearly drowned," Cynthia said. "Didn't she? Meg nearly drowned."

"I don't know how it could have happened," said the lifeguard. "One moment she was there, and the next she wasn't."

What had happened was that Meg had climbed out of the water at the shallow end and run along the edge of the pool toward the deep end. She saw a comb that somebody had dropped lying on the bottom. She crouched down and reached in to pick it up, quite deceived about the depth of the water. She went over the edge and slipped into the pool, making such a light splash that nobody heard—not the lifeguard, who was kissing her boyfriend, or Cynthia, who was watching them. That must have been the moment under the trees when I thought, Where are the children? It must have been the same moment. At that moment, Meg was slipping, surprised, into the treacherously clear blue water.

"It's okay," I said to the lifeguard, who was nearly crying. "She can move pretty fast." (Though that wasn't what we usually said about Meg at all. We said she thought everything over and took her time.)

"You swam, Meg," said Cynthia, in a congratulatory way. (She told us about the kissing later.)

"I didn't know it was deep," Meg said. "I didn't drown."

WE HAD lunch at a takeout place, eating hamburgers and fries at a picnic table not far from the highway. In my excitement, I forgot to get Meg a plain hamburger, and had to scrape off the relish and mustard with plastic spoons, then wipe the meat with a paper napkin, before she would eat it. I took advantage of the trash can there to clean out the car. Then we resumed driving east, with the car windows open in front. Cynthia and Meg fell asleep in the back seat.

Andrew and I talked quietly about what had happened. Suppose I hadn't had the impulse just at that moment to check on the children? Suppose we had gone uptown to get drinks, as we had thought of doing? How had Andrew got over the fence? Did he jump or climb? (He couldn't remember.) How had he reached Meg so quickly? And think of the lifeguard not watching. And Cynthia, taken up with the kissing. Not seeing anything else. Not seeing Meg drop over the edge.

Disappeared.

But she swam. She held her breath and came up swimming.

What a chain of lucky links.

That was all we spoke about—luck. But I was compelled to picture the opposite. At this moment, we could have been filling out forms. Meg removed from us, Meg's body being prepared for shipment. To Vancouver—where we had never noticed such a thing as a graveyard—or to Ontario? The scribbled drawings she had made this morning would still be in the back seat of the car. How could this be borne all at once, how did people bear it? The plump, sweet shoulders and hands and feet, the fine brown hair, the rather satisfied, secretive expression—all exactly the same as when she had been alive. The most ordinary tragedy. A child drowned in a swimming pool at noon on a sunny day. Things tidied up quickly. The pool opens as usual at two o'clock. The lifeguard is a bit shaken up and gets the afternoon off. She drives away with her boyfriend in the Roto-Rooter truck. The body sealed away in some kind of shipping coffin. Sedatives, phone calls, arrangements. Such a sudden vacancy, a blind sinking and shifting. Waking up groggy from the pills, thinking for a moment it wasn't true. Thinking if only we hadn't stopped, if only we hadn't taken this route, if only they hadn't let us use the pool. Probably no one would ever have known about the comb.

There's something trashy about this kind of imagining, isn't there? Something shameful. Laying your finger on the wire to get the safe shock, feeling a bit of what it's like, then pulling back. I believed that Andrew was more scrupulous than I about such things, and that at this moment he was really trying to think about something else.

When I stood apart from my parents at Steve Gauley's funeral and watched them, and had this new, unpleasant feeling about them, I thought that I was understanding something about them for the first time. It was a deadly serious thing. I was understanding that they were implicated. Their big, stiff, dressed-up bodies did not stand between me and sudden death, or any kind of death. They gave consent. So it seemed. They gave consent to the death of children and to my death not by anything they said or thought but by the very fact that they had made children—they had made me. They had made me, and for that reason my death—however grieved they were, however they carried on—would seem to them anything but impossible or unnatural. This was a fact, and even then I knew they were not to blame.

But I did blame them. I charged them with effrontery, hypocrisy. On Steve Gauley's behalf, and on behalf of all children, who knew that by rights they should have sprung up free, to live a new, superior kind of life, not to be caught in the snares of vanquished grownups, with their sex and funerals.

Steve Gauley drowned, people said, because he was next thing to an orphan and was let run free. If he had been warned enough and given chores to do and kept in check, he wouldn't have fallen from an untrustworthy tree branch into a spring pond, a full gravel pit near the river—he wouldn't have drowned. He was neglected, he was free, so he drowned. And his father took it as an accident, such as might happen to a dog. He didn't have a good suit for the funeral, and he didn't bow his head for the prayers. But he was the only grownup that I let off the hook. He was the only one I didn't see giving consent. He couldn't prevent anything, but he wasn't implicated in anything, either—not like the others, saying the Lord's Prayer in their unnaturally weighted voices, oozing religion and dishonor.

AT GLENDIVE, not far from the North Dakota border, we had a choice—either to continue on the interstate or head northeast, toward Williston, taking Route 16, then some secondary roads that would get us back to Highway 2.

We agreed that the interstate would be faster, and that it was important for us not to spend too much time—that is, money—on the road. Nevertheless we decided to cut back to Highway 2.

"I just like the idea of it better," I said.

Andrew said, "That's because it's what we planned to do in the beginning."

"We missed seeing Kalispell and Havre. And Wolf Point. I like the name."

"We'll see them on the way back."

Andrew's saying "on the way back" was a surprising pleasure to me. Of course, I had believed that we would be coming back, with our car and our lives and our family intact, having covered all that distance, having dealt somehow with those loyalties and problems, held ourselves up for inspection in such a foolhardy way. But it was a relief to hear him say it.

"What I can't get over," said Andrew, "is how you got the signal. It's got to be some kind of extra sense that mothers have."

Partly I wanted to believe that, to bask in my extra sense. Partly I wanted to warn him—to warn everybody—never to count on it.

"What I can't understand," I said, "is how you got over the fence."

"Neither can I."

So we went on, with the two in the back seat trusting us, because of no choice, and we ourselves trusting to be forgiven, in time, for everything that had first to be seen and condemned by those children: whatever was flippant, arbitrary, careless, callous—all our natural, and particular, mistakes.

# *Fits*

THE TWO PEOPLE who died were in their early sixties. They were both tall and well built, and carried a few pounds of extra weight. He was gray-haired, with a square, rather flat face. A broad nose kept him from looking perfectly dignified and handsome. Her hair was blond, a silvery blond that does not strike you as artificial anymore—though you know it is not natural—because so many women of that age have acquired it. On Boxing Day, when they dropped over to have a drink with Peg and Robert, she wore a pale-gray dress with a fine, shiny stripe in it, gray stockings, and gray shoes. She drank gin-and-tonic. He wore brown slacks and a cream-colored sweater, and drank rye-and-water. They had recently come back from a trip to Mexico. He had tried parachute-riding. She hadn't wanted to. They had gone to see a place in Yucatán—it looked like a well—where virgins were supposed to have been flung down, in the hope of good harvests.

"Actually, though, that's just a nineteenth-century notion," she said. "That's just the nineteenth-century notion of being so preoccupied with virginity. The truth probably is that they threw people down sort of indiscriminately. Girls or men or old people or whoever they could get their hands on. So not being a virgin would be no guarantee of safety!"

Across the room, Peg's two sons—the older one, Clayton, who was a virgin, and the younger one, Kevin, who was not—watched this breezy-talking silvery-blond woman with stern, bored expressions. She had said that she used to be a high-school English teacher. Clayton remarked afterward that he knew the type.

· · · ·

ROBERT and Peg have been married for nearly five years. Robert was never married before, but Peg married for the first time when she was eighteen. Her two boys were born while she and her husband lived with his parents on a farm. Her husband had a job driving trucks of livestock to the Canada Packers Abattoir in Toronto. Other truck-driving jobs followed, taking him farther and farther away. Peg and the boys moved to Gilmore, and she got a job working in Kuiper's store, which was called the Gilmore Arcade. Her husband ended up in the Arctic, driving trucks to oil rigs across the frozen Beaufort Sea. She got a divorce.

Robert's family owned the Gilmore Arcade but had never lived in Gilmore. His mother and sisters would not have believed you could survive a week in such a place. Robert's father had bought the store, and two other stores in nearby towns, shortly after the Second World War. He hired local managers, and drove up from Toronto a few times during the year to see how things were getting on.

For a long time, Robert did not take much interest in his father's various businesses. He took a degree in civil engineering, and had some idea of doing work in underdeveloped countries. He got a job in Peru, travelled through South America, gave up engineering for a while to work on a ranch in British Columbia. When his father became ill, it was necessary for him to come back to Toronto. He worked for the Provincial Department of Highways, in an engineering job that was not a very good one for a man of his age. He was thinking of getting a teaching degree and maybe going up North to teach Indians, changing his life completely, once his father died. He was getting close to forty then, and having his third major affair with a married woman.

Now and then, he drove up to Gilmore and the other towns to keep an eye on the stores. Once, he brought Lee with him, his third—and, as it turned out, his last—married woman. She brought a picnic lunch, drank Pimm's No. 1 in the car, and treated the whole trip as a merry excursion, a foray into hillbilly country. She had counted on making love in the open fields, and was incensed to find they were all full of cattle or uncomfortable cornstalks.

Robert's father died, and Robert did change his life, but instead of becoming a teacher and heading for the wilderness, he came to live in Gilmore to manage the stores himself. He married Peg.

IT WAS entirely by accident that Peg was the one who found them.

On Sunday evening, the farm woman who sold the Kuipers their eggs knocked on the door.

"I hope you don't mind me bringing these tonight instead of tomorrow morning," she said. "I have to take my daughter-in-law to Kitchener to have her ultrasound. I brought the Weebles theirs too, but I guess they're not home. I wonder if you'd mind if I left them here with you? I have to leave early in the morning. She was going to drive herself but I didn't think that was such a good idea. She's nearly five months but still vomiting. Tell them they can just pay me next time."

"No problem," said Robert. "No trouble at all. We can just run over with them in the morning. No problem at all!" Robert is a stocky, athletic-looking man, with curly, graying hair and bright brown eyes. His friendliness and obligingness are often emphatic, so that people might get the feeling of being buffeted from all sides. This is a manner that serves him well in Gilmore, where assurances are supposed to be repeated, and in fact much of conversation is repetition, a sort of dance of good intentions, without surprises. Just occasionally, talking to people, he feels something else, an obstruction, and isn't sure what it is (malice, stubbornness?) but it's like a rock at the bottom of a river when you're swimming—the clear water lifts you over it.

For a Gilmore person, Peg is reserved. She came up to the woman and relieved her of the eggs she was holding, while Robert went on assuring her it was no trouble and asking about the daughter-in-law's pregnancy. Peg smiled as she would smile in the store when she gave you your change—a quick transactional smile, nothing personal. She is a small slim woman with a cap of soft brown hair, freckles, and a scrubbed, youthful look. She wears pleated skirts, fresh neat blouses buttoned to the throat, pale sweaters, sometimes a black ribbon tie. She moves gracefully and makes very little noise. Robert once told her he had never met anyone so self-contained as she was. (His women have usually been talkative, stylishly effective, though careless about some of the details, tense, lively, "interesting.")

Peg said she didn't know what he meant.

He started to explain what a self-contained person was like. At that time, he had a very faulty comprehension of Gilmore vocabulary—he could still make mistakes about it—and he took too seriously the limits that were usually observed in daily exchanges.

"I know what the words mean," Peg said, smiling. "I just don't understand how you mean it about me."

Of course she knew what the words meant. Peg took courses, a different course each winter, choosing from what was offered at the local high school. She took a course on the History of Art, one on Great Civilizations of the East, one on Discoveries and Explorations Through the Ages. She went to class one night a week, even if she was very tired or had a cold. She wrote tests and prepared papers. Sometimes Robert would find a page covered with her small neat handwriting on top of the refrigerator or the dresser in their room.

*Therefore we see that the importance of Prince Henry the Navigator was in the inspiration and encouragement of other explorers for Portugal, even though he did not go on voyages himself.*

He was moved by her earnest statements, her painfully careful small handwriting, and angry that she never got more than a B-plus for these papers she worked so hard at.

"I don't do it for the marks," Peg said. Her cheekbones reddened under the freckles, as if she was making some kind of personal confession. "I do it for the enjoyment."

ROBERT was up before dawn on Monday morning, standing at the kitchen counter drinking his coffee, looking out at the fields covered with snow. The sky was clear, and the temperatures had dropped. It was going to be one of the bright, cold, hard January days that come after weeks of west wind, of blowing and falling snow. Creeks, rivers, ponds frozen over. Lake Huron frozen over as far as you could see. Perhaps all the way this year. That had happened, though rarely.

He had to drive to Keneally, to the Kuiper store there. Ice on the roof was causing water underneath to back up and leak through the ceiling. He would have to chop up the ice and get the roof clear. It would take him at least half the day.

All the repair work and upkeep on the store and on this house is done by Robert himself. He has learned to do plumbing and wiring. He enjoys the feeling that he can manage it. He enjoys the difficulty, and the difficulty of winter, here. Not much more than a hundred miles from Toronto, it is a different country. The snowbelt. Coming up here to live was not unlike heading into the wilderness, after all. Blizzards still isolate the towns and villages. Winter comes down hard on the country, settles down just the way the two-mile-high ice did thousands of years ago. People live within the winter in a way outsiders do not understand. They are watchful, provident, fatigued, exhilarated.

A thing he likes about this house is the back view, over the open country. That makes up for the straggling dead-end street without trees or sidewalks. The street was opened up after the war, when it was taken for granted that everybody would be using cars, not walking anywhere. And so they did. The houses are fairly close to the street and to each other, and when everybody who lives in the houses is home, cars take up nearly all the space where sidewalks, boulevards, shade trees might have been.

Robert, of course, was willing to buy another house. He assumed they would do that. There were—there are—fine old houses for sale in Gilmore, at prices that are a joke, by city standards. Peg said she couldn't see herself living in those places. He offered to build her a new house in the subdivision on the other side of town. She didn't want that either. She wanted to stay in this house, which was the first house she and the boys had lived in on their own. So Robert bought it—she was only renting—and built on the master bedroom and another bathroom, and made a television room in the basement. He got some help from Kevin, less from Clayton. The house still looked, from the street, like the house he had parked in front of the first time he drove Peg home from work. One and a half stories high, with a steep roof and a living-room window divided into square panes like the window on a Christmas card. White aluminum siding, narrow black shutters, black trim. Back in Toronto, he had thought of Peg living in this house. He had thought of her patterned, limited, serious, and desirable life.

He noticed the Weebles' eggs sitting on the counter. He thought of taking them over. But it was too early. The door would be locked. He didn't want to wake them. Peg could take the eggs when she left to open up the store. He took the Magic Marker that was sitting on the ledge under her reminder pad, and wrote on a paper towel, *Don't forget eggs to W's. Love, Robert.* These eggs were no cheaper than the ones you bought at the supermarket. It was just that Robert liked getting them from a farm. And they were brown. Peg said city people all had a thing about brown eggs—they thought brown eggs were more natural somehow, like brown sugar.

When he backed his car out, he saw that the Weebles' car was in their carport. So they were home from wherever they had been last night. Then he saw that the snow thrown up across the front of their driveway by the town snowplow had not been cleared. The plow must have gone by during the night. But he himself hadn't had to shovel any snow; there hadn't been any fresh snow overnight and the plow hadn't been out. The snow was from yesterday. They couldn't have been out last night. Unless they were walking. The sidewalks were not cleared, except along the main street and the school streets, and it was difficult to walk along the narrowed streets with their banks of snow, but, being new to town, they might have set out not realizing that.

He didn't look closely enough to see if there were footprints.

HE PICTURED what happened. First from the constable's report, then from Peg's.

Peg came out of the house at about twenty after eight. Clayton had already gone off to school, and Kevin, getting over an ear infection, was down in the basement room playing a Billy Idol tape and watching a game show on television. Peg had not forgotten the eggs. She got into her car and turned on the engine to warm it up, then walked out to the street, stepped over the Weebles' uncleared snow, and went up their driveway to the side door. She was wearing her white knitted scarf and tam and her lilac-colored, down-filled coat. Those coats made most of the women in Gilmore look like barrels, but Peg looked all right, being so slender.

The houses on the street were originally of only three designs. But by now most of them had been so altered, with new windows, porches, wings, and decks, that it was hard to find true mates anymore. The Weebles' house had been built as a mirror image of the Kuipers', but the front window had been changed, its Christmas-card panes taken out, and the roof had been lifted, so that there was a large upstairs window overlooking the street. The siding was pale green and the trim white, and there were no shutters.

The side door opened into a utility room, just as Peg's door did at home. She knocked lightly at first, thinking that they would be in the kitchen, which was only a few steps up from the utility room. She had noticed the car, of course, and wondered if they had got home late and were sleeping in. (She hadn't thought yet about the snow's not having been shovelled, and the fact that the plow hadn't been past in the night. That was something that occurred to her later on when she got into her own car and backed it out.) She knocked louder and louder. Her face was stinging already in the bright cold. She tried the door and found that it wasn't locked. She opened it and stepped into shelter and called.

The little room was dark. There was no light to speak of coming down from the kitchen, and there was a bamboo curtain over the side door. She set the eggs on the clothes dryer, and was going to leave them there. Then she thought she had better take them up into the kitchen, in case the Weebles wanted eggs for breakfast and had run out. They wouldn't think of looking in the utility room.

(This, in fact, was Robert's explanation to himself. She didn't say all that, but he forgot she didn't. She just said, "I thought I might as well take them up to the kitchen.")

The kitchen had those same bamboo curtains over the sink window and over the breakfast-nook windows, which meant that though the room faced east, like the Kuipers' kitchen, and though the sun was fully up by this time, not much light could get in. The day hadn't begun here.

But the house was warm. Perhaps they'd got up a while ago and turned up the thermostat, then gone back to bed. Perhaps they left it up all night—though they had seemed to Peg to be thriftier than that. She set the eggs on the counter by the sink. The layout of the kitchen was almost exactly the same as her own. She noticed a few dishes stacked, rinsed, but not washed, as if they'd had something to eat before they went to bed.

She called again from the living-room doorway.

The living room was perfectly tidy. It looked to Peg somehow too per-fectly tidy, but that—as she said to Robert—was probably the way the liv-ing room of a retired couple was bound to look to a woman used to having children around. Peg had never in her life had quite as much tidi-ness around her as she might have liked, having gone from a family home where there were six children to her in-laws' crowded farmhouse, which was crowded further with her own babies. She had told Robert a story about once asking for a beautiful bar of soap for Christmas, pink soap with a raised design of roses on it. She got it, and she used to hide it after every use so that it wouldn't get cracked and moldy in the cracks, the way soap always did in that house. She was grown up at that time, or thought she was.

She had stamped the snow off her boots in the utility room. Neverthe-less she hesitated to walk across the clean, pale-beige living-room carpet. She called again. She used the Weebles' first names, which she barely knew. Walter and Nora. They had moved in last April, and since then they had been away on two trips, so she didn't feel she knew them at all well, but it seemed silly to be calling, "Mr. and Mrs. Weeble. Are you up yet, Mr. and Mrs. Weeble?"

No answer.

They had an open staircase going up from the living room, just as Peg and Robert did. Peg walked now across the clean, pale carpet to the foot of the stairs, which were carpeted in the same material. She started to climb. She did not call again.

She must have known then or she would have called. It would be the normal thing to do, to keep calling the closer you got to where people might be sleeping. To warn them. They might be deeply asleep. Drunk. That wasn't the custom of the Weebles, so far as anybody knew, but no-body knew them that well. Retired people. Early retirement. He had been an accountant; she had been a teacher. They had lived in Hamilton. They had chosen Gilmore because Walter Weeble used to have an aunt and uncle here, whom he visited as a child. Both dead now, the aunt and uncle, but the place must have held pleasant memories for him. And it was cheap; this was surely a cheaper house than they could have afforded. They meant to spend their money travelling. No children.

She didn't call; she didn't halt again. She climbed the stairs and didn't look around as she came up; she faced straight ahead. Ahead was the bath-room, with the door open. It was clean and empty.

She turned at the top of the stairs toward the Weebles' bedroom. She had never been upstairs in this house before, but she knew where that would be. It would be the extended room at the front, with the wide window overlooking the street.

The door of that room was open.

PEG CAME downstairs and left the house by the kitchen, the utility room, the side door. Her footprints showed on the carpet and on the linoleum tiles, and outside on the snow. She closed the door after herself. Her car had been running all this time and was sitting in its own little cloud of steam. She got in and backed out and drove to the police station in the Town Hall.

"It's a bitter cold morning, Peg," the constable said.

"Yes, it is."

"So what can I do for you?"

ROBERT got more, from Karen.

Karen Adams was the clerk in the Gilmore Arcade. She was a young married woman, solidly built, usually good-humored, alert without particularly seeming to be so, efficient without a lot of bustle. She got along well with the customers; she got along with Peg and Robert. She had known Peg longer, of course. She defended her against those people who said Peg had got her nose in the air since she married rich. Karen said Peg hadn't changed from what she always was. But after today she said, "I always believed Peg and me to be friends, but now I'm not so sure."

Karen started work at ten. She arrived a little before that and asked if there had been many customers in yet, and Peg said no, nobody.

"I don't wonder," Karen said. "It's too cold. If there was any wind, it'd be murder."

Peg had made coffee. They had a new coffeemaker, Robert's Christmas present to the store. They used to have to get takeouts from the bakery up the street.

"Isn't this thing marvellous?" Karen said as she got her coffee.

Peg said yes. She was wiping up some marks on the floor.

"Oh-oh," said Karen. "Was that me or you?"

"I think it was me," Peg said.

"So I didn't think anything of it," Karen said later. "I thought she must've tracked in some mud. I didn't stop to think, Where would you get down to mud with all this snow on the ground?"

After a while, a customer came in, and it was Celia Simms, and she had heard. Karen was at the cash, and Peg was at the back, checking some invoices. Celia told Karen. She didn't know much; she didn't know how it had been done or that Peg was involved.

Karen shouted to the back of the store. "Peg! Peg! Something terrible has happened, and it's your next-door neighbors!"

Peg called back, "I know."

Celia lifted her eyebrows at Karen—she was one of those who didn't like Peg's attitude—and Karen loyally turned aside and waited till Celia went out of the store. Then she hurried to the back, making the hangers jingle on the racks.

"Both the Weebles are shot dead, Peg. Did you know that?"

Peg said, "Yes. I found them."

"You did! When did you?"

"This morning, just before I came in to work."

"They were murdered!"

"It was a murder-suicide," Peg said. "He shot her and then he shot himself. That's what happened."

"When she told me that," Karen said, "I started to shake. I shook all over and I couldn't stop myself." Telling Robert this, she shook again, to demonstrate, and pushed her hands up inside the sleeves of her blue plush jogging suit.

"So I said, 'What did you do when you found them,' and she said, 'I went and told the police.' I said, 'Did you scream, or what?' I said didn't her legs buckle, because I know mine would've. I can't imagine how I would've got myself out of there. She said she didn't remember much about getting out, but she did remember closing the door, the outside door, and thinking, Make sure that's closed in case some dog could get in. Isn't that awful? She was right, but it's awful to think of. Do you think she's in shock?"

"No," Robert said. "I think she's all right."

This conversation was taking place at the back of the store in the afternoon, when Peg had gone out to get a sandwich.

"She had not said one word to me. Nothing. I said, 'How come you never said a word about this, Peg,' and she said, 'I knew you'd find out pretty soon.' I said yes, but she could've told me. 'I'm sorry,' she says. 'I'm sorry.' Just like she's apologizing for some little thing like using my coffee mug. Only, Peg would never do that."

ROBERT had finished what he was doing at the Keneally store around noon, and decided to drive back to Gilmore before getting anything to eat. There was a highway diner just outside of town, on the way in from Keneally, and he thought that he would stop there. A few truckers and travellers were usually eating in the diner, but most of the trade was local—farmers on the way home, business and working men who had driven out from town. Robert liked this place, and he had entered it today with a feeling of buoyant expectation. He was hungry from his work in the cold air, and aware of the brilliance of the day, with the snow on the fields looking sculpted, dazzling, as permanent as marble. He had the sense he had fairly often in Gilmore, the sense of walking onto an informal stage, where a rambling, agreeable play was in progress. And he knew his lines—or knew, at least, that his improvisations would not fail. His whole life in Gilmore sometimes seemed to have this quality, but if he ever tried to describe it that way, it would sound as if it was an artificial life, something contrived, not entirely serious. And the very opposite was true. So when he met somebody from his old life, as he sometimes did when he went to Toronto, and was asked how he liked living in Gilmore, he would say, "I can't tell you how much I like it!" which was exactly the truth.

"WHY DIDN'T you get in touch with me?"

"You were up on the roof."

"You could have called the store and told Ellie. She would have told me."

"What good would that have done?"

"I could at least have come home."

He had come straight from the diner to the store, without eating what he had ordered. He did not think he would find Peg in any state of collapse—he knew her well enough for that—but he did think she would want to go home, let him fix her a drink, spend some time telling him about it.

She didn't want that. She wanted to go up the street to the bakery to get her usual lunch—a roll with ham and cheese.

"I let Karen go out to eat, but I haven't had time. Should I bring one back for you? If you didn't eat at the diner, I might as well."

When she brought him the sandwich, he sat and ate it at the desk where she had been doing invoices. She put fresh coffee and water into the coffeemaker.

"I can't imagine how we got along without this thing."

He looked at Peg's lilac-colored coat hanging beside Karen's red coat on the washroom door. On the lilac coat there was a long crusty smear of reddish-brown paint, down to the hemline.

Of course that wasn't paint. But on her coat? How did she get blood on her coat? She must have brushed up against them in that room. She must have got close.

Then he remembered the talk in the diner, and realized she wouldn't have needed to get that close. She could have got blood from the door frame. The constable had been in the diner, and he said there was blood everywhere, and not just blood.

"He shouldn't ever have used a shotgun for that kind of business," one of the men at the diner said.

Somebody else said, "Maybe a shotgun was all he had."

IT WAS busy in the store most of the afternoon. People on the street, in the bakery and the café and the bank and the Post Office, talking. People wanted to talk face to face. They had to get out and do it, in spite of the cold. Talking on the phone was not enough.

What had gone on at first, Robert gathered, was that people had got on the phone, just phoned anybody they could think of who might not have heard. Karen had phoned her friend Shirley, who was at home in bed with the flu, and her mother, who was in the hospital with a broken hip. It turned out her mother knew already—the whole hospital knew. And Shirley said, "My sister beat you to it."

It was true that people valued and looked forward to the moment of breaking the news—Karen was annoyed at Shirley's sister, who didn't work and could get to the phone whenever she wanted to—but there was real kindness and consideration behind this impulse, as well. Robert thought so. "I knew she wouldn't want not to know," Karen said, and that was true. Nobody would want not to know. To go out into the street, not knowing. To go around doing all the usual daily things, not knowing. He himself felt troubled, even slightly humiliated, to think that he hadn't known; Peg hadn't let him know.

Talk ran backward from the events of the morning. Where were the Weebles seen, and in what harmlessness and innocence, and how close to the moment when everything was changed?

She had stood in line at the Bank of Montreal on Friday afternoon.

He had got a haircut on Saturday morning.

They were together, buying groceries, in the I.G.A. on Friday evening at about eight o'clock.

What did they buy? A good supply? Specials, advertised bargains, more than enough to last for a couple of days?

More than enough. A bag of potatoes, for one thing.

Then reasons. The talk turned to reasons. Naturally. There had been no theories put forward in the diner. Nobody knew the reason, nobody could imagine. But by the end of the afternoon there were too many explanations to choose from.

Financial problems. He had been mixed up in some bad investment scheme in Hamilton. Some wild money-making deal that had fallen through. All their money was gone and they would have to live out the rest of their lives on the old-age pension.

They had owed money on their income taxes. Being an accountant, he thought he knew how to fix things, but he had been found out. He would be exposed, perhaps charged, shamed publicly, left poor. Even if it was only cheating the government, it would still be a disgrace when that kind of thing came out.

Was it a lot of money?

Certainly. A lot.

It was not money at all. They were ill. One of them or both of them. Cancer. Crippling arthritis. Alzheimer's disease. Recurrent mental problems. It was health, not money. It was suffering and helplessness they feared, not poverty.

A division of opinion became evident between men and women. It was nearly always the men who believed and insisted that the trouble had been money, and it was the women who talked of illness. Who would kill themselves just because they were poor, said some women scornfully. Or even because they might go to jail? It was always a woman too who suggested unhappiness in the marriage, who hinted at the drama of a discovered infidelity or the memory of an old one.

Robert listened to all these explanations but did not believe any of them. Loss of money, cancer, Alzheimer's disease. Equally plausible, these seemed to him, equally hollow and useless. What happened was that he believed each of them for about five minutes, no longer. If he could have believed one of them, hung on to it, it would have been as if something had taken its claws out of his chest and permitted him to breathe.

("They weren't Gilmore people, not really," a woman said to him in the bank. Then she looked embarrassed. "I don't mean like you.")

Peg kept busy getting some children's sweaters, mitts, snowsuits ready for the January sale. People came up to her when she was marking the tags, and she said, "Can I help you," so that they were placed right away in the position of being customers, and had to say that there was something they were looking for. The Arcade carried ladies' and children's clothes, sheets, towels, knitting wool, kitchenware, bulk candy, magazines, mugs, artificial flowers, and plenty of other things besides, so it was not hard to think of something.

What was it they were really looking for? Surely not much in the way of details, description. Very few people actually want that, or will admit they do, in a greedy and straightforward way. They want it, they don't want it. They start asking, they stop themselves. They listen and they back away. Perhaps they wanted from Peg just some kind of acknowledgment, some word or look that would send them away, saying, "Peg Kuiper is absolutely shattered." "I saw Peg Kuiper. She didn't say much but you could tell she was absolutely shattered."

Some people tried to talk to her, anyway.

"Wasn't that terrible what happened down by you?"

"Yes, it was."

"You must have known them a little bit, living next door."

"Not really. We hardly knew them at all."

"You never noticed anything that would've led you to think this could've happened?"

"We never noticed anything at all."

ROBERT pictured the Weebles getting into and out of their car in the driveway. That was where he had most often seen them. He recalled their Boxing Day visit. Her gray legs made him think of a nun. Her mention of virginity had embarrassed Peg and the boys. She reminded Robert a little of the kind of women he used to know. Her husband was less talkative, though not shy. They talked about Mexican food, which it seemed the husband had not liked. He did not like eating in restaurants.

Peg had said, "Oh, men never do!"

That surprised Robert, who asked her afterward did that mean she wanted to eat out more often?

"I just said that to take her side. I thought he was glaring at her a bit."

Was he glaring? Robert had not noticed. The man seemed too self-controlled to glare at his wife in public. Too well disposed, on the whole, perhaps in some way too indolent, to glare at anybody anywhere.

But it wasn't like Peg to exaggerate.

Bits of information kept arriving. The maiden name of Nora Weeble. Driscoll. Nora Driscoll. Someone knew a woman who had taught at the same school with her in Hamilton. Well-liked as a teacher, a fashionable dresser, she had some trouble keeping order. She had taken a French Conversation course, and a course in French cooking.

Some women here had asked her if she'd be interested in starting a book club, and she had said yes.

He had been more of a joiner in Hamilton than he was here. The Rotary Club. The Lions Club. Perhaps it had been for business reasons.

They were not churchgoers, as far as anybody knew, not in either place.

(ROBERT was right about the reasons. In Gilmore everything becomes known, sooner or later. Secrecy and confidentiality are seen to be against the public interest. There is a network of people who are married to or related to the people who work in the offices where all the records are kept.

There was no investment scheme, in Hamilton or anywhere else. No income-tax investigation. No problem about money. No cancer, tricky heart, high blood pressure. She had consulted the doctor about headaches, but the doctor did not think they were migraines, or anything serious.

At the funeral on Thursday, the United Church minister, who usually took up the slack in the cases of no known affiliation, spoke about the pressures and tensions of modern life but gave no more specific clues. Some people were disappointed, as if they expected him to do that—or thought that he might at least mention the dangers of falling away from faith and church membership, the sin of despair. Other people thought that saying anything more than he did say would have been in bad taste.)

ANOTHER person who thought Peg should have let him know was Kevin. He was waiting for them when they got home. He was still wearing his pajamas.

Why hadn't she come back to the house instead of driving to the police station? Why hadn't she called to him? She could have come back and phoned. Kevin could have phoned. At the very least, she could have called him from the store.

He had been down in the basement all morning, watching television. He hadn't heard the police come; he hadn't seen them go in or out. He had not known anything about what was going on until his girlfriend, Shanna, phoned him from school at lunch hour.

"She said they took the bodies out in garbage bags."

"How would she know?" said Clayton. "I thought she was at school."

"Somebody told her."

"She got that from television."

"She *said* they took them out in garbage bags."

"Shanna is a cretin. She is only good for one thing."

"Some people aren't good for anything."

Clayton was sixteen, Kevin fourteen. Two years apart in age but three years apart at school, because Clayton was accelerated and Kevin was not.

"Cut it out," Peg said. She had brought up some spaghetti sauce from the freezer and was thawing it in the double boiler. "Clayton. Kevin. Get busy and make me some salad."

Kevin said, "I'm sick. I might contaminate it."

He picked up the tablecloth and wrapped it around his shoulders like a shawl.

"Do we have to eat off that?" Clayton said. "Now he's got his crud on it?"

Peg said to Robert, "Are we having wine?"

Saturday and Sunday nights they usually had wine, but tonight Robert had not thought about it. He went down to the basement to get it. When he came back, Peg was sliding spaghetti into the cooker and Kevin had discarded the tablecloth. Clayton was making the salad. Clayton was small-boned, like his mother, and fiercely driven. A star runner, a demon examination writer.

Kevin was prowling around the kitchen, getting in the way, talking to Peg. Kevin was taller already than Clayton or Peg, perhaps taller than Robert. He had large shoulders and skinny legs and black hair that he wore in the nearest thing he dared to a Mohawk cut—Shanna cut it for him. His pale skin often broke out in pimples. Girls didn't seem to mind.

"So was there?" Kevin said. "Was there blood and guck all over?"

"Ghoul," said Clayton.

"Those were human beings, Kevin," Robert said.

"Were," said Kevin. "I know they *were* human beings. I mixed their drinks on Boxing Day. She drank gin and he drank rye. They were human beings then, but all they are now is chemicals. Mom? What did you see first? Shanna said there was blood and guck even out in the hallway."

"He's brutalized from all the TV he watches," Clayton said. "He thinks it was some video. He can't tell real blood from video blood."

"Mom? Was it splashed?"

Robert has a rule about letting Peg deal with her sons unless she asks for his help. But this time he said, "Kevin, you know it's about time you shut up."

"He can't help it," Clayton said. "Being ghoulish."

"You too, Clayton. You too."

But after a moment Clayton said, "Mom? Did you scream?"

"No," said Peg thoughtfully. "I didn't. I guess because there wasn't anybody to hear me. So I didn't."

"I might have heard you," said Kevin, cautiously trying a comeback.

"You had the television on."

"I didn't have the sound on. I had my tape on. I might have heard you through the tape if you screamed loud enough."

Peg lifted a strand of the spaghetti to try it. Robert was watching her, from time to time. He would have said he was watching to see if she was in any kind of trouble, if she seemed numb, or strange, or showed a quiver, if she dropped things or made the pots clatter. But in fact he was watching her just because there was no sign of such difficulty and because he knew there wouldn't be. She was preparing an ordinary meal, listening to the boys in her usual mildly censorious but unruffled way. The only thing more apparent than usual to Robert was her gracefulness, lightness, quickness, and ease around the kitchen.

Her tone to her sons, under its severity, seemed shockingly serene.

"Kevin, go and get some clothes on, if you want to eat at the table."

"I can eat in my pajamas."

"No."

"I can eat in bed."

"Not spaghetti, you can't."

WHILE they were washing up the pots and pans together—Clayton had gone for his run and Kevin was talking to Shanna on the phone—Peg told Robert her part of the story. He didn't ask her to, in so many words. He started off with "So when you went over, the door wasn't locked?" and she began to tell him.

"You don't mind talking about it?" Robert said.

"I knew you'd want to know."

She told him she knew what was wrong—at least, she knew that something was terribly wrong—before she started up the stairs.

"Were you frightened?"

"No. I didn't think about it like that—being frightened."

"There could have been somebody up there with a gun."

"No. I knew there wasn't. I knew there wasn't anybody but me alive in the house. Then I saw his leg, I saw his leg stretched out into the hall, and I knew then, but I had to go on in and make sure."

Robert said, "I understand that."

"It wasn't the foot he had taken the shoe off that was out there. He took the shoe off his other foot, so he could use that foot to pull the trigger when he shot himself. That was how he did it."

Robert knew all about that already, from the talk in the diner.

"So," said Peg. "That's really about all."

She shook dishwater from her hands, dried them, and, with a critical look, began rubbing in lotion.

Clayton came in at the side door. He stamped the snow from his shoes and ran up the steps.

"You should see the cars," he said. "Stupid cars all crawling along this street. Then they have to turn around at the end and crawl back. I wish they'd get stuck. I stood out there and gave them dirty looks, but I started to freeze so I had to come in."

"It's natural," Robert said. "It seems stupid but it's natural. They can't believe it, so they want to see where it happened."

"I don't see their problem," Clayton said. "I don't see why they can't believe it. Mom could believe it all right. Mom wasn't surprised."

"Well, of course I was," Peg said, and this was the first time Robert had noticed any sort of edge to her voice. "Of course I was surprised, Clayton. Just because I didn't break out screaming."

"You weren't surprised they could do it."

"I hardly knew them. We hardly knew the Weebles."

"I guess they had a fight," said Clayton.

"We don't know that," Peg said, stubbornly working the lotion into her skin. "We don't know if they had a fight, or what."

"When you and Dad used to have those fights?" Clayton said. "Remember, after we first moved to town? When he would be home? Over by the car wash? When you used to have those fights, you know what I used to think? I used to think one of you was going to come and kill me with a knife."

"That's not true," said Peg.

"It is true. I did."

Peg sat down at the table and covered her mouth with her hands. Clayton's mouth twitched. He couldn't seem to stop it, so he turned it into a little, taunting, twitching smile.

"That's what I used to lie in bed and think."

"Clayton. We would never either one of us ever have hurt you."

Robert believed it was time that he said something.

"What this is like," he said, "it's like an earthquake or a volcano. It's that kind of happening. It's a kind of fit. People can take a fit like the earth takes a fit. But it only happens once in a long while. It's a freak occurrence."

"Earthquakes and volcanoes aren't freaks," said Clayton, with a certain dry pleasure. "If you want to call that a fit, you'd have to call it a periodic fit. Such as people have, married people have."

"We don't," said Robert. He looked at Peg as if waiting for her to agree with him.

But Peg was looking at Clayton. She who always seemed pale and silky and assenting, but hard to follow as a watermark in fine paper, looked dried out, chalky, her outlines fixed in steady, helpless, unapologetic pain.

"No," said Clayton. "No, not you."

ROBERT told them that he was going for a walk. When he got outside, he saw that Clayton was right. There were cars nosing along the street, turning at the end, nosing their way back again. Getting a look. Inside those cars were just the same people, probably the very same people, he had been talking to during the afternoon. But now they seemed joined to their cars, making some new kind of monster that came poking around in a brutally curious way.

To avoid them, he went down a short dead-end street that branched off theirs. No houses had ever been built on this street, so it was not plowed. But the snow was hard, and easy to walk on. He didn't notice how easy it was to walk on until he realized that he had gone beyond the end of the street and up a slope, which was not a slope of land at all, but a drift of snow. The drift neatly covered the fence that usually separated the street from the field. He had walked over the fence without knowing what he was doing. The snow was that hard.

He walked here and there, testing. The crust took his weight without a whisper or a crack. It was the same everywhere. You could walk over the snowy fields as if you were walking on cement. (This morning, looking at the snow, hadn't he thought of marble?) But this paving was not flat. It rose and dipped in a way that had not much to do with the contours of the ground underneath. The snow created its own landscape, which was sweeping, in a grand and arbitrary style.

Instead of walking around on the plowed streets of town, he could walk over the fields. He could cut across to the diner on the highway, which stayed open until midnight. He would have a cup of coffee there, turn around, and walk home.

ONE NIGHT, about six months before Robert married Peg, he and Lee were sitting drinking in his apartment. They were having an argument about whether it was permissible, or sickening, to have your family initial on your silverware. All of a sudden, the argument split open—Robert couldn't remember how, but it split open, and they found themselves saying the cruellest things to each other that they could imagine. Their voices changed from the raised pitch and speed of argument, and they spoke quietly with a subtle loathing.

"You always make me think of a dog," Lee said. "You always make me think of one of those dogs that push up on people and paw them, with their big disgusting tongues hanging out. You're so eager. All your friendliness and eagerness—that's really aggression. I'm not the only one who thinks this about you. A lot of people avoid you. They can't stand you. You'd be surprised. You push and paw in that eager pathetic way, but you have a calculating look. That's why I don't care if I hurt you."

"Maybe I should tell you one of the things I don't like, then," said Robert reasonably. "It's the way you laugh. On the phone particularly. You laugh at the end of practically every sentence. I used to think it was a nervous tic, but it always really annoyed me. And I've figured out why. You're always telling somebody about what a raw deal you're getting somewhere or some unkind thing a person said to you—that's about two-thirds of your horrendously boring self-centered conversation. And then you laugh. Ha-ha, you can take it, you don't expect anything better. That laugh is sick."

After some more of this, they started to laugh themselves, Robert and Lee, but it was not the laughter of a breakthrough into reconciliation; they did not fall upon each other in relief, crying, "What rot, I didn't mean it, did you mean it?" ("No, of course not, of course I didn't mean it.") They laughed in recognition of their extremity, just as they might have laughed at another time, in the middle of quite different, astoundingly tender declarations. They trembled with murderous pleasure, with the excitement of saying what could never be retracted; they exulted in wounds inflicted but also in wounds received, and one or the other said at some point, "This is the first time we've spoken the truth since we've known each other!" For even things that came to them more or less on the spur of the moment seemed the most urgent truths that had been hardening for a long time and pushing to get out.

It wasn't so far from laughing to making love, which they did, all with no retraction. Robert made barking noises, as a dog should, and nuzzled Lee in a bruising way, snapping with real appetite at her flesh. Afterward they were enormously and finally sick of each other but no longer disposed to blame.

"THERE are things I just absolutely and eternally want to forget about," Robert had told Peg. He talked to her about cutting his losses, abandoning old bad habits, old deceptions and self-deceptions, mistaken notions about life, and about himself. He said that he had been an emotional spendthrift, had thrown himself into hopeless and painful entanglements as a way of avoiding anything that had normal possibilities. That was all experiment and posturing, rejection of the ordinary, decent contracts of life. So he said to her. Errors of avoidance, when he had thought he was running risks and getting intense experiences.

"Errors of avoidance that I mistook for errors of passion," he said, then thought that he sounded pretentious when he was actually sweating with sincerity, with the effort and the relief.

In return, Peg gave him facts.

We lived with Dave's parents. There was never enough hot water for the baby's wash. Finally we got out and came to town and we lived beside the car wash. Dave was only with us weekends then. It was very noisy, especially at night. Then Dave got another job, he went up North, and I rented this place.

Errors of avoidance, errors of passion. She didn't say.

Dave had a kidney problem when he was little and he was out of school a whole winter. He read a book about the Arctic. It was probably the only book he ever read that he didn't have to. Anyway, he always dreamed about it; he wanted to go there. So finally he did.

A man doesn't just drive farther and farther away in his trucks until he disappears from his wife's view. Not even if he has always dreamed of the Arctic. Things happen before he goes. Marriage knots aren't going to slip apart painlessly, with the pull of distance. There's got to be some wrenching and slashing. But she didn't say, and he didn't ask, or even think much about that, till now.

HE WALKED very quickly over the snow crust, and when he reached the diner he found that he didn't want to go in yet. He would cross the highway and walk a little farther, then go into the diner to get warmed up on his way home.

By the time he was on his way home, the police car that was parked at the diner ought to be gone. The night constable was in there now, taking his break. This was not the same man Robert had seen and listened to when he dropped in on his way home from Keneally. This man would not have seen anything at first hand. He hadn't talked to Peg. Nevertheless he would be talking about it; everybody in the diner would be talking about it, going over the same scene and the same questions, the possibilities. No blame to them.

When they saw Robert, they would want to know how Peg was.

There was one thing he was going to ask her, just before Clayton came in. At least, he was turning the question over in his mind, wondering if it would be all right to ask her. A discrepancy, a detail, in the midst of so many abominable details.

And now he knew it wouldn't be all right; it would never be all right. It had nothing to do with him. One discrepancy, one detail—one lie—that would never have anything to do with him.

Walking on this magic surface, he did not grow tired. He grew lighter, if anything. He was taking himself farther and farther away from town, although for a while he didn't realize this. In the clear air, the lights of Gilmore were so bright they seemed only half a field away, instead of half a mile, then a mile and a half, then two miles. Very fine flakes of snow, fine as dust, and glittering, lay on the crust that held him. There was a glitter too around the branches of the trees and bushes that he was getting closer to. It wasn't like the casing around twigs and delicate branches that an ice storm leaves. It was as if the wood itself had altered and begun to sparkle.

This is the very weather in which noses and fingers are frozen. But nothing felt cold.

He was getting quite close to a large woodlot. He was crossing a long slanting shelf of snow, with the trees ahead and to one side of him. Over there, to the side, something caught his eye. There was a new kind of glitter under the trees. A congestion of shapes, with black holes in them, and unmatched arms or petals reaching up to the lower branches of the trees. He headed toward these shapes, but whatever they were did not become clear. They did not look like anything he knew. They did not look like anything, except perhaps a bit like armed giants half collapsed, frozen in combat, or like the jumbled towers of a crazy small-scale city—a space-age, small-scale city. He kept waiting for an explanation, and not getting one, until he got very close. He was so close he could almost have touched one of these monstrosities before he saw that they were just old cars. Old cars and trucks and even a school bus that had been pushed in under the trees and left. Some were completely overturned, and some were tipped over one another at odd angles. They were partly filled, partly covered, with snow. The black holes were their gutted insides. Twisted bits of chrome, fragments of headlights, were glittering.

He thought of himself telling Peg about this—how close he had to get before he saw that what amazed him and bewildered him so was nothing but old wrecks, and how he then felt disappointed, but also like laughing. They needed some new thing to talk about. Now he felt more like going home.

AT NOON, when the constable in the diner was giving his account, he had described how the force of the shot threw Walter Weeble backward. "It blasted him partways out of the room. His head was laying out in the hall. What was left of it was laying out in the hall."

Not a leg. Not the indicative leg, whole and decent in its trousers, the shod foot. That was not what anybody turning at the top of the stairs would see and would have to step over, step through, in order to go into the bedroom and look at the rest of what was there.

# Friend of My Youth

WITH THANKS TO R.J.T.

I USED TO DREAM about my mother, and though the details in the dream varied, the surprise in it was always the same. The dream stopped, I suppose, because it was too transparent in its hopefulness, too easy in its forgiveness.

In the dream I would be the age I really was, living the life I was really living, and I would discover that my mother was still alive. (The fact is, she died when I was in my early twenties and she in her early fifties.) Sometimes I would find myself in our old kitchen, where my mother would be rolling out piecrust on the table, or washing the dishes in the battered cream-colored dishpan with the red rim. But other times I would run into her on the street, in places where I would never have expected to see her. She might be walking through a handsome hotel lobby, or lining up in an airport. She would be looking quite well—not exactly youthful, not entirely untouched by the paralyzing disease that held her in its grip for a decade or more before her death, but so much better than I remembered that I would be astonished. Oh, I just have this little tremor in my arm, she would say, and a little stiffness up this side of my face. It is a nuisance but I get around.

I recovered then what in waking life I had lost—my mother's liveliness of face and voice before her throat muscles stiffened and a woeful, impersonal mask fastened itself over her features. How could I have forgotten this, I would think in the dream—the casual humor she had, not ironic but merry, the lightness and impatience and confidence? I would say that I was sorry I hadn't been to see her in such a long time—meaning not that I felt guilty but that I was sorry I had kept a bugbear in my mind, instead of this reality—and the strangest, kindest thing of all to me was her matter-of-fact reply.

Oh, well, she said, better late than never. I was sure I'd see you someday.

WHEN my mother was a young woman with a soft, mischievous face and shiny, opaque silk stockings on her plump legs (I have seen a photograph of her, with her pupils), she went to teach at a one-room school, called Grieves School, in the Ottawa Valley. The school was on a corner of the farm that belonged to the Grieves family—a very good farm for that country. Well-drained fields with none of the Precambrian rock shouldering through the soil, a little willow-edged river running alongside, a sugar bush, log barns, and a large, unornamented house whose wooden walls had never been painted but had been left to weather. And when wood weathers in the Ottawa Valley, my mother said, I do not know why this is, but it never turns gray, it turns black. There must be something in the air, she said. She often spoke of the Ottawa Valley, which was her home—she had grown up about twenty miles away from Grieves School—in a dogmatic, mystified way, emphasizing things about it that distinguished it from any other place on earth. Houses turn black, maple syrup has a taste no maple syrup produced elsewhere can equal, bears amble within sight of farmhouses. Of course I was disappointed when I finally got to see this place. It was not a valley at all, if by that you mean a cleft between hills; it was a mixture of flat fields and low rocks and heavy bush and little lakes—a scrambled, disarranged sort of country with no easy harmony about it, not yielding readily to any description.

The log barns and unpainted house, common enough on poor farms, were not in the Grieveses' case a sign of poverty but of policy. They had the money but they did not spend it. That was what people told my mother. The Grieveses worked hard and they were far from ignorant, but they were very backward. They didn't have a car or electricity or a telephone or a tractor. Some people thought this was because they were Cameronians—they were the only people in the school district who were of that religion—but in fact their church (which they themselves always called the Reformed Presbyterian) did not forbid engines or electricity or any inventions of that sort, just cardplaying, dancing, movies, and, on Sundays, any activity at all that was not religious or unavoidable.

My mother could not say who the Cameronians were or why they were called that. Some freak religion from Scotland, she said from the perch of her obedient and lighthearted Anglicanism. The teacher always boarded with the Grieveses, and my mother was a little daunted at the thought of going to live in that black board house with its paralytic Sundays and coal-oil lamps and primitive notions. But she was engaged by that time, she wanted to work on her trousseau instead of running around the country having a good time, and she figured she could get home one Sunday out of three. (On Sundays at the Grieveses' house, you could light a fire for heat but not for cooking, you could not even boil the kettle to make tea, and you were not supposed to write a letter or swat a fly. But it turned out that my mother was exempt from these rules. "No, no," said Flora Grieves, laughing at her. "That doesn't mean you. You must just go on as you're used to doing." And after a while my mother had made friends with Flora to such an extent that she wasn't even going home on the Sundays when she'd planned to.)

Flora and Ellie Grieves were the two sisters left of the family. Ellie was married, to a man called Robert Deal, who lived there and worked the farm but had not changed its name to Deal's in anyone's mind. By the way people spoke, my mother expected the Grieves sisters and Robert Deal to be middle-aged at least, but Ellie, the younger sister, was only about thirty, and Flora seven or eight years older. Robert Deal might be in between.

The house was divided in an unexpected way. The married couple didn't live with Flora. At the time of their marriage, she had given them the parlor and the dining room, the front bedrooms and staircase, the winter kitchen. There was no need to decide about the bathroom, because there wasn't one. Flora had the summer kitchen, with its open rafters and uncovered brick walls, the old pantry made into a narrow dining room and sitting room, and the two back bedrooms, one of which was my mother's. The teacher was housed with Flora, in the poorer part of the house. But my mother didn't mind. She immediately preferred Flora, and Flora's cheerfulness, to the silence and sickroom atmosphere of the front rooms. In Flora's domain it was not even true that all amusements were forbidden. She had a crokinole board—she taught my mother how to play.

The division had been made, of course, in the expectation that Robert and Ellie would have a family, and that they would need the room. This hadn't happened. They had been married for more than a dozen years and there had not been a live child. Time and again Ellie had been pregnant, but two babies had been stillborn, and the rest she had miscarried. During my mother's first year, Ellie seemed to be staying in bed more and more of the time, and my mother thought that she must be pregnant again, but there was no mention of it. Such people would not mention it. You could not tell from the look of Ellie, when she got up and walked around, because she showed a stretched and ruined though slack-chested shape. She carried a sickbed odor, and she fretted in a childish way about everything. Flora took care of her and did all the work. She washed the clothes and tidied up the rooms and cooked the meals served in both sides of the house, as well as helping Robert with the milking and separating. She was up before daylight and never seemed to tire. During the first spring my mother was there, a great housecleaning was embarked upon, during which Flora climbed the ladders herself and carried down the storm windows, washed and stacked them away, carried all the furniture out of one room after another so that she could scrub the woodwork and varnish the floors. She washed every dish and glass that was sitting in the cupboards supposedly clean already. She scalded every pot and spoon. Such need and energy possessed her that she could hardly sleep—my mother would wake up to the sound of stovepipes being taken down, or the broom, draped in a dish towel, whacking at the smoky cobwebs. Through the washed uncurtained windows came a torrent of unmerciful light. The cleanliness was devastating. My mother slept now on sheets that had been bleached and starched and that gave her a rash. Sick Ellie complained daily of the smell of varnish and cleansing powders. Flora's hands were raw. But her disposition remained top-notch. Her kerchief and apron and Robert's baggy overalls that she donned for the climbing jobs gave her the air of a comedian—sportive, unpredictable.

My mother called her a whirling dervish.

"You're a regular whirling dervish, Flora," she said, and Flora halted. She wanted to know what was meant. My mother went ahead and explained, though she was a little afraid lest piety should be offended. (Not piety exactly—you could not call it that. Religious strictness.) Of course it wasn't. There was not a trace of nastiness or smug vigilance in Flora's observance of her religion. She had no fear of heathens—she had always lived in the midst of them. She liked the idea of being a dervish, and went to tell her sister.

"Do you know what the teacher says I am?"

Flora and Ellie were both dark-haired, dark-eyed women, tall and narrow-shouldered and long-legged. Ellie was a wreck, of course, but Flora was still superbly straight and graceful. She could look like a queen, my mother said—even riding into town in that cart they had. For church they used a buggy or a cutter, but when they went to town they often had to transport sacks of wool—they kept a few sheep—or of produce, to sell, and they had to bring provisions home. The trip of a few miles was not made often. Robert rode in front, to drive the horse—Flora could drive a horse perfectly well, but it must always be the man who drove. Flora would be standing behind holding on to the sacks. She rode to town and back standing up, keeping an easy balance, wearing her black hat. Almost ridiculous but not quite. A gypsy queen, my mother thought she looked like, with her black hair and her skin that always looked slightly tanned, and her lithe and bold serenity. Of course she lacked the gold bangles and the bright clothes. My mother envied her her slenderness, and her cheekbones.

RETURNING in the fall for her second year, my mother learned what was the matter with Ellie.

"My sister has a growth," Flora said. Nobody then spoke of cancer.

My mother had heard that before. People suspected it. My mother knew many people in the district by that time. She had made particular friends with a young woman who worked in the Post Office; this woman was going to be one of my mother's bridesmaids. The story of Flora and Ellie and Robert had been told—or all that people knew of it—in various versions. My mother did not feel that she was listening to gossip, because she was always on the alert for any disparaging remarks about Flora—she would not put up with that. But indeed nobody offered any. Everybody said that Flora had behaved like a saint. Even when she went to extremes, as in dividing up the house—that was like a saint.

Robert came to work at Grieveses' some months before the girls' father died. They knew him already, from church. (Oh, that church, my mother said, having attended it once, out of curiosity—that drear building miles on the other side of town, no organ or piano and plain glass in the windows and a doddery old minister with his hours-long sermon, a man hitting a tuning fork for the singing.) Robert had come out from Scotland and was on his way west. He had stopped with relatives or people he knew, members of the scanty congregation. To earn some money, probably, he came to Grieveses'. Soon he and Flora were engaged. They could not go to dances or to card parties like other couples, but they went for long walks. The chaperone—unofficially—was Ellie. Ellie was then a wild tease, a long-haired, impudent, childish girl full of lolloping energy. She would run up hills and smite the mullein stalks with a stick, shouting and prancing and pretending to be a warrior on horseback. That, or the horse itself. This when she was fifteen, sixteen years old. Nobody but Flora could control her, and generally Flora just laughed at her, being too used to her to wonder if she was quite right in the head. They were wonderfully fond of each other. Ellie, with her long skinny body, her long pale face, was like a copy of Flora—the kind of copy you often see in families, in which because of some carelessness or exaggeration of features or coloring, the handsomeness of one person passes into the plainness—or almost plainness—of the other. But Ellie had no jealousy about this. She loved to comb out Flora's hair and pin it up. They had great times, washing each other's hair. Ellie would press her face into Flora's throat, like a colt nuzzling its mother. So when Robert laid claim to Flora, or Flora to him— nobody knew how it was—Ellie had to be included. She didn't show any spite toward Robert, but she pursued and waylaid them on their walks; she sprung on them out of the bushes or sneaked up behind them so softly that she could blow on their necks. People saw her do it. And they heard of her jokes. She had always been terrible for jokes and sometimes it had got her into trouble with her father, but Flora had protected her. Now she put thistles in Robert's bed. She set his place at the table with the knife and fork the wrong way around. She switched the milk pails to give him the old one with the hole in it. For Flora's sake, maybe, Robert humored her.

The father had made Flora and Robert set the wedding day a year ahead, and after he died they did not move it any closer. Robert went on living in the house. Nobody knew how to speak to Flora about this being scandalous, or looking scandalous. Flora would just ask why. Instead of putting the wedding ahead, she put it back—from next spring to early fall, so that there should be a full year between it and her father's death. A year from wedding to funeral—that seemed proper to her. She trusted fully in Robert's patience and in her own purity.

So she might. But in the winter a commotion started. There was Ellie, vomiting, weeping, running off and hiding in the haymow, howling when they found her and pulled her out, jumping to the barn floor, running around in circles, rolling in the snow. Ellie was deranged. Flora had to call the doctor. She told him that her sister's periods had stopped—could the backup of blood be driving her wild? Robert had had to catch her and tie her up, and together he and Flora had put her to bed. She would not take food, just whipped her head from side to side, howling. It looked as if she would die speechless. But somehow the truth came out. Not from the doctor, who could not get close enough to examine her, with all her thrashing about. Probably, Robert confessed. Flora finally got wind of the truth, through all her high-mindedness. Now there had to be a wedding, though not the one that had been planned.

No cake, no new clothes, no wedding trip, no congratulations. Just a shameful hurry-up visit to the manse. Some people, seeing the names in the paper, thought the editor must have got the sisters mixed up. They thought it must be Flora. A hurry-up wedding for Flora! But no—it was Flora who pressed Robert's suit—it must have been—and got Ellie out of bed and washed her and made her presentable. It would have been Flora who picked one geranium from the window plant and pinned it to her sister's dress. And Ellie hadn't torn it out. Ellie was meek now, no longer flailing or crying. She let Flora fix her up, she let herself be married, she was never wild from that day on.

Flora had the house divided. She herself helped Robert build the necessary partitions. The baby was carried full term—nobody even pretended that it was early—but it was born dead after a long, tearing labor. Perhaps

Ellie had damaged it when she jumped from the barn beam and rolled in the snow and beat on herself. Even if she hadn't done that, people would have expected something to go wrong, with that child or maybe one that came later. God dealt out punishment for hurry-up marriages—not just Presbyterians but almost everybody else believed that. God rewarded lust with dead babies, idiots, harelips and withered limbs and clubfeet.

In this case the punishment continued. Ellie had one miscarriage after another, then another stillbirth and more miscarriages. She was constantly pregnant, and the pregnancies were full of vomiting fits that lasted for days, headaches, cramps, dizzy spells. The miscarriages were as agonizing as full-term births. Ellie could not do her own work. She walked around holding on to chairs. Her numb silence passed off, and she became a complainer. If anybody came to visit, she would talk about the peculiarities of her headaches or describe her latest fainting fit, or even—in front of men, in front of unmarried girls or children—go into bloody detail about what Flora called her "disappointments." When people changed the subject or dragged the children away, she turned sullen. She demanded new medicine, reviled the doctor, nagged Flora. She accused Flora of washing the dishes with a great clang and clatter, out of spite, of pulling her—Ellie's—hair when she combed it out, of stingily substituting water-and-molasses for her real medicine. No matter what she said, Flora soothed her. Everybody who came into the house had some story of that kind to tell. Flora said, "Where's my little girl, then? Where's my Ellie? This isn't my Ellie, this is some crosspatch got in here in place of her!"

In the winter evenings after she came in from helping Robert with the barn chores, Flora would wash and change her clothes and go next door to read Ellie to sleep. My mother might invite herself along, taking whatever sewing she was doing, on some item of her trousseau. Ellie's bed was set up in the big dining room, where there was a gas lamp over the table. My mother sat on one side of the table, sewing, and Flora sat on the other side, reading aloud. Sometimes Ellie said, "I can't hear you." Or if Flora paused for a little rest Ellie said, "I'm not asleep yet."

What did Flora read? Stories about Scottish life—not classics. Stories about urchins and comic grandmothers. The only title my mother could remember was *Wee Macgregor*. She could not follow the stories very well, or laugh when Flora laughed and Ellie gave a whimper, because so much was in Scots dialect or read with that thick accent. She was surprised that Flora could do it—it wasn't the way Flora ordinarily talked, at all.

(But wouldn't it be the way Robert talked? Perhaps that is why my mother never reports anything that Robert said, never has him contributing to the scene. He must have been there, he must have been sitting there in the room. They would only heat the main room of the house. I see him black-haired, heavy-shouldered, with the strength of a plow horse, and the same kind of sombre, shackled beauty.)

Then Flora would say, "That's all of that for tonight." She would pick up another book, an old book written by some preacher of their faith. There was in it such stuff as my mother had never heard. What stuff? She couldn't say. All the stuff that was in their monstrous old religion. That put Ellie to sleep, or made her pretend she was asleep, after a couple of pages.

All that configuration of the elect and the damned, my mother must have meant—all the arguments about the illusion and necessity of free will. Doom and slippery redemption. The torturing, defeating, but for some minds irresistible pileup of interlocking and contradictory notions. My mother could resist it. Her faith was easy, her spirits at that time robust. Ideas were not what she was curious about, ever.

But what sort of thing was that, she asked (silently), to read to a dying woman? This was the nearest she got to criticizing Flora.

The answer—that it was the only thing, if you believed it—never seemed to have occurred to her.

BY SPRING a nurse had arrived. That was the way things were done then. People died at home, and a nurse came in to manage it.

The nurse's name was Audrey Atkinson. She was a stout woman with corsets as stiff as barrel hoops, marcelled hair the color of brass candlesticks, a mouth shaped by lipstick beyond its own stingy outlines. She drove a car into the yard—her own car, a dark-green coupé, shiny and smart. News of Audrey Atkinson and her car spread quickly. Questions were asked. Where did she get the money? Had some rich fool altered his will on her behalf? Had she exercised influence? Or simply helped herself to a stash of bills under the mattress? How was she to be trusted?

Hers was the first car ever to sit in the Grieveses' yard overnight.

Audrey Atkinson said that she had never been called out to tend a case in so primitive a house. It was beyond her, she said, how people could live in such a way.

"It's not that they're poor, even," she said to my mother. "It isn't, is it? That I could understand. Or it's not even their religion. So what is it? They do not care!"

She tried at first to cozy up to my mother, as if they would be natural allies in this benighted place. She spoke as if they were around the same age—both stylish, intelligent women who liked a good time and had modern ideas. She offered to teach my mother to drive the car. She offered her cigarettes. My mother was more tempted by the idea of learning to drive than she was by the cigarettes. But she said no, she would wait for her husband to teach her. Audrey Atkinson raised her pinkish-orange eyebrows at my mother behind Flora's back, and my mother was furious. She disliked the nurse far more than Flora did.

"I knew what she was like and Flora didn't," my mother said. She meant that she caught a whiff of a cheap life, maybe even of drinking establishments and unsavory men, of hard bargains, which Flora was too unworldly to notice.

Flora started into the great housecleaning again. She had the curtains spread out on stretchers, she beat the rugs on the line, she leapt up on the stepladder to attack the dust on the molding. But she was impeded all the time by Nurse Atkinson's complaining.

"I wondered if we could have a little less of the running and clattering?" said Nurse Atkinson with offensive politeness. "I only ask for my patient's sake." She always spoke of Ellie as "my patient" and pretended that she was the only one to protect her and compel respect. But she was not so respectful of Ellie herself. "Allee-oop," she would say, dragging the poor creature up on her pillows. And she told Ellie she was not going to stand for fretting and whimpering. "You don't do yourself any good that way," she said. "And you certainly don't make me come any quicker. What you just as well might do is learn to control yourself." She exclaimed at Ellie's bedsores in a scolding way, as if they were a further disgrace of the house. She demanded lotions, ointments, expensive soaps—most of them, no doubt, to protect her own skin, which she claimed suffered from the hard water. (How could it be hard, my mother asked her—sticking up for the household when nobody else would—how could it be hard when it came straight from the rain barrel?)

Nurse Atkinson wanted cream too—she said that they should hold some back, not sell it all to the creamery. She wanted to make nourishing soups and puddings for her patient. She did make puddings, and jellies, from packaged mixes such as had never before entered this house. My mother was convinced that she ate them all herself.

Flora still read to Ellie, but now it was only short bits from the Bible. When she finished and stood up, Ellie tried to cling to her. Ellie wept, sometimes she made ridiculous complaints. She said there was a horned cow outside, trying to get into the room and kill her.

"They often get some kind of idea like that," Nurse Atkinson said. "You mustn't give in to her or she won't let you go day or night. That's what they're like, they only think about themselves. Now, when I'm here alone with her, she behaves herself quite nice. I don't have any trouble at all. But after you been in here I have trouble all over again because she sees you and she gets upset. You don't want to make my job harder for me, do you? I mean, you brought me here to take charge, didn't you?"

"Ellie, now, Ellie dear, I must go," said Flora, and to the nurse she said, "I understand. I do understand that you have to be in charge and I admire you, I admire you for your work. In your work you have to have so much patience and kindness."

My mother wondered at this—was Flora really so blinded, or did she hope by this undeserved praise to exhort Nurse Atkinson to the patience and kindness that she didn't have? Nurse Atkinson was too thick-skinned and self-approving for any trick like that to work.

"It is a hard job, all right, and not many can do it," she said. "It's not like those nurses in the hospital, where they got everything laid out for them." She had no time for more conversation—she was trying to bring in "Make-Believe Ballroom" on her battery radio.

My mother was busy with the final exams and the June exercises at the school. She was getting ready for her wedding in July. Friends came in cars and whisked her off to the dressmaker's, to parties, to choose the invitations and order the cake. The lilacs came out, the evenings lengthened, the birds were back and nesting, my mother bloomed in everybody's attention, about to set out on the deliciously solemn adventure of marriage. Her dress was to be appliquéd with silk roses, her veil held by a cap of seed pearls. She belonged to the first generation of young women who saved their money and paid for their own weddings—far fancier than their parents could have afforded.

On her last evening, the friend from the Post Office came to drive her away, with her clothes and her books and the things she had made for her trousseau and the gifts her pupils and others had given her. There was great fuss and laughter about getting everything loaded into the car. Flora came out and helped. This getting married is even more of a nuisance than I thought, said Flora, laughing. She gave my mother a dresser scarf, which she had crocheted in secret. Nurse Atkinson could not be shut out of an important occasion—she presented a spray bottle of cologne. Flora stood on the slope at the side of the house to wave goodbye. She had been invited to the wedding, but of course she had said she could not come, she could not "go out" at such a time. The last my mother ever saw of her was this solitary, energetically waving figure in her housecleaning apron and bandanna, on the green slope by the black-walled house, in the evening light.

"Well, maybe now she'll get what she should've got the first time round," the friend from the Post Office said. "Maybe now they'll be able to get married. Is she too old to start a family? How old is she, anyway?"

My mother thought that this was a crude way of talking about Flora and replied that she didn't know. But she had to admit to herself that she had been thinking the very same thing.

WHEN she was married and settled in her own home, three hundred miles away, my mother got a letter from Flora. Ellie was dead. She had died firm in her faith, Flora said, and grateful for her release. Nurse Atkinson was staying on for a little while, until it was time for her to go off to her next case. This was late in the summer.

News of what happened next did not come from Flora. When she wrote at Christmas, she seemed to take for granted that information would have gone ahead of her.

*You have in all probability heard*, wrote Flora, *that Robert and Nurse Atkinson have been married. They are living on here, in Robert's part of the house. They are fixing it up to suit themselves. It is very impolite of me to call her Nurse Atkinson, as I see I have done. I ought to have called her Audrey.*

Of course the Post Office friend had written, and so had others. It was a great shock and scandal and a matter that excited the district—the wedding as secret and surprising as Robert's first one had been (though surely not for the same reason), Nurse Atkinson permanently installed in the community, Flora losing out for the second time. Nobody had been aware of any courtship, and they asked how the woman could have enticed him. Did she promise children, lying about her age?

The surprises were not to stop with the wedding. The bride got down to business immediately with the "fixing up" that Flora mentioned. In came the electricity and then the telephone. Now Nurse Atkinson—she would always be called Nurse Atkinson—was heard on the party line lambasting painters and paperhangers and delivery services. She was having everything done over. She was buying an electric stove and putting in a bathroom, and who knew where the money was coming from? Was it all hers, got in her deathbed dealings, in shady bequests? Was it Robert's, was he claiming his share? Ellie's share, left to him and Nurse Atkinson to enjoy themselves with, the shameless pair?

All these improvements took place on one side of the house only. Flora's side remained just as it was. No electric lights there, no fresh wallpaper or new venetian blinds. When the house was painted on the outside—cream with dark-green trim—Flora's side was left bare. This strange open statement was greeted at first with pity and disapproval, then with less sympathy, as a sign of Flora's stubbornness and eccentricity (she could have bought her own paint and made it look decent), and finally as a joke. People drove out of their way to see it.

There was always a dance given in the schoolhouse for a newly married couple. A cash collection—called "a purse of money"—was presented to them. Nurse Atkinson sent out word that she would not mind seeing this custom followed, even though it happened that the family she had married into was opposed to dancing. Some people thought it would be a disgrace to gratify her, a slap in the face to Flora. Others were too curious to hold back. They wanted to see how the newlyweds would behave. Would Robert dance? What sort of outfit would the bride show up in? They delayed a while, but finally the dance was held, and my mother got her report.

The bride wore the dress she had worn at her wedding, or so she said. But who would wear such a dress for a wedding at the manse? More than likely it was bought specially for her appearance at the dance. Pure-white satin with a sweetheart neckline, idiotically youthful. The groom was got up in a new dark-blue suit, and she had stuck a flower in his buttonhole. They were a sight. Her hair was freshly done to blind the eye with brassy reflections, and her face looked as if it would come off on a man's jacket, should she lay it against his shoulder in the dancing. Of course she did dance. She danced with every man present except the groom, who sat scrunched into one of the school desks along the wall. She danced with every man present—they all claimed they had to do it, it was the custom—and then she dragged Robert out to receive the money and to thank everybody for their best wishes. To the ladies in the cloakroom she even hinted that she was feeling unwell, for the usual newlywed reason. Nobody believed her, and indeed nothing ever came of this hope, if she really had it. Some of the women thought that she was lying to them out of malice, insulting them, making them out to be so credulous. But nobody challenged her, nobody was rude to her—maybe because it was plain that she could summon a rudeness of her own to knock anybody flat.

Flora was not present at the dance.

"My sister-in-law is not a dancer," said Nurse Atkinson. "She is stuck in the olden times." She invited them to laugh at Flora, whom she always called her sister-in-law, though she had no right to do so.

My mother wrote a letter to Flora after hearing about all these things. Being removed from the scene, and perhaps in a flurry of importance due to her own newly married state, she may have lost sight of the kind of person she was writing to. She offered sympathy and showed outrage, and said blunt disparaging things about the woman who had—as my mother saw it—dealt Flora such a blow. Back came a letter from Flora saying that she did not know where my mother had been getting her information, but that it seemed she had misunderstood, or listened to malicious people, or jumped to unjustified conclusions. What happened in Flora's family was nobody else's business, and certainly nobody needed to feel sorry for her or angry on her behalf. Flora said that she was happy and satisfied in her life, as she always had been, and she did not interfere with what others did or wanted, because such things did not concern her. She wished my mother all happiness in her marriage and hoped that she would soon be too busy with her own responsibilities to worry about the lives of people that she used to know.

This well-written letter cut my mother, as she said, to the quick. She and Flora stopped corresponding. My mother did become busy with her own life and finally a prisoner in it.

But she thought about Flora. In later years, when she sometimes talked about the things she might have been, or done, she would say, "If I could have been a writer—I do think I could have been; I could have been a writer—then I would have written the story of Flora's life. And do you know what I would have called it? 'The Maiden Lady.' "

*The Maiden Lady.* She said these words in a solemn and sentimental tone of voice that I had no use for. I knew, or thought I knew, exactly the value she found in them. The stateliness and mystery. The hint of derision turning to reverence. I was fifteen or sixteen years old by that time, and I believed that I could see into my mother's mind. I could see what she would do with Flora, what she had already done. She would make her into a noble figure, one who accepts defection, treachery, who forgives and stands aside, not once but twice. Never a moment of complaint. Flora goes about her cheerful labors, she cleans the house and shovels out the cow byre, she removes some bloody mess from her sister's bed, and when at last the future seems to open up for her—Ellie will die and Robert will beg forgiveness and Flora will silence him with the proud gift of herself—it is time for Audrey Atkinson to drive into the yard and shut Flora out again, more inexplicably and thoroughly the second time than the first. She must endure the painting of the house, the electric lights, all the prosperous activity next door. "Make-Believe Ballroom," "Amos 'n' Andy." No more Scottish comedies or ancient sermons. She must see them drive off to the dance—her old lover and that coldhearted, stupid, by no means beautiful woman in the white satin wedding dress. She is mocked. (And of course she has made over the farm to Ellie and Robert, of course he has inherited it, and now everything belongs to Audrey Atkinson.) The wicked flourish. But it is all right. It is all right—the elect are veiled in patience and humility and lighted by a certainty that events cannot disturb.

That was what I believed my mother would make of things. In her own plight her notions had turned mystical, and there was sometimes a hush, a solemn thrill in her voice that grated on me, alerted me to what seemed a personal danger. I felt a great fog of platitudes and pieties lurking, an incontestable crippled-mother power, which could capture and choke me. There would be no end to it. I had to keep myself sharp-tongued and cynical, arguing and deflating. Eventually I gave up even that recognition and opposed her in silence.

This is a fancy way of saying that I was no comfort and poor company to her when she had almost nowhere else to turn.

I had my own ideas about Flora's story. I didn't think that I could have written a novel but that I would write one. I would take a different tack. I saw through my mother's story and put in what she left out. My Flora would be as black as hers was white. Rejoicing in the bad turns done to her and in her own forgiveness, spying on the shambles of her sister's life. A Presbyterian witch, reading out of her poisonous book. It takes a rival ruthlessness, the comparatively innocent brutality of the thick-skinned nurse, to drive her back, to flourish in her shade. But she is driven back; the power of sex and ordinary greed drive her back and shut her up in her own part of the house with the coal-oil lamps. She shrinks, she caves in, her bones harden and her joints thicken, and—oh, this is it, I see the bare beauty of the ending I will contrive!—she becomes crippled herself, with arthritis, hardly able to move. Now Audrey Atkinson comes into her full power—she demands the whole house. She wants those partitions knocked out that Robert put up with Flora's help when he married Ellie. She will provide Flora with a room, she will take care of her. (Audrey Atkinson does not wish to be seen as a monster, and perhaps she really isn't one.) So one day Robert carries Flora—for the first and last time he carries her in his arms—to the room that his wife Audrey has prepared for her. And once Flora is settled in her well-lit, well-heated corner Audrey Atkinson undertakes to clean out the newly vacated rooms, Flora's rooms. She carries a heap of old books out into the yard. It's spring again, house-cleaning time, the season when Flora herself performed such feats, and now the pale face of Flora appears behind the new net curtains. She has dragged herself from her corner, she sees the light-blue sky with its high skidding clouds over the watery fields, the contending crows, the flooded creeks, the reddening tree branches. She sees the smoke rise out of the incinerator in the yard, where her books are burning. Those smelly old books, as Audrey has called them. Words and pages, the ominous dark spines. The elect, the damned, the slim hopes, the mighty torments—up in smoke. There was the ending.

To me the really mysterious person in the story, as my mother told it, was Robert. He never has a word to say. He gets engaged to Flora. He is walking beside her along the river when Ellie leaps out at them. He finds Ellie's thistles in his bed. He does the carpentry made necessary by his and Ellie's marriage. He listens or does not listen while Flora reads. Finally he sits scrunched up in the school desk while his flashy bride dances by with all the men.

So much for his public acts and appearances. But he was the one who started everything, in secret. He *did it to* Ellie. He did it to that skinny wild girl at a time when he was engaged to her sister, and he did it to her again and again when she was nothing but a poor botched body, a failed child-bearer, lying in bed.

He must have done it to Audrey Atkinson, too, but with less disastrous results.

Those words, *did it to*—the words my mother, no more than Flora, would never bring herself to speak—were simply exciting to me. I didn't feel any decent revulsion or reasonable indignation. I refused the warning. Not even the fate of Ellie could put me off. Not when I thought of that first encounter—the desperation of it, the ripping and striving. I used to sneak longing looks at men in those days. I admired their wrists and their necks and any bit of their chests a loose button let show, and even their ears and their feet in shoes. I expected nothing reasonable of them, only to be engulfed by their passion. I had similar thoughts about Robert.

What made Flora evil in my story was just what made her admirable in my mother's—her turning away from sex. I fought against everything my mother wanted to tell me on this subject; I despised even the drop in her voice, the gloomy caution, with which she approached it. My mother had grown up in a time and in a place where sex was a dark undertaking for women. She knew that you could die of it. So she honored the decency, the prudery, the frigidity, that might protect you. And I grew up in horror of that very protection, the dainty tyranny that seemed to me to extend to all areas of life, to enforce tea parties and white gloves and all other sorts of tinkling inanities. I favored bad words and a breakthrough, I teased myself with the thought of a man's recklessness and domination. The odd thing is that my mother's ideas were in line with some progressive notions of her times, and mine echoed the notions that were favored in my time. This in spite of the fact that we both believed ourselves independent, and lived in backwaters that did not register such changes. It's as if tendencies that seem most deeply rooted in our minds, most private and singular, have come in as spores on the prevailing wind, looking for any likely place to land, any welcome.

NOT LONG before she died, but when I was still at home, my mother got a letter from the real Flora. It came from that town near the farm, the town that Flora used to ride to, with Robert, in the cart, holding on to the sacks of wool or potatoes.

Flora wrote that she was no longer living on the farm.

*Robert and Audrey are still there,* she wrote. *Robert has some trouble with his back but otherwise he is very well. Audrey has poor circulation and is often short of breath. The doctor says she must lose weight but none of the diets seem to work. The farm has been doing very well. They are out of sheep*

*entirely and into dairy cattle. As you may have heard, the chief thing now-*
*adays is to get your milk quota from the government and then you are set.*
*The old stable is all fixed up with milking machines and the latest modern*
*equipment, it is quite a marvel. When I go out there to visit I hardly know*
*where I am.*

She went on to say that she had been living in town for some years now,
and that she had a job clerking in a store. She must have said what kind of
a store this was, but I cannot now remember. She said nothing, of course,
about what had led her to this decision—whether she had in fact been put
off her own farm, or had sold out her share, apparently not to much advantage. She stressed the fact of her friendliness with Robert and Audrey.
She said her health was good.

*I hear that you have not been so lucky in that way,* she wrote. *I ran into*
*Cleta Barnes who used to be Cleta Stapleton at the post office out at home,*
*and she told me that there is some problem with your muscles and she said*
*your speech is affected too. This is sad to hear but they can do such wonderful*
*things nowadays so I am hoping that the doctors may be able to help you.*

An unsettling letter, leaving so many things out. Nothing in it about
God's will or His role in our afflictions. No mention of whether Flora still
went to that church. I don't think my mother ever answered. Her fine
legible handwriting, her schoolteacher's writing, had deteriorated, and she
had difficulty holding a pen. She was always beginning letters and not finishing them. I would find them lying around the house. *My dearest Mary,*
they began. *My darling Ruth, My dear little Joanne (though I realize you are*
*not little anymore), My dear old friend Cleta, My lovely Margaret.* These
women were friends from her teaching days, her Normal School days, and
from high school. A few were former pupils. I have friends all over the
country, she would say defiantly. I have dear, dear friends.

I remember seeing one letter that started out: *Friend of my Youth.* I
don't know whom it was to. They were all friends of her youth. I don't
recall one that began with *My dear and most admired Flora.* I would always
look at them, try to read the salutation and the few sentences she had written,
and because I could not bear to feel sadness I would feel an impatience
with the flowery language, the direct appeal for love and pity. She would
get more of that, I thought (more from myself, I meant), if she could
manage to withdraw with dignity, instead of reaching out all the time to
cast her stricken shadow.

I had lost interest in Flora by then. I was always thinking of stories, and
by this time I probably had a new one on my mind.

But I have thought of her since. I have wondered what kind of a store. A
hardware store or a five-and-ten, where she has to wear a coverall, or a
drugstore, where she is uniformed like a nurse, or a Ladies' Wear, where

she is expected to be genteelly fashionable? She might have had to learn about food blenders or chain saws, negligees, cosmetics, even condoms. She would have to work all day under electric lights, and operate a cash register. Would she get a permanent, paint her nails, put on lipstick? She must have found a place to live—a little apartment with a kitchenette, overlooking the main street, or a room in a boardinghouse. How could she go on being a Cameronian? How could she get to that out-of-the-way church unless she managed to buy a car and learned to drive it? And if she did that she might drive not only to church but to other places. She might go on holidays. She might rent a cottage on a lake for a week, learn to swim, visit a city. She might eat meals in a restaurant, possibly in a restaurant where drinks were served. She might make friends with women who were divorced.

She might meet a man. A friend's widowed brother, perhaps. A man who did not know that she was a Cameronian or what Cameronians were. Who knew nothing of her story. A man who had never heard about the partial painting of the house or the two betrayals, or that it took all her dignity and innocence to keep her from being a joke. He might want to take her dancing, and she would have to explain that she could not go. He would be surprised but not put off—all that Cameronian business might seem quaint to him, almost charming. So it would to everybody. She was brought up in some weird religion, people would say. She lived a long time out on some godforsaken farm. She is a little bit strange but really quite nice. Nice-looking too. Especially since she went and got her hair done.

I might go into a store and find her.

No, no. She would be dead a long time now.

But suppose I had gone into a store—perhaps a department store. I see a place with the brisk atmosphere, the straightforward displays, the old-fashioned modern look of the fifties. Suppose a tall, handsome woman, nicely turned out, had come to wait on me, and I had known, somehow, in spite of the sprayed and puffed hair and the pink or coral lips and fingernails—I had known that this was Flora. I would have wanted to tell her that I knew, I knew her story, though we had never met. I imagine myself trying to tell her. (This is a dream now, I understand it as a dream.) I imagine her listening, with a pleasant composure. But she shakes her head. She smiles at me, and in her smile there is a degree of mockery, a faint, self-assured malice. Weariness, as well. She is not surprised that I am telling her this, but she is weary of it, of me and my idea of her, my information, my notion that I can know anything about her.

Of course it's my mother I'm thinking of, my mother as she was in those dreams, saying, It's nothing, just this little tremor; saying with such astonishing lighthearted forgiveness, Oh, I knew you'd come someday.

My mother surprising me, and doing it almost indifferently. Her mask, her fate, and most of her affliction taken away. How relieved I was, and happy. But I now recall that I was disconcerted as well. I would have to say that I felt slightly cheated. Yes. Offended, tricked, cheated, by this welcome turnaround, this reprieve. My mother moving rather carelessly out of her old prison, showing options and powers I never dreamed she had, changes more than herself. She changes the bitter lump of love I have carried all this time into a phantom—something useless and uncalled for, like a phantom pregnancy.

THE CAMERONIANS, I have discovered, are or were an uncompromising remnant of the Covenanters—those Scots who in the seventeenth century bound themselves, with God, to resist prayer books, bishops, any taint of popery or interference by the King. Their name comes from Richard Cameron, an outlawed, or "field," preacher, soon cut down. The Cameronians—for a long time they have preferred to be called the Reformed Presbyterians—went into battle singing the seventy-fourth and the seventy-eighth Psalms. They hacked the haughty Bishop of St. Andrews to death on the highway and rode their horses over his body. One of their ministers, in a mood of firm rejoicing at his own hanging, excommunicated all the other preachers in the world.

# *Meneseteung*

~

### I

*Columbine, bloodroot,*
*And wild bergamot,*
*Gathering armfuls,*
*Giddily we go.*

*Offerings*, the book is called. Gold lettering on a dull-blue cover. The author's full name underneath: Almeda Joynt Roth. The local paper, the *Vidette*, referred to her as "our poetess." There seems to be a mixture of respect and contempt, both for her calling and for her sex—or for their predictable conjuncture. In the front of the book is a photograph, with the photographer's name in one corner, and the date: 1865. The book was published later, in 1873.

The poetess has a long face; a rather long nose; full, sombre dark eyes, which seem ready to roll down her cheeks like giant tears; a lot of dark hair gathered around her face in droopy rolls and curtains. A streak of gray hair plain to see, although she is, in this picture, only twenty-five. Not a pretty girl but the sort of woman who may age well, who probably won't get fat. She wears a tucked and braid-trimmed dark dress or jacket, with a lacy, floppy arrangement of white material—frills or a bow—filling the deep V at the neck. She also wears a hat, which might be made of velvet, in a dark color to match the dress. It's the untrimmed, shapeless hat, something like a soft beret, that makes me see artistic intentions, or at least a shy and stubborn eccentricity, in this young woman, whose long neck and forward-inclining head indicate as well that she is tall and slender and somewhat awkward. From the waist up, she looks like a young nobleman of another century. But perhaps it was the fashion.

"In 1854," she writes in the preface to her book, "my father brought us—my mother, my sister Catherine, my brother William, and me—to the wilds of Canada West (as it then was). My father was a harness-maker by trade, but a cultivated man who could quote by heart from the Bible, Shakespeare, and the writings of Edmund Burke. He prospered in this newly opened land and was able to set up a harness and leather-goods store, and after a year to build the comfortable house in which I live (alone) today. I was fourteen years old, the eldest of the children, when we came into this country from Kingston, a town whose handsome streets I have not seen again but often remember. My sister was eleven and my brother nine. The third summer that we lived here, my brother and sister were taken ill of a prevalent fever and died within a few days of each other. My dear mother did not regain her spirits after this blow to our family. Her health declined, and after another three years she died. I then became housekeeper to my father and was happy to make his home for twelve years, until he died suddenly one morning at his shop.

"From my earliest years I have delighted in verse and I have occupied myself—and sometimes allayed my griefs, which have been no more, I know, than any sojourner on earth must encounter—with many floundering efforts at its composition. My fingers, indeed, were always too clumsy for crochetwork, and those dazzling productions of embroidery which one sees often today—the overflowing fruit and flower baskets, the little Dutch boys, the bonneted maidens with their watering cans—have likewise proved to be beyond my skill. So I offer instead, as the product of my leisure hours, these rude posies, these ballads, couplets, reflections."

Titles of some of the poems: "Children at Their Games," "The Gypsy Fair," "A Visit to My Family," "Angels in the Snow," "Champlain at the Mouth of the Meneseteung," "The Passing of the Old Forest," and "A Garden Medley." There are other, shorter poems, about birds and wildflowers and snowstorms. There is some comically intentioned doggerel about what people are thinking about as they listen to the sermon in church.

"Children at Their Games": The writer, a child, is playing with her brother and sister—one of those games in which children on different sides try to entice and catch each other. She plays on in the deepening twilight, until she realizes that she is alone, and much older. Still she hears the (ghostly) voices of her brother and sister calling. *Come over, come over, let Meda come over.* (Perhaps Almeda was called Meda in the family, or perhaps she shortened her name to fit the poem.)

"The Gypsy Fair": The Gypsies have an encampment near the town, a "fair," where they sell cloth and trinkets, and the writer as a child is afraid that she may be stolen by them, taken away from her family. Instead, her family has been taken away from her, stolen by Gypsies she can't locate or bargain with.

"A Visit to My Family": A visit to the cemetery, a one-sided conversation.

"Angels in the Snow": The writer once taught her brother and sister to make "angels" by lying down in the snow and moving their arms to create wing shapes. Her brother always jumped up carelessly, leaving an angel with a crippled wing. Will this be made perfect in Heaven, or will he be flying with his own makeshift, in circles?

"Champlain at the Mouth of the Meneseteung": This poem celebrates the popular, untrue belief that the explorer sailed down the eastern shore of Lake Huron and landed at the mouth of the major river.

"The Passing of the Old Forest": A list of all the trees—their names, appearance, and uses—that were cut down in the original forest, with a general description of the bears, wolves, eagles, deer, waterfowl.

"A Garden Medley": Perhaps planned as a companion to the forest poem. Catalogue of plants brought from European countries, with bits of history and legend attached, and final Canadianness resulting from this mixture.

The poems are written in quatrains or couplets. There are a couple of attempts at sonnets, but mostly the rhyme scheme is simple—*a b a b* or *a b c b*. The rhyme used is what was once called "masculine" ("shore"/ "before"), though once in a while it is "feminine" ("quiver"/"river"). Are those terms familiar anymore? No poem is unrhymed.

II

*White roses cold as snow*
*Bloom where those "angels" lie.*
*Do they but rest below*
*Or, in God's wonder, fly?*

In 1879, Almeda Roth was still living in the house at the corner of Pearl and Dufferin streets, the house her father had built for his family. The house is there today; the manager of the liquor store lives in it. It's covered with aluminum siding; a closed-in porch has replaced the veranda. The woodshed, the fence, the gates, the privy, the barn—all these are gone. A photograph taken in the 1880s shows them all in place. The house and fence look a little shabby, in need of paint, but perhaps that is just because of the bleached-out look of the brownish photograph. The lace-curtained windows look like white eyes. No big shade tree is in sight, and, in fact, the tall elms that overshadowed the town until the 1950s, as well as the maples that shade it now, are skinny young trees with rough fences around them to protect them from the cows. Without the shelter of those trees, there is a great exposure—back yards, clotheslines, woodpiles, patchy sheds and barns and privies—all bare, exposed, provisional-looking. Few houses would have anything like a lawn, just a patch of plantains and anthills and raked dirt. Perhaps petunias growing on top of a stump, in a round box. Only the main street is gravelled; the other streets are dirt roads, muddy or dusty according to season. Yards must be fenced to keep animals out. Cows are tethered in vacant lots or pastured in back yards, but sometimes they get loose. Pigs get loose too, and dogs roam free or nap in a lordly way on the boardwalks. The town has taken root, it's not going to vanish, yet it still has some of the look of an encampment. And, like an encampment, it's busy all the time—full of people, who, within the town, usually walk wherever they're going; full of animals, which leave horse buns, cow pats, dog turds that ladies have to hitch up their skirts for; full of the noise of building and of drivers shouting at their horses and of the trains that come in several times a day.

I read about that life in the *Vidette*.

The population is younger than it is now, than it will ever be again. People past fifty usually don't come to a raw, new place. There are quite a few people in the cemetery already, but most of them died young, in accidents or childbirth or epidemics. It's youth that's in evidence in town. Children—boys—rove through the streets in gangs. School is compulsory for only four months a year, and there are lots of occasional jobs that even a child of eight or nine can do—pulling flax, holding horses, delivering groceries, sweeping the boardwalk in front of stores. A good deal of time they spend looking for adventures. One day they follow an old woman, a drunk nicknamed Queen Aggie. They get her into a wheelbarrow and trundle her all over town, then dump her into a ditch to sober her up. They also spend a lot of time around the railway station. They jump on shunting cars and dart between them and dare each other to take chances, which once in a while result in their getting maimed or killed. And they keep an eye out for any strangers coming into town. They follow them, offer to carry their bags, and direct them (for a five-cent piece) to a hotel. Strangers who don't look so prosperous are taunted and tormented. Speculation surrounds all of them—it's like a cloud of flies. Are they coming to town to start up a new business, to persuade people to invest in some scheme, to sell cures or gimmicks, to preach on the street corners? All these things are possible any day of the week. Be on your guard, the *Vidette* tells people. These are times of opportunity and danger. Tramps, confidence men, hucksters, shysters, plain thieves are travelling the roads, and particularly the railroads. Thefts are announced: money invested and never seen again, a pair of trousers taken from the clothesline, wood from the woodpile, eggs from the henhouse. Such incidents increase in the hot weather.

Hot weather brings accidents too. More horses run wild then, upsetting buggies. Hands caught in the wringer while doing the washing, a man lopped in two at the sawmill, a leaping boy killed in a fall of lumber at the lumberyard. Nobody sleeps well. Babies wither with summer complaint, and fat people can't catch their breath. Bodies must be buried in a hurry. One day a man goes through the streets ringing a cowbell and calling, "Repent! Repent!" It's not a stranger this time, it's a young man who works at the butcher shop. Take him home, wrap him in cold wet cloths, give him some nerve medicine, keep him in bed, pray for his wits. If he doesn't recover, he must go to the asylum.

Almeda Roth's house faces on Dufferin Street, which is a street of considerable respectability. On this street, merchants, a mill owner, an operator of salt wells have their houses. But Pearl Street, which her back windows overlook and her back gate opens onto, is another story. Workmen's houses are adjacent to hers. Small but decent row houses—that is all right. Things deteriorate toward the end of the block, and the next, last one becomes dismal. Nobody but the poorest people, the unrespectable and undeserving poor, would live there at the edge of a boghole (drained since then), called the Pearl Street Swamp. Bushy and luxuriant weeds grow there, makeshift shacks have been put up, there are piles of refuse and debris and crowds of runty children, slops are flung from doorways. The town tries to compel these people to build privies, but they would just as soon go in the bushes. If a gang of boys goes down there in search of adventure, it's likely they'll get more than they bargained for. It is said that even the town constable won't go down Pearl Street on a Saturday night. Almeda Roth has never walked past the row housing. In one of those houses lives the young girl Annie, who helps her with her housecleaning. That young girl herself, being a decent girl, has never walked down to the last block or the swamp. No decent woman ever would.

But that same swamp, lying to the east of Almeda Roth's house, presents a fine sight at dawn. Almeda sleeps at the back of the house. She keeps to the same bedroom she once shared with her sister Catherine— she would not think of moving to the large front bedroom, where her mother used to lie in bed all day, and which was later the solitary domain of her father. From her window she can see the sun rising, the swamp mist filling with light, the bulky, nearest trees floating against that mist and the trees behind turning transparent. Swamp oaks, soft maples, tamarack, butternut.

### III

*Here where the river meets the
  inland sea,
Spreading her blue skirts from the
  solemn wood,
I think of birds and beasts and
  vanished men,
Whose pointed dwellings on these
  pale sands stood.*

One of the strangers who arrived at the railway station a few years ago was Jarvis Poulter, who now occupies the next house to Almeda Roth's—separated from hers by a vacant lot, which he has bought, on Dufferin Street. The house is plainer than the Roth house and has no fruit trees or flowers planted around it. It is understood that this is a natural result of Jarvis Poulter's being a widower and living alone. A man may keep his house decent, but he will never—if he is a proper man—do much to decorate it. Marriage forces him to live with more ornament as well as sentiment, and it protects him, also, from the extremities of his own nature—from a frigid parsimony or a luxuriant sloth, from squalor, and from excessive sleeping or reading, drinking, smoking, or freethinking.

> *In the interests of economy, it is believed, a certain estimable gentleman of our town persists in fetching water from the public tap and supplementing his fuel supply by picking up the loose coal along the railway track. Does he think to repay the town or the railway company with a supply of free salt?*

This is the *Vidette*, full of sly jokes, innuendo, plain accusation that no newspaper would get away with today. It's Jarvis Poulter they're talking about—though in other passages he is spoken of with great respect, as a civil magistrate, an employer, a churchman. He is close, that's all. An eccentric, to a degree. All of which may be a result of his single condition, his widower's life. Even carrying his water from the town tap and filling his coal pail along the railway track. This is a decent citizen, prosperous: a tall—slightly paunchy?—man in a dark suit with polished boots. A beard? Black hair streaked with gray. A severe and self-possessed air, and a large pale wart among the bushy hairs of one eyebrow? People talk about a young, pretty, beloved wife, dead in childbirth or some horrible accident, like a house fire or a railway disaster. There is no ground for this, but it adds interest. All he has told them is that his wife is dead.

He came to this part of the country looking for oil. The first oil well in the world was sunk in Lambton County, south of here, in the 1850s. Drilling for oil, Jarvis Poulter discovered salt. He set to work to make the most of that. When he walks home from church with Almeda Roth, he tells her about his salt wells. They are twelve hundred feet deep. Heated water is pumped down into them, and that dissolves the salt. Then the brine is pumped to the surface. It is poured into great evaporator pans over slow, steady fires, so that the water is steamed off and the pure, excellent salt remains. A commodity for which the demand will never fail.

"The salt of the earth," Almeda says.

"Yes," he says, frowning. He may think this disrespectful. She did not intend it so. He speaks of competitors in other towns who are following his lead and trying to hog the market. Fortunately, their wells are not drilled so deep, or their evaporating is not done so efficiently. There is salt everywhere under this land, but it is not so easy to come by as some people think.

Does this not mean, Almeda says, that there was once a great sea?

Very likely, Jarvis Poulter says. Very likely. He goes on to tell her about other enterprises of his—a brickyard, a limekiln. And he explains to her how this operates, and where the good clay is found. He also owns two farms, whose woodlots supply the fuel for his operations.

> *Among the couples strolling home from church on a recent, sunny Sabbath morning we noted a certain salty gentleman and literary lady, not perhaps in their first youth but by no means blighted by the frosts of age. May we surmise?*

This kind of thing pops up in the *Vidette* all the time.

May they surmise, and is this courting? Almeda Roth has a bit of money, which her father left her, and she has her house. She is not too old to have a couple of children. She is a good enough housekeeper, with the tendency toward fancy iced cakes and decorated tarts that is seen fairly often in old maids. (Honorable mention at the Fall Fair.) There is nothing wrong with her looks, and naturally she is in better shape than most married women of her age, not having been loaded down with work and children. But why was she passed over in her earlier, more marriageable years, in a place that needs women to be partnered and fruitful? She was a rather gloomy girl—that may have been the trouble. The deaths of her brother and sister, and then of her mother, who lost her reason, in fact, a year before she died, and lay in her bed talking nonsense—those weighed on her, so she was not lively company. And all that reading and poetry—it seemed more of a drawback, a barrier, an obsession, in the young girl than in the middle-aged woman, who needed something, after all, to fill her time. Anyway, it's five years since her book was published, so perhaps she has got over that. Perhaps it was the proud, bookish father encouraging her?

Everyone takes it for granted that Almeda Roth is thinking of Jarvis

Poulter as a husband and would say yes if he asked her. And she is think-ing of him. She doesn't want to get her hopes up too much, she doesn't want to make a fool of herself. She would like a signal. If he attended church on Sunday evenings, there would be a chance, during some months of the year, to walk home after dark. He would carry a lantern. (There is as yet no street lighting in town.) He would swing the lantern to light the way in front of the lady's feet and observe their narrow and deli-cate shape. He might catch her arm as they step off the boardwalk. But he does not go to church at night.

Nor does he call for her, and walk with her *to* church on Sunday morn-ings. That would be a declaration. He walks her home, past his gate as far as hers; he lifts his hat then and leaves her. She does not invite him to come in—a woman living alone could never do such a thing. As soon as a man and woman of almost any age are alone together within four walls, it is assumed that anything may happen. Spontaneous combustion, instant fornication, an attack of passion. Brute instinct, triumph of the senses. What possibilities men and women must see in each other to infer such dangers. Or, believing in the dangers, how often they must think about the possibilities.

When they walk side by side, she can smell his shaving soap, the bar-ber's oil, his pipe tobacco, the wool and linen and leather smell of his manly clothes. The correct, orderly, heavy clothes are like those she used to brush and starch and iron for her father. She misses that job—her fa-ther's appreciation, his dark, kind authority. Jarvis Poulter's garments, his smell, his movements all cause the skin on the side of her body next to him to tingle hopefully, and a meek shiver raises the hairs on her arms. Is this to be taken as a sign of love? She thinks of him coming into her— *their*—bedroom in his long underwear and his hat. She knows this outfit is ridiculous, but in her mind he does not look so; he has the solemn ef-frontery of a figure in a dream. He comes into the room and lies down on the bed beside her, preparing to take her in his arms. Surely he removes his hat? She doesn't know, for at this point a fit of welcome and submis-sion overtakes her, a buried gasp. He would be her husband.

One thing she has noticed about married women, and that is how many of them have to go about creating their husbands. They have to start ascribing preferences, opinions, dictatorial ways. Oh, yes, they say, my husband is very particular. He won't touch turnips. He won't eat fried meat. (Or he will only eat fried meat.) He likes me to wear blue (brown) all the time. He can't stand organ music. He hates to see a woman go out bareheaded. He would kill me if I took one puff of tobacco. This way, be-wildered, sidelong-looking men are made over, made into husbands, heads of households. Almeda Roth cannot imagine herself doing that. She wants a man who doesn't have to be made, who is firm already and determined and mysterious to her. She does not look for companionship. Men—except for her father—seem to her deprived in some way, incurious. No doubt that is necessary, so that they will do what they have to do. Would she herself, knowing that there was salt in the earth, discover how to get it out and sell it? Not likely. She would be thinking about the ancient sea. That kind of speculation is what Jarvis Poulter has, quite properly, no time for.

Instead of calling for her and walking her to church, Jarvis Poulter might make another, more venturesome declaration. He could hire a horse and take her for a drive out to the country. If he did this, she would be both glad and sorry. Glad to be beside him, driven by him, receiving this attention from him in front of the world. And sorry to have the countryside removed for her—filmed over, in a way, by his talk and preoccupations. The countryside that she has written about in her poems actually takes diligence and determination to see. Some things must be disregarded. Manure piles, of course, and boggy fields full of high, charred stumps, and great heaps of brush waiting for a good day for burning. The meandering creeks have been straightened, turned into ditches with high, muddy banks. Some of the crop fields and pasture fields are fenced with big, clumsy uprooted stumps; others are held in a crude stitchery of rail fences. The trees have all been cleared back to the woodlots. And the woodlots are all second growth. No trees along the roads or lanes or around the farmhouses, except a few that are newly planted, young and weedy-looking. Clusters of log barns— the grand barns that are to dominate the countryside for the next hundred years are just beginning to be built—and mean-looking log houses, and every four or five miles a ragged little settlement with a church and school and store and a blacksmith shop. A raw countryside just wrenched from the forest, but swarming with people. Every hundred acres is a farm, every farm has a family, most families have ten or twelve children. (This is the country that will send out wave after wave of settlers—it's already starting to send them—to Northern Ontario and the West.) It's true that you can gather wildflowers in spring in the woodlots, but you'd have to walk through herds of horned cows to get to them.

IV

*The Gypsies have departed.*
*Their camping-ground is bare.*
*Oh, boldly would I bargain now*
*At the Gypsy Fair.*

Almeda suffers a good deal from sleeplessness, and the doctor has given her bromides and nerve medicine. She takes the bromides, but the drops gave her dreams that were too vivid and disturbing, so she has put the bottle by for an emergency. She told the doctor her eyeballs felt dry, like hot glass, and her joints ached. Don't read so much, he said, don't study; get yourself good and tired out with housework, take exercise. He believes that her troubles would clear up if she got married. He believes this in spite of the fact that most of his nerve medicine is prescribed for married women.

So Almeda cleans house and helps clean the church, she lends a hand to friends who are wallpapering or getting ready for a wedding, she bakes one of her famous cakes for the Sunday-school picnic. On a hot Saturday in August, she decides to make some grape jelly. Little jars of grape jelly will make fine Christmas presents, or offerings to the sick. But she started late in the day and the jelly is not made by nightfall. In fact, the hot pulp has just been dumped into the cheesecloth bag to strain out the juice. Almeda drinks some tea and eats a slice of cake with butter (a childish indulgence of hers), and that's all she wants for supper. She washes her hair at the sink and sponges off her body to be clean for Sunday. She doesn't light a lamp. She lies down on the bed with the window wide open and a sheet just up to her waist, and she does feel wonderfully tired. She can even feel a little breeze.

When she wakes up, the night seems fiery hot and full of threats. She lies sweating on her bed, and she has the impression that the noises she hears are knives and saws and axes—all angry implements chopping and jabbing and boring within her head. But it isn't true. As she comes further awake, she recognizes the sounds that she has heard sometimes before—the fracas of a summer Saturday night on Pearl Street. Usually the noise centers on a fight. People are drunk, there is a lot of protest and encouragement concerning the fight, somebody will scream, "Murder!" Once, there was a murder. But it didn't happen in a fight. An old man was stabbed to death in his shack, perhaps for a few dollars he kept in the mattress.

She gets out of bed and goes to the window. The night sky is clear, with no moon and with bright stars. Pegasus hangs straight ahead, over the swamp. Her father taught her that constellation—automatically, she counts its stars. Now she can make out distinct voices, individual contributions to the row. Some people, like herself, have evidently been wakened from sleep. "Shut up!" they are yelling. "Shut up that caterwauling or I'm going to come down and tan the arse off yez!"

But nobody shuts up. It's as if there were a ball of fire rolling up Pearl Street, shooting off sparks—only the fire is noise; it's yells and laughter and shrieks and curses, and the sparks are voices that shoot off alone. Two voices gradually distinguish themselves—a rising and falling howling cry and a steady throbbing, low-pitched stream of abuse that contains all those words which Almeda associates with danger and depravity and foul smells and disgusting sights. Someone—the person crying out, "Kill me! Kill me now!"—is being beaten. A woman is being beaten. She keeps crying, "Kill me! Kill me!" and sometimes her mouth seems choked with blood. Yet there is something taunting and triumphant about her cry. There is something theatrical about it. And the people around are calling out, "Stop it! Stop that!" or "Kill her! Kill her!" in a frenzy, as if at the theatre or a sporting match or a prizefight. Yes, thinks Almeda, she has noticed that before—it is always partly a charade with these people; there is a clumsy sort of parody, an exaggeration, a missed connection. As if anything they did—even a murder—might be something they didn't quite believe but were powerless to stop.

Now there is the sound of something thrown—a chair, a plank?—and of a woodpile or part of a fence giving way. A lot of newly surprised cries, the sound of running, people getting out of the way, and the commotion has come much closer. Almeda can see a figure in a light dress, bent over and running. That will be the woman. She has got hold of something like a stick of wood or a shingle, and she turns and flings it at the darker figure running after her.

"Ah, go get her!" the voices cry. "Go baste her one!"

Many fall back now; just the two figures come on and grapple, and break loose again, and finally fall down against Almeda's fence. The sound they make becomes very confused—gagging, vomiting, grunting, pounding. Then a long, vibrating, choking sound of pain and self-abasement, self-abandonment, which could come from either or both of them.

Almeda has backed away from the window and sat down on the bed. Is that the sound of murder she has heard? What is to be done, what is she to do? She must light a lantern, she must go downstairs and light a lantern—she must go out into the yard, she must go downstairs. Into the yard. The lantern. She falls over on her bed and pulls the pillow to her face. In a minute. The stairs, the lantern. She sees herself already down there, in the back hall, drawing the bolt of the back door. She falls asleep.

She wakes, startled, in the early light. She thinks there is a big crow sitting on her windowsill, talking in a disapproving but unsurprised way about the events of the night before. "Wake up and move the wheelbarrow!" it says to her, scolding, and she understands that it means something else by "wheelbarrow"—something foul and sorrowful. Then she is awake and sees that there is no such bird. She gets up at once and looks out the window.

Down against her fence there is a pale lump pressed—a body.
*Wheelbarrow.*

She puts a wrapper over her nightdress and goes downstairs. The front rooms are still shadowy, the blinds down in the kitchen. Something goes *plop, plup*, in a leisurely, censorious way, reminding her of the conversation of the crow. It's just the grape juice, straining overnight. She pulls the bolt and goes out the back door. Spiders have draped their webs over the doorway in the night, and the hollyhocks are drooping, heavy with dew. By the fence, she parts the sticky hollyhocks and looks down and she can see.

A woman's body heaped up there, turned on her side with her face squashed down into the earth. Almeda can't see her face. But there is a bare breast let loose, brown nipple pulled long like a cow's teat, and a bare haunch and leg, the haunch showing a bruise as big as a sunflower. The unbruised skin is grayish, like a plucked, raw drumstick. Some kind of nightgown or all-purpose dress she has on. Smelling of vomit. Urine, drink, vomit.

Barefoot, in her nightgown and flimsy wrapper, Almeda runs away. She runs around the side of her house between the apple trees and the veranda; she opens the front gate and flees down Dufferin Street to Jarvis Poulter's house, which is the nearest to hers. She slaps the flat of her hand many times against the door.

"There is the body of a woman," she says when Jarvis Poulter appears at last. He is in his dark trousers, held up with braces, and his shirt is half unbuttoned, his face unshaven, his hair standing up on his head. "Mr. Poulter, excuse me. A body of a woman. At my back gate."

He looks at her fiercely. "Is she dead?"

His breath is dank, his face creased, his eyes bloodshot.

"Yes. I think murdered," says Almeda. She can see a little of his cheerless front hall. His hat on a chair. "In the night I woke up. I heard a racket down on Pearl Street," she says, struggling to keep her voice low and sensible. "I could hear this—pair. I could hear a man and a woman fighting."

He picks up his hat and puts it on his head. He closes and locks the front door, and puts the key in his pocket. They walk along the boardwalk and she sees that she is in her bare feet. She holds back what she feels a need to say next—that she is responsible, she could have run out with a lantern, she could have screamed (but who needed more screams?), she could have beat the man off. She could have run for help then, not now.

They turn down Pearl Street, instead of entering the Roth yard. Of course the body is still there. Hunched up, half bare, the same as before.

Jarvis Poulter doesn't hurry or halt. He walks straight over to the body and looks down at it, nudges the leg with the toe of his boot, just as you'd nudge a dog or a sow.

"You," he says, not too loudly but firmly, and nudges again.

Almeda tastes bile at the back of her throat.

"Alive," says Jarvis Poulter, and the woman confirms this. She stirs, she grunts weakly.

Almeda says, "I will get the doctor." If she had touched the woman, if she had forced herself to touch her, she would not have made such a mistake.

"Wait," says Jarvis Poulter. "Wait. Let's see if she can get up."

"Get up, now," he says to the woman. "Come on. Up, now. Up."

Now a startling thing happens. The body heaves itself onto all fours, the head is lifted—the hair all matted with blood and vomit—and the woman begins to bang this head, hard and rhythmically, against Almeda Roth's picket fence. As she bangs her head, she finds her voice and lets out an openmouthed yowl, full of strength and what sounds like an anguished pleasure.

"Far from dead," says Jarvis Poulter. "And I wouldn't bother the doctor."

"There's blood," says Almeda as the woman turns her smeared face.

"From her nose," he says. "Not fresh." He bends down and catches the horrid hair close to the scalp to stop the head-banging.

"You stop that, now," he says. "Stop it. Gwan home, now. Gwan home, where you belong." The sound coming out of the woman's mouth has stopped. He shakes her head slightly, warning her, before he lets go of her hair. "Gwan home!"

Released, the woman lunges forward, pulls herself to her feet. She can walk. She weaves and stumbles down the street, making intermittent, cautious noises of protest. Jarvis Poulter watches her for a moment to make sure that she's on her way. Then he finds a large burdock leaf, on which he wipes his hand. He says, "There goes your dead body!"

The back gate being locked, they walk around to the front. The front gate stands open. Almeda still feels sick. Her abdomen is bloated; she is hot and dizzy.

"The front door is locked," she says faintly. "I came out by the kitchen." If only he would leave her, she could go straight to the privy. But he follows. He follows her as far as the back door and into the back hall. He speaks to her in a tone of harsh joviality that she has never before heard from him. "No need for alarm," he says. "It's only the consequences of drink. A lady oughtn't to be living alone so close to a bad neighborhood." He takes hold of her arm just above the elbow. She can't open her mouth to speak to him, to say thank you. If she opened her mouth, she would retch.

What Jarvis Poulter feels for Almeda Roth at this moment is just what he has not felt during all those circumspect walks and all his own solitary calculations of her probable worth, undoubted respectability, adequate comeliness. He has not been able to imagine her as a wife. Now that is possible. He is sufficiently stirred by her loosened hair—prematurely gray but thick and soft—her flushed face, her light clothing, which nobody but a husband should see. And by her indiscretion, her agitation, her foolishness, her need?

"I will call on you later," he says to her. "I will walk with you to church."

> At the corner of Pearl and Dufferin streets last Sunday morning there was discovered, by a lady resident there, the body of a certain woman of Pearl Street, thought to be dead but only, as it turned out, dead drunk. She was roused from her heavenly—or otherwise—stupor by the firm persuasion of Mr. Poulter, a neighbour and a Civil Magistrate, who had been summoned by the lady resident. Incidents of this sort, unseemly, troublesome, and disgraceful to our town, have of late become all too common.

### V

> *I sit at the bottom of sleep,*
> *As on the floor of the sea.*
> *And fanciful Citizens of the Deep*
> *Are graciously greeting me.*

As soon as Jarvis Poulter has gone and she has heard her front gate close, Almeda rushes to the privy. Her relief is not complete, however, and she realizes that the pain and fullness in her lower body come from an accumulation of menstrual blood that has not yet started to flow. She closes and locks the back door. Then, remembering Jarvis Poulter's words about church, she writes on a piece of paper, *I am not well, and wish to rest today.* She sticks this firmly into the outside frame of the little window in the front door. She locks that door too. She is trembling, as if from a great shock or danger. But she builds a fire, so that she can make tea. She boils water, measures the tea leaves, makes a large pot of tea, whose steam and smell sicken her further. She pours out a cup while the tea is still quite weak and adds to it several dark drops of nerve medicine. She sits to drink it without raising the kitchen blind. There, in the middle of the floor, is the cheesecloth bag hanging on its broom handle between the two chairbacks. The grape pulp and juice has stained the swollen cloth a dark purple. *Plop, plup,* into the basin beneath. She can't sit and look at such a thing. She takes her cup, the teapot, and the bottle of medicine into the dining room.

She is still sitting there when the horses start to go by on the way to church, stirring up clouds of dust. The roads will be getting hot as ashes.

She is there when the gate is opened and a man's confident steps sound on her veranda. Her hearing is so sharp she seems to hear the paper taken out of the frame and unfolded—she can almost hear him reading it, hear the words in his mind. Then the footsteps go the other way, down the steps. The gate closes. An image comes to her of tombstones—it makes her laugh. Tombstones are marching down the street on their little booted feet, their long bodies inclined forward, their expressions preoccupied and severe. The church bells are ringing.

Then the clock in the hall strikes twelve and an hour has passed.

The house is getting hot. She drinks more tea and adds more medicine. She knows that the medicine is affecting her. It is responsible for her extraordinary languor, her perfect immobility, her unresisting surrender to her surroundings. That is all right. It seems necessary.

Her surroundings—some of her surroundings—in the dining room are these: walls covered with dark-green garlanded wallpaper, lace curtains and mulberry velvet curtains on the windows, a table with a crocheted cloth and a bowl of wax fruit, a pinkish-gray carpet with nosegays of blue and pink roses, a sideboard spread with embroidered runners and holding various patterned plates and jugs and the silver tea things. A lot of things to watch. For every one of these patterns, decorations seems charged with life, ready to move and flow and alter. Or possibly to explode. Almeda Roth's occupation throughout the day is to keep an eye on them. Not to prevent their alteration so much as to catch them at it—to understand it, to be a part of it. So much is going on in this room that there is no need to leave it. There is not even the thought of leaving it.

Of course, Almeda in her observations cannot escape words. She may think she can, but she can't. Soon this glowing and swelling begins to suggest words—not specific words but a flow of words somewhere, just about ready to make themselves known to her. Poems, even. Yes, again, poems. Or one poem. Isn't that the idea—one very great poem that will contain everything and, oh, that will make all the other poems, the poems she has written, inconsequential, mere trial and error, mere rags? Stars and flowers and birds and trees and angels in the snow and dead children at twilight—that is not the half of it. You have to get in the obscene racket on Pearl Street and the polished toe of Jarvis Poulter's boot and the plucked-chicken haunch with its blue-black flower. Almeda is a long way now from human sympathies or fears or cozy household considerations. She doesn't think about what could be done for that woman or about keeping Jarvis Poulter's dinner warm and hanging his long underwear on the line. The basin of grape juice has overflowed and is running over her kitchen floor, staining the boards of the floor, and the stain will never come out.

She has to think of so many things at once—Champlain and the naked

Indians and the salt deep in the earth, but as well as the salt the money, the money-making intent brewing forever in heads like Jarvis Poulter's. Also the brutal storms of winter and the clumsy and benighted deeds on Pearl Street. The changes of climate are often violent, and if you think about it there is no peace even in the stars. All this can be borne only if it is channelled into a poem, and the word *channelled* is appropriate, because the name of the poem will be—it *is*—"The Meneseteung." The name of the poem is the name of the river. No, in fact it is the river, the Meneseteung, that is the poem—with its deep holes and rapids and blissful pools under the summer trees and its grinding blocks of ice thrown up at the end of winter and its desolating spring floods. Almeda looks deep, deep into the river of her mind and into the tablecloth, and she sees the crocheted roses floating. They look bunchy and foolish, her mother's crocheted roses— they don't look much like real flowers. But their effort, their floating independence, their pleasure in their silly selves do seem to her so admirable. A hopeful sign. *Meneseteung.*

She doesn't leave the room until dusk, when she goes out to the privy again and discovers that she is bleeding, her flow has started. She will have to get a towel, strap it on, bandage herself up. Never before, in health, has she passed a whole day in her nightdress. She doesn't feel any particular anxiety about this. On her way through the kitchen, she walks through the pool of grape juice. She knows that she will have to mop it up, but not yet, and she walks upstairs leaving purple footprints and smelling her escaping blood and the sweat of her body that has sat all day in the closed hot room.

No need for alarm.

For she hasn't thought that crocheted roses could float away or that tombstones could hurry down the street. She doesn't mistake that for reality, and neither does she mistake anything else for reality, and that is how she knows that she is sane.

### VI

*I dream of you by night,*
*I visit you by day.*
*Father, Mother,*
*Sister, Brother,*
*Have you no word to say?*

*April 22, 1903. At her residence, on Tuesday last, between three and four o'clock in the afternoon, there passed away a lady of talent and refinement whose pen, in days gone by, enriched our local literature with a volume of sensitive, eloquent verse. It is a sad misfortune that in later years the mind of this fine person had become somewhat clouded and her behaviour, in consequence, somewhat rash and unusual. Her attention to decorum and to the care and adornment of her person had suffered, to the degree that she had become, in the eyes of those unmindful of her former pride and daintiness, a familiar eccentric, or even, sadly, a figure of fun. But now all such lapses pass from memory and what is recalled is her excellent published verse, her labours in former days in the Sunday school, her dutiful care of her parents, her noble womanly nature, charitable concerns, and unfailing religious faith. Her last illness was of mercifully short duration. She caught cold, after having become thoroughly wet from a ramble in the Pearl Street bog. (It has been said that some urchins chased her into the water, and such is the boldness and cruelty of some of our youth, and their observed persecution of this lady, that the tale cannot be entirely discounted.) The cold developed into pneumonia, and she died, attended at the last by a former neighbour, Mrs. Bert (Annie) Friels, who witnessed her calm and faithful end.*

*January, 1904. One of the founders of our community, an early maker and shaker of this town, was abruptly removed from our midst on Monday morning last, whilst attending to his correspondence in the office of his company. Mr. Jarvis Poulter possessed a keen and lively commercial spirit, which was instrumental in the creation of not one but several local enterprises, bringing the benefits of industry, productivity, and employment to our town.*

So the *Vidette* runs on, copious and assured. Hardly a death goes undescribed, or a life unevaluated.

I LOOKED for Almeda Roth in the graveyard. I found the family stone. There was just one name on it—ROTH. Then I noticed two flat stones in the ground, a distance of a few feet—six feet?—from the upright stone. One of these said PAPA, the other MAMA. Farther out from these I found two other flat stones, with the names WILLIAM and CATHERINE on them. I had to clear away some overgrowing grass and dirt to see the full name of Catherine. No birth or death dates for anybody, nothing about being dearly beloved. It was a private sort of memorializing, not for the world. There were no roses, either—no sign of a rosebush. But perhaps it was taken out. The groundskeeper doesn't like such things; they are a nuisance to the lawnmower, and if there is nobody left to object he will pull them out.

I thought that Almeda must have been buried somewhere else. When this plot was bought—at the time of the two children's deaths—she would still have been expected to marry, and to lie finally beside her husband. They might not have left room for her here. Then I saw that the stones in the ground fanned out from the upright stone. First the two for the parents, then the two for the children, but these were placed in such a way that there was room for a third, to complete the fan. I paced out from CATHERINE the same number of steps that it took to get from CATHERINE to WILLIAM, and at this spot I began pulling grass and scrabbling in the dirt with my bare hands. Soon I felt the stone and knew that I was right. I worked away and got the whole stone clear and I read the name MEDA. There it was with the others, staring at the sky.

I made sure I had got to the edge of the stone. That was all the name there was—Meda. So it was true that she was called by that name in the family. Not just in the poem. Or perhaps she chose her name from the poem, to be written on her stone.

I thought that there wasn't anybody alive in the world but me who would know this, who would make the connection. And I would be the last person to do so. But perhaps this isn't so. People are curious. A few people are. They will be driven to find things out, even trivial things. They will put things together. You see them going around with notebooks, scraping the dirt off gravestones, reading microfilm, just in the hope of seeing this trickle in time, making a connection, rescuing one thing from the rubbish.

And they may get it wrong, after all. I may have got it wrong. I don't know if she ever took laudanum. Many ladies did. I don't know if she ever made grape jelly.

# *Differently*

~

GEORGIA ONCE took a creative-writing course, and what the instructor told her was: Too many things. Too many things going on at the same time; also too many people. Think, he told her. What is the important thing? What do you want us to pay attention to? Think.

Eventually she wrote a story that was about her grandfather killing chickens, and the instructor seemed to be pleased with it. Georgia herself thought that it was a fake. She made a long list of all the things that had been left out and handed it in as an appendix to the story. The instructor said that she expected too much, of herself and of the process, and that she was wearing him out.

The course was not a total loss, because Georgia and the instructor ended up living together. They still live together, in Ontario, on a farm. They sell raspberries, and run a small publishing business. When Georgia can get the money together, she goes to Vancouver to visit her sons. This fall Saturday she has taken the ferry across to Victoria, where she used to live. She did this on an impulse that she doesn't really trust, and by midafternoon, when she walks up the driveway of the splendid stone house where she used to visit Maya, she has already been taken over some fairly shaky ground.

When she phoned Raymond, she wasn't sure that he would ask her to the house. She wasn't sure that she even wanted to go there. She had no notion of how welcome she would be. But Raymond opens the door before she can touch the bell, and he hugs her around the shoulders and kisses her twice (surely he didn't use to do this?) and introduces his wife,

Anne. He says he has told her what great friends they were, Georgia and Ben and he and Maya. Great friends.

Maya is dead. Georgia and Ben are long divorced.

They go to sit in what Maya used to call, with a certain flat cheerfulness, "the family room."

(One evening Raymond had said to Ben and Georgia that it looked as if Maya wasn't going to be able to have any children. "We try our best," he said. "We use pillows and everything. But no luck."

"Listen, old man, you don't do it with pillows," Ben said boisterously. They were all a little drunk. "I thought you were the expert on all the apparatus, but I can see that you and I are going to have to have a little talk."

Raymond was an obstetrician and gynecologist.

By that time Georgia knew all about the abortion in Seattle, which had been set up by Maya's lover, Harvey. Harvey was also a doctor, a surgeon. The bleak apartment in the run-down building, the bad-tempered old woman who was knitting a sweater, the doctor arriving in his shirtsleeves, carrying a brown-paper bag that Maya hysterically believed must contain the tools of his trade. In fact, it contained his lunch—an egg-and-onion sandwich. Maya had the smell of that in her face all the time he and Mme. Defarge were working her over.

Maya and Georgia smiled at each other primly while their husbands continued their playful conversation.)

Raymond's curly brown hair has turned into a silvery fluff, and his face is lined. But nothing dreadful has happened to him—no pouches or jowls or alcoholic flush or sardonic droop of defeat. He is still thin, and straight, and sharp-shouldered, still fresh-smelling, spotless, appropriately, expensively dressed. He'll make a brittle, elegant old man, with an obliging boy's smile. There's that sort of shine on both of them, Maya once said glumly. She was speaking of Raymond and Ben. Maybe we should soak them in vinegar, she said.

The room has changed more than Raymond has. An ivory leather sofa has replaced Maya's tapestry-covered couch, and of course all the old opium-den clutter, Maya's cushions and pampas grass and the gorgeous multicolored elephant with the tiny sewn-on mirrors—that's all gone. The room is beige and ivory, smooth and comfortable as the new blond wife, who sits on the arm of Raymond's chair and maneuvers his arm around her, placing his hand on her thigh. She wears slick-looking white pants and a cream-on-white appliquéd sweater, with gold jewelry. Raymond gives her a couple of hearty and defiant pats.

"Are you going someplace?" he says. "Possibly shopping?"

"Righto," says the wife. "Old times." She smiles at Georgia. "It's okay," she says. "I really do have to go shopping."

When she has gone, Raymond pours drinks for Georgia and himself. "Anne is a worrywart about the booze," he says. "She won't put salt on the table. She threw out all the curtains in the house to get rid of the smell of Maya's cigarettes. I know what you may be thinking: Friend Raymond has got hold of a luscious blonde. But this is actually a very serious girl, and a very steady girl. I had her in my office, you know, quite a while before Maya died. I mean, I had her *working* in my office. I don't mean that the way it sounds! She isn't as young as she looks, either. She's thirty-six."

Georgia had thought forty. She is tired of the visit already, but she has to tell about herself. No, she is not married. Yes, she works. She and the friend she lives with have a farm and a publishing business. Touch and go, not much money. Interesting. A male friend, yes.

"I've lost all track of Ben somehow," Raymond says. "The last I heard, he was living on a boat."

"He and his wife sail around the West Coast every summer," Georgia says. "In the winter they go to Hawaii. The Navy lets you retire early."

"Marvellous," says Raymond.

Seeing Raymond has made Georgia think that she has no idea what Ben looks like now. Has he gone white-haired, has he thickened around the middle? Both of these things have happened to her—she has turned into a chunky woman with a healthy olive skin, a crest of white hair, wearing loose and rather splashy clothes. When she thinks of Ben, she sees him still as a handsome Navy officer, with a perfect Navy look—keen and serious and self-effacing. The look of someone who longed, bravely, to be given orders. Her sons must have pictures of him around—they both see him, they spend holidays on his boat. Perhaps they put the pictures away when she comes to visit. Perhaps they think of protecting these images of him from one who did him hurt.

On the way to Maya's house—Raymond's house—Georgia walked past another house, which she could easily have avoided. A house in Oak Bay, which in fact she had to go out of her way to see.

It was still the house that she and Ben had read about in the real-estate columns of the Victoria *Colonist*. Roomy bungalow under picturesque oak trees. Arbutus, dogwood, window seats, fireplace, diamond-paned windows, character. Georgia stood outside the gate and felt a most predictable pain. Here Ben had cut the grass, here the children had made their paths and hideaways in the bushes, and laid out a graveyard for the birds and snakes killed by the black cat, Domino. She could recall the inside of the house perfectly—the oak floors she and Ben had laboriously sanded, the walls they had painted, the room where she had lain in drugged misery after having her wisdom teeth out. Ben had read aloud to her, from *Dublin-*

*ers.* She couldn't remember the title of the story. It was about a timid poetic sort of young man, with a mean pretty wife. Poor bugger, said Ben when he'd finished it.

Ben liked fiction, which was surprising in a man who also liked sports, and had been popular at school.

She ought to have stayed away from this neighborhood. Everywhere she walked here, under the chestnut trees with their flat gold leaves, and the red-limbed arbutus, and the tall Garry oaks, which suggested fairy stories, European forests, woodcutters, witches—everywhere her footsteps reproached her, saying *what-for, what-for, what-for.* This reproach was just what she had expected—it was what she courted—and there was something cheap about doing such a thing. Something cheap and useless. She knew it. But *what-for, what-for, what-for, wrong-and-waste, wrong-and-waste* went her silly, censorious feet.

Raymond wants Georgia to look at the garden, which he says was made for Maya during the last months of her life. Maya designed it; then she lay on the tapestry couch (setting fire to it twice, Raymond says, by dozing off with a cigarette lit), and she was able to see it all take shape.

Georgia sees a pond, a stone-rimmed pond with an island in the middle. The head of a wicked-looking stone beast—a mountain goat?—rears up on the island, spouting water. Around the pond a jungle of Shasta daisies, pink and purple cosmos, dwarf pines and cypresses, some other miniature tree with glossy red leaves. On the island, now that she looks more closely, are mossy stone walls—the ruins of a tiny tower.

"She hired a young chap to do the work," Raymond says. "She lay there and watched him. It took all summer. She just lay all day and watched him making her garden. Then he'd come in and they'd have tea, and talk about it. You know, Maya didn't just design that garden. She imagined it. She'd tell him what she'd been imagining about it, and he'd take off from there. I mean, this to them was not just a garden. The pond was a lake in this country they had some name for, and all around the lake were forests and territories where different tribes and factions lived. Do you get the picture?"

"Yes," says Georgia.

"Maya had a dazzling imagination. She could have written fantasy or science fiction. Whatever. She was a creative person, without any doubt about it. But you could not get her to seriously use her creativity. That goat was one of the gods of that country, and the island was like a sacred place with a former temple on it. You can see the ruins. They had the religion all worked out. Oh, and the literature, the poems and the legends and the history—everything. They had a song that the queen would sing. Of course it was supposed to be a translation, from that language. They had some of that figured out too. There had been a queen that was shut up in that ruin. That temple. I forget why. She was getting sacrificed, probably. Getting her heart torn out or some gruesome thing. It was all complicated and melodramatic. But think of the effort that went into it. The creativity. The young chap was an artist by profession. I believe he thought of himself as an artist. I don't know how she got hold of him, actually. She knew people. He supported himself doing this kind of thing, I imagine. He did a good job. He laid the pipes, everything. He showed up every day. Every day he came in when he was finished and had tea and talked to her. Well, in my opinion, they didn't have just tea. To my knowledge, not just tea. He would bring a little substance, they would have a little smoke. I told Maya she should write it all down.

"But you know, the instant he was finished, off he went. Off he went. I don't know. Maybe he got another job. It didn't seem to me that it was my place to ask. But I did think that even if he had got a job he could have come back and visited her now and then. Or if he'd gone off on a trip somewhere he could have written letters. I thought he could have. I expected that much of him. It wouldn't have been any skin off his back. Not as I see it. It would have been nice of him to make her think that it hadn't been just a case of—of hired friendship, you know, all along."

Raymond is smiling. He cannot repress, or perhaps is not aware of, this smile.

"For that was the conclusion she must have come to," he says. "After all that nice time and imagining together and egging each other on. She must have been disappointed. She must have been. Even at that stage, such a thing would matter a lot to her. You and I know it, Georgia. It would have mattered. He could have treated her a little more kindly. It wouldn't have had to be for very long."

MAYA DIED a year ago, in the fall, but Georgia did not hear about it until Christmas. She got the news in Hilda's Christmas letter. Hilda, who used to be married to Harvey, is now married to another doctor, in a town in the interior of British Columbia. A few years ago she and Georgia, both visitors, met by chance on a Vancouver street, and they have written occasional letters since.

*Of course you knew Maya so much better than I did,* Hilda wrote. *But I've been surprised how often I've thought about her. I've been thinking of all of us, really, how we were, fifteen or so years ago, and I think we were just as vulnerable in some ways as the kids with their acid trips and so on, that were supposed to be marked for life. Weren't we marked—all of us smashing up our marriages and going out looking for adventure? Of course, Maya didn't smash up her marriage, she of all people stayed where she was, so I suppose it doesn't make much sense what I'm saying. But Maya seemed the most vulnerable person of all to me, so gifted and brittle. I remember I could hardly bear to look at that vein in her temple where she parted her hair.*

What an odd letter for Hilda to write, thought Georgia. She remembered Hilda's expensive pastel plaid shirtdresses, her neat, short, fair hair, her good manners. Did Hilda really think she had smashed up her marriage and gone out looking for adventure under the influence of dope and rock music and revolutionary costumes? Georgia's impression was that Hilda had left Harvey, once she found out what he was up to—or some of what he was up to—and gone to the town in the interior where she sensibly took up her old profession of nursing and in due time married another, presumably more trustworthy doctor. Maya and Georgia had never thought of Hilda as a woman like themselves. And Hilda and Maya had not been close—they had particular reason not to be. But Hilda had kept track; she knew of Maya's death, she wrote these generous words. Without Hilda, Georgia would not have known. She would still have been thinking that someday she might write to Maya, there might come a time when their friendship could be mended.

THE FIRST time that Ben and Georgia went to Maya's house, Harvey and Hilda were there. Maya was having a dinner party for just the six of them. Georgia and Ben had recently moved to Victoria, and Ben had phoned Raymond, who had been a friend of his at school. Ben had never met Maya, but he told Georgia that he had heard that she was very clever, and weird. People said that she was weird. But she was rich—an heiress—so she could get away with it.

Georgia groaned at the news that Maya was rich, and she groaned again at the sight of the house—the great stone-block house with its terraced lawns and clipped bushes and circular drive.

Georgia and Ben came from the same small town in Ontario, and had the same sort of families. It was a fluke that Ben had been sent to a good private school—the money had come from a great-aunt. Even in her teens, when she was proud of being Ben's girl and prouder than she liked to let on about being asked to the dances at that school, Georgia had a low opinion of the girls she met there. She thought rich girls were spoiled and brainless. She called them twits. She thought of herself as a girl—and then a woman—who didn't much like other girls and women. She called the other Navy wives "the Navy *ladies*." Ben was sometimes entertained by her opinions of people and at other times asked if it was really necessary to be so critical.

He had an inkling, he said, that she was going to like Maya. This didn't predispose Georgia in Maya's favor. But Ben turned out to be right. He was very happy then, to have come up with somebody like Maya as an offering to Georgia, to have found a couple with whom he and Georgia could willingly link up as friends. "It'll be good for us to have some non-Navy friends," he was to say. "Some wife for you to knock around with who isn't so conventional. You can't say Maya's conventional."

Georgia couldn't. The house was more or less what she had expected—soon she learned that Maya called it "your friendly neighborhood fortress"—but Maya was a surprise. She opened the door herself, barefoot, wearing a long shapeless robe of coarse brown cloth that looked like burlap. Her hair was long and straight, parted high at one temple. It was almost the same dull-brown color as the robe. She did not wear lipstick, and her skin was rough and pale, with marks like faint bird tracks in the hollows of her cheeks. This lack of color, this roughness of texture about her seemed a splendid assertion of quality. How indifferent she looked, how arrogant and indifferent, with her bare feet, her unpainted toenails, her queer robe. The only thing that she had done to her face was to paint her eyebrows blue—to pluck out all the hairs of her eyebrows, in fact, and paint the skin blue. Not an arched line—just a little daub of blue over each eye, like a swollen vein.

Georgia, whose dark hair was teased, whose eyes were painted in the style of the time, whose breasts were stylishly proffered, found all this disconcerting, and wonderful.

Harvey was the other person there whose looks Georgia found impressive. He was a short man with heavy shoulders, a slight potbelly, puffy blue eyes, and a pugnacious expression. He came from Lancashire. His gray hair was thin on top but worn long at the sides—combed over his ears in a way that made him look more like an artist than a surgeon. "He doesn't even look to me exactly clean enough to be a surgeon," Georgia said to Ben afterward. "Wouldn't you think he'd be something like a sculptor? With gritty fingernails? I expect he treats women badly." She was recalling how he had looked at her breasts. "Not like Raymond," she said. "Raymond worships Maya. And he is extremely clean."

(Raymond has the kind of looks everybody's mother is crazy about, Maya was to say to Georgia, with slashing accuracy, a few weeks after this.)

The food that Maya served was no better than you would expect at a family dinner, and the heavy silver forks were slightly tarnished. But Raymond poured good wine that he would have liked to talk about. He did not manage to interrupt Harvey, who told scandalous and indiscreet hospital stories, and was blandly outrageous about necrophilia and masturbation. Later, in the living room, the coffee was made and served with some ceremony. Raymond got everybody's attention as he ground the beans in a Turkish cylinder. He talked about the importance of the aromatic oils.

Harvey, halted in mid-anecdote, watched with an unkindly smirk, Hilda with patient polite attention. It was Maya who gave her husband radiant encouragement, hung about him like an acolyte, meekly and gracefully assisting. She served the coffee in beautiful little Turkish cups, which she and Raymond had bought in a shop in San Francisco, along with the coffee grinder. She listened demurely to Raymond talking about the shop, as if she recalled other holiday pleasures.

Harvey and Hilda were the first to leave. Maya hung on Raymond's shoulder, saying goodbye. But she detached herself once they were gone, her slithery grace and wifely demeanor discarded. She stretched out casually and awkwardly on the sofa and said, "Now, don't you go yet. Nobody gets half a chance to talk while Harvey is around—you have to talk after."

And Georgia saw how it was. She saw that Maya was hoping not to be left alone with the husband whom she had aroused—for whatever purposes—by her showy attentions. She saw that Maya was mournful and filled with a familiar dread at the end of her dinner party. Raymond was happy. He sat down on the end of the sofa, lifting Maya's reluctant feet to do so. He rubbed one of her feet between his hands.

"What a savage," Raymond said. "This is a woman who won't wear shoes."

"Brandy!" said Maya, springing up. "I knew there was something else you did at dinner parties. You drink brandy!"

"He loves her but she doesn't love him," said Georgia to Ben, just after she had remarked on Raymond's worshipping Maya and being very clean. But Ben, perhaps not listening carefully, thought she was talking about Harvey and Hilda.

"No, no, no. There I think it's the other way round. It's hard to tell with English people. Maya was putting on an act for them. I have an idea about why."

"You have an idea about everything," said Ben.

GEORGIA and Maya became friends on two levels. On the first level, they were friends as wives; on the second as themselves. On the first level, they had dinner at each other's houses. They listened to their husbands talk about their school days. The jokes and fights, the conspiracies and disasters, the bullies and the victims. Terrifying or pitiable schoolfellows and teachers, treats and humiliations. Maya asked if they were sure they hadn't read all that in a book. "It sounds just like a story," she said. "A boys' story about school."

They said that their experiences were what the books were all about. When they had talked enough about school, they talked about movies, politics, public personalities, places they had travelled to or wanted to travel to. Maya and Georgia could join in then. Ben and Raymond did not believe in leaving women out of the conversation. They believed that women were every bit as intelligent as men.

On the second level, Georgia and Maya talked in each other's kitchens, over coffee. Or they had lunch downtown. There were two places, and only two, where Maya liked to have lunch. One was the Moghul's Court— a seedy, grandiose bar in a large, grim railway hotel. The Moghul's Court had curtains of moth-eaten pumpkin-colored velvet, and desiccated ferns, and waiters who wore turbans. Maya always dressed up to go there, in droopy, silky dresses and not very clean white gloves and amazing hats that she found in secondhand stores. She pretended to be a widow who had served with her husband in various outposts of the Empire. She spoke in fluty tones to the sullen young waiters, asking them, "Could you be so good as to . . ." and then telling them they had been terribly, terribly kind.

She and Georgia worked out the history of the Empire widow, and Georgia was added to the story as a grumpy, secretly Socialistic hired companion named Miss Amy Jukes. The widow's name was Mrs. Allegra Forbes-Bellyea. Her husband had been Nigel Forbes-Bellyea. Sometimes Sir Nigel. Most of one rainy afternoon in the Moghul's Court was spent in devising the horrors of the Forbes-Bellyea honeymoon, in a damp hotel in Wales.

The other place that Maya liked was a hippie restaurant on Blanshard Street, where you sat on dirty plush cushions tied to the tops of stumps and ate brown rice with slimy vegetables and drank cloudy cider. (At the Moghul's Court, Maya and Georgia drank only gin.) When they lunched at the hippie restaurant, they wore long, cheap, pretty Indian cotton dresses and pretended to be refugees from a commune, where they had both been the attendants or concubines of a folksinger named Bill Bones. They made up several songs for Bill Bones, all mild and tender blue-eyed songs that contrasted appallingly with his greedy and licentious ways. Bill Bones had very curious personal habits.

When they weren't playing these games, they talked in a headlong fashion about their lives, childhoods, problems, husbands.

"That was a horrible place," Maya said. "That school."

Georgia agreed.

"They were poor boys at a rich kids' school," Maya said. "So they had to try hard. They had to be a credit to their families."

Georgia would not have thought Ben's family poor, but she knew that there were different ways of looking at such things.

Maya said that whenever they had people in for dinner or the evening, Raymond would pick out beforehand all the records he thought suitable and put them in a suitable order. "I think sometime he'll hand out conversational topics at the door," Maya said.

Georgia revealed that Ben wrote a letter every week to the great-aunt who had sent him to school.

"Is it a nice letter?" said Maya.

"Yes. Oh, yes. It's very nice."

They looked at each other bleakly, and laughed. Then they announced—they admitted—what weighed on them. It was the innocence of these husbands—the hearty, decent, firm, contented innocence. That is a wearying and finally discouraging thing. It makes intimacy a chore.

"But do you feel badly," Georgia said, "talking like this?"

"Of course," said Maya, grinning and showing her large perfect teeth—the product of expensive dental work from the days before she had charge of her own looks. "I have another reason to feel badly," she said. "But I don't know whether I do. I do and I don't."

"I know," said Georgia, who up until that moment hadn't known, for sure.

"You're very smart," Maya said. "Or I'm very obvious. What do you think of him?"

"A lot of trouble," Georgia said judiciously. She was pleased with that answer, which didn't show how flattered she felt by the disclosure, or how heady she found this conversation.

"You aren't just a-whistlin' 'Dixie,' " Maya said, and she told the story about the abortion. "I am going to break up with him," she said. "Any day now."

But she kept on seeing Harvey. She would relate, at lunch, some very disillusioning facts about him, then announce that she had to go, she was meeting him at a motel out on the Gorge Road, or at the cabin he had on Prospect Lake.

"Must scrub," she said.

She had left Raymond once. Not for Harvey. She had run away with, or to, a musician. A pianist—Nordic and sleepy-looking but bad-tempered—from her society-lady, symphony-benefit days. She travelled with him for five weeks, and he deserted her in a hotel in Cincinnati. She then developed frightful chest pains, appropriate to a breaking heart. What she really had was a gallbladder attack. Raymond was sent for, and he came and got her out of the hospital. They had a little holiday in Mexico before they came home.

"That was it, for me," Maya said. "That was your true and desperate love. Nevermore."

What, then, was Harvey?

"Exercise," said Maya.

GEORGIA got a part-time job in a bookstore, working several evenings a week. Ben went away on his yearly cruise. The summer turned out to be unusually hot and sunny for the West Coast. Georgia combed her hair out and stopped using most of her makeup and bought a couple of short halter dresses. Sitting on her stool at the front of the store, showing her bare brown shoulders and sturdy brown legs, she looked like a college girl—clever but full of energy and bold opinions. The people who came into the store liked the look of a girl—a woman—like Georgia. They liked to talk to her. Most of them came in alone. They were not exactly lonely people, but they were lonely for somebody to talk to about books. Georgia plugged in the kettle behind the desk and made mugs of raspberry tea. Some favored customers brought in their own mugs. Maya came to visit and lurked about in the background, amused and envious.

"You know what you've got?" she said to Georgia. "You've got a salon! Oh, I'd like to have a job like that! I'd even like an ordinary job in an ordinary store, where you fold things up and find things for people and make change and say thank you very much, and colder out today, will it rain?"

"You could get a job like that," said Georgia.

"No, I couldn't. I don't have the discipline. I was too badly brought up. I can't even keep house without Mrs. Hanna and Mrs. Cheng and Sadie."

It was true. Maya had a lot of servants, for a modern woman, though they came at different times and did separate things and were nothing like an old-fashioned household staff. Even the food at her dinner parties, which seemed to show her own indifferent touch, had been prepared by someone else.

Usually, Maya was busy in the evenings. Georgia was just as glad, because she didn't really want Maya coming into the store, asking for crazy titles that she had made up, making Georgia's employment there a kind of joke. Georgia took the store seriously. She had a serious, secret liking for it that she could not explain. It was a long, narrow store with an old-fashioned funnelled entryway between two angled display windows. From her stool behind the desk Georgia was able to see the reflections in one window reflected in the other. This street was not one of those decked out to receive tourists. It was a wide east-west street filled in the early evening with a faintly yellow light, a light reflected off pale stucco buildings that were not very high, plain storefronts, nearly empty sidewalks. Georgia found this plainness liberating after the winding shady streets, the flowery yards and vine-framed windows of Oak Bay. Here the books could come into their own, as they never could in a more artful and enticing suburban bookshop. Straight long rows of paperbacks. (Most of the Penguins then still had their orange-and-white or blue-and-white covers, with no designs or pictures, just the unadorned, unexplained titles.) The store was a straight avenue of bounty, of plausible promises. Certain books that Georgia had never read, and probably never would read, were important to her, because of the stateliness or mystery of their titles. *In Praise of Folly. The Roots of Coincidence. The Flowering of New England. Ideas and Integrities.*

Sometimes she got up and put the books in stricter order. The fiction was shelved alphabetically, by author, which was sensible but not very interesting. The history books, however, and the philosophy and psychology and other science books were arranged according to certain intricate and delightful rules—having to do with chronology and content—that Georgia grasped immediately and even elaborated on. She did not need to read much of a book to know about it. She got a sense of it easily, almost at once, as if by smell.

At times the store was empty, and she felt an abundant calm. It was not even the books that mattered then. She sat on the stool and watched the street—patient, expectant, by herself, in a finely balanced and suspended state.

She saw Miles' reflection—his helmeted ghost parking his motorcycle at the curb—before she saw him. She believed that she had noted his valiant profile, his pallor, his dusty red hair (he took off his helmet and shook out his hair before coming into the store), and his quick, slouching, insolent, invading way of moving, even in the glass.

It was no surprise that he soon began to talk to her, as others did. He told her that he was a diver. He looked for wrecks, and lost airplanes, and dead bodies. He had been hired by a rich couple in Victoria who were planning a treasure-hunting cruise, getting it together at the moment. Their names, the destination were all secrets. Treasure-hunting was a lunatic business. He had done it before. His home was in Seattle, where he had a wife and a little daughter.

Everything he told her could easily have been a lie.

He showed her pictures in books—photographs and drawings, of mollusks, jellyfish, the Portuguese man-of-war, sargasso weed, the Caribbean flying fish, the girdle of Venus. He pointed out which pictures were accurate, which were fakes. Then he went away and paid no more attention to her, even slipping out of the store while she was busy with a customer. Not a hint of a goodbye. But he came in another evening, and told her about a drowned man wedged into the cabin of a boat, looking out the watery window in an interested way. By attention and avoidance, impersonal conversations in close proximity, by his oblivious prowling, and unsmiling, lengthy, gray-eyed looks, he soon had Georgia in a disturbed and not disagreeable state. He stayed away two nights in a row, then came in and asked her, abruptly, if she would like a ride home on his motorcycle.

Georgia said yes. She had never ridden on a motorcycle in her life. Her car was in the parking lot; she knew what was bound to happen.

She told him where she lived. "Just a few blocks up from the beach," she said.

"We'll go to the beach, then. We'll go and sit on the logs."

That was what they did. They sat for a while on the logs. Then, though the beach was not quite dark or completely deserted, they made love in the imperfect shelter of some broom bushes. Georgia walked home, a strengthened and lightened woman, not in the least in love, favored by the universe.

"My car wouldn't start," she told the baby-sitter, a grandmother from down the street. "I walked all the way home. It was lovely, walking. Lovely. I enjoyed it so much."

Her hair was wild, her lips were swollen, her clothes were full of sand.

HER LIFE filled up with such lies. Her car would be parked beside outlying beaches, on the logging roads so conveniently close to the city, on the wandering back roads of the Saanich Peninsula. The map of the city that she had held in her mind up till now, with its routes to shops and work and friends' houses, was overlaid with another map, of circuitous routes followed in fear (not shame) and excitement, of flimsy shelters, temporary hiding places, where she and Miles made love, often within hearing distance of passing traffic or a hiking party or a family picnic. And Georgia herself, watching her children on the roundabout, or feeling the excellent shape of a lemon in her hand at the supermarket, contained another woman, who only a few hours before had been whimpering and tussling on the ferns, on the sand, on the bare ground, or, during a rainstorm, in her own car—who had been driven hard and gloriously out of her mind and drifted loose and gathered her wits and made her way home again. Was this a common story? Georgia cast an eye over the other women at the supermarket. She looked for signs—of dreaminess or flaunting, a sense of drama in a woman's way of dressing, a special rhythm in her movements.

How many, she asked Maya.

"God knows," said Maya. "Do a survey."

Trouble began, perhaps, as soon as they said that they loved each other. Why did they do that—defining, inflating, obscuring whatever it was they did feel? It seemed to be demanded, that was all—just the way changes, variations, elaborations in the lovemaking itself might be demanded. It was a way of going further. So they said it, and that night Georgia couldn't sleep. She did not regret what had been said or think that it was a lie, though she knew that it was absurd. She thought of the way Miles sought to have her look into his eyes during lovemaking—something Ben expressly did not do—and she thought of how his eyes, at first bright and challenging, became cloudy and calm and sombre. That way she trusted him—it was the only way. She thought of being launched out on a gray, deep, baleful, magnificent sea. Love.

"I didn't know this was going to happen," she said in Maya's kitchen the next day, drinking her coffee. The day was warm, but she had put on a sweater to huddle in. She felt shaken, and submissive.

"No. And you don't know," said Maya rather sharply. "Did he say it too? Did he say he loved you too?"

Yes, said Georgia, yes, of course.

"Look out, then. Look out for next time. Next time is always pretty tricky when they've said that."

And so it was. Next time a rift opened. At first they simply tested it, to see if it was there. It was almost like a new diversion to them. But it widened, it widened. Before any words were said to confirm that it was there, Georgia felt it widen, she coldly felt it widen, though she was desperate for it to close. Did he feel the same thing? She didn't know. He too seemed cold—pale, deliberate, glittering with some new malicious intent.

They were sitting recklessly, late at night, in Georgia's car among the other lovers at Clover Point.

"Everybody here in these cars doing the same thing we're doing," Miles had said. "Doesn't that idea turn you on?"

He had said that at the very moment in their ritual when they had been moved, last time, to speak brokenly and solemnly of love.

"You ever think of that?" he said. "I mean, we could start with Ben and Laura. You ever imagine how it would be with you and me and Ben and Laura?"

Laura was his wife, at home in Seattle. He had not spoken of her before, except to tell Georgia her name. He had spoken of Ben, in a way that Georgia didn't like but passed over.

"What does Ben think you do for fun," he'd said, "while he is off cruising the ocean blue?"

"Do you and Ben usually have a big time when he gets back?"

"Does Ben like that outfit as much as I do?"

He spoke as if he and Ben were friends in some way, or at least partners, co-proprietors.

"You and me and Ben and Laura," he said, in a tone that seemed to Georgia insistently and artificially lecherous, sly, derisive. "Spread the joy around."

He tried to fondle her, pretending not to notice how offended she was, how bitterly stricken. He described the generous exchanges that would take place among the four of them abed. He asked whether she was getting excited. She said no, disgusted. Ah, you are but you won't give in to it, he said. His voice, his caresses grew more bullying. What is so special about you, he asked softly, despisingly, with a hard squeeze at her breasts. Georgia, why do you think you're such a queen?

"You are being cruel and you know you're being cruel," said Georgia, pulling at his hands. "Why are you being like this?"

"Honey, I'm not being cruel," said Miles, in a slippery mock-tender voice. "I'm being horny. I'm horny again is all." He began to pull Georgia around, to arrange her for his use. She told him to get out of the car.

"Squeamish," he said, in that same artificially and hatefully tender voice, as if he were licking fanatically at something loathsome. "You're a squeamish little slut."

Georgia told him that she would lean on the horn if he didn't stop. She would lean on the horn if he didn't get out of the car. She would yell for somebody to call the police. She did lean against the horn as they struggled. He pushed her away, with a whimpering curse such as she'd heard from him at other times, when it meant something different. He got out.

She could not believe that such ill will had erupted, that things had so stunningly turned around. When she thought of this afterward—a good long time afterward—she thought that perhaps he had acted for conscience' sake, to mark her off from Laura. Or to blot out what he had said to her last time. To humiliate her because he was frightened. Perhaps. Or perhaps all this seemed to him simply a further, and genuinely interesting, development in lovemaking.

She would have liked to talk it over with Maya. But the possibility of talking anything over with Maya had disappeared. Their friendship had come suddenly to an end.

THE NIGHT after the incident at Clover Point, Georgia was sitting on the living-room floor playing a bedtime card game with her sons. The phone rang, and she was sure that it was Miles. She had been thinking all day that he would call, he would have to call to explain himself, to beg her pardon, to say that he had been testing her, in a way, or had been temporarily deranged by circumstances that she knew nothing about. She would not forgive him immediately. But she would not hang up.

It was Maya.

"Guess what weird thing happened," Maya said. "Miles phoned me.

Your Miles. It's okay, Raymond isn't here. How did he even know my name?"

"I don't know," said Georgia.

She had told him it, of course. She had offered wild Maya up for his entertainment, or to point out what a novice at this game she herself was—a relatively chaste prize.

"He says he wants to come and talk to me," Maya said. "What do you think? What's the matter with him? Did you have a fight? . . . Yes? Oh, well, he probably wants me to persuade you to make up. I must say he picked the right night. Raymond's at the hospital. He's got this balky woman in labor; he may have to stay and do a section on her. I'll phone and tell you how it goes. Shall I?"

After a couple of hours, with the children long asleep, Georgia began to expect Maya's call. She watched the television news, to take her mind off expecting it. She picked up the phone to make sure there was a dial tone. She turned off the television after the news, then turned it on again. She started to watch a movie; she watched it through three commercial breaks without going to the kitchen to look at the clock.

At half past midnight she went out and got into her car and drove to Maya's house. She had no idea what she would do there. And she did not do much of anything. She drove around the circular drive with the lights off. The house was dark. She could see that the garage was open and Raymond's car was not there. The motorcycle was nowhere in sight.

She had left her children alone, the doors unlocked. Nothing happened to them. They didn't wake up and discover her defection. No burglar, or prowler, or murderer surprised her on her return. That was a piece of luck that she did not even appreciate. She had gone out leaving the door open and the lights on, and when she came back she hardly recognized her folly, though she closed the door and turned out some lights and lay down on the living-room sofa. She didn't sleep. She lay still, as if the smallest movement would sharpen her suffering, until she saw the day getting light and heard the birds waking. Her limbs were stiff. She got up and went to the phone and listened again for the dial tone. She walked stiffly to the kitchen and put on the kettle and said to herself the words *a paralysis of grief*.

*A paralysis of grief.* What was she thinking of? That was what she would feel, how she might describe the way she would feel, if one of her children had died. Grief is for serious matters, important losses. She knew that. She would not have bartered away an hour of her children's lives to have had the phone ring at ten o'clock last night, to have heard Maya say, "Georgia, he's desperate. He's sorry; he loves you very much."

No. But it seemed that such a phone call would have given her a happiness that no look or word from her children could give her. Than anything could give her, ever again.

She phoned Maya before nine o'clock. As she was dialling, she thought that there were still some possibilities to pray for. Maya's phone had been temporarily out of order. Maya had been ill last night. Raymond had been in a car accident on his way home from the hospital.

All these possibilities vanished at the first sound of Maya's voice, which was sleepy (pretending to be sleepy?) and silky with deceit. "Georgia? Is that Georgia? Oh, I thought it was going to be Raymond. He had to stay over at the hospital in case this poor wretched woman needed a C-section. He was going to call me—"

"You told me that last night," said Georgia.

"He was going to call me—Oh, Georgia, I was supposed to call you! Now I remember. Yes. I was supposed to call you, but I thought it was probably too late. I thought the phone might wake up the children. I thought, Oh, better just leave it till morning!"

"How late was it?"

"Not awfully. I just thought."

"What happened?"

"What do you mean, what happened?" Maya laughed, like a lady in a silly play. "Georgia, are you in a state?"

"What happened?"

"Oh, Georgia," said Maya, groaning magnanimously but showing an edge of nerves. "Georgia, I'm sorry. It was nothing. It was just nothing. I've been rotten, but I didn't mean to be. I offered him a beer. Isn't that what you do when somebody rides up to your house on a motorcycle? You offer him a beer. But then he came on very lordly and said he only drank Scotch. And he said he'd only drink Scotch if I would drink with him. I thought he was pretty high-handed. Pretty high-handed pose. But I really was doing this for you, Georgia—I was wanting to find out what was on his mind. So I told him to put the motorcycle behind the garage, and I took him to sit in the back garden. That was so if I heard Raymond's car I could chase him out the back way and he could walk the motorcycle down the lane. I am not about to unload anything *new* onto Raymond at this point. I mean even something innocent, which this started out to be."

Georgia, with her teeth chattering, hung up the phone. She never spoke to Maya again. Maya appeared at her door, of course, a little while later, and Georgia had to let her in, because the children were playing in the yard. Maya sat down contritely at the kitchen table and asked if she could smoke. Georgia did not answer. Maya said she would smoke anyway and she hoped it was all right. Georgia pretended that Maya wasn't there.

SELECTED STORIES

While Maya smoked, Georgia cleaned the stove, dismantling the elements and putting them back together again. She wiped the counters and polished the taps and straightened out the cutlery drawer. She mopped the floor around Maya's feet. She worked briskly, thoroughly, and never quite looked at Maya. At first she was not sure whether she could keep this up. But it got easier. The more earnest Maya became—the further she slipped from sensible remonstrance, half-amused confession, into true and fearful regret—the more fixed Georgia was in her resolve, the more grimly satisfied in her heart. She took care, however, not to appear grim. She moved about lightly. She was almost humming.

She took a knife to scrape out the grease from between the counter tiles by the stove. She had let things get into a bad way.

Maya smoked one cigarette after another, stubbing them out in a saucer that she fetched for herself from the cupboard. She said, "Georgia, this is so stupid. I can tell you, he's not worth it. It was nothing. All it was was Scotch and opportunity."

She said, "I am really sorry. Truly sorry. I know you don't believe me. How can I say it so you will?"

And, "Georgia, listen. You are humiliating me. Fine. Fine. Maybe I deserve it. I do deserve it. But after you've humiliated me enough we'll go back to being friends and we'll laugh about this. When we're old ladies, I swear we'll laugh. We won't be able to remember his name. We'll call him the motorcycle sheikh. We will."

Then, "Georgia, what do you want me to do? Do you want me to throw myself on the floor? I'm about ready to. I'm trying to keep myself from snivelling, and I can't. I'm snivelling, Georgia. Okay?"

She had begun to cry. Georgia put on her rubber gloves and started to clean the oven.

"You win," said Maya. "I'll pick up my cigarettes and go home."

She phoned a few times. Georgia hung up on her. Miles phoned, and Georgia hung up on him too. She thought he sounded cautious but smug. He phoned again and his voice trembled, as if he were striving just for candor and humility, bare love. Georgia hung up at once. She felt violated, shaken.

Maya wrote a letter, which said, in part, *I suppose you know that Miles is going back to Seattle and whatever home fires he keeps burning there. It seems the treasure thing has fallen through. But you must have known he was bound to go sometime and you'd have felt rotten then, so now you've got the rotten feeling over with. So isn't that okay? I don't say this to excuse myself. I know I was weak and putrid. But can't we put it behind us now?*

She went on to say that she and Raymond were going on a long-planned holiday to Greece and Turkey, and that she hoped very much that she would get a note from Georgia before she left. But if she didn't get any word she would try to understand what Georgia was telling her, and she would not make a nuisance of herself by writing again.

She kept her word. She didn't write again. She sent, from Turkey, a pretty piece of striped cloth large enough for a tablecloth. Georgia folded it up and put it away. She left it for Ben to find after she moved out, several months later.

"I'M HAPPY," Raymond tells Georgia. "I'm very happy, and the reason is that I'm content to be an ordinary sort of person with an ordinary calm life. I am not looking for any big revelation or any big drama or any messiah of the opposite sex. I don't go around figuring out how to make things more interesting. I can say to you quite frankly I think Maya made a mistake. I don't mean she wasn't very gifted and intelligent and creative and so on, but she was looking for something—maybe she was looking for something that just is not there. And she tended to despise a lot that she had. It's true. She didn't want the privileges she had. We'd travel, for example, and she wouldn't want to stay in a comfortable hotel. No. She had to go on some trek that involved riding on poor, miserable donkeys and drinking sour milk for breakfast. I suppose I sound very square. Well, I suppose I am. I am square. You know, she had such beautiful silver. Magnificent silver. It was passed down through her family. And she couldn't be bothered to polish it or get the cleaning woman to polish it. She wrapped it all up in plastic and hid it away. She hid it away—you'd think it was a disgrace. How do you think she envisaged herself? As some kind of hippie, maybe? Some kind of free spirit? She didn't even realize it was her money that kept her afloat. I'll tell you, some of the free spirits I've seen pass in and out of this house wouldn't have been long around her without it.

"I did all I could," said Raymond. "I didn't scoot off and leave her, like her Prince of Fantasy Land."

GEORGIA got a vengeful pleasure out of breaking with Maya. She was pleased with the controlled manner in which she did it. The deaf ear. She was surprised to find herself capable of such control, such thoroughgoing punishment. She punished Maya. She punished Miles, through Maya, as much as she could. What she had to do, and she knew it, was to scrape herself raw, to root out all addiction to the gifts of those two pale prodigies. Miles and Maya. Both of them slippery, shimmery—liars, seducers, finaglers. But you would have thought that after such scourging she'd have scuttled back into her marriage and locked its doors, and appreciated what she had there as never before.

That was not what happened. She broke with Ben. Within a year, she was gone. Her way of breaking was strenuous and unkind. She told him about Miles, though she spared her own pride by leaving out the part about Miles and Maya. She took no care—she had hardly any wish—to avoid unkindness. On the night when she waited for Maya to call, some bitter, yeasty spirit entered into her. She saw herself as a person surrounded by, living by, sham. Because she had been so readily unfaithful, her marriage was a sham. Because she had gone so far out of it, so quickly, it was a sham. She dreaded, now, a life like Maya's. She dreaded just as much a life like her own before this happened. She could not but destroy. Such cold energy was building in her she had to blow her own house down.

She had entered with Ben, when they were both so young, a world of ceremony, of safety, of gestures, concealment. Fond appearances. More than appearances. Fond contrivance. (She thought when she left that she would have no use for contrivance anymore.) She had been happy there, from time to time. She had been sullen, restless, bewildered, and happy. But she said most vehemently, Never, never. I was never happy, she said.

People always say that.

People make momentous shifts, but not the changes they imagine.

JUST THE SAME, Georgia knows that her remorse about the way she changed her life is dishonest. It is real and dishonest. Listening to Raymond, she knows that whatever she did she would have to do again. She would have to do it again, supposing that she had to be the person she was.

Raymond does not want to let Georgia go. He does not want to part with her. He offers to drive her downtown. When she has gone, he won't be able to talk about Maya. Very likely Anne has told him that she does not want to hear any more on the subject of Maya.

"Thank you for coming," he says on the doorstep. "Are you sure about the ride? Are you sure you can't stay to dinner?"

Georgia reminds him again about the bus, the last ferry. She says no, no, she really wants to walk. It's only a couple of miles. The late afternoon so lovely, Victoria so lovely. I had forgotten, she says.

Raymond says once more, "Thank you for coming."

"Thank you for the drinks," Georgia says. "Thank you too. I guess we never believe we are going to die."

"Now, now," says Raymond.

"No. I mean we never behave—we never behave as if we believed we were going to die."

Raymond smiles more and more and puts a hand on her shoulder. "How should we behave?" he says.

"Differently," says Georgia. She puts a foolish stress on the word, meaning that her answer is so lame that she can offer it only as a joke.

Raymond hugs her, then involves her in a long chilly kiss. He fastens onto her with an appetite that is grievous but unconvincing. A parody of passion, whose intention neither one of them, surely, will try to figure out.

She doesn't think about that as she walks back to town through the yellow-leafed streets with their autumn smells and silences. Past Clover Point, the cliffs crowned with broom bushes, the mountains across the water. The mountains of the Olympic Peninsula, assembled like a blatant backdrop, a cutout of rainbow tissue paper. She doesn't think about Raymond, or Miles, or Maya, or even Ben.

She thinks about sitting in the store in the evenings. The light in the street, the complicated reflections in the windows. The accidental clarity.

# Carried Away

❦

## LETTERS

IN THE DINING ROOM of the Commercial Hotel, Louisa opened the letter that had arrived that day from overseas. She ate steak and potatoes, her usual meal, and drank a glass of wine. There were a few travellers in the room, and the dentist who ate there every night because he was a widower. He had shown an interest in her in the beginning but had told her he had never before seen a woman touch wine or spirits.

"It is for my health," said Louisa gravely.

The white tablecloths were changed every week and in the meantime were protected by oilcloth mats. In winter, the dining room smelled of these mats wiped by a kitchen rag, and of coal fumes from the furnace, and beef gravy and dried potatoes and onions—a smell not unpleasant to anybody coming in hungry from the cold. On each table was a little cruet stand with the bottle of brown sauce, the bottle of tomato sauce, and the pot of horseradish.

The letter was addressed to "The Librarian, Carstairs Public Library, Carstairs, Ontario." It was dated six weeks before—January 4, 1917.

> *Perhaps you will be surprised to hear from a person you don't know and that doesn't remember your name. I hope you are still the same Librarian though enough time has gone by that you could have moved on.*
>
> *What has landed me here in Hospital is not too serious. I see worse all around me and get my mind off of all that by picturing things and wondering for instance if you are still there in the Library. If you are the one I mean, you are about of medium size or perhaps not quite, with light brownish hair. You came a few months before it*

was time for me to go in the Army following on Miss Tamblyn who had been there since I first became a user aged nine or ten. In her time the books were pretty much every which way, and it was as much as your life was worth to ask her for the least help or anything since she was quite a dragon. Then when you came what a change, it was all put into sections of Fiction and Non-Fiction and History and Travel and you got the magazines arranged in order and put out as soon as they arrived, not left to molder away till everything in them was stale. I felt gratitude but did not know how to say so. Also I wondered what brought you there, you were an educated person.

My name is Jack Agnew and my card is in the drawer. The last book I took out was very good—H. G. Wells, Mankind in the Making. My education was to Second Form in High School, then I went into Douds as many did. I didn't join up right away when I was eighteen so you will not see me as a Brave Man. I am a person tending to have my own ideas always. My only relative in Carstairs, or anyplace, is my father Patrick Agnew. He works for Douds not at the factory but at the house doing the gardening. He is a lone wolf even more than me and goes out to the country fishing every chance he gets. I write him a letter sometimes but I doubt if he reads it.

After supper Louisa went up to the Ladies' Parlor on the second floor, and sat down at the desk to write her reply.

I am very glad to hear you appreciated what I did in the Library though it was just the normal organization, nothing special.

I am sure you would like to hear news of home, but I am a poor person for the job, being an outsider here. I do talk to people in the Library and in the hotel. The travellers in the hotel mostly talk about how business is (it is brisk if you can get the goods) and a little about sickness, and a lot about the War. There are rumors on rumors and opinions galore, which I'm sure would make you laugh if they didn't make you angry. I will not bother to write them down because I am sure there is a Censor reading this who would cut my letter to ribbons.

You ask how I came here. There is no interesting story. My parents are both dead. My father worked for Eaton's in Toronto in the Furniture Department, and after his death my mother worked there too in Linens. And I also worked there for a while in Books. Perhaps you could say Eaton's was our Douds. I graduated from Jarvis Collegiate. I had some sickness which put me in hospital for a long time, but I am quite well now. I had a great deal of time to read and my favorite authors are Thomas Hardy, who is accused of being gloomy but I think is very true to life—and Willa Cather. I just happened to be in this town when I heard the Librarian had died and I thought, perhaps that is the job for me.

.    .    .

A good thing your letter reached me today as I am about to be discharged from here and don't know if it would have been sent on to where I am going. I am glad you did not think my letter was too foolish.

If you run into my father or anybody you do not need to say anything about the fact we are writing to each other. It is nobody's business and I know there are plenty of people would laugh at me writing to the Librarian as they did at me going to the Library even, why give them the satisfaction?

I am glad to be getting out of here. So much luckier than some I see that will never walk or have their sight and will have to hide themselves away from the world.

You asked where did I live in Carstairs. Well, it was not anyplace to be proud of. If you know where Vinegar Hill is and you turned off on Flowers Road it is the last house on the right, yellow paint once upon a time. My father grows potatoes, or did. I used to take them around town with my wagon, and every load I sold got a nickel to keep.

You mention favorite authors. At one time I was fond of Zane Grey, but I drifted away from reading fiction stories to reading History or Travel. I sometimes read books away over my head, I know, but I do get something out of them. H. G. Wells I mentioned is one and Robert Ingersoll who writes about religion. They have given me a lot to think about. If you are very religious I hope I have not offended you.

One day when I got to the Library it was a Saturday afternoon and you had just unlocked the door and were putting the lights on as it was dark and raining out. You had been caught out with no hat or umbrella and your hair had got wet. You took the pins out of it and let it come down. Is it too personal a thing to ask if you have it long still or have you cut it? You went over and stood by the radiator and shook your hair on it and the water sizzled like grease in the frying pan. I was sitting reading in the London Illustrated News about the War. We exchanged a smile. (I didn't mean to say your hair was greasy when I wrote that!)

I have not cut my hair though I often think about it. I do not know if it is vanity or laziness that prevents me.

I am not very religious.

I walked up Vinegar Hill and found your house. The potatoes are looking healthy. A police dog disputed with me, is he yours?

The weather is getting quite warm. We have had the flood on the river, which I gather is an annual Spring event. The water got into the hotel basement and somehow contaminated our drinking supply so that we were given free beer or ginger ale. But only if we lived or were staying there. You can imagine there were plenty of jokes.

I should ask if there is anything that I could send you.

*I am not in need of anything particular. I get the tobacco and other bits of things the ladies in Carstairs do up for us. I would like to read some books by the authors you have mentioned but I doubt whether I would get the chance here.*

*The other day there was a man died of a heart attack. It was the News of all time. Did you hear about the man who died of a heart attack? That was all you heard about day and night here. Then everybody would laugh which seems hard-hearted but it just seemed so strange. It was not even a hot time so you couldn't say maybe he was scared. (As a matter of fact he was writing a letter at the time so I had better look out.) Before and after him others have died being shot up or blown up but he is the famous one, to die of a heart attack. Everybody is saying what a long way to come and a lot of expense for the Army to go to, for that.*

*The summer has been so dry the watering tank has been doing the streets every day, trying to lay the dust. The children would dance along behind it. There was also a new thing in town—a cart with a little bell that went along selling ice cream, and the children were pretty attentive to this as well. It was pushed by the man who had an accident at the factory—you know who I mean, though I can't recall his name. He lost his arm to the elbow. My room at the hotel, being on the third floor, it was like an oven, and I often walked about till after midnight. So did many other people, sometimes in pajamas. It was like a dream. There was still a little water in the river, enough to go out in a rowboat, and the Methodist minister did that on a Sunday in August. He was praying for rain in a public service. But there was a small leak in the boat and the water came in and wet his feet and eventually the boat sank and left him standing in the water, which did not nearly reach his waist. Was it an accident or a malicious trick? The talk was all that his prayers were answered but from the wrong direction.*

*I often pass the Douds' place on my walks. Your father keeps the lawns and hedges looking beautiful. I like the house, so original and airy-looking. But it may not have been cool even there, because I heard the voice of the mother and baby daughter late at night as if they were out on the lawn.*

*Though I told you there is nothing I need, there is one thing I would like. That is a photograph of you. I hope you will not think I am overstepping the bounds to ask for it. Maybe you are engaged to somebody or have a sweetheart over here you are writing to as well as me. You are a cut above the ordinary and it would not surprise me if some Officer had spoken for you. But now that I have asked I cannot take it back and will just leave it up to you to think what you like of me.*

Louisa was twenty-five years old and had been in love once, with a doctor she had known in the sanitorium. Her love was returned, eventually, costing the doctor his job. There was some harsh doubt in her mind about whether he had been told to leave the sanitorium or had left of his own accord, being weary of the entanglement. He was married, he had children. Letters had played a part that time too. After he left, they were still writing to one another. And once or twice after she was released. Then she asked him not to write anymore and he didn't. But the failure of his letters to arrive drove her out of Toronto and made her take the travelling job. Then there would be only the one disappointment in the week, when she got back on Friday or Saturday night. Her last letter had been firm and stoical, and some consciousness of herself as a heroine of love's tragedy went with her around the country as she hauled her display cases up and down the stairs of small hotels and talked about Paris styles and said that her sample hats were bewitching, and drank her solitary glass of wine. If she'd had anybody to tell, though, she would have laughed at just that notion. She would have said love was all hocus-pocus, a deception, and she believed that. But at the prospect she still felt a hush, a flutter along the nerves, a bowing down of sense, a flagrant prostration.

She had a picture taken. She knew how she wanted it to be. She would have liked to wear a simple white blouse, a peasant girl's smock with the string open at the neck. She did not own a blouse of that description and in fact had only seen them in pictures. And she would have liked to let her hair down. Or if it had to be up, she would have liked it piled very loosely and bound with strings of pearls.

Instead she wore her blue silk shirtwaist and bound her hair as usual. She thought the picture made her look rather pale, hollow-eyed. Her expression was sterner and more foreboding than she had intended. She sent it anyway.

*I am not engaged, and do not have a sweetheart. I was in love once and it had to be broken off. I was upset at the time but I knew I must bear it, and now I believe that it was all for the best.*

She had wracked her brains, of course, to remember him. She could not remember shaking out her hair, as he said she had done, or smiling at any young man when the raindrops fell on the radiator. He might as well have dreamed all that, and perhaps he had.

She had begun to follow the war in a more detailed way than she had done previously. She did not try to ignore it anymore. She went along the street with a sense that her head was filled with the same exciting and troubling information as everybody else's. Saint-Quentin, Arras, Montdidier, Amiens, and then there was a battle going on at the Somme River, where surely there had been one before? She laid open on her desk the maps of the war that appeared as double-page spreads in the magazines. She saw in colored lines the German drive to the Marne, the first thrust of the Americans at Château-Thierry. She looked at the artist's brown pictures of a horse rearing up during an air attack, of some soldiers in East Africa drinking out of coconuts, and of a line of German prisoners with bandaged heads or limbs and bleak, sullen expressions. Now she felt what everybody else did—a constant fear and misgiving and at the same time this addictive excitement. You could look up from your life of the moment and feel the world crackling beyond the walls.

*I am glad to hear you do not have a sweetheart though I know that is selfish of me. I do not think you and I will ever meet again. I don't say that because I've had a dream about what will happen or am a gloomy person always looking for the worst. It just seems to me it is the most probable thing to happen, though I don't dwell on it and go along every day doing the best I can to stay alive. I am not trying to worry you or get your sympathy either but just explain how the idea I won't ever see Carstairs again makes me think I can say anything I want. I guess it's like being sick with a fever. So I will say I love you. I think of you up on a stool at the Library reaching to put a book away and I come up and put my hands on your waist and lift you down, and you turning around inside my arms as if we agreed about everything.*

Every Tuesday afternoon the ladies and girls of the Red Cross met in the Council Chambers, which was just down the hall from the Library. When the Library was empty for a few moments, Louisa went down the hall and entered the room full of women. She had decided to knit a scarf. At the sanitorium she had learned how to knit a basic stitch, but she had never learned or had forgotten how to cast on or off.

The older women were all busy packing boxes or cutting up and folding bandages from sheets of heavy cotton that were spread on the tables. But a lot of girls near the door were eating buns and drinking tea. One was holding a skein of wool on her arms for another to wind.

Louisa told them what she needed to know.

"So what do you want to knit, then?" said one of the girls with some bun still in her mouth.

Louisa said, a muffler. For a soldier.

"Oh, you'll want the regulation wool," another said, more politely, and jumped off the table. She came back with some balls of brown wool, and fished a spare pair of needles out of her bag, telling Louisa they could be hers.

"I'll just get you started," she said. "It's a regulation width too."

Other girls gathered around and teased this girl, whose name was Corrie. They told her she was doing it all wrong.

"Oh, I am, am I?" said Corrie. "How would you like a knitting needle in your eye? Is it for a friend?" she said solicitously to Louisa. "A friend overseas?"

"Yes," said Louisa. Of course they would think of her as an old maid, they would laugh at her or feel sorry for her, according to whatever show they put on, of being kind or brazen.

"So knit up good and tight," said the one who'd finished her bun. "Knit up good and tight to keep him warm!"

ONE OF THE GIRLS in this group was Grace Horne. She was a shy but resolute-looking girl, nineteen years old, with a broad face, thin lips often pressed together, brown hair cut in a straight bang, and an attractively mature body. She had become engaged to Jack Agnew before he went overseas, but they had agreed not to say anything about it.

### SPANISH FLU

Louisa had made friends with some of the travellers who stayed regularly at the hotel. One of these was Jim Frarey, who sold typewriters and office equipment and books and all sorts of stationery supplies. He was a fair-haired, rather round-shouldered but strongly built man in his middle forties. You would think by the look of him that he sold something heavier and more important in the masculine world, like farm implements.

Jim Frarey kept travelling all through the Spanish flu epidemic, though you never knew then if stores would be open for business or not. Occasionally the hotels too would be closed, like the schools and movie houses and even—Jim Frarey thought this a scandal—the churches.

"They ought to be ashamed of themselves, the cowards," he said to Louisa. "What good does it do anybody to lurk around home and wait for it to strike? Now you never closed the Library, did you?"

Louisa said only when she herself was sick. A mild case, hardly lasting a week, but of course she had to go to the hospital. They wouldn't let her stay in the hotel.

"Cowards," he said. "If you're going to be taken, you'll be taken. Don't you agree?"

They discussed the crush in the hospitals, the deaths of doctors and nurses, the unceasing drear spectacle of the funerals. Jim Frarey lived down the street from an undertaking establishment in Toronto. He said they still got out the black horses, the black carriage, the works, to bury such personages as warranted a fuss.

"Day and night they went on," he said. "Day and night." He raised his glass and said, "Here's to health, then. You look well yourself."

He thought that in fact Louisa was looking better than she used to. Maybe she had started putting on rouge. She had a pale-olive skin, and it seemed to him that her cheeks used to be without color. She dressed with more dash too, and took more trouble to be friendly. She used to be very on-again, off-again, just as she chose. She was drinking whisky now too, though she would not try it without drowning it in water. It used to be only a glass of wine. He wondered if it was a boyfriend that had made the difference. But a boyfriend might perk up her looks without increasing her interest in all and sundry, which was what he was pretty sure had happened. It was more likely time running out and the husband prospects thinned out so dreadfully by the war. That could set a woman stirring. She was smarter and better company and better-looking too than most of the married ones. What happened with a woman like that? Sometimes just bad luck. Or bad judgment at a time when it mattered. A little too sharp and self-assured, in the old days, making the men uneasy?

"Life can't be brought to a standstill all the same," he said. "You did the right thing, keeping the Library open."

This was in the early winter of 1919, when there had been a fresh outbreak of flu after the danger was supposed to be past. They seemed to be all alone in the hotel. It was only about nine o'clock but the hotelkeeper had gone to bed. His wife was in the hospital with the flu. Jim Frarey had brought the bottle of whisky from the bar, which was closed for fear of contagion—and they sat at a table beside the window, in the dining room. A winter fog had collected outside and was pressing against the window. You could barely see the streetlights or the few cars that trundled cautiously over the bridge.

"Oh, it was not a matter of principle," Louisa said. "That I kept the Library open. It was a more personal reason than you think."

Then she laughed and promised him a peculiar story. "Oh, the whisky must have loosened my tongue," she said.

"I am not a gossip," said Jim Frarey.

She gave him a hard laughing look and said that when a person announced they weren't a gossip, they almost invariably were. The same when they promised never to tell a soul.

"You can tell this where and when you like just as long as you leave out the real names and don't tell it around here," she said. "That I hope I can trust you not to do. Though at the moment I don't feel as if I cared. I'll probably feel otherwise when the drink wears off. It's a lesson, this story.

It's a lesson in what fools women can make of themselves. So, you say, what's new about that, you can learn it every day!"

She began to tell him about a soldier who had started writing letters to her from overseas. The soldier remembered her from when he used to go into the Library. But she didn't remember him. However, she replied in a friendly way to his first letter and a correspondence sprang up between them. He told her where he had lived in the town and she walked past the house so that she could tell him how things looked there. He told her what books he'd read and she gave some of the same kind of information. In short, they both revealed something of themselves and feelings warmed up on either side. On his side first, as far as any declarations went. She was not one to rush in like a fool. At first, she thought she was simply being kind. Even later, she didn't want to reject and embarrass him. He asked for a picture. She had one taken, it was not to her liking, but she sent it. He asked if she had a sweetheart and she replied truthfully that she did not. He did not send any picture of himself nor did she ask for one, though of course she was curious as to what he looked like. It would be no easy matter for him to have a picture taken in the middle of a war. Furthermore, she did not want to seem like the sort of woman who would withdraw kindness if looks did not come up to scratch.

He wrote that he did not expect to come home. He said he was not so afraid of dying as he was of ending up like some of the men he had seen when he was in the hospital, wounded. He did not elaborate, but she supposed he meant the cases they were just getting to know about now— the stumps of men, the blinded, the ones made monstrous with burns. He was not whining about his fate, she did not mean to imply that. It was just that he expected to die and picked death over some other options and he thought about her and wrote to her as men do to a sweetheart in such a situation.

When the war ended, it was a while since she had heard from him. She went on expecting a letter every day and nothing came. Nothing came. She was afraid that he might have been one of those unluckiest of soldiers in the whole war—one of those killed in the last week, or on the last day, or even in the last hour. She searched the local paper every week, and the names of new casualties were still being printed there till after New Year's but his was not among them. Now the paper began to list as well the names of those returning home, often printing a photo with the name, and a little account of rejoicing. When the soldiers were returning thick and fast there was less room for these additions. And then she saw his name, another name on the list. He had not been killed, he had not been wounded—he was coming home to Carstairs, perhaps was already there.

It was then that she decided to keep the Library open, though the flu was raging. Every day she was sure he would come, every day she was prepared for him. Sundays were a torment. When she entered the Town Hall she always felt he might be there before her, leaning up against the wall awaiting her arrival. Sometimes she felt it so strongly she saw a shadow that she mistook for a man. She understood now how people believed they had seen ghosts. Whenever the door opened she expected to look up into his face. Sometimes she made a pact with herself not to look up till she had counted to ten. Few people came in, because of the flu. She set herself jobs of rearranging things, else she would have gone mad. She never locked up until five or ten minutes after closing time. And then she fancied that he might be across the street on the Post Office steps, watching her, being too shy to make a move. She worried of course that he might be ill, she always sought in conversation for news of the latest cases. No one spoke his name.

It was at this time that she entirely gave up on reading. The covers of books looked like coffins to her, either shabby or ornate, and what was inside them might as well have been dust.

She had to be forgiven, didn't she, she had to be forgiven for thinking, after such letters, that the one thing that could never happen was that he wouldn't approach her, wouldn't get in touch with her at all? Never cross her threshold, after such avowals? Funerals passed by her window and she gave no thought to them, as long as they were not his. Even when she was sick in the hospital her only thought was that she must get back, she must get out of bed, the door must not stay locked against him. She staggered to her feet and back to work. On a hot afternoon she was arranging fresh newspapers on the racks and his name jumped out at her like something in her feverish dreams.

She read a short notice of his marriage to a Miss Grace Horne. Not a girl she knew. Not a Library user.

The bride wore fawn silk crêpe with brown-and-cream piping, and a beige straw hat with brown velvet streamers.

There was no picture. Brown-and-cream piping. Such was the end, and had to be, to her romance.

But on her desk at the Library, a matter of a few weeks ago, on a Saturday night after everybody had gone and she had locked the door and was turning out the lights, she discovered a scrap of paper. A few words written on it. *I was engaged before I went overseas.* No name, not his or hers. And there was her photograph, partly shoved under the blotter.

He had been in the Library that very evening. It had been a busy time, she had often left the desk to find a book for somebody or to straighten up the papers or to put some books on the shelves. He had been in the same room with her, watched her, and taken his chance. But never made himself known.

*I was engaged before I went overseas.*

"Do you think it was all a joke on me?" Louisa said. "Do you think a man could be so diabolical?"

"In my experience, tricks like that are far more often indulged in by the women. No, no. Don't you think such a thing. Far more likely he was sincere. He got a little carried away. It's all just the way it looks on the surface. He was engaged before he went overseas, he never expected to get back in one piece but he did. And when he did, there is the fiancée waiting—what else could he do?"

"What indeed?" said Louisa.

"He bit off more than he could chew."

"Ah, that's so, that's so!" Louisa said. "And what was it in my case but vanity, which deserves to get slapped down!" Her eyes were glassy and her expression roguish. "You don't think he'd had a good look at me any one time and thought the original was even worse than that poor picture, so he backed off?"

"I do not!" said Jim Frarey. "And don't you so belittle yourself."

"I don't want you to think I am stupid," she said. "I am not so stupid and inexperienced as that story makes me sound."

"Indeed I don't think you are stupid at all."

"But perhaps you think I am inexperienced?"

This was it, he thought—the usual. Women after they have told one story on themselves cannot stop from telling another. Drink upsets them in a radical way, prudence is out the window.

She had confided in him once before that she had been a patient in a sanitorium. Now she told about being in love with a doctor there. The sanitorium was on beautiful grounds up on Hamilton Mountain, and they used to meet there along the hedged walks. Shelves of limestone formed the steps and in sheltered spots there were such plants as you do not commonly see in Ontario—azaleas, rhododendrons, magnolias. The doctor knew something about botany and he told her this was the Carolinian vegetation. Very different from here, lusher, and there were little bits of woodland too, wonderful trees, paths worn under the trees. Tulip trees.

"Tulips!" said Jim Frarey. "Tulips on the trees!"

"No, no, it is the shape of their leaves!"

She laughed at him challengingly, then bit her lip. He saw fit to continue the dialogue, saying, "Tulips on the trees!" while she said no, it is the leaves that are shaped like tulips, no, I never said that, stop! So they passed into a state of gingerly evaluation—which he knew well and could only hope she did—full of small pleasant surprises, half-sardonic signals, a welling-up of impudent hopes, and a fateful sort of kindness.

"All to ourselves," Jim Frarey said. "Never happened before, did it? Maybe it never will again."

She let him take her hands, half lift her from her chair. He turned out the dining-room lights as they went out. Up the stairs they went, that they had so often climbed separately. Past the picture of the dog on his master's grave, and Highland Mary singing in the field, and the old King with his bulgy eyes, his look of indulgence and repletion.

"It's a foggy, foggy night, and my heart is in a fright," Jim Frarey was half singing, half humming as they climbed. He kept an assured hand on Louisa's back. "All's well, all's well," he said as he steered her round the turn of the stairs. And when they took the narrow flight of steps to the third floor he said, "Never climbed so close to Heaven in this place before!"

But later in the night Jim Frarey gave a concluding groan and roused himself to deliver a sleepy scolding. "Louisa, Louisa, why didn't you tell me that was the way it was?"

"I told you everything," said Louisa in a faint and drifting voice.

"I got a wrong impression, then," he said. "I never intended for this to make a difference to you."

She said that it hadn't. Now without him pinning her down and steadying her, she felt herself whirling around in an irresistible way, as if the mattress had turned into a child's top and was carrying her off. She tried to explain that the traces of blood on the sheets could be credited to her period, but her words came out with a luxurious nonchalance and could not be fitted together.

## ACCIDENTS

When Arthur came home from the factory a little before noon he shouted, "Stay out of my way till I wash! There's been an accident over at the works!" Nobody answered. Mrs. Feare, the housekeeper, was talking on the kitchen telephone so loudly that she could not hear him, and his daughter was of course at school. He washed, and stuffed everything he had been wearing into the hamper, and scrubbed up the bathroom, like a murderer. He started out clean, with even his hair slicked and patted, to drive to the man's house. He had had to ask where it was. He thought it was up Vinegar Hill but they said no, that was the father—the young fellow and his wife live on the other side of town, past where the Apple Evaporator used to be, before the war.

He found the two brick cottages side by side, and picked the left-hand one, as he'd been told. It wouldn't have been hard to pick which house, anyway. News had come before him. The door to the house was open, and children too young to be in school yet hung about in the yard. A small girl sat on a kiddie car, not going anywhere, just blocking his path. He stepped around her. As he did so an older girl spoke to him in a formal way—a warning.

"Her dad's dead. Hers!"

A woman came out of the front room carrying an armload of curtains, which she gave to another woman standing in the hall. The woman who received the curtains was gray-haired, with a pleading face. She had no upper teeth. She probably took her plate out, for comfort, at home. The woman who passed the curtains to her was stout but young, with fresh skin.

"You tell her not to get up on that stepladder," the gray-haired woman said to Arthur. "She's going to break her neck taking down curtains. She thinks we need to get everything washed. Are you the undertaker? Oh, no, excuse me! You're Mr. Doud. Grace, come out here! Grace! It's Mr. Doud!"

"Don't trouble her," Arthur said.

"She thinks she's going to get the curtains all down and washed and up again by tomorrow, because he's going to have to go in the front room. She's my daughter. I can't tell her anything."

"She'll quiet down presently," said a sombre but comfortable-looking man in a clerical collar, coming through from the back of the house. Their minister. But not from one of the churches Arthur knew. Baptist? Pentecostal? Plymouth Brethren? He was drinking tea.

Some other woman came and briskly removed the curtains.

"We got the machine filled and going," she said. "A day like this, they'll dry like nobody's business. Just keep the kids out of here."

The minister had to stand aside and lift his teacup high, to avoid her and her bundle. He said, "Aren't any of you ladies going to offer Mr. Doud a cup of tea?"

Arthur said, "No, no, don't trouble."

"The funeral expenses," he said to the gray-haired woman. "If you could let her know—"

"Lillian wet her pants!" said a triumphant child at the door. "Mrs. Agnew! Lillian peed her pants!"

"Yes. Yes," said the minister. "They will be very grateful."

"The plot and the stone, everything," Arthur said. "You'll make sure they understand that. Whatever they want on the stone."

The gray-haired woman had gone out into the yard. She came back with a squalling child in her arms. "Poor lamb," she said. "They told her she wasn't supposed to come in the house so where could she go? What could she do but have an accident!"

The young woman came out of the front room dragging a rug.

"I want this put on the line and beat," she said.

"Grace, here is Mr. Doud come to offer his condolences," the minister said.

"And to ask if there is anything I can do," said Arthur.

The gray-haired woman started upstairs with the wet child in her arms and a couple of others following.

Grace spotted them.

"Oh, no, you don't! You get back outside!"

"My mom's in here."

"Yes and your mom's good and busy, she don't need to be bothered with you. She's here helping me out. Don't you know Lillian's dad's dead?"

"Is there anything I can do for you?" Arthur said, meaning to clear out.

Grace stared at him with her mouth open. Sounds of the washing machine filled the house.

"Yes, there is," she said. "You wait here."

"She's overwhelmed," the minister said. "It's not that she means to be rude."

Grace came back with a load of books.

"These here," she said. "He had them out of the Library. I don't want to have to pay fines on them. He went every Saturday night so I guess they are due back tomorrow. I don't want to get in trouble about them."

"I'll look after them," Arthur said. "I'd be glad to."

"I just don't want to get in any trouble about them."

"Mr. Doud was saying about taking care of the funeral," the minister said to her, gently admonishing. "Everything including the stone. Whatever you want on the stone."

"Oh, I don't want anything fancy," Grace said.

*On Friday morning last there occurred in the sawmill operation of Douds Factory a particularly ghastly and tragic accident. Mr. Jack Agnew, in reaching under the main shaft, had the misfortune to have his sleeve caught by a setscrew in an adjoining flunge, so that his arm and shoulder were drawn under the shaft. His head in consequence was brought in contact with the circular saw, that saw being about one foot in diameter. In an instant the unfortunate young man's head was separated from his body, being severed at an angle below the left ear and through the neck. His death is believed to have been instantaneous. He never spoke or uttered a cry so it was not by any sound of his but by the spurt and shower of his blood that his fellow-workers were horribly alerted to the disaster.*

This account was reprinted in the paper a week later for those who might have missed it or who wished to have an extra copy to send to friends or relations out of town (particularly to people who used to live in Carstairs and did not anymore). The misspelling of *flange* was corrected. There was a note apologizing for the mistake. There was also a description of a very large funeral, attended even by people from neighboring towns and as far away as Walley. They came by car and train, and some by horse and buggy. They had not known Jack Agnew when he was alive, but, as the paper said, they wished to pay tribute to the sensational and tragic manner of his death. All the stores in Carstairs were closed for two hours that afternoon. The hotel did not close its doors but that was because all the visitors needed somewhere to eat and drink.

The survivors were a wife, Grace, and a four-year-old daughter, Lillian. The victim had fought bravely in the Great War and had only been wounded once, not seriously. Many had commented on this irony.

The paper's failure to mention a surviving father was not deliberate. The editor of the paper was not a native of Carstairs, and people forgot to tell him about the father until it was too late.

The father himself did not complain about the omission. On the day of the funeral, which was very fine, he headed out of town as he would have done ordinarily on a day he had decided not to spend at Douds. He was wearing a felt hat and a long coat that would do for a rug if he wanted to take a nap. His overshoes were neatly held on his feet with the rubber rings from sealing jars. He was going out to fish for suckers. The season hadn't opened yet, but he always managed to be a bit ahead of it. He fished through the spring and early summer and cooked and ate what he caught. He had a frying pan and a pot hidden out on the riverbank. The pot was for boiling corn that he snatched out of the fields later in the year, when he was also eating the fruit of wild apple trees and grapevines. He was quite sane but abhorred conversation. He could not altogether avoid it in the weeks following his son's death, but he had a way of cutting it short.

"Should've watched out what he was doing."

Walking in the country that day, he met another person who was not at the funeral. A woman. She did not try to start any conversation and in fact seemed as fierce in her solitude as himself, whipping the air past her with long fervent strides.

THE PIANO factory, which had started out making pump organs, stretched along the west side of town, like a medieval town wall. There were two long buildings like the inner and outer ramparts, with a closed-in bridge between them where the main offices were. And reaching up into the town and the streets of workers' houses you had the kilns and the sawmill and the lumberyard and storage sheds. The factory whistle dictated the time for many to get up, blowing at six o'clock in the morning. It blew again for work to start at seven and at twelve for dinnertime and at one in the afternoon for work to recommence, and then at five-thirty for the men to lay down their tools and go home.

Rules were posted beside the time clock, under glass. The first two rules were:

> ONE MINUTE LATE IS FIFTEEN MINUTES PAY. BE PROMPT.
> DON'T TAKE SAFETY FOR GRANTED. WATCH OUT FOR
> YOURSELF AND THE NEXT MAN.

There had been accidents in the factory and in fact a man had been killed when a load of lumber fell on him. That had happened before Arthur's time. And once, during the war, a man had lost an arm, or part of an arm. On the day that happened, Arthur was away in Toronto. So he had never seen an accident—nothing serious, anyway. But it was often at the back of his mind now that something might happen.

Perhaps he did not feel so sure that trouble wouldn't come near him, as he had felt before his wife died. She had died in 1919, in the last flurry of the Spanish flu, when everyone had got over being frightened. Even she had not been frightened. That was nearly five years ago and it still seemed to Arthur like the end of a carefree time in his life. But to other people he had always seemed very responsible and serious—nobody had noticed much difference in him.

In his dreams of an accident there was a spreading silence, everything was shut down. Every machine in the place stopped making its customary noise and every man's voice was removed, and when Arthur looked out of the office window he understood that doom had fallen. He never could remember any particular thing he saw that told him this. It was just the space, the dust in the factory yard, that said to him *now*.

THE BOOKS stayed on the floor of his car for a week or so. His daughter Bea said, "What are those books doing here?" and then he remembered.

Bea read out the titles and the authors. *Sir John Franklin and the Romance of the Northwest Passage*, by G. B. Smith. *What's Wrong with the World?*, G. K. Chesterton. *The Taking of Quebec*, Archibald Hendry. *Bolshevism: Practice and Theory*, by Lord Bertrand Russell.

"Bol-*shev*-ism," Bea said, and Arthur told her how to pronounce it correctly. She asked what it was, and he said, "It's something they've got in Russia that I don't understand so well myself. But from what I hear of it, it's a disgrace."

Bea was thirteen at this time. She had heard about the Russian Ballet and also about dervishes. She believed for the next couple of years that Bolshevism was some sort of diabolical and maybe indecent dance. At least this was the story she told when she was grown up.

She did not mention that the books were connected with the man who had had the accident. That would have made the story less amusing. Perhaps she had really forgotten.

THE LIBRARIAN was perturbed. The books still had their cards in them, which meant they had never been checked out, just removed from the shelves and taken away.

"The one by Lord Russell has been missing a long time."

Arthur was not used to such reproofs, but he said mildly, "I am returning them on behalf of somebody else. The chap who was killed. In the accident at the factory."

The Librarian had the Franklin book open. She was looking at the picture of the boat trapped in the ice.

"His wife asked me to," Arthur said.

She picked up each book separately, and shook it as if she expected something to fall out. She ran her fingers in between the pages. The bottom part of her face was working in an unsightly way, as if she was chewing at the inside of her cheeks.

"I guess he just took them home as he felt like it," Arthur said.

"I'm sorry?" she said in a minute. "What did you say? I'm sorry."

It was the accident, he thought. The idea that the man who had died in such a way had been the last person to open these books, turn these pages. The thought that he might have left a bit of his life in them, a scrap of paper or a pipe cleaner as a marker, or even a few shreds of tobacco. That unhinged her.

"No matter," he said. "I just dropped by to bring them back."

He turned away from her desk but did not immediately leave the Library. He had not been in it for years. There was his father's picture between the two front windows, where it would always be.

> A. V. Doud, founder of the Doud Organ Factory
> and Patron of this Library. A Believer in Progress,
> Culture, and Education. A True Friend of the Town
> of Carstairs and of the Working Man.

The Librarian's desk was in the archway between the front and back rooms. The books were on shelves set in rows in the back room. Green-shaded lamps, with long pull cords, dangled down in the aisles between. Arthur remembered years ago some matter brought up at the Council

Meeting about buying sixty-watt bulbs instead of forty. This Librarian was the one who had requested that, and they had done it.

In the front room, there were newspapers and magazines on wooden racks, and some round heavy tables, with chairs, so that people could sit and read, and rows of thick dark books behind glass. Dictionaries, probably, and atlases and encyclopedias. Two handsome high windows looking out on the main street, with Arthur's father hanging between them. Other pictures around the room hung too high, and were too dim and crowded with figures for the person down below to interpret them easily. (Later, when Arthur had spent many hours in the Library and had discussed these pictures with the Librarian, he knew that one of them represented the Battle of Flodden Field, with the King of Scotland charging down the hill into a pall of smoke, one the funeral of the Boy King of Rome, and one the Quarrel of Oberon and Titania, from *A Midsummer Night's Dream*.)

He sat down at one of the reading tables, where he could look out the window. He picked up an old copy of the *National Geographic* which was lying there. He had his back to the Librarian. He thought this the tactful thing to do, since she seemed somewhat wrought-up. Other people came in, and he heard her speak to them. Her voice sounded normal enough now. He kept thinking he would leave, but did not.

He liked the high bare window full of the light of the spring evening, and he liked the dignity and order of these rooms. He was pleasantly mystified by the thought of grown people coming and going here, steadily reading books. Week after week, one book after another, a whole life long. He himself read a book once in a while, when somebody recommended it, and usually he enjoyed it, and then he read magazines, to keep up with things, and never thought about reading a book until another one came along, in this almost accidental way.

There would be little spells when nobody was in the Library but himself and the Librarian.

During one of these, she came over and stood near him, replacing some newspapers on the rack. When she finished this, she spoke to him, with a controlled urgency.

"The account of the accident that was printed in the paper—I take it that was more or less accurate?"

Arthur said that it was possibly too accurate.

"Why? Why do you say that?"

He mentioned the public's endless appetite for horrific details. Ought the paper to pander to that?

"Oh, I think it's natural," the Librarian said. "I think it's natural to want to know the worst. People do want to picture it. I do myself. I am very ignorant of machinery. It's hard for me to imagine what happened. Even with the paper's help. Did the machine do something unexpected?"

"No," Arthur said. "It wasn't the machine grabbing him and pulling him in, like an animal. He made a wrong move or at any rate a careless move. Then he was done for."

She said nothing, but did not move away.

"You have to keep your wits about you," Arthur said. "Never let up for a second. A machine is your servant and it is an excellent servant, but it makes an imbecile master."

He wondered if he had read that somewhere, or had thought it up himself.

"And I suppose there are no ways of protecting people?" the Librarian said. "But you must know all about that."

She left him then. Somebody had come in.

The accident was followed by a rush of warm weather. The length of the evenings and the heat of the balmy days seemed sudden and surprising, as if this were not the way winter finally ended in that part of the country, almost every year. The sheets of floodwater shrank magically back into the bogs, and the leaves shot out of the reddened branches, and barnyard smells drifted into town and were wrapped in the smell of lilacs.

Instead of wanting to be outdoors on such evenings, Arthur found himself thinking of the Library, and he would often end up there, sitting in the spot he had chosen on his first visit. He would sit for half an hour, or an hour. He looked at the London *Illustrated News*, or the *National Geographic* or *Saturday Night* or *Collier's*. All of these magazines arrived at his own house and he could have been sitting there, in the den, looking out at his hedged lawns, which old Agnew kept in tolerable condition, and the flower beds now full of tulips of every vivid color and combination. It seemed that he preferred the view of the main street, where the occasional brisk-looking new Ford went by, or some stuttering older-model car with a dusty cloth top. He preferred the Post Office, with its clock tower telling four different times in four different directions—and, as people liked to say, all wrong. Also the passing and loitering on the sidewalk. People trying to get the drinking fountain to work, although it wasn't turned on till the first of July.

It was not that he felt the need of sociability. He was not there for chat, though he would greet people if he knew them by name, and he did know most. And he might exchange a few words with the Librarian, though often it was only "Good evening" when he came in, and "Good night" when he went out. He made no demands on anybody. He felt his presence to be genial, reassuring, and, above all, natural. By sitting here, reading and reflecting, here instead of at home, he seemed to himself to be providing something. People could count on it.

There was an expression he liked. *Public servant.* His father, who looked out at him here with tinted baby-pink cheeks and glassy blue eyes and an old man's petulant mouth, had never thought of himself so. He had thought of himself more as a public character and benefactor. He had operated by whims and decrees, and he had got away with it. He would go around the factory when business was slow, and say to one man and another, "Go home. Go on home now. Go home and stay there till I can use you again." And they would go. They would work in their gardens or go out shooting rabbits and run up bills for whatever they had to buy, and accept that it couldn't be otherwise. It was still a joke with them, to imitate his bark. *Go on home!* He was their hero more than Arthur could ever be, but they were not prepared to take the same treatment today. During the war, they had got used to the good wages and to being always in demand. They never thought of the glut of labor the soldiers had created when they came home, never thought about how a business like this was kept going by luck and ingenuity from one year to the next, even from one season to the next. They didn't like changes—they were not happy about the switch now to player pianos, which Arthur believed were the hope of the future. But Arthur would do what he had to, though his way of proceeding was quite the opposite of his father's. Think everything over and then think it over again. Stay in the background except when necessary. Keep your dignity. Try always to be fair.

They expected all to be provided. The whole town expected it. Work would be provided just as the sun would rise in the mornings. And the taxes on the factory raised at the same time rates were charged for the water that used to come free. Maintenance of the access roads was now the factory's responsibility instead of the town's. The Methodist Church was requesting a hefty sum to build the new Sunday school. The town hockey team needed new uniforms. Stone gateposts were being erected for the War Memorial Park. And every year the smartest boy in the senior class was sent to university, courtesy of Douds.

Ask and ye shall receive.

Expectations at home were not lacking either. Bea was agitating to go away to private school and Mrs. Feare had her eye on some new mixing apparatus for the kitchen, also a new washing machine. All the trim on the house was due to be painted this year. All that wedding-cake decoration that consumed paint by the gallon. And in the midst of this what had Arthur done but order himself a new car—a Chrysler sedan.

It was necessary—he had to drive a new car. He had to drive a new car, Bea had to go away to school, Mrs. Feare had to have the latest, and the trim had to be as fresh as Christmas snow. Else they would lose respect, they would lose confidence, they would start to wonder if things were going downhill. And it could be managed, with luck it could all be managed.

For years after his father's death, he had felt like an impostor. Not steadily, but from time to time he had felt that. And now the feeling was gone. He could sit here and feel that it was gone.

HE HAD BEEN in the office when the accident happened, consulting with a veneer salesman. Some change in noise registered with him, but it was more of an increase than a hush. It was nothing that alerted him—just an irritation. Because it happened in the sawmill, nobody would know about the accident immediately in the shops or in the kilns or in the yard, and work in some places continued for several minutes. In fact Arthur, bending over the veneer samples on his desk, might have been one of the last people to understand that there had been an intervention. He asked the salesman a question, and the salesman did not answer. Arthur looked up and saw the man's mouth open, his face frightened, his salesman's assurance wiped away.

Then he heard his own name being called—both "Mr. Doud!" as was customary and "Arthur, Arthur!" by such of the older men as had known him as a boy. Also he heard "saw" and "head" and "Jesus, Jesus, Jesus!"

Arthur could have wished for the silence, the sounds and objects drawing back in that dreadful but releasing way, to give him room. It was nothing like that. Yelling and questioning and running around, himself in the midst being propelled to the sawmill. One man had fainted, falling in such a way that if they had not got the saw turned off a moment before, it would have got him too. It was his body, fallen but entire, that Arthur briefly mistook for the body of the victim. Oh, no, no. They pushed him on. The sawdust was scarlet. It was drenched, brilliant. The pile of lumber here was all merrily spattered, and the blades. A pile of work clothes soaked in blood lay in the sawdust and Arthur realized that it was the body, the trunk with limbs attached. So much blood had flowed as to make its shape not plain at first—to soften it, like a pudding.

The first thing he thought of was to cover that. He took off his jacket and did so. He had to step up close, his shoes squished in it. The reason no one else had done this would be simply that no one else was wearing a jacket.

"Have they gone a-get the doctor?" somebody was yelling. "Gone a-get the doctor!" a man quite close to Arthur said. "Can't sew his head back on—doctor. Can he?"

But Arthur gave the order to get the doctor; he imagined it was necessary. You can't have a death without a doctor. That set the rest in motion.

Doctor, undertaker, coffin, flowers, preacher. Get started on all that, give them something to do. Shovel up the sawdust, clean up the saw. Send the men who had been close by to wash themselves. Carry the man who had fainted to the lunchroom. Is he all right? Tell the office girl to make tea.

Brandy was what was needed, or whisky. But he had a rule against it, on the premises.

Something still lacking. Where was it? There, they said. Over there. Arthur heard the sound of vomiting, not far away. All right. Either pick it up or tell somebody to pick it up. The sound of vomiting saved him, steadied him, gave him an almost lighthearted determination. He picked it up. He carried it delicately and securely as you might carry an awkward but valuable jug. Pressing the face out of sight, as if comforting it, against his chest. Blood seeped through his shirt and stuck the material to his skin. Warm. He felt like a wounded man. He was aware of them watching him and he was aware of himself as an actor must be, or a priest. What to do with it, now that he had it against his chest? The answer to that came too. Set it down, put it back where it belongs, not of course fitted with exactness, not as if a seam could be closed. Just more or less in place, and lift the jacket and tug it into a new position.

He couldn't now ask the man's name. He would have to get it in some other way. After the intimacy of his services here, such ignorance would be an offense.

But he found he did know it—it came to him. As he edged the corner of his jacket over the ear that had lain and still lay upward, and so looked quite fresh and usable, he received a name. Son of the fellow who came and did the garden, who was not always reliable. A young man taken on again when he came back from the war. Married? He thought so. He would have to go and see her. As soon as possible. Clean clothes.

THE LIBRARIAN often wore a dark-red blouse. Her lips were reddened to match, and her hair was bobbed. She was not a young woman anymore, but she maintained an eye-catching style. He remembered that years ago when they had hired her, he had thought that she got herself up very soberly. Her hair was not bobbed in those days—it was wound around her head, in the old style. It was still the same color—a warm and pleasant color, like leaves—oak leaves, say, in the fall. He tried to think how much she was paid. Not much, certainly. She kept herself looking well on it. And where did she live? In one of the boardinghouses—the one with the schoolteachers? No, not there. She lived in the Commercial Hotel.

And now something else was coming to mind. No definite story that he could remember. You could not say with any assurance that she had a bad reputation. But it was not quite a spotless reputation, either. She was said to take a drink with the travellers. Perhaps she had a boyfriend among them. A boyfriend or two.

Well, she was old enough to do as she liked. It wasn't quite the same as the way it was with a teacher—hired partly to set an example. As long as she did her job well, and anybody could see that she did. She had her life to live, like everyone else. Wouldn't you rather have a nice-looking woman in here than a crabby old affair like Mary Tamblyn? Strangers might drop in, they judge a town by what they see, you want a nice-looking woman with a nice manner.

Stop that. Who said you didn't? He was arguing in his head on her behalf just as if somebody had come along who wanted her chucked out, and he had no intimation at all that that was the case.

What about her question, on the first evening, regarding the machines? What did she mean by that? Was it a sly way of bringing blame?

He had talked to her about the pictures and the lighting and even told her how his father had sent his own workmen over here, paid them to build the Library shelves, but he had never spoken of the man who had taken the books out without letting her know. One at a time, probably. Under his coat? Brought back the same way. He must have brought them back, or else he'd have had a houseful, and his wife would never stand for that. Not stealing, except temporarily. Harmless behavior, but peculiar. Was there any connection? Between thinking you could do things a little differently that way and thinking you could get away with a careless move that might catch your sleeve and bring the saw down on your neck?

There might be, there might be some connection. A matter of attitude.

"That chap—you know the one—the accident—" he said to the Librarian. "The way he took off with the books he wanted. Why do you think he did that?"

"People do things," the Librarian said. "They tear out pages. On account of something they don't like or something they do. They just do things. I don't know."

"Did he ever tear out some pages? Did you ever give him a lecture? Ever make him scared to face you?"

He meant to tease her a little, implying that she would not be likely to scare anybody, but she did not take it that way.

"How could I when I never spoke to him?" she said. "I never saw him. I never saw him, to know who he was."

She moved away, putting an end to the conversation. So she did not like to be teased. Was she one of those people full of mended cracks that you could only see close up? Some old misery troubling her, some secret? Maybe a sweetheart had been lost in the war.

. . .

ON A LATER evening, a Saturday evening in the summer, she brought the subject up herself, that he would never have mentioned again.

"Do you remember our talking once about the man who had the accident?"

Arthur said he did.

"I have something to ask you and you may think it strange."

He nodded.

"And my asking it—I want you to—it is confidential."

"Yes, indeed," he said.

"What did he look like?"

Look like? Arthur was puzzled. He was puzzled by her making such a fuss and secret about it—surely it was natural to be interested in what a man might look like who had been coming in and making off with her books without her knowing about it—and because he could not help her, he shook his head. He could not bring any picture of Jack Agnew to mind.

"Tall," he said. "I believe he was on the tall side. Otherwise I cannot tell you. I am really not such a good person to ask. I can recognize a man easily but I can't ever give much of a physical description, even when it's someone I see on a daily basis."

"But I thought you were the one—I heard you were the one—" she said. "Who picked him up. His head."

Arthur said stiffly, "I didn't think that you could just leave it lying there." He felt disappointed in the woman, uneasy and ashamed for her. But he tried to speak matter-of-factly, keeping reproach out of his voice.

"I could not even tell you the color of his hair. It was all—all pretty much obliterated, by that time."

She said nothing for a moment or two and he did not look at her. Then she said, "It must seem as if I am one of those people—one of those people who are fascinated by these sorts of things."

Arthur made a protesting noise, but it did, of course, seem to him that she must be like that.

"I should not have asked you," she said. "I should not have mentioned it. I can never explain to you why I did. I would like just to ask you, if you can help it, never to think that that is the kind of person I am."

Arthur heard the word "never." She could never explain to him. He was never to think. In the midst of his disappointment he picked up this suggestion, that their conversations were to continue, and perhaps on a less haphazard basis. He heard a humility in her voice, but it was a humility that was based on some kind of assurance. Surely that was sexual.

Or did he only think so, because this was the evening it was? It was the Saturday evening in the month when he usually went to Walley. He was going there tonight, he had only dropped in here on his way, he had not meant to stay as long as he had done. It was the night when he went to visit a woman whose name was Jane MacFarlane. Jane MacFarlane lived apart from her husband, but she was not thinking of getting a divorce. She had no children. She earned her living as a dressmaker. Arthur had first met her when she came to his house to make clothes for his wife. Nothing had gone on at that time, and neither of them had thought of it. In some ways Jane MacFarlane was a woman like the Librarian—good-looking, though not so young, plucky and stylish and good at her work. In other ways, not so like. He could not imagine Jane ever presenting a man with a mystery, and following that up with the information that it would never be solved. Jane was a woman to give a man peace. The submerged dialogue he had with her—sensual, limited, kind—was very like the one he had had with his wife.

The Librarian went to the switch by the door, and turned out the main light. She locked the door. She disappeared among the shelves, turning out the lights there too, in a leisurely way. The town clock was striking nine. She must think that it was right. His own watch said three minutes to.

It was time to get up, time for him to leave, time to go to Walley.

When she had finished dealing with the lights, she came and sat down at the table beside him.

He said, "I would never think of you in any way that would make you unhappy."

Turning out the lights shouldn't have made it so dark. They were in the middle of summer. But it seemed that heavy rain clouds had moved in. When Arthur had last paid attention to the street, he had seen plenty of daylight left: country people shopping, boys squirting each other at the drinking fountain, and young girls walking up and down in their soft, cheap, flowery summer dresses, letting the young men watch them from wherever the young men congregated—the Post Office steps, the front of the feed store. And now that he looked again he saw the street in an uproar from the loud wind that already carried a few drops of rain. The girls were shrieking and laughing and holding their purses over their heads as they ran to shelter, store clerks were rolling up awnings and hauling in the baskets of fruit, the racks of summer shoes, the garden implements that had been displayed on the sidewalks. The doors of the Town Hall banged as the farm women ran inside, grabbing on to packages and children, to cram themselves into the Ladies' Rest Room. Somebody tried the Library door. The Librarian looked over at it but did not move. And soon the rain was sweeping like curtains across the street, and the wind battered the Town Hall roof, and tore at the treetops. That roaring and danger lasted a few minutes, while the power of the wind went by. Then the sound left was the sound of the rain, which was now falling vertically and so heavily they might have been under a waterfall.

If the same thing was happening at Walley, he thought, Jane would know enough not to expect him. This was the last thought he had of her for a long while.

"Mrs. Feare wouldn't wash my clothes," he said, to his own surprise. "She was afraid to touch them."

The Librarian said, in a peculiarly quivering, shamed, and determined voice, "I think what you did—I think that was a remarkable thing to do."

The rain made such a constant noise that he was released from answering. He found it easy then to turn and look at her. Her profile was dimly lit by the wash of rain down the windows. Her expression was calm and reckless. Or so it seemed to him. He realized that he knew hardly anything about her—what kind of person she really was or what kind of secrets she could have. He could not even estimate his own value to her. He only knew that he had some, and it wasn't the usual.

He could no more describe the feeling he got from her than you can describe a smell. It's like the scorch of electricity. It's like burnt kernels of wheat. No, it's like a bitter orange. I give up.

He had never imagined that he would find himself in a situation like this, visited by such a clear compulsion. But it seemed he was not unprepared. Without thinking over twice or even once what he was letting himself in for, he said, "I wish—"

He had spoken too quietly, she did not hear him.

He raised his voice. He said, "I wish we could get married."

Then she looked at him. She laughed but controlled herself.

"I'm sorry," she said. "I'm sorry. It's just what went through my mind."

"What was that?" he said.

"I thought—that's the last I'll see of him."

Arthur said, "You're mistaken."

### TOLPUDDLE MARTYRS

The passenger train from Carstairs to London had stopped running during the Second World War and even the rails were taken up. People said it was for the War Effort. When Louisa went to London to see the heart specialist, in the mid-fifties, she had to take the bus. She was not supposed to drive anymore.

The doctor, the heart specialist, said that her heart was a little wonky and her pulse inclined to be jumpy. She thought that made her heart sound like a comedian and her pulse like a puppy on a lead. She had not come fifty-seven miles to be treated with such playfulness but she let it pass, because she was already distracted by something she had been reading in the doctor's waiting room. Perhaps it was what she had been reading that had made her pulse jumpy.

On an inside page of the local paper she had seen the headline LOCAL MARTYRS HONORED, and simply to put in the time she had read further. She read that there was to be some sort of ceremony that afternoon at Victoria Park. It was a ceremony to honor the Tolpuddle Martyrs. The paper said that few people had heard of the Tolpuddle Martyrs, and certainly Louisa had not. They were men who had been tried and found guilty for administering illegal oaths. This peculiar offense, committed over a hundred years ago in Dorset, England, had got them transported to Canada and some of them had ended up here in London, where they lived out the rest of their days and were buried without any special notice or commemoration. They were considered now to be among the earliest founders of the Trade Union movement, and the Trade Unions Council, along with representatives of the Canadian Federation of Labor and the ministers of some local churches, had organized a ceremony taking place today on the occasion of the hundred-and-twentieth anniversary of their arrest.

*Martyrs* is laying it on somewhat, thought Louisa. They were not executed, after all.

The ceremony was to take place at three o'clock and the chief speakers were to be one of the local ministers, and Mr. John (Jack) Agnew, a union spokesman from Toronto.

It was a quarter after two when Louisa came out of the doctor's office. The bus to Carstairs did not leave until six o'clock. She had thought she would go and have tea and something to eat on the top floor of Simpsons, then shop for a wedding present, or if the time fitted go to an afternoon movie. Victoria Park lay between the doctor's office and Simpsons, and she decided to cut across it. The day was hot and the shade of the trees pleasant. She could not avoid seeing where the chairs had been set up, and a small speakers' platform draped in yellow cloth, with a Canadian flag on the one side and what she supposed must be a Labor Union flag on the other. A group of people had collected and she found herself changing course in order to get a look at them. Some were old people, very plainly but decently dressed, the women with kerchiefs around their heads on the hot day, Europeans. Others were factory workers, men in clean short-sleeved shirts and women in fresh blouses and slacks, let out early. A few women must have come from home, because they were wearing summer dresses and sandals and trying to keep track of small children. Louisa thought that they would not care at all for the way she was dressed—fashionably, as always, in beige shantung with a crimson silk tam—but she noticed, just then, a woman more elegantly got up than she was, in green silk with her dark hair drawn tightly back, tied with a green-and-gold scarf. She might have been forty—her face was worn, but beautiful. She came over to Louisa at once, smiling, showed her a chair and gave her a mimeographed paper. Louisa could not read the purple printing. She tried to get a look at some men who were talking beside the platform. Were the speakers among them?

The coincidence of the name was hardly even interesting. Neither the first name nor the last was all that unusual.

She did not know why she had sat down, or why she had come over here in the first place. She was beginning to feel a faintly sickening, familiar agitation. She could feel that over nothing. But once it got going, telling herself that it was over nothing did no good. The only thing to do was to get up and get away from here before any more people sat down and hemmed her in.

The green woman intercepted her, asked if she was all right.

"I have to catch a bus," said Louisa in a croaky voice. She cleared her throat. "An out-of-town bus," she said with better control, and marched away, not in the right direction for Simpsons. She thought in fact that she wouldn't go there, she wouldn't go to Birks for the wedding present or to a movie either. She would just go and sit in the bus depot until it was time for her to go home.

WITHIN half a block of the bus depot she remembered that the bus had not taken her there that morning. The depot was being torn down and re-built—there was a temporary depot several blocks away. She had not paid quite enough attention to which street it was on—York Street, east of the real depot, or King? At any rate, she had to detour, because both of these streets were being torn up, and she had almost decided she was lost when she realized she had been lucky enough to come upon the temporary depot by the back way. It was an old house—one of those tall yellow-gray brick houses dating from the time when this was a residential district. This was probably the last use it would be put to before being torn down. Houses all around it must have been torn down to make the large gravelled lot where the buses pulled in. There were still some trees at the edge of the lot and under them a few rows of chairs that she had not noticed when she got off the bus before noon. Two men were sitting on what used to be the veranda of the house, on old car seats. They wore brown shirts with the bus company's insignia but they seemed to be halfhearted about their work, not getting up when she asked if the bus to Carstairs was leaving at six o'clock as scheduled and where could she get a soft drink?

Six o'clock, far as they knew.

Coffee shop down the street.

Cooler inside but only Coke and orange left.

She got herself a Coca-Cola out of the cooler in a dirty little indoor waiting room that smelled of a bad toilet. Moving the depot to this dilapidated house must have thrown everyone into a state of indolence and fecklessness. There was a fan in the room they used as an office, and she saw, as she went by, some papers blow off the desk. "Oh, shit," said the office girl, and stamped her heel on them.

The chairs set up in the shade of the dusty city trees were straight-backed old wooden chairs originally painted different colors—they looked as if they had come from various kitchens. Strips of old carpet and rubber bathroom mats were laid down in front of them, to keep your feet off the gravel. Behind the first row of chairs she thought she saw a sheep lying on the ground, but it turned into a dirty-white dog, which trotted over and looked at her for a moment in a grave semi-official way—gave a brief sniff at her shoes, and trotted away. She had not noticed if there were any drinking straws and did not feel like going back to look. She drank Coke from the bottle, tilting back her head and closing her eyes.

When she opened them, a man was sitting one chair away, and was speaking to her.

"I got here as soon as I could," he said. "Nancy said you were going to catch a bus. As soon as I finished with the speech, I took off. But the bus depot is all torn up."

"Temporarily," she said.

"I knew you right away," he said. "In spite of—well, many years. When I saw you, I was talking to somebody. Then I looked again and you'd disappeared."

"I don't recognize you," said Louisa.

"Well, no," he said. "I guess not. Of course. You wouldn't."

He was wearing tan slacks, a pale-yellow short-sleeved shirt, a cream-and-yellow ascot scarf. A bit of a dandy, for a union man. His hair was white but thick and wavy, the sort of springy hair that goes in ripples, up and back from the forehead, his skin was flushed and his face was deeply wrinkled from the efforts of speechmaking—and from talking to people privately, she supposed, with much of the fervor and persuasiveness of his public speeches. He wore tinted glasses, which he took off now, as if willing that she should see him better. His eyes were a light blue, slightly bloodshot and apprehensive. A good-looking man, still trim except for a little authoritative bulge over the belt, but she did not find these service-able good looks—the careful sporty clothes, the display of ripply hair, the effective expressions—very attractive. She preferred the kind of looks

Arthur had. The restraint, the dark-suited dignity that some people could call pompous, that seemed to her admirable and innocent.

"I always meant to break the ice," he said. "I meant to speak to you. I should have gone in and said goodbye at least. The opportunity to leave came up so suddenly."

Louisa did not have any idea what to say to this. He sighed. He said, "You must have been mad at me. Are you still?"

"No," she said, and fell back, ridiculously, on the usual courtesies. "How is Grace? How is your daughter? Lillian?"

"Grace is not so well. She had some arthritis. Her weight doesn't help it. Lillian is all right. She's married but she still teaches high school. Mathematics. Not too usual for a woman."

How could Louisa begin to correct him? Could she say, No, your wife Grace got married again during the war, she married a farmer, a widower. Before that she used to come in and clean our house once a week. Mrs. Feare had got too old. And Lillian never finished high school, how could she be a high-school teacher? She married young, she had some children, she works in the drugstore. She had your height and your hair, dyed blond. I often looked at her and thought she must be like you. When she was growing up, I used to give her my stepdaughter's outgrown clothes.

Instead of this, she said, "Then the woman in the green dress—that was not Lillian?"

"Nancy? Oh, no! Nancy is my guardian angel. She keeps track of where I'm going, and when, and have I got my speech, and what I drink and eat and have I taken my pills. I tend toward high blood pressure. Nothing too serious. But my way of life's no good. I'm on the go constantly. Tonight I've got to fly out of here to Ottawa, tomorrow I've got a tough meeting, tomorrow night I've got some fool banquet."

Louisa felt it necessary to say, "You knew that I got married? I married Arthur Doud."

She thought he showed some surprise. But he said, "Yes, I heard that. Yes."

"We worked hard too," said Louisa sturdily. "Arthur died six years ago. We kept the factory going all through the thirties even though at times we were down to three men. We had no money for repairs and I remember cutting up the office awnings so that Arthur could carry them up on a ladder and patch the roof. We tried making everything we could think of. Even outdoor bowling alleys for those amusement places. Then the war came and we couldn't keep up. We could sell all the pianos we could make but also we were making radar cases for the Navy. I stayed in the office all through."

"It must have been a change," he said, in what seemed a tactful voice. "A change from the Library."

"Work is work," she said. "I still work. My stepdaughter Bea is divorced, she keeps house for me after a fashion. My son has finally finished university—he is supposed to be learning about the business, but he has some excuse to go off in the middle of every afternoon. When I come home at suppertime, I am so tired I could drop, and I hear the ice tinkling in their glasses and them laughing behind the hedge. Oh, Mud, they say when they see me, Oh, poor Mud, sit down here, get her a drink! They call me Mud because that was my son's name for me when he was a baby. But they are neither of them babies now. The house is cool when I come home—it's a lovely house if you remember, built in three tiers like a wedding cake. Mosaic tiles in the entrance hall. But I am always thinking about the factory, that is what fills my mind. What should we do to stay afloat? There are only five factories in Canada making pianos now, and three of them are in Quebec with the low cost of labor. No doubt you know all about that. When I talk to Arthur in my head, it is always about the same thing. I am very close to him still but it is hardly in a mystical way. You would think as you get older your mind would fill up with what they call the spiritual side of things, but mine just seems to get more and more practical, trying to get something settled. What a thing to talk to a dead man about."

She stopped, she was embarrassed. But she was not sure that he had listened to all of this, and in fact she was not sure that she had said all of it.

"What started me off—" he said. "What got me going in the first place, with whatever I have managed to do, was the Library. So I owe you a great deal."

He put his hands on his knees, let his head fall.

"Ah, rubbish," he said.

He groaned, and ended up with a laugh.

"My father," he said. "You wouldn't remember my father?"

"Oh, yes."

"Well. Sometimes I think he had the right idea."

Then he lifted his head, gave it a shake, and made a pronouncement.

"Love never dies."

She felt impatient to the point of taking offense. This is what all the speechmaking turns you into, she thought, a person who can say things like that. Love dies all the time, or at any rate it becomes distracted, overlaid—it might as well be dead.

"Arthur used to come and sit in the Library," she said. "In the beginning I was very provoked with him. I used to look at the back of his neck and think, Ha, what if something should hit you there! None of that would make sense to you. It wouldn't make sense. And it turned out to be something else I wanted entirely. I wanted to marry him and get into a normal life.

"A normal life," she repeated—and a giddiness seemed to be taking over, a widespread forgiveness of folly, alerting the skin of her spotty hand, her dry thick fingers that lay not far from his, on the seat of the chair between them. An amorous flare-up of the cells, of old intentions. *Oh, never dies.*

Across the gravelled yard came a group of oddly dressed folk. They moved all together, a clump of black. The women did not show their hair—they had black shawls or bonnets covering their heads. The men wore broad hats and black braces. The children were dressed just like their elders, even to the bonnets and hats. How hot they all looked in those clothes—how hot and dusty and wary and shy.

"The Tolpuddle Martyrs," he said, in a faintly joking, resigned, and compassionate voice. "Ah, I guess I'd better go over. I'd better go over there and have a word with them."

That edge of a joke, the uneasy kindness, made her think of somebody else. Who was it? When she saw the breadth of his shoulders from behind, and the broad flat buttocks, she knew who.

Jim Frarey.

Oh, what kind of a trick was being played on her, or what kind of trick was she playing on herself! She would not have it. She pulled herself up tightly, she saw all those black clothes melt into a puddle. She was dizzy and humiliated. She would not have it.

But not all black, now that they were getting closer. She could see dark blue, those were the men's shirts, and dark blue and purple in some of the women's dresses. She could see faces—the men's behind beards, the women's in their deep-brimmed bonnets. And now she knew who they were. They were Mennonites.

Mennonites were living in this part of the country, where they never used to be. There were some of them around Bondi, a village north of Carstairs. They would be going home on the same bus as she was.

He was not with them, or anywhere in sight.

A traitor, helplessly. A traveller.

Once she knew that they were Mennonites and not some lost unidentifiable strangers, these people did not look so shy or dejected. In fact, they seemed quite cheerful, passing around a bag of candy, adults eating candy with the children. They settled on the chairs all around her.

No wonder she was feeling clammy. She had gone under a wave, which nobody else had noticed. You could say anything you liked about what had happened—but what it amounted to was going under a wave. She had gone under and through it and was left with a cold sheen on her skin, a beating in her ears, a cavity in her chest, and revolt in her stomach. It was anarchy she was up against—a devouring muddle. Sudden holes and impromptu tricks and radiant vanishing consolations.

But these Mennonite settlings are a blessing. The plop of behinds on chairs, the crackling of the candy bag, the meditative sucking and soft conversations. Without looking at Louisa, a little girl holds out the bag, and Louisa accepts a butterscotch mint. She is surprised to be able to hold it in her hand, to have her lips shape thank-you, then to discover in her mouth just the taste that she expected. She sucks on it as they do on theirs, not in any hurry, and allows that taste to promise her some reasonable continuance.

Lights have come on, though it isn't yet evening. In the trees above the wooden chairs someone has strung lines of little colored bulbs that she did not notice until now. They make her think of festivities. Carnivals. Boats of singers on the lake.

"What place is this?" she said to the woman beside her.

ON THE DAY of Miss Tamblyn's death it happened that Louisa was staying in the Commercial Hotel. She was a traveller then for a company that sold hats, ribbons, handkerchiefs and trimmings, and ladies' underwear to retail stores. She heard the talk in the hotel, and it occurred to her that the town would soon need a new Librarian. She was getting very tired of lugging her sample cases on and off trains, and showing her wares in hotels, packing and unpacking. She went at once and talked to the people in charge of the Library. A Mr. Doud and a Mr. Macleod. They sounded like a vaudeville team but did not look it. The pay was poor, but she had not been doing so well on commission, either. She told them that she had finished high school, in Toronto, and had worked in Eaton's Book Department before she switched to travelling. She did not think it necessary to tell them that she had only worked there five months when she was discovered to have t.b., and that she had then spent four years in a sanitorium. The t.b. was cured, anyway, her spots were dry.

The hotel moved her to one of the rooms for permanent guests, on the third floor. She could see the snow-covered hills over the rooftops. The town of Carstairs was in a river valley. It had three or four thousand people and a long main street that ran downhill, over the river, and uphill again. There was a piano and organ factory.

The houses were built for lifetimes and the yards were wide and the streets were lined with mature elm and maple trees. She had never been here when the leaves were on the trees. It must make a great difference. So much that lay open now would be concealed.

She was glad of a fresh start, her spirits were hushed and grateful. She had made fresh starts before and things had not turned out as she had hoped, but she believed in the swift decision, the unforeseen intervention, the uniqueness of her fate.

The town was full of the smell of horses. As evening came on, big blinkered horses with feathered hooves pulled the sleighs across the bridge, past the hotel, beyond the streetlights, down the dark side roads. Somewhere out in the country they would lose the sound of each other's bells.

# Vandals

I

"LIZA, MY DEAR, I have never written you yet to thank you for going out to our house (poor old Dismal, I guess it really deserves the name now) in the teeth or anyway the aftermath of the storm last February and for letting me know what you found there. Thank your husband too, for taking you there on his snowmobile, also if as I suspect he was the one to board up the broken window to keep out the savage beasts, etc. Lay not up treasure on earth where moth and dust not to mention teenagers doth corrupt. I hear you are a Christian now, Liza, what a splendid thing to be! Are you born again? I always liked the sound of that!

"Oh, Liza, I know it's boring of me but I still think of you and poor little Kenny as pretty sunburned children slipping out from behind the trees to startle me and leaping and diving in the pond.

"Ladner had not the least premonition of death on the night before his operation—or maybe it was the night before that, whenever I phoned you. It is not very often nowadays that people die during a simple bypass and also he really did not think about being mortal. He was just worried about things like whether he had turned the water off. He was obsessed more and more by that sort of detail. The one way his age showed. Though I suppose it is not such a detail if you consider the pipes bursting, that would be a calamity. But a calamity occurred anyway. I have been out there just once to look at it and the odd thing was it just looked natural to me. On top of Ladner's death, it seemed almost the right way for things to be. What would seem unnatural would be to get to work and clean it up, though I suppose I shall have to do that, or hire somebody. I am tempted just to light a match and let everything go up in smoke, but I imagine that if I did that I would find myself locked up.

"I wish in a way that I had had Ladner cremated, but I didn't think of it. I just put him here in the Doud plot to surprise my father and my stepmother. But now I must tell you, the other night I had a dream! I dreamed that I was around behind the Canadian Tire Store and they had the big plastic tent up as they do when they are selling bedding-plants in the spring. I went and opened up the trunk of my car, just as if I were getting my annual load of salvia or impatiens. Other people were waiting as well and men in green aprons were going back and forth from the tent. A woman said to me, 'Seven years sure goes by in a hurry!' She seemed to know me but I didn't know her and I thought, Why is this always happening? Is it because I did a little schoolteaching? Is it because of what you might politely call the conduct of my life?

"Then the significance of the seven years struck me and I knew what I was doing there and what the other people were doing there. They had come for the bones. I had come for Ladner's bones; in the dream it was seven years since he had been buried. But I thought, Isn't this what they do in Greece or somewhere, why are we doing it here? I said to some people, Are the graveyards getting overcrowded? What have we taken up this custom for? Is it pagan or Christian or what? The people I spoke to looked rather sullen and offended and I thought, What have I done now. I've lived around here all my life but I can still get this look—is it the word *pagan*? Then one of the men handed me a plastic bag and I took it gratefully and held it, thinking of Ladner's strong leg bones and wide shoulder bones and intelligent skull all washed and polished by some bath-and-brush apparatus no doubt concealed in the plastic tent. This seemed to have something to do with my feelings for him and his for me being purified but the idea was more interesting and subtle than that. I was so happy, though, to receive my load and other people were happy too. In fact some of them became quite jolly and were tossing their plastic bags in the air. Some of the bags were bright blue, but most were green, and mine was one of the regular green ones.

" 'Oh,' someone said to me. 'Did you get the little girl?'

"I understood what was meant. The little girl's bones. I saw that my bag was really quite small and light, to contain Ladner. I mean, Ladner's bones. What little girl? I thought, but I was already getting confused about everything and had a suspicion that I might be dreaming. It came into my mind, Do they mean the little boy? Just as I woke up I was thinking of Kenny and wondering, Was it seven years since the accident? (I hope it doesn't hurt you, Liza, that I mention this—also I know that Kenny was no longer little when the accident happened.) I woke up and thought that I must ask Ladner about this. I always know even before I am awake that Ladner's body is not beside me and that the sense of him I have, of his weight and heat and smell, are memories. But I still have the feeling—when I wake—that he is in the next room and I can call him and tell him my dream or whatever. Then I have to realize that isn't so, every morning, and I feel a chill. I feel a shrinking. I feel as if I had a couple of wooden planks lying across my chest, which doesn't incline me to get up. A common experience I'm having. But at the moment I'm not having it, just describing it, and in fact I am rather happy sitting here with my bottle of red wine."

This was a letter Bea Doud never sent and in fact never finished. In her big, neglected house in Carstairs, she had entered a period of musing and drinking, of what looked to everybody else like a slow decline, but to her seemed, after all, sadly pleasurable, like a convalescence.

Bea Doud had met Ladner when she was out for a Sunday drive in the country with Peter Parr. Peter Parr was a science teacher, also the Principal of the Carstairs High School, where Bea had for a while done some substitute teaching. She did not have a teacher's certificate, but she had an M.A. in English and things were more lax in those days. Also, she would be called upon to help with school excursions, herding a class to the Royal Ontario Museum or to Stratford for their annual dose of Shakespeare. Once she became interested in Peter Parr, she tried to keep clear of such involvements. She wished things to be seemly, for his sake. Peter Parr's wife was in a nursing home—she had multiple sclerosis, and he visited her faithfully. Everyone thought he was an admirable man, and most understood his need to have a steady girlfriend (a word Bea said she found appalling), but some perhaps thought that his choice was a pity. Bea had had what she herself referred to as a checkered career. But she settled down with Peter—his decency and good faith and good humor had brought her into an orderly life, and she thought that she enjoyed it.

When Bea spoke of having had a checkered career, she was taking a sarcastic or disparaging tone that did not reflect what she really felt about her life of love affairs. That life had started when she was married. Her husband was an English airman stationed near Walley during the Second World War. After the war she went to England with him, but they were soon divorced. She came home and did various things, such as keeping house for her stepmother, and getting her M.A. But love affairs were the main content of her life, and she knew that she was not being honest when she belittled them. They were sweet, they were sour; she was happy in them, she was miserable. She knew what it was to wait in a bar for a man who never showed up. To wait for letters, to cry in public, and on the other hand to be pestered by a man she no longer wanted. (She had been obliged to resign from the Light Opera Society because of a fool who directed baritone solos at her.) But still she felt the first signal of a love affair like the warmth of the sun on her skin, like music through a doorway, or the moment, as she had often said, when the black-and-white television commercial bursts into color. She did not think that her time was being wasted. She did not think it had been wasted.

She did think, she did admit, that she was vain. She liked tributes and attention. It irked her, for instance, when Peter Parr took her for a drive in the country, that he never did it for the sake of her company alone. He was a well-liked man and he liked many people, even people that he had just met. He and Bea would always end up dropping in on somebody, or talking for an hour with a former student now working at a gas station, or joining an expedition that had been hatched up with some people they had run into when they stopped at a country store for ice-cream cones. She had fallen in love with him because of his sad situation and his air of gallantry and loneliness and his shy, thin-lipped smile, but in fact he was compulsively sociable, the sort of person who could not pass a family volleyball game in somebody's front yard without wanting to leap out of the car and get into the action.

On a Sunday afternoon in May, a dazzling, freshly green day, he said to her that he wanted to drop in for a few minutes on a man named Ladner. (With Peter Parr, it was always a few minutes.) Bea thought that he had already met this man somewhere, since he called him by a single name and seemed to know a great deal about him. He said that Ladner had come out here from England soon after the war, that he had served in the Royal Air Force (yes, like her husband!), had been shot down and had received burns all down one side of his body. So he had decided to live like a hermit. He had turned his back on corrupt and warring and competitive society, he had bought up four hundred acres of unproductive land, mostly swamp and bush, in the northern part of the county, in Stratton Township, and he had created there a remarkable sort of nature preserve, with bridges and trails and streams dammed up to make ponds, and exhibits along the trails of lifelike birds and animals. For he made his living as a taxidermist, working mostly for museums. He did not charge people anything for walking along his trails and looking at the exhibits. He was a man who had been wounded and disillusioned in the worst way and had withdrawn from the world, yet gave all he could back to it in his attention to Nature.

Much of this was untrue or only partly true, as Bea discovered. Ladner was not at all a pacifist—he supported the Vietnam War and believed that nuclear weapons were a deterrent. He favored a competitive society. He had been burned only on the side of his face and neck, and that was from an exploding shell during the ground fighting (he was in the Army) near

Caen. He had not left England immediately but had worked for years there, in a museum, until something happened—Bea never knew what—that soured him on the job and the country.

It was true about the property and what he had done with it. It was true that he was a taxidermist.

Bea and Peter had some trouble finding Ladner's house. It was just a basic A-frame in those days, hidden by the trees. They found the driveway at last and parked there and got out of the car. Bea was expecting to be introduced and taken on a tour and considerably bored for an hour or two, and perhaps to have to sit around drinking beer or tea while Peter Parr consolidated a friendship.

Ladner came around the house and confronted them. It was Bea's impression that he had a fierce dog with him. But this was not the case. Ladner did not own a dog. He was his own fierce dog.

Ladner's first words to them were "What do you want?"

Peter Parr said that he would come straight to the point. "I've heard so much about this wonderful place you've made here," he said. "And I'll tell you right off the bat, I am an educator. I educate high-school kids, or try to. I try to give them a few ideas that will keep them from mucking up the world or blowing it up altogether when their time comes. All around them what do they see but horrible examples? Hardly one thing that is positive. And that's where I'm bold enough to approach you, sir. That's what I've come here to ask you to consider."

Field trips. Selected students. See the difference one individual can make. Respect for nature, cooperation with the environment, opportunity to see at first hand.

"Well, I am not an educator," said Ladner. "I do not give a fuck about your teenagers, and the last thing I want is a bunch of louts shambling around my property smoking cigarettes and leering like half-wits. I don't know where you got the impression that what I've done here I've done as a public service, because that is something in which I have zero interest. Sometimes I let people go through but they're the people I decide on."

"Well, I wonder just about us," said Peter Parr. "Just us, today—would you let us have a look?"

"Out of bounds today," said Ladner. "I'm working on the trail."

Back in the car, heading down the gravel road, Peter Parr said to Bea, "Well, I think that's broken the ice, don't you?"

This was not a joke. He did not make that sort of joke. Bea said something vaguely encouraging. But she realized—or had realized some minutes before, in Ladner's driveway—that she was on the wrong track with Peter Parr. She didn't want any more of his geniality, his good intentions, his puzzling and striving. All the things that had appealed to her and comforted her about him were now more or less dust and ashes. Now that she had seen him with Ladner.

She could have told herself otherwise, of course. But such was not her nature. Even after years of good behavior, it was not her nature.

She had a couple of friends then, to whom she wrote and actually sent letters that tried to investigate and explain this turn in her life. She wrote that she would hate to think she had gone after Ladner because he was rude and testy and slightly savage, with the splotch on the side of his face that shone like metal in the sunlight coming through the trees. She would hate to think so, because wasn't that the way in all the dreary romances— some brute gets the woman tingling and then it's goodbye to Mr. Fine-and-Decent?

No, she wrote, but what she did think—and she knew that this was very regressive and bad form—what she did think was that some women, women like herself, might be always on the lookout for an insanity that could contain them. For what was living with a man if it wasn't living inside his insanity? A man could have a very ordinary, a very unremarkable, insanity, such as his devotion to a ball team. But that might not be enough, not big enough—and an insanity that was not big enough simply made a woman mean and discontented. Peter Parr, for instance, displayed kindness and hopefulness to a fairly fanatical degree. But in the end, for me, Bea wrote, that was not a suitable insanity.

What did Ladner offer her, then, that she could live inside? She didn't mean just that she would be able to accept the importance of learning the habits of porcupines and writing fierce letters on the subject to journals that she, Bea, had never before heard of. She meant also that she would be able to live surrounded by implacability, by ready doses of indifference which at times might seem like scorn.

So she explained her condition, during the first half-year.

Several other women had thought themselves capable of the same thing. She found traces of them. A belt—size 26—a jar of cocoa butter, fancy combs for the hair. He hadn't let any of them stay. Why them and not me? Bea asked him.

"None of them had any money," said Ladner.

A joke. *I am slit top to bottom with jokes.* (Now she wrote her letters only in her head.)

BUT DRIVING out to Ladner's place during the school week, a few days after she had first met him, what was her state? Lust and terror. She had to feel sorry for herself, in her silk underwear. Her teeth chattered. She pitied herself for being a victim of such wants. Which she had felt before—she would not pretend she hadn't. This was not yet so different from what she had felt before.

She found the place easily. She must have memorized the route well. She had thought up a story: She was lost. She was looking for a place up here that sold nursery shrubs. That would suit the time of year. But Ladner was out in front of his trees working on the road culvert, and he greeted her in such a matter-of-fact way, without surprise or displeasure, that it was not necessary to trot out this excuse.

"Just hang on until I get this job done," he said. "It'll take me about ten minutes."

For Bea there was nothing like this—nothing like watching a man work at some hard job, when he is forgetful of you and works well, in a way that is tidy and rhythmical, nothing like it to heat the blood. There was no waste about Ladner, no extra size or unnecessary energy and certainly no elaborate conversation. His gray hair was cut very short, in the style of his youth—the top of his head shone silver like the metallic-looking patch of skin.

Bea said that she agreed with him about the students. "I've done some substitute teaching and taken them on treks," she said. "There have been times when I felt like setting Dobermans on them and driving them into a cesspit.

"I hope you don't think I'm here to persuade you of anything," she said. "Nobody knows I'm here."

He took his time answering her. "I expect you'd like a tour," he said when he was ready. "Would you? Would you like a tour of the place yourself?"

That was what he said and that was what he meant. A tour. Bea was wearing the wrong shoes—at that time in her life she did not own any shoes that would have been right. He did not slow down for her or help her in any way to cross a creek or climb a bank. He never held out a hand, or suggested that they might sit and rest on any appropriate log or rock or slope.

He led her first on a boardwalk across a marsh to a pond, where some Canada geese had settled and a pair of swans were circling each other, their bodies serene but their necks mettlesome, their beaks letting out bitter squawks. "Are they mates?" said Bea.

"Evidently."

Not far from these live birds was a glass-fronted case containing a stuffed golden eagle with its wings spread, a gray owl, and a snow owl. The case was an old gutted freezer, with a window set in its side and a camouflage of gray and green swirls of paint.

"Ingenious," said Bea.

Ladner said, "I use what I can get."

He showed her the beaver meadow, the pointed stumps of the trees the beavers had chewed down, their heaped, untidy constructions, the two richly furred beavers in their case. Then in turn she looked at a red fox, a golden mink, a white ferret, a dainty family of skunks, a porcupine, and a fisher, which Ladner told her was intrepid enough to kill porcupines. Stuffed and lifelike raccoons clung to a tree trunk, a wolf stood poised to howl, and a black bear had just managed to lift its big soft head, its melancholy face. Ladner said that was a small bear. He couldn't afford to keep the big ones, he said—they brought too good a price.

Many birds as well. Wild turkeys, a pair of ruffed grouse, a pheasant with a bright-red ring around its eye. Signs told their habitat, their Latin names, food preferences, and styles of behavior. Some of the trees were labelled too. Tight, accurate, complicated information. Other signs presented quotations.

> *Nature does nothing uselessly.*        *—Aristotle*

> *Nature never deceives us; it is always we who deceive ourselves.*
>        *—Rousseau*

When Bea stopped to read these, it seemed to her that Ladner was impatient, that he scowled a little. She no longer made comments on anything she saw.

She couldn't keep track of their direction or get any idea of the layout of the property. Did they cross different streams, or the same stream several times? The woods might stretch for miles, or only to the top of a near hill. The leaves were new and couldn't keep out the sun. Trilliums abounded. Ladner lifted a mayapple leaf to show her the hidden flower. Fat leaves, ferns just uncurling, yellow skunk cabbage bursting out of bogholes, all the sap and sunshine around, and the treacherous tree rot underfoot, and then they were in an old apple orchard, enclosed by woods, and he directed her to look for mushrooms—morels. He himself found five, which he did not offer to share. She confused them with last year's rotted apples.

A steep hill rose up in front of them, cluttered with little barbed hawthorn trees in bloom. "The kids call this Fox Hill," he said. "There's a den up here."

Bea stood still. "You have children?"

He laughed. "Not to my knowledge. I mean the kids from across the road. Mind the branches, they have thorns."

By this time lust was lost to her altogether, though the smell of the hawthorn blossoms seemed to her an intimate one, musty or yeasty. She had long since stopped fixing her eyes on a spot between his shoulder blades and willing him to turn around and embrace her. It occurred to her that this tour, so strenuous physically and mentally, might be a joke on her, a punishment for being, after all, such a tiresome vamp and fraud. So she roused her pride and acted as if it were exactly what she had come for. She questioned, she took an interest, she showed no fatigue. As later on—but not on this day—she would learn to match him with some of the same pride in the hard-hearted energy of sex.

She did not expect him to ask her into the house. But he said, "Would you like a cup of tea? I can make you a cup of tea," and they went inside. A smell of hides greeted her, of Borax soap, wood shavings, turpentine. Skins lay in piles, folded flesh-side out. Heads of animals, with empty eyeholes and mouth holes, were set on stands. What she thought at first was the skinned body of a deer turned out to be only a wire armature with bundles of what looked like glued straw tied to it. He told her the body would be built up with papier-mâché.

There were books in the house—a small section of books on taxidermy, the others mostly in sets. The History of the Second World War. The History of Science. The History of Philosophy. The History of Civilization. The Peninsular War. The Peloponnesian Wars. The French and Indian Wars. Bea thought of his long evenings in the winter—his orderly solitude, his systematic reading and barren contentment.

He seemed a little nervous, getting the tea. He checked the cups for dust. He forgot that he had already taken the milk out of the refrigerator, and he forgot that she had already said she did not take sugar. When she tasted the tea, he watched her, asked her if it was all right. Was it too strong, would she like a little hot water? Bea reassured him and thanked him for the tour and mentioned things about it that she had particularly appreciated. Here is this man, she was thinking, not so strange a man after all, nothing so very mysterious about him, maybe nothing even so very interesting. The layers of information. The French and Indian Wars.

She asked for a bit more milk in her tea. She wanted to drink it down faster and be on her way.

He said that she must drop in again if she was ever out in this part of the country with nothing particular to do. "And feel the need of a little exercise," he said. "There is always something to see, whatever the time of year." He spoke of the winter birds and the tracks on the snow and asked if she had skis. She saw that he did not want her to go. They stood in the open doorway and he told her about skiing in Norway, about the tramcars with ski racks on top of them and the mountains at the edge of town.

She said that she had never been to Norway but she was sure she would like it.

She looked back on this moment as their real beginning. They both seemed uneasy and subdued, not reluctant so much as troubled, even sorry for each other. She asked him later if he had felt anything important at the time, and he said yes—he had realized that she was a person he could live with. She asked him if he couldn't say wanted to live with, and he said yes, he could say that. He could say it, but he didn't.

She had many jobs to learn which had to do with the upkeep of this place and also with the art and skill of taxidermy. She would learn, for instance, how to color lips and eyelids and the ends of noses with a clever mixture of oil paint and linseed and turpentine. Other things she had to learn concerned what he would say and wouldn't say. It seemed that she had to be cured of all her froth and vanity and all her old notions of love.

*One night I got into his bed and he did not take his eyes from his book or move or speak a word to me even when I crawled out and returned to my own bed, where I fell asleep almost at once because I think I could not bear the shame of being awake.*

*In the morning he got into my bed and all went as usual.*

*I come up against blocks of solid darkness.*

She learned, she changed. Age was a help to her. Drink also.

And when he got used to her, or felt safe from her, his feelings took a turn for the better. He talked to her readily about what he was interested in and took a kinder comfort from her body.

On the night before the operation they lay side by side on the strange bed, with all available bare skin touching—legs, arms, haunches.

## II

Liza told Warren that a woman named Bea Doud had phoned from Toronto and asked if they—that is, Warren and Liza—could go out and check on the house in the country, where Bea and her husband lived. They wanted to make sure that the water had been turned off. Bea and Ladner (not actually her husband, said Liza) were in Toronto waiting for Ladner to have an operation. A heart bypass. "Because the pipes might burst," said Liza. This was on a Sunday night in February during the worst of that winter's storms.

"You know who they are," said Liza. "Yes, you do. Remember that couple I introduced you to? One day last fall on the square outside of Radio Shack? He had a scar on his cheek and she had long hair, half black and half gray. I told you he was a taxidermist, and you said, 'What's that?' "

Now Warren remembered. An old—but not too old—couple in flannel shirts and baggy pants. His scar and English accent, her weird hair and rush of friendliness. A taxidermist stuffs dead animals. That is, animal skins. Also dead birds and fish.

He had asked Liza, "What happened to the guy's face?" and she had said, "W.W. Two."

"I know where the key is—that's why she called me," Liza said. "This is up in Stratton Township. Where I used to live."

"Did they go to your same church or something?" Warren said.

"Bea and *Ladner*? Let's not be funny. They just lived across the road.

"It was her gave me some money." Liza continued, as if it was something he ought to know, "To go to college. I never asked her. She just phones up out of the blue and says she wants to. So I think, Okay, she's got lots."

WHEN she was little, Liza had lived in Stratton Township with her father and her brother Kenny, on a farm. Her father wasn't a farmer. He just rented the house. He worked as a roofer. Her mother was already dead. By the time Liza was ready for high school—Kenny was a year younger and two grades behind her—her father had moved them to Carstairs. He met a woman there who owned a trailer home, and later on he married her. Later still, he moved with her to Chatham. Liza wasn't sure where they were now—Chatham or Wallaceburg or Sarnia. By the time they moved, Kenny was dead—he had been killed when he was fifteen, in one of the big teenage car crashes that seemed to happen every spring, involving drunk, often unlicensed drivers, temporarily stolen cars, fresh gravel on the country roads, crazy speeds. Liza finished high school and went to college in Guelph for one year. She didn't like college, didn't like the people there. By that time she had become a Christian.

That was how Warren met her. His family belonged to the Fellowship of the Saviour Bible Chapel, in Walley. He had been going to the Bible Chapel all his life. Liza started going there after she moved to Walley and got a job in the government liquor store. She still worked there, though she worried about it and sometimes thought that she should quit. She never drank alcohol now, she never even ate sugar. She didn't want Warren eating a Danish on his break, so she packed him oat muffins that she made at home. She did the laundry every Wednesday night and counted the strokes when she brushed her teeth and got up early in the morning to do knee bends and read Bible verses.

She thought she should quit, but they needed the money. The small-engines shop where Warren used to work had closed down, and he was retraining so that he could sell computers. They had been married a year.

. . .

IN THE MORNING, the weather was clear, and they set off on the snow-mobile shortly before noon. Monday was Liza's day off. The plows were working on the highway, but the back roads were still buried in snow.

Snowmobiles had been roaring through the town streets since before dawn and had left their tracks across the inland fields and on the frozen river.

Liza told Warren to follow the river track as far as Highway 86, then head northeast across the fields so as to half-circle the swamp. All over the river there were animal tracks in straight lines and loops and circles. The only ones that Warren knew for sure were dog tracks. The river with its three feet of ice and level covering of snow made a wonderful road. The storm had come from the west, as storms usually did in that country, and the trees along the eastern bank were all plastered with snow, clotted with it, their branches spread out like wicker snow baskets. On the western bank, drifts curled like waves stopped, like huge lappings of cream. It was exciting to be out in this, with all the other snowmobiles carving the trails and assaulting the day with such roars and swirls of noise.

The swamp was black from a distance, a long smudge on the northern horizon. But close up, it too was choked with snow. Black trunks against the snow flashed by in a repetition that was faintly sickening. Liza directed Warren with light blows of her hand on his leg to a back road full as a bed, and finally hit him hard to stop him. The change of noise for silence and speed for stillness made it seem as if they had dropped out of streaming clouds into something solid. They were stuck in the solid middle of the winter day.

On one side of the road was a broken-down barn with old gray hay bulging out of it. "Where we used to live," said Liza. "No, I'm kidding. Actually, there was a house. It's gone now."

On the other side of the road was a sign, "Lesser Dismal," with trees behind it, and an extended A-frame house painted a light gray. Liza said that there was a swamp somewhere in the United States called Great Dismal Swamp, and that was what the name referred to. A joke.

"I never heard of it," said Warren.

Other signs said "No Trespassing," "No Hunting," "No Snowmobiling," "Keep Out."

The key to the back door was in an odd place. It was in a plastic bag inside a hole in a tree. There were several old bent trees—fruit trees, probably—close to the back steps. The hole in the tree had tar around it—Liza said that was to keep out squirrels. There was tar around other holes in other trees, so the hole for the key didn't in any way stand out. "How did you find it, then?" Liza pointed out a profile—easy to see, when you looked closely—emphasized by a knife following cracks in the bark. A long nose, a down-slanting eye and mouth, and a big drop—that was the tarred hole—right at the end of the nose.

"Pretty funny?" said Liza, stuffing the plastic bag in her pocket and turning the key in the back door. "Don't stand there," she said. "Come on in. Jeepers, it's cold as the grave in here." She was always very conscientious about changing the exclamation "Jesus" to "Jeepers" and "Hell" to "help," as they were supposed to do in the Fellowship.

She went around twirling thermostats to get the baseboard heating going.

Warren said, "We aren't going to hang around here, are we?"

"Hang around till we get warmed up," said Liza.

Warren was trying the kitchen taps. Nothing came out. "Water's off," he said. "It's okay."

Liza had gone into the front room. "What?" she called. "What's okay?"

"The water. It's turned off."

"Oh, is it? Good."

Warren stopped in the front-room doorway. "Shouldn't we ought to take our boots off?" he said. "Like, if we're going to walk around?"

"Why?" said Liza, stomping on the rug. "What's the matter with good clean snow?"

Warren was not a person who noticed much about a room and what was in it, but he did see that this room had some things that were usual and some that were not. It had rugs and chairs and a television and a sofa and books and a big desk. But it also had shelves of stuffed and mounted birds, some quite tiny and bright, and some large and suitable for shooting. Also a sleek brown animal—a weasel?—and a beaver, which he knew by its paddle tail.

Liza was opening the drawers of the desk and rummaging in the paper she found there. He thought that she must be looking for something the woman had told her to get. Then she started pulling the drawers all the way out and dumping them and their contents on the floor. She made a funny noise—an admiring cluck of her tongue, as if the drawers had done this on their own.

"Christ!" he said. (Because he had been in the Fellowship all his life, he was not nearly so careful as Liza about his language.) "Liza? What do you think you're doing?"

"Nothing that is remotely any of your business," said Liza. But she spoke cheerfully, even kindly. "Why don't you relax and watch TV or something?"

She was picking up the mounted birds and animals and throwing them down one by one, adding them to the mess she was making on the floor. "He uses balsa wood," she said. "Nice and light."

Warren did go and turn on the television. It was a black-and-white set, and most of its channels showed nothing but snow or ripples. The only thing he could get clear was a scene from the old series with the blond girl in the harem outfit—she was a witch—and the J. R. Ewing actor when he was so young he hadn't yet become J. R.

"Look at this," he said. "Like going back in time."

Liza didn't look. He sat down on a hassock with his back to her. He was trying to be like a grownup who won't watch. Ignore her and she'll quit. Nevertheless he could hear behind him the ripping of books and paper. Books were being scooped off the shelves, torn apart, tossed on the floor. He heard her go out to the kitchen and yank out drawers, slam cupboard doors, smash dishes. She came back to the front room after a while, and a white dust began to fill the air. She must have dumped out flour. She was coughing.

Warren had to cough too, but he did not turn around. Soon he heard stuff being poured out of bottles—thin, splashing liquid and thick glug-glug-glugs. He could smell vinegar and maple syrup and whisky. That was what she was pouring over the flour and the books and the rugs and the feathers and fur of the bird and animal bodies. Something shattered against the stove. He bet it was the whisky bottle.

"Bull's-eye!" said Liza.

Warren wouldn't turn. His whole body felt as if it was humming, with the effort to be still and make this be over.

Once, he and Liza had gone to a Christian rock concert and dance in St. Thomas. There was a lot of controversy about Christian rock in the Fellowship—about whether there could even be such a thing. Liza was bothered by this question. Warren wasn't. He had gone a few times to rock concerts and dances that didn't even call themselves Christian. But when they started to dance, it was Liza who slid under, right away, it was Liza who caught the eye—the vigilant, unhappy eye—of the Youth Leader, who was grinning and clapping uncertainly on the sidelines. Warren had never seen Liza dance, and the crazy, slithery spirit that possessed her amazed him. He felt proud rather than worried, but he knew that whatever he felt did not make the least difference. There was Liza, dancing, and the only thing he could do was wait it out while she tore her way through the music, supplicated and curled around it, kicked loose, and blinded herself to everything around her.

That's what she's got in her, he felt like saying to them all. He thought that he had known it. He had known something the first time he had seen her at the Fellowship. It was summer and she was wearing the little summer straw hat and the dress with sleeves that all the Fellowship girls had to wear, but her skin was too golden and her body too slim for a Fellowship girl's. Not that she looked like a girl in a magazine, a model or a show-off. Not Liza, with her high, rounded forehead and deep-set brown eyes, her expression that was both childish and fierce. She looked unique, and she was. She was a girl who wouldn't say, "Jesus!" but who would, in moments of downright contentment and meditative laziness, say, "Well, *fuck*!"

She said she had been wild before becoming a Christian. "Even when I was a kid," she said.

"Wild in what way?" he had asked her. "Like, with guys?"

She gave him a look, as if to say, Don't be dumb.

Warren felt a trickle now, down one side of his scalp. She had sneaked up behind him. He put a hand to his head and it came away green and sticky and smelling of peppermint.

"Have a sip," she said, handing him a bottle. He took a gulp, and the strong mint drink nearly strangled him. Liza took back the bottle and threw it against the big front window. It didn't go through the window but it cracked the glass. The bottle hadn't broken—it fell to the floor, and a pool of beautiful liquid streamed out from it. Dark-green blood. The window glass had filled with thousands of radiating cracks, and turned as white as a halo. Warren was standing up, gasping from the liquor. Waves of heat were rising through his body. Liza stepped delicately among the torn, spattered books and broken glass, the smeared, stomped birds, the pools of whisky and maple syrup and the sticks of charred wood dragged from the stove to make black tracks on the rugs, the ashes and gummed flour and feathers. She stepped delicately, even in her snowmobile boots, admiring what she'd done, what she'd managed so far.

Warren picked up the hassock he had been sitting on and flung it at the sofa. It toppled off; it didn't do any damage, but the action had put him in the picture. This was not the first time he'd been involved in trashing a house. Long ago, when he was nine or ten years old, he and a friend had got into a house on their way home from school. It was his friend's aunt who lived in this house. She wasn't home—she worked in a jewelry store. She lived by herself. Warren and his friend broke in because they were hungry. They made themselves soda-cracker-and-jam sandwiches and drank some ginger ale. But then something took over. They dumped a bottle of ketchup on the tablecloth and dipped their fingers in, and wrote on the wallpaper, *"Beware! Blood!"* They broke plates and threw some food around.

They were strangely lucky. Nobody had seen them getting into the house and nobody saw them leaving. The aunt herself put the blame on some teenagers whom she had recently ordered out of the store.

Recalling this, Warren went to the kitchen looking for a bottle of ketchup. There didn't seem to be any, but he found and opened a can of tomato sauce. It was thinner than ketchup and didn't work as well, but he tried to write with it on the wooden kitchen wall. *"Beware! This is your blood!"*

The sauce soaked into or ran down the boards. Liza came up close to read the words before they blotted themselves out. She laughed. Somewhere in the rubble she found a Magic Marker. She climbed up on a chair and wrote above the fake blood, *"The Wages of Sin is Death."*

"I should have got out more stuff," she said. "Where he works is full of paint and glue and all kinds of crap. In that side room."

Warren said, "Want me to get some?"

"Not really," she said. She sank down on the sofa—one of the few places in the front room where you could still sit down. "Liza Minnelli," she said peacefully. "Liza Minnelli, stick it in your belly!"

Was that something kids at school sang at her? Or something she made up for herself?

Warren sat down beside her. "So what did they do?" he said. "What did they do that made you so mad?"

"Who's mad?" said Liza, and hauled herself up and went to the kitchen. Warren followed, and saw that she was punching out a number on the phone. She had to wait a little. Then she said, "Bea?" in a soft, hurt, hesitant voice. "Oh, Bea!" She waved at Warren to turn off the television.

He heard her saying, "The window by the kitchen door . . . I think so. Even maple syrup, you wouldn't believe it. . . . Oh, and the beautiful big front window, they threw something at that, and they got sticks out of the stove and the ashes and those birds that were sitting around and the big beaver. I can't tell you what it looks like. . . ."

He came back into the kitchen, and she made a face at him, raising her eyebrows and setting her lips blubbering as she listened to the voice on the other end of the phone. Then she went on describing things, commiserating, making her voice quiver with misery and indignation. Warren didn't like watching her. He went around looking for their helmets.

When she had hung up the phone, she came and got him. "It was her," she said. "I already told you what she did to me. She sent me to college!" That started them both laughing.

But Warren was looking at a bird in the mess on the floor. Its soggy feathers, its head hanging loose, showing one bitter red eye. "It's weird doing that for a living," he said. "Always having dead stuff around."

"They're weird," Liza said.

Warren said, "Do you care if he croaks?"

Liza made croaking noises to stop him being thoughtful. Then she touched her teeth, her pointed tongue to his neck.

### III

Bea asked Liza and Kenny a lot of questions. She asked them what their favorite TV shows and colors and ice-cream flavors were, and what kind of animals they would be if they could turn into animals, and what was the earliest thing they remembered. "Eating boogers," said Kenny. He did not mean to be funny.

Ladner and Liza and Bea all laughed—Liza the loudest. Then Bea said, "You know, that's one of the earliest things I can remember myself!"

She's lying, Liza thought. Lying for Kenny's sake, and he doesn't even know it.

"This is Miss Doud," Ladner had told them. "Try to be decent to her."

"Miss Doud," said Bea, as if she had swallowed something surprising. "Bea. Bzzz. My name is Bea."

"Who is that?" Kenny said to Liza, when Bea and Ladner were walking ahead of them. "Is she going to live with him?"

"It's his girlfriend," Liza said. "They are probably going to get married." By the time Bea had been at Ladner's place for a week, Liza could not stand the thought of her ever going away.

THE FIRST time that Liza and Kenny had ever been on Ladner's property, they had sneaked in under a fence, as all the signs and their own father had warned them not to do. When they had got so far into the trees that Liza was not sure of the way out, they heard a sharp whistle.

Ladner called them: "You two!" He came out like a murderer on television, with a little axe, from behind a tree. "Can you two read?"

They were about six and seven at this time. Liza said, "Yes."

"So did you read my signs?"

Kenny said faintly, "A fox run in here." When they were driving with their father, one time, they had seen a red fox run across the road and disappear into the trees here. Their father had said, "Bugger's living in Ladner's bush."

Foxes do not live in the bush, Ladner told them. He took them to see where the fox did live. A den, he called it. There was a pile of sand beside a hole on a hillside covered with dry, tough grass and little white flowers. "Pretty soon those are going to turn into strawberries," Ladner said.

"What will?" said Liza.

"You are a pair of dumb kids," Ladner said. "What do you do all day—watch TV?"

That was the beginning of their spending Saturdays—and, when summer came, nearly all days—with Ladner. Their father said it was all right, if Ladner was fool enough to put up with them. "But you better not cross him or he'll skin you alive," their father said. "Like he does with his other stuff. You know that?"

They knew what Ladner did. He had let them watch. They had seen him clean out a squirrel's skull and fix a bird's feathers to best advantage with delicate wire and pins. Once he was sure that they would be careful enough, he let them fit the glass eyes in place. They had watched him skin animals, scrape the skins and salt them, and set them to dry inside out before he sent them to the tanner's. Tanning put a poison in them so they would never crack, and the fur would never fall out.

Ladner fitted the skin around a body in which nothing was real. A bird's body could be all of one piece, carved of wood, but an animal's larger body was a wonderful construction of wires and burlap and glue and mushed-up paper and clay.

Liza and Kenny had picked up skinned bodies that were tough as rope. They had touched guts that looked like plastic tubing. They had squished eyeballs to jelly. They told their father about that. "But we won't get any diseases," Liza said. "We wash our hands in Borax soap."

Not all the information they had was about dead things: What does the red-winged blackbird say? *Compan-ee!* What does the Jenny wren say? *Pleasa-pleasa-please, can I have a piece of cheese?*

"Oh, can it!" said their father.

Soon they knew much more. At least Liza did. She knew birds, trees, mushrooms, fossils, the solar system. She knew where certain rocks came from and that the swelling on a goldenrod stem contains a little white worm that can live nowhere else in the world.

She knew not to talk so much about all she knew.

Bea was standing on the bank of the pond, in her Japanese kimono. Liza was already swimming. She called to Bea, "Come on in, come in!" Ladner was working on the far side of the pond, cutting reeds and clearing the weeds that clogged the water. Kenny was supposed to be helping him. Liza thought, Like a family.

Bea dropped her kimono and stood in her yellow, silky bathing suit. She was a small woman with dark hair, lightly grayed, falling heavily around her shoulders. Her eyebrows were thick and dark and their arched shape, like the sweet sulky shape of her mouth, entreated kindness and consolation. The sun had covered her with dim freckles, and she was just a bit too soft all over. When she lowered her chin, little pouches collected along her jaw and under her eyes. She was prey to little pouches and sags, dents and ripples in the skin or flesh, sunbursts of tiny purplish veins, faint discolorations in the hollows. And it was in fact this collection of flaws, this shadowy damage, that Liza especially loved. Also she loved the dampness that was often to be seen in Bea's eyes, the tremor and teasing and playful pleading in Bea's voice, its huskiness and artificiality. Bea was not measured or judged by Liza in the way that other people were. But this did not mean that Liza's love for Bea was easy or restful—her love was one of expectation, but she did not know what it was that she expected.

Now Bea entered the pond. She did this in stages. A decision, a short run, a pause. Knee-high in the water, she hugged herself and squealed.

"It's not cold," said Liza.

"No, no, I love it!" Bea said. And she continued, with noises of appreciation, to a spot where the water was up to her waist. She turned around to face Liza, who had swum around behind her with the intention of splashing.

"Oh, no, you don't!" Bea cried. And she began to jump in place, to pass her hands through the water, fingers spread, gathering it as if it were flower petals. Ineffectually, she splashed Liza.

Liza turned over and floated on her back and gently kicked a little water toward Bea's face. Bea kept rising and falling and dodging the water Liza kicked, and as she did so she set up some sort of happy silly chant. *Oh-woo, oh-woo, oh-woo.* Something like that.

Even though she was lying on her back, floating on the water, Liza could see that Ladner had stopped working. He was standing in waist-deep water on the other side of the pond, behind Bea's back. He was watching Bea. Then he too started jumping up and down in the water. His body was stiff but he turned his head sharply from side to side, skimming or patting the water with fluttery hands. Preening, twitching, as if carried away with admiration for himself.

He was imitating Bea. He was doing what she was doing but in a sillier, ugly way. He was most intentionally and insistently making a fool of her. See how vain she is, said Ladner's angular prancing. See what a fake. Pretending not to be afraid of the deep water, pretending to be happy, pretending not to know how we despise her.

This was thrilling and shocking. Liza's face was trembling with her need to laugh. Part of her wanted to make Ladner stop, to stop at once, before the damage was done, and part of her longed for that very damage, the damage Ladner could do, the ripping open, the final delight of it.

Kenny whooped out loud. He had no sense.

Bea had already seen the change in Liza's face, and now she heard Kenny. She turned to see what was behind her. But Ladner had dropped into the water again, he was pulling up weeds.

Liza at once kicked up a distracting storm. When Bea didn't respond to this, she swam out into the deep part of the pond and dived down. Deep, deep, to where it's dark, where the carp live, in the mud. She stayed down there as long as she could. She swam so far that she got tangled in the weeds near the other bank and came up gasping, only a yard or so away from Ladner.

"I got caught in the reeds," she said. "I could have drowned."

"No such luck," said Ladner. He made a pretend grab at her, to get her between the legs. At the same time he made a pious, shocked face, as if the person in his head was having a fit at what his hand might do.

Liza pretended not to notice. "Where's Bea?" she said.

Ladner looked at the opposite bank. "Maybe up to the house," he said. "I didn't see her go." He was quite ordinary again, a serious work-man, slightly fed up with all their foolishness. Ladner could do that. He could switch from one person to another and make it your fault if you remembered.

Liza swam in a straight line as hard as she could across the pond. She splashed her way out and heavily climbed the bank. She passed the owls and the eagle staring from behind glass. The "Nature does nothing uselessly" sign.

She didn't see Bea anywhere. Not ahead on the boardwalk over the marsh. Not in the open space under the pine trees. Liza took the path to the back door of the house. In the middle of the path was a beech tree you had to go around, and there were initials carved in the smooth bark. One "L" for Ladner, another for Liza, a "K" for Kenny. A foot or so below were the letters "P.D.P." When Liza had first shown Bea the initials, Kenny had banged his fist against P.D.P. "Pull down pants!" he shouted, hopping up and down. Ladner gave him a serious pretend-rap on the head. "Proceed down path," he said, and pointed out the arrow scratched in the bark, curving around the trunk. "Pay no attention to the dirty-minded juveniles," he said to Bea.

Liza could not bring herself to knock on the door. She was full of guilt and foreboding. It seemed to her that Bea would have to go away. How could she stay after such an insult—how could she put up with any of them? Bea did not understand about Ladner. And how could she? Liza herself couldn't have described to anybody what he was like. In the secret life she had with him, what was terrible was always funny, badness was mixed up with silliness, you always had to join in with dopey faces and voices and pretending he was a cartoon monster. You couldn't get out of it, or even want to, any more than you could stop an invasion of pins and needles.

Liza went around the house and out of the shade of the trees. Barefoot, she crossed the hot gravel road. There was her own house sitting in the middle of a cornfield at the end of a short lane. It was a wooden house with the top half painted white and the bottom half a glaring pink, like lipstick. That had been Liza's father's idea. Maybe he thought it would perk the place up. Maybe he thought pink would make it look as if it had a woman inside it.

There is a mess in the kitchen—spilled cereal on the floor, puddles of milk souring on the counter. A pile of clothes from the Laundromat overflowing the corner armchair, and the dishcloth—Liza knows this without looking—all wadded up with the garbage in the sink. It is her job to clean all this up, and she had better do it before her father gets home.

She doesn't worry about it yet. She goes upstairs where it is baking hot under the sloping roof and gets out her little bag of precious things. She keeps this bag stuffed in the toe of an old rubber boot that is too small for her. Nobody knows about it. Certainly not Kenny.

In the bag there is a Barbie-doll evening dress, stolen from a girl Liza used to play with (Liza doesn't much like the dress anymore, but it has an importance because it was stolen), a blue snap-shut case with her mother's glasses inside, a painted wooden egg that was her prize for an Easter picture-drawing contest in Grade 2 (with a smaller egg inside it and a still smaller egg inside that). And the one rhinestone earring that she found on the road. For a long time she believed the rhinestones to be diamonds. The design of the earring is complicated and graceful, with teardrop rhinestones dangling from loops and scallops of smaller stones, and when hung from Liza's ear it almost brushes her shoulders.

She is wearing only her bathing suit, so she has to carry the earring curled up in her palm, a blazing knot. Her head feels swollen with the heat, with leaning over her secret bag, with her resolution. She thinks with longing of the shade under Ladner's trees, as if that were a black pond.

There is not one tree anywhere near this house, and the only bush is a lilac with curly, brown-edged leaves, by the back steps. Around the house nothing but corn, and at a distance the leaning old barn that Liza and Kenny are forbidden to go into, because it might collapse at any time. No divisions over here, no secret places—everything is bare and simple.

But when you cross the road—as Liza is doing now, trotting on the gravel—when you cross into Ladner's territory, it's like coming into a world of different and distinct countries. There is the marsh country, which is deep and jungly, full of botflies and jewelweed and skunk cabbage. A sense there of tropical threats and complications. Then the pine plantation, solemn as a church, with its high boughs and needled carpet, inducing whispering. And the dark rooms under the down-swept branches of the cedars—entirely shaded and secret rooms with a bare earth floor. In different places the sun falls differently and in some places not at all. In some places the air is thick and private, and in other places you feel an energetic breeze. Smells are harsh or enticing. Certain walks impose decorum and certain stones are set a jump apart so that they call out for craziness. Here are the scenes of serious instruction where Ladner taught them how to tell a hickory tree from a butternut and a star from a planet, and places also where they have run and hollered and hung from branches and performed all sorts of rash stunts. And places where Liza thinks there is a bruise on the ground, a tickling and shame in the grass.

*P.D.P.*
*Squeegey-boy.*
*Rub-a-dub-dub.*

When Ladner grabbed Liza and squashed himself against her, she had a sense of danger deep inside him, a mechanical sputtering, as if he would exhaust himself in one jab of light, and nothing would be left of him but black smoke and burnt smells and frazzled wires. Instead, he collapsed heavily, like the pelt of an animal flung loose from its flesh and bones. He lay so heavy and useless that Liza and even Kenny felt for a moment that it was a transgression to look to him. He had to pull his voice out of his groaning innards, to tell them they were bad.

He clucked his tongue faintly and his eyes shone out of ambush, hard and round as the animals' glass eyes.

*Bad-bad-bad.*

"The loveliest thing," Bea said. "Liza, tell me—was this your mother's?"

Liza said yes. She could see now that this gift of a single earring might be seen as childish and pathetic—perhaps intentionally pathetic. Even keeping it as a treasure could seem stupid. But if it was her mother's, that would be understandable, and it would be a gift of some importance. "You could put it on a chain," she said. "If you put it on a chain you could wear it around your neck."

"But I was just thinking that!" Bea said. "I was just thinking it would look lovely on a chain. A silver chain—don't you think? Oh, Liza, I am just so proud you gave it to me!"

"You could wear it in your nose," said Ladner. But he said this without any sharpness. He was peaceable now—played out, peaceable. He spoke of Bea's nose as if it might be a pleasant thing to contemplate.

Ladner and Bea were sitting under the plum trees right behind the house. They sat in the wicker chairs that Bea had brought out from town. She had not brought much—just enough to make islands here and there among Ladner's skins and instruments. These chairs, some cups, a cushion. The wineglasses they were drinking out of now.

Bea had changed into a dark-blue dress of very thin and soft material. It hung long and loose from her shoulders. She trickled the rhinestones through her fingers, she let them fall and twinkle in the folds of her blue dress. She had forgiven Ladner, after all, or made a bargain not to remember.

Bea could spread safety, if she wanted to. Surely she could. All that is needed is for her to turn herself into a different sort of woman, a hard-and-fast, draw-the-line sort, clean-sweeping, energetic, and intolerant.

*None of that. Not allowed. Be good.* The woman who could rescue them—who could make them all, keep them all, good.

What Bea has been sent to do, she doesn't see.

Only Liza sees.

IV

Liza locked the door as you had to, from the outside. She put the key in the plastic bag and the bag in the hole in the tree. She moved towards the snowmobile, and when Warren didn't do the same she said, "What's the matter with you?"

Warren said, "What about the window by the back door?"

Liza breathed out noisily. "Ooh, I'm an idiot!" she said. "I'm an idiot ten times over!"

Warren went back to the window and kicked at the bottom pane. Then he got a stick of firewood from the pile by the tin shed and was able to smash the glass out. "Big enough so a kid could get in," he said.

"How could I be so stupid?" Liza said. "You saved my life."

"Our life," Warren said.

The tin shed wasn't locked. Inside it he found some cardboard boxes, bits of lumber, simple tools. He tore off a piece of cardboard of a suitable size. He took great satisfaction in nailing it over the pane that he had just smashed out. "Otherwise animals could get in," he said to Liza.

When he was all finished with this job, he found that Liza had walked down into the snow between the trees. He went after her.

"I was wondering if the bear was still in there," she said.

He was going to say that he didn't think bears came this far south, but she didn't give him the time. "Can you tell what the trees are by their bark?" she said.

Warren said he couldn't even tell from their leaves. "Well, maples," he said. "Maples and pines."

"Cedar," said Liza. "You've got to know cedar. There's a cedar. There's a wild cherry. Down there's birch. The white ones. And that one with the bark like gray skin? That's a beech. See, it had letters carved on it, but they've spread out, they just look like any old blotches now."

Warren wasn't interested. He only wanted to get home. It wasn't much after three o'clock, but you could feel the darkness collecting, rising among the trees, like cold smoke coming off the snow.

# THE HISTORY OF VINTAGE

The famous American publisher Alfred A. Knopf (1892–1984) founded Vintage Books in the United States in 1954 as a paperback home for the authors published by his company. Vintage was launched in the United Kingdom in 1990 and works independently from the American imprint although both are part of the international publishing group, Random House.

Vintage in the United Kingdom was initially created to publish paperback editions of books acquired by the prestigious hardback imprints in the Random House Group such as Jonathan Cape, Chatto & Windus, Hutchinson and later William Heinemann, Secker & Warburg and The Harvill Press. There are many Booker and Nobel Prize-winning authors on the Vintage list and the imprint publishes a huge variety of fiction and non-fiction. Over the years Vintage has expanded and the list now includes great authors of the past – who are published under the Vintage Classics imprint – as well as many of the most influential authors of the present.

For a full list of the books Vintage publishes, please visit our website
www.vintage-books.co.uk

For book details and other information about the classic authors we publish, please visit the Vintage Classics website
www.vintage-classics.info